THE TEUTONIC KNIGHTS

THE
TEUTONIC
KNIGHTS

Henryk Sienkiewicz

Translated by
Alicia Tyszkiewicz

Newly Edited and Revised by
Miroslaw Lipinski

HIPPOCRENE BOOKS
New York

Library of Congress Cataloging-in-Publication Data
Sienkiewicz, Henryk, 1846-1916
    [Krzyzacy. English]
    The Teutonic Knights / Henryk Sienkiewicz ; translated by
  Alicia Tyszkiewicz ; newly editied and revised by
  Miroslaw Lipinski.
       p. cm.
    ISBN 0-7818-0121-4
    1. Poland—History—Vladislaus II Jagiello, 1386-1434—
  Fiction. 2. Teutonic Knights—Fiction.   I. Tyszkiewicz, Alicia.
  II. Lipinski, Miroslaw.   III. Title.
  PG7158.S4K73   1993
  891.8'536—dc20   93-23033
                                                              CIP

For information, address:
HIPPOCRENE BOOKS, INC.
171 Madison Avenue
New York, NY 10016

Printed in the United States of America

THE TEUTONIC
KNIGHTS

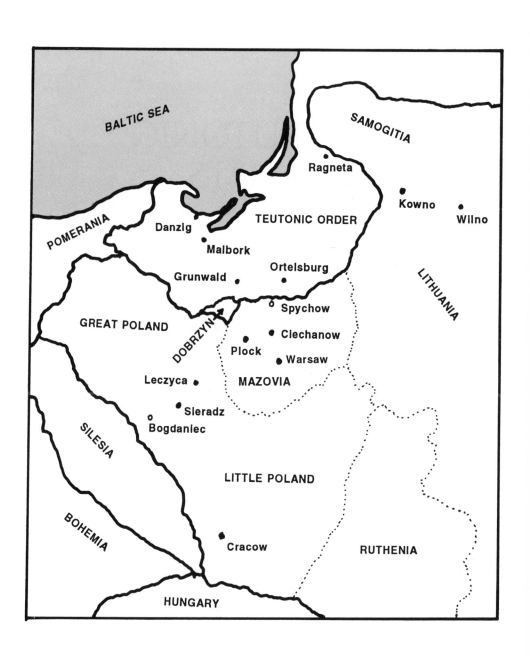

INTRODUCTION

The Teutonic Knights stands as one of the most splendid achievements of Polish literature. Henryk Sienkiewicz himself considered it to be his best novel. It directly followed his internationally popular *Quo Vadis?* and was the last major work to issue forth from his impressive imagination. Here the author's pace is stately, his artistic vision concentrated, his plot finely detailed and lean. Sienkiewicz spent over four years writing *The Teutonic Knights*, struggling continually to purify its style. Serialization commenced in Poland in 1897, and the completed book was offered to the public to commemorate the author's literary silver jubilee in 1900.

Historically, the time period Sienkiewicz chose for his canvas was of vital importance to the Polish people. Twenty-nine years before the events of the novel (the novel begins in 1399 and ends, except for a brief final chapter, in 1410), Poland had lost its last king from the Piast line, Kazimierz the Great. A new ruling dynasty was formed through the marriage of Queen Jadwiga, daughter of Louis of Hungary, and Jagiello, Grand Duke of Lithuania. This merger had a tremendous impact on that part of the world. Its immediate effect was to unite two, at times conflicting nations— Poland and Lithuania, and to Christianize the pagan Lithuania. But it also threatened the existence of the Teutonic Knights, a military order that resided along the Baltic coast. This German religious brotherhood was formed in Palestine in 1190 during the Crusades, and was invited into the Baltic Sea area thirty-five years later by Conrad, a duke of adjacent Mazovia, an important Polish state. Conrad wanted the Knights to quell the Prussian population to his north. The destruction of paganism would be the pretext for domination. The Knights carried out their task with methodical ruthlessness and were overwhelmingly successful in subjugating the populace. But what had started out as an expedient, albeit naive political move by a Polish duke backfired with disastrous results. The power of the Teutonic Knights grew as they became firmly entrenched in the Baltic area. They assimilated another monastic order to their east, the Brethren of the Sword, and their rule began to expand into Polish and Lithuanian territories.

By the time the novel opens, the Order of the Teutonic Knights was a powerful military institution well-known in the region for its unchristian practices and cruelty. Politically shrewd, the German brotherhood was able to attract foreign knights to its "religious" cause, and it had the military strength to influence alliances in an atmosphere where alliances continually changed. Even the legendary Witold, who succeeded Jagiello as Grand Duke of Lithuania, and who is a strong though mostly unseen presence in Sienkiewicz's book, sided with the Knights against Jagiello after the latter wrested power for the Lithuanian Grand Dukedom from Kiejstut, Witold's father and Jagiello's uncle. (Family rivalries were, of course, nothing new in the medieval era, nor were the uses of matrimony to unite formerly warring peoples. Both of the Polish dukes of Mazovia, Janusz and Ziemowit, married women related to Witold and Jagiello.) With Lithuania now Christianized, the Knights lost their major propaganda tool for political control, though this did not stop them from making religious claims by simply sneering at the Christianization of Lithuania. Likewise, the merger of Poland and Lithuania did little to check the military conceits of the Teutonic Knights.

For Sienkiewicz the German brotherhood represented a direct link to contemporary issues. Sienkiewicz wrote *The Teutonic Knights* in a Poland partitioned by Russia, Austria, and German Prussia. The Prussian rule was particularly harsh: Polish land was being turned over to German settlers, Polish culture was being systematically eradicated, the Polish language was being suppressed. The parallels between the medieval German lords and the contemporary ones were certainly evident to the Polish populace, and also to the international readership when the book was translated worldwide after its publication in Poland.

While this attack on Germanism is a strong current running through the novel, there are other vigorous impulses that are vital to its substance. The importance of land, family, national unity, the value of honor and strength and constancy, the Romantic dream of personal salvation through a stirring ideal—all these are to be found within *The Teutonic Knights*. And there's something else to be said of this novel: it is a rousing adventure of epic proportions whose images will remain with the reader through the years. Truly, they don't write them like this anymore.

A few words about this translation: As editor and revisor of the Alicia Tyszkiewicz translation, first published in Great Britain in 1943, I have gone through the Polish original and the Tyszkiewicz version with the intent of accurately representing the original. Sienkiewicz's lengthy sentences and paragraphs, as well as several stylistic touches, have been retained. In keeping with the principle of fidelity, and underscoring a personal anathema to transliterations, I have also retained the Polish spelling of most names and towns, but accent marks I have eliminated as they are of no use to the English-speaking reader. Most of these editorial decisions had been made in the fine Tyszkiewicz translation. Of course, any rule can and should be broken for the balance of the whole, and occasionally I've veered from strict fidelity when a circumstance would mandate it. Ultimately, much thought was given in the Tyszkiewicz version, and in this revision, as to how everything would be presented, and much effort was expended in rendering the full flavor of this epic's Romantic spirit, a spirit which still evokes wonder and determination in hearts eager for the full scope and vitality of life.

I dedicate this revised translation to my father, Jan, and my mother, Milada.

—Miroslaw Lipinski

CHAPTER I

AT the Wild Aurochs, an inn belonging to the abbey at Tyniec, several men were sitting, listening to the tales of war and travel being related by a veteran knight who had come from distant parts.

The man was bearded, sturdy, broad-shouldered, almost gigantic in stature, but lean; his hair was confined by a net ornamented with beads, and he wore a leather jacket, dented by the pressure of his cuirass, and over it a belt made of bronze buckles; from his belt hung a knife in a horn sheath and at his side was a short traveller's sword.

Next to him at the table sat a youth with long golden hair and playful eyes, evidently his companion, or perhaps his esquire, for he was also in travelling dress and also wore a leather jacket marked by a cuirass. The remainder of the company consisted of two landowners from the neighborhood of Cracow and three burghers in red folding caps, the pointed ends of which hung down at the side to their elbows.

The innkeeper, a German in a sandy hood and a serrated collar, poured spiced beer for them from a flagon into earthenware mugs and listened eagerly to the veteran warrior.

The burghers, however, listened still more eagerly. In those times the hatred which divided the towns from the knightly landowners in the reign of Wladyslaw the Short had for the most part died out, and the burgher class carried their heads higher than they would in later centuries. They still were praised for their readiness *ad concessionem pecuniarum*; and so, because of this liberality in loaning money, it not infrequently happened that one might see merchants sitting in the inns, drinking companionably with the gentry. They were even welcome, for, being persons who had usually enough ready cash, they generally paid for what the armigers consumed.

Thus they were sitting and talking and from time to time motioning to the host to fill up their mugs.

"So, noble knight, you've seen something of the world!" commented one of the merchants.

"Not many of those now coming to Cracow from all over have seen as much," replied the newly-arrived knight.

"And many are coming," continued the burgher. "Great festivities and great rejoicings for the kingdom! It is said, and for sure it's true, that the king ordered for the queen a bed of cloth-of-gold embroidered with pearls and a similar baldachin over it. There will be entertainments and tournaments such as the world has never seen!"

"Gamroth, don't interrupt the knight," said the second merchant.

"I am not interrupting him, Eyertreter; I merely think that he will be glad to know what is being said, for I am sure he is going to Cracow himself. Anyway, we shall not be able to make it back to town before they shut the gates; and since at night the fleas around here will not let us sleep, we have time for everything."

"You answer one word with twenty. You're getting old, Gamroth!"

"But I still can carry a bale of damp cloth under one arm."

"That's true! Cloth like a sieve, through which one can see plenty of light!"

But further contention was interrupted by the travelling warrior, who said:

"I will certainly be staying at Cracow, for I have heard of the tournaments, and I will gladly try my strength in the lists, as will this nephew of mine. Though young and beardless, he has left more than one armed man on the ground."

The guests looked at the youth, who smiled cheerfully and smoothed his long hair back behind his ears, before raising a mug of beer to his lips.

The veteran knight added:

"Even if we wanted to go back, we have nowhere to go to."

"How so?" asked one of the gentry. "Where are you from? What are your names?"

"I am Macko of Bogdaniec, and this youth, my brother's son, is Zbyszko. Our family's coat-of-arms is the Blunt Horseshoe, and our motto is 'Hailstones!'"

"Where is your Bogdaniec?"

"Ha! It would be better to ask, brothers, where it was, for it's not there any more. During the war between the clans of Grzymala and Nalecz, they burned our Bogdaniec to the ground so that nothing but the old house remained. Whatever there was, they carried off; and the servants ran away. Only bare ground was left. Even the yeomen in the neighborhood went farther into the wilderness. We rebuilt Bogdaniec, I and my brother, the father of this youth here, but a year later a flood swept it away. Then my brother died, leaving me alone with an orphan. So I thought: I won't stay here! Right at that time there was talk of war and how Jasko of Olesnica—whom King Wladyslaw sent after Nicholas of Moskorzowo to Wilno—was seeking knights throughout Poland. So I pledged my land to a worthy abbot, a kinsman of ours, Janko of Tulcza, and with that money bought a suit of armor and a horse. I equipped myself for a military expedition; the boy, who was twelve years old, I put on a riding horse—and off to Jasko of Olesnica!"

"You and this youth?"

"He wasn't a youth at that time, of course. But he's been robust since he was a little boy. When he was twelve years old he could rest a crossbow on the ground, press it against his stomach, turn the crank, and draw the bow better than any of the Englishmen we saw at Wilno."

"He was that strong?"

"He carried my helmet and, when he passed his thirteenth year, my lance as well."

"You had no lack of war over there."

"Because of Witold. He was living among the Teutonic Knights, and every year they made expeditions against Wilno. Various nationalities went with them: Germans, Frenchmen, Englishmen, who were the best at the bow, Czechs, Swiss, and Burgundians. They cut through the forests, built castles on the road, and then mercilessly ravaged Lithuania with fire and sword, so that the entire population that lives on that land wanted to leave it and seek another, even were it to be in some corner of the world, even among the sons of Belial, just as long as it was far from the Germans."

"We heard even here that all the Lithuanians wanted to leave with their wives and children, but we did not believe it."

"I was there and saw everything. Listen, if it had not been for Nicholas of Moskorzowo and Jasko of Olesnica, and, without boasting, if it had not been for us, there would be no Wilno."

"That we know. You did not surrender the castle."

"We did not. Mark what I say, for I have been in service and have seen combat. The old people still say: 'Fierce Lithuania'—and it's true! They fight well, but they cannot measure themselves with the Knights in the open field. Of course, it's another matter when the Germans' horses sink in the marshes or when the forest is thick."

"The Germans are splendid knights!" called out the burghers.

"They stand like a wall side by side in their iron mail, so protected that you can scarcely see their dog-eyes through their visors. And they advance in line. The Lithuanians attack and scatter like sand, and if they don't scatter, they are mown down and trampled underfoot. Not all of the Teutonic Knights are German; every nation in the world is represented among them. And they are valiant. Even before a battle, a single knight often will crouch with his lance poised in front of him and charge a whole army, like a hawk swooping down on a flock of sheep."

"Christ!" called out Gamroth. "Who are the best among them?"

"That depends on the weapon. With the crossbow the best are the English; they can pierce a cuirass with an arrow and hit a pigeon at a hundred paces. The Czechs are very fierce with their axes. For the double-handed battle-axe no one can surpass the Germans. The Swiss like to smash helmets with their iron flails. But the greatest knights are those who come from the land of France. They will fight on horseback and on foot, and all the time shout tremendously valiant words, which you won't understand at all, for their language sounds like the beating of tin dishes. Yet they are pious people. They told us through the Germans that we were defending pagans and Saracens against the Cross, and pledged themselves to prove it in knightly combat. There is indeed to be such a trial between four of them and four of our knights at the court of Waclaw, King of Rome and Bohemia."

At this point the landowners and the merchants showed still greater curiosity, craning their necks over their mugs towards Macko of Bogdaniec, and asking:

"Who are our knights? Tell us quickly!"

But Macko put the mug to his lips, drank, and only afterwards spoke:

"Ah, do not fear for them. There is the Dobrzyn castellan, Jan of Wloszczowa, there is Nicholas of Waszmuntow, there is Jasko of Zdakow, and Jarosz of Czechow: all valiant knights and stout lads. They can fight with lance or sword or axe—no weapon is unknown to them. People will have something to look at and something to listen to, for, as I said, if you squeeze a Frenchman's throat with your foot, he will still utter knightly words. So help me God, they will win the talking and our men will win the fighting!"

"We shall win fame, if only God will bless us," said one of the gentry.

"And St. Stanislaw!" added the second.

Then, turning to Macko again, he asked further:

"Well! tell us! You have praised the Germans and the other knights, saying that they are valiant and have easily routed the Lithuanians. But wasn't it more difficult for the Germans against you? Did they advance as readily? How did God decide it? Say something in praise of our men!"

"Those knights who had recently arrived from distant lands attacked us readily, but after they tried once or twice they lost some of their courage, for our people are hard. This hardness is often made a reproach against us: 'You despise death'—they said—'but you help the Saracens, and for that you will be damned.' But our men's obstinacy only increases at this kind of talk, for it is not true. The king and queen baptized Lithuania, and every man there confesses Christ our Lord, though not everyone knows who He is. It is well known that our gracious lord, when they threw a devil to the ground in the cathedral at Plock, ordered a candle lit for him—and the priests had to tell him that it wasn't proper to do such a thing. So how can you blame the common man! Not just one person says: 'The duke had himself baptized, so I was baptized; he ordered us to do homage to Christ, so I do homage; but why should I not leave some bits of cheese for our old pagan devils, or throw them some roast turnips, or pour them out some froth from the beer? If I don't, my horses will fall, or my cows will become mangy, or their milk will be mixed with blood, or something will spoil the harvest.' And many do these things, and they make themselves suspect. But they do this out of ignorance and fear of the devils. Ah, those devils used to be well off. They had their own groves, large dwellings, and horses to ride on, and took tithes. But now the groves are cut down, there is nothing to eat, the church bells ring in the towns, and so the wretched creatures have taken refuge in the depths of the forests and howl there with longing for what they have lost. If a Lithuanian goes to the forest, then in the undergrowth one devil or another will pluck him by his sheepskin coat and say, 'Give me something!' Some of them do give, but there are some bold fellows who don't want to give anything, or who even catch them. One of these Lithuanians put roast peas in an ox bladder, and thirteen devils immediately crept into it. Then he tied it up with a rowan twig and took them to the Franciscan friars at Wilno for sale, and they gladly gave him twenty coins so that these enemies of Christ could be destroyed. I myself saw the bladder, from which emanated a horrid stink, for that is how these disgusting spirits show their fear of holy water."

"And who counted that there were thirteen of them?" asked Gamroth shrewdly.

"The Lithuanian counted them as they crawled in. It was clear that they were there, for you could tell from the mere smell and no one wanted to undo the twig."

"It's strange, very strange," said one of the gentry.

"I've seen many things that are very strange, since one cannot say that these Lithuanians are good, but everything about them is strange. They are shaggy and hardly anyone but the duke combs his hair; they give you roast turnips, preferring them to everything else, for they say the turnips produce courage. They live in their dwellings along with their domestic animals and snakes, and know no restraint in eating and drinking. They don't think much of married women, but prize virgins most highly and ascribe to them powers of healing: they say that if a virgin rubs a man's stomach with dried galingale, his colic will pass."

"If their women are beautiful, it wouldn't be bad to get the colic!" exclaimed Eyertreter.

"You should ask Zbyszko," replied Macko of Bogdaniec.

Zbyszko laughed until the bench began to shake under him. "Beautiful they are!" he exclaimed. "Wasn't Ryngalla beautiful?"

"Ryngalla? Who is she, some penitent or what? Speak!"

"What? Have you never heard of Ryngalla?" asked Macko.

"Not a word."

"Why, she's the sister of Duke Witold and the wife of Henry, Duke of Mazovia."

"You don't say! What Duke Henry? There was only one Duke of Mazovia by that name, the bishop elect of Plock, but he is dead."

"That is the same man. He was to get a dispensation from Rome; but death gave him a dispensation first, since evidently he did not please God too much by his doings. I was sent at that time with a letter from Jasko of Olesnica to Duke Witold, when Duke Henry, the bishop elect of Plock, came from the king to Ritterswerder. By then Witold had wearied of war precisely because he could not capture Wilno, while our king was weary of his own brothers and their dissolute life. So the king, recognizing that Witold had more resourcefulness than his own brothers and more intelligence, sent the bishop to him to persuade him to leave the Teutonic Knights and promise fealty to him, in return for which the government of Lithuania was to be put in his hands. And Witold, always eager for change, readily listened to the envoy. There were banquets and a tournament. The bishop elect gladly mounted a horse, although the other bishops did not approve, and showed his knightly strength in the lists. All the dukes of Mazovia are powerful—it is well known that even little girls from this bloodline can easily break horseshoes in two. The duke unhorsed three knights, at another time, five—and of our men, he overthrew me, and Zbyszko's horse sat on its haunches under the force of his charge. He received his prizes from the hands of the fair Ryngalla, before whom he knelt in full armor. They became so infatuated with each other that at the banquets the *clerici*, who had arrived with him, had to pull him away from her by the sleeve, and Witold had to restrain his sister. Finally the duke said: 'I will give myself a dispensation, and the pope will confirm it; if not the one at Rome, then the one at Avignon, and the marriage must take place immediately, or I will burn up!' The sacrilege was great, but Witold did not want to object and insult a royal envoy—so the marriage took place. After that, the couple went to Surazo and then to Sluck, to the great sorrow of Zbyszko here, who had chosen the Duchess Ryngalla, according to the German custom, for the lady of his heart and had vowed to be faithful to her till death."

"Yes! it's true!" Zbyszko interrupted. "But afterwards people said that the Duchess Ryngalla, realizing that it was not proper for her to marry the bishop elect—for he, though he had married, was unwilling to resign his ecclesiastical office—and that a divine blessing was not to be expected on such a union, poisoned her husband. When I heard this, I begged a holy hermit near Lublin to absolve me from my vow."

"He was certainly a hermit," replied Macko, laughing, "but whether he was holy I don't know, for we came upon him on a Friday in the forest breaking bears' bones with an axe and sucking the marrow so vigorously that music was coming out of his throat!"

"But he said that marrow is not meat and, moreover, that he had received permission to eat it because afterwards wonderful visions came to him in his sleep and he could prophesy on the following day till noon."

"Well, well!" said Macko. "Now the fair Ryngalla is a widow and may call on you to fulfill your vow."

"She would call in vain, for I will choose another lady whom I will serve till death—I will also find a wife."

"First you must find your knight's belt."

"Ah, but won't there be a tournament when the queen's child is born? And sooner or later the king will dub several knights. I will challenge every one of them. The duke would not have overthrown me if my horse had not sat on its haunches."

"There will be better men there than you."

Now the landowners from the neighborhood of Cracow began to shout:

"Great heavens! those who appear before the queen will not be youths like you but the most famous knights in the world. Zawisza of Garbowo will joust, and Farurey, and Dobko of Olesnica, and such a man as Powala of Taczewo, or such a one as Paszko the Thief of Biskupice, or Jasko Naszan, and Abdank of Gory and Andrew of Brochocice and Christian of Ostrow and James of Kobylany! How can you measure yourself with them, when there is no one who can, either here or at the Bohemian court or at the Hungarian? What are you saying? Are you better than they? How old are you?"

"Eighteen," answered Zbyszko.

"Then any one of them can crush you with one hand."

"We shall see."

But Macko said:

"I have heard that the king is generously rewarding knights who are returning from the Lithuanian war. Tell me, you who live here, is this true?"

"Upon my word, it is true!" replied one of the gentry. "The king's generosity is known throughout the world; but it will not be easy to make one's way to him now, for Cracow is swarming with guests who have come for the queen's lying-in and the christening, and want either to honor our lord or pay homage to him. The King of Hungary is to be there and the Roman Emperor also, they say, and various dukes, and counts and knights as numerous as poppy-seeds, and every one of them hopes that he will not go away empty-handed. They said even that Pope Boniface himself is coming, because he needs the favor and help of our lord against his enemy of Avignon. In such a throng it will not be easy to get access to the king, but if one does succeed in approaching him and embracing his legs, then he will generously reward those who have served."

"Then I will embrace his legs also, for I have served him well, and if there is war, I will go again. A little booty was taken, and Witold gave a little reward—we are not poor. But my winter years are coming on, and one would gladly have a quiet corner in one's old age, when the strength leaves one's bones."

"The king welcomed those who came back from Lithuania under Jasko of Olesnica, and they all now are feeding on the fat of the land."

"You see! But I didn't come back at that time; I went on fighting. You should know that the Germans bore the brunt of the agreement between the king and Duke Witold. The duke cunningly got back his hostages—and then, off against the Germans! He destroyed and burned castles, slew knights, and cut down swarms of people. The Germans wanted vengeance, as did Swidrigiello, who fled to them. There was another great expedition. Grand Master Conrad himself went on it with a large number of people. They besieged Wilno, they tried to destroy the castle with the aid of huge towers, they tried treachery—they accomplished nothing! And on their return so many fell that half of them did not escape. We went into the field against Ulrich von Jungingen, brother of the grand master and governor of Sambia. But the governor was afraid of the duke and fled in tears, and from that time there has been peace, and the town is being rebuilt. A holy monk, who could walk barefoot on red-hot iron, prophesied that from that moment until the end of the world Wilno would never again see a German soldier under its walls. But if it is to be so, whose hands have brought it about?"

Saying this, Macko of Bogdaniec spread out his broad and unusually powerful hands, while the others nodded their heads in assent.

"Yes, yes! There is truth in what he says. Yes!"

But further talk was interrupted by a confused noise which came through the window, the shutter of which had been taken down, for the night had fallen warm and pleasant. A jingling could be heard in the distance, men's voices, the snorting of horses, and singing. The company was surprised, for the hour was late, and the moon already high in the heavens. The German innkeeper ran into the yard, and before the guests were able to down their last mugs, he came back in still greater haste, exclaiming:

"Some members of the court have arrived!"

A moment later in the doorway appeared an esquire dressed in a blue jacket, a red folding cap on his head. He stood still, looked around at the company, and, seeing the innkeeper, said:

"Wipe the tables and bring in lights. Duchess Anna Danuta is stopping here for a rest."

Then he withdrew. There was a stir in the inn: the innkeeper began to call the servants, and the guests looked at one another in astonishment.

"Duchess Anna Danuta," said one of the burghers; "why, that is Kiejstut's daughter, the wife of Janusz of Mazovia. She was in Cracow for two weeks, but went to Zator to pay a visit to Duke Waclaw, and now must be returning."

"Gamroth," said the second burgher, "let us go and sleep on hay in the barn. This company is too high for us."

"It doesn't surprise me that they should travel by night," said Macko, "for it is hot in the daytime, but why do they stop at an inn when they have a monastery nearby?"

He turned to Zbyszko.

"She is the fair Ryngalla's own sister—do you understand?"

And Zbyszko answered:

"There must be a crowd of young Mazovian ladies with her—hey!"

CHAPTER II

AND then the duchess came in through the door—a middle-aged lady with a smiling face, clad in a red cloak and a tight-fitting green gown, with a gilt belt around her hips that sank along her groin to a large buckle below. Behind the lady came the young women of the court, some of them older, some of them not yet grown-up, with wreaths of roses and lilies adorning their heads, and the majority of them holding lutes in their hands. A few carried whole bunches of fresh flowers, evidently plucked by the wayside. The inn quickly became filled with people, for, after the young women, there appeared several courtiers and boy pages. They all came in merrily, with joyous faces, talking aloud or singing, as if intoxicated with the beauty of the night and the bright moonlight. Among the courtiers were two minstrels—one with a lute, the other with a fiddle hanging from his belt. One of the girls, still very young, perhaps twelve years old, walked behind the duchess, carrying a small lute studded with bronze nails.

"Jesus Christ be praised!" said the duchess, standing in the middle of the room.

"For ever and ever, amen!" answered those present, while making low bows.

"Where is the innkeeper?"

The German, hearing himself called, came forward and knelt down according to German custom.

"We are stopping here for rest and food," said the lady. "Spread the table quickly, for we are hungry."

The burghers had already gone; now the two local gentry, together with Macko of Bogdaniec and the young Zbyszko, bowed again and prepared to leave the room, not wanting to disturb the court people.

But the duchess stopped them.

"You are nobles. You will not disturb us! Make yourselves acquainted with the members of my court. Where has God brought you from?"

They began to mention their names, their coats-of-arms, their mottoes, and the villages after which they were named. As soon as the lady heard where Macko came from, she clapped her hands and said:

"How fortunate! Tell us about Wilno, about my brother and sister? Is it true that Duke Witold is coming here for the queen's lying-in and the christening?"

"He would like to, but he doesn't know if he will be able; that is why he has sent a silver cradle in advance with the priests and boyars as a gift for the queen. I and my nephew also have come with the cradle, guarding it along the way."

"Is it here? I should like to see it. Is it all silver?"

"It is all silver, but it isn't here. They have taken it to Cracow."

"What are you doing at Tyniec, then?"

"We turned back here to see the proctor of the monastery, a kinsman of ours, to leave under the protection of the honorable monks what the war has given us and what the duke has presented to us."

"Then God has favored you. Is it good booty? But tell me, why is my brother uncertain whether he is coming?"

"Because he's preparing an expedition against the Tartars."

"That I know. One thing worries me, however. The queen has not prophesied a happy ending for that expedition, and what she prophesies always comes true."

Macko smiled.

"Ah, our lady is holy, there is no denying that, but Duke Witold will be taking many of our knights with him, good fellows all, against whom no one will get much advantage."

"You will not be going?"

"I was sent with the others with the cradle, and I haven't taken off my armor for five years," said Macko, pointing to the dents left on his elk-skin jacket by his cuirass; "but as soon as I've had some rest I will go; and if I don't go myself, I will give this nephew of mine, Zbyszko, to Lord Spytko of Melsztyn, under whose leadership all our knights will be going."

Duchess Danuta looked at the handsome figure of Zbyszko, but further talk was interrupted by the arrival of a monk from the monastery, who, after greeting the duchess, began to humbly reproach her for not having sent a messenger to announce her arrival and for not having stopped at the monastery, but at a common inn, unworthy of her majesty. After all, he stated, there was no lack of houses and buildings in the monastery precincts, in which even the common man might find hospitality, much more therefore majesty, especially the majesty of the wife of a duke from whose ancestors and kinsmen the abbey had received so many benefactions.

But the duchess answered merrily:

"We have only stepped in here to stretch our legs, and in the morning we must be on our way to Cracow. We slept in the daytime and are travelling by night for the sake of cool weather; and since the cocks have already crowed, I did not want to wake the good monks, especially with such a company, which thinks more of singing and of dancing than of rest."

However, as the monk continued to press her, she added: "No. We will stay here. The time will pass pleasantly in listening to worldly songs, but we will come to church for Matins so as to begin the day with God."

"There will be a Mass for the prosperity of the worshipful duke and the worshipful duchess," said the monk.

"The duke, my husband, will not arrive for four or five days."

"God can bestow happiness even from afar; in the meantime, allow us, poor folk, to bring at least some wine from our monastery."

"You will have my gratitude," said the duchess.

As soon as the monk had gone, she called out:

"Danusia! Danusia! Jump on the bench and rejoice our hearts with that song which you sang at Zator."

Hearing that, some members of the court quickly placed a bench in the middle of the room. The minstrels sat down on either end of it, and between them stood the young girl who had carried the lute studded with bronze nails in the duchess's train. On her head she had a little wreath; her hair hung loosely onto her shoulders; and she wore a blue dress and red shoes with long points. Standing on the bench, she looked like a little child, but also a very beautiful one, as if she were a statuette from a church, or a figure from a nativity play. Apparently it was not the first time that she had had to stand thus and sing to the duchess, for she did not show the slightest sign of confusion.

"Go on, Danusia! go on!" called the young women of the court.

So she took her lute, lifted her head, like a bird which is about to sing, and, closing her eyes, began in a silvery voice:

> *"Oh, if I but had*
> *Little wings like a dove,*
> *Away I would fly,*
> *Away, away to my love*
> *In Silesia."*

The minstrels immediately accompanied her, one on the fiddle, the other on a large lute; the duchess, who liked worldly songs more than anything, began to sway her head from side to side, while the little girl went on singing in a high, lively voice which seemed like the singing of birds in the forest in springtime:

> *"Down I would light*
> *On the fence of his glade.*
> *Look, O my Jack,*
> *At a poor orphan maid*
> *In Silesia!"*

And again the minstrels accompanied her. The young Zbyszko of Bogdaniec, who had been accustomed from childhood to war and its harsh scenes and had never in his life seen anything like this, touched the arm of a Mazovian standing next to him, and asked:

"Who is that girl?"

"That is a maiden from the duchess's court. We have no lack of minstrels to cheer the court, but she is the sweetest little minstrel of all, and the duchess listens to nobody's songs with such pleasure as to hers."

"That doesn't surprise me. I thought she was an angel, and I cannot come to my senses. What is her name?"

"Didn't you hear?—Danusia. Her father is Jurand of Spychow, a rich and valiant count, who is part of the advance troops."

"She is a sight to behold!"

"Everyone loves her for her singing and her charm."

"And who is her knight?"

"Why, she is only a child."

Further talk was interrupted by the renewal of Danusia's song. Zbyszko, standing to the side, looked at her bright hair, her lifted head, her closed eyes, and at her entire figure, which was illuminated both by the light of the wax candles and by the moonbeams streaming through the open window—and he became more and more entranced. It seemed to him that he had once seen her before, but he could not remember whether it was in a dream, or somewhere in Cracow, in a stained-glass window.

And again touching the courtier's arm, he whispered:

"So she is from your court?"

"Her mother came from Lithuania with the Duchess Anna Danuta. The duchess gave the mother in marriage to Count Jurand of Spychow. She was beautiful and came from a powerful family; she was beloved by the duchess above all the other maidens, and was herself devoted to the duchess. That is why she gave her daughter the same name—Anna Danuta. But five years ago, when the Germans fell upon our court at Zlotorya, she died of terror. Then the duchess took the little girl—and from that time has brought her up. Her father often comes to the court and rejoices to see how his daughter is growing up in good health, under the duchess's care and love. But whenever he looks at her, his eyes are filled with tears at the memory of his dead wife, and then he goes back to seek vengeance on the Germans for the terrible wrong done him. He loved that wife of his as no one has ever loved a wife in the whole of Mazovia—and he has slain many Germans for her."

Zbyszko's eyes suddenly flashed and the veins on his forehead swelled.

"So the Germans killed her mother?" he asked.

"Yes and no. She died of fright. Five years ago there was peace, no one thought of war and everyone walked in safety. The duke had gone to build a tower at Zlotorya, without any army, but only with his court, as usual in time of peace. Meanwhile the treacherous Germans fell upon them without declaring war, without any cause.

They tied the duke to a horse and carried him off, with no regard for divine displeasure, nor for the fact that they had received all benefits from his ancestors; his people they slew. The duke remained long in captivity among them, and it was only when King Wladyslaw threatened them with war that they let him go. But Danusia's mother died during that attack, for her heart rose to her throat and choked her."

"And you, sir, were you there? What is your name, for I have forgotten?"

"I am Nicholas of Longwood, but my nickname is Broadaxe. I was at the attack. I saw how a German with peacock feathers on his helmet tried to tie Danusia's mother to his saddle—and how she turned white right before his eyes. I myself received a halberd cut, and still bear its mark."

He showed Zbyszko a deep scar on his head, extending from under his hair to his eyebrows.

A moment of silence followed. Zbyszko began again to look at Danusia. Then he asked:

"And you said, sir, that she has no knight?"

But at that moment Danusia's song came to an end, and one of the minstrels, a fat and heavy man, rose suddenly and the bench tipped up. Danusia swayed and stretched out her hands. Before she could fall or jump, Zbyszko leapt like a wild cat and caught her in his arms.

The duchess, who at first had cried out in fear, now burst into merry laughter and called out:

"There is Danusia's knight! Hail, young knight, and give us back our wonderful little songstress!"

"He caught her gallantly!" said voices among the courtiers.

So Zbyszko went up to the duchess, holding Danusia to his breast, while she embraced his neck with one arm, and with the other held up her lute in fear that it might get crushed. Her face was smiling and joyous, though a little frightened.

Meanwhile the youth, having made his way to the duchess, set down Danusia before her, while he himself knelt and, lifting his head, said with a boldness unusual for his age:

"Let it be according to your words, worshipful lady! It is time for this fair maiden to have her knight, and it is time for me to have my lady, whose charm and virtue I will profess. So, with your permission, I wish to make my vow to her here and to remain faithful to her in every adventure until death."

The duchess's face showed surprise, not because of Zbyszko's words, but because everything had happened so suddenly. The custom of making knightly vows was not, it is true, a Polish one, yet Mazovia, adjoining as it did the German border and frequently seeing knights even from distant countries, knew it better than other districts and imitated it often enough. The duchess had heard of it long before, at the court of her great father, where all Western customs were regarded as laws and models for the more noble warriors, and for these reasons she did not find anything in Zbyszko's desire that might be insulting to her or to Danusia. Rather, she rejoiced that a girl of her court who was so dear to her heart was beginning to draw the hearts and eyes of knights.

So she turned with an amused face to the girl.

"Danusia, Danusia! Do you want to have a knight of your own?"

The golden-haired Danusia skipped forward three times in her red shoes and, embracing the duchess around the neck, cried out joyously, as if she had been offered leave to go to some entertainment, open only to grown-ups:

"Yes, yes, yes!"

The duchess laughed until tears came to her eyes, and all the courtiers laughed along. But at last the lady, freeing herself from Danusia's arms, said to Zbyszko:

"Come then, make your vow! make your vow! And what will you promise her on your oath?"

But Zbyszko, who amid all the laughter had preserved a firm seriousness, declared equally seriously, without rising from his knees:

"I vow to her that when I am at Cracow I will hang a lance in front of my quarters, with a card fastened to it, on which a cleric, versed in writing, shall have inscribed beautifully for me the statement that the Lady Danuta, Jurand's daughter, is the most charming and virtuous of maidens in all kingdoms. And if any man denies this, I will fight with him until he or I perish—unless he prefers captivity."

"Good! I see you know the knightly custom. And what more?"

"And then, having learned from Sir Nicholas of Longwood how the mother of Jurand's daughter breathed her last because of a

German with a peacock crest on his helmet, I vow to tear three such peacock crests from German heads and lay them at my lady's feet."

Hearing that, the duchess turned serious.

"You're not making your vow for fun?" she asked.

"So help me God," replied Zbyszko, "I will repeat my vow in church before a priest."

"It is praiseworthy to fight against the mighty foe of our race, but I am sorry for you, for you are young and may easily perish."

Then Macko of Bogdaniec came forward. He had been listening to everything with a certain indifference, but now he considered it fitting to speak:

"As for that, don't be afraid, worshipful lady. Death in battle may happen to everyone, and for a noble, old or young, it is even praiseworthy. But this youth is not inexperienced in war, for although he has not yet reached full age, he has fought not just once on horseback and on foot, with pike and axe, with long sword or short, with lance or without it. The custom of a knight making a vow to a lady who pleases his eye is a modern one, but I have nothing against Zbyszko promising peacock crests to his girl. He has already hated the Germans, let him still hate them, and if a few heads are broken because of this hatred—then his fame will grow."

"I see, then, that the affair is not a mere whim," said the duchess. And then to Danusia: "Sit down in my place, as the first person today—but do not laugh, for it is not fitting."

Danusia sat down in the lady's place. She wanted to look serious, but her blue eyes smiled at the kneeling Zbyszko, and she could not help swinging her feet from joy.

"Give him your gloves," said the duchess.

Danusia took out her gloves and gave them to Zbyszko, who received them with great respect, and, pressing them to his lips, said:

"I will fasten them to my helmet and whoever reaches for them—woe to him!"

He kissed Danusia's hands and, after her hands, her feet. Then he stood up. His seriousness left him, for his heart was filled with great joy that now he would pass for a mature man in the eyes of the whole court. So he waved Danusia's gloves, and called out half-merrily and half-haughtily:

"Over here, you curs with peacock crests! Over here!"

At that moment the same monk entered the inn who had been there before, accompanied now by two older monks. The monastery servants followed them with wicker baskets containing kegs of wine and various dainties picked in haste. Like the other monk, the two monks greeted the duchess and reproached her for not having come to the abbey, but she explained once again that she and her court had slept in the daytime and travelled by night for the coolness, and so did not need any rest; and that, not wanting to wake either the distinguished abbot or the honorable monks, she preferred to stop and stretch her legs at the inn.

After many polite words, it was finally decided that after Mantins and the Mass the duchess and her court would take breakfast and a short rest in the monastery. The courteous monks also invited the Cracow landowners and Macko of Bogdaniec, who, in any case, had intended to go to the abbey to deposit the wealth he had won in the war or had received as presents from the generous Witold, with which he hoped to buy back Bogdaniec. But the young Zbyszko did not hear the invitations. He had dashed off to his own and his uncle's wagons, guarded by their servants, to change his clothes and present himself to the duchess and Danusia in more handsome apparel. So he took the baggage from one wagon and ordered it carried to the servants' room, where he began to undress. After first hastily combing his hair, he confined it in a silk net adorned with amber beads and fronted with pearls. Next, he put on a white silk jacket embroidered with golden griffins and lined at the bottom with a gold fringe. Over that, he girthed himself with a golden double girdle, from which hung a small sword with a silver and ivory hilt. Everything was new and glittering and unstained with blood, although it had been taken as booty from a young Frisian knight serving with the Teutonic Knights. Next, Zbyszko put on beautiful hose. One leg had long stripes of green and red; the other, of violet and yellow; while both were topped by a bright checker pattern. After that, having put on a pair of purple shoes with long pointed toes, he went, handsome and fresh, into the public room.

As he stood in the doorway, his appearance made a powerful impression on everyone. The duchess, seeing now how handsome was the knight who had made his vow to her dear Danusia, rejoiced still more, while Danusia immediately sprang towards him like a fawn. But either the beauty of the youth or the surprised exclamations of the courtiers restrained her before she reached him. She stopped a pace in front of him, suddenly lowered her eyes and folded her hands and twisted her fingers, blushing and confused.

But others came up behind her: the duchess herself, the courtiers and court girls, the minstrels and the monks, for they all wished to have a better view of him. The Mazovian maidens looked at him as at a rainbow, each of them now regretting that he had not chosen her, and the elder women admired the costliness of his attire. A circle of curious spectators soon formed around him. Zbyszko, meanwhile, stood in the middle with a proud smile on his youthful face, and turned himself about a little, so that they might see him the better.

"Who is he?" asked one of the monks.

"He is a young knight, the nephew of that nobleman there," replied the duchess, pointing to Macko. "He has just made his vow to Danusia."

But the monks showed no surprise, for such a vow carried no obligations. Vows were frequently made to married women, and in distinguished families, where the Western custom was well known, almost every woman had her knight. If a knight made a vow to a maiden, he did not thereby become her betrothed; on the contrary, most frequently she took another for her husband, while he, in so far as he possessed the virtue of constancy, did not cease to be faithful to her, though he married another.

The monks were a little more surprised at Danusia's young age, but not very much even at that, since in those times sixteen-year-old youths were frequently castellans. The great Queen Jadwiga herself, when she arrived from Hungary, was fifteen, and girls of thirteen married. They looked more at Zbyszko than at Danusia, and listened to the words of Macko, who was proud of his nephew and was relating how the young man had come into possession of such splendid garments.

"A year and nine weeks ago," he said, "we were invited to an inn by some Saxon knights. With them at the inn was also a certain knight from the distant nation of the Frisians, who live far away, on the edge of the sea, and he had with him his son, a youth three years older than Zbyszko. At the banquet that son of his began to improperly reproach Zbyszko for not having a moustache or a beard. Zbyszko, impetuous as he is, did not like that, and immediately caught him by the chin and pulled out all his hairs—on account of which we later fought till death or captivity."

"How's that—you fought?" asked the Lord of Longwood.

"Because the father took up the cause of his son, and I took up Zbyszko's. So we fought, the four of us, in the presence of the guests, on trodden ground. Our agreement was that whoever won should take the wagons and horses and servants of the vanquished. And God decided. We overcame those Frisians, though with no little trouble, for they lacked neither valor nor strength; and we took splendid booty: there were four wagons, with a pair of horses to each, and four enormous stallions and nine servants, and two splendid suits of Milan mail, such as you will seldom find among us. Their helmets, it is true, we broke in the fight, but the Lord Jesus pleased us with something else, for there was a whole chest, beautifully studded, full of costly garments, including those which Zbyszko has just put on."

The two landowners from Cracow and all the Mazovians began to look with greater respect at the uncle and nephew, and the Lord of Longwood, called Broadaxe, said:

"I see you are fierce fellows, eager for a fight."

"Now we believe that that youth will get the peacock crests!"

And Macko laughed, while in his stern face there was truly something ravenous.

In the meantime, the monastery servants had distributed wine and dainties from the wicker baskets, and servant girls brought dishes of smoking buttered eggs from the kitchen, ringed with sausages, from which a strong but appetizing smell of pork fat spread throughout the room. At the sight of the food, everyone felt a desire to eat, and all moved towards the table.

No one, however, took a seat before the duchess, and she, when she had sat down in the middle, bade Zbyszko and Danusia sit side by side opposite her. Then she addressed Zbyszko:

"It is proper for you to eat out of one dish with Danusia, but don't press her foot under the table, and don't pat her knee, as other knights do, for she is too young."

He replied: "I will not do that, worshipful lady, unless perhaps after two or three years, if Jesus allows me to fulfill my vow, and when this berry is ripe; and as for pressing her feet, I cannot even if I wanted to, for they are dangling in the air."

"That is true," answered the duchess. "I am glad to know that you have good manners."

Then silence fell, for they all began to eat. Zbyszko cut off the fattest pieces of sausage and gave them to Danusia, or put them straight into her mouth, and she, glad to be waited on by such an elegant knight, ate with puffed-out cheeks, half shutting her eyes and smiling now at him and now at the duchess.

After removing the dishes, the monastery servants began to pour out sweet, fragrant wine—plentifully for the men and sparingly for the ladies. But Zbyszko's knightly manners were especially evident when full bowls of nuts from the monastery were brought in. There were wild nuts and Italian nuts, rare at that time, since they were imported from afar; and the banqueters threw themselves upon them most eagerly, so that for a while no sound could be heard in the room except the crunching of nutshells. But one would be wrong in thinking that Zbyszko looked only after himself, for he preferred to show his knightly strength and temperance to the duchess and Danusia, rather than lower himself in their eyes by gluttonous pleasure in eating rare dainties. Taking a handful of nuts, whether wild or Italian, he did not put them between his teeth like the others, but squeezed them in his iron fingers, cracked them, and then gave Danusia the kernels picked from the shells. He even invented a game for her. After taking out the kernels, he would bring his closed hand to his mouth and suddenly take a deep breath and blow the nutshells to the roof-beams. Danusia laughed so much that the duchess was afraid she would choke, so she told him not to go on with his game. However, seeing the girl's pleasure, she asked her:

"Well, Danusia? Is it good to have a knight of your own?"

"Oh, yes!" the girl answered. And then, extending her rosy finger, she touched Zbyszko's white silk jacket and, withdrawing it at once, asked him: "Will you also be mine tomorrow?"

"Tomorrow and next week and till death," replied Zbyszko.

The supper was prolonged, for after the nuts, sweet flat-cakes were served, full of raisins. Some of the courtiers wanted to dance; others wished to hear the singing of the minstrels or Danusia. But Danusia's eyes began to close, and her head to nod. Once or twice she looked at the duchess and then at Zbyszko; then she rubbed her eyelids with her small fists, and immediately afterwards, leaning with great confidence on the knight's arm, she fell asleep.

"Is she sleeping?" asked the duchess. "There you have your 'lady'!"

"She is dearer to me in sleep than another would be in dance," replied Zbyszko, sitting erect and motionless so as not to wake the girl.

But she was not waked even by the playing and singing of the minstrels. Some beat time to the music with their feet, others accompanied it by clashing dishes. But the greater the noise, the sounder she slept, her mouth open like a little goldfish.

She woke up at last when the cocks were crowing and the church bells ringing, and everyone was getting up from their benches exclaiming: "To Matins! To Matins!"

"Let us go on foot, to the glory of God," said the duchess.

And taking the wakened Danusia by the hand, she went out of the inn first, followed by the whole court.

The night was already paling. A delicate glow was to be seen in the eastern sky, green above and rosy below, and under that a narrow golden ribbon that expanded as one watched. In the west the moon seemed to withdraw before this brightness. The dawn grew ever rosier and brighter. The world awoke wet from abundant dew, joyous and rested.

"God has given a clear day, but the heat will be dreadful," said the ducal courtiers.

"No matter," the Lord of Longwood consoled them. "We will sleep at the abbey and reach Cracow towards evening."

"For another banquet, to be sure."

"Banquets are held there every day now; and after the queen's lying-in and after the tournaments, there will be still larger ones."

"We shall see how Danusia's knight shows himself."

"Eh, those must be sturdy fellows! Did you hear what they said about that battle of two against two?"

"Maybe they will join our court, for they are discussing something together."

They were in fact having a discussion, for Macko, none too pleased with what had happened, had purposefully fallen to the rear of the procession, where he paused now and then to speak freely to Zbyszko:

"In truth, you will gain nothing by it. I myself will make my way somehow to the king's presence, perhaps with this court here, and maybe I shall get something. I should greatly like some little castle or fort. . . . Well, we shall see. In any case, I will redeem Bogdaniec, for what our ancestors had we ought to have. But where shall I get peasants from? Those whom the abbot put there he will take back, and land without peasants is as good as nothing. So mark what I tell you: you can make a vow, or not make a vow, to whomsoever you wish, but go with the Lord of Melsztyn to Duke Witold and join his expedition against the Tartars. If they proclaim it before the queen's lying-in, don't wait for that event nor for the knightly tournaments, but go where there may be profit. You know how generous Duke Witold is, and he knows you already. If you distinguish yourself, he will reward you bountifully. But above all, God willing, you can take innumerable captives. The Tartars are like swarms of ants. In case of victory, one knight can get threescore."

Here Macko, who was greedy for land and labor, began to dream. "Dear God! To get, say, fifty men and settle them at Bogdaniec! They would clear a fine piece of forest. Both of us would get rich. And be very sure, you'll never take as many anywhere as you can there!"

But Zbyszko shook his head. "Bah! All I should take would be riders who feed on the flesh of dead horses and are unaccustomed to tilling the soil. What good would they be at Bogdaniec? Besides, I have vowed three German crests. Where shall I find them among the Tartars?"

"You vowed that because you're stupid, but such vows are not worth much."

"And my knightly honor? What of that?"

"What happened with Ryngalla?"

"Ryngalla poisoned the duke—and the hermit absolved me."

"Then the abbot at Tyniec will absolve you. The abbot is better than the hermit, who looked more like a robber than a monk."

"But I don't want him to absolve me."

Macko stopped and asked with obvious anger: "Well, then how is it to be?"

"Go yourself to Witold, for I will not."

"You little German mercenary! And who will pay homage to the king? Are you not sorry for my old bones?"

"If a tree would fall on your bones, it would not break them. And even if I were sorry for you, I wouldn't go to Witold."

"Then what will you do? Will you become a falconer or a minstrel at the Mazovian court?"

"Is a falconer so bad? Since you prefer to grumble rather than to listen to me, well, go ahead and grumble."

"Where will you go? Is Bogdaniec nothing to you? Will you plough it with your nails? Without peasants?"

"Not at all! A fine lot of good you would do with your Tartars. You heard what the Ruthenians said, that you would find just as many Tartars as lay dead on the field and that you would never take a captive, for you could never catch a Tartar in the steppe. With what shall I pursue them? With those heavy stallions that we took from the Germans? You see! And what booty shall I take? Mangy sheepskins and nothing more. Oh, I shall arrive in Bogdaniec a rich man! I will be called a count! Ha!"

Macko was silent, for there was much truth in what Zbyszko said. It was a while before he answered: "But Duke Witold would reward you."

"Bah, you know. He gives too much to one and nothing to another."

"Then speak: where are you going?"

"To Jurand of Spychow."

Macko angrily pulled at the belt on his leather coat and said: "You must be mad."

"Listen," replied Zbyszko calmly. "I talked with Nicholas of Longwood, and he says that Jurand is looking for vengeance on the Germans because of his wife. I will go and help him. Firstly, you yourself said that I am not without some experience at fighting Germans, for we know them, and we know methods for dealing with them; secondly, I shall get those peacock crests sooner on the border; and thirdly, you know that it's not every German soldier who wears a peacock crest on his head, and so if the Lord Jesus grants the crests, He will grant booty as well. Finally: a captive from there will not be a Tartar. To settle such in the forest would surely be worthwhile."

"Have you lost your senses, boy? Why, there is no war now, and God knows when there will be one."

"Oh, my dear uncle! The bears have made peace with the bee-keepers and won't spoil the hives in the forests nor eat honey! Ha, ha! And is it news to you that, although large forces are not fighting, and though the king and the grand master put their seal to a piece of parchment, there are always disturbances on the border? They carry off cattle and flocks, and for every cow's head, they burn a few villages and besiege a few castles. What about the kidnapping of peasants and girls? Of merchants on the highways? Remember the old times, of which you told me yourself. Was it bad for that Nalecz who captured forty knights on their way to join the Teutonic Knights, put them in a dungeon, and did not let them go until the grand master sent him a wagon-load of marks? Jurand of Spychow also does nothing else and always has plenty of work on the border."

They walked in silence. Meanwhile it grew quite light, and the bright rays of the sun lit up the rocks on which the abbey was built.

"God can always prosper us," said Macko at last, calmly. "Pray to Him to bless us."

"It is certain that everything is a result of His grace."

"And think of Bogdaniec, for you will not convince me that you want to go to Jurand at Spychow for the sake of Bogdaniec and not for the sake of that little bird."

"Don't talk like that, for I shall get angry. I like to see her, and that I don't deny. This is a different kind of vow from that which I made to Ryngalla. Have you ever met a more charming girl!"

"What do I care for her charms! Better marry her when she grows up, if she is the daughter of a rich count."

Zbyszko's youthful face lighted up with a bright smile.

"That may happen, too. No other lady and no other wife for me! When old age makes your bones grow brittle, you will nurse the grandchildren she and I will give you."

At that, Macko smiled also, and answered in good spirits: "Hailstones! Hailstones! May they be like hail! A joy in one's old age and, after death, salvation. Jesus grant us that!"

CHAPTER III

DUCHESS Danuta, Macko, and Zbyszko had already been at Tyniec before, but in their train were courtiers who were now seeing it for the first time; and these, raising their eyes, looked with amazement at the splendid abbey, at its indented walls running along the rocks over the precipices, at its buildings—some on the slopes of the hill, some within the fortifications—towering up, lofty and shining golden in the rising sun. From these imposing walls and buildings, from the houses and outbuildings, destined for the most varied uses, from the gardens lying at the foot of the hill and from the carefully tilled fields which the eye could see from above, one could perceive at first glance the ancient, uninterrupted wealth to which the people from poor Mazovia were unaccustomed and which they had to look at with surprise. There were, it is true, rich and ancient Benedictine abbeys in other parts of the country—as, for example, at Lubiaz on the Oder River, at Plock, in Great Poland at Mogilno and in other places—but none could compare with Tyniec, whose possessions exceeded those of more than one independent duchy, and whose revenues might rouse the envy of the kings of those days.

Accordingly, the courtiers' amazement increased, and some could scarcely believe their eyes. Meanwhile the duchess, to make the road seem shorter and to entertain the young women accompanying her, asked one of the monks to relate the old and terrible tale of Walgierz the Charming, which she had heard already, though not too accurately, at Cracow.

Hearing that, the young women flocked close around the lady

and went slowly uphill, looking like walking flowers in the early rays of the sun.

"Let brother Hidulf tell the story of Walgierz, who appeared to him one night," said one of the monks, glancing at another, a stooped man advanced in years, walking alongside Nicholas of Longwood.

"Did you see him with your own eyes, pious father?" asked the duchess.

"I saw him," answered the monk gloomily. "There are times when he is allowed by the will of God to leave his hellish subterranean prison and show himself on earth."

"When does this happen?"

The monk looked at the two others and said nothing, for there was a saying that the ghost of Walgierz appeared when the manners of the religious order were corrupt and when the monks thought more than they should of worldly ways and pleasures.

No one was willing to admit to this, but it was also said that the vision foretold war or some other misfortune, so brother Hidulf, after a moment's silence, said:

"His appearance foreshadows nothing good."

"I certainly would not like to see him," said the duchess, crossing herself. "But why is he in hell, since, as I heard, he only took vengeance for a terrible wrong done to him?"

"Even though he had been virtuous his whole life long," answered the monk sternly, "he would still have been damned, for he lived in pagan times, and was not washed clean of original sin by Holy Baptism."

At these words, the duchess's brows contracted in pain, for she thought how her great father, whom she had loved with her whole heart, had also died in pagan error—and so had to roast throughout eternity.

"We are listening," she said, after a moment's silence.

And brother Hidulf began his tale.

"There was in pagan times a rich count, who because of his great beauty was called Walgierz the Charming. This whole country, as far as the eye could see, belonged to him. On expeditions, besides the foot folk, he led a hundred pikemen, for all the gentry—as far as Opole in the west and Sandomierz in the east—were his vassals. No one could count his flocks and herds, and at Tyniec he had a whole tower filled with money, as the Teutonic Knights now have at Malbork."

"I know they have!" interrupted Duchess Danuta.

"He was like a giant," continued the monk, "and could tear up oaks by the roots; and in beauty, in lute playing, and in singing no one in the whole world compared with him. Then one day, when he was at the court of the King of France, the Princess Helgunda fell in love with him. Her father wanted to give her to a nunnery for the glory of God, so she eloped with Walgierz to Tyniec, where the two lived in sin, since no priest would give them a Christian marriage. At Wislica lived Wislas the Beautiful of the line of King Popiel. During the absence of Walgierz the Charming, he had laid waste the county of Tyniec. Walgierz defeated him and brought him captive to Tyniec, not heeding that whatever woman set eyes on Wislas was ready to immediately leave father, mother, and husband to satisfy her desires. So it was with Helgunda. She invented such bonds for Walgierz that, giant though he was and able to uproot oaks, he could not burst them—and she gave him up to Wislas, who took him to Wislica. But Rynga, Wislas's sister, hearing Walgierz singing in his dungeon, straightaway fell in love with him and freed him—whereupon he cut to pieces Wislas and Helgunda with his sword and left their bodies to the crows, and himself returned to Tyniec with Rynga."

"Did he not do right?" asked the duchess.

And brother Hidulf answered:

"If he had received Baptism and given Tyniec to the Benedictines, God would have pardoned his sins, but since he did not do this, the earth swallowed him up."

"The Benedictines were already in his kingdom?"

"There were no Benedictines in the kingdom, for in those days only pagans lived here."

"Then how could he receive baptism, or give Tyniec to the Benedictines?"

"He could not and, for that very reason, is condemned to hell, to everlasting torment," replied the monk gravely.

"Certainly! He is right!" said several voices.

Meanwhile they were approaching the main gate of the monastery, where the abbot, at the head of a numerous group of monks and gentry, was waiting for the duchess. There were always a large number of laymen in the monastery: "economists," "advocates," "proctors," and various officials serving the monks. Many land-owners, and even rich knights, held the immeasurable lands of the monastery by feudal tenure, a system uncommon in Poland—and they, as "vassals," gladly came to the court of their "suzerain," where, at the high altar, it was easy to obtain gifts, favors, and benefits of all kinds, sometimes for quite small services, or for a clever word, or because the powerful abbot was in a momentary good mood. The festivities being prepared at the capital also at-tracted many such vassals from distant parts, and since, because of the crowds, it would have been difficult to find quarters at Cracow, they were accommodated at Tyniec. For these reasons, the *abbas centum villarum* could greet the duchess with a more numerous train than usual.

He was a man of tall stature, with a dry, intelligent face, and a head shaven on the top and, lower down, surrounded with a wreath of greying hair. On his forehead he had a scar from a wound received in his younger, knightly days. His eyes were penetrating and looked out haughtily from under black eyebrows. He was dressed in the habit of his order, but over it had a black cloak lined with purple; around his neck was a gold chain, at the end of which hung a gold cross set with precious stones—the emblem of his dignity as abbot. His whole figure revealed a man proud, accus-tomed to command, and confident of himself.

He greeted the duchess courteously, however, and even humbly, for he remembered that her husband came from the same line of Mazovian dukes as kings Wladyslaw and Kazimierz, and, on the distaff side, the reigning queen of one of the largest states in the world. So he stepped over the threshold of the gateway, bowed low, and then, after blessing Anna Danuta and the whole court with a small gold box which he held in the fingers of his right hand, he said:

"Welcome, gracious lady, at the poor threshold of our monas-tery. May St. Benedict of Nursia, St. Maurus, St. Boniface and St. Benedict of Aniane, and also John of Ptolomeus, our patrons living in everlasting glory, grant you health and happiness and bless you seven times a day, all the days of your life!"

"They would be deaf if they did not hear the words of so great an abbot," replied the duchess courteously; "the more so, that we've come here for Mass, during which we will give ourselves over to their protection."

Thus saying she extended her hand, which he kissed, knightly fashion, kneeling on one knee, and then they went together through the gateway. Evidently the Mass had been kept waiting, for the bells, large and small, began to ring at that exact moment. Trumpeters blew great trumpets at the church doors in honor of the duchess, while other musicians beat enormous kettledrums, hammered out of red bronze and covered with skin, which produced a loud resonance. The duchess, who had not been born in a Christian country, and who was always powerfully impressed by every church, was impressed even more than usual by the one at Tyniec, for few others could compare with it for splendor. Darkness filled most of the sanctuary. On the high altar, flickering little lines of lights mingled with the glow of candles illuminating the sculpture and gold. A monk, wearing a chasuble, came out with the Sacrament, bowed to the duchess, and began the service. Soon there arose perfumed clouds of rich incense that veiled the priest and the altar and rose in gentle clouds aloft, increasing the mysterious solemnity of the church. Anna Danuta bent her head back and, spreading out her arms to the level of her face, began to pray devoutly. But when the organ sounded, an instrument which at that time was still rare in churches, and began to shake the whole nave with its splendid thunder, filling it now with angel voices and now with songs like that of nightingales, the duchess's eyes were cast up and on her face, beside piety and fear, was painted boundless delight—and anyone looking at her might have thought that she was some blessed one, who in a miraculous vision saw heaven opening up before her.

Thus prayed Kiejstut's daughter, born in paganism. Like all the people of those times, she mentioned the name of God in a friendly and intimate fashion in daily life, yet in the house of the Lord, she raised her eyes to the mysterious and immeasurable power with childish awe and humility.

And equally piously, though with less awe, prayed the whole court. Zbyszko knelt in front of the stalls among the Mazovians, for only the court ladies sat in the stalls with the duchess, and recommended himself to divine protection. At times he looked at Danusia, sitting with eyes closed near the duchess, and he thought that it would indeed be worthwhile to become the knight of such a girl, but also that it was no small thing which he had promised her. So now, when the beer and wine which he had drunk at the inn had left his head, he was not a little anxious as to how he would perform the vow. There was no war. In the border disturbances it would be easy, for sure, to engage an armed German and either break his bones or lose one's own head. He had said so much to Macko. And he knew that not every German wore a peacock or ostrich-feather crest on his helmet. Of the foreigners serving with the Teutonic Knights, maybe some counts, and of the Teutonic Knights themselves, maybe a commander—but not everyone. If there should be no war, years might pass before he got his three crests; and it further occurred to him that, not being yet dubbed a knight, he could challenge only such as were not yet dubbed. He hoped indeed to obtain a knight's belt from the hands of the king during the tournaments that were proclaimed for the christening, for he had long deserved it, but then what? He would go to Jurand of Spychow, he would help him, he would knock down all the soldiers there—and that would be all. The mercenary soldiers of the Teutonic Order were not knights with peacock feathers on their heads.

So, in his anxiety and uncertainty—and seeing that he would not get much without the special favor of God—he began to pray:

"O Jesus, grant war with the Teutonic Knights and with the Germans, who are the enemies of this kingdom and of all the nations who confess Thy sacred name in our language. And bless us, but wipe out those who serve rather the Lord of Hell than Thee, who bear rage against us in their hearts and are most angry because our king and queen, having baptized Lithuania, forbid them to slay Thy Christian servants with the sword. For which anger, punish them.

"And I, sinful Zbyszko, kneel before Thee and beg Thee by Thy five wounds for help, to send me three distinguished Germans with peacock crests on their helmets as soon as possible, and in Thy grace permit me to overthrow and slay them. It is because I have promised those crests to Lady Danuta, Jurand's daughter and Thy servant, and have vowed it on my knightly honor.

"And as for what is found on the slain, I will faithfully give a tithe of it to Thy holy Church, that Thou also, sweet Jesus, may have some use and praise of me, and that Thou mayest recognize that I have promised Thee with a sincere heart and not in vain. This is the truth, so help me. Amen!"

But as he prayed, his heart melted more and more in piety, and he added a fresh promise: that after redeeming Bogdaniec, he would also give the Church all the wax which the bees made in their hives in a whole year. He hoped that his uncle Macko would not be against that, while the Lord Jesus would be especially pleased with the wax for candles—and wanting to get it more quickly, would the more quickly help him. This idea seemed so just that his whole heart was filled with joy, and he was now certain that his prayer would be heard and that war would begin soon, or even if it did not, that at least he would fulfill his vow. He felt such great strength in his arms and legs that at that moment he would have attacked a whole company alone. He even thought that after performing his promises to God, he might add another two Germans for Danusia! The young man's ardor urged him to that, but this time prudence gained the upper hand, for he feared that he might exhaust God's patience by demanding too much.

Nevertheless, his confidence grew still more when, after Prime and the long rest which the whole court took, he heard the conversation which the abbot carried on at breakfast with Anna Danuta.

The wives of the dukes and kings in those days, out of piety and also because of the splendid gifts which the grand masters of the Order did not spare to give them, showed great friendship to the Teutonic Knights. Even the holy Jadwiga, as long as her life lasted, restrained the hand of her powerful husband against them. Anna Danuta alone hated them with her whole heart for the cruel wrongs they had done her family. Accordingly, when the abbot asked her about Mazovia and its affairs, she began to complain most bitterly of the Order: "Anything may happen in a duchy with such neighbors. There is supposed to be peace: envoys and letters pass, and despite that, one can never feel safe. If a man goes to sleep in the evening in the border country, he never knows whether he will wake up in chains, or with the edge of a sword at his throat, or with the roof burning over his head. There is no assurance against treachery in vows, seals, and parchment. It was the same at Zlotorya, where the duke was carried off into captivity in a time of the greatest peace. The Teutonic Knights declared that the castle there might be a threat to them, but castles are built for defence and not for attack. And what duke has not the right to erect them or to rebuild them in his own land? Neither the weak nor the strong can become reconciled with the Order, for the weak they despise and the strong they strive to bring to a fall. Whoever does them good, they repay with evil. Is there another Order on the earth which has received such benefits in other kingdoms as they have received from the Polish dukes—and how have they repaid them? By hatred, by the ravaging of lands, by war and treachery. And it is vain to complain, it is vain even to accuse them to the Apostolic See, since, living in hardness of heart and pride, they do not obey even the Pope of Rome. They have now indeed sent an embassy for the queen's lying-in and for the expected christening, but only because they wish to turn away the wrath of the powerful king for what they did in Lithuania. In their hearts they are still thinking of the destruction of the kingdom and of the whole Polish race."

The abbot listened attentively, nodding his head in agreement, and then said:

"I know that the commander Lichtenstein has come to Cracow at the head of an embassy, a brother greatly respected in the Order for his distinguished birth, his valor, and his intelligence. Perhaps you will see him here soon, gracious lady, for he sent me word yesterday that he was coming to visit us at Tyniec, desiring to pray before our relics."

When she heard that, the duchess began to make fresh complaints:

"Men say, and God grant it may be true, that a great war will shortly break out, in which on one side will be the kingdom of Poland, and all the nations who speak languages akin to Polish, and on the other all the Germans and the Order. There is, so they say, a prophecy of some saint concerning the war—"

"St. Bridget," interrupted the learned abbot. "Eight years ago she was canonized. The pious Peter of Alvastro and Matthew of Linkoping wrote down her visions, in which a great war is actually foretold."

Zbyszko quivered with joy at these words and could not restrain himself from asking: "Is it to be soon?"

But the abbot, occupied with the duchess, did not hear, or perhaps pretended not to hear, the question.

The duchess went on:

"The young knights among us rejoice at this war, but the older and more circumspect say this: 'We are not afraid of the Germans, although their power and pride is great, nor of their lances and swords, but'—they say—'we are afraid of the relics which they possess, for against them all human power is of no avail.'"

Here Anna Danuta looked at the abbot with fear, and added in a lower voice:

"They are said to have an actual piece of the Holy Cross: how can one fight against them?"

"The King of France sent it to them," replied the abbot.

There followed a few moments of silence, after which Nicholas of Longwood, called Broadaxe, began to speak, a man much travelled and experienced.

"I was in captivity among the Teutonic Knights," he said, "and I saw the processions in which they carried that most sacred object. But besides that, they have a number of other very valuable relics in the monastery at Oliva, without which the Order would not have attained such power."

The Benedictines stretched their heads toward the speaker and began to ask him with great curiosity:

"Tell us, what do they have?"

"There is a piece of the garment of the Most Holy Virgin," replied the Lord of Longwood; "there is the molar tooth of Mary Magdalene, and some cinders from the burning bush in which God the Father appeared to Moses; there is an arm of St. Liborius, and bones of other saints whom you cannot count on your fingers and toes."

"How can one fight against them?" asked the duchess again, this time with a sigh.

But the abbot frowned and, after some moments' consideration, replied:

"It is hard to fight against them, if only because they are monks and wear the Cross on their cloaks; but if they overpass the measure in their sins, then even the relics may become disgusted with dwelling among them. In that case, the relics will not only not give them strength, but will take it from them in order to get into more pious hands. May God spare Christian blood, but if there does come a great war, our kingdom also possesses relics which will fight for us. A voice in the vision of St. Bridget says: 'I appointed them to be bees of usefulness and established them on the edge of Christian lands, but lo! they rose up against Me. For they have no care for the souls and no compassion for the bodies of a people who have turned from their error to the Catholic faith and to Me. They made thralls of them, and do not teach them the divine commandments, and by taking from them the Holy Sacraments, they condemn them to still greater pains in hell than if they had remained in paganism. And they wage wars for the satisfaction of their greed. Therefore the time will come when their teeth shall be broken, and their right hand cut off, and their right leg lamed, that they may acknowledge their sins.'"

"God grant it!" exclaimed Zbyszko.

The other knights and monks were also of good cheer when they heard the words of the prophecy, and the abbot turned to the duchess and said:

"Therefore, have confidence in God, gracious lady, for their days are numbered sooner than yours; meanwhile, receive with a grateful heart this little box, in which you will find a toe of St. Ptolomeus, one of our patron saints."

The duchess put out her hand, trembling from happiness, and, kneeling down, received the box, which she immediately pressed to her lips. The joy of the lady was shared by the men and women of her court, for no one doubted that blessing and prosperity would flow from such a gift on all, and perhaps on the whole duchy. Zbyszko also felt happy, for it seemed to him that war ought to begin immediately after the Cracow festivities.

CHAPTER IV

IT was well past noon when the duchess and her train went on their way from hospitable Tyniec to Cracow. The knights of those days, when travelling to larger towns or visiting distinguished people in their castles, frequently put on full armor. It was indeed the custom to take it off on passing through the gateway, the lord of the castle summoning them to do so in the consecrated words: "Take off your armor, noble lord, for you have come to friends." None the less, a warlike entrance was regarded as more imposing and raised the status of the knight. For this reason, both Macko and Zbyszko had put on the splendid breastplates and hauberks—bright, glittering, and ornamented at the edges with an inlaid thread of gold—which they had taken from the Frisian knights. Nicholas of Longwood, who in the course of his life had seen much of the world and many knights, and was no mean connoisseur of military things, recognized at once that this was armor made by the Milanese, the most famous armorers in the world, and that only the richest knights could afford it, since each suit represented a fortune. He concluded that the Frisians must have been distinguished men among their nation, and began to look at Macko and Zbyszko with greater respect. Their helmets, though also not insignificant, were not as costly; but their enormous stallions, beautifully caparisoned, aroused admiration and envy among the courtiers.

Seated on their unusually high horses, Macko and Zbyszko looked down on the whole court. Each of them held in his hand a long lance, each had a sword at his side and an axe at his saddle-bow. For convenience they had, it is true, placed their shields in the wagons, but even without them they looked as though they were riding to battle, not to town.

They both rode near to the duchess's carriage, on the back seat of which sat the duchess and Danusia; and on the front, old Nicholas of Longwood and the dignified court lady Ofka, widow of Christian of Jarzabkowo. Danusia looked with great attention at the iron-clad knights, while the duchess repeatedly took out the little box with the relic of St. Ptolomeus from the bosom of her dress and raised it to her lips.

"I am most curious to see what the bones inside look like," she said at last, "but I will not open it myself, so as not to offend the saint. Let the bishop at Cracow open it."

The cautious knight of Longwood replied:

"You should not let it leave your hands; it's too coveted an item."

"Maybe you are right," said the duchess after a moment's consideration, and then added: "It has been long time since anyone gave me such joy as that honorable abbot by this gift and by relieving my fears of the Teutonic Knights' relics."

"He spoke wisely and honestly," said Macko of Bogdaniec. "They also had various relics at Wilno, particularly because they wanted to convince their foreign guests that the war was against the pagans. Well, and what of it? Our people saw that if you merely spat on your hands and swung an axe round your head, their helmets would fall and their heads with them. The saints can help—it would be a sin to say otherwise—but they help only the honest man who goes to battle for a just cause in the name of God. So I think, worshipful lady, that should a great war come, even if all the Germans would help the Teutonic Knights, we shall decimate them, for our nation is greater and the Lord Jesus has put greater strength into our bones. And as for relics—is there not a piece of the Holy Cross here among us in the Monastery of the Cross?"

"True, as I love God!" said the duchess. "But our relic will stay in the monastery, whereas they carry theirs with them in case of need."

"It doesn't matter! The power of God knows no distance."

"Is that true? Tell me how it is," said the duchess, turning to the wise Nicholas of Longwood, and he replied:

"Every bishop will testify to that. It is far to Rome too, but the pope governs the world—how much more God!"

These words finally consoled the duchess, so she turned the conversation to Tyniec and its magnificence. The Mazovians were amazed in general, not only by the wealth of the abbey, but also by the wealth and beauty of the whole countryside through which they were now riding. In all directions were many prosperous villages surrounded by orchards full of fruit trees, linden groves, with storks' nests in the treetops and straw skeps for bees underneath. Along the highway on both sides stretched wide fields of grain. The wind at times bent this still greenish sea of corn ears, amid which twinkled in profusion, like stars in heaven, the heads of blue cornflowers and bright red poppies. Far away beyond the cornfields rose a line of black forests. Here and there the eye rested with delight on oak and alder trees, on moist meadows full of grass and with peewits hovering over the marshy spots, and then on hills dotted with cottages, and on fields of corn. This land was obviously inhabited by a swarming and industrious people, in love with the soil—as far as the eye could see, the land appeared flowing with milk and honey, and full of happiness and peace.

"This is the royal domain of King Kazimierz," said the duchess. "Here one would like to live and never die."

"The Lord Jesus smiles on such a land," replied Nicholas of Longwood, "and the blessing of God is on it; but how can it be otherwise, since here, when the bells begin to ring, the sound reaches every corner! It is well known, of course, that evil spirits, not being able to bear the sound of church bells, have to flee to the silent forests on the Hungarian border."

"I am surprised," declared the Lady Ofka, widow of Christian of Jarzabkowo, "that Walgierz the Charming, of whom the monk told, is able to show himself at Tyniec, where the bells ring seven times a day."

This question perplexed Nicholas for a while, and it was only after some moments' thought that he replied:

"Firstly, the judgments of God are inscrutable, and secondly, don't forget that he gets special permission every time."

"That may be, but I'm glad that we're not spending the night in the monastery. I should die of fright if such a hellish giant appeared to me."

"Hey! one never knows; they say he is quite charming."

"Even if he were the most handsome of men, I should not like a kiss from a mouth breathing sulphur."

"How do you know that he would insist on kissing you?"

At these words the duchess, and with her Sir Nicholas and both the knights of Bogdaniec, began to laugh. Following their example, Danusia laughed too, though she didn't understand the joke; but Ofka of Jarzabkowo turned an angry face to Nicholas of Long-wood, and said:

"I'd rather have him than you."

"Ah, don't call a wolf from the forest," answered the Mazovian cheerfully, "for evil spirits frequently walk on the high road between Cracow and Tyniec, particularly towards evening. Supposing he hears you and shows himself to you in the form of a giant!"

"Heaven forbid!" replied Ofka.

At that moment Macko of Bogdaniec, who was mounted on a large stallion and could see further than those who were sitting in the carriage, drew rein and said:

"Oh, as I love God, what is that?"

"What is what?"

"Some giant is riding out from behind that hill to our front."

"And the word became flesh!" exclaimed the duchess. "Be careful what you say!"

Zbyszko rose in his stirrups and said:

"Indeed—a giant, Walgierz, no one else!"

The frightened coachman stopped his horse and began to cross himself without letting the reins slip from his hands, for he also saw from his position the enormous figure of a rider on the hill.

The duchess stood up—and immediately sat down again, her face altered by fear, while Danusia hid her head in the folds of the duchess's dress. The courtiers, the young women, and the minstrels, who were riding on horseback behind the carriage, began to gather around it when they heard the ill-omened name. The men still tried to laugh, but their eyes betrayed concern; the girls turned pale, and only Nicholas of Longwood, who had eaten bread from more than one oven, preserved a cheerful countenance and said, to console the duchess:

"Don't be afraid, worshipful lady. The sun has not yet set, and even if it were night, St. Ptolomeus would be able to deal with Walgierz."

Meanwhile the unknown rider, having reached the crest of the hill, checked his horse and stood motionless. In the rays of the setting sun, he was clearly visible—and indeed his figure seemed to surpass the usual dimensions of a man. The space between him and the duchess's company was not more than three hundred paces.

"Why has he stopped?" asked one of the minstrels.

"Because we have stopped," answered Macko.

"He's looking at us as if he wanted to pick someone for himself," remarked the second minstrel. "If I knew that he was a human being and not an evil spirit, I would ride up to him and hit him on the head with my lute."

The women were now thoroughly frightened and began to pray aloud, while Zbyszko, anxious to acquire a reputation for courage with the duchess and Danusia, said:

"I will ride up to him in any case. What do I care for Walgierz?"

At that Danusia began to call out, half-weeping: "Zbyszko! Zbyszko!" But he started his horse and rode faster and faster, confident that even if he found the real Walgierz, he would transfix him with his lance.

But Macko, who had keen sight, said:

"He looks like a giant because he is standing on a hill. He's a big fellow, but an ordinary mortal—nothing more. Here! I will ride up myself to prevent a quarrel between him and Zbyszko."

Meanwhile Zbyszko, riding fast, was thinking whether to couch his lance or observe from close-by what the fellow on the hill looked like. He decided first to observe him, and immediately realized that it had been the better idea, for as he approached him, the unknown rider began to lose his superhuman proportions. The man was huge and was mounted on an enormous horse, bigger even than Zbyszko's stallion—but he did not overpass the dimensions of a man. He was, moreover, unarmed, with a bell-shaped samite cap on his head, and a white linen dust-cape, beneath which a green garment could be seen. Standing on the hill, he had raised his head and was praying. Evidently he had stopped his horse in order to finish his evening prayers.

"Hey, some Walgierz!" thought the young lad.

He had now come so near that he could have reached the

unknown rider with his lance; but the latter, seeing a splendidly armed knight before him, smiled at him in a friendly manner and said:

"Jesus Christ be praised!"

"For ever and ever."

"Is not that the court of the Duchess of Mazovia down there?"

"It is."

"Then you come from Tyniec?"

But Zbyszko made no answer. He saw something which so astounded him that he did not even hear the question. He stood frozen for a few moments, not believing his own eyes, for there, a quarter of a furlong behind the unknown man, he saw ten or fifteen mounted soldiers, at the head of whom, considerably in front, rode a knight clad all in shining armor, and wearing a white linen cloak with a black cross on it, and a steel helmet with a magnificent tuft of peacock feathers.

"A Teutonic Knight!" exclaimed Zbyszko under his breath.

At that sight, he thought his prayers had been answered. Surely God in His mercy had sent him such a German as he had prayed for at Tyniec, and he ought to make the most of the divine favor. So, without a moment's hesitation—before all this had time pass through his head, before he could recover from his amazement—he leaned forward on his horse, set his lance at the height of his horse's ears, and uttering his family war-cry, "Hailstones! Hailstones!" dashed full gallop at the Teutonic Knight.

The latter was also astounded. He checked his horse and looked straight forward without lowering his lance, which was sticking up from his stirrup, apparently uncertain whether the attack was meant for him.

"Lower your lance!" cried out Zbyszko, striking the iron points of his stirrups into his horse's sides. "Hailstones! Hailstones!"

The space dividing them began to diminish. The Teutonic Knight, seeing that the attack was really directed at him, reined in his horse and poised his weapon, and Zbyszko's lance was just about to smash against his breast when a powerful hand suddenly broke it off near Zbyszko's fist as if were a dry reed, and then the same hand drew the reins of his horse with such tremendous strength that the charger dug all four feet into the ground and stood as if rooted to the ground.

"Madman, what are you doing?" called a deep, threatening voice. "You are attacking an envoy, you are showing contempt of the king!"

Zbyszko looked around and recognized the same gigantic man who had been taken for Walgierz and had frightened the duchess's court ladies.

"Let me get at the German! Who are you?" he called out, grasping the handle of his axe.

"Put away your axe, in God's name! Put away your axe, I say, or I will hurl you from your horse!" called out the unknown rider, more threateningly than before. "You have insulted the majesty of the king and you will be called to judgment."

Then he turned to the men who were riding behind the Teutonic Knight and shouted: "Everything is all right!"

Meanwhile Macko had ridden up with a disquieted and ill-boding face. He understood clearly that Zbyszko had acted like a madman and that the results might be fatal for him, but none the less he was ready for battle. The whole train of the unknown knight and of the Teutonic Knight amounted to scarcely fifteen men, armed partly with pikes and partly with crossbows—so two knights in full armor might meet them with some hope of victory. Macko also thought that if later they were to be threatened with a court of justice, it might be better to avoid it by riding over these men and then hiding somewhere until the storm blew over. So his face immediately twitched, like the jaws of a wolf ready to bite, and forcing his horse between Zbyszko and the unknown man, he asked, grasping his sword at the same time:

"Who are you? Whence have you your right?"

"My right is from this," replied the stranger; "that the king has commanded me to watch over the safety of this neighborhood, and my name is Powala of Taczewo."

At these words Macko and Zbyszko looked at the knight and then sheathed their already half-drawn swords and lowered their heads. It was not fear which overcame them; they bowed their heads before a famous name which they knew very well, for Powala of Taczewo, a nobleman of a distinguished family and a rich lord, possessing wide lands near Radom, was at the time one of the most renowned knights in the kingdom. Minstrels celebrated him in their songs as a model of honor and valor, praising his name equally

with those of Zawisza of Garbowo, and Farurej, and Skarbek of
Gory, and Dobko of Olesnica, and Jasko Naszan, and Nicholas of
Moskorzowo, and Zyndram of Maszkowice. At that moment,
moreover, he represented to some extent the person of the king,
and so to attack him meant as much as to put one's head under the
executioner's axe.

Macko therefore, having cooled down, called out to him with
much respect:

"Honor and greeting to you, lord, and to your fame and valor!"

"Greeting to you also, lord," answered Powala, "though I would
have preferred not to make your acquaintance in so grave an affair."

"Why so?" asked Macko.

But Powala turned to Zbyszko:

"Whatever have you done, rash youth? On the public highway,
in the king's neighborhood, you have attacked an envoy. Do you
know what awaits you for that?"

"He attacked the envoy because he is young and foolish, and it's
easier for him to act than to think," said Macko. "But do not judge
him too harshly. I will tell you the whole story."

"It is not I who will judge him. It is my business only to put
fetters on him."

"How so?" called Macko, casting another gloomy glance at the
whole party of men.

"By the king's command."

At these words silence fell.

"He is a nobleman," said Macko at last.

"Then let him promise on his knightly honor that he will come
for judgment whenever he is called."

"I promise on my honor!" exclaimed Zbyszko.

"Good. What is your name?"

Macko mentioned his name and coat-of-arms.

"If you belong to the court of Duke Janusz's wife, then beg her
to intervene on your behalf with the king."

"We are not of the court. We come from Duke Witold in
Lithuania. Would to God that we had never met any court! This
meeting has brought misfortune to the lad."

And Macko began to relate what had occurred at the inn. He
spoke of the meeting with the duchess's court and of Zbyszko's
vow, but finally he was seized with sudden anger against Zbyszko,

through whose rashness they had fallen into such a difficult situation. So he turned to him and exclaimed:

"Would you had fallen at Wilno! Whatever were you thinking of, you wild boar?"

"After my vow," replied Zbyszko, "I prayed to the Lord Jesus to grant me Germans—and I promised Him a gift—so when I saw peacock feathers and with them a cloak with a black cross, a voice immediately exclaimed within me: 'Strike at the German, for it's a miracle!' Well—I rode at him. Who would not have done the same?"

"Listen," interrupted Powala. "I wish you no evil, for I see clearly that this youth is at fault more through the thoughtlessness typical of his age than through wickedness. I would be glad to pay no attention at all to what he has done and to ride on as if nothing had happened. But I cannot do this unless that German commander will promise not to complain to the king. Ask him to do that: perhaps he will take pity on the youth."

"I would rather go before the court than have to humiliate myself before a Teutonic Knight!" exclaimed Zbyszko. "It is not in keeping with my knightly honor."

Powala of Taczewo looked at him sternly.

"You are behaving unwisely," he said. "Elder men know better than you what is in keeping and what is not in keeping with knightly honor. Men have heard of me, and I tell you that if I had done such a deed, I should not hesitate to ask for forgiveness."

Zbyszko was ashamed, but he looked around him and replied:

"The ground would be level here if it were only trodden a little. Rather than beg the German's pardon, I would prefer to meet him on horseback or on foot, till death or captivity."

"Fool!" interrupted Macko. "How can you fight an envoy? You can neither fight him, nor will he fight such a young stag." Macko turned to Powala. "Excuse him, noble lord. The boy has been completely corrupted by the war, and it would be better that he not speak to the German, for he would call him evil names. I will speak to him; I will beg his pardon; and if after the conclusion of his embassy, the commander is willing to engage in single combat in the lists, I will meet him."

"He is a knight of high birth who will not meet everyone," replied Powala.

"What? Do I not wear a belt and spurs? Even the duke may meet me in combat."

"That is true, but don't speak of it to him, unless he mentions it himself; otherwise, he may bear you a grudge. Well, God help you in this affair."

"I will go and take the shame upon myself," said Macko to Zbyszko. "You wait here!"

So saying, he approached the Teutonic Knight, who had stopped some paces away and was sitting motionless on his huge horse, as if he were a statue made of iron, and listening with the greatest indifference to the preceding dialogue. Macko, in the course of long years of warfare, had learned a little German, so he now began to explain to the commander in his native language what had happened, and to lay the blame on the youthfulness and impetuosity of the lad, who thought that God Himself had sent him a knight with a peacock crest, and finally to beg him to forgive Zbyszko's offence.

The commander's face did not even twitch. He sat stiff and straight, with raised head, and looked at the talking Macko with his steely eyes as indifferently and, at the same time, as scornfully, as if he been looking at, not a knight, not even a human being, but a post in a fence. The Lord of Bogdaniec perceived this, and although his words did not cease to be courteous, his heart began to storm within. He spoke with ever greater constraint, and red spots appeared on his burning cheeks. It was obvious that, confronted with the German's cold pride, he was making a strong effort not to gnash his teeth and burst out in anger.

Powala saw this and, having a good heart, resolved to come to his aid. In his younger days at the Hungarian, Austrian, Burgundian, and Bohemian courts, when seeking the knightly adventures that would cover his name in glory, he had learned German, so now he spoke in that language to Macko in a conciliatory and intentionally light tone:

"You see, lord, that the noble commander regards the whole affair as not worth even a single word. Not only in our kingdom, but everywhere, young men are lacking in good sense, but a knight like him does not fight against children, either with the sword or with the law."

At that Lichtenstein blew out his sandy moustache and moved on, passing Macko and Zbyszko without a word.

Mad rage began to lift their hair beneath their helmets, and their hands trembled with eagerness to seize their swords.

"Wait, you Teutonic dog," said the older knight of Bogdaniec through set teeth; "now I will make a vow, and I will find you when you have ceased to be an envoy."

Powala, whose blood also began to boil, said:

"Do that afterwards. Now let the duchess speak for you, else it will go badly for the boy."

Then he rode after the Teutonic Knight, stopped him, and for some time talked animatedly with him. Both Macko and Zbyszko noticed that the German knight did not look at Powala with the same proud face as at them—and this made them even angrier than before. After a while Powala returned to them and, waiting a moment for the Teutonic Knight to move out of hearing range, said:

"I spoke for you, but the fellow is hopeless. He says he will make no complaint only if you do what he demands."

"What does he demand?"

"He said this: 'I shall stop to greet the Duchess of Mazovia. Let them,' he said, 'ride up, dismount, take off their helmets, and beg me from the ground with bare heads—then I will answer them.'"

Powala looked sharply at Zbyszko and added: "This is a hard thing to do for men of noble line—I understand. But I must warn you that if you do not do this, who knows what awaits you—maybe the executioner's sword."

Both the faces of Macko and Zbyszko seemed turned to stone. Silence fell again.

"Well?" asked Powala.

Zbyszko answered calmly and with such gravity that he might have grown twenty years older in that one moment:

"Well? The divine power is over men!"

"What do you mean?"

"Even if I had two heads and the executioner had to cut off both—I have only one honor. That honor I cannot disgrace."

Powala grew grave and, turning to Macko, asked him:

"And what do you say?"

"I say," replied Macko gloomily, "that I have brought up this boy

from childhood. Our family line depends on him too, because I am
old. But this he cannot do, even if he has to die."

Here his stern face began to quiver, and his love for his nephew
suddenly burst out in him with such strength that he took him in
his iron-clad arms and cried out:

"Zbyszko! Zbyszko!"

The young knight became quite astonished and, returning his
uncle's embrace, said:

"I did not know that you loved me so!"

"I see that you are true knights," said Powala, moved by the
scene before him. "And since the young man has promised on his
honor to come for judgment, I will not fetter him. People like you
can be trusted. And be of good cheer. The German will spend a day
or so at Tyniec, so I shall see the king first and will tell him of the
affair in such a way as to anger him as little as possible. It was
fortunate that I was able to break the lance—quite fortunate!"

But Zbyszko said:

"If I do have to lose my head, I wish at least I had had the
pleasure of breaking his Teutonic bones."

"It is amazing that you can defend your own honor, but do not
understand how you would bring shame on our whole nation!"
replied Powala impatiently.

"I do understand," said Zbyszko, "and this is why I regret—"

Powala turned to Macko:

"You know, sir, if this youth somehow succeeds in getting out of
trouble, you ought to put a hood over his head, as they do with
falcons. Otherwise, he will not die a natural death."

"He could get out of trouble, if you, sir, were willing to conceal
what has happened from the king."

"And what am I to do with the German? I cannot put a gag over
his mouth!"

"True! true! . . ."

Talking thus, they started towards the duchess's court. Powala's
attendants, who before had been mixed with Lichtenstein's people,
now rode behind them. From a distance, one could see among the
Mazovian caps the Teutonic Knight's peacock feathers waving in
the breeze, and his bright helmet shining in the sun.

"The nature of a Teutonic Knight is strange," reflected Powala
of Taczewo. "When things are not going well for a Teutonic

Knight, he will be as forebearing as a Franciscan friar, as humble as a lamb and as sweet as honey—so that you won't find anyone better in the world. But if he feels strong, no one will be more puffed up, and in no one will you find less mercy. One can see that the Lord Jesus has given them flints instead of hearts. I have observed various nations and frequently I have seen how a true knight will spare another who is weaker, saying to himself: 'I shall get no honor if I trample someone who is down.' But a Teutonic Knight becomes fiercer precisely at that moment. Hold onto him by the neck and do not let go—otherwise, woe to you! Look at that envoy! He demanded not only your apology but also your dishonor. I am glad that that will not happen."

"Never, never!" exclaimed Zbyszko.

"By the way, don't let him see any sign of worry on your part, for he will immediately rejoice."

They reached the procession and rejoined the duchess's court. Seeing them, the Teutonic envoy put on an expression of haughtiness and scorn, but they appeared not to notice him at all. Zbyszko rode at Danusia's side and began to tell her cheerfully that there would be a good view of Cracow from the top of the hill, while Macko told one of the minstrels of the extraordinary strength of the Lord of Taczewo, who had broken Zbyszko's lance with one hand as if it were a dry stalk.

"Why did he break it?" asked the minstrel.

"Because the boy had levelled it at the German, but only in fun."

The minstrel, who was a nobleman and a travelled man, did not think such a joke very appropriate, but seeing that Macko spoke lightly of the affair, he also did not take it to heart. Meanwhile their behavior began to annoy the German. He looked twice at Zbyszko and then at Macko. At last he understood that they were not going to dismount and were purposely taking no notice of him. Then something like steel glittered in his eyes—and he immediately began to take his leave.

At the moment, however, when he was moving off, the Lord of Taczewo could not contain himself and said to him at parting:

"Ride safely, valiant knight. The land is peaceful and no one will fall upon you, unless some playful boy."

"Although the customs in this land are strange, it was not

defence but your company which I sought," replied Lichtenstein. "I hope we shall meet again, here at the court, or elsewhere. . . ."

The last words sounded as if they contained a hidden threat, so Powala answered gravely:

"God will grant it."

And he bowed and turned away. Then he shrugged his shoulders and said in an undertone, but loud enough to be heard by those who were near:

"Weakling! I could lift you from your saddle on the point of my lance and hold you in the air for three paternosters."

And he began to talk with the duchess, whom he knew well. Anna Danuta asked him what he was doing on the highway, and he explained to her that he was riding by the king's command to maintain public safety in a district in which, because of the large number of guests converging to Cracow from all directions, some quarrel might easily arise. He gave, as an example, the incident he had just been a witness to. Thinking, however, that there would be plenty of time to ask for the duchess's intervention on Zbyszko's behalf when the need for it should arrive, he did not give the episode too great importance, not desiring to spoil the cheerful atmosphere. So the duchess even laughed at Zbyszko for being so eager to get his peacock crests, and others, hearing of the breaking of the lance, marvelled at the Lord of Taczewo, who could do it so easily with one hand.

The latter, being somewhat boastful, was pleased by this praise, and soon began to tell of the deeds which had made his name famous, particularly in Burgundy at the court of Philip the Bold. Once, at a tournament there, after his lance broke, he took a certain Ardennes knight by the waist, dragged him from his saddle, and threw him a lance-length in the air, though the man was all clad in iron. Philip the Bold gave him a golden chain for that, and the duchess her velvet slipper, which he wore afterwards on his helmet.

Hearing that, everyone was greatly amazed, with the exception of Nicholas of Longwood, who said:

"There are no such men in these present effeminate times as there were in my youth, and none such as my father told me of. If a nobleman now can tear open a cuirass, or draw a crossbow without the crank, or twist an iron chopper between his fingers, he calls himself a strong man and boasts that he is superior to others. But in days of yore even girls used to do these things."

"I do not deny that men used to be stronger," answered Powala, "but stout fellows are to be found even today. The Lord Jesus was not sparing of the strength He gave my bones, and yet I do not call myself the strongest in the kingdom. Did you ever see Zawisza of Garbowo? He could overpower me."

"I have seen him. His shoulders are as broad as the beam of the Cracow bell."

"And what about Dobko of Olesnica? Once at a tournament held by the Teutonic Knights at Torun, he overthrew twelve knights, to the great glory of himself and our nation."

"But our Mazovian, Staszko Ciolek, was stronger, my lord, than you or Zawisza or Dobko. They say that he took in his hand a newly-made stake and squeezed the sap out of it."

"I, too, can squeeze out sap!" exclaimed Zbyszko.

And before anyone asked him to prove it, he spurred his horse to the side of the road, plucked a thick branch from a tree and then squeezed the end of it before the eyes of the duchess and Danusia so strongly that the sap really began to drip onto the road.

"O Jesus!" exclaimed Ofka of Jarzabkowo at the sight; "don't go to war, for it would be a pity for such a man to die before marrying."

"It would be a pity!" repeated Macko, growing suddenly dejected.

But Nicholas of Longwood began to laugh, and the duchess with him. The others loudly praised the strength of Zbyszko, for in those days an iron hand was valued above all else. The girls called to Danusia: "Be glad!" And she was glad, although she did not well understand what she might get from that crushed piece of wood. Zbyszko, completely forgetting the Teutonic Knight, looked so superior that Nicholas of Longwood, desiring to bring him back to earth, said:

"You would boast of your strength in vain, for there are better men than you. I myself did not see him, but my father witnessed something better, which happened at the court of Charles, the Roman Emperor. Our King Kazimierz went to visit him with many courtiers, among whom there was that knight I spoke of—the one renowned for his strength, Staszko Ciolek, son of Viovode Andrew.

The emperor began to boast that among his people he had a certain Czech who could seize a bear by the middle and strangle him on the spot. They arranged a spectacle, and the Czech strangled two bears, one after the other. Our king was very concerned by this, fearing that he would have to go away disgraced, so he said: 'My Ciolek will not let himself be shamed.' A day was set for them to wrestle. Many ladies and important knights came to see the match, and three days later the Czech and Ciolek faced each other in the castle yard. But the match did not last long. Scarcely had they taken hold of each other when Ciolek broke the Czech's back, crushed all his ribs, and only let him go when he was dead, to the great praise of the king. From that time he was called Bone-breaker. Once, all by himself, he carried an enormous bell up to a tower, though twenty townsmen could not move it from its place."

"How old was he?" asked Zbyszko.

"He was young!"

Meanwhile Powala of Taczewo, riding on the duchess's right, bent towards her ear and finally told her the whole truth about the seriousness of what had happened. At the same time, he begged her to support him when he should intervene on behalf of Zbyszko, who might have to pay dearly for his action. The duchess, who liked Zbyszko, received the news with sorrow and became very upset.

"The Bishop of Cracow is always glad to see me," said Powala. "I may entreat him, and the queen too, for the more people there are who speak on his behalf, the better it will be for the rash youth."

"If the queen were to take his part, no hair would fall from his head," said Anna Danuta. "The king honors her greatly for her holiness and for her dowry, and particularly now, when the shame of barrenness is taken from her. But there is also a beloved sister of the king at Cracow, Duke Ziemowit's wife. Go to her too. I will do what I can, but she is his sister and I only his cousin."

"The king loves you too, gracious lady."

"Ah, but not so much," the duchess answered with a certain sorrow. "For me a small link, for her a whole chain; for me a fox-skin, for her a sable. The king loves none of his brothers and sisters as he loves Alexandra. There is never a day that she goes away with empty hands."

Amid this talk, they approached Cracow. The highway, which had been swarming with people all the way from Tyniec, now swarmed still more. They passed landowners travelling to the city at the head of retinues of servants. Some were in arms, some in summer garments and straw hats; some rode on horseback, some sat in carriages with their wives and daughters, who were eager to see the long-proclaimed tournaments. In places the whole road was blocked by merchants' wagons, which were forbidden to bypass Cracow, and so defraud the town of numerous dues. These wagons carried salt, wax, grain, fish, hides, hemp, and wood. Others were coming from the town laden with cloth, barrels of beer, and various urban goods. Cracow could now be clearly seen: the gardens belonging to the king, the lords, and the townsfolk, surrounding the city, and behind them the walls and church towers. The nearer they came, the greater was the congestion, and at the gates it was difficult to make way through the traffic at all.

"Now this is a city!" said Macko. "There's none other like it in all the world."

"It's always like a fair," replied a fat minstrel. "Has it been long since you were here, sir?"

"Long. And I am as amazed as if I were seeing it for the first time, for we are coming from a primitive region."

"They say that Cracow has grown tremendously under King Jagiello."

This was true. Since the Grand Duke of Lithuania mounted the throne, the immeasurable lands of Lithuania and Ruthenia had been thrown open to Cracow trade, in consequence of which the town had grown from day to day in population, in wealth, and in buildings—and had become one of the most important in the world.

"The cities of the Teutonic Knights are also fine," continued the corpulent minstrel.

"If one could get to them, the booty would be plentiful," answered Macko.

But Powala was thinking of something else, namely, that the young Zbyszko, whose offence was due only to foolish impetuosity, was going into the wolf's mouth. The Lord of Taczewo, stern and obstinate as he was in time of war, had, nevertheless, in his power-

ful breast the true heart of a dove. He knew better than others the
fate awaiting the guilty youth, and so he had pity for him.

"I have been thinking and thinking," he said now to the duchess, "whether to tell the king what has happened or not. If the
Teutonic Knight does not complain, then there will be no trouble,
but if he is going to complain it may be better to tell everything
first, so that the king may not blow up in anger."

"If a Teutonic Knight has the power to ruin anyone, he will ruin
him," replied the duchess. "But I will tell the young man to attach
himself to our court. Perhaps the king will not punish a courtier of
ours so severely."

She called Zbyszko, who, when he heard what was proposed,
leapt from his horse, embraced her knees, and agreed with the
greatest joy to be her courtier, not only for greater safety, but
because he might in this way remain near Danusia.

Meanwhile Powala asked Macko: "Where are you going to stay?"

"At an inn."

"There has been no room in the inns for quite some time."

"Then we will go to a merchant we know—Amylej. Perhaps he
will put us up for the night."

"I will tell you what: come to my house. Your nephew could stay
in the castle with the duchess's court, but it would be better for him
not to be nearby the king. The king, if he gets angry, might act
without thinking; given time, he might cool down. No doubt you
will divide your wealth, wagons, and servants, and for that you
need time. Both of you will be comfortable and safe with me—I
assure you!"

Although somewhat disquieted that Powala took such thought
for their safety, Macko thanked him warmly, and they entered the
city. Here he and Zbyszko forgot their anxieties for a while at the
sight of the marvels which surrounded them. In Lithuania and on
the border they had seen only single castles and, of more important
towns, only Wilno—ill-built and burnt, all of it in ashes and
ruins—but here the merchants' houses were frequently more imposing than the castle of the grand duke over there. Many houses,
it is true, were built of wood, but even these surprised them by the
height of their walls and roofs and by their windows with glass
panes framed in lead, which reflected the rays of the setting sun in
such a way that one might think a fire blazed inside. In the streets

nearer to the marketplace there were, however, nothing but houses of red brick or solid stone, tall, ornamented along the walls with oriels and black cross-patterns. These houses stood side by side like soldiers in the ranks, some broad, others perhaps only nine cubits wide, but shooting upwards, with vaulted porches and often a crucifix or a picture of the Most Holy Virgin over the front door. There were streets in which one might see two rows of buildings and a strip of sky above; and down below, a roadway entirely paved with stones; and on both sides, as far as the eye could see, shops and shops—rich, full of gorgeous, mostly unknown wares, at which Macko, accustomed as he was to constant warfare and the taking of booty, looked at with a somewhat greedy eye. But Macko and Zbyszko were still more amazed by the public buildings: the Church of Our Lady on the marketplace, the Cloth Hall, the Town Hall with its huge cellar in which Swidnice beer and gin were sold, as well as other churches, and cloth shops, and the enormous *mercatorium* intended for foreign merchants, and the building where the municipal weights and scales were locked up, and the hairdresser shops, baths, bronze foundries, wax-melting establishments, goldsmiths and silversmiths, breweries, and the whole mountains of barrels around the so-called *Schrotamt*—in a word, such wealth and riches as a man who was unfamiliar with the city could not imagine, even if he were the rich owner of a "little castle."

Powala took Macko and Zbyszko to his own house on St. Anne's Street, gave them a spacious room, and recommended them to the care of his esquires, while he himself went to the castle, from which he returned for supper quite late at night. With him arrived some of his friends, and partaking abundantly of wine and meat, they feasted merrily, though their host remained somewhat anxious. When the guests finally went home, Powala said to Macko:

"I spoke to one of the canons, practised in writing and in the law, who tells me that insulting an envoy is a crime punishable by death. So pray to God that the Teutonic Knight does not bring forth a complaint."

So both knights, although they had somewhat exceeded the measure at the feast, retired with less cheerful hearts.

Macko could not even sleep, and after some time, when they had already lain down to bed, he called to his nephew:

"Zbyszko!"

"Yes?"

"After thinking everything over, I believe that they will cut off your head."

"Do you?" asked Zbyszko in a sleepy voice. And turning to the wall, he fell soundly asleep, for he was immensely tired. . . .

CHAPTER V

THE next day the two knights of Bogdaniec, together with Powala, went to early Mass at the cathedral, both for the sake of the service and to see the court and the guests who were coming to the castle. On the way there, Powala met a number of acquaintances, among them many knights famous at home and abroad, at whom the young Zbyszko looked with admiration, promising himself that if the affair with Lichtenstein went off all right, he would strive to equal them in valor and in all other virtues. One of these knights, Toporczyk, a kinsman of the Castellan of Cracow, told them the news of the return from Rome of Wojciech Jastrzebiec, the scholastic, who had gone to Pope Boniface IX with a letter from the king inviting him to the christening at Cracow. Boniface accepted the invitation, although he expressed doubt whether he could come in person. He therefore empowered an envoy to hold the newborn child in his name at the christening and, moreover, requested that, in token of his special love for both the king and the queen, the child should be given the name of Boniface or Bonifacia, depending on its sex.

They spoke also of the approaching arrival of the King of Hungary, Sigismund. He was expected for certain, for he always came, invited or not, to every occasion where the opportunity existed for visits, feasts, and tournaments, in which he loved to take part, desiring to shine before the world as a ruler, as a singer, and as a premier knight. Powala, Zawisza of Garbowo, Dobko of Olesnica, Naszan, and other men of like measure cheerfully reminded one another how, the last time Sigismund had been present, King Wladyslaw had secretly begged them not to press too hard upon him in the tourney, and to spare the "Hungarian guest," whose well-known vanity was so great that tears used to flow from his eyes if he had ill-success. But the greatest curiosity was raised among the knights by the affairs of Witold. Marvelous things were related about the splendor of the cradle, cast out of pure silver, which the Lithuanian dukes and boyars were bringing as a gift from Witold and his wife Anna. Groups of people gathered, as usual before divine service, telling one another the latest news. In one of them Macko, hearing talk of the cradle, began to describe the costliness of the gift, but he told still more about the huge expedition planned by Witold against the Tartars, about which he was overwhelmed with questions. The preparations for it were almost complete; huge armies were already moving to the east of White Ruthenia. If the expedition succeeded, it would extend the sovereignty of King Jagiello over almost half the world, to the unknown plains of Asia, to the borders of Persia and the coasts of the Aral Sea. Macko, who once had been near to the person of Witold and therefore knew his designs, described them with such detail and even eloquence that, before the bells rang for Mass, a circle of curious listeners had gathered around him at the foot of the cathedral steps. "At issue is a crusade," he said. "Witold, although he is called grand duke, rules Lithuania under Jagiello, and is just a viceroy, so the merit would fall on the king. And what glory it would be for newly-baptized Lithuania and for the power of Poland if their united armies bore the standard of the Cross to lands where, if they mention the name of the Redeemer at all, it is only to blaspheme Him, and where the foot of neither Pole and Lithuanian has ever been set! When the Polish and Lithuanian armies will put him on the Tartar throne again, the exiled Tochtamysz will acknowledge himself as 'son' of King Jagiello, and as he has promised, he will bow before the Cross together with the whole of the Golden Horde."

They listened to these words with close attention, but many did not know what it was all about, whom Witold was to help, or against whom he was to fight—so some of them asked:

"Tell us clearly against whom the war will be?"

"Against whom? Against Timur the Lame," replied Macko.

A moment of silence followed. The Western knights had, it is true, repeatedly heard the name of the Golden, Blue, and Azo hordes and various others, but Tartar affairs and the civil wars between particular hordes were not well known to them. On the other hand, you would not have found a single man in Europe in those days who had not heard of the terrible Timur the Lame, or Tamerlaine the Great, whose name was mentioned with as much dread as formerly that of Attila. He was "lord of the world" and "lord of ages"—ruler of twenty-seven conquered countries, ruler of Muscovite Russia, ruler of Siberia, of China up to the border of India, of Baghdad, Ispahan, Aleppo, and Damascus—whose shadow fell across the sands of Arabia onto Egypt and across the Bosphorus onto the Greek Empire—the exterminator of the human race, a monstrous builder of pyramids made of human skulls, the victor in all his battles, unconquered in any, "the lord of souls and bodies."

Tochtamysz had been placed by him on the throne of the Golden and the Blue hordes, and recognized by him as his "son." But when his rule had come to extend from the Urals to the Crimea, over more lands than existed in the rest of Europe, the "son" desired to be an independent ruler. For this he was deprived of his throne by "one finger" of his terrible father, and he escaped to the Lithuanian viceroy, whom he begged for help. It was he whom Witold proposed to bring back to his kingdom, but in order to do that it was necessary first to measure forces with the lame Timur, the ruler of the world.

Accordingly, his name made a strong impression on the listeners, and after a moment of silence one of the oldest knights, Wojciech of Jaglowo, said:

"It is no small person with whom you propose to deal."

"But it is over a small matter," remarked Nicholas of Longwood prudently. "For what is it to us whether Tochtamysz or some Tartar rules over the sons of Belial far away in the tenth kingdom?"

"Tochtamysz would receive the Christian faith," answered Macko.

"He might receive it, or he might not. Can we believe these curs who do not acknowledge Christ?"

"But it is fitting to die for the name of Christ," replied Powala.

"And for one's knightly honor," added Toporczyk, kinsman of the castellan. "There are some among us who are going. Lord

Spytko of Melsztyn has a young and beloved wife, yet he has gone to Duke Witold."

"It's not to be wondered at," remarked Jasko of Naszan. "Though you have the most ignoble sin on your conscience, your pardon after such a war is certain, and so is your redemption."

"And fame for ever and ever," said Powala. "War is war, and if it is with an important person, all the better. Timur has conquered the world and has twenty-seven kingdoms under him. Our nation would be bathed in glory if we were to wipe him out."

"Why not?" said Toporczyk. "Though he possessed a hundred kingdoms, others may fear him, but not we! You speak well! If we collect only ten thousand good lancers, we can go through the world."

"And what nation is to defeat the Lame One, if not ours?"

Thus the knights talked with one another, and Zbyszko was surprised that he had never before felt the desire to go with Witold into the wild steppes. But during his stay at Wilno he had wanted to see Cracow and the court, and to take part in the tournaments of knights; whereas now he thought that here he could find disgrace and judgment, and there—in the worst case—a glorious death.

But the centenarian Wojciech of Jaglowo, whose neck trembled with age, but whose understanding corresponded to his years, threw cold water on the eagerness of the knights.

"You are fools," he said. "Has none of you heard that the figure of Christ has spoken to the queen, and if the Redeemer himself admits her to such intimacy, why should the Holy Ghost, who is the third person of the Trinity, be less gracious to her? Because of this, she sees future events as if they were happening before her very eyes, and she said that—"

Here he stopped and shook his head for a moment, and then said:

"I have forgotten what she said, but I shall remember in a moment."

And he began to think, while they waited with eager attention, for the belief was widespread that the queen foresaw the future.

"Aha!" he said at last, "now I know! The queen said that if all our knights were to go with Duke Witold against the Lame One, the pagan power would be crushed. But that cannot be, because of the rancor amongst the Christian lords. The borders have to be guarded against the Czechs, against the Hungarians, against the Order—for no one can be trusted. And if only a handful of Poles goes with Witold, he will be defeated by Timur the Lame or his voivodes, who lead innumerable hosts."

"But now there is peace," declared Toporczyk, "and the Order itself is said to be giving help of some kind to Witold. The Teutonic Knights can hardly do otherwise, or they'll face disgrace. They have to show the Holy Father that they are ready to fight against pagans. The courtiers even say that Kuno Lichtenstein is staying here not only for the christening but also to take counsel with the king. . . ."

"And here he is!" exclaimed Macko in surprise.

"True!" said Powala, looking around. "It is indeed he! He stayed but a short time with the abbot and must have left Tyniec at dawn."

"He seems to have been in a great hurry," said Macko glumly.

Meanwhile Kuno Lichtenstein passed near them. Macko recognized him by the cross embroidered on his cloak, but the German recognized neither him nor Zbyszko, since he had seen them previously in their helmets, and under a helmet, even if the visor was open, only a small part of a knight's face was visible. As he passed he nodded to Powala of Taczewo and to Toporczyk, after which he went gravely and majestically up the steps to the cathedral, followed by his esquires.

All of a sudden the bells rang out, disturbing a flock of jackdaws and pigeons nesting in the towers while announcing that Mass would shortly begin. Macko and Zbyszko went into the church with the others, somewhat troubled by the swift return of Lichtenstein. But the older knight was more troubled, for Zbyszko's attention became entirely taken up by the royal court. Zbyszko had never in his life seen anything so splendid as that church and that gathering. To the right and the left of him he had the most distinguished men in the kingdom, famous in council or in fight. Many whose intelligence had brought about the marriage of the Grand Duke of Lithuania with the young and beautiful Queen of Poland had already died, but some were left and were looked on with unusual respect. The young knight could not look enough at the wonderful figure of Jasko of Teczyn, castellan of Cracow, in which astuteness was united with gravity and righteousness; he admired the wise and dignified faces of the other town councillors,

and the powerful countenances of the knights, with their hair cut
straight over their eyebrows and hanging in long locks at the sides
and back of the head. Some wore nets over their heads, others only
bands to keep their hair in order. The foreign guests, the envoys of
the kings of Rome, Bohemia, Hungary, and Austria, with their
attendants, caused amazement by the magnificent elegance of their
costumes; the Lithuanian dukes and boyars, standing beside the
king, wore for the occasion imposing cloaks lined with costly fur,
despite the summer and the hot weather; the Ruthenian dukes, in
stiff, wide garments, looked like Byzantine pictures against the
background of church walls and gilding. But Zbyszko waited with
the greatest curiosity for the entrance of the king and queen, and
pushed as far as he could towards the stalls, beyond which, near the
altar, two red velvet cushions were to be seen, for the royal pair
always heard Mass on their knees. He did not have to wait long:
the king entered first, emerging through the sacristy door, and
before he reached the altar it was possible to get a good look at him.
He had long black hair, ruffled and thinning somewhat over his
forehead and pushed back over his ears at the sides; his face was
dark and clean-shaven, his nose aquiline and pointed; there were
wrinkles around his mouth, and his small, black, flashing eyes
threw rapid glances in all directions, as if he wanted to count all
the people in the church before he reached the altar. His countenance had a good-natured and sensitive expression—that of a man
who, having been raised by fortune to heights above his own
expectations, had constantly to think whether his actions corresponded with his dignity, and who was afraid of malicious criti-
cism. But for that very reason there was a certain impatience in his
face and movements. It was easy to guess that his anger must be
sudden and terrible, and that he still was the same duke who in his
time, impatient of the scheming tactics of the Teutonic Knights,
called out to their envoys: "You come to me with parchment, but
I to you with spear!"

But now his innate impetuosity was restrained by a great and
sincere piety. Not only were the newly-converted Lithuanian dukes
edified at the sight of the king in church, but also the Polish
magnates whose fathers and grandfathers had been Christians.
Frequently he threw aside the cushion and, for greater penance,
knelt on the bare stones; frequently he lifted his hands and held

them up until they fell through sheer weariness. He heard at least three Masses daily, and heard them most often with eagerness. The uncovering of the chalice and the sound of the Sanctus bell always filled his heart with excitement, joy and fear. After Mass he would emerge from church as if awakened from sleep, calm and gentle; and the courtiers had learned early on that that was the best time to beg him either for forgiveness or for gifts.

Jadwiga entered through the sacristy door. When they saw her, the knights nearer to the stalls, although Mass had not yet begun, immediately knelt down, involuntarily paying her the homage of a saint. Zbyszko did the same, for in the whole of that gathering no one doubted that she was a real saint, whose pictures would in the course of time adorn church altars. Particularly for the last few years the stern, penitent life of Jadwiga had caused her to receive almost religious honors in addition to the homage due a queen. Stories passed from mouth to mouth among the lords and the populace of the miracles she had performed. It was said that the touch of her hand healed the sick, that people who had lost the use of their arms and legs recovered it after putting on old garments which had belonged to her. Reliable witnesses asserted that they had heard with their own ears how once Christ had spoken to her from the altar. Foreign monarchs honored her on their knees, and even the proud Teutonic Order honored her and feared to offend her. Pope Boniface IX called her the holy and elect daughter of the Church. The world looked at her actions and remembered that this child of the house of Anjou and of the Polish Piasts, this daughter of the powerful Louis, brought up at the most splendid court, and this most beautiful of maidens on the earth, had renounced happiness, had renounced her first maiden love and had married, as queen, the "wild" Duke of Lithuania in order to bring with him to the foot of the Cross the last pagan nation in Europe. What the strength of all the Germans had not accomplished, nor the power of the Order, nor the crusades, nor a sea of blood—had been accomplished by one word from her. Never had the glory of apostleship radiated from a younger and more beautiful brow; never had apostleship been united with such devotion; never had feminine beauty been illuminated by such angelic goodness and such silent sorrow.

She was also celebrated by minstrels at all the courts of Europe;

knights came to Cracow from the most distant lands to see the Polish queen; she was loved by her own nation as the apple of its eye, for by her union with Jagiello she had increased its power and glory. Only one grave anxiety lay upon her and upon the nation— for long years God had denied issue to her, His elect.

But now that this misfortune had finally passed, the joyful news of the desired blessing spread like lightning from the Baltic to the Black Sea and the Carpathian Mountains, and filled all the peoples of the enormous kingdom with good cheer. Except at the capital of the Teutonic Knights, the news was received with joy even in foreign courts. At Rome the *Te Deum* was sung. In the Polish lands the opinion took firm root that whatever the "blessed lady" asked of God would certainly be granted.

So people came to ask her to pray for their health; envoys came from the various provinces and districts asking her, according to their needs, to pray for rain, or fine weather for the harvest, or satisfactory hay-making, or a prosperous honey-flow; for an abundance of fish in the lakes and for game in the forests. Threatening knights from the border castles and forts, who, by a custom adopted from the Germans, occupied themselves with robbery or war among themselves, at a word from her sheathed their swords, let go their captives without ransom, returned the flocks and herds which they had driven off, and gave each other their hands in mutual agreement. Every misfortune, every kind of poverty pressed to the gates of Wawel Castle. Jadwiga's pure spirit penetrated to the hearts of men, softened the fate of captives, the pride of lords, the sternness of judges—and hung like the dawn of happiness, like an angel of justice and peace, over the whole land.

Accordingly, everyone awaited with heartfelt anticipation the day of benediction.

The knights looked eagerly at the figure of the queen, to judge from her appearance how long they would have to wait for a future heir or a future heiress to the throne. Wysz, the Bishop of Cracow, who was the most skilled physician in the country, and famous even abroad, did not yet foretell a speedy delivery, and if preparations were made it was because the custom of the age was to begin all festivities as early as possible and prolong them for many weeks. The figure of the lady, though somewhat advanced, preserved its slender line. Her clothing was simple to the extreme. Formerly—

brought up as she had been at a splendid court, and being the most beautiful of all the princesses of her time—she had loved costly textiles, chains, pearls, gold bracelets and rings, but now, for some years, she had not only worn the garments of a nun but had even veiled her face in fear lest the thought of her own beauty might arouse in her worldly pride. In vain Jagiello, when he learned of her pregnancy, instructed in his joyous excitement her bed adorned with cloth-of-gold and jewels. She told him that the moment of childbirth was very often the moment of death, and therefore she ought to receive the favor God was granting her, not in the midst of jewels, but in silent humility.

And so the gold and jewels went to the University of Cracow and to pay the expenses of newly baptized Lithuanian youths at foreign schools.

The queen agreed to alter her nun's attire only in so far that, when the hope of maternity had become a complete certainty, she ceased to veil her face, considering very properly that the dress of a penitent was not suitable at such a time.

All eyes now rested with affection on that beautiful face, which could not be further embellished with gold or precious stones. The queen passed slowly from the sacristy door to the altar, her eyes cast upwards, in one hand a book, in the other a rosary. Zbyszko looked at her lily face, her blue eyes, and her truly angelic features, full of peace, goodness, and charity, and his heart began to beat like a hammer. He knew that by divine command he ought to love both his king and queen, and he did love them after his own fashion. But now his heart suddenly boiled over with that great affection which arises, not by command, but of itself like a flame, and consists at one and the same time of a feeling of the highest honor, humility and self-sacrifice. Zbyszko was young and impetuous, so he was immediately possessed by the desire to display the love and faith of a subject-knight, to do something for her, to rush off somewhere, to cut up someone, to win something, and to risk his neck in doing so. "I should go with Duke Witold," he said to himself, "for how shall I serve the holy lady, if there is no war nearby?" It never even came to his head that he could serve her other than with sword or lance or axe; instead, he was ready to strike alone against the whole might of Timur the Lame. He wanted immediately after Mass to mount his horse and begin some

undertaking. What undertaking?—he did not know. He knew only
that he could not restrain himself, that his hands were itching and
his whole heart was aflame.

Once again he entirely forgot the danger threatening him. He
even momentarily forgot about Danusia—and when she came into
his mind because of the young voices which suddenly began to sing
in the church, he had a feeling that "that was something different."
He had sworn faith to Danusia, he had promised her three Germans, and he would keep his word; but the queen was above all
women—and when he thought about the number of the enemy he
would like to kill for the queen, he pictured whole armies of
coats-of-mail, helmets, ostrich and peacock feathers, and felt that
even that would be too little to satisfy him.

Meanwhile he did not take his eyes off Jadwiga for a moment,
pondering in his loving heart with what prayer he might honor her,
for he thought that one could not pray for the queen just anyhow.
He knew how to say, *"Pater noster, qui es in coelis, sanctificetur
nomen Tuum,"* for that he had learned from a certain Franciscan
friar at Wilno. But whether it was that the friar himself did not
know any more or that Zbyszko had forgotten the rest, in any case
he could not repeat the whole of the Lord's Prayer. Now, however,
he began to repeat those few words over and over again, and in his
heart they meant: "Give our beloved lady health and life and
happiness, and care for her before all else." And since these were
the thoughts of a man over whose own head judgment and punishment were hanging, there was no more sincere prayer in the whole
church.

At the end of Mass, Zbyszko thought that if he might only stand
before the queen, fall on his face before her and embrace her feet,
then the world could end and it wouldn't matter. But after the first
Mass there followed a second, and then a third, and after that the
lady went to her apartments, for she usually fasted until midday
and purposely took no part in the merry breakfast, at which jesters
and jugglers amused the king and his guests. However, the old
knight of Longwood came to Zbyszko and called him to the
duchess.

"At breakfast you will wait upon me and Danusia as my courtier," said the duchess, "and it would be well if you could entertain
the king with some witticism or some deed that might win his

heart. The Teutonic Knight, if he recognizes you, will not be able to make his complaint when he sees you serving me at the royal table."

Zbyszko kissed the duchess's hand. Then he turned to Danusia, and though he was accustomed more to war and battles than to court customs, it was yet evident that he knew what a knight ought to do when he sees the lady of his thoughts in the morning, for he stepped back and, assuming an expression of amazement, exclaimed, crossing himself: "In the name of the Father and of the Son and of the Holy Ghost!"

Raising her blue eyes to his, Danusia asked:

"Why do you cross yourself, Zbyszko, when Mass is already over?"

"Because during the last night, fair lady, your beauty has so increased that I am astonished."

But Nicholas of Longwood, being an old man and not liking these modern, foreign knightly customs, shrugged his shoulders and said:

"Why do you waste your time talking about her charms? She's only a little chick, just barely hatched."

Zbyszko shot a fierce glance at him:

"Beware to call her a little chick," he said, paling with wrath; "and know that if you were younger I would immediately have the ground behind this castle trodden smooth and we would fight till your death or mine!"

"Silence, boy! I could deal with you even at my age."

"Silence!" repeated the duchess. "Instead of thinking of your own head, will you look for more quarrels? It would have been better to have a more serious knight for Danusia. But I tell you that if you want to get angry, you may go and do it elsewhere; here such men are not wanted."

Zbyszko was ashamed at the duchess's words and began to beg her pardon. At the same time he thought that if Lord Nicholas of Longwood had a grown-up son he would some day challenge him to fight on foot or on horseback, for he would not overlook that "little chick" remark. Meanwhile, however, he determined to be as quiet as a mouse in the royal apartments and not challenge anybody, unless his knightly honor made it absolutely necessary.

A blare of trumpets announced that breakfast was ready, so

Duchess Anna, taking Danusia by the hand, went into the royal apartment, in front of which the worldly dignitaries and knights stood waiting for her. Duke Ziemowit's wife had gone in first, since, as the king's own sister, she took a higher place at the table. The room was soon swarming with foreign guests and the local dignitaries and knights who had been invited. The king sat at the higher end of the table with the Bishop of Cracow and Wojciech Jastrzebiec, who, although lower in rank than the prelates, sat on the king's right because he was a papal envoy. The two duchesses occupied the next places. Beyond Anna Danuta the former Archbishop of Gniezno, Jan, sprawled at his ease in a wide chair; he was a descendent of the Silesian Piasts and the son of Bolko III, Duke of Opole. Zbyszko had heard of him at the court of Witold, and now, standing behind the duchess and Danusia, he recognized him immediately by his unusually thick hair, which was wound in curls and made his head look like a holy-water sprinkler. He was therefore nicknamed Sprinkler at the courts of the Polish dukes, and even the Teutonic Knights used the same Polish nickname. He was famed for his merriment and his wayward values. Having received the pallium as Archbishop of Gniezno contrary to the king's will, he wanted to occupy his diocese by force; when he was deprived of his dignity for this and driven out, he joined the Teutonic Knights, who gave him the poor bishopric of Kamieniec in Pomerania. Then, finally understanding that it is better to be on good terms with a powerful king, he begged his pardon, returned to the country and waited until some archbishop's throne should become vacant, hoping that he would receive it from the hands of his good-natured lord. He was not to be disappointed in the future. But in the meantime he endeavored to win the king's heart by his witty remarks. However, he kept his old hankering for the Teutonic Knights. Even now, at the court of Jagiello—to the annoyance of the dignitaries and the knighthood—he sought the company of Lichtenstein and gladly sat beside him at the table.

Zbyszko, standing behind the duchess's chair, found himself so near the Teutonic Knight that he might have touched him with his hand. Indeed, his fingers began at once to itch and cramp, but involuntarily, and he restrained his impetuosity and did not permit himself a wicked thought. None the less, he could not refrain from throwing somewhat greedy glances from time to time at Lichtenstein's sandy head, which was growing rather bald at the back, and at his neck and shoulders and arms, to see whether he would have much trouble with him if he should ever meet him in the future, either in battle or in single combat. It seemed to him that he would not have too much difficulty, for though the Teutonic Knight's shoulder-blades were outlined powerfully enough under a tight-fitting garment of thin grey cloth, he was, nevertheless, a weakling in comparison with Powala, Paszko the Thief of Biskupice, the two famous Sulimczyks, Krzon of Goat's Head and many other knights who were sitting at the royal table.

Zbyszko looked at these knights with amazement and envy, but his main attention was given to the king himself, who, casting his eyes in all directions, pushed his hair behind his ears at every moment, as if impatient that breakfast had not yet begun. His glance rested for a split second on Zbyszko, and then the young knight experienced a feeling of fear, and at the thought that he would certainly have to stand before the angry face of the king, he was overcome with fierce anxiety. For the first time he really thought of the account he would have to give and the punishment that might await him, which until now had seemed far off and indistinct, and therefore not worth concern.

But the German had no idea that the knight who had attacked him so audaciously on the highway was now so near to him. Breakfast began. Wine soup was brought in, so strongly flavored with eggs, cinnamon, cloves, ginger, and saffron that the whole room became filled with the aroma. At the same time the jester Ciaruszek, sitting in the doorway on a three-legged stool began to imitate the song of the nightingale, which apparently cheered the king. Another jester then went around the table with the servants carrying the food, approached each guest unobserved and imitated the nearby buzzing of a bee so well that one and another laid down his spoon and began to pass his hand through his hair. At this sight everyone else burst out laughing. Zbyszko was attentively serving the duchess and Danusia, but when Lichtenstein in his turn began to pat his baldish head, he forgot his danger and laughed until tears came to his eyes, and the young Lithuanian Duke Jamont, son of the Governor of Smolensk, who was standing near him, helped him along in this so sincerely that he dropped food from the dishes.

The Teutonic Knight, finally realizing his mistake, reached for his purse, and turning to Bishop Sprinkler, spoke a few words to him in German, which the bishop immediately repeated in Polish.

"The noble lord says this to you," he said, turning to the fool: "'You will get two coins, but do not buzz too near, for bees get driven away and drones get killed.'"

The jester put away the two coins which the Teutonic Knight had given him and availing himself of the privileged freedom which fools enjoyed at all courts, he answered:

"There is much honey in the Land of Dobrzyn, and that is why the drones have occupied it. Kill them, King Jagiello!"

"There you have a grosz from me too, for you have spoken well," said Sprinkler; "only remember that if the ladder gives way, the beekeeper breaks his neck. Those Malbork drones which have occupied Dobrzyn have stings, and it is dangerous to climb up to their hives."

"Bah!" exclaimed Zyndram of Maszkowice, sword-bearer of Cracow; "one may smoke them out!"

"With what?"

"With powder!"

"Or split open the hive with an axe!" said the huge Paszko the Thief of Biskupice.

Zbyszko's heart swelled, for he thought that such words must promise war. But Kuno Lichtenstein, who had been long at Torun and Chelmno, and had learned Polish, but did not use it because of his arrogance, understood them too. Now, irritated by Zyndram's words, he turned his grey eyes to him and said:

"We shall see."

"Our fathers have seen at Plowce, and we have seen at Wilno," replied Zyndram.

"*Pax vobiscum!*" exclaimed Sprinkler. "*Pax, pax!* Just let Father Nicholas of Kurowo resign the bishopric of Kuyavia and the gracious king appoint me in his place, and I will preach to you such a beautiful sermon on love between Christian nations that it will transform you completely. For what is hatred, if not *ignis*, and what is more, *ignis infernalis*, a fire so fierce that water cannot put it out—only wine can extinguish it. Bring wine, there! Let us go to the land of Hops, as the late Bishop Zawisza of Kurozwek used to say."

"And from Hops to hell, as the devil said," added the jester Ciaruszek.

"May he carry you off!"

"It will be a miracle if he carries you off. Nobody has ever seen a devil with a Sprinkler; but I think we shall have that pleasure soon."

"First I will sprinkle you. Bring wine, and long live love between Christians!"

"Between real Christians," repeated Kuno Lichtenstein with emphasis.

"What?" exclaimed the Bishop of Cracow, Wysz, raising his head. "Are you not in an ancient Christian kingdom? Are the churches here not older than at Malbork?"

"I don't know," replied the Teutonic Knight.

The king was particularly sensitive when Christianity was in question. It seemed to him that the Teutonic Knight wanted to annoy him, and so his protruding cheeks were immediately covered with red spots and his eyes began to flash.

"What!" he exclaimed in a deep voice. "Am I not a Christian king? What!"

"The kingdom calls itself Christian," replied the Teutonic Knight coldly, "but its customs are pagan."

At this, ominous knights sprang up: Martin of Wrocimowice, whose escutcheon was a half-goat, Florian of Korytnica, Bartosz of Wodzinko, Domarat of Kobylany, Powala of Taczewo, Paszko the Thief of Biskupice, Zyndram of Maszkowice, Lis of Fair-Ground, Krzon of Goat's Head, Sigismund of Bobowa, and Staszko of Charbimowice—powerful, famous, victors in many battles and in many tournaments, burning with rage, or pale, or gnashing their teeth; and they began to shout one after another:

"Woe to us! for he is a guest and cannot be challenged!"

Zawisza the Black, the most famous of all the famous, the model of knighthood, turned his wrinkled brow to Lichtenstein and said:

"I do not understand you, Kuno. How can you, being a knight, call shame upon a splendid nation, when you know that as an envoy no punishment can fall upon you for it?"

Kuno calmly bore his threatening look.

"Our Order," he answered slowly and emphatically, "before it came to Prussia, waged war in Palestine, but even the Saracens respected envoys. You alone do not respect them—that is why I call your customs pagan."

At that the noise became still greater. Again shouts were heard around the table: "Woe! woe!"

But silence fell when the king, whose face was burning with rage, clapped his hands several times according to the Lithuanian custom. Then old Jasko Topor of Teczyno, Castellan of Cracow, grey-haired, grave, arousing fear by the dignity of this office, stood up and said:

"Noble knight of Lichtenstein, if some insult has been done to you as envoy, speak, and stern justice shall speedily be done."

"Such a thing would never have happened to me in any other Christian country," replied Kuno. "Yesterday on the road to Tyniec a knight of yours attacked me, and although he could easily recognize from the cross on my cloak who I am, he aimed at my life."

Hearing these words, Zbyszko turned pale and glanced involuntarily at the king, whose face was indeed terrible.

"Can that be?" asked Jasko of Teczyno in amazement.

"Ask the Lord of Taczewo, who was a witness."

All eyes turned to Powala, who stood for a while gloomy, with lowered eyelids.

"It is so!" he finally said.

The knights began to shout: "Disgrace! Disgrace! May the earth open up under whoever did this!" And from shame some of them beat their thighs and breasts with their fists, while others twisted pewter dishes between their fingers, not knowing what else to do.

"Why did you not slay him?" thundered the king.

"Because his head belongs to the court," replied Powala.

"Did you throw him into prison?" asked Jasko of Teczyno.

"No, for he swore on his honor as a knight to present himself."

"He will not do so!" said Kuno mockingly, raising his head.

Then a young, sad voice was heard not far behind the Teutonic Knight's back:

"God forbid that I should prefer disgrace to death. I did it: Zbyszko of Bogdaniec."

At these words the knights threw themselves towards the unhappy Zbyszko, but they were restrained by a threatening nod from the king, who stood up, sparks of fire flashing from his eyes, and shouted in a rumbling voice:

"Cut off his head! Cut off his head! Let the Teutonic Knight send his head to the grand master at Malbork!"

Then he called to the young Lithuanian duke, the son of the Governor of Smolensk, standing near Zbyszko:

"Hold him, Jamont!"

Terrified by the king's wrath, Jamont laid trembling hands on Zbyszko's shoulders; the latter turned a pale face to him and said:

"I will not try to escape."

The white-bearded Castellan of Cracow, Jasko of Teczyno, raised his hand as a sign that he wished to speak, and when silence fell he said:

"Your Majesty! let the commander convince himself that not your impetuosity but our laws impose death as a penalty for attacking the person of an envoy. Otherwise he might properly suppose that there are no Christian laws in this kingdom. The court alone will deal with the guilty!"

The last words he uttered in loud voice, and apparently not imagining for a moment that that voice would not be obeyed, he nodded to Jamont:

"Shut him in prison. You, Lord of Taczewo, will be a witness."

"I will relate the entire offence of this boy, which no mature man among us would ever have committed," replied Powala, looking gloomily at Lichtenstein.

"He speaks well!" repeated the others immediately. "This is just a youth! Why should all of us be disgraced because of him?"

There followed a moment of silence when they looked with displeasure at the Teutonic Knight; meanwhile, Jamont led Zbyszko away to give him into the hands of the bowmen posted in the castle court. He felt in his young heart pity for the prisoner, which was strengthened by his ingrained hatred of the Germans. But as a Lithuanian, accustomed blindly to carry out the will of the grand duke, and himself afraid of the king's wrath, he began to whisper to the young knight, in the way of friendly advice:

"Do you know what I say: hang yourself! It will be best to hang yourself at once. The king is enraged, and in any case they will cut off your head. Why not make the king happy? Hang yourself, friend! Such is our custom."

Zbyszko, only half-conscious through shame and fear, did not at first understand the young duke's words, but at last he did understand, so that he stopped in amazement:

"What did you say?"

"Hang yourself! Why should they have to judge you? You will make the king happy," repeated Jamont.

"You hang yourself!" exclaimed the young knight. "You've been baptized, but your skin has remained pagan. You don't even understand that it's a sin for a Christian to do such a thing."

The young duke shrugged his shoulders.

"It would not be voluntarily. They will cut off your head anyhow."

The thought passed through Zbyszko's head that for such words he ought to immediately challenge the young boyar to combat on foot or on horseback, with swords or axes, but he stifled the idea, remembering that he had no time for that now. So he bent his head sadly and allowed himself in silence to be given into the hands of the leader of the palace archers.

Meanwhile in the banquet hall the general attention had turned in another direction. Danusia, when she saw what had been happening, was at first so terrified that her breath stopped in her breast. Her little face turned white as a sheet, her eyes became round with fear—and, motionless like a wax figurine in church, she stared at the king. But when at last she heard that her Zbyszko's head was to be cut off, when they took him and led him out of the room, she was seized with immeasurable sorrow; her lips and eyebrows began to quiver; nothing helped, neither her fear of the king, nor biting her lips with her teeth—and suddenly she burst out weeping so grievously that every face turned towards her, and the king himself asked:

"What is the matter?"

"Your Majesty!" exclaimed Duchess Anna. "This is the daughter of Jurand of Spychow, to whom that unfortunate knight made a vow. He vowed to tear off three peacock crests from helmets for her—and seeing such a crest on the helmet of this commander, he thought that God himself had sent it for him. He did not do it out of wickedness, Sire, only through folly; so be gracious to him and do not punish him, we beg you on our knees."

So saying, she stood up, and taking Danusia by the hand, hastened with her to the king, who, seeing this, began to draw back. But they both knelt down before him, and Danusia, embracing the king's legs with her arms, began to cry:

"Pardon Zbyszko, Your Majesty; pardon Zbyszko!"

And in excitement and, at the same time, in fear, she hid her bright little head in the folds of the king's dark robe, kissing his knees and shaking like a leaf. Duchess Alexandra knelt down on the other side and, folding her hands, looked imploringly at the king, whose face showed great embarrassment. He drew back, it is true, with his chair; but he did not forcibly push away Danusia; he only waved both hands, as if driving away flies.

"Leave me in peace!" he exclaimed. "He has brought guilt and shame on the whole kingdom! Let them cut off his head!"

But the small arms embraced his knees ever more tightly, and the childish voice called ever more sadly:

"Pardon Zbyszko, Your Majesty; pardon Zbyszko!"

Suddenly the voices of the knights were heard:

"Jurand of Spychow, the famous knight, terror of the Germans!"

"And that boy deserves much for his service at Wilno," added Powala.

Although touched by the sight of Danusia, the king continued to defend himself:

"Leave me in peace! His fault was not against me, and it is not I who can pardon him. Let the envoy of the Order pardon him, and then I will pardon him; but if not, then let them cut off his head."

"Pardon him, Kuno!" said Zawisza the Black. "The grand master himself will not blame you for it."

"Pardon him, lord!" called out both the duchesses.

"Pardon him; pardon!" repeated the voices of the knights.

Kuno closed his eyes and sat with head raised, as if taking delight in the fact that the two duchesses and such distinguished knights were thus entreating him. Suddenly he became a different man: he lowered his head, crossed his hands on his breast, became humble instead of proud, and spoke in a low, gentle voice:

"Christ, our Redeemer, pardoned the thief on the cross and his enemies."

"The knight speaks the truth!" exclaimed Bishop Wysz.

"True! true!"

"How could I not pardon," continued Kuno, "who am not only

a Christian but also a monk? So I pardon him from the bottom of my heart, as a servant of Christ and as a monk!"

"Praise be to him!" shouted Powala of Taczewo.

"Praise!" repeated the others.

"But," said the Teutonic Knight, "I am here among you as an envoy and bear in myself the majesty of the whole Order, which is Christ's Order. So he who has wronged me as an envoy, has wronged the Order, and he who has insulted the Order has insulted Christ himself, and such a wrong I cannot forgive in the face of God and man—and if your law forgives it, then let all Christian lords hear that this is so."

At these words a dull silence fell. After a while there were heard, here and there, gnashings of teeth, heavy sighs of stifled rage, and the sobbing of Danusia.

Towards evening all hearts turned to Zbyszko. Those same knights who in the morning had been ready to cut him to pieces with their swords at a single nod from the king now racked their brains to find some way of coming to his aid. The duchesses determined to entreat the queen to try and persuade Lichtenstein to withdraw his complaint, or, in case of need, to write to the grand master, asking him to order Kuno to drop the affair. This path seemed a sure one, for Jadwiga was surrounded with such unusual respect and honor that the grand master would draw down upon himself the wrath of the pope and the blame of all Christian dukes if he refused her. That would probably not happen, for Conrad von Jungingen was a peaceful man and much more gentle than his predecessors. Unfortunately, the Bishop of Cracow, Wysz, who was at the same time the queen's chief physician, strictly forbade a single word to be said to her about the matter. "She does not like hearing of death sentences," he said. "Even the fate of a simple robber touches her heart; how much more therefore the life of a youth who might very properly expect her mercy. Any disturbance may easily bring her to a serious crisis, and her health means more to the whole kingdom than the heads of ten knights." Finally he swore that if anyone dared to disturb the lady against his orders, he would draw down on that person the terrible wrath of the king—and an excommunication.

The two duchesses were terrified by this threat and determined to say nothing to the queen, but to importune the king until he promised to show some mercy. The whole court and all the knights now stood on Zbyszko's side. Powala of Taczewo declared that he would tell the whole truth, but at the same time he would give evidence favorable to the youth and represent the whole affair as due to boyish impetuosity. None the less, everyone foresaw, and Castellan Jasko of Teczyno declared aloud, that if the Teutonic Knight insisted, stern justice must be done.

Therefore, the hearts of the knights raged against Lichtenstein all the more, and many of them thought, or even openly said: "He is an envoy and cannot be challenged to the lists, but when he has returned to Malbork, God grant that he may not die a natural death." And those were not vain threats, for belted knights were forbidden to waste words, and he who made a promise had to carry it out or perish. The threatening Powala showed himself the most intent of all, for at Taczewo he had a beloved daughter of Danusia's age, and consequently Danusia's tears completely broke his heart.

So the very same day he visited Zbyszko in his dungeon and bade him be of good cheer, and told him of the requests of the two duchesses and of Danusia's tears. Zbyszko, when he learned that the girl had thrown herself at the king's feet for him, was moved to tears, and not knowing how to give expression to his gratitude and longing, he said, wiping his eyes with the back of his hand:

"May God bless her! And may He permit me as soon as possible to engage in some fight for her on foot or horse! I promised her too few Germans—I ought to have vowed her as many as she has years. If the Lord Jesus saves me from this plight, I will not be stingy with her." And he raised his most grateful eyes to Heaven.

"First promise the Church something," replied the Lord of Taczewo, "for if your promise pleases God, most certainly you will soon be free. And secondly, listen: Your uncle has gone to Lichtenstein, and presently I am going too. It will be no shame to you to beg his pardon, for you were at fault, and it will not be Lichtenstein, but an envoy whose pardon you beg. Are you willing to do this?"

"Since such a knight as your grace says that it is fitting, I will do it! But if he wants me to beg his pardon in the same way as he did on the road from Tyniec, then let them cut off my head. My uncle will remain and my uncle will repay him when his envoy work is finished."

"We shall see what he will say to Macko," said Powala.

Macko did indeed go to see the German in the evening, but the latter received him insolently: he did not even have the lights lit but talked to him in the dusk. So the old knight came back from the visit sombre as night, and went to seek an audience with the king. The king, in the company of the castellan Jasko of Teczyno, received him kindly, for he was now quite calm again. When Macko knelt down, he bade him rise at once, asking what he desired.

"Your Majesty," said Macko, "there was a fault and there must be punishment—otherwise there would be no law on the earth. But the fault is partly mine, for I have never restrained the natural impetuosity of that youth, and I have even praised it. I brought him up that way, and afterwards war brought him up. It is my fault, Sire. More than once, I have said to him: 'Strike first, and then see whom you have cut in two.' This was a good rule for war, though a bad one at court! But he is a youth of pure gold, the last of his line, and I am most grieved for him."

"He brought shame on me, he brought shame on the kingdom," said the king. "Shall I give him honey for this?"

Macko said nothing. Grief suddenly took him by the throat at the memory of Zbyszko, and it was only after a considerable while that he began to speak, this time in a broken voice:

"I did not know that I loved him so—only now do I see it, when misfortune has come upon us. I am old, and he is the last of his line. If he is no more, we shall be no more. Your Majesty, Sire, have pity upon our family!"

Here Macko knelt down again and, spreading out before him his war-worn hands, he said with tears in his eyes:

"We defended Wilno. God gave us rich booty. To whom shall I leave it? The Teutonic Knight demands punishment, Sire; let there be punishment, but let me give my own head. What would life be for me without Zbyszko! He is young, let him redeem his land and beget offspring, as God commanded man. Not even the Teutonic Knight will ask whose head fell, if only a head has fallen. No shame will fall upon our family for this. It is hard for a man to meet death, but if one thinks about it, it is better for a man to perish than for his line to die out."

He embraced the king's legs, and the king began to blink his eyes, a sign of emotion in him, and he finally said:

"It cannot be that I should order the head of a belted knight to be cut off when he is innocent! It cannot be, it cannot be!"

"And there would be no justice in it," added the castellan. "The law crushes the guilty, but it is not a dragon which laps the blood of man without looking whose it is. And consider this: shame would indeed fall upon your line, for if your nephew agreed to what you say, everyone would regard him, and his children after him, as dishonored."

To that Macko replied:

"He would not agree to this. But if it happened without his knowledge, then he would avenge me, as I shall avenge him."

"Ha!" said the castellan. "Go to the Teutonic Knight and ask him to withdraw his complaint."

"I have already been to him."

"And?" asked the king. "What did he say?"

"He said this: 'You ought to have asked pardon on the road from Tyniec. You were unwilling, and now so am I.'"

"And why were you unwilling?"

"Because he wanted us to dismount from our horses and beg his pardon on foot."

The king smoothed his hair back behind his ears and was about to say something when a courtier came in to announce that the knight of Lichtenstein was asking for an audience.

Hearing that, Jagiello looked at Jasko of Teczyno and then at Macko, but told them to stay, perhaps in the hope that he would reconcile the matter by virtue of his royal dignity.

Meanwhile the Teutonic Knight came in, bowed to the king, and said:

"Your Majesty! here is a written complaint of the insult I received in your kingdom."

"Make your complaint to him," replied the king, pointing to Jasko of Teczyno.

But, looking straight in the king's face, the Teutonic Knight said:

"I do not know your laws, nor your courts; I know only that an envoy of the Order can make a complaint only to the king himself."

Jagiello's small eyes flashed with impatience, but he stretched out his hand, took the complaint and gave it to the Lord of Teczyno.

The latter unrolled it and began to read, but as he read his face became ever more concerned and sad.

"Lord," he said at last, "you insist on the death of this youth as if he were a terror to the whole Order. Do you Teutonic Knights now fear children?"

"We Teutonic Knights fear no one," replied the commander proudly.

To which the old castellan added in a whisper:

"Least of all God."

The next day Powala of Taczewo did everything in his power before the castellan's court to diminish the enormity of Zbyszko's guilt. But in vain did he ascribe his deed to childishness and inexperience; in vain did he say that even an older man, if he had vowed three peacock crests and had prayed that they might be sent to him, and then suddenly saw such a crest before him, might have thought that it was a divine dispensation. One thing the honorable knight could not deny, and that was that if it had not been for him, Zbyszko's lance would have struck the Teutonic Knight's breast. Kuno had the suit of armor he had been wearing that day brought before the court. It was shown to be made of thin metal plate, such as was used only for solemn visits, so that Zbyszko, considering his unusual strength, would assuredly have pierced it with his point and have deprived the envoy of his life. Accordingly, Zbyszko was asked whether he had intended to slay the Teutonic Knight, and he would not deny it. "I called to him from a distance to lower his lance," he said, "for I knew he would not let his helmet be torn from his head as long as he lived. But if he had called out from a distance that he was an envoy, I would have left him in peace."

These words pleased the knights, who had come in crowds to the court, wishing the young man well, and numerous voices were immediately raised. "True! why did he not call out?" But the castellan's face remained stern and gloomy. Bidding the others keep silence, he himself also was silent for a while, and then fixed his eyes piercingly on Zbyszko and asked him:

"Can you swear on the Passion of our Lord that you did not see his cloak and the cross?"

"I cannot!" answered Zbyszko. "If I had not seen the cross, I should have thought that he was one of our knights, and as such I should certainly not have attacked him."

"And how could there be any other Teutonic Knight near Cracow except an envoy or one of his train?"

To that Zbyszko had no answer, for there was no answer possible. It was too clear to everyone that if it had not been for the Lord of Taczewo, not the envoy's suit of armor but the envoy himself would have been lying before the court, his breast pierced to the everlasting shame of the Polish nation. So even those who sympathized with Zbyszko wholeheartedly understood that the sentence could not be in his favor.

So the castellan said after a while:

"Since in your impetuosity you did not think whom you were attacking and you did it without ill intent, our Redeemer will take this into consideration and forgive you. But, poor fellow, recommend yourself to our Most Holy Lady, for the law cannot forgive you."

Although he expected some such words, Zbyszko paled a little, but soon afterwards he shook his long hair back, crossed himself, and said:

"God's will! Well, it cannot be helped!"

Then he turned to Macko and gave him a sign by glancing at Lichtenstein, as if recommending him not to forget, while Macko nodded in token that he understood and would remember. That glance and that movement Lichtenstein also understood; and although his heart beat courageously and fiercely in his breast, a shiver passed through him momentarily from head to foot, so gruesome and sinister was the old warrior's expression. The Teutonic Knight saw that between him and that old knight, whose entire face he could not see clearly under his helmet, there would be now a deadly feud, and that even if he wished to hide from him, he would not be able, and that when he had ceased to be an envoy, they would meet somewhere, even were it at Malbork.

Meanwhile the castellan went into the adjoining room to dictate the sentence on Zbyszko to his secretary, who was skilled in writing. During this interval, one and another knight approached the Teutonic Knight, saying:

"God grant that you may be judged more mercifully on the last day! Are you happy that this blood must flow?"

But Lichtenstein cared for none of them, only for Zawisza the Black, who, because of his deeds of arms, his knowledge of the laws of chivalry, and his immeasurable sternness in protecting them, was known far and wide throughout the world. In the most complicated cases in which knightly honor was at stake, men came to consult him, sometimes from afar, and no one ever dared to contradict him, not only because single combat with him was unwise, but also because he was regarded as "a mirror of honor." A single word of blame or praise from his mouth quickly spread throughout the knighthood of Poland, Hungary, Bohemia, and Germany, and might be decisive for the good or ill fame of a knight.

So Lichtenstein approached him and, as if wishing to justify himself for his obstinacy, said:

"Only the grand master himself and the chapter could show him mercy; I cannot."

"Your grand master has nothing to do with our laws. Mercy may be shown not by him, but by our king," replied Zawisza.

"As an envoy, I had to demand punishment."

"You were a knight before you were an envoy, Lichtenstein."

"Do you think that I have stained my honor?"

"You know our books of chivalry and you know that a knight is instructed to imitate two animals: the lion and the lamb. Which of them have you imitated in this affair?"

"You are not my judge."

"You asked me whether you stained your honor, and so I told you what I thought."

"I cannot swallow what you say."

"You will choke with your own rage, not with mine."

"Christ bids me to care more for the majesty of the Order than for your praise."

"He will judge us all."

Further talk was hindered by the entry of the castellan and his secretary. It was already known that the sentence would be unfavorable, but all the same a dull silence fell. The castellan took his place at the table and, holding a crucifix in his hand, ordered Zbyszko to kneel down.

The secretary began to read out the sentence in Latin. Neither

Zbyszko nor any of the knights present understood it, yet all guessed that it was a sentence of death. At the end of the reading, Zbyszko struck his breast several times with his fist, repeating: "God be merciful to me, a sinner!"

Then he got up and threw himself into Macko's arms, while the latter silently began to kiss his head and eyes.

That evening a herald proclaimed at the four corners of the marketplace, to the sound of trumpets, to knights, guests, and townspeople, that the noble Zbyszko of Bogdaniec was condemned by sentence of the castellan to be beheaded with the sword.

But Macko asked for a delay in the execution, and his request was easily granted, since noble prisoners in those days, fond of disposing of their property in minute detail, were given time to conclude agreements with their families, and also to reconcile themselves with God. Even Lichtenstein did not press for a swift execution of the sentence, understanding that since the injured majesty of the Order was receiving satisfaction, it was not advisable to annoy further the powerful monarch to whom he had been sent, not merely to take part in the christening festivities, but also to conclude an agreement about the Land of Dobrzyn. The most important consideration, however, was the queen's health. Bishop Wysz would not hear of an execution before her delivery, considering quite properly that such an event could not be concealed from the lady and that once she heard of it, she would fall into a "perturbation" which might seriously affect her health. So Zbyszko was given perhaps a few months of life to make his last dispositions and to take leave of his acquaintances.

Macko visited him every day and cheered him as best he could. They spoke mournfully of Zbyszko's inevitable death, and still more mournfully of the probable extinction of their line.

"It cannot be otherwise—you will have to get some woman to marry you," said Zbyszko one day.

"I would rather find some kinsman, however distant," replied the distressed Macko. "How can I think of women when your head is to be cut off? And even if I would have to take a wife, I would not do it until I had sent Lichtenstein a knightly challenge and taken vengeance on him. Have no fear about that!"

"God reward you! Let me have at least that pleasure! I knew you would not forgive him. What will you do?"

"When his mission ends, there will be either war or peace, do you understand? If there is war, I will send him a challenge to engage in single combat with me before the battle."

"On trodden ground?"

"On trodden ground, on horseback or on foot, but only till death, not captivity. But if there is peace I will go to Malbork and strike my lance on the castle gate and bid a trumpeter proclaim that I summon him to mortal combat. He will not be able to hide himself."

"He certainly will not be able to hide himself. I see that you will be able to deal with him."

"Deal with him? I could not deal with Zawisza, I could not deal with Paszko, or with Powala; but, without boasting, I could deal with two Lichtensteins. He will see! Was that Frisian knight not stronger than he? Yet when I split his head, where did my axe stop? It stopped at his teeth—did it not?"

Zbyszko took a deep breath of relief.

"Now it will be easier for me to die," he said.

And they both began to sigh, after which the old nobleman said with emotion:

"Don't worry. Your bones will not have to look for one another on the Judgment Day. I have ordered an oak coffin made for you that even the canons of St. Mary's would envy. You shall not perish like some small landholder. No! I won't even allow them to behead you on the same cloth as they use for the townspeople. I have already arranged with Amylej for you to have a brand new cloth, a cloth good enough for the king to line his fur coat with. And I won't begrudge you Masses—never fear!"

Zbyszko's heart rejoiced at that, so he took his uncle in his arms and said again:

"God reward you!"

At times, however, despite all the cheer, he was seized with heavy longing; so one day when Macko came to visit him, Zbyszko scarcely greeted him before he asked, looking out through the grating in the wall:

"How is it outside?"

"The weather is golden, and the sun's warmth makes the whole world quite pleasant."

Zbyszko put both his hands on the nape of his neck.

"Ah, Almighty God!" he said, throwing his head back. "To have a horse under one and ride over the wide fields! It is hard for a young man to die! Terribly hard!"

"Men die even on horseback," replied Macko.

"Ha! but how many men do they kill first!"

Zbyszko began to ask about the knights whom he had seen at the king's court—about Zawisza, about Farurej, about Powala of Taczewo, about Lis of Fair-Ground, and all the others: what they were doing, how they were amusing themselves, in what honorable exercises they were passing their time. And he listened greedily to Macko's answers as the old warrior told how in the morning they leapt over their horses in full armor, how they pulled ropes, how they practiced axe and sword with leaden edges, and finally how they feasted and what songs they sang. Zbyszko longed with heart and soul to join them, and when he heard that immediately after the christening Zawisza was going somewhere far away into the depths of Hungary to fight the Turks, he could not refrain from crying out:

"If they would only let me go with him! If I might only perish in battle against the pagans!"

But that could not be, and meanwhile something else happened. The two Mazovian duchesses did not cease to think of Zbyszko, who had won their hearts by his youth and charm. Finally Duchess Alexandra thought of sending a letter to the grand master. The master, it was true, could not change the sentence passed by the castellan, but he might intervene on the young man's behalf with the king. It was not fitting for Jagiello himself to show mercy, since it was a question of an attack on an envoy; yet it seemed indubitable that he would gladly show it on the intervention of the grand master. So hope rose again in the hearts of both ladies. Duchess Alexandra, having herself a weakness for the polished knights of the Teutonic Order, was highly respected by them. On more than one occasion rich gifts had come for her from Malbork, and letters in which the master called her the honored holy benefactress and special protectress of the Order. Her words were really influential, and it was very probable that she would not be met with a refusal. It was a question only of finding a messenger who would use his utmost efforts to deliver the letter as quickly as possible and return with an answer. Hearing that, old Macko undertook the mission without any hesitation.

The castellan was summoned, and he set a date up to which he promised to put off the execution of the sentence. Full of hope, Macko busied himself the same day with preparations for departure, and then went to Zbyszko to tell him the happy news.

At first Zbyszko exhibited great joy, as if the doors of the prison were already open. Afterwards, however, he took thought and grew suddenly gloomy.

"Who can expect anything good from a German?" he said. "Lichtenstein might have asked the king for mercy—and it would have been to his advantage, for he would have avoided your vengeance—but for that very reason he did not."

"He was displeased because we were unwilling to ask his pardon on the road from Tyniec. People don't speak ill of Grand Master Conrad. Besides, you won't lose anything by this."

"That's true," said Zbyszko, "but don't bow low before him."

"Why should I have to bow? I shall bear a letter from Duchess Alexandra—and that's all."

"Ha! since you are so good, may God help you!"

Suddenly he looked keenly at his uncle and said:

"But if the king pardons me, Lichtenstein will be mine and not yours. Don't forget."

"You're not yet certain of your own neck, so don't make any promises. You've had enough of stupid vows," answered the old man angrily.

They threw themselves into one another's arms—then Zbyszko remained alone. Hope and uncertainty tore apart his soul, but when the night came, and with it a storm, when the barred window began to be lit by ill-boding lightning flashes and the walls to shake with thunder, when at last a strong wind whistled through the tower and the dim oil-lamp by his bed went out, Zbyszko, plunged in darkness, again lost all hope—and was unable to close his eyes throughout the entire night.

"I shall not escape death," he thought; "nothing can save me."

The next day the honorable Duchess Anna Danuta visited him, accompanied by Danusia with her little lute hanging on a strap. Zbyszko fell at their feet in turn, and though he was worn-out after a sleepless night, though he was weighed down by misery and uncertainty, he did not forget his knightly duty of showing Danusia surprise at her charms.

But the duchess raised to him eyes full of sadness.

"Don't admire her," she said, "for if Macko doesn't bring a favorable answer, or does not return at all, you, poor lad, will soon be admiring better things in heaven."

After that she began to shed tears, thinking of the future uncertain fate of the young knight, and Danusia immediately cried along with her. Zbyszko bent again to their feet, for his heart was softened by their weeping like wax in heat. He did not love Danusia as a man loves a woman, yet he felt that he loved her from the bottom of his heart and that at the sight of her something happened to him: he became, as it were, another man, someone less severe, less impetuous, less eager for war, but desirous instead of sweet love. A terrible grief overcame him at the thought that he would have to leave her without being able to keep the vow he had made.

"I shall not be able to lay any peacock crests at your feet, my poor thing," he said. "But if I stand before the face of God, I will say: 'Pardon me, Lord, my sins, and grant that everything good on earth is given to no one else but to the lady of Spychow, Jurand's daughter.'"

"The both of you met not too long ago," said the duchess. "God will not allow your meeting to have been in vain."

Zbyszko began to recall all that had happened in the inn at Tyniec and became completely overcome with emotion. In the end he begged Danusia to sing the same song which she had sung that time when he had caught her from the bench and carried her to the duchess.

So Danusia, though she was in no mood for singing, straight-away raised her head towards the vaulted ceiling, and closing her eyes like a little bird, began:

> *"Oh, if I but had*
> *Little wings like a dove,*
> *Away I would fly,*
> *Away, away to my love*
>   *In Silesia.*
> *"Down I would light*
> *On the fence of his glade.*
> *Look, O my Jack—"*

Suddenly tears began to flow copiously from under her shut

eyelids—and she could not sing any more. Zbyszko caught her in his arms as he had done before in the Tyniec inn, and began to walk up and down with her in his cell, repeating with excitement:

"I should have sought not just a lady in you. If God had saved me—and had your father allowed it—then, when you would have been older, I would have married you, my maiden! Oh, yes, yes!"

Danusia, putting her arms around his neck, hid her tear-stained face on his shoulder, while his grief grew and grew, and flowing as it did from the depth of his wild Slavonic nature, it evolved in his simple heart almost into a folk song:

> *"I would have married you,*
> *my maiden!*
> *I would have married you. . . ."*

CHAPTER VI

WITHOUT warning, an event occurred that rendered all other matters insignificant. Towards evening, on the twenty-first of June, the news spread throughout the castle of the sudden illness of the queen. Doctors were summoned and, along with Bishop Wysz, they stayed the whole night in her apartment. Meanwhile it was learned from the servant women that the lady was threatened with a premature delivery. The Castellan of Cracow, Jasko Topor of Teczyno, sent messengers that night to the absent king. On the following morning the news spread like wildfire through the town and the surrounding neighborhood. It was a Sunday, so crowds filled all the churches, and priests enjoined the people to pray for the queen's health. Then all doubt ceased. After service, the nobility, the deputations of merchants, and the visiting knights, who had come in expectation of festivities, all proceeded to the castle; the gilds and brotherhoods came with their standards. From midday countless masses of people surrounded Wawel Castle, order being maintained among them by the royal archers, who enforced peace and quiet. The town became almost completely depopulated. From time to time groups of peasants from the neighboring regions passed through the empty streets, for they also had already heard of the sickness of their adored lady, and were making for the castle. Finally, at the main gateway, the bishop and the castellan appeared, accompanied by the cathedral canons, the royal councillors, and the knights. They spread out along the walls, their faces revealing that they bore important information. They began by strictly prohibiting any shouts and cries, since these might negatively effect the sick lady's health. Then they announced that the queen had borne a daughter. The news filled all hearts with joy, particularly since it was also announced that, although the delivery had been premature, there was no obvious danger either for the mother or the child. The crowds began to disperse, since they were not allowed to shout near the castle, and each person wanted to give free expression to his or her joy. So, when the streets leading to the market had filled with people, songs and joyous calls were heard. No one was distressed by the fact that it was a daughter who had been born into the world. "Was it bad," said the merchants, "that King Louis had no sons and that the kingdom passed to Jadwiga? It was by her marriage to Jagiello that the power of our nation was doubled. So it will be now. Where can we find such a heiress as will be our princess, when neither the Roman emperor nor any of the other kings possesses so great a state, such wide lands, and so numerous a knighthood? The most powerful monarchs on the earth will want to marry her, they will do homage to the queen and the king, they will ride to Cracow, and we shall profit. And let us not forget that some other state, maybe Bohemia or Hungry, will unite with our kingdom." So said the merchants among themselves—and the joy became every moment more general. Banquets were held in private houses and inns. The marketplace teemed with lanterns and torches. In the suburbs the yeomen from the adjacent regions, arriving in ever greater numbers to town, formed camps with their wagons. The Jews conferred in their synagogue on Kazimierz Street. The marketplace was alive with noise and people until late at night, almost until dawn, particularly near the town hall and the office of weights and measures, just as if it were a great fair. People exchanged information with each other; messengers were sent to the castle for the latest news, and curious crowds surrounded them when they returned.

The worst piece of news was that Bishop Peter had baptized the child the same night, from which it was deduced that it must be very weak. Experienced townswomen quoted cases in which children born half-dead had gained strength immediately after being baptized. So hope grew, and this hope was strengthened by the name given to the child. It was said that no Bonifacia could die immediately after birth, since, as the name implied, the child was destined to do something good, and a child could neither do good or evil during the first years of life, and all the more in the first months of life.

The next day, however, unfavorable news of the child and its mother came from the castle—and it greatly upset the town. The churches were packed throughout the day, as at the time of Absolution. Numerous ex-votos were offered for the health of the queen and the princess. People were touched to see poor peasants offering measures of grain, lambs, fowls, strings of dried mushrooms, or birchen bowls of nuts. Important offerings flowed in from the knighthood, the merchants, and the craftsmen. Messengers were sent to places where miracles had occurred. Astrologers studied the stars. At Cracow itself solemn processions were ordered. All the gilds and all the brotherhoods took part in them. The whole town was decorated with flags. There was also a procession of children, for it was thought that innocent creatures would more easily be able to obtain God's favor by their prayers. New crowds came continually through the city gates from the surrounding country.

So day after day passed, amid the unceasing ringing of bells, the bustle of people in churches, processions, and divine services. When a week had passed and both the sick queen and the child were still alive, everyone became optimistic. It seemed impossible that God should prematurely take away a queen who had done so much for Him, and who would have to leave her enormous work unfinished—a female apostle, who by the sacrifice of her own happiness had brought the last pagan nation in Europe within the Christian fold. Scholars recalled how much she had done for the university, clerics how much for the glory of God, politicians how much for peace among Christian monarchs, lawyers how much for justice, and poor folk how much for the poor—and none of them could believe that a life so necessary for the kingdom and the whole world could be cut off before its time.

Meanwhile, on the thirteenth of July, the tolling of bells announced the death of the child. The town went into an upheaval, and people were alarmed. Once again crowds besieged Wawel, inquiring after the queen's health. But this time no one came out with good news. On the contrary, the faces of the lords who rode into the castle or rode out through the gateway were gloomy, and became gloomier with each new day. It was said that Father Stanislaw of Skarbimierz, Master of Liberal Arts at Cracow, now never left the queen, who received communion daily. It was also said that each time she received the sacrament her apartment became filled with celestial light. Some even saw it through the window. But the sight inspired fear in hearts devoted to the lady, for it was interpreted as a sign that the other world had already begun for her.

Some, however, did not believe that so dreadful a thing could happen, and cherished the hope that a just heaven would be content with one victim. Meanwhile, on Friday morning, the seventeenth of July, the report flew among the people that the queen was dying. Every living person hastened to the castle. The town was so depopulated that only the lame were left, for even mothers with infant children hastened to the castle gates. Shops were shut; meals were not prepared. All business was interrupted, while a massive sea of humanity waited outside Wawel—tense, frightened, but silent.

Then, at one o'clock in the afternoon, the bell tolled in the cathedral tower. Its meaning was not immediately understood, yet a growing panic began to seize people. Every head and every eye turned towards the turret where the bell was swinging with ever greater impetus, and its melancholy sound was taken up by others in the town—at the church of the Franciscans, at Holy Trinity, St. Mary's, and far beyond throughout the length and breadth of the city. Finally the tolling was understood, and the souls of the people became filled with terror and with such pain as if the bronze clappers of the bells were striking directly upon their hearts.

Suddenly on the tower there appeared a black flag with a large skull in the middle, under which were two white, crossed human bones. All doubt vanished. The queen had rendered up her soul to God.

Around the castle hundreds of thousands of people began to howl and weep, mingling their lamentations with the gloomy tolling of the bells. Some threw themselves on the earth, others tore their garments or scratched their faces; others looked at the walls in dumb stupefaction, some sobbed dully, while others, stretching out their hands towards the church and the queen's apartment, called for a miracle and divine mercy. But there were also angry voices which began to blaspheme in their excitement and despair. "Our beloved queen has been taken away from us. What was the good of our processions, our prayers and implorations? Our silver and gold votive offerings were gladly received, but what was given in return? All was taken, nothing was given!" Others, however, repeated, with floods of tears and sobs: "Jesus! Jesus! Jesus!" The crowds wanted to enter the castle to look one more time on the queen's beloved face. They were not admitted, but were promised that the body would shortly lie in state in the church, and then everyone might look at it and pray beside it. Accordingly, towards evening, gloomy crowds began to return to the town, telling one another of the queen's final moments, of her upcoming funeral, and of the miracles which all were absolutely certain would occur near her body and around her grave. It was also widely said that the queen would be canonized soon, and when some doubted whether that could happen, others became indignant and threatened to turn to the pope at Avignon.

A morose sadness fell over the town and the whole country. Not only the common people but everyone thought that along with the queen a favorable star for the whole kingdom had expired. Even among the Cracow lords were some to whom the future seemed dark. They began to ask themselves and others what would happen next—whether Jagiello had the right to continue ruling in the kingdom after the queen's death, whether he would have to return to his own Lithuania and content himself with the grand-ducal throne. Some foresaw—and as it turned out, not without justification—that he himself would desire to abdicate, and that in such case wide lands would fall away from the crown, and incursions from Lithuania would begin again, and bloody retaliation would be made by the inhabitants of the kingdom. The Order would increase in strength; the Roman emperor and the Hungarian king would increase in strength; and the kingdom, up to yesterday one of the most powerful in the world, would be brought to shame and disgrace.

The merchants, to whose trade the wide lands of Lithuania and Ruthenia stood open, foresaw serious loss and made pious vows if only Jagiello should remain on the throne. But in that case they foretold speedy warfare with the Order, for it was known that only the queen had prevented it hitherto. People reminded themselves how once, indignant at their greed and lust for plunder, she had told the Teutonic Knights of a prophetic vision: "As long as I live I will restrain the hand and righteous anger of my husband, but remember that after my death punishment will fall on you for your sins!"

The Teutonic Knights, in their pride and blindness, were not afraid of war, reckoning that after the queen's death the influence of her holiness should no longer check the influx of volunteers from the Western states, and, therefore, thousands of warriors from Germany, Burgundy, France, and still more distant lands, would come to their aid. Yet the death of Jadwiga was so serious an event that Lichtenstein, the Teutonic Knight's envoy, without even waiting for the return of the absent king, went off as quickly as he could to Malbork, to announce as soon as possible to the grand master and the chapter the important, and somewhat threatening, news.

The Hungarian, Austrian, Imperial, and Bohemian envoys also departed or sent messengers to their monarchs. Jagiello arrived at Cracow in deep despair. He immediately declared to the lords that he did not wish to be king anymore without the queen and that he would depart to his own inheritance of Lithuania, and then he fell into a kind of numbness, not desiring to decide any matter and not answering questions. At other times he became terribly angry with himself for having gone away and not having been present at the queen's deathbed, for not having taken leave of her and not having heard her last words and instructions. In vain Stanislaw of Skarbimierz and Bishop Wysz explained to him that the queen's illness had come unexpectedly and that according to human calculations he would have had plenty of time to return if her delivery had been at the proper time. This brought him no comfort, nor did it soothe his grief. "Without her, I am not a king," he would repeat to the bishop. "I am only a repentant sinner who finds no comfort." Then he would cast he eyes on the ground and no one could get another word out of him.

Meanwhile everyone's thoughts were occupied with the queen's funeral. New crowds of lords, gentry, and people began to come from all over the country, particularly of poor folk who expected great profit from the alms they could get at the funeral ceremonies, set to last a whole month. The queen's body lay in state in the cathedral on a raised bier, so arranged that the broader part of the coffin, where the head rested, was considerably higher than the feet. This was done purposely, that the people might better see the face of the queen. In the cathedral, divine service was celebrated continually; by the catafalque burned thousands of wax candles, and amidst this candlelight and amidst the flowers lay She—peaceful, smiling, like a white, mystic rose, her hands crossed on her azure dress. The people saw in her a saint; they brought to her the possessed, the lame, and sick children, and from time to time in the midst of the church there was heard the cry of some mother who saw the flush of health returning to the face of her sick child or the cry of some paralytic who suddenly regained the use of his withered limbs. Then the hearts of the people were thrilled, the news of the miracle flew through the church, the castle, and the town, and drew still greater swarms of pitiful humanity who could expect alleviation only from a miracle.

Meanwhile Zbyszko had been completely forgotten—for who, in the face of so immense a misfortune, could remember an ordinary noble squire and his imprisonment in a castle dungeon? Zbyszko, however, had known from the jailers of the queen's sickness. When he had heard their weeping and the tolling of the bells, he threw himself on his knees and, forgetting his own fate, began to weep wholeheartedly at the death of his adored lady. It seemed to him that something had also died within him and that in face of a death like this, life on earth became purposeless for all.

The echo of the funeral, the sound of the church bells, the singing of the processions, and the weeping of the crowds continued to reach him for a whole week. During that time he became gloomy, lost his desire to eat and sleep, and paced up and down in his dungeon like a wild beast behind bars. His loneliness weighed upon him, for there were days when even the jailer failed to bring him fresh food and water, so much was everyone occupied with the royal funeral. Since the time of her death no one came to see him: neither the duchess, nor Danusia, nor Powala of Taczewo, who before had shown him so much kindness, nor Macko's acquaintance, the merchant Amylej. Zbyszko thought bitterly that without Macko around he was forgotten. Sometimes the thought came into his head that perhaps even the law had forgotten him, in which case he would rot to death in prison. At such times he prayed for a speedy death.

Finally, when a month had passed since the queen's funeral and a second month was beginning, he began to doubt whether Macko would return. Macko had promised to ride quickly and not spare

his horse. Malbork was not at the end of the world. The entire
journey should have taken no more than twelve weeks—particularly if one was on an urgent quest. "But perhaps he did not think
it urgent!" thought Zbyszko sadly. "Perhaps he's found a woman for
himself somewhere on the road and is gladly taking her to Bogdaniec to get issue of his own, while I shall wait here for divine
mercy for ages."

At last he lost count of time, ceased to talk to the jailer, and only
noted from the cobwebs, which were covering the iron grating in
the window ever more thickly, that autumn was arriving in the
world. Now he used to sit for hours at a time upon his bed with his
elbows on his knees and his fingers in his hair, which had grown
far down over his shoulders. In a dreamy daze, he did not raise his
head even when the jailer spoke to him when he brought his food.
Until one day the hinges creaked and a familiar voice called from
the threshold of the prison:

"Zbyszko!"

"Uncle!" called out Zbyszko, leaping from his bed.

Macko caught him in his arms and then took his blond head in
his hands and began to kiss it. Grief, bitterness, and longing so
affected the heart of the young man that he began to weep on his
uncle's breast like a small child.

"I thought you were never going to come back," he said, crying.

"I very nearly did not," replied Macko.

Then Zbyszko raised his head and, looking at him, exclaimed:

"What's happened to you?"

And he looked with amazement at the haggard, sunken and pale
face of the old warrior, at his bent figure and his grey hair.

"What's happened to you?" he repeated.

Macko sat on the bed and breathed heavily for a while.

"What has happened?" he said at last. "I had scarcely passed the
border when, going through a forest, Germans shot me with arrows
from crossbows. Robber-knights, do you know? It's still difficult
for me to breathe. . . . God sent me help—otherwise you would not
be seeing me here."

"Who helped you?"

"Jurand of Spychow," replied Macko.

A moment of silence followed.

"They fell upon me, and that same day he fell upon them.

Scarcely half escaped. He took me to his fortalice, and there at Spychow for three weeks I wrestled with death. God did not let me die—and though it's still hard for me to get around, I have returned."

"Then you were not at Malbork?"

"What should I go with? They robbed me thoroughly and took the letter together with my other things. I returned to ask Duchess Alexandra for another letter, but I missed her on the road, and whether I shall overtake her I don't know, for I'm more likely to go to the other world."

Macko spat into his palm and showed Zbyszko the pure blood on it, saying:

"Do you see?" Then he added: "It's God's will."

For some time they both were silent, lost in pensive thoughts. Finally Zbyszko said:

"Do you spit blood all the time?"

"How could I not, when there is a two-inch splinter sticking between my ribs! You would do likewise, never fear! But I felt better at Spychow. Now I am terribly weary again, for the way was long and I rode in a hurry."

"Why such haste?"

"Because I wanted to catch up to Duchess Alexandra and get a second letter from her. Jurand of Spychow said, 'Ride, and return to Spychow with the letter. I have several Germans under the floor, and I will free one of them on his word as a knight, and he will carry the letter to the grand master.' He always keeps a few of them as revenge for his wife's death, and he likes to hear them moaning at night and rattling their chains, for he is a determined fellow. Do you understand?"

"I understand. Only I wonder how you could have lost the letter. If Jurand captured those that fell upon you, the letter ought to have been on them."

"He did not capture all of them. About five escaped. That was our misfortune."

Macko cleared his throat, spat blood again, and groaned a little from the pain in his chest.

"They really wounded you with their arrows," said Zbyszko. "How did it happen? From an ambush?"

"From behind bushes so thick you could hardly see through

them. And I was riding without arms, because the merchants told me the country was safe. And the weather was hot."

"Who was the leader of the robbers? A Teutonic Knight?"

"Not a monk but a German, a Chelmno man from Lentz, famous for robbery and plunder."

"What happened to him?"

"He is at Jurand's, on a chain. But he himself has two Mazovian nobles in a dungeon, whom he wants to exchange for himself."

Silence fell anew.

"Dear Jesus!" said Zbyszko at last. "Lichtenstein will live, and the knight of Lentz will live, but we must perish without vengeance. They will cut off my head, and you surely will not survive the winter."

"I shall not even make it to winter! If I could only save you somehow. . . ."

"Have you seen anyone here?"

"I went to the Castellan of Cracow. When I had learned that Lichtenstein had gone, I thought they might be lenient with you."

"Then Lichtenstein has gone?"

"Immediately after the queen's death, to Malbork. So I went to the castellan, and he said this: 'They are not cutting off your nephew's head to please Lichtenstein but only because such is the sentence, and whether Lichtenstein is here or not makes no difference. Even if he were to die, it would change nothing, for the law is according to justice—not like a jacket you can turn inside out. The king may show mercy, but no one else.'"

"And where is the king?"

"After the funeral he went to Ruthenia."

"Well, then nothing can be done."

"Nothing. The castellan said further: 'I am sorry for him, for Duchess Anna pleads for him, but if I cannot do anything, I cannot.'"

"Is Duchess Anna still here?"

"May God reward her! She is a good lady. She is still here, for Jurand's daughter fell sick, and the duchess loves her like her own child."

"Oh, Dear God! So Danusia is ill! What's wrong with her?"

"Do I know? The duchess says that someone has cast a spell on her."

"Certainly Lichtenstein! No one else but Lichtenstein—accursed dog!"

"Maybe it was he. But what will you do to him? Nothing."

"So that is why everyone forgot me here—because she was sick."

Zbyszko began to walk up and down the cell with long strides; finally he grabbed Macko's hand, kissed it, and said:

"May God reward you for everything. Because of me, you will die. But since you rode as far as Prussia, and as long as you are not worn out by your sickness, do one thing more for me. Go to the castellan and beg him to let me go free for twelve weeks on my word of honor as a knight. After that I will come back, and they can cut off my head, but—it really cannot be that we should perish without any vengeance. I will go to Malbork and send Lichtenstein a challenge. It cannot be otherwise—his death or mine!"

Macko began to wipe his brow.

"I can go to the castellan, but will he allow this?"

"I will give my word of honor. Twelve weeks—more I do not need."

"What are you talking about? Twelve weeks! And if you are wounded and do not return, what will they say?"

"Even if I have to crawl on all fours, I will return. But don't worry! And maybe in the meantime the king will return from Ruthenia, and I shall be able to beg him for mercy."

"That's true," admitted Macko. "But," he added, after a while, "the castellan told me this as well: 'We forgot your nephew because of the queen's death, but now we must finish this affair.'"

"Eh, he will give me permission," replied Zbyszko cheerfully. "He knows very well that a nobleman will keep his word, and whether they cut off my head now or after Michaelmas makes no difference to him."

"I will go to him this very day!"

"Today go to Amylej and lie down a little. Let them put some kind of balsam on your wound. Go to the castellan tomorrow."

"Well then, God be with you!"

"And with you too!"

They embraced and Macko turned to the door, but on the threshold he stopped and frowned, as if he had suddenly remembered something.

"Why, you haven't yet got your knight's belt. Lichtenstein will tell you that he does not fight with unbelted men—and what will you do then?"

Zbyszko was troubled, but only for a moment.

"And how is it in war?" he asked. "Does a belted knight choose only belted knights to fight against?"

"War is war, but single combat is something else."

"True, but wait—we must think this over. . . . Ah, there is a way! Duke Janusz will dub me a knight. If the duchess and Danusia beg him, he will dub me a knight. And along the way, once I'm in Mazovia, I shall fight the son of Nicholas of Longwood."

"What for?"

"Because Nicholas—you know, the one who attends the duchess and is called Broadaxe—called Danusia 'a little chick.'"

Macko looked at him with amazement, and Zbyszko, apparently wishing to explain himself more clearly, went on:

"I cannot forgive him for that, but I cannot fight with Nicholas, for he must be eighty years old."

Macko replied:

"Listen, boy! It will be a pity for you to lose your head, but not your brains. You are as stupid as a goat!"

"Why are you angry?"

Macko made no reply and wanted to leave, but Zbyszko blocked his way.

"How is Danusia? Is she well? Don't get angry over nothing. It's been a long time since I've seen you."

And he bent again over the old man's hand. His uncle shrugged his shoulders, though he answered gently:

"Jurand's daughter is well, only they don't yet let her leave her apartment. Farewell."

Zbyszko remained alone, but he seemed reborn in body and spirit. He was glad to think that he would still have three more months of life before him, that he would go into distant lands, seek out Lichtenstein and engage the German in mortal combat. The mere thought of it brought joy into his heart. It would be good to feel a horse under him for twelve weeks, to ride through the wide world, to fight and not to perish unavenged. And afterwards, let happen what may! for twelve weeks was a very long time. The king may return from Ruthenia and grant a pardon; the war that everybody has been foretelling for so long may break out; perhaps the castellan himself, seeing, after three months, the victor over the haughty Lichtenstein will say: "Off you go to the forests! to the woods!" For Zbyszko felt clearly that no one cherished ill feeling against him except the Teutonic Knight, and that the stern castellan had only condemned him to death because his hands had been tied.

So he grew more and more hopeful, for he did not doubt that they would not refuse him the three months. Indeed, he thought they would give him even more time, for it certainly would not enter the head of the old Lord of Teczyno that a nobleman who had given his word of honor could possibly break it.

Accordingly, when Macko came to the prison the next day at nightfall, Zbyszko, who could scarcely sit still, sprang to meet him at the threshold.

"Has he given permission?" he asked.

Macko sat down on the bed, for he could not stand owing to his great weakness. He breathed heavily for a while, and finally said:

"The castellan said as follows: 'If you need to divide your land or your property, then I will release your nephew for one or two weeks on his knightly word, but not for longer.'"

Zbyszko was so taken aback that for some time he could not speak.

"For two weeks?" he asked after a while. "Why, I could not even reach the border in two weeks! What does this mean? Didn't you tell the castellan why I want to go to Malbork?"

"I not only begged him on your behalf, but the Duchess Anna did too."

"And?"

"And the old man told her that he didn't want your head and that he himself grieved for you. 'If I could find some law in his favor,' he said, 'or even some precedent—I would let him go altogether, but if I cannot, I cannot. It would be bad for this kingdom if people begin to shut their eyes to the law and be lenient because of friendship; that I would not do, even if it were a question of my relative, Toporczyk, or my own brother.' People are so useless here! He went on to say: 'We pay no special regard to the Teutonic Knights, but we cannot bring shame upon ourselves before them. What would they think, and their guests who come from the whole world, if I were to release a nobleman sentenced to

death because he wanted to go and fight them? Would they believe
that he would ever be punished, or that there is any justice in our
country? I would rather cut off one head than have the king and
the kingdom ridiculed.' To that the duchess replied that she was
surprised at a justice where a kinswoman of the king has her pleas
fall on deaf ears, but the old man replied: 'The king himself may
show mercy, but he may not show it against the law.' And they
began to quarrel, for the duchess was carried away by anger. 'Then
at least do not let him rot in prison,' she said. And the castellan
replied: 'Very well! tomorrow I will have the scaffold put up in the
marketplace.' And with that, they parted. Now, poor lad, only the
Lord Jesus can save you."

A long period of silence followed.

"So?" said Zbyszko in a dull voice. "It will be soon now?"

"In two or three days. If it can't be helped, it can't be helped.
What I could do, I did. I fell at the castellan's feet and begged for
mercy, but he repeated what he had said before: 'Find me some law
or some precedent!' What can I find? I went to see Father Stanislaw
of Skarbimierz and asked him to come to you with the Holy
Sacrament. You should have this at least to boast of, that the same
priest who heard the queen's last confession, also heard yours. But
I didn't find him at home, for he was with Duchess Anna."

"Maybe with Danusia?"

"Not at all. The girl is getting stronger and stronger. I'm going
to see him early tomorrow morning. They say that after a confession by him, one's redemption is as certain as if it were in the bag."

Zbyszko sat down, rested his elbows on his knees and bowed his
head so low that his hair covered his face. The older man gazed at
him for some time and finally exclaimed in a low voice: "Zbyszko!
Zbyszko!"

The youth looked up, showing a face which was full of irritation
and cold fury rather than of pain.

"What?"

"Listen carefully, for perhaps I have found an answer." He drew
near and began almost to whisper: "You've heard how Duke Witold, once upon a time, when he was imprisoned by our present
king at Krewo, escaped from prison disguised in woman's clothes.
No woman will stay in prison here for you, but take my leather
jacket, take my hood, and go out—you know what I mean. No one

will notice you. And the way is clear. It's dark beyond the door. No one will throw a light in your face. They saw me yesterday when I was going out, but no one took a good look at me. Be quiet and listen: They will find me tomorrow—and then what? Will they cut off my head? Much good that would do them, for I'm fated to die in two or three weeks. When you get out of here, mount a horse and ride straight to Duke Witold. Recall yourself to his memory, pay your respects to him, and he will accept you, and you will be as safe as behind a stove in heaven. People here say that the ducal armies have been destroyed by the Tartars. One does not know if it is true, but it may be, for the deceased queen prophesied it. If it is true, the duke will need knights all the more and will be glad to see you. Stick to him, for there is no better service in the world. If any other king loses a war, it's all over with him, but Duke Witold is so clever that after a loss he makes himself stronger than he was before. And he is generous, and loves our people mightily. Tell him everything as it happened. Tell him that you wanted to march with him against the Tartars but could not because you were in prison. If God grants it, he may give you land and peasants—and dub you a knight and speak on your behalf with the king. He will be a good advocate—you will see!"

Zbyszko listened in silence, and Macko, as if excited by his own words, went on:

"Don't die when you're young, but return to Bogdaniec. And when you've returned you must immediately take a wife so that our line may not die out. Only when you have begotten children may you challenge Lichtenstein to combat to the death. Beware of seeking vengeance before that, for it they were to shoot at you somewhere in Prussia as they did me, there would be no help for you. Now take my leather jacket, take my hood, and go in God's name."

Macko stood up and began to take off his jacket, but Zbyszko got up also, stopped him, and said:

"I won't do what you want, as God and the Holy Cross may help me."

"Why not?" asked Macko in amazement.

"Because I won't."

Macko paled with emotion and anger.

"I wish you had never been born."

"You already told the castellan," said Zbyszko, "that you would give your head for mine."

"How do you know?"

"The Lord of Taczewo told me."

"Well, and what of it?"

"What of it! The castellan told you that shame would fall on me and our whole line. Would it not be a still greater shame if I escaped from here and left you to the vengeance of the law?"

"What vengeance? Be sensible, for God's sake! What will the law do to me, when I shall die in any case?"

"All the more reason that I should not do this. May God punish me if I abandon you when you are old and sick. What dishonor!"

Silence followed: nothing but the hard, loud breathing of Macko was to be heard—and the calls of the archers, standing guard at the gates. Deep night had already fallen over the outside world.

"Listen," said Macko at last in a broken voice, "it was not dishonorable for Duke Witold to escape from Krewo in the way that he did. And it will not be dishonorable for you. . . ."

"Ha!" replied Zbyszko with a certain melancholy. "The duke is a Grand Duke! He has a crown received from the king's hands; he has wealth and lordship—and I, poor nobleman, have nothing but my honor." Then, after a pause, he exclaimed, as if in a sudden outburst of anger: "Don't you understand that I love you also, and that I won't give your head for mine?"

Macko got up on his shaky legs, stretched out his hands before him, and—although the natures of men at that time were hard, as if cast in iron—roared suddenly in a heartrending voice: "Zbyszko!"

The next day the court servants began to transport to the marketplace beams for the scaffold which was to be erected opposite the main gate of the town hall.

The duchess was still taking counsel with Wojciech Jastrzebiec, with Stanislaw of Skarbimierz, and other learned canons, skilled alike in written laws and in customs. She was induced to make these efforts by the words of the castellan, who had declared that if they could find some "law or precedent," he would not fail to set Zbyszko free. Consequently they deliberated long and hard to find something, and although Father Stanislaw had prepared Zbyszko for death and given him the Last Sacrament, none the less he returned directly from the dungeon to take his place again at the council, which lasted nearly until dawn.

Meanwhile the day of execution arrived. From early morning, crowds made their way to the marketplace, for the head of a nobleman awakened greater curiosity than that of an ordinary man, and the weather was beautiful. Furthermore, the news spread among the women that the condemned man was young and extraordinarily handsome, so the entire road from the castle blossomed with groups of elegantly dressed townswomen. In the windows looking onto the marketplace and the projecting oriels one could see women's caps, gold and velvet headbands, or blond heads of girls adorned only with chaplets of roses and lilies. Although the business had really nothing to do with them, the town councillors all came out to show their own importance and took up a position near the scaffold immediately behind the knights, who, wishing to show their sympathy with the youth, had assembled in the front. Behind them was a motley crowd, composed of the smaller merchants, and craftsmen in the colors of their gilds. Young students and children, pushed to the back, darted about like vexatious flies amidst the crowd, forcing their way into any freely available space. Above the compact mass of human heads towered the scaffold, overspread with new cloth, on which stood three men: the executioner—a broad-shouldered, ominous German, dressed in a red jacket and hood, with a heavy, double-edged sword in his hand—and his two attendants with bare arms and halters at their belts. At their feet was a block and a coffin, also covered with cloth. The bells in the towers of St. Mary's tolled, filling the town with a booming sound and frightening flocks of jackdaws and pigeons. The people looked at the road running from the castle, and then at the scaffold and the executioner standing up on it with his sword glowing in the sunshine, and then again at the knights, who they always regarded with envy and respect. This time there was indeed something to look at, for the most famous in the country were standing in a square around the scaffold. They admired the broad shoulders and the dignity of Zawisza the Black, and his raven hair falling down to his shoulders; they admired the short stocky figure and bowlegs of Zyndram of Maszkowice and the huge, almost superhuman stature of Paszko the Thief of Biskupice; the threatening face of Bartosz of Wodzinko, and the handsome figure of Dobko of Olesnica, who had overthrown twelve German knights at a tournament at Torun, and Sigismund of Bobowa, who was famous for having done the same to Hungarians at Koszyce, and Krzon of Goat's Head, and Lis of Fair-Ground, terrible in hand-to-hand combat, and Staszko of Charbimowice, who could catch up to a galloping horse. Attention was also paid to the pale-faced Macko of Bogdaniec, who was accompanied by Florian of Korytnica and Martin of Wrocimowice. It was generally supposed that he was the father of the condemned man.

But the greatest interest of all was aroused by Powala of Taczewo, who, standing in the front row, held in his mighty arms Danusia, dressed all in white, with a green chaplet of rue on her fair hair. People did not understand what it meant and why the white-clad girl had to witness the execution of the condemned. Some said it was his sister, others guessed that it was the lady of the young knight's thoughts, but even they could not explain either her dress or her presence near the scaffold. However, the sight of her face, ruddy like an apple but all wet with tears, awakened sympathy and emotion in every heart. The close-packed crowds of people began to whisper against the sternness of the castellan and the severity of the law—and their whisper gradually grew into a threatening murmur—and at last voices began to be raised here and there, shouting that if the scaffold were wrecked, the execution would have to be put off.

The crowds came to life and swayed. Word went from mouth to mouth that if the king had been present, he would have undoubtedly shown mercy to the youth, who, it was asserted, had not committed any offence.

But everything quieted down when distant shouts proclaimed the approach of the royal archers and halberdiers, with the condemned man in the midst of them. Presently the procession appeared on the marketplace. At the head of it walked the funeral brotherhood, dressed in black cloaks reaching to the ground, with black veils over their faces, leaving only holes for the eyes. The populace were afraid of these sombre figures and fell silent at the sight of them. Behind them came a company of crossbow men, composed of chosen Lithuanians clad in jackets of untanned elk-skin. This was a company of the royal guard. At the rear of the procession could be seen the halberds of a second company, in the midst of which, between the clerk of the court, who had to read the sentence, and Father Stanislaw of Skarbimierz, carrying the crucifix, walked Zbyszko.

All eyes now turned to him, and from every window and oriel leaned out women. Zbyszko was clad in his captured white jacket, embroidered with golden griffins and with a gold fringe at the bottom—and in this splendid attire he seemed to the eyes of the crowd like some young duke or an esquire of a great house. From his stature and the breadth of his shoulders, visible under his tight garment, from his powerful thighs and broad chest, he might have seemed to be a fully grown man, but above this man's figure was the face of a boy, with the first down on his upper lip—a beautiful face, the face of a royal page with golden hair, cut in a straight line above the eyebrows and hanging down over the shoulders. He walked with an even, energetic step, yet he was pale. At times he looked at the crowd, as if he were in a dream; at times he raised his eyes to the church towers, to the flocks of jackdaws and the swinging bells, which were ringing out his last hour; and at other times a certain surprise was mirrored on his face that these sounds and the sobbing of women and the whole ceremony should all be for him. On the marketplace he finally caught sight of the scaffold in the distance, and on it the red silhouette of the executioner. He shuddered and crossed himself, and the priest at the same moment gave him the crucifix to kiss. A few steps further a bunch of cornflowers fell at his feet, thrown by a young girl of the people. Zbyszko bent and picked it up and smiled at the girl, who burst into loud weeping. But he apparently thought that, in the face of these crowds, and in the face of the women waving their kerchiefs from the windows, he ought to die bravely and leave behind him at least the memory of a "valiant youth." So he exerted all his courage and willpower, and with a sudden movement, he tossed his hair back, raised his head still higher, and walked proudly, almost as if he were a victor in a tournament going to receive his prize. Progress was slow, however, because the crowd in front of them became denser and denser and gave way unwillingly. In vain the Lithuanian bowmen, walking in the first rank, called out every moment: *"Eyk shalin! Eyk shalin!"* (Out of the way!) The crowd refused to guess the meaning of these words, and only drew closer together. Although the citizenry of Cracow in those days was composed two-thirds of Germans, threatening curses were widely uttered against the Teutonic Knights: "Disgrace! Disgrace! May those black-crossed wolves perish if children are to be executed here because of them! Shame on the king and the kingdom!" The Lithuanians, seeing the resistance, took their bent bows from their shoulders and began to look frowningly at the populace, but they did not dare to shoot into the close-packed multitude without an order. The captain sent forward the halberdiers, for whom it was easier to force a way, and at last they reached the knights standing around the scaffold.

These made way without opposition. The halberdiers passed first, then Zbyszko behind them with the priest and the clerk. But then something unexpected happened. Suddenly from the midst of the knights stepped forward Powala with Danusia on his arm, and he cried out: "Stop!" with such a thunderous voice that the whole procession stopped as if rooted to the ground. Neither the captain nor any of the soldiers was inclined to oppose a lord and a belted knight, whom they were accustomed to see every day at the castle, sometimes in confidential talk with the king. Other knights, too, equally distinguished, began to shout in tones of command: "Stop! Stop!"—while the Lord of Taczewo approached Zbyszko and gave him the white-clad Danusia.

He, thinking that it was a last farewell, seized her, embraced her, and pressed her to his breast—but Danusia, instead of nestling in his arms and throwing her own about his neck, hastily tore her white veil from her fair hair, from under her chaplet of rue, and covered Zbyszko's head with it, at the same time calling with the entire strength of her tearful, childish voice:

"He's mine! He's mine!"

"He is hers!" repeated the powerful voices of the knights. "To the castellan!"

They were answered by a thundering shout from the populace: "To the castellan! To the castellan!" The father confessor raised his eyes, the clerk of the court became confused, the captain and the halberdiers lowered their weapons, for they all understood what had happened.

There was an old Polish and Slavic custom, as valid as any law, known in the foothills of the Carpathians, in the province of Cracow, and even in other lands, that if a virgin threw her veil over a lad being led to death, as a sign that she was ready to marry him, she thereby redeemed him from death and punishment. The custom was known to the knights, to the yeomen, and to the Polish urban population—and even the Germans who had long inhabited Polish towns had heard of its validity. Old Macko nearly fainted from emotion at the sight; the knights, quickly dispersing the crossbow men, surrounded Zbyszko and Danusia; the populace, touched and delighted, shouted ever more loudly: "To the castellan! To the castellan!" The crowds surged suddenly, resembling huge waves of a sea. The executioner and his helpers ran quickly from the scaffold. There was general confusion. It became clear to all that if Jasko of Teczyno now wished to oppose this consecrated custom a serious uproar would begin. A wave of people immediately threw themselves upon the scaffold. In the twinkling of an eye the cloth was torn off and rent in pieces, and then the beams and planks, dragged by strong hands, or chopped with axes, began to bend, to crack, and to break—and a few paternosters later not a trace of the scaffold was left on the square.

Zbyszko, still holding Danusia on his arm, returned to the castle as if he were a conquering hero. For around him went the first knights of the kingdom, their faces joyous, and on either side, in front and behind, jostled thousands of men, women, and children, yelling, singing, stretching their hands towards Danusia and praising the valor and the charm of the couple. From the windows rich townswomen clapped their white hands; everywhere eyes were wet with tears of joy. A rain of chaplets of roses and lilies, a rain of ribbons and even of golden headbands and hairnets fell at the feet of the happy youth, while he, radiant as the sun, his heart filled with gratitude, kept lifting up his lady in white and, occasionally, kissing her knees when absolute joy overcame him. At this sight some of the townswomen were so moved that they threw themselves into the arms of their lovers, declaring that should their men deserve death, they would be freed in the same manner. Thus Zbyszko and Danusia became, as it were, the beloved children of the knights, the burghers, and the common folk. Old Macko, whom Florian of Korytnica and Martin of Wrocimowice led all the time by hand, almost went out of his mind with joy—and with amazement that such a means of saving his nephew had never even entered his head. In his powerful voice, Powala of Taczewo related amid the general uproar how the means had been thought out, or rather recalled, by Wojciech Jastrzebiec and Stanislaw of Skarbimierz, both well versed in written law and custom, when they were taking counsel with the duchess. The knights had marvelled at its simplicity, saying that if none remembered the custom, it was because for a long time it had not been practised in a city where Germans lived.

Everything, however, still depended on the castellan. The knights and people made their way toward the castle, in which the Lord of Teczyno lived in the absence of the king. The clerk of the court, Father Stanislaw of Skarbimierz, Zawisza, Farurej, Zyndram of Maszkowice, and Powala of Taczewo went straight to him, to represent to him the validity of the custom and to remind him how he had said himself that if they found a "law or precedent," he would quickly liberate the condemned man. And could there be a better law than an ancient custom which had never been broken? The Lord of Teczyno answered that the custom was more suited to the simple folk and to the robbers in the Carpathian foothills than to the nobility, but he was himself too learned in all fields of law to be able to deny its force. At the same time he covered his silver beard with his hands and smiled behind his fingers, being obviously glad. At last he came out onto a low terrace, with Duchess Anna Danuta and a few clergy and knights by his side.

Seeing him, Zbyszko lifted Danusia up once again—and the Lord of Teczyno put his wrinkled hand on her golden hair, kept it there for a moment, and then nodded his grey head solemnly and kindly.

The sign was understood, and the cheers of the populace were so loud that the walls of the castle shook. "May God always assist you! Long live, the just lord! Live and judge us!"—rang from all sides. Then new shouts were raised for Danusia and Zbyszko, and a moment later the pair, coming out onto the terrace, fell at the feet of the good Duchess Anna Danuta, to whom Zbyszko owed his life, for she had thought out the means with the learned men and had instructed Danusia on what to do.

"Long live the young couple!" exclaimed Powala of Taczewo at the sight of the kneeling pair.

"Long live the young couple!" repeated the others.

The grey castellan turned to the duchess and said:

"The betrothal must now take place at once, gracious duchess, for the custom so bids."

"I will celebrate the betrothal at once," the good lady answered with a beaming face, "but the marriage I will not allow without the consent of her father, Jurand of Spychow."

CHAPTER VII

AT the residence of the merchant Amylej, Macko and Zbyszko were considering what they should do next. The old knight expected early death, and since the Franciscan, Father Cybek, who was versed in the treatment of wounds, also predicted it for him, he desired to return to Bogdaniec, to be buried with his forefathers in the cemetery at Ostrow.

However, not all his forefathers lay there. Theirs had once been a numerous family. In time of war they had shouted their war-cry: "Hailstones!" And on their coat-of-arms, thinking themselves better than other small landowners, who had not always a right to an escutcheon, they bore a Blunt Horseshoe. In the year 1331, at the battle of Plowce, seventy-four warriors of Bogdaniec had been shot in a march by German bowmen, one alone having been saved, Wojciech, nicknamed the Aurochs, to whom King Wladyslaw the Short, after the defeat of the Germans, had confirmed the special privilege of a coat-of-arms and the lands of Bogdaniec. The bones of the others had lain from that time bleaching on the field of Plowce, while Wojciech had returned home, only to see the complete ruin of his line.

For, while the men of Bogdaniec had been dying under German arrows, robber knights from neighboring Silesia had fallen upon their nest, burned the settlement to the ground, and cut down the people or carried them off to be sold in distant German lands. Wojciech was left alone in the old house, which had been saved from the fire, the heir of wide but empty lands, which had before belonged to the whole of his family. Five years later he married, and having begotten two sons, Jasko and Macko, he was killed by an aurochs while hunting in the forest.

The sons grew up under the care of their mother, Kachna of Spalenica, who in two campaigns avenged her old wrongs on the Silesian Germans, but fell in the third. Jasko, when he grew up, united in marriage with Jagienka of Mocarzewo, by whom he had a son, Zbyszko; while Macko, remaining in the bachelor state, looked after the property and his nephew as much as war expeditions allowed.

But when, during the civil war between the Grzymala and the Nalecz clans, the buildings at Bogdaniec were burned for the second time and the yeomen scattered, the lone Macko strove in vain to raise them again. After spending several years in poverty, he finally pledged his land to an abbot who was a kinsman of his, and went himself with Zbyszko, still a boy, to Lithuania to fight the Germans.

However, he never lost sight of Bogdaniec. He went to Lithuania precisely to enrich himself with booty and then return, redeem his land, populate it with prisoners of war, rebuild the castelet and settle Zbyszko in it. And so now, after the happy rescue of the young man, he only thought of Bogdaniec and consulted with him about it at Amylej's house.

They had the means to redeem their land. They had amassed large enough resources from booty, from the ransoms which captured knights had paid them, and from the gifts of Witold. They had profited particularly well from that battle to the death with the two Frisian knights. The suits of armor alone, which they had taken from them, constituted a real fortune in those days, and aside from the armor, they had taken wagons, horses, men, garments, money, and a rich supply of war implements. Much of this booty was now bought by the merchant Amylej, among other things two pieces of fine Flanders cloth which the prudent and wealthy Frisians had had with them in their wagons.

Macko also sold the costly suit of armor he had captured, thinking that in view of his approaching death it would now no longer be of use to him. The armorer who bought it sold it the following day with considerable profit to Martin of Wrocimowice, who had the Half-Goat as his escutcheon, for Milan armor was at that time valued above any other in the world.

Zbyszko regretted the sale of the armor with all his heart.

"If God gives you back your health," he said to his uncle, "where will you find another armor like that?"

"Where I found the first one—on some German," answered Macko. "But I shall not escape death this time. The iron cracked between my ribs and a splinter remained in me. When I wanted to take it in my fingers and pull it out, I only pushed it in deeper. And now nothing can be done."

"You ought to drink a pot or two of bear's fat!"

"Ha! Father Cybek also says that it would be a good thing, for perhaps the chip would slip out somehow. But where am I to get any here? At Bogdaniec one could take an axe and wait at night under a honey-tree."

"Then we must go to Bogdaniec. Just don't die on the road."

Old Macko looked at his nephew with a certain affection.

"I know where you would like to go: to the court of Duke Janusz, or to Jurand of Spychow, to ride against the Chelmno Germans."

"That I do not deny. I should be glad to go with the duchess's court to either Warsaw or Ciechanow, in order to be as long as possible with Danusia. Life is nothing without her now, for she is not only my lady but also my love. I am so taken by her that when I think of her I get the shivers. I will go after her even to the end of the world, but now my first duty is to you. You did not abandon me, so I will not abandon you. If we are to go to Bogdaniec, then let's go!"

"You're a good lad," said Macko.

"God would punish me if I behaved otherwise to you. Look, they are already loading the wagons; I've ordered one to be spread with hay for you. Amylej's wife has also given us a fine feather bed, but I don't know whether you won't be too hot lying on it. We will go slowly, together with the duchess and her court, that you may not lack care. Then they will return to Mazovia and we to our own place—so help us God!"

"I should like to live long enough to build up the castelet again," said Macko, "for I know that after my death you won't think much about Bogdaniec."

"Why should I not think about it?"

"Because your head will be full of combat and of love."

"Was not your head full of war? Why, I see clearly what I have to do—and the first thing will be to build the castelet more strongly of oak and then to have a moat dug around it for defence."

"You think so?" asked Macko with interest. "Well, and when the castelet is built? Go on!"

"When the castelet is built, I will go to the duke's court either at Warsaw or Ciechanow."

"After my death?"

"If you die soon, then after your death, though first I will bury you properly; but if the Lord Jesus gives you health, then you will stay at Bogdaniec. The duchess promised me that I should get a knight's belt from the duke. Otherwise Lichtenstein would not be willing to fight with me."

"So after that you will go to Malbork?"

"To Malbork, or to the end of the world if need be, only I must find Lichtenstein."

"For that I don't blame you. Your death or his!"

"I will bring you his gloves and belt to Bogdaniec—never fear!"

"Just beware of treachery. Treachery is second nature to them."

"I will pay my respects to Duke Janusz and ask him to get a safe conduct from the grand master. Now there is peace. I will ride with the safe conduct to Malbork, where there are always a number of guests of the Order. Then you know what I will do? First comes Lichtenstein; then I will seek out any others who have peacock crests on their helmets, and I will challenge them in turn. Dear God! If the Lord Jesus grants me victory, then I will fulfill my vow at the same time!"

So saying, Zbyszko smiled at his own thoughts, and his face at that moment resembled that of a boy who promises what knightly deeds he will do when he grows up.

"Hey!" said Macko, nodding his head, "if you overthrow three knights of distinguished family, you will not only fulfill your vow but will take some booty from them—dear God!"

"Three knights!" exclaimed Zbyszko. "I told myself in prison that I would not be stingy with Danusia. As many as I have fingers on my hands—not just three!"

Macko shrugged his shoulders.

"You may be surprised, or you many even not believe me," said Zbyszko, "but I am going from Malbork to Jurand of Spychow.

How should I not pay my respects to him, when he is Danusia's father? And I will ride with him against the Germans from Chelmno. You said yourself that there isn't a greater werewolf against the Germans to be found in the whole of Mazovia."

"And if he refuses you Danusia?"

"That's not likely! He seeks his own vengeance, and I mine. Where would he find a better ally? And since the duchess allowed the betrothal, he will not object to it."

"I see one thing already," said Macko. "You will take all the people away from Bogdaniec, so as to provide yourself with a retinue worthy of a knight, and the land will be left without hands. As long as I live I won't give them, but after my death I see that you will take them."

"God will provide me with a retinue; and, after all, Abbot Janko of Tulcza is a kinsman of ours, so he will be generous."

Suddenly the door opened, and as if to prove that God would provide Zbyszko with a retinue, two men entered. Dark-complexioned, short and thick, wearing yellow Jewish-like caftans, red Crimean caps and extraordinarily wide breeches, they stood just inside the doorway and laid their fingers on their forehead, their lips, and their breasts, while making low bows.

"Who are these odd fellows?" asked Macko; then, addressing the pair: "Who are you?"

"Your slaves," answered the newcomers in broken Polish.

"How so? Where from? Who has sent you here?"

"Lord Zawisza has sent us as a gift to the young knight, to be his slaves."

"Oh, God be praised! Two more men for us!" exclaimed Macko joyfully. "Of what nation are you?"

"We are Turks."

"Turks?" repeated Zbyszko. "I shall have two Turks in my retinue. Have you ever seen any Turks?"

And springing towards them he began to turn them around and look at them as if they were strange creatures from overseas. Macko, however, said:

"No, I never saw any, but I've heard that Zawisza has Turks in his service, whom he took when he was fighting on the Danube with the Roman Emperor Sigismund. So? Are you pagans, you curs?"

"Our lord commanded us to be baptized," said one of the prisoners of war.

"And had you nothing to ransom yourselves with?"

"We come from far, from the Asiatic coast, from Brussa."

Zbyszko, who was always eager to hear all kinds of war stories, and particularly when they dealt with the deeds of the famous Zawisza the Black, began to ask them in what way they had come to be taken prisoner. But there was nothing unusual in their stories: Zawisza had fallen upon thirty or forty of them in a ravine three years before, had slain some and taken others—and afterwards had given many away. Zbyszko's and Macko's hearts were filled with joy at the sight of such a wonderful gift, particularly since it was difficult to get men in those times, and the possession of them constituted real wealth.

A moment later Zawisza himself came in, accompanied by Powala and Paszko the Thief of Biskupice. Since they had all worked to save Zbyszko's life and were glad they had succeeded, each now brought him some gift in farewell and remembrance. The generous Lord of Taczewo gave him an embroidered horse-cloth, wide and rich, with a gold fringe hanging over the breast; Paszko, on the other hand, gave him a Hungarian sword worth several marks. Afterwards there came Lis of Fair-Ground, Farurej and Krzon of Goat's Head, and Martin of Wrocimowice, and, last of all, Zyndram of Maszkowice—each of them with full hands.

Zbyszko greeted them with an overflowing heart, for he was doubly happy—at receiving the gifts and at having the most famous knights in the kingdom show him their friendship. For their part, they asked him about his departure and about Macko's health, advising the old warrior, as they were experienced in these matters though comparatively young, to try various ointments and balsams, marvellous for healing wounds.

But Macko enjoined them to think only of Zbyszko, for he himself was bound for the other world. He stated that it was difficult to live with an iron splinter under one's ribs. He also complained that he was constantly spitting blood and could not eat. A bowl of shelled nuts, two spans of sausage, and a dish of butter eggs was all he could eat in a day. Father Cybek had let his blood several times, thinking that thus he would draw the fever from under his heart and give him back his appetite for food—but even this did not help.

However, he was so glad at the gifts his nephew had received that he immediately felt better, and when the merchant Amylej ordered a keg of wine to be brought into the room in honor of such distinguished guests, he sat down to drink alongside them. They began to talk about Zbyszko's escape from death and his betrothal to Danusia. The knights were sure that Jurand of Spychow would be disinclined to opposed the will of the duchess, particularly if Zbyszko should avenge the memory of Danusia's mother and present the promised peacock crests.

"As regards Lichtenstein," said Zawisza, "I do not know if he will be willing to fight you, since he is a monk and also one of the elders of the Order. Indeed! His attendants said that if he waits long enough, he will eventually become grand master."

"If he refuses to fight, he loses his honor," said Lis of Fair-Ground.

"That is not the case," replied Zawisza, "for, unlike a secular knights, monks are forbidden to engage in single combat."

"Yet many do so."

"Because the practices in the Order have become corrupt. They make various vows and then boast, to the great indignation of the whole Christian world, that they break them from time to time. But a Teutonic Knight, and particularly a commander, is forbidden to engage in a fight to the death."

"Ha! then you must get him in wartime."

"But they say there won't be any war," said Zbyszko, "because the Teutonic Knights are now afraid of our nation."

At that Zyndram of Maszkowice said:

"Peace will not last long. There can be no harmony with a wolf, for he has to live on what others have."

"Meanwhile we might have to grapple with Timur the Lame," said Powala. "Duke Witold suffered a defeat at the hands of Edyga—so much is certain."

"Yes, and Voivode Spytko did not return," noted Paszko the Thief of Biskupice.

"And many Lithuanian dukes were left on the field."

"The deceased queen foretold that it would be so," said the Lord of Taczewo.

"Ha! then maybe we shall move against Timur."

Here the conversation turned to the Lithuanian expedition against the Tartars. There was no longer any doubt that Duke Witold, a leader more impetuous than skillful, had suffered a terrible defeat on the Worskla, in which a large number of Lithuanian and Ruthenian boyars had fallen and, along with them, a handful of auxiliary Polish knights and even some Teutonic Knights. The company gathered at Amylej's house complained particularly of the fate of the young Spytko of Melsztyn, the greatest lord in the kingdom, who had gone on the expedition as a volunteer and after the battle was missing. They also praised to the skies his truly chivalrous behavior in that, having received from the enemy leader a Tartar cap conferring safety, he refused to put it on during the battle, preferring a glorious death to life by favor of the pagan chief. It was, however, still uncertain whether he had fallen or had been taken captive. He had the means to ransom himself from captivity, for his wealth was immeasurable, and, moreover, King Wladyslaw had allowed him to hold the whole of Podolia as a fief from the Crown.

The defeat of the Lithuanians might be dangerous for the whole of the Jagiellonian state. No one knew exactly whether the Tartars, encouraged by their victory over Witold, would not throw themselves on the lands and strongholds belonging to the grand duchy. In such case the kingdom would be drawn into the war. Accordingly, many knights like Zawisza, Farurej, Dobko, and even Powala, accustomed to seek adventures and combats at foreign courts, purposely remained at Cracow, not knowing what the near future might bring. If Tamerlane, lord of twenty-seven kingdoms, were to move the whole Mongolian world, then the danger might be enormous. And there were people who foresaw that it might be so.

"If there be need, we will measure our strength with the Lame One himself. It will not be as easy for him to deal with our nation as it was with all those whom he has conquered and overrun hitherto. And other Christian princes will come to our aid."

Zyndram of Maszkowice, who burned with especial hatred against the Order, replied bitterly:

"Princes—I don't know, but the Teutonic Knights are ready to ally themselves with the Tartars and attack us from the other side."

"Then there will be war!" exclaimed Zbyszko. "I will go against the Teutonic Knights!"

But the other knights began to dispute Zyndram's statement. It was true, they said, that the Teutonic Knights did not know the fear of God and regarded only their own interests, but they would not go so far as to help pagans against a Christian nation. Besides, Timur was waging war somewhere in Asia, and the Tartar chief Edyga had lost so many men in the battle that he was said to have become alarmed at the cost of his victory. Duke Witold was resourceful and was sure to have supplied his strongholds well; and although the Lithuanians had not succeeded this time, it was nothing new for them to defeat the Tartars.

"Our fight to the death is with the Germans, not the Tartars," said Zyndram of Maszkowice. "If we do not wipe them out, they will be our ruin."

Then he turned to Zbyszko.

"But Mazovia would perish first. You will always find work there—never fear!"

"If my uncle were well, I would go there at once!"

"May God help you!" said Powala, raising his cup.

"To your health and Danusia's!"

"And to the destruction of the Germans!" added Zyndram.

And they began to take their leave. Meanwhile one of the duchess's courtiers came in, a falcon on his fist. Bowing to the knights present, he turned with an odd smile to Zbyszko.

"The lady duchess instructed me to tell you," he said, "that she is spending tonight at Cracow and will start tomorrow morning."

"Good," said Zbyszko, "but why is that? Has someone fallen ill?"

"No. The duchess has a guest from Mazovia."

"Has the duke arrived?"

"Not the duke, but Jurand of Spychow," replied the courtier.

Hearing that, Zbyszko became perturbed. His heart began to beat as violently in his breast as once before, when his death-sentence had been read out.

CHAPTER VIII

DUCHESS Anna was not too surprised at Jurand's arrival. In the midst of his constant expeditions, inroads, and battles with neighboring German knights, he was seized frequently with a sudden yearning for Danusia. Then he appeared unexpectedly, at either Warsaw or Ciechanow, or wherever the court of Duke Janusz might be. At the sight of his child he always broke out into great grief. For Danusia, as the years went by, became so like her mother that it seemed to him that he saw his deceased wife as he had once known her at Duchess Anna's court in Warsaw. People sometimes thought that this grief would finally soften an iron heart devoted only to vengeance. Accordingly, the duchess often tried to persuade him to leave his blood-stained Spychow and stay at the court, near Danusia. The duke himself, valuing his courage and his distinction, and desiring to avoid the trouble to which the continual border incidents exposed his own person and land, offered him the office of sword-bearer. But always in vain. The sight of Danusia reopened his old wounds. After a few days he lost the desire to eat, or sleep, or talk. His heart began to storm and swell with blood, and finally he would vanish from the court and return to his Spychow marshes to drown his grief and anger in blood. Then people said: "Woe to the Germans! Indeed they are not sheep, but for Jurand they are sheep, and he is their wolf." After a certain time had passed, stories spread, sometimes of the capture of volunteers passing through the border lands to take service with the Teutonic Knights, sometimes of burned houses, sometimes of peasants seized, or of fights to the death in which the terrible Jurand always emerged victorious. Since both the Mazovians and those German knights who held adjacent land and fortalices on behalf of the Order were so fond of preying on each other, warlike disturbances on the frontier never ceased, even in times of profound peace between the Mazovian dukes and the Teutonic Order. The inhabitants used to take crossbows or pikes even when they went to cut wood in the forests or to reap their harvests. Men lived in uncertainty of the morrow, in constant preparation for war, in hardness of heart. No one was satisfied merely with self-defence, but repaid robbery with robbery, arson with arson, and inroad with inroad. And it happened that when the Germans were stealing quietly through the border forests to fall upon some fortalice and to carry off peasants or cattle, the Mazovians were doing the same thing at the same time. So they frequently met and fought to the death, or sometimes it was only the leaders who challenged one another to mortal combat, the victor taking the whole troop of his defeated antagonist. Accordingly, when complaints were made against Jurand at the Warsaw court, the duke answered by complaints against the inroads made in other directions by the German knights. Thus, with both sides demanding justice and being unwilling or unable to satisfy it, all these robberies, burnings, and inroads passed completely unpunished.

But Jurand, sitting in his marshy, rush-grown Spychow, and burning with unquenchable lust for vengeance, became such a burden to his foreign neighbors that eventually their fear became greater than their hatred. The fields adjacent to Spychow lay uncultivated, the forests were overgrown with wild hop and hazel bushes, and the meadows with coarse bents. More than one German knight, accustomed to the law of the fist in his homeland, tried to settle in the neighborhood of Spychow, but each one after a certain time preferred to abandon fief, cattle, and villeins rather than live at the side of such an implacable man. Often the knights agreed to make a common attack against Spychow, but each incursion ended in defeat. They tried various methods. Once they brought in a knight from the banks of the River Main, well known for his strength and fierceness, a victor in all his fights, to challenge Jurand to combat on trodden ground. But when they stood in the lists, the German, as if bewitched, lost heart at the sight of the terrible Mazovian and turned his horse to flee. Jurand pierced his unarmed back with his lance and thus deprived him of both honor and the light of day. From that time onwards his neighbors were possessed with still greater fear, and if a German caught sight of the smoke of Spychow, even from a considerable distance, he immediately crossed himself and began to pray to his patron in heaven, for the belief established itself that Jurand had sold his soul to the Evil One for the sake of vengeance.

Terrible things were also said of Spychow: that the path leading to it, running through soft bogs and dreamy pools overgrown with pondweed and knotgrass, was so narrow that two men on horseback could not ride it abreast; that on both sides of this path German bones were rotting, while at night the heads of drowned men walked along it on spiders' legs, howling and drawing riders and horses into the depths of the swamp. It was reported that the palisade of the fortalice was adorned with human skulls. The truth was that in the grated dungeons, dug beneath the lord's quarters at Spychow, there were always a larger or smaller number of groaning captives, and that the name of Jurand was more terrible than those tales of skeletons and water-spirits.

Zbyszko, when he learned of Jurand's arrival, hastened at once to see him, but since Jurand was Danusia's father he went with a certain disquiet in his heart. No one could complain that he had taken Danusia for the lady of his thoughts and made a vow to her, but later the duchess had celebrated his betrothal with Danusia. What would Jurand say to that? Would he agree or would he not? And what would happen if, as her father, he were to declare that he would never allow the marriage? These questions filled Zbyszko with anxiety, for he cared more for Danusia than for anything else in the world. One thought alone gave him hope, and that was that Jurand would look upon his attack on Lichtenstein with favor and not with reproach, for he had done it to avenge Danusia's mother—and had almost lost his own head.

Meanwhile he began to question the courtier who had come for him.

"Where are you taking me?" he asked. "To the castle?"

"Of course to the castle. Jurand is staying with the duchess's court."

"Tell me, what sort of man is he? I'd like to know how to speak to him?"

"What can I tell you! He is a man completely different from other men. They say that he used to be merry until the blood in his liver congealed."

"Is he wise?"

"He's cunning, for he strikes but doesn't get hit. He has only one eye, because the Germans shot out the other with a crossbow. But with that eye he looks into your very soul. No one gets his own way with him. But he loves the duchess, our lady, for he took her lady-in-waiting to be his wife, and now his daughter is being raised by us."

Zbyszko sighed out.

"So you don't think he will oppose the duchess's will?"

"I know what you would like to know, and I will tell you what I have heard. The duchess spoke with him about your betrothal, for it would not have been nice to conceal it. But what he said in reply, nobody knows."

Amid this talk, they arrived at the gate. The captain of the royal archers, the same man who before had conducted Zbyszko to the executioner's sword, now nodded to him in friendly fashion. They passed the guards and found themselves in the courtyard, and then went to the annex on the right where the duchess had her quarters.

The courtier, meeting a page before the door, asked him:

"Where is Jurand of Spychow?"

"In the Crooked Chamber with his daughter."

"In there," said the courtier, pointing to a door.

Zbyszko crossed himself and, raising the curtain that hung across the open doorway, went in with beating heart. But he did not immediately see Jurand and Danusia, for the chamber was not only "crooked" but dark as well. Only after a moment did he perceive the fair head of the girl, who was sitting on her father's knee. They did not hear him come in, so he stood by the curtain, cleared his throat, and finally said:

"May the Lord be praised!"

"For ever and ever," replied Jurand, standing up.

Danusia sprang towards the young knight and, catching him by the hand, began to cry out:

"Zbyszko! Daddy has come!"

Zbyszko knelt and kissed her hands; then, rising, he went up to Jurand with Danusia, and said:

"I have come to pay my respects to you. Do you know who I am?"

Then he bowed slightly and made a movement as if he wanted to embrace Jurand's legs. But Jurand caught his hand, turned him towards the light, and began to look at him in silence.

Zbyszko had already regained some measure of self-control, so he raised his eyes in curiosity to Jurand and saw before him a man of enormous stature with sandy hair and an equally sandy moustache, a pockmarked face, and one eye the color of iron. It seemed to him that that eye wanted to pierce him straight through, and he became confused again. Finally, not knowing what to say, yet wanting desperately to say something in order to break the painful silence, he asked:

"So you are Jurand of Spychow, Danusia's father?"

But Jurand merely pointed to a bench next to the oak chair he sat on, and went on looking at him without saying a word.

At last Zbyszko grew impatient.

"You know," he said, "it's not pleasant to sit like this, as if in a court of judgment."

Then Jurand spoke.

"You wanted to fight with Lichtenstein?"

"Well, yes," replied Zbyszko.

A strange gleam flashed in Jurand's eye, and his fierce face brightened up a bit. After a moment, he looked at Danusia and asked again:

"Was it for her?"

"For whom else? My uncle must have told you how I vowed to tear three peacock crests from German heads. But now there will be not only three; there will be at least as many as I have fingers on both hands. Thus I shall aid you in your vengeance, for this concerns Danusia's mother, after all."

"Woe to them!" replied Jurand.

And silence fell once more. Zbyszko, noticing that by showing his hatred of the Germans he had found the way to Jurand's heart, said:

"I will not forgive them my own wrongs, for I nearly lost my head through them." He turned to Danusia and added: "She saved my life."

"I know," said Jurand.

"This does not displease you?"

"Since you made a vow to her, serve her, for that is the knightly custom."

Zbyszko hesitated a little and then spoke with evident unease.

"For, you see . . . she covered my head with her veil. . . . All the knighthood heard—as did the Franciscan by my side who held the cross—how she said: 'He's mine!' It is certain that I will be no one else's till death, so help me God."

He knelt down again, and wanting to show that he knew the knightly custom, he kissed with great respect both of Danusia's shoes as she sat on the arm of the chair. Then he got up and, turning to Jurand, asked him:

"Have you ever seen anyone like her?"

Jurand suddenly put his terrible, murderous hands on his head and, lowering his eyelids, said in a dull tone:

"I did, but the Germans killed her."

"Then listen," said Zbyszko passionately. "We have one wrong and one vengeance. Those curs also killed a number of our men from Bogdaniec with crossbows while their horses' feet sank in marshy ground. . . . You won't find anyone better than I for your work. I'm not new at this. Ask my uncle. Whether with lance, or axe, with long or short sword, it makes no difference to me. And did my uncle tell you of those Frisians? I will slay you Germans like sheep, and as for the girl, I vow to you on my knees that I will fight for her even with the Lord of Hell himself; and I won't renounce her either for land or cattle or any kind of gear, and even if they gave me a castle with glass windows, if it were without her, I would refuse the castle and would go after her to the end of the world."

Jurand sat for some time with his head in his hands, but at last he roused himself, as if from sleep, and said with grief and sadness:

"You please me, lad, but I will not give her to you, for she is not destined for you, poor soul!"

Zbyszko was dumbfounded and looked at Jurand with round eyes, unable to say a single world.

But Danusia came to his aid. She was very fond of Zbyszko, and she liked very much to be treated as a "ripe maiden" and not a "young chick." She also liked the betrothal and the sweetmeats which her young knight brought her every day; so now when she understood that all could be taken away from her, she leapt from the arm of the chair and, hiding her head on her father's knees, began to lament:

"Daddy! Daddy! I shall cry!"

He obviously loved her above everything else. He laid his hand gently on her head, and in his face there was neither hate nor anger, only sorrow.

Zbyszko in the meantime grew calmer, and said:

"How is this possible? Do you want to oppose the will of God?"

To that Jurand replied:

"If it be the will of God, you will get her, only I cannot bend my will. Indeed, I would gladly bend it for you, but I cannot."

So saying, he raised Danusia and, taking her by the hand, led her to the door. When Zbyszko wanted to block his way, he stopped for a moment and said:

"I shall not take it ill if you serve her like a knight; but don't ask me more questions, for I cannot tell you anything."

And he went out.

CHAPTER IX

THE next day Jurand did not avoid Zbyszko in the least, nor did he prevent him from doing various services for Danusia on the road, services which as a knight he ought to do. On the contrary, Zbyszko, though greatly distressed, noticed that the gloomy Lord of Spychow looked at him with goodwill and, as it were, with sorrow that he had given him so cruel an answer. So the young knight tried more than once to approach him and enter into a conversation. After leaving Cracow, it was not hard to find an opportunity, for both of them accompanied the duchess on horseback. Although usually silent, Jurand talked willingly enough. But as soon as Zbyszko tried to learn something of the obstacles separating him from Danusia, the conversation was suddenly broken off, and Jurand's face became clouded over. Zbyszko thought that the duchess might know something, so he looked for a suitable moment and tried to get any kind of information from her, but she could not tell him much.

"It is a secret," she said. "Jurand himself told me as much and asked me not to question him about it. Undoubtedly he is bound by some vow, as is the custom among men. God, however, will bring everything to light in due time."

"Without Danusia I should feel like a dog on a chain or like a bear in a trap," replied Zbyszko. "No joy, no delight. Nothing but sorrow and sighing. I would go to Tawania with Duke Witold. Let the Tartars kill me there. But first I must take my uncle home, and then I must tear those peacock crests from German heads, as I swore to do. Maybe I will be killed in trying. I would prefer that to seeing Danusia taken by another."

The duchess raised her kind blue eyes to him and asked with a certain surprise:

"And would you let anyone do that?"

"I? As long as I breathe, I will not! Unless my hand would wither and I could not swing an axe!"

"So, you see!"

"Ha! but how can I take her against her father's will?"

At that the duchess said, as if to herself: "Almighty God! But it happens sometimes. . . ." And then to Zbyszko: "Is the will of God not more powerful than that of a father? And what did Jurand say? 'If it be the will of God, he will get her.'"

"He said the same thing to me!" exclaimed Zbyszko. "He said: 'If it be the will of God, you will get her.'"

"You see?"

"That, and your favor, worshipful lady, are my only comforts."

"You have my favor, and Danusia will be loyal to you. Just yesterday I asked her: 'Danusia, will you be loyal to Zbyszko?' And she said, 'I will be Zbyszko's or no one's.' She's only a green berry, but if she says something she will keep her word, for she's a noble child and not a common gadabout. The same was true of her mother."

"God grant it!" said Zbyszko.

"Only remember to be loyal yourself—for more than one youth is fickle. He promises to be faithful, but immediately afterwards prances and rears so that you cannot even tie him down. I speak the truth."

"May the Lord Jesus punish me first!" exclaimed Zbyszko ardently.

"Well, just keep it in mind. And after seeing your uncle home, come to our court. There will be an opportunity to get your spurs there, and after that we shall see what God will grant. In the meantime Danusia will ripen and will feel the urge. She is terribly fond of you, it is true—one cannot deny it—but she does not yet love you as grown-up girls love. Maybe also Jurand will incline his heart to you, for I think he would be glad to do so. If you go to Spychow and ride with Jurand against the Germans, it may happen that you will do him some service and win him completely."

"That is exactly what I myself thought of doing, worshipful duchess, but it will be easier if I get permission."

This talk cheered up Zbyszko considerably. Meanwhile, at the first stop, old Macko fell so sick that it was necessary to stay and wait for him to recover a little strength for the further journey. The good duchess Anna Danuta left him all her medicines and balsams, for she had to go on, and so the two knight of Bogdaniec had to part company with the Mazovian court. Zbyszko fell full length at the feet of the duchess and then at the feet of Danusia. Once again he promised her faithful knightly service, and pledged to come quickly to Ciechanow, or to Warsaw. Finally he took her in his strong arms and lifted her up, exclaiming in an emotional voice:

"Don't forget me, my dearest little flower! Don't forget me, my little goldfish!"

And Danusia, taking him in her arms just as if she were his younger sister, pressed her little turned-up nose to his cheek and wept great pea-like tears, repeating:

"I don't want to go to Ciechanow without Zbyszko! I don't want to go!"

Jurand saw this but did not burst out in anger. On the contrary, he himself took leave of the youth very kindly, and when he was mounted on his horse, he turned to him once again and said:

"God be with you, and bear me no grudge."

"How can I bear you a grudge, when you are Danusia's father?" exclaimed Zbyszko sincerely, and he leaned toward him.

Jurand grasped his hand.

"May God bless you in everything!" he said. "Do you understand?"

And he rode away.

Zbyszko understood what great goodwill was expressed in his last words, and returning to the wagon on which Macko lay, he said:

"Do you know, he is on my side, but there is some obstacle in the way. You've been at Spychow, and your mind is sharp, so try to figure out what it can be."

But Macko was too sick. The fever that had been tormenting him since the morning increased towards evening to such a degree that he began to lose consciousness; so instead of answering Zbyszko, he looked at him as if in surprise, and asked:

"Where is that ringing coming from?"

Zbyszko became frightened. It occurred to him that when a sick man hears bells, it is obvious that death is approaching. He also thought that the old man might die without a priest and without confession and therefore might go, if not straight to hell, then, at the very least, to purgatory for a long time. So he decided to go on, and try and reach some parish as soon as possible, where Macko might receive the Last Sacrament.

Therefore they travelled all night. Zbyszko sat in the wagon where the sick man was lying on the hay, and watched over him until daylight. From time to time he gave him some of the wine that the merchant Amylej had provided for them, and the thirsty Macko drank the wine greedily, for it obviously brought him relief. After the second quart he even recovered consciousness, but after the third he fell so soundly asleep that Zbyszko had to bend over him occasionally to make sure he was not dead.

And at that thought he was seized with deep grief. Until his imprisonment at Cracow he had not fully realized how fond he was of that uncle who had been both a father and a mother to him. But now he knew it very well, and he felt that after his uncle's death he would be frightfully lonely in the world, without any kinsmen save that abbot who held Bogdaniec in pledge, without any friends, and without anyone to help him. It also occurred to him that if Macko died it would be because of the Germans, through whom he himself had nearly lost his head, through whom all his forefathers and Danusia's mother had perished, as well as many, many innocent people whom he knew or of whom he had heard from his acquaintances. And he was overcome with amazement. "Is there," he said to himself, "in the whole kingdom a single person who has not suffered a wrong at their hands and who does not long for vengeance?" He recalled the Germans with whom he had fought at Wilno, and he thought that surely even the Tartars did not wage war more fiercely than they. Yes, there was no other such nation in the whole world.

The dawn interrupted his thoughts. The day broke bright but cool. Macko was apparently better, for he breathed evenly and quietly. He did not wake until the sun was already hot; opening his eyes, he said:

"The fever has passed. Where are we?"

"We're approaching Olkusz. You know, where they dig silver and send ingots to the Treasury."

"Oh, if we only had what is in the ground here! Then we could rebuild Bogdaniec!"

"I see that you indeed are feeling better!" replied Zbyszko, laughing. "Hey, with the silver here we could even build a stone castle. But let us drive up to the parish church, for there they will make us welcome, and you will be able to have your confession heard. Everything is in God's hands, but all the same it is better to have one's conscience in order."

"I am a sinful man, I will gladly repent," replied Macko. "I dreamt in the night that devils were pulling my leather boots from my legs, and they were jabbering German to one another. God is good; my fever has passed. And you, did you sleep a bit?"

"How could I sleep when I was attending to you?"

"Then lie down for a while. When we arrive, I will wake you."

"How can I sleep?"

"What is there to prevent you?"

Zbyszko looked at his uncle with the eyes of a child.

"What, if not love? I actually feel the colic in my stomach from sighing. I will ride my horse for a little while. That will relieve me."

Getting out of the wagon, he mounted a horse that had been efficiently brought forward by one of the Turks given to him by Zawisza. Meanwhile Macko, in some pain, put his hand on his side. But he was apparently thinking of something else, not of his own sickness, for he shook his head, smacked his lips, and finally said:

"I am surprised; I am surprised and I can't get over my surprise, how you come to be so passionate for this love thing, for neither your father was like that, nor am I."

Instead of answering, Zbyszko suddenly straightened himself on his horse, put his hands on his hips, threw up his head, and shouted with the whole force of his lungs:

> *"I wept through the night,*
> *I wept in the morning,*
> *Where have you gone to,*
> *my beloved girl?*
> *Nothing will help me,*
> *though I weep my eyes out,*
> *For you, my dear maiden,*
> *never more shall I see.*
> *Hey!"*

And this "hey!" rang through the forests, resounded from the tree-trunks by the roadside, raised a distant echo, and died away in the thickets.

Macko touched his side again, where the German iron resided, and said, groaning a little:

"Men were wiser of yore—do you understand?"

He took thought, however, as if actually recalling old times, and added:

"Though one and another was stupid, even of yore."

Meanwhile they emerged from the forest and saw before them the huts of the miners and, farther on, the battlemented walls of Olkusz, raised by King Kazimierz, and the tower of the parish church, built by Wladyslaw the Short.

CHAPTER X

THE canon from the parish church heard Macko's confession, and kept him and Zbyszko hospitably for the night. They continued their journey the following morning. Beyond Olkusz they turned towards Silesia, whose border they had to follow until they came to Great Poland. The way led for the most part through virgin forest, in which, towards sunset, they heard the roaring of aurochs and bison, like subterranean thunder, and where at night the eyes of wolves gleamed through the hazel thickets. On this road, however, greater danger than from wild beasts threatened wayfarers and merchants from the German, or Germanized, knights of Silesia, whose castelets rose here and there on the border. It is true that, as a result of the war with Naderspan, Duke of Opole—who was aided by his Silesian sons-in-law against King Wladyslaw—the majority of these little castles had been destroyed by Polish hands, yet it was always necessary to be vigilant and, particularly after sunset, not to let one's weapons out of one's hands.

However, they rode in peace, so that Zbyszko grew tired of the road. But when they were only a day's journey from Bogdaniec, they heard at night the snorting and hoofbeats of horses to their rear.

"Some people are riding behind us," said Zbyszko.

Macko, not yet asleep, looked at the stars and replied, as a man of experience:

"The dawn is not far off. Robbers would not fall upon us now, for they have to be home early."

Nevertheless, Zbyszko stopped the wagon and drew up his men

across the road, facing the approaching riders, while he rode forward a little and waited.

Soon he caught sight of ten or fifteen horsemen in the dusk. One of them was riding ahead, a few paces in advance of the rest, with no apparent intention of concealment, for he was singing loudly. Zbyszko could not make out the words, but his ears caught the merry refrain—"Heh! Heh!"—that the unknown rider concluded every verse of his song with.

"Our people!" he said to himself. But then he shouted: "Stand!"

"And you sit!" replied a jesting voice.

"What sort of ones are you?"

"What sort of twos are you?"

"Why are you following us?"

"Why are you stopping us?"

"Answer, for our crossbows are drawn."

"And ours are real—so shoot!"

"Answer like a normal human being, or you'll be in trouble."

A merry song answered Zbyszko:

> *"One trouble and another trouble,*
> *Went to dance where roads*
> *   are double.*
> *Heh! heh! heh!*
> *"What good to them is a dance*
> *   in the rubble?*
> *A dance is good, even in trouble.*
> *Heh! heh! heh!"*

Zbyszko was amazed to hear such an answer. When the song ceased, the same voice asked:

"And how's old Macko? Still breathing?"

Macko lifted himself up in the wagon.

"Great heavens, they are friends!" he exclaimed.

Zbyszko, however, rode forward.

"Who is asking about Macko?"

"A neighbor, Zych of Zgorzelice. I've been riding after you for a week now and asking about you along the road."

"Heavens! Uncle! Zych of Zgorzelice is here!" Zbyszko shouted.

And they began to greet one another joyfully, for Zych was

indeed their neighbor, and, besides, he was a good fellow, liked for his great cheerfulness.

"Well, how are you?" he asked, shaking Macko's hand. "Still up and about?"

"Not up," replied Macko. "But I'm glad to see you. Dear God, it's as if I were already at Bogdaniec!"

"What's wrong with you? I heard that the Germans had shot you."

"Those curs did shoot me! There's a splinter of iron between my ribs."

"Great heavens! And what did you do for it? Did you try drinking bear's fat?"

"You see!" said Zbyszko. "Everyone recommends bear's fat. As soon as we get to Bogdaniec, I will take an axe and wait by a honey-tree."

"Maybe Jagienka will have some bear's fat; if not, I'll send someone around to ask."

"What Jagienka? Your woman's name was Malgochna, wasn't it?" asked Macko.

"Oh, poor Malgochna! Come Michaelmas it will be the third autumn that she is lying in the priest's lump of ground. She was a fine woman, Lord rest her soul! Jagienka is like her, only she's young.

> *"Here the fields, there the water,*
> *As the mother, so the daughter.*
> *Heh! heh! heh!"*

"I told Malgochna: 'Don't climb up pine trees; you're fifty-years-old.' But she wouldn't listen! She climbed up a pine tree. The branch broke and—wham! I tell you, she made a hole in the ground. Three days later she breathed her last."

"May God rest her soul!" said Macko. "I remember, I remember. When she put her hands on her hips and began to scold, the farm lads would hide themselves in the hay! But for running the house and the farm she was excellent. And she fell off a pine tree? Dear, dear!"

"She fell like a fir-cone to the ground. . . . Oh, there was grief. Do you know, after the funeral I got so drunk to drown out my grief that they couldn't wake me for three days? They thought that

I had croaked. And the tears I cried after that, you couldn't have carried them away in twenty buckets! But Jagienka is also excellent at running the house and the farm. Everything now rests on her shoulders."

"I barely remember her. When I went away she was no bigger than an axe-handle. She could walk under a horse without touching its belly with her head. Yes, that was long ago, and she must have grown up by now."

"She was fifteen on St. Agnes's Day. I haven't seen her in almost a year."

"And what have you been doing? Where are you coming from?"

"From the war. Am I a slave, to sit at home when I have Jagienka?"

Macko, sick though he was, pricked up his ears at the mention of war.

"Were you perhaps with Duke Witold at the Worskla?" he asked.

"I was," answered Zych of Zgorzelice cheerfully. "Well, God did not bless him. We suffered a cruel defeat at the hands of Edyga. They shot our horses first. Your Tartar does not attack you directly, like a Christian knight, but shoots arrows at you from a distance. You charge him, but he slips away, then shoots again. You can't do anything with him! The knights in our army were immoderately boastful and said: 'We won't even lower our lances or draw our swords, we will scatter those vermin with our horses' hooves.' Thus they boasted, when suddenly the arrows began to whiz so thick that the sky became dark. And after the battle? Scarcely one in ten was left alive. Can you believe it? More than half of the army and seventy Lithuanian and Ruthenian dukes were left on the field, and as for the boyars and various courtiers, or *otroki* as they call them, you wouldn't have been able to count them in two weeks."

"So I heard," interrupted Macko. "And many of our auxiliary knights also fell."

"Yes, even nine Teutonic Knights, since they had to serve the power of Witold. And of ours also a considerable number fell, for as you know, when others look behind them, ours do not. The grand duke trusted our knights most of all. He didn't want to have any other guard around him, but only Poles. Truly they fell in heaps around him, and he was not touched! There fell Lord Spytko of Melsztyn, and the sword-bearer Bernat, and the cup-bearer

Nicholas, and Procopius, and Przeclaw, and Dobrogost, and Jasko of Lazewice, and Pilik the Mazovian, and Warsz of Michowo, and Voivode Socha, and Zasko of Oak Grove, and Pietro of Miloslaw, Szczepiecki, and Oderski, and Tomko Lagoda. Who could count them all? Some of them I saw so stuck with arrows that they looked like porcupines. It made one laugh to see them!"

Here he really burst out laughing, as if he had told the merriest story, and suddenly began to sing:

> *"You'll know what a Tartar can be*
> *When he hits you and makes you flee!"*

"Well, then what happened?" asked Zbyszko.

"Then the grand duke fled, but he quickly recovered, as he usually does. The harder you push him, the harder he rebounds, like a hazelnut twig. We hastened to the ford at Tawania to defend the crossing. A handful of fresh knights from Poland came with us. Well, nothing happened! Good! The next day Edyga advanced with a swarm of Tartars, but this time he got nothing. Hey, it was splendid fun! Whenever he wanted to cross the ford, we smacked him in the mouth. There was nothing he could do. We slew and captured many of his men. I grabbed five myself, whom I'm bringing with me to Zgorzelice. You will see in the daytime what dog faces they have."

"At Cracow they were saying that the war might come to the kingdom."

"Do you take Edyga for a fool? He knew very well what kind of knights we had. He also knew that the greatest knights had remained at home because of the queen's displeasure with Witold for starting war on his own. Eh, that old Edyga is cunning! He noticed immediately at Tawania that the duke was growing in strength, and away he went, far off to some remote corner."

"And you have returned?"

"Yes, I have returned. There was nothing more to do there. At Cracow I heard of you, that you had left only a short time before me."

"So that's how you knew it was we?"

"I knew it was you, for I had asked about you at every stop."

Here he turned to Zbyszko.

"Dear God, the last time I saw you, you were a little boy, but now, though it's dark, I can see that you're built like an ox. And so eager to shoot! One can see that you've been to war."

"War has brought me up from childhood. My uncle will tell you whether I'm lacking in experience."

"Your uncle doesn't have to tell me anything. At Cracow I saw the Lord of Taczewo, who told me much about you. He says that the Mazovian doesn't want to give you his daughter, but I would not be so obstinate about it, for I like you. You will forget that one as soon as you see my Jagienka. Now that's a girl for you!"

"It's not true! I shall never forget, even if I see ten girls like Jagienka."

"She will get Moczydoly, where there is a mill. When I left, there were also ten good mares with foal in the pastures. More than one man will ask me for Jagienka's hand—never fear!"

Zbyszko was about to answer, "But not I!" when Zych began to sing again:

> *"I will always bow low and carry water,*
> *If you'll give me your lovely daughter.*
> *Praise the Lord!"*

"You are always merry and full of song," observed Macko.

"Yes, and what do the blessed souls in heaven do?"

"They sing."

"Well, you see! And the damned weep. I would rather join the singers than the weepers. Furthermore, Saint Peter will say: 'We must let him into heaven, for otherwise the rascal will sing in hell, and that won't do.' Look—it's dawn already."

And, in fact, the day had dawned. They rode out into a wide clearing, where it was already quite light. Some men were catching fish in a lake that took up the larger part of the clearing. At the sight of armed men, they threw down their nets and, dashing out of the water, grasped their gaffs and staves, and stood in threatening poses, ready to fight.

"They take us for robbers," said Zych, laughing. "Hey, fishermen! Whose people are you?"

For some time they stood in silence, looking at him distrustfully, but at last the oldest of them recognized the knights and said:

"Abbot Janko's."

"Our kinsman," said Macko, "who is holding Bogdaniec in

pledge. These must be his forests, but he must have bought them recently."

"Bought them, indeed!" answered Zych. "He quarrelled with Wolf of Birchwood over them and apparently was successful in getting them. A year ago they were even proposing to meet on horseback with lances and long swords for all this district, but I don't know how it all ended, for I went away."

"Well, we're all on the same side," said Macko. "He will not quarrel with us, and maybe he will give us back something of the pledge."

"Maybe. If he's in good humor, he may even add something of his own. He's a knightly abbot, for whom it's nothing new to cover his head with a helmet. Besides, he is pious and celebrates Mass very beautifully. Surely you must remember! When he roars the swallows fly out of their nests under the roof. Well, it's all for the greater glory of God."

"How could I not remember? Why, he blew out a candle on the altar from ten paces away. Did he ever visit Bogdaniec?"

"Of course. He settled five villeins with their wives on some cleared land. He also saw us at Zgorzelice, for as you know he christened Jagienka, and loves her very much, calling her his little daughter."

"God grant that he may leave me the villeins!" said Macko.

"Don't worry! What are five peasants to such a rich man? Anyway, if Jagienka asks him, he will leave them."

The conversation stopped for a while. Over the dark forest and the red dawn rose the bright sun, lighting up the surrounding country. The knights greeted it with the usual "May the Lord be praised!" and then, crossing themselves, began their morning prayers.

Zych finished first, and striking his chest several times, he called out to his companions:

"Now I can get a good look at you. Hey, how you both have changed! You, Macko, must first recover your health. Jagienka will have to look after you because you have no woman at your place. . . . Well, it's obvious you've got a splinter sticking between your ribs. That's not good." Here he turned to Zbyszko. "You, too, show yourself. Almighty God! I remember you as a little boy, climbing up a colt's tail onto its back, but now, dear me, what a young knight! Your face is quite boyish, but you are a sturdy fellow. Why, you could even wrestle with a bear."

"What is a bear to him!" said Macko. "He was younger than he is today when that Frisian called him a beardless boy. He didn't like that too much, so he pulled out his moustache hairs!"

"I know," interrupted Zych. "And afterwards you fought and took their retinue. The Lord of Taczewo told me everything.

> *"A German came, with a mighty mace;*
> *They buried him with a hairless face.*
> *Heh! heh! heh!"*

And he looked at Zbyszko with an amused glance, while the latter looked with great curiosity at his tall, stick-like figure, his lean face and huge nose, and his round eyes full of laughter.

"Oh!" he said, "with such a neighbor, if only God gives my uncle back his health, we shall not be sad."

"It's better to have a cheerful neighbor, for with a cheerful one there can be no quarrels," replied Zych. "Now listen to what I am going to tell you with good Christian intentions. You haven't been at home in a long while, so you won't find everything in order at Bogdaniec. I'm not talking about the farm and the lands, for the abbot has managed those well. He has cleared a piece of forest and settled new peasants. But since he himself comes only from time to time, the food stock will be short, and there's barely a bench in the house or a bundle of pea-straw to sleep on, and a sick man needs comfort. So you know what? Ride with me to Zgorzelice. Stay a month or two there. That will make me happy, and meanwhile Jagienka will look after Bogdaniec. All you have to do is to rely on her and not worry about a thing. Zbyszko will go and attend to the farming, and the abbot will come and see you at Zgorzelice, so you can make your accounts with him right away. My girl will take as much care of you, Macko, as if you were her father. When one is sick a woman's care is better than any other. Well, my dear friends, do as I ask of you."

"It is well known that you are a good fellow, and always were," answered Macko with emotion; "but, you see, if I have to die through this cursed splinter under my ribs, I'd rather die in my own rubbish. And at home, even if one is sick, one can attend to this or that, ask after this and that, and bring this and that to order.

If God bids me to go to the other world—well, it can't be helped! Whether greater care is taken of one, or less—it doesn't matter. We have been accustomed to discomfort in the war. Even pea-straw is pleasant for a man who has slept for years on bare ground. But I thank you sincerely for your good heart, and if I do not show my gratitude, God grant that Zbyszko may show his."

Zych of Zgorzelice, well-known indeed for his good nature and readiness to help, began to press Macko anew, but the latter insisted that if he had to die he would die on his own piece of land. He had longed for Bogdaniec for so many years, that now, when its border was so near, he would not renounce it for anything, even if it were to be his last night's lodging. In any case, God was gracious in allowing him to drag himself back home.

Here he wiped away with his fists the tears glistening under his eyelids, looked around and said:

"If these are Wolf of Birchwood's forests, we shall reach home this afternoon."

"They are not Wolf of Birchwood's forests, they are now the abbot's," remarked Zych.

The sick Macko smiled at that.

"If they are the abbot's," he said, after a while, "some day they may be ours."

"Why, you've just been speaking of death!" exclaimed Zych merrily. "And now you want to outlive the abbot!"

"I shall not outlive him, Zbyszko will."

Further talk was interrupted by the sound of horns in the forest, somewhere far away to their front. Zych immediately checked his horse and listened.

"Someone must be hunting here," he said. "Wait!"

"Maybe the abbot. It would be a good thing if we were to meet him now."

"Quiet!" Then he turned to his attendants. "Halt!"

They stopped. The horns sounded nearer, and a moment later the baying of hounds reached their ears.

"Halt!" repeated Zych. "They're coming towards us."

Zbyszko, however, leapt from his horse and shouted:

"Give me my crossbow! Maybe the beast will charge us! Quick! Quick!"

And grabbing a crossbow from the hand of a servant, he rested it on the ground, pressed it against his stomach, bent down, strained his back like a bow, and taking the bow-string between the fingers of his two hands, drew it in the twinkling of an eye to the iron notch, laid an arrow in place, and rushed forward into the forest.

"He has bent it! He has bent it without the crank," whispered Zych, amazed at such a proof of strength.

"Ha! he's a stalwart fellow," whispered Macko proudly in reply.

Meanwhile the horns and the baying of the dogs sounded still nearer, until suddenly from the forest on the right there came the sound of heavy trampling, accompanied by the cracking of broken bushes and branches—and like a thunderbolt an old, bearded bison rushed onto the road from the thickets, with blood-shot eyes and protruding tongue, breathless and terrible, its enormous head lowered. Coming to a deep ditch by the roadside, it crossed it with a single leap and fell on its knees, but immediately got up and was just about to take cover in the thickets on the other side of the road when suddenly the ominous twang of a crossbow string and the whiz of an arrow were heard. The beast reared up, twisted, roared horribly, and fell, as if struck by lightning, to the ground.

Zbyszko came out from behind a tree, bent his bow again, and holding it ready to shoot, approached the prostrate bull, whose hind legs were still kicking the ground.

But after looking at it for a moment, he started slowly toward his attendants, shouting from a distance: "He got it so bad, that he's lying in his own excrement!"

"Can you believe it!" called Zych, riding up. "With one arrow!"

"It was nothing. The distance wasn't great, and besides, the arrow's flight was very swift. Take a look! Not only the shaft but the feathers have gone right in under its shoulder-blade."

"The hunters must be near now. They will certainly take it from you."

"I won't give it up!" answered Zbyszko. "It was killed on the road, and the road belongs to no one."

"But if it is the abbot who is hunting?"

"If it is the abbot, well, he can have it."

Meanwhile ten or fifteen dogs rushed out of the forest. Seeing the beast, they threw themselves on it with a frightful uproar. Soon they were biting one another.

"The huntsmen will be here directly," said Zych. "Look! there they are, only they've come out some distance in front of us, and they don't yet see the beast. Hallo! hallo! Over here! over here! The beast is down! It's down!"

Suddenly he stopped and shaded his eyes with his hand.

"Dear God!" he said presently. "Who is that? Am I blind or is it. . . ."

"There's somebody in front on a black-and-white horse," said Zbyszko.

Zych suddenly exclaimed: "Dear Jesus! Why, surely it's Jagienka!" And he immediately began to shout, "Jagna! Jagna!"

Then he moved forward, but before he could put his horse to a gallop, Zbyszko saw the strangest sight in the world. On a swift piebald horse, seated astride like a man, rushed towards them a girl with a crossbow in her hand and a javelin at her back. In her hair, flying in the wind, hop-cones had stuck. Her face was as red as the dawn; her shirt was open at her bosom, and over her shirt she wore a sleeveless leather jacket with the wool outside. When she reached them, she checked her horse on the spot. Her face reflected disbelief, amazement, and joy; finally, not being able to deny the evidence of her eyes and ears, she cried out in a high, still somewhat childish voice:

"Papa! My dearest papa!"

In the twinkling of an eye, she slipped down from her horse, and when Zych also leapt to the ground to greet her, she threw herself on his neck. For a long time Zbyszko heard nothing but the sound of kisses and two words repeated in joyous intoxication: "Papa!" "Jagna!" "Papa!" "Jagna!"

Both retinues rode up, and Macko in his wagon drove up too, but they still went on repeating, "Papa!" "Jagna!" And still kept their arms around each other's necks. When at last they had had enough of greetings and exclamations, Jagienka began to question him:

"So you're returning from the war? Are you well?"

"Yes, from the war. And why should I not be well? And you? And the boys? Are they both well? They must be, else you would not be riding through the forest. But whatever are you doing, girl?"

"Well, can't you see? I'm hunting," replied Jagienka, laughing.

"In other people's forests?"

"The abbot gave me permission, and he sent me servants skilled in the chase, and dogs."

Here she turned to her retinue:

"Drive away those dogs, or they will tear the hide!" Then to Zych: "Oh, I'm glad, I'm so very glad to see you! Everything is all right with us."

"I'm glad too!" replied Zych. "Give me your face again, girl."

And they began to kiss anew. When they had finished, Jagienka said:

"It's a long way home. We rode far after that beast. We must have chased him two leagues, and the horses are exhausted. But it's a fine bison. Did you see it? It has three of my arrows in it, and it must have fallen from the last one."

"It fell from the last one, but not from yours. That young knight shot it."

Jagienka pushed back her hair, which had fallen over her eyes, and looked keenly, but not too kindly, at Zbyszko.

"Do you know who that is?" asked Zych.

"No."

"No wonder you don't recognize him; he has grown. But maybe you will recognize old Macko of Bogdaniec?"

"Heavens! is that Macko?" exclaimed Jagienka.

And approaching the wagon, she kissed Macko's hand.

"Is that you?"

"It is I. The Germans shot me; that's why I'm in this wagon."

"What Germans? Wasn't the war with the Tartars? I know, for I begged papa many times to take me with him."

"There was war with the Tartars, but we were not in it. Zbyszko and I had been fighting in Lithuania before that one occurred."

"And where is Zbyszko?"

"Did you not recognize him?" asked Macko with a smile.

"Is that Zbyszko?" exclaimed the girl, looking afresh at the young knight.

"Of course!"

"Give him a kiss for old times' sake," said Zych merrily.

Jagienka turned eagerly to Zbyszko, but suddenly drew back and, covering her eyes with her hands, said:

"I'm embarrassed."

"Why, we have known each other since we were little!" said Zbyszko.

"Yes, we know each other well! I remember, I remember! Eight years ago you and Macko came to visit us, and my poor mother gave us nuts and honey. But no sooner had the elders left the room, when you hit me on the nose and ate the nuts yourself."

"He would not do that now!" said Macko. "He has been with Duke Witold; he has been at the castle at Cracow; and he has learned courtly manners."

But something else occurred to Jagienka. She turned to Zbyszko and asked:

"Then it was you who killed the bison?"

"Yes."

"Let me see where the arrow went in."

"You won't see, for it's buried under the shoulder-blade."

"Let it be; don't quarrel," said Zych. "We all saw how he shot it, and we saw something better. Within a second he drew the crossbow without the crank."

Jagienka looked for the third time at Zbyszko, but this time with admiration.

"You bent the crossbow without the crank?" she asked.

Zbyszko sensed a certain disbelief in her tone, so he rested the bow on the ground, and since it was now unbent, drew it in the twinkling of an eye until the iron frame creaked; then, wanting to show that he had courtly manners, he knelt down on one knee and offered it to Jagienka.

Instead of taking it from his hand, the girl blushed, not knowing why, and drew her homespun shirt together at the neck, for it had opened up during her swift ride through the forest.

CHAPTER XI

THE day after their arrival at Bogdaniec, Macko and Zbyszko began to look around their old home, and they soon found that Zych of Zgorzelice had been right when he said that they would have problems in the beginning.

The land was still more or less in order. There were a few manses cultivated by peasants who had been there before or who had been freshly settled by the abbot. Formerly there had been far more cultivated land at Bogdaniec, but ever since the family of the Hailstones had been almost completely extirpated at the battle of Plowce there had been a lack of workers, and after the inroads of the Silesian Germans and the war between the Grzymala and Nalecz clans, the once fertile fields of Bogdaniec had been over-grown for the most part with forest. Macko had not been able to deal with it by himself. He had tried in vain, some fifteen years before, to attract yeomen from Krzesnia and to lease them parcels of land for rent in kind; but they had preferred to dwell on their own little plots rather than cultivate strips belonging to someone else. He had, however, lured a few homeless people; and in various wars he had taken some ten or fifteen prisoners, whom he married off and settled in cottages. In this way, the village had begun to rise up again. But it had been done with great difficulty, and so when he found an opportunity to pledge his land, Macko had gladly pledged the whole of Bogdaniec, thinking, firstly, that it would be easier for a wealthy abbot to administer it, and secondly, that in the meantime he and Zbyszko would get men and money by war. The abbot had managed it with firm hand. The number of workers at

Bogdaniec had been increased by five peasant families; the herds of cattle and horses had been enlarged; besides which, a barn, a cattle-shed of woven branches, and a similar stable had been built. On the other hand, as he did not live permanently at Bogdaniec, he had neglected the house, and Macko, who had dreamed at times that when he came home he would find it surrounded with a moat and palisade, found everything as he had left it, with this difference, that the corner beams had warped a little and the walls seemed lower, for they had settled and sunk into the ground.

The house was composed of an enormous entrance-hall and two large rooms with bed-alcoves and a kitchen. The rooms had membrane windows, and in the middle of room was a hearth in the clay floor, the smoke issuing through openings in the roof. The roof, completely black, had been in better times used for smoke-drying meat. In the pegs driven into the beams there had formerly hung hams of pig and wild boar, of bear and elf, loins of stag and fawn, sirloins of beef, and whole strings of sausages. However, the hooks at Bogdaniec were now empty, and so were the shelves around the walls, which in other houses were laden with metal and earthenware dishes. Only the walls under the shelves did not appear too bare. Zbyszko had ordered his men to hang on them breastplates, helmets, short and long swords, javelins, forks, crossbows, lances, shields and axes and rump-armor for horses. The weapons would turn black from being hung up thus in the smoke, and they had to be cleaned often, but everything was at hand, and worms did not eat the wood of the lances, crossbows, or axe-handles. The solicitous Macko had all the costly garments placed in his bed-alcove.

In the front rooms, near the membrane windows, were tables made of pine-boards and benches on which the lords sat down to eat along with the servants. These men, accustomed to discomfort in long years of war, did not need much. But at Bogdaniec there was a shortage of bread, flour, and various other stores, and particularly utensils. The peasants brought what they could, but Macko counted most on his neighbors coming to his help, as was usual in such cases—and, in fact, he was not disappointed, at least as far as Zych of Zgorzelice was concerned.

On the day after their arrival the old warrior was sitting on a log before the house, making the most of the beautiful autumn weather, when Jagienka rode into the yard on her pied horse. A man chopping wood near the fence offered to help her dismount, but she leaped to the ground with ease and came up to Macko, somewhat out of breath from her swift ride and ruddy like an apple.

"May the Lord be praised! I have come to greet you from papa and to ask after your health."

"No worse than it was on the road," replied Macko. "One can at least sleep in one's own rubbish."

"But you must be very uncomfortable, and a sick man needs care."

"We are hardened fellows. It is true there is no comfort now, but we are not hungry. I have had an ox and two sheep slaughtered, so there is enough meat. The peasant women have also brought a little flour and eggs, though not much. The worst thing is that we have no utensils."

"I've ordered two wagons loaded. The first has bedding for two people and utensils, and the second contains various provisions. There are flat cakes and flour, and bacon, and dried mushrooms; there is a keg of beer and another of mead. A bit of everything that we had at home."

Macko, always pleased with any addition to the house, put out his hand and stroked Jagienka's head, saying:

"God reward you and your father! When we are settled, we will give all this back to you."

"Oh, no! Do you think we are Germans, to take back what we have given?"

"Well, God will reward you all the more. Your father told me what a good manager you are. So you administered the whole of Zgorzelice for a year?"

"Of course! If you need anything more, send someone for it; only send a man who knows what is wanted—for sometimes a stupid servant comes around forgetting what he has been sent for."

Here Jagienka began to look about a little, and Macko, noticing this, smiled and asked:

"Whom are you looking for?"

"For no one!"

"I will send Zbyszko to thank you and Zych for me. Did you like Zbyszko when you saw him the other day?"

"Oh, I wasn't looking."

"Well, have a look at him now, for there he is."

Zbyszko was walking from the watering-place, and when he saw Jagienka he hastened his steps. He was dressed in an elk-skin jacket with a round felt cap on his head, such as was worn under a helmet. His hair, unconfined by a net, and cut in a straight line over his eyebrows, fell in golden curls at the sides onto his shoulders. He approached them quickly, tall and fresh, looking like an esquire of a great house.

Jagienka turned away from him to Macko, to show that she had come to see only him, but Zbyszko greeted her cheerfully, and then took her hand and raised it to his lips despite her resistance.

"Why do you kiss my hand?" she asked. "Am I a priest?"

"Don't resist! Such is the custom."

"If he were also to kiss your other hand," Macko remarked, "it would not be too much for what you have brought."

"What has she brought?" asked Zbyszko, looking around the yard and seeing nothing but the pied horse tied to a post.

"The wagons haven't arrived yet, but they will come," replied Jagienka.

Macko began to enumerate the things she had brought, omitting nothing, and when he mentioned the bedding for two, Zbyszko said:

"I'm quite content to lie on my bison skin, but I thank you for thinking of me."

"It wasn't I; it was papa," the girl replied, blushing. "If you prefer to lie on a skin, do so; no one is forcing you."

"I like to lie on whatever there is. Sometimes in a field after a battle I have slept with a dead Teutonic Knight under my head."

"Oh, so you killed a Teutonic Knight? I'm sure you didn't!"

Instead of answering, Zbyszko began to laugh. Macko, however, exclaimed:

"Good heavens, girl, you don't know him! Why, he's done nothing else but fight Germans till the sparks flew. He's ready to use lance or axe or anything, and when he sees a German in the distance, even if you hold him on a leash, he will break loose and rush at him. At Cracow he wanted even to attack the envoy Lichtenstein, for which he nearly lost his head. That's the kind of fellow he is! And I will tell you of the two Frisians, from whom we took attendants and such rich booty that we could redeem Bogdaniec with half of it."

Macko then began to tell of the combat with the Frisians, and after that of other adventures which had happened to them and other deeds they had done. They had fought from behind walls and in the open fields against the greatest knights from foreign countries. They had fought Germans and Frenchmen, they had fought Englishmen and Burgundians. They had been in the midst of battles where horses, men, arms, Germans, and plumed crests had all been tangled up together. And what had they not seen! They had seen Teutonic castles of red brick, Lithuanian fortalices of wood, and churches such as were not to be found near Bogdaniec; they had seen towns, and wild primeval forests where at night one could hear the lamentation of Lithuanian gods, expelled from their temples; and they had seen many, many strange things. And at every battle Zbyszko had been in the forefront, to the amazement of even the greatest of knights.

Jagienka, sitting on the log by Macko's side, listened to these tales with an open mouth, screwing her head now towards Macko and now towards Zbyszko, and looking at the young knight with increasing wonder. At last, when Macko had finished, she sighed and said:

"If only I had been born a boy!"

But Zbyszko, who had been looking attentively at her while his uncle was talking, was apparently thinking of something else, for he suddenly said:

"What a beautiful girl you are!"

Jagienka answered half-reluctantly, half-sadly:

"I'm sure you've seen girls more beautiful than I."

However, Zbyszko could tell her without lying that he had not seen many such, for Jagienka was really glowing with health, youth, and strength. The old abbot had said of her, justly, that she looked half like a whitten, half like a young pine. Everything about her was beautiful: her slender figure, her broad shoulders, her breasts which seemed to be hewn out of rock, her red lips, and her keen blue eyes. Today she was dressed more carefully than she had been previously for the hunt in the forest. Around her neck she had a necklace of colorful beads, and she wore a sheepskin coat open in front, covered with green cloth, a skirt of striped home-

spun fabric, and new boots. Even old Macko noticed her lovely
attire, and after looking at her for a while, he asked her:

"Why have you dressed as if for a church fair?"

Instead of answering, she called out:

"The wagons are coming, they're coming!"

When the wagons arrived she dashed towards them, and
Zbyszko followed her. The unloading lasted until sunset, to
Macko's great satisfaction. He looked at everything in detail and
praised Jagienka for everything. Dusk had already fallen when the
girl made ready to go home. She was about to mount her horse,
when Zbyszko suddenly caught her by the waist. Before she could
say a word, he lifted her up and placed her in the saddle. She
blushed like the dawn and, turning her face towards him, said in a
half-stifled voice:

"You are a strong lad!"

But he, not noticing her blushes and her confusion in the dark,
burst out laughing.

"Aren't you afraid of wild beasts?" he asked. "It is already night."

"There's a spear on the wagon. Give it to me."

Zbyszko went to the wagon, took the spear and handed it to
Jagienka.

"Farewell!"

"Farewell!"

"God will reward you! I'll come tomorrow or the next day to
Zgorzelice, to thank Zych and you for your neighborliness."

"Do come! We shall be glad to see you! Gee-up!"

Her horse started forward, and Jadwiga was soon lost to sight
behind the roadside scrub.

Zbyszko turned to his uncle.

"It's time for you to go indoors."

But Macko didn't move from the log.

"Hey! what a girl!" he said. "She lighted up the whole yard!"

"She did indeed!"

There followed a few moments' silence. Macko seemed to be
thinking of something as he gazed at the rising stars. Then he said,
as if to himself:

"She's plucky and capable of looking after house and farm,
though she is no more than fifteen."

"True!" said Zbyszko. "Old Zych loves her like the apple of his eye."

"And he said that Moczydoly will be hers, and that there is a herd of mares with foal in the meadows."

"Aren't there terrible bogs in the forests of Moczydoly?"

"Yes, but there are beaver lodges in them."

Silence fell once more. Macko looked askance at Zbyszko for a time. Finally he asked:

"What are you brooding over? What are you thinking about?"

"Well, you see . . . Jagienka reminded me of Danusia. I feel a pain in my heart."

"Let's go inside," responded the old man. "It's getting late."

And rising with difficulty he leaned on Zbyszko, who brought him into his sleeping-chamber.

The very next day Zbyszko rode to Zgorzelice, for Macko urged him to do so. He also persuaded his nephew to take with him two attendants for show, and to dress in his best clothes, in order thus to show honor to Zych and express due gratitude. Zbyszko agreed and went dressed as for a wedding, in his handsome jacket of white atlas, edged with a golden fringe and embroidered with gold griffins. Zych received him with open arms, with joy and with singing, but Jagienka, coming into the doorway, stood as if turned to stone, and almost dropped the jug of wine she was carrying at the sight of the young man, for she thought some prince must have arrived. She immediately lost her confidence and sat in silence, sometimes rubbing her eyes as if to wake herself from a dream. Zbyszko, who had not much experience, thought that for some reason or other she was not pleased to see him, so he spoke only with Zych, praising his neighborly generosity and admiring the house at Zgorzelice, which, in fact, was nothing like the one at Bogdaniec.

The whole place spoke of wealth and riches. The windows of the rooms had panes of horn, planed thin until they were almost as transparent as glass. There were no hearths in the middle of the rooms, but only great hooded chimneys in the corners. The floor was made of larch boards, washed clean, and on the walls were weapons and a number of dishes, shining like the sun, and beautifully carved racks, with rows of spoons, of which two were of silver. Here and there were tapestries, captured in war or bought from wandering merchants. Under the table lay huge sand-colored skins of aurochs, bison, and wild boar. Zych took delight in showing his riches, repeating every moment that they were due to Jagienka's management. He also took Zbyszko to an alcove smelling with resin and mint, from the roof timber of which hung whole bundles of wolf, fox, marten, and beaver furs. He showed him the cheese closet, the stores of wax and honey, the kegs of flour, and the stores of biscuits, hemp, and dried mushrooms. Then he took him to the granaries, the cattle stalls, the stables, and the pigsties, and to the sheds in which were wagons, hunting gear, and nets, and so dazzled his eyes with all this wealth that Zbyszko, when he came back to supper, could not help expressing his amazement.

"One can live here forever!" he exclaimed.

"Moczydoly is almost the same," replied Zych. "You remember Moczydoly. It lies in the direction of Bogdaniec. In times of yore our fathers even quarrelled about the boundaries, and sent one another challenges to single combat, but I shall not quarrel with you."

They touched their mugs of mead together, and Zych asked:

"Maybe you'd like to sing something?"

"No," said Zbyszko, "but I would gladly listen to you."

"This place, you know, will be taken by my cubs. If only they don't tear themselves up over it."

"What cubs?"

"Why, the boys, Jagienka's brothers."

"They won't need to suck on their paws in wintertime!"

"For certain! But Jagienka at Moczydoly will not be short of bacon to put in her mouth either."

"Indeed not!"

"Why do you not eat and drink? Jagienka, pour out some mead for the lad and me."

"I'm eating and drinking as much as I can."

"If you can't eat and drink more, then unbuckle. . . . That's a beautiful belt! You must have taken good booty in Lithuania?"

"We're not complaining," replied Zbyszko, glad of the opportunity to show that the lords of Bogdaniec were not mere small landholders. "A part of the booty we sold at Cracow for forty marks of silver."

"Heavens! for that you could buy a village."

"There was a suit of Milan armor, which uncle sold, since he expected to die soon, and that, you know—"

"I know! Well! It was worthwhile going to Lithuania. I wanted to, in my time, but I was afraid."

"What? Of the Teutonic Knights?"

"Ha! who would be afraid of them? As long as they don't kill you, what is there to be afraid of? And if you're dead, you're dead. I was afraid of those pagan gods, or devils. Apparently the Lithuanian forests are swarming with them."

"Where are they to stay, when their temples have been burnt? Of yore they were rich, but now they live only on mushrooms and ants."

"Have you ever seen them?"

"I haven't seen them myself, but I have heard of people who have seen them. This one and that one stretches out a hairy paw from behind a tree and shakes it, asking you to give him something."

"Macko said the same thing," replied Jagienka.

"Yes, he told us about them on the road," added Zych. "Of course, there's nothing strange in all this. Why, even among us, although the country has been Christian for a long while, you may sometimes hear laughing in the marshes, and at home, although the priests raise their voices against it, it's always better to leave the goblins a dish of food for the night, or they'll scratch the walls so that you won't be able to fall asleep. Jagienka! leave a dish before the threshold."

Jagienka took an earthenware dish full of cheese dumplings and put it at the threshold, while Zych said:

"The priests cry out and scold, but the Lord Jesus will not lose glory because of a few dumplings, and the goblin, if only it is well fed and well disposed, will protect us from fire and thieves."

Then he turned to Zbyszko:

"Maybe you'd like to unbuckle your belt and sing a little."

"You sing. I see that you've long been wanting to, and maybe the young Lady Jagienka will sing too?"

"We will sing in turn," said Zych joyfully. "And there's a servant in the house who will accompany us on a wooden pipe. Call him."

They called the servant, who sat down on a stool, put his "whistle" to his lips, spread his fingers over it, and looked at the company, wondering whom he was to accompany.

Meanwhile they began to argue, for none of them wished to be first. At last Zych told Jagienka to set the example, so, although she was very embarrassed in front of Zbyszko, she rose from her seat, put her hands under her apron, and began:

"Oh, if I but had
Little wings like a dove,
Away I would fly,
Away, away to my love
In Silesia. . . ."

Zbyszko opened his eyes wide and sprang to his feet, exclaiming in a loud voice:

"Wherever did you learn to sing that?"

Jagienka looked at him in amazement.

"Why, everybody sings it. What's the matter with you?"

Thinking that Zbyszko must be tipsy, Zych turned a joyous face to him.

"Unbuckle yourself!" he said. "You'll feel better at once!"

But Zbyszko stood for a while, his face changing colors. Then, mastering his emotion, he said to Jagienka:

"I beg your pardon. Something suddenly came to my mind. Go on singing."

"Perhaps you feel sad when you listen to this song."

"Of course not!" he replied with a quivering voice. "I could listen to it all night long."

He sat down and, shading his eyes with his hand, listened carefully, not wishing to miss a single word.

Jagienka sang the second verse. When she had finished it, she saw a great tear running down Zbyszko's fingers.

So she went up to him quickly and, sitting down beside him, nudged him with her elbow:

"Well? What's wrong? I don't want you to weep. Tell me what's the matter?"

"Nothing, nothing!" replied Zbyszko with a sigh. "It would be a long story. What's happened has happened. I feel more cheerful now."

"Maybe you would like to drink some sweet wine?"

"Good girl!" exclaimed Zych. "Why do you not call one another by your forenames? Call him 'Zbyszko,' and you call her 'Jagienka.' After all, you've known one another from childhood."

Then he turned to his daughter:

"It's nothing that he beat you up once! He won't do it now."

"I won't!" said Zbyszko. "She can beat me for it now if she wants."

Jagienka, wanting to make him merry, clenched her fist and pretended, as she laughed, that she was hitting him:

"That's for my broken nose! And that! And that!"

"Wine!" called out the delighted owner of Zgorzelice.

Jagienka dashed to the store-cupboard and presently brought over a stone jug of wine, two beautiful mugs, ornamented with silver flowers and the work of Wroclaw goldsmiths, and a few pieces of cheese whose aroma preceded them.

Already affected by the mead, Zych became completely moved by this sight. So he took the jug, pressed it to his stomach, and, apparently thinking that it was Jagienka, began to say:

"Oh, my little daughter! Oh, you poor orphan! What shall I, poor fellow, do at Zgorzelice when they take you away from me? What shall I do?"

"You'll have to let her go soon!" exclaimed Zbyszko.

In the twinkling of an eye, Zych passed from sentimentality to laughter:

"Ha! ha! The girl is only fifteen and already attracted to the boys! As soon as she sees one in the distance, she rubs one knee against the other."

"Papa, I shall leave," said Jagienka.

"Don't go! It's good to have you here."

Then he winked mysteriously at Zbyszko.

"Two young fellows come here: one is young Wolf, the son of old Wolf of Birchwood, and the other is Cztan of Rogow. If they found you here they would immediately begin to gnash their teeth at you, just as they do at one another."

"Bah!" said Zbyszko.

Then he turned to Jagienka, and calling her informally by her forename, as Zych had recommended, he asked her:

"Which of them do you prefer, Jagienka?"

"Neither."

"Wolf is a sturdy lad," remarked Zych.

"He can howl someplace else!"

"And Cztan?"

Jagienka began to laugh.

"Cztan," she said, turning to Zbyszko, "has such shaggy hair on his face, like a he-goat, that one can't see his eyes, and there is as much fat on him as on a bear."

Zbyszko suddenly slapped his forehead, as if he had remembered something.

"Oh! Since you are so good, I will ask you for one more thing. Have you no bear's fat in the house? My uncle needs it as medicine, and I could not get any at Bogdaniec."

"We did have some," said Jagienka, "but the boys carried it into the yard to grease their bows—and the dogs ate it all up. . . . It's a pity!"

"Was there none left?"

"They licked the pot clean!"

"Well, then I'll have to go to the forest to look for some."

"Arrange a hunt, for there are many bears around here. If you need any hunting gear, we will give you some."

"Why waste time! I will go at night to a honey-tree."

"Take five of our helpers. There are some experienced lads among them."

"I won't go with a crowd. They would frighten the beast away."

"What then? Will you go with a crossbow?"

"What should I do with a crossbow in the forest at night? The moon isn't shining now. I will take a barbed fork and a good axe and will go by myself tomorrow."

Jagienka was silent for a while, her face betraying concern.

"Last year," she said, "a hunter, Bezduch, went out from our house, and a bear tore him to pieces. It's always dangerous, for as soon as he sees a man at night, and particularly near a honey-tree, a bear will immediately stand on his hind legs."

"If he'd run away, I wouldn't be able to get him," replied Zbyszko.

Meanwhile Zych, who had been dozing, suddenly woke and began to sing:

> *"You are Kub, a man of work,*
> *While I, Mat, all labor shirk.*
> *You tomorrow take your spade.*
> *I'll to the rye with my merry maid.*
>   *Heh! heh!"*

Then he said to Zbyszko:

"You know there are two of them: Wolf of Birchwood and Cztan of Rogow. . . . And you—"

Fearing that Zych would say too much, Jagienka quickly went up to Zbyszko.

"When are you going?" she asked him. "Tomorrow?"

"Tomorrow at sunset."

"And to which tree-hives?"

"To ours, at Bogdaniec, not far from your piece of land, near the Radzikowo marshes. They tell me it's easier to find bears there."

CHAPTER XII

ZBYSZKO went after the bear as he had proposed, for Macko felt worse and worse. At first the old warrior had been sustained by joy and the initial domestic tasks, but on the third day the fever and the pain in his side returned with such force that he had to lie down. Before doing anything else, Zbyszko went in the daytime and looked at the tree-hives, observing that there was an enormous track in the mud nearby. He had a talk with the beekeeper, Wawrek, who slept at night in a shack not far away, with a pair of fierce Carpathian sheep-dogs, but who was about to move to the village because of the autumn cold.

The two men pulled down and scattered the shack, took the dogs, and smeared a little honey here and there on the tree-trunks to attract a bear. That accomplished, Zbyszko returned home and prepared himself. He dressed warmly in his sleeveless elk-skin jacket. He put a steel-wire cap on his head to prevent the bear from scalping him, and then took a strong two-pronged fork with barbs and a broad steel axe with an oak handle a bit longer than carpenters use. By milking-time in the evening, he was already at the spot he had earlier selected. There he crossed himself, made himself as comfortable as possible, and waited.

The red rays of the setting sun shone between the branches of the pines. On the treetops the crows gathered noisily, cawing and flapping their wings. Here and there hares darted to the water, rustling through the yellowing bilberry bushes and the fallen leaves. At times a marten scurried swiftly along a beech bough.

From thickets, there still came the twitter of birds, gradually dying away.

There was no quiet in the forest at sunset. Soon a herd of wild boars passed not far from Zbyszko with much trampling and grunting, and later a long row of elks trotted past, each holding its head to the next one's tail. Dry branches cracked under their hooves, so that the forest echoed with the sound, while they, their red coats shining in the sun, made for the marshes, where they felt safe and secure at night. Then the glow of sunset overspread the sky. The tops of the pines seemed afire, and everything gradually grew still. The forest went to sleep. The dusk rose from the earth and floated upwards until the russet glow itself grew pale and faint, and darkened, and went out.

"Now, it will be quiet until the wolves start to howl," thought Zbyszko.

He regretted that he had not taken his crossbow, for he might easily have shot a boar or an elk. Meanwhile, there came occasionally from the marshes stifled sounds like heavy groaning and whistling. Zbyszko looked uneasily towards that direction, for the peasant Radzik, who had once lived here in a mud hut, had vanished with his family as if the earth had swallowed him. Some said that robbers had carried them off, but there were others who later saw strange tracks near the hut, neither of men nor of animals, and who puzzled over them, and even debated whether a priest from Krzesnia should not be brought over to exorcize the spot. It did not come to that, for no one could be found willing to live there, and the hut, or rather the daub on the wattle walls, slowly decomposed from the rains. But the place did not have good name thereafter. It is true that Wawrek, the beekeeper, who used to spend nights here in the summer in his shack, paid no attention to these stories—but, then again, various things were said of Wawrek himself. Zbyszko, having a fork and an axe, was not afraid of wild beasts, but he was concerned about evil spirits and was glad when the noises finally died away.

The last glow disappeared from the sky and night fell. The wind ceased. There was not even the usual soughing in the tops of the pines. From time to time the crash of a falling pinecone sounded loud and penetrating amidst the general silence, but otherwise it was so quiet that Zbyszko heard his own breathing.

In this way he passed a long time, thinking first of the bear which might come, and then of Danusia, who had gone far away with the Mazovian court. He remembered how he had held her when parting from the duchess and how her tears had fallen on his cheek. He remembered her bright face, her golden hair, her chaplets of cornflowers, and her singing, and her red slippers with long toes, which he had kissed at parting. He remembered everything which had happened since they met, and he was overcome with such grief for her absence and such longing for her presence that he forgot that he was in the forest, lying in wait for a wild beast, and he said to himself:

"I will go to you, for I cannot live without you."

And he felt that it was so—that he must go to Mazovia, or else he would languish away at Bogdaniec. He thought of Jurand and his strange opposition, and then it seemed to him that he must go all the more, to find out what mystery, what obstacles there were, and whether some challenge to a life-and-death combat might not serve to remove them. Finally, it seemed to him that Danusia was stretching out her hands to him and calling out, "Come, Zbyszko, come!" How could he fail to go to her?

He did not sleep, yet he saw her as clearly as in a vision or in a dream. There was Danusia riding beside the duchess, touching her lute and singing, but thinking of him—thinking that she would see him before long, and perhaps looking around to make sure he was not hastening behind her. Meanwhile he was far away in a dark forest.

Then Zbyszko came to himself—not only because he remembered that he was in a dark forest, but also because he heard a distant rustling behind him.

He grasped his fork more firmly in his hands, pricked his ears, and began to listen.

The rustling came nearer and, after a certain time, grew quite distinct. Dry branches crackled under cautious feet, and the fallen leaves and bilberry bushes rustled. . . . Something was approaching.

At times the rustling ceased, as if the animal had stopped among the trees, and the silence became so profound that Zbyszko's ears began to ring. Then the slow and wary steps were heard again. Altogether there was something so cautious about this approach that Zbyszko was overcome with astonishment.

"The old bear must be afraid of the dogs that were here by the shack," he said to himself, "or perhaps it's a wolf that has scented me."

Meanwhile the sound of the steps ceased. Zbyszko, however, heard clearly that something had stopped twenty or thirty paces behind him and seemed to sit down. He looked around once or twice, but although the tree-trunks were outlined well enough in the night, he could perceive nothing. There was nothing else to do but wait.

And he waited so long that he was overcome with surprise for a second time.

"A bear would not have come to sleep under the hive, and a wolf would have scented me already and would not wait till morning."

Suddenly pins and needles seemed to prick him from head to foot.

What if something "uncanny" had emerged from the marshes and was creeping up behind him? What if the slimy hands of some drowned corpse were to seize him unexpectedly, or if the green eyes of some phantom were to look into his face? What if frightful laughter would burst out behind him, or if a livid head on spider legs happened to crawl out between the pines!

He felt his hair beginning to stand on end under his steel cap.

Then he heard the rustling to his front, this time still more distinctly than before. Zbyszko breathed freely. He supposed that the strange monster had gone around him and was now approaching from the front. But he preferred that. He grasped his fork firmly, got up noiselessly, and waited.

Suddenly over his head he heard the soughing of the pines, on his face he felt a strong gust of wind from the direction of the marshes—and the smell of a bear came to his nostrils.

There was not the least doubt. A bear was approaching!

Zbyszko ceased to be afraid, and lifting his head, looked and listened intently. Heavy, distinct steps came nearer, the smell became sharper, and soon he could hear snuffing and growling.

"I hope there's only one!" thought Zbyszko.

And then he saw before him the great dark figure of the animal, which coming from the windward side, had not scented him until the last moment, particularly as it was taken up with the smell of the honey smeared on the tree-trunks.

"Come on, grandpa!" called Zbyszko, emerging from behind a pine.

The bear gave a sharp growl, as if alarmed by the unexpected sight, but it was already too near to save itself by flight, so it immediately rose on its hind feet and extended its front legs as if to embrace him. This was what Zbyszko had been waiting for. He gathered all his strength, sprang as quick as lightning, and drove his fork into the animal's chest with the whole force of his powerful arms and the whole weight of his body.

The entire forest reverberated with its terrifying roar. The bear seized the fork it its paws, trying to pull it out, but the barbs on the points held, and feeling the pain, it thundered still more terribly. Striving to reach Zbyszko, it leaned on the fork and thus drove it in still deeper. Zbyszko kept hold of the handle, not knowing whether the prongs had yet gone in deep enough. Man and beast began to struggle. The forest shook with the animal's roaring, full of rage and despair.

Zbyszko was unable to seize his axe until he had driven the pointed handle-end of the fork into the ground, while the bear, seizing the butt in its paws, shook it, and Zbyszko with it, as if understanding what he was trying to do. Despite the pain that every movement of the deep-plunged prongs caused it, the bear would not allow itself to be "propped." So the terrible struggle continued, and Zbyszko realized that his strength would finally be exhausted. He might also fall, and then he would be lost, so he gathered all his strength, strained his arms, planted his feet firmly on the ground, bent his back like a bow so as not to be overthrown, and muttered through set teeth:

"It's either you or I!"

Finally he became seized with such rage and determination that he would really have rather perished than let go of the animal. Suddenly his foot caught the root of a pine, and he lost his balance. And he would have fallen had it not been that at that moment a dark figure appeared beside him, and a second fork "propped" the beast, while at the same time a voice called close to his ear:

"Use your axe!"

In the excitement of the struggle, Zbyszko did not lose a second wondering from where this unexpected help had come, but immediately seized his axe and attacked savagely. The fork now cracked under the weight and the last convulsions of the beast, which fell as if struck by lightning to the ground and began to give its death-rattle. But it stopped almost at once. Silence followed, broken only by the loud breathing of Zbyszko, leaning against a pine, his knees threatening to give way under him. Only after a while did he raise his head and look at the figure standing beside him—and he became terrified, thinking that perhaps it was not human.

"Who are you?" he asked uneasily.

"Jagienka," answered a high-pitched feminine voice.

Zbyszko was struck dumb with surprise, not believing his own ears. But his doubt did not last long, for Jagienka's voice spoke again:

"Let us kindle a fire."

The sound of steel on flint was heard, sparks began to leap, and in their twinkling light Zbyszko saw the white forehead, the dark brows, and the pouting lips of the girl who was blowing at the lighted tinder. Only then did he think that she had come to the forest to help him, and he realized that without her fork it might have gone badly for him. So he felt such gratitude to her that without thinking he caught her by the waist and kissed both her cheeks.

Her tinder and steel fell to the ground.

"Let me go! What are you doing?" she said in a stifled voice. But she did not take her face away. On the contrary, her lips touched Zbyszko's lips, as if by chance.

Then he let her go and said:

"May God reward you! I don't know what would have happened without you."

Jagienka, squatting in the dark to look for her steel and tinder, began to explain:

"I was afraid for you. Bezduch also went with a fork and an axe, and the bear tore him to pieces. Macko would have been grieved. As it is, he is barely alive. . . . So I took a fork and went after you."

"Then it was you who was under the pines?"

"Yes."

"And I thought it was some evil spirit."

"I was also afraid, for it's no good to be by the Radzikowo marshes at night without a fire."

"Why didn't you call out?"

"Because I was afraid you would drive me away."

She began to strike sparks again, and then laid a handful of dry hemp fibres on the tinder, which soon burned with a bright flame.

"I have two slivers of wood," she said. "Go and quickly gather some dry branches. We'll have a fire."

Soon there was a merry blaze, which illuminated the huge ginger-haired carcass of the bear, lying in a pool of its own blood.

"Hey, what a fierce creature!" exclaimed Zbyszko with a certain boastfulness.

"You almost completely split its head! Oh, Jesus!"

Jagienka bent down and plunged her hand into the bear's shaggy fur to make sure whether the animal had much fat. She got up with a cheerful face.

"There will be fat for two years or more!"

"But the fork is broken, look!"

"That's a pity. What shall I say at home?"

"Why?"

"Because papa wouldn't have let me go to the forest. I had to wait until they had all gone to bed." Then she added: "Don't tell anyone that I was here, for they might have something to say about it."

"But I will take you home, for wolves may attack you, and you have no fork."

"Well—all right!"

Thus they talked for some time in the cheerful light of the fire, by the carcass of the bear, and they looked like two young forest sprites.

Zbyszko gazed at Jagienka's pleasant face, lit up by the flames, and said impulsively:

"There's not another girl like you in the world. You could go to war!"

She looked in his eyes for a moment.

"I know," she replied, almost sadly, "but do not laugh at me."

CHAPTER XIII

JAGIENKA herself melted a large pot of bear's fat, the first quart of which Macko drank with satisfaction, for it was fresh, not burned, and had the smell of angelica, which the girl, knowledgeable about medicines, had dropped into the pot. Macko's spirits rose at once, and he began to hope he would get well.

"That was what I needed," he said. "When everything in one gets properly covered with fat, then perhaps that cursed splinter will slip out."

The following quarts, however, did not taste as good as the first, but he drank them because his good sense told him to. Jagienka tried to cheer him up, saying:

"You will be well. Bilud of Ostrog had a link from his coat of mail driven deep into the back of his neck, but it came out with fat. When the wound opens up though, you must stop it with beaver-fat."

"Have you any?"

"We have. And if you need any fresh fat, Zbyszko and I will go to the beaver lodges. It's not hard to find beavers. Yet it would do no harm to make a vow to some saint, someone who is a patron of wounds."

"I've already thought of that, but I don't really know to whom I should make a vow. St. George is the patron of knights. He protects a warrior from misadventure and always gives him courage in case of need, and they say that he often stands on the side of justice and helps to defeat those whom God dislikes. But the one who likes to fight seldom likes to heal, and besides, there may be another on whose terrain he would not want to trespass. Every saint has his own office and his special business in heaven—that is known! And one never interferes with another, for that might lead to quarrels, and it is not fitting for saints to dispute or fight in heaven. . . . There are also Cosmas and Damian, great saints, to whom doctors pray that diseases may not die out on the earth, for otherwise they would have nothing to eat. There is also St. Apollonia for teeth and St. Liborius for kidneys. But these saints are not what I want. The abbot will come and tell me to whom I have to address myself, for not just any old cleric knows all the divine secrets, and not everyone knows such things, even if he has a shaven head."

"What if you were to make a vow to the Lord Jesus himself?"

"Certainly, He is above all. But that would be as if your father, let's say, were to beat a peasant of mine, and I were to make my complaint to the king at Cracow. What would the king say to me? He would say: 'I am administrator of the whole kingdom, and you come to me with your peasant. Have you no officials in your land? Can you not go to my castellan and representative?' The Lord Jesus is administrator of the whole world, do you understand? For minor matters he has his saints."

"I will tell you what," said Zbyszko, who had come in at the end of this talk. "Make a vow to our deceased queen, that if she helps you, you will make a pilgrimage to her grave at Cracow. Many miracles have already occurred there. Why look for foreign saints when our own lady is better than others?"

"Ha! If I only knew that she was for wounds!"

"So what if she is not! Ordinary saints will not dare to take issue with her, and if they do, they will get a scolding from God himself, for she is not just a common maid, but the Queen of Poland."

"Who brought a pagan country to the Christian faith," added Macko. "There is sense in what you say. She must have a high seat in the divine council, and it is certain that no common little saint can oppose her. In order to regain my health I will do what you advise!"

The advice pleased Jagienka also, and she could not help admiring Zbyszko's intelligence. Macko made the solemn vow that same evening, and thereafter drank his bear's fat every day with greater confidence and the sure expectation of recovery. However, after a week he began to lose hope. He said that the fat was "storming" in his stomach and that some type of lump was growing on his skin near his last rib. After ten days, his condition worsened. The lump had grown in size and become red, and he himself weakened considerably. When his temperature rose, he began once more to prepare for death.

One night he suddenly awakened Zbyszko.

"Light some wood quickly," he said, "for something is happening to me, but I don't know whether it's good or bad."

Zbyszko sprang to his feet and speedily returned with a burning tarry sliver he had gotten from the hearth in the other room.

"What's the matter with you?"

"What's the matter with me? Something has pierced the lump. It must be the splinter! I'm holding it, but I can't get it out! I can only feel it clink and grate when my nails touch it. . . ."

"It's the splinter, for sure! Catch hold of it firmly and pull."

Macko began to twist and hiss with pain, but he plunged his fingers deeper and deeper, until he had got firm hold of the hard object. Then he jerked it out.

"Oh, Jesus!"

"Is that it?" asked Zbyszko.

"Yes. I thought I'd pass out. But this is it—look!"

He showed Zbyszko a long sharp splinter, which had broken off from a badly forged arrowhead and had remained in his body for several months.

"Praise be to God and Queen Jadwiga! Now you will be well."

"Maybe it has given me relief, but it really hurts," said Macko, pressing the lump from which blood flowed freely, mingled with pus. "Well, the less of this disgusting stuff in a man, the better. Jagienka said that the wound must now be stopped with beaver-fat."

"We'll go for a beaver tomorrow."

The very next day Macko felt remarkably better. He slept late, and upon awakening, he called for food. He could not look at bear's fat any more, but they broke twenty eggs for him into a skillet. Jagienka, being cautious, would not allow him more eggs. He ate them greedily with half a loaf of bread and drank a mug of beer, and then called to them to bring him Zych, for he was in a happy mood.

So Zbyszko sent one of his Turks, given him by Zawisza, to fetch

Zych, who mounted a horse and arrived in the afternoon, just as the young people were leaving for the little lake of Odstajan to hunt beaver.

At first the old men laughed and jested and sang over their mead to their hearts' content, but later they began to talk of their children, each praising his own.

"What a lad that Zbyszko is!" said Macko. "There's no one else like him in the whole world. Valiant, swift as a wild cat, skillful. Do you know, when they were conducting him at Cracow to the executioner, the girls at the windows began to scream as if someone behind them had pricked them with a needle. And what girls! Knights' and castellans' daughters, to say nothing of various beautiful townswomen."

"Even if they are castellans' daughters and beautiful, they are no better than my Jagienka," replied Zych of Zgorzelice.

"Did I say they were better? You couldn't find anywhere a girl more pleasing than Jagienka."

"Nothing bad can be said about Zbyszko, either. He actually bends a crossbow without a crank!"

"And he propped a bear all by himself. Did you see how he struck it? He severed the whole head and one paw!"

"He severed its head, but he the didn't prop it by himself. Jagienka helped him."

"She helped him? He didn't tell me anything about it."

"Because he promised her he wouldn't. The girl was ashamed of having gone to the forest at night. She told me at once what had happened. Others gladly lie, but she can never hide the truth. Speaking frankly, I was none too happy, for who knows. . . . I wanted to scold her, but she said: 'Only I can protect my maidenhead; you can't do it for me, papa. But don't worry. Zbyszko knows what is knightly honor.'"

"That's true! They've even gone out together today."

"But they will return before evening. The devil is worst at night, and when it is dark a girl doesn't need to be ashamed."

Macko thought for a while; then he said, as if to himself:

"Yet they are glad to see one another. . . ."

"If only he hadn't made a vow to another!"

"That, you know, is the knightly custom. Any young man who doesn't have a lady is taken for a simpleton. He vowed the peacock crests, and he will have to pluck them from German heads since he has promised on his knightly honor. He must get Lichtenstein too. But the abbot can absolve him from his other vows."

"The abbot is due to arrive any day now."

"You think so?" asked Macko, and then went on. "Anyway, what is the use of such vows when Jurand told him quite simply that he would not give him the girl? Whether he has promised her to another or dedicated her to the service of God, I don't know—but he said that he would not give her to Zbyszko."

"Did I tell you," asked Zych, "that the abbot loves Jagienka as if she were his own daughter? The last time he saw her, he said: 'Kinsmen I have only on my mother's side of the family, but you will get more than they will.'"

Macko glanced uneasily, and even suspiciously, at Zych, and replied only after a short while:

"You wouldn't want us wronged. . . ."

"Jagienka will get Moczydoly," said Zych evasively.

"Immediately when she marries?"

"Immediately. I wouldn't do this for anyone else but her."

"Bogdaniec is already half Zbyszko's, and if God grant me health, I will administer it for him as befits. Do you like Zbyszko?"

Zych winked.

"The thing is," he said, "that if anyone mentions his name, Jagienka turns her face away."

"And if you mention someone else's name?"

"If I mention someone else, she laughs and says, 'Not him!'"

"Ah, you see. God grant that near such a girl Zbyszko may forget the other one! I am old, but I would forget. . . . Will you drink some mead?"

"I will."

"So, the abbot . . . he's a wise's man! Some abbots, as you know, are quite worldly men, but he, though he doesn't sit among his monks, is a priest—and a priest always gives better advice than an ordinary man, for he knows how to read and is close to the Holy Ghost. . . . But you, that you will give the girl Moczydoly immediately—that is right. On my part, if the Lord Jesus helps me to regain my health, I will try to entice away as many of Wolf of Birchwood's yeomen as I can. I will give each of them good land. At Bogdaniec there is no lack of it. Let them give notice to Wolf at

Christmas, and come to me. Can they not do as they wish? As time goes on, I will build a castelet at Bogdaniec, a worthy little castle of oak, with a moat around it. . . . Let Zbyszko and Jagienka go hunting together. . . . I don't think we shall have to wait long for snow. . . . Let them get accustomed to one another, and let the boy forget the other girl. Let them go about together. . . . But let's get to the heart of the matter! Would you give him Jagienka, or would you not?"

"I would give her. We've always thought that they were made for one another, and that Moczydoly and Bogdaniec would be for our grandchildren."

"Hailstones!" exclaimed Macko joyfully. "God grant that they may be as numerous as hailstones. The abbot will christen them for us."

"If he gets here on time!" said Zych merrily. "Hey, I haven't seen you so happy in a long while."

"Because my heart is full of joy. The splinter has come out. And as for Zbyszko, don't worry about him. Yesterday, when Jagienka mounted her horse—you know—the wind was blowing. . . . So I asked Zbyszko: 'Did you see that?' And he immediately got the shivers. I noticed that at first they talked together but little, but now when they go about together, they're constantly turning their heads to one another, and yak, yak, yak! . . . Have another drink."

"I will. . . ."

"To the health of Zbyszko and Jagienka!"

CHAPTER XIV

OLD Macko was not mistaken when he said that Zbyszko and Jagienka liked to be together, and even that they longed for one another. In the beginning, Jagienka frequently came to Bogdaniec under the pretext of visiting the sick Macko, either with her father or alone; and Zbyszko dropped in at Zgorzelice from time to time, if only through mere gratitude. So as the days went by there grew up between them a close familiarity and friendship. They began to grow fond of one another and to like "yaking" together, that is, talking about anything of possible concern. There was also a lot of mutual admiration in this friendship, for the young and handsome Zbyszko, who had already gained fame in war and had taken part in tournaments and had been in the chambers of the king, seemed to the girl, in comparison with a Cztan of Rogow or a Wolf of Birchwood, a real knight of the court and almost a prince, while he at times marvelled at her beauty. He thought faithfully of his Danusia, but sometimes, when he glanced at Jagienka, whether in the forest or in the house, he involuntarily said to himself: "Hey! what a fine girl she is!" And when he took her by the waist and placed her in the saddle, feeling her firm, robust body under his hands, he was overcome with disquiet and, as Macko said, was taken with the shivers, and at the same time something seemed to pass through his bones, making him languid and weak.

Jagienka, proud by nature, quick to laugh scornfully, and even bold, became gradually more humble with him, just like a servant girl who looks into her master's eyes to see how she can serve and please him. For his part, Zbyszko noticed her great friendliness and was grateful to her, and he liked more and more to be with her. Finally, especially from the time when Macko began to drink bear's fat, they saw each other almost every day; and after the splinter had come out of his wound, they went together after beaver, whose fresh fat was very necessary for healing the wound.

They took their crossbows, mounted their horses, and rode first to Moczydoly, Jagienka's dowry in the future, and then to the forest, where they left their horses in charge of a servant. Further progress had to be made on foot, for it would have been difficult to ride through the thickets and morasses. Along the way Jagienka pointed to an extensive meadow covered with coarse bents and a bluish strip of forest.

"Those are Cztan of Rogow's forests," she said.

"The man who would like to marry you?"

She began to laugh:

"He would like to if only I would let him!"

"You can easily defend yourself against him with the help of Wolf, who, as I've heard, bares his fangs at him. I'm surprised that they haven't challenged one another yet to mortal combat."

"That's because papa, when he was going to the war, said to them: 'If you fight each other, I don't want to set eyes on either of you again.' So what were they to do? When they are at Zgorzelice, they huff and puff at one another, but afterwards they drink together in the inn at Krzesnia until they fall to the floor."

"Stupid fellows!"

"Why?"

"Because when Zych was not at home one or the other ought to have come to Zgorzelice and taken you by force. What could Zych have done if he had come back and found you with a child in your arms?"

Jagienka's blue eyes flashed immediately:

"You think I would have let myself be taken? You think there are no men at Zgorzelice, or that I don't know how to grasp a spear or a crossbow? If they would have attempted anything, I would have driven each of them home again, and then raided Rogow or Birchwood! Papa knew that he could go to the war without any worries."

So saying, she knit her beautiful eyebrows and shook her crossbow so threateningly that Zbyszko burst out laughing.

"Why, you ought to have been a knight and not a girl!" he exclaimed.

She calmed down and replied:

"Cztan protected me from Wolf, and Wolf from Cztan. Anyway, I was under the abbot's guardianship, and it's not good to run afoul of the abbot."

"Ah, yes," replied Zbyszko, "everybody here is afraid of the abbot! But, believe me, I would not have been afraid either of the abbot, or of Zych, or of the Zgorzelice huntsmen, or of you—I would have taken you."

Hearing that, Jagienka stopped and raised her eyes to Zbyszko, asking in a strange, soft, and dreamy voice:

"You would have?"

Then her lips parted, and she waited for the answer, blushing like the dawn.

But he was only thinking of what he would have done had he been Cztan or Wolf, for he shook his golden head and went on:

"Why should a girl fight with lads when she ought to get married? If a third one doesn't come along, you must take one of them, mustn't you?"

"Don't you tell me that," the girl replied sadly.

"Why? I haven't been here long, so I don't know whether there is anyone in the neighborhood of Zgorzelice whom you like better."

"Hey!" replied Jagienka. "Leave me alone!"

They went on in silence, forcing their way through thickets, which were the more difficult to pass since the bushes and trees were overgrown with wild hop. Zbyszko went first, tearing a way through the green tangle and breaking boughs here and there, while Jagienka, looking like some hunting goddess, followed him, her crossbow on her back.

"Beyond the thickets," she said, "there will be a broad stream, but I know a place where there is a ford."

"I won't get wet; I have knee-boots on," replied Zbyszko.

After some time they came to the stream. Jagienka, knowing the Moczydoly forests well, had no difficulty in finding the ford, but it turned out that the brook was swollen from the rains, and therefore the water was fairly deep. So Zbyszko, without asking, took the girl in his arms.

"I can get across by myself," said Jagienka.

"Hold on to my neck!" ordered Zbyszko.

He went slowly through the flood water, feeling with his foot for any depressions, while the girl clung to him as she had been told. Then, when they were near to the other side, she said:

"Zbyszko!"

"Yes?"

"I will not marry either Cztan or Wolf."

He reached the bank and put her down carefully.

"God give you the best man possible!" he replied, somewhat perturbed. "You will be worthy of him."

The little Odstajan lake was not far off now. Jagienka went first, turning around from time to time and putting her fingers on her lips to warn Zbyszko to keep silent. They went among clusters of osiers and grey willows over wet, low-lying land. From the right, there came the sound of birds to their ears, and Zbyszko was surprised, as it was already time for them to migrate.

"There's a warm spring there," whispered Jagienka, "where the wild ducks spend the winter. But even in the lake the water freezes only at the sides in hard frosts. Look how it is steaming. . . ."

Zbyszko glanced through the osiers and saw before him what seemed to be one massive cloud of mist. It was the Odstajan lake.

Jagienka again put her finger to her lips. After a while they reached the shore. The girl crawled onto a thick old willow leaning over the water, and Zbyszko followed her example. For a long time they lay silent, seeing nothing because of the mist and hearing only the melancholy call of the pewits and the kingfishers over their heads. At length, however, a wind blew, rustled the osiers and the yellowing leaves of the willows, and revealed the lake, ruffled by the breeze and empty.

"You see nothing?" whispered Zbyszko.

"There's nothing. Be quiet!"

The breeze fell and the silence became profound. Then one black head appeared on the surface of the water, and then another. Finally, close-by, a large beaver entered the water carrying a fresh-cut branch in his mouth. The beaver began to swim through the pondweed and marsh marigolds, holding his head up and pushing the branch before him. Zbyszko, lying on the willow-trunk below Jagienka, suddenly saw her elbows moving quietly and her head leaning forward. Evidently she was aiming at the animal, which, suspecting no danger, was swimming no more than half a bow-shot from her, towards the open water.

At last the bowstring twanged, and at the same moment Jagienka's voice called out:

"I've got him! I've got him!"

Zbyszko quickly crawled higher up and looked through the branches. The beaver now dived and now floated on the surface, turning over and over and at times showing his belly, which was lighter in color than his back.

"He got it good! He will soon be still," said Jagienka.

And she was right, for the beaver's movements became weaker and weaker, and after a single Ave Maria had passed, the animal was floating belly upwards.

"I'm going for it," said Zbyszko.

"Don't. The mud here is deep. If anyone doesn't know how to deal with it, he will certainly drown."

"Then how will we get him?"

"He'll be at Bogdaniec by evening, don't trouble your head about that. Now it's time for us to go home."

"That was a good shot!"

"Bah! I've done this before."

"Other girls are afraid even to look at a crossbow, but with a companion like you one might range the forest for a lifetime."

Hearing this praise, Jagienka smiled with joy, but made no reply, and they went back the same way through the osiers. Zbyszko began to question her about the beavers' lodges, and she told him how many beavers there were at Moczydoly and how many at Zgorzelice, and how they busied themselves on the lakes and streams.

Suddenly, however, she struck her hip with her hand.

"Oh!" she exclaimed. "I've left my arrows on the willow. Wait!"

And before he could answer that he would go for them himself, she dashed back like a fawn, disappearing quickly from his sight. Zbyszko waited and waited, until at last he began to wonder why she was so long.

"She probably lost her arrows and is looking for them," he said to himself. "But I'll go and see whether anything has happened to her."

He had hardly gone a few steps when the girl appeared before him with her crossbow in her hand, smiling and flushed, and the beaver on her back.

"Heavens!" exclaimed Zbyszko. "However did you get him out?"

"How? I went into the water, that's all! It's not the first time I have done it, and I didn't want to let you go, for if anyone doesn't know how to swim there, the mud will drag him down."

"And here I was waiting for you like an idiot! You're a cunning girl."

"Well, so what? Was I suppose to undress in front of you?"

"Then you didn't forget your arrows?"

"No, I only wanted to get you away from the bank."

"Ah! and if I'd only gone after you, I would have seen a wondrous sight! There would have been something to marvel at. Hey!"

"Be quiet!"

"As God is dear to me, I was just about to go after you."

"Be quiet!"

Then, evidently wanting to change the conversation, she said:

"Squeeze out my plait of hair. It's wetting my back badly."

Zbyszko caught hold of her plait with one hand close to her head, and began to wring it out with the other, saying:

"It would be better to unplait it, for then the wind will dry it quickly."

But she would not do that because of the thickets through which they had to force their way. Zbyszko now took the beaver on his back, while Jagienka went first.

"Macko will get well soon," she said, "for nothing is better for wounds than bear's fat for the inside and beaver's fat for the outside. In a couple of weeks he should be able to sit on a horse."

"God grant it!" replied Zbyszko. "I am desperately waiting for his recovery, for it is difficult for me to leave a sick man, yet it is hard for me to stay here."

"Hard for you to stay here?" asked Jagienka. "Why?"

"Did not Zych tell you anything about Danusia?"

"He told me a little. . . . I know that she covered you with her veil. . . . Yes, that I know! He also told me that every knight vows to do some deed for his lady. But he told me that such service is nothing, for some make such vows even though they are married.

But this Danusia, Zbyszko, what is she to you? Tell me! Who is this Danusia?"

And coming nearer to him, she raised her eyes and began to look uneasily at his face, while he, without noticing in the least her anxious tone and look, said:

"She is my lady, but also she is my dearest love. I do not tell that to anyone, but I will tell you as I would my own sister, for we have known each other since we were little. For her sake I would go anywhere, to Germany or Tartary. There is no girl like her in all the world. My uncle can stay at Bogdaniec and I will set out after her. . . . What is Bogdaniec to me without her! What are its buildings, its flocks and herds and the abbot's wealth! I will mount my horse—yes, I will—and ride to Mazovia and, so help me God, fulfill that which I have vowed to her, unless I fall first."

"I didn't know this," replied Jagienka dully.

Then Zbyszko began to tell her how he had first met Danusia at Tyniec, and how he had immediately made a vow to her, and he related all that had happened afterwards, that is to say, his imprisonment, how Danusia rescued him, Jurand's refusal, their parting, his longing, and finally his joy that when Macko was well again he would be able to ride to his beloved girl and fulfill what he had promised her. He broke off his story only when he saw the servant with the horses, waiting at the edge of the forest.

Jagienka immediately mounted her horse and began to take leave of Zbyszko.

"My servant can ride after you with the beaver and I will go back to Zgorzelice."

"Won't you come to Bogdaniec? Zych is there."

"No. Papa was to return and told me to do likewise."

"Well, may God reward you for the beaver!"

"God be with you!"

Then Jagienka was left alone. Riding homewards through the heather she looked around from time to time towards the distancing Zbyszko, and when he had at last vanished among the trees, she covered her eyes with her hand as if shading them from the light of the sun.

Soon great tears began to roll down her cheeks and fall one after another, like peas, onto her saddle and her horse's mane.

CHAPTER XV

AFTER her talk with Zbyszko, Jagienka did not show herself at Bogdaniec for three days, but on the fourth she dropped in with the news that the abbot had come to Zgorzelice. Macko received it with some emotion. He possessed, it is true, the means to repay the sum pledged, and he even calculated that enough would be left over to increase the number of settlers and to purchase flocks and herds and other items necessary for the administration of Bogdaniec. None the less, much depended on the goodwill of his rich kinsman, who might, for example, take away the villeins whom he had settled on parcels of land, or might leave them, thereby diminishing or increasing the value of the estate.

Accordingly, Macko questioned Jagienka very closely about the abbot. He wanted to know in what mood he had arrived: cheerful or morose; what he said about them, and when he was coming to Bogdaniec. She answered his questions prudently, endeavoring to inspire him with hope and to calm his anxieties.

She told him the abbot was well and in good spirits, and that he had arrived with a considerable troop of followers, including both armed retainers and a few wandering clerics and minstrels; that he sometimes sang with Zych and listened gladly not only to spiritual but also to worldly songs. She remarked also that he had inquired with much solicitude about Macko, and that he eagerly listened to Zych's stories of Zbyszko's adventures at Cracow.

"You yourself know best what you ought to do," said the shrewd girl in conclusion. "But I think it would be well for Zbyszko to ride at once and pay his respects to his old kinsman, without waiting for him to come to Bogdaniec first."

Macko found this advice convincing, so he sent for Zbyszko and said to him:

"Dress yourself handsomely and ride to Zgorzelice to embrace the abbot's knees and do him honor, so that he may take to you." Then he turned to Jagienka. "It wouldn't have surprised me had you been stupid, because that's what women are, but it does surprise me that you have brains. Tell me how best I can entertain the abbot and how I can please him when he comes here."

"As for food, he will tell you himself what he is fond of. He likes to eat well, but he will not complain if there is plenty of saffron."

Macko grabbed his head.

"Where am I to get saffron from!"

"I have brought some," said Jagienka.

"If only there were more girls like you!" exclaimed Macko joyfully. "Pleasing to the eye, and good administrators, and sagacious, and well-disposed to people! Hey, if only I were young I would take you at once!"

Jagienka glanced imperceptibly at Zbyszko and, sighing quietly, went on:

"I have also brought you dice, a dice-box and a piece of cloth, for he likes a game of dice after every meal."

"He had that custom of yore, and he used to get terribly angry when playing."

"He gets angry now too. Sometimes he flings the dice-box on the ground and storms out of the house. But afterwards he returns laughing and is himself the first to be surprised at his anger. You know him. As long as you don't oppose him, there's no better fellow in the world."

"Who would oppose him, when he has more sense than anyone else?"

Thus they talked with one another, while Zbyszko was changing his clothes in the alcove. When he finally came out, he was so handsome that Jagienka became quite dazzled, just as she had been when he came that first time to Zgorzelice in his white jacket. But this time she was overcome with deep melancholy at the thought that his charms were not for her and that he loved another.

Macko, however, was joyful, for he thought that the abbot

would most surely like Zbyszko and therefore make no difficulties in the negotiations over Bogdaniec. This pleased him so much that he decided to go with him.

"Have my wagon made ready," he said to Zbyszko. "If I could travel from Cracow as far as Bogdaniec with a splinter between my ribs, I can now go to Zgorzelice without it."

"As long as you don't faint," said Jagienka.

"Oh, nothing will be wrong. I feel strong already. And even if I do feel a little faint, the abbot will see how speedily I've come to him, and will show himself all the more generous because of that."

"I prefer your health to his generosity," replied Zbyszko.

But Macko insisted on having his own way. On the road, he groaned a little, but he did not cease to give Zbyszko instructions as to how to behave at Zgorzelice, and particularly recommended him to be obedient and humble with his powerful kinsman, since the abbot could not endure the least opposition.

When they arrived at Zgorzelice, they found Zych and the abbot sitting on a terrace, looking at God's beautiful world in front of them and drinking wine. Behind them, on a bench by the wall, sat six of the abbot's retinue, including two minstrels and a pilgrim, easily recognizable by his twisted staff, the drinking-cup at his belt, and the shells sewn to his dark gown. The others looked like clerics, for they had their heads shaven on the top, though they wore worldly garb, belts of bull's hide, and swords at their sides.

At the sight of Macko, arriving on his wagon, Zych sprang up; but the abbot, evidently anxious to preserve his spiritual dignity, remained sitting, and said something to his clerics, a few more of whom came pouring out through the open door of the house. Zbyszko and Zych led the weak Macko to the terrace.

"I still cannot walk around that much," said Macko, kissing the abbot's hand, "but I have come to pay my respects to you, my benefactor, to thank you for administering Bogdaniec and to beg you for your blessing, which a sinful man greatly needs."

"I heard that you were better," said the abbot, embracing him, "and that you have promised to visit the grave of our deceased queen."

"Not knowing to which saint to turn, I turned to her."

"You did well!" said the abbot fervently. "She is better than the others, and let anyone dare object!"

His face grew angry, his cheeks flushed with blood, and his eyes began to flash.

The others knew his fiery temperament, and Zych began to laugh.

"Strike, whoever believes in God!" he exclaimed.

The abbot heaved out a loud sigh and rolled his eyes at the company. Then he burst out laughing, just as suddenly as he had previously burst into wrath. Looking at Zbyszko, he asked:

"I suppose this is your nephew and my kinsman?"

Zbyszko bowed and kissed his hand.

"I saw you last when you were a small boy," said the the abbot. "I should not have recognized you! Show yourself to me!"

And he began to look at him from head to foot with keen eyes.

"Too handsome!" he said finally. "A young lady rather than a knight!"

"The Germans danced with this young lady," replied Macko, "but whoever took her soon fell down and didn't get up again."

"And he bends a crossbow without a crank!" exclaimed Jagienka suddenly.

The abbot turned to her.

"What are you doing here?"

She blushed so strongly that her neck and ears reddened, and she became quite flustered:

"I—I saw him. . . ."

"Beware that he doesn't shoot you by chance, for it would take you nine months to get over it."

The minstrels, the pilgrim, and the wandering clerics burst into roars of laughter, and Jagienka was so embarrassed that the abbot took pity on her and lifting his arm, showed her the enormous sleeve of his dress.

"Hide yourself here, girl," he said, "or the blood will spurt from your cheeks."

Meanwhile Zych gave Macko a seat on the bench and called for wine, which Jagienka hastened to bring. The abbot turned to Zbyszko.

"Enough jests!" he said. "I didn't compare you to a girl to shame you, but only for merriment's sake, because of your good looks, which many a girl might begrudge you. I know you are a sturdy lad!

I have heard of your deeds at Wilno, and of the Frisians, and of Cracow. Zych told me everything—do you understand?"

He looked sharply into Zbyszko's eyes, then spoke again:

"You've vowed three peacock crests, so go and look for them! It is praiseworthy and pleasing to God to hunt the enemies of our race. But if you've vowed anything else, then know that I can absolve you from those vows straightaway, for I have such power."

"Hey!" said Zbyszko; "when one has made a promise to the Lord Jesus in one's heart, what power can absolve one from it?"

Hearing that, Macko glanced with some anxiety at the abbot, but he was obviously in an excellent humor, for instead of bursting into anger, he threatened Zbyszko merrily with his finger, saying:

"What a clever fellow you are! Be careful you do not meet the same fate that befell that German, Beyhard."

"What happened to him?" asked Zych.

"He was burned at the stake."

"What for?"

"For saying that a layman can understand the divine secrets as well as a clergyman."

"His punishment was severe."

"But quite just!" thundered the abbot. "He blasphemed against the Holy Ghost! What do you think? Can a layman know anything of the divine secrets?"

"Most certainly he cannot!" exclaimed the clerics in chorus.

"You gleemen, be quiet!" said the abbot. "Even though you have shaven heads, you are not yet clergymen."

"But we are not gleemen anymore, nor goliards; we are courtiers of your grace," replied one of them, glancing at the same time at a great flagon, from which came the smell of malt and hops, though it was some distance away.

"Look! he talks as if from a barrel!" exclaimed the abbot. "Hey, you shaggy fellow! What are you looking at that flagon for? You won't find any Latin at the bottom of it."

"It's not Latin I'm looking for, only beer, which I can't find."

The abbot turned to Zbyszko, who was looking at these courtiers in amazement, and said:

"They are all *clerici scholares*, though each of them would rather fling down his book and grasp a lute and wander with it through the world. I've got hold of them and feed them, for what am I to do? They are ne'er-do-wells and vagabonds, but they know how to sing, and they have picked up a little of divine service, so I have some use of them in church, and in case of need, I have protection, for some of them are sturdy lads! That pilgrim there says he's been to the Holy Land, but you would ask him in vain what seas or what countries he has crossed. He does not even know the name of the Greek emperor, nor the city in which he lives."

"I did know once," replied the pilgrim in a hoarse voice, "but when a fever seized and shook me on the Danube, it shook everything out of me."

"I am most astonished at their swords," said Zbyszko. "I have never seen wandering clerics wearing swords before."

"They are allowed to wear them," said the abbot, "because they haven't been ordained yet. As for me, it's not surprising that I wear a sword at my side. A year ago I challenged Wolf of Birchwood to single combat for those forests through which you passed on the way to Bogdaniec. He did not take up my challenge."

"How could he engage in combat with a clergyman?" interrupted Zych.

The abbot exploded and, striking his fist on the table, shouted:

"When wearing armor I'm not a priest but a nobleman! . . . He did not face me, for he preferred to fall upon me with his men at Tulcza by night. That's why I wear a sword at my side! *Omnes leges, omniaque iura vim vi repellere cunctisque sese defensare permittunt!* And that's why I have given them swords too."

Zych, Macko, and Zbyszko were silent when they heard the Latin, and bowed their heads before the wisdom of the abbot, for none of them understood a single word. He, however, looked around angrily for some time, and finally said:

"Who knows whether he won't fall upon me here?"

"Let him just try!" exclaimed the wandering clerics, grasping the hilts of their swords.

"Yes, let him try! I'm itching for a fight."

"He will not do that," said Zych. "More likely he will come with greetings, and peacefully. He has already renounced the forests, but he's concerned for his son. You know what I mean! But he'll be disappointed!"

Meanwhile the abbot had calmed down, and he said:

"I saw young Wolf drinking with Cztan of Rogow in the inn at

Krzesnia. They didn't recognize me at first, for it was dark—and they talked all the time about Jagienka." Here he turned to Zbyszko. "And about you."

"What did they want of me?"

"They didn't want anything of you. They are displeased that there should be a third young man in the neighborhood of Zgorzelice. Cztan said to Wolf: 'When I've tanned his hide, he won't be so smooth anymore.' And Wolf said: 'Maybe he will be afraid of us, and if not, I will break his bones in a flash.' And then they began to assure one another that you would be afraid of them."

Macko looked at Zych, and Zych at him, and both their faces took on an expression of cunning and delight. Neither of them were sure whether the abbot had really heard such a conversation or whether he had invented it to spur Zbyszko on. But both of them, and particularly Macko, who knew Zbyszko so well, understood that there was no better way in the world to push him towards Jagienka.

And the abbot, as if intentionally, added:

"And, to tell the truth, they are sturdy fellows."

Zbyszko's face betrayed nothing, but he began to ask Zych in a strange, unnatural tone:

"Tomorrow will be Sunday?"

"Yes, Sunday."

"Are you going to Mass?

"Of course!"

"Where? At Krzesnia?"

"That's the nearest place. Where else should we go?"

"Good!"

CHAPTER XVI

ZBYSZKO, catching up to Zych and Jagienka as they were riding in the company of the abbot and his clerics to Krzesnia, joined them and rode at their side, for he wanted to show the abbot that he was not afraid of Wolf of Birchwood or of Cztan of Rogow, and would not hide from them. He was struck again by Jagienka's beauty. Although he had seen her several times exquisitely dressed to receive guests, both at Zgorzelice and at Bogdaniec, he had never yet seen her dressed as she was now for church. She wore a gown of red cloth, lined with skins of ermine, red gloves, and an ermine hood embroidered with gold, from beneath which her two plaits of hair hung down her back. She was not sitting astride her horse but on a high saddle with a back-rest and support for her feet, which were scarcely visible under her long, evenly pleated skirt. Zych, though he allowed his girl to dress in a sheepskin jacket and untanned leather boots at home, was concerned that everyone at church should see that she was the daughter of no ordinary small landholder but of a well-to-do knightly house. So her horse was led by two pages attired in tight hose and puffed jackets, the typical dress of their kind. Four retainers brought up the rear; accompanying them were the abbot's clerics, their swords and lutes at their belts. Zbyszko admired the whole train, but particularly Jagienka, who looked like a picture, and the abbot, who in his red robe with its enormous sleeves looked to him like some travelling prince. The most modestly dressed of all was Zych himself. He cared that others should make an impression, but liked only merriment and singing for himself.

They rode four abreast: the abbot, Jagienka, Zbyszko, and Zych. The abbot at first bade his gleemen sing pious songs—but he soon had enough of that, and began to talk to Zbyszko, who was looking with a smile at his hefty sword, a weapon as large as a two-handed German blade.

"I see," he said solemnly, "that you are surprised at my sword. Know, therefore, that the synods allow the clergy to carry swords, and even ballistas and catapults, when on a journey—and we are on a journey. When the Holy Father forbade priests to carry swords or wear red robes, he must assuredly have been thinking of people of lower station, for God created the nobleman to bear arms, and whoever should wish to take them from him, would be opposing His everlasting judgments."

"I have seen Henry, Duke of Mazovia, jousting in the lists," replied Zbyszko.

"He is not to be blamed for jousting," replied the abbot, lifting his finger, "but for marrying and, what is more, for marrying unhappily. For he took a fornicaria and *bibula mulier*, who, as they say, *Bacchum adorabat* from her youth, and, furthermore, was an *adultera*, so that nothing good could possibly come of her."

Here he actually stopped his horse and began to instruct Zbyszko still more gravely:

"Whoever, therefore, is about to marry, or to take an *uxor*, must take care that she is God-fearing, of good manners, a good administrator, and of orderly habits; all of which is recommended, not only by the Church fathers but also by a certain pagan sage called Seneca. And how are you to know that you have made a good choice unless you know the nest from which you are choosing your life's companion? Another Christian sage says: '*Pomus non cadit absque arbore.*' As the ox, so the hide; as the mother, so the daughter. . . . Therefore, sinful man, learn not to seek a wife far away but near at hand, for if you get one who is bad-tempered and bold, you will some day weep, as that philosopher wept when his quarrelsome wife in her anger threw *aqua sordida* on his head."

"*In saecula saeculorum, amen!*" thundered the wandering clerics with one voice, for they always answered the abbot thus, without caring much whether it made sense or not.

The entire company listened with great attention to the abbot's words, admiring his eloquence and his knowledge of the Scriptures. Yet he did not just speak to Zbyszko. In fact, he turned more frequently to Zych and Jagienka, as if for their particular edification. Jagienka evidently understood his intention, for she looked keenly from under her long eyelashes at the youth, who frowned and bend his head as if deeply pondering what he had heard.

The company moved forward again, but this time in silence. It was only when Krzesnia was already in view that the abbot felt for his belt and pulled it around, so that it would be easy to grasp the hilt of his sword.

"Old Wolf Birchwood will certainly come with a large retinue," he stated.

"Certainly," agreed Zych, "but the servants were saying something about his being sick."

"One of my clerics heard that he is going to fall upon us in front of the inn, after church."

"He would not do that without a challenge—and particularly after Holy Mass."

"May God give him self-control. I seek war with no one and bear wrongs patiently." Here he looked around at his gleemen, saying: "Don't draw your swords and remember that you are clerkly retainers. But if they draw first, strike!"

Meanwhile Zbyszko, riding at Jagienka's side, questioned her about the things which concerned him most.

"I shall certainly find Cztan and young Wolf at Krzesnia," he said. "Point them out to me, so that I may know who they are."

"Yes, Zbyszko," replied Jagienka.

"Undoubtedly they see you before and after Mass. What do they do on those occasions?"

"Attend on me as best they can."

"They will not attend on you today, do you understand?"

And she answered again, almost with humility:

"Yes, Zbyszko."

Further talk was interrupted by the sound of wooden rattles, there being no bells as yet at Krzesnia. Soon they reached the town. Young Wolf and Cztan of Rogow immediately came forward from the crowds waiting before the church. But Zbyszko anticipated them: He leapt from his horse before they could run up, and catching Jagienka by the waist, he lifted her from the saddle; then he took her by the hand and, glancing provocatively at them, led her into church.

In the church vestibule a fresh disappointment awaited the two suitors. Both hastened to the holy-water basin, dipped their hands in it, and extended them to the girl. But Zbyszko did the same, and she touched his fingers, crossed herself, and went into the church with him. Then not only young Wolf but also Cztan of Rogow, with his limited intelligence, understood that all had been done on purpose, and they were both seized with such wild rage that their hair began to bristle under their nets. However, they still possessed enough sense not to enter the church in their rage and provoke divine retribution. Instead, Wolf rushed out of the vestibule and ran like a madman between the trees of the churchyard, scarcely knowing where he was going. Cztan ran after him, also without knowing to what end he did it.

They stopped at the corner of the fence, where some large rocks were lying ready for use as a foundation for a bell-tower. Wishing to release the rage that was nearly choking him, Wolf seized one of the boulders and began to rock it with all his strength. Seeing this, Cztan grasped it also, and after a few moments both of them began to roll it angrily through the churchyard, right up to the church gate.

People looked at them with amazement, supposing they were fulfilling some vow and that they wished thus to contribute to the building of the bell-tower. Their physical efforts gave them considerable relief, and they both came to their senses, standing pale from their exertions, breathing heavily, and looking uncertainly at one another.

The silence was broken first by Cztan of Rogow.

"Well, what now?" he asked.

"What?" answered Wolf.

"Shall we attack him at once?"

"How can you attack him in church?"

"Not in church, but after Mass."

"He is with Zych—and with the abbot. Have you forgotten what Zych said? That if we started a fight he would banish us both from Zgorzelice. If it were not for that, I would have broken your ribs long ago."

"Or I yours," replied Cztan, clenching his powerful fists.

Their eyes began to flash ominously, but they quickly realized that now they needed to agree together more than ever before. They had fought one another several times but had always become reconciled afterwards, for although they were divided by their love for Jagienka, they could not live without one another. Now they had a common enemy, and both felt that he was an extremely dangerous one.

So Cztan asked:

"What shall we do? Send a challenge to Bogdaniec?"

Wolf, the wiser of the two, did not know yet what to do. Luckily the rattles came to his aid, sounding again as a sign that divine service was about to begin. So he said:

"What shall we do? Go to Mass, and afterwards God will decide."

Cztan of Rogow was pleased with this sensible answer.

"Maybe the Lord Jesus will inspire us," he said.

"And bless us," added Wolf.

"In accordance with what is just."

They went to church, where they heard divine service piously and had their spirits uplifted. After Mass they did not lose their heads even when Jagienka again took holy water from Zbyszko's hand. In the churchyard by the gate they fell at the feet of Zych, Jagienka, and even the abbot, though he was the enemy of the old Wolf of Birchwood. They looked askance at Zbyszko, it is true, but neither of them growled at him, although their hearts were burning in their breasts with pain, wrath, and jealousy, for Jagienka had never appeared to them so beautiful and so like a princess. Only after the splendid company had set out on its return, and the cheerful sound of the singing of the wandering clerics came to their ears form a distance, did Cztan begin to wipe the sweat from his hairy cheeks and to snort like a horse, while Wolf exclaimed, grinding his teeth:

"To the inn! to the inn! Woe is me!"

Then, remembering what had given them relief before, they got hold of the boulder again and energetically rolled it back to its former place.

In the meantime Zbyszko rode by Jagienka's side, listening to the songs of the abbot's gleemen. When they had gone five or six furlongs, he suddenly checked his horse and said:

"Oh, I forgot! I had to pay the priest for a Mass for my uncle's health. I will go back."

"Don't go back!" exclaimed Jagienka. "I will send someone from Zgorzelice."

"I shall return. Don't wait for me. God be with you!"

"And with you too!" said the abbot. "Go!"

And the abbot's face brightened up. When Zbyszko had disappeared from sight, he nudged Zych.

"Do you understand?" he asked.

"What have I to understand?"

"He will fight at Krzesnia with Wolf and Cztan as surely as an amen follows a prayer. But that is what I wanted, and that is what I've achieved."

"They are sturdy fellows! They might wound him—and what then?"

"What do you mean, what then? If he fights for Jagienka, how can he afterwards think of Jurand's daughter? Jagienka will be his lady from that time on, not the other. That is what I want, for he is my kinsman and I like him!"

"And what about his vow?"

"I will release him from it immediately. Didn't you hear me promise that already?"

"You think of everything," replied Zych.

The abbot was pleased to be praised. He turned to Jagienka and asked her:

"Why are you so sad?"

She leaned forward in the saddle and taking the abbot's hand, raised it to her lips:

"Godfather, maybe you could send a few gleemen to Krzesnia?"

"What for? They will get drunk in the inn, and that's all."

"Maybe they will prevent some quarrel."

The abbot looked her keenly in the eyes.

"Suppose they killed him there?" he said suddenly.

"Let them kill me too!" exclaimed Jagienka.

And the bitterness which had united with the grief in her breast since she had had her last talk with Zbyszko found expression now in a sudden flood of tears. Seeing that, the abbot put his arm around the girl, covering her almost completely with his enormous sleeve.

"Never fear, little daughter," he said. "There may be a quarrel, but they, too, are noblemen, and will not fall upon him in a band but only challenge him to the field according to knightly custom, and then he will be able to deal with them, even if he has to fight both at once. And as for Jurand's daughter, of whom you have heard, I will tell you only this, that the wood for her marriage-bed is not growing in any forest."

"Since he loves her more, I don't care for him," replied Jagienka through her tears.

"Then why are you crying?"

"Because I'm afraid for him."

"Woman's wit!" said the abbot, laughing.

Then, leaning over to Jagienka's ear, he said:

"Remember, girl, that even if he takes you, he will sometimes have to fight, for that is the duty of a nobleman." He bent still nearer and added: "And he will take you—and before very long, as sure as God is in heaven!"

"Would that he might!" replied Jagienka.

And she smiled through her tears and looked at the abbot as if she wanted to ask him how he knew.

Meanwhile Zbyszko, having reached Krzesnia, went straight to the priest, for he really did wish to pay for a Mass for Macko's health. But after settling that business he went straight to the inn, where he hoped to find young Wolf of Birchwood and Cztan of Rogow.

He came upon both of them, and also a huge crowd of people—nobles, small landholders, yeomen, and a few jugglers, who were showing the company various German tricks. At first, however, he could not recognize anybody, since the windows of the inn, made of ox-bladder, did not let through much light. Only when the servingman had thrown a few pine chips on the fire did he perceive in the corner behind tankards of beer the hairy mug of Cztan and the stern, fiery face of Wolf of Birchwood.

Then he went up slowly to them, pushing aside anyone in his way, and when he got to them, he struck his fist on the table so powerfully that the whole inn resounded with the noise.

They immediately got up and began hastily to pull around their leather belts, but before they could grasp the hilts of their swords, Zbyszko threw his glove to the table, and speaking through his nose, as was the custom for knights when uttering a challenge, he uttered the following words, expected by none:

"If either of you two, or any other knight in this room, denies that the most beautiful and virtuous girl in the world is the Lady Danuta of Spychow, Jurand's daughter, I challenge him to fight on horseback or on foot till one of us kneels or until death."

Wolf and Cztan were amazed, just as the abbot would have been if he had heard anything like that. For a while they couldn't say a word. "What lady is this?" they thought. They cared for Jagienka, not for her. . . . And if this wildcat did not care for Jagienka, what did he want with them? Why had he angered them in front of the church? Why had he come here and sought a quarrel with them? These questions made such a mess in their heads that they opened their mouths wide—while Cztan also opened his eyes as if it were not a man which stood before him but some German monster.

But the sharper-witted Wolf, who knew something of knightly customs, was aware that sometimes knights vow service to one woman and marry another. He thought, therefore, that it might be so in this case, and considered that if an opportunity presented itself of taking Jagienka's part, they ought immediately to take advantage of it.

So he came around the table and approached Zbyszko with a threatening expression, and then asked:

"What, you dog, is not Jagienka, Zych's daughter, the most beautiful?"

Cztan also left the table—and people began to gather around the three, for all now saw that this was no trifling matter.

CHAPTER XVII

WHEN she reached home, Jagienka immediately sent a servant to Krzesnia to find out whether there had been a fight in the inn or whether at least a challenge had been issued. The servant, however, having received some money for the way, began to drink with the priest's servants, and did not think of coming back. A second messenger, sent to Bogdaniec to announce to Macko the abbot's visit, returned from his errand and declared that he had seen Zbyszko playing dice with the old landowner.

This calmed Jagienka a little. She knew Zbyszko's experience and skill, and had therefore not feared a challenge for him so much as some unexpected serious adventure at the inn. Now she wanted to ride to Bogdaniec with the abbot, but he would not let her, desiring to talk with Macko about the pledge and another still more important matter he did not wish her to hear.

Anyway, he wanted to travel by night. When her learned of Zbyszko's happy return, he fell into an excellent humor and bade his wandering clerics sing and shout, which they did so loudly that the forest resounded with their noise and the yeomen in Bogdaniec itself looked out from their huts to see if there was a fire or a hostile attack. The pilgrim, riding in front with his twisted staff, calmed them by saying that a churchman of high dignity was riding by. So they bowed before the abbot and some even made the sign of the cross on their breasts; and he, seeing how they respected him, rode on in joyful pride, pleased with the world and full of goodwill to men.

Hearing the shouts and singing, Macko and Zbyszko came to

the gate to meet him. Some of the clerics had already been with the abbot at Bogdaniec, but there were others who had joined his company recently and had never seen it until now. Their hearts fell at the sight of the miserable house, which could bear no comparison with the spacious mansion at Zgorzelice. None the less, they were cheered by the sight of the smoke making its way through the straw thatch of the roof, and they were particularly filled with good hope when they went into the front room and smelled the odor of saffron and various meats, and saw two tables covered with metal dishes—still empty, it is true, but so large that every eye was cheered at the sight of them. On a smaller table shone a dish of pure silver, prepared for the abbot, and a beautifully carved silver flagon, both of which had been won, with other treasures, from the Frisians.

Macko and Zbyszko immediately asked the company to take their seats at table, but the abbot, who had eaten a lot before leaving Zgorzelice, declined, particularly as he was occupied with something else. From the first moment of his arrival he had looked attentively, and at the same time uneasily, at Zbyszko, to see if he bore any trace of a fight. But when he saw the calm bearing of the young man, he became impatient and finally could not restrain his great curiosity anymore.

"Let us go to the alcove," he said, "and talk about the mortgage. Do as I say or I shall get angry!"

Then he turned to his clerics and thundered:

"And you, sit quietly and don't listen at the door!"

He opened the door to the alcove, where there was scarcely room for him, and went in, followed by Zbyszko and Macko. They all sat down on chests, and the abbot turned to the young knight.

"You went back to Krzesnia?" he asked.

"Yes."

"Well, what happened?"

"I paid for a Mass for my uncle's health, that was all."

The abbot shifted restlessly on his chest. "Ha!" he thought, "he did not meet either Cztan or Wolf. Maybe they were not there, or maybe he did not look for them. I was wrong."

But he became angry at being wrong and at having his plans thwarted. So his face grew red, and he began to breathe heavily.

"Let's talk of the mortgage," he said. "Do you have the money? If not, then the estate is mine."

Macko, who knew how to deal with him, got up in silence, opened the chest on which he had been siting, and took out a bag of money, evidently already prepared.

"We are poor people," he said, "but we have money, and what we owe, we pay, as it stands in the mortgage deed, and as I have declared myself with the sign of the Holy Cross. If you want further payment for the implements and the cattle, we will not dispute it but will pay what you bid us, and will embrace your knees, our benefactor."

He bowed to the abbot's knees, and Zbyszko followed his example. Having expected disputes and bargaining, the abbot was greatly surprised by such behavior, and indeed was not very pleased, for he had wanted to make various conditions when they were bargaining, and now the opportunity was gone.

So he gave back the receipt for the mortgage on which Macko had signed with a cross, and said:

"Why do you talk about further payment?"

"Because I don't want to take something for nothing," replied Macko cunningly, knowing that the more he opposed him in this case, the more he would profit.

The abbot exploded in the twinkling of an eye:

"Look at them! They don't want to take something for nothing from their kin! Bread makes them proud. I did not take waste land, so I will not give back waste land. And if it pleases me to throw this bag away, I will!"

"You won't do that!" exclaimed Macko.

"Won't I? Your mortgage money means nothing to me! Your fines mean nothing to me! I can do whatever I please with this bag. If I choose to leave it on the road, it's none of your business. I won't throw this bag away, eh? Just watch!"

He took the bag by the neck and hurled it on the floor. It burst and the money scattered.

"God reward you! God reward you, father and benefactor!" cried out Macko, who had been waiting for precisely this moment. "I would not have taken it from another, but from a kinsman and a churchman I will take it."

The abbot looked threateningly at him, at Zbyszko, and finally said:

"Even though I'm angry, I know what I'm doing. So keep what you've got, for I tell you that you won't get anything more from me."

"We did not expect to."

"But bear in mind that when I die, all I have will go to Jagienka."

"The land too?" asked Macko naively.

"The land too!" shouted the abbot.

Macko's face lengthened, but he mastered himself and said:

"Eh, why should we think of death? May the Lord Jesus give you a hundred years or more, and before that an honorable bishopric."

"And suppose He did! Am I worse than others?" replied the abbot.

"Not worse, but better."

These words calmed the abbot, and indeed his anger was generally short-lived.

"Well," he said, "you are my kinsmen, and she is only my god-daughter; but I have loved her and Zych for many years. A better fellow than Zych is not to be found, nor a better girl than Jagienka. Does anyone have anything to say against them?"

And he rolled his eyes challengingly. Macko not only did not deny it but eagerly avouched that it would be vain to look for a better neighbor in the whole kingdom.

"And as for the girl," he said, "I could not have loved my own daughter more than I love her. It was through her that I recovered my health, and I shall never forget that as long as I live."

"Both of you will be damned if you do forget," said the abbot, "and I shall be the first to curse you for it. I wish you no harm, for you are my kinsmen, and therefore I have thought out a way by which my inheritance may be both Jagienka's and yours—do you understand?"

"God grant it may happen so!" replied Macko. "Dear Jesus! I would go on foot to the queen's grave at Cracow and to Bald Hill to bow before the wood of the Holy Cross."

The abbot was pleased with the sincerity of Macko's words. He smiled and said:

"The girl has the right to choose. She is beautiful and has a worthy dowry and her family is honorable. What would a Cztan of a Wolf be for her, when even a voivode's son would not be too good for her? But she would marry anyone I would recommend, for she loves me and knows that I would not give her bad advice."

"Whomever you recommend will be fortunate," said Macko.

The abbot turned to Zbyszko:

"And what do you think?"

"Well, I think the same as my uncle."

The abbot's countenance brightened still more. He slapped Zbyszko's back so hard that the alcove rang, and asked:

"Why did you not let either Cztan or Wolf come near Jagienka in front of the church?"

"I did not want them to think that I was afraid of them, and I did not want you to think so either."

"But you gave her holy water."

"I did."

The abbot slapped his back a second time:

"Well, then—take her!"

"Take her!" echoed Macko.

Zbyszko pushed his hair under his net and answered calmly:

"How can I take her when I have made a vow at Tyniec to Danusia?"

"You swore to get peacock crests for her, so look for them, but take Jagienka now."

"No," replied Zbyszko. "After Danusia threw her veil over me, I swore to marry her."

The abbot's face flushed. His ears turned blue, and his eyes began to bulge out of his head. He came up to Zbyszko and said in a voice half-choked with rage:

"Your vows are chaff and I am the wind—do you understand? Like this!"

And he blew on Zbyszko's head so strongly that the young knight's net few off, and his hair fell in disorder on his shoulders and down his back. Zbyszko frowned and, looking the abbot straight in the eye, said:

"In my vow is my honor, and I alone am the guardian of that!"

Unaccustomed as he was to opposition, the abbot lost his breath to such an extent that for some time he could not speak. An ominous silence followed, finally broken by Macko.

"Zbyszko!" he exclaimed, "control yourself! What's the matter with you?"

Meanwhile the abbot raised his arm and, pointing at the young man, began to shout:

"What's the matter with him? I know what's the matter with him! His heart is not the heart of a knight—nor is it that of a nobleman. It is the heart of a chicken. This is what's the matter with him: he is afraid of Cztan and Wolf!"

But Zbyszko, who had not lost his composure even for a moment, shrugged his shoulders.

"Bah!" he replied. "I broke their heads for them at Krzesnia."

"Great heavens!" exclaimed Macko.

The abbot looked for some time at Zbyszko with wide-open eyes. Anger fought with admiration within him, while his innate sense told him that he might be able to gain some advantage for his plans from this beating of Wolf and Cztan. So he calmed down somewhat and shouted at Zbyszko:

"Why did you not say so?"

"Because I was ashamed. I thought they would challenge me, as befits knights, to fight on horseback or on foot, but they are robbers, not knights. Wolf first tore a plank from a table, and Cztan torn another one—and both of them went at me! What was I to do? I seized a bench—well, you can guess the rest!"

"Are they alive?" asked Macko.

"Alive, but dazed. They began to recover before I left them."

The abbot listened, wiped his brow, and then suddenly sprang up from the chest on which he had sat down to collect his thoughts.

"Wait!" he exclaimed. "Let me tell you something!"

"What will you tell me?" asked Zbyszko.

"I will tell you that if you fought for Jagienka and broke men's heads for her sake, then you are in truth her knight and no one else's, and you must take her."

So saying, he put his hands on his hips and began to look at Zbyszko triumphantly. But the young man merely smiled and said:

"Ha! I knew very well why you wanted to set me against them. But you missed your mark."

"How so? Speak?"

"Because I told them to acknowledge that the most beautiful

and virtuous girl in the world is Danusia, Jurand's daughter. They took Jagienka's part, however. That's why there was a fight."

The abbot stood for a while petrified. Only from the blinking of his eyes could one tell that he was still alive. Suddenly he turned where he stood, kicked open the door of the alcove, burst into the room, seized the twisted staff from the hands of the pilgrim and began to lay it on the backs of his gleemen, roaring like a wounded aurochs:

"To horse, you buffoons! To horse, you dogs! I will never set foot in this house again! To horse, whoever believes in God! To horse!"

And kicking open another door, he went out into the yard, his terrified clerics behind him. They went in a body to the stable and saddled their horses in a flash. In vain Macko ran after the abbot; in vain he begged and implored him, swearing that it was not his fault. Nothing helped! The abbot cursed the house, the people, the fields. And when they gave him a horse, he leapt on its back without putting his feet in the stirrups and left the place at a gallop, his sleeves streaming behind him, so that he looked like an enormous red bird. The clerics rode after him in fear, like a herd following its leader.

Macko looked after them for some time, and when they had vanished into forest, he returned slowly to the house and said to Zbyszko, nodding his head gloomily:

"Whatever have you done!"

"This wouldn't have happened if I'd gone away earlier, and that I didn't do because of you."

"Because of me?"

"Yes. I didn't want to leave you when you were sick."

"And what will happen now?"

"Now I shall go."

"Where?"

"To Mazovia, to Danusia—and to look for peacock crests among the Germans."

Macko was silent for a while.

"He gave me back the deed," he finally said, "but the mortgage is also entered in the court register. Now the abbot will not let us off without some payment."

"Well, then let him not let us off. You have money, and I don't need any for the road. They will receive me everywhere and give my horses food. And as long as I have armor on my back and a sword in my hand, I care for nothing."

Macko thought for a while and considered everything that had happened. Nothing had gone according to his wishes, nothing according to his heart's desire. He also had wished from the bottom of his heart that Jagienka might be Zbyszko's. Yet he understood that no bread could be made of this flour. Finally, in view of the quarrel with Cztan and Wolf, it would be better for Zbyszko to go rather than be the cause of further disputes and quarrels.

"Ha!" he said at last, "you must in any case seek the heads of Teutonic Knights, so go. May the Lord's will be done! . . . But I must go at once to Zgorzelice; maybe I shall be able to patch things up with Zych and the abbot. I am particularly sorry for Zych." He suddenly looked Zbyszko in the eyes and asked: "Are you not sorry for Jagienka?"

"God grant her health and all the best!" replied Zbyszko.

CHAPTER XVIII

MACKO waited patiently for several days to see whether news might not arrive from Zgorzelice or whether the abbot might not recover his good humor, but at last the uncertainty and waiting were too much for him and he decided to visit Zych himself. Nothing that had happened was his fault; even so, he wanted to know whether Zych was offended with him. As for the abbot, Macko was certain that henceforth his anger would weigh on Zbyszko and himself.

None the less, he wished to do everything in his power to soften the abbot's anger, so on his ride he thought and planned what to say to each person at Zgorzelice in order to diminish the offence and preserve the friendship of his old neighbor. However, his thoughts somehow failed to be clear, so he was glad to find Jagienka alone. She received him as of old with a greeting and a kiss of the hand—in a word, kindly, though rather sadly.

"Is your father at home?" he asked.

"The abbot and he have gone out hunting. I expect them back soon."

She took him into the large room, where they sat down and both said nothing for a long time. The girl was the first to speak:

"Is it lonely for you at Bogdaniec?"

"Yes," replied Macko. "So you know that Zbyszko has gone?"

Jagienka sighed gently.

"I knew on that very day—and I thought . . . he would have come in to say good-bye, but he did not."

"How could he?" said Macko. "Why, the abbot would have torn

him in two, and your father also would not have been glad to see him."

She shook her head.

"You may be sure I wouldn't have let anyone harm him," she said.

Although his heart was well-hardened, Macko was moved by her words. He drew the girl to him.

"God be with you, girl!" he said. "You are sad, but I, too, am sad, for I tell you that neither the abbot nor your own father loves you more than I. It would have been better for me to have died of that wound which you healed, if only he could have taken you and not another."

Jagienka was overcome for a time with grief and longing, wherein the secrets of the human heart are often revealed.

"I shall never see him again," she said, "and if I do, he will be with Jurand's daughter. I would rather cry my eyes out first."

And taking the corner of her apron she wiped her eyes, which were overflowing with tears.

"Talk no more about it," said Macko. "He has gone, because he had to go, but by God's grace he will not come back with Jurand's daughter."

"Why should he not?" asked Jagienka from behind her apron.

"Because Jurand refuses to give him the girl."

Jagienka suddenly uncovered her face and turned to Macko.

"He told me that—but is it true?" she asked eagerly.

"As God is in heaven."

"But why?"

"Who knows? Some vow or something, and there's no help for a vow. He liked Zbyszko because Zbyszko had promised to assist him in his vengeance against the Germans, but even that was of no avail. Nor was Duchess Anna's recommendation. Jurand refused to listen to prayers or persuasions or commands. He said that he could not. Well, evidently the cause is such that he cannot, and he is an obstinate fellow, who will not change what he has once said. You must not lose hope, girl; be of good cheer. Justice requires the youth to go, for he vowed those peacock crests in church. Besides, the girl covered him with her veil as a sign that she was ready to marry him, and for that reason they did not cut off his head. He owes his life to her, there's no denying that. God grant that she will not be his, but according to law he is hers. Zych is angry with him, the abbot undoubtedly will take vengeance and make him suffer, and I am angry too. Yet if one considers the whole thing, what could he do? Since he was under an obligation to her, he had to go. He's a nobleman. But I tell you this: that if the Germans do not give him a thrashing somewhere over there, he will come back as he left—and he will come back not only to an old man like me, not only to Bogdaniec, but also to you, for he has always been very glad to see you."

"Ha! Zbyszko glad to see me!" exclaimed Jagienka. But at the same time she moved nearer to Macko and nudged him with her elbow, asking: "How do you know? What? Surely it's not true?"

"How do I know?" replied Macko. "I saw how difficult it was for him to ride away. Furthermore, when he had decided that he must go, I asked him: 'And are not sorry for Jagienka?' And he replied: 'God grant her health and all the best!' Then he began to sigh as if he had a blacksmith's bellows in his chest."

"I'm sure it's not true," Jagienka repeated softly. "But tell me more. . . ."

"As I love God, it is true! Danusia will not seem the same to him now that he knows you. You know yourself that one can't find a more robust and beautiful girl in the world than you. He felt the urge toward you—never fear—maybe even more than you felt it towards him."

"May it be so! God grant it!" exclaimed Jagienka.

Realizing what she had so hastily expressed, she covered her blushing face with her sleeve. Macko smiled, stroked his moustache, and said:

"Ah, if only I were young again! . . . But be of good cheer, for I see how it will be: he will ride, he will get his spurs at the Mazovian court, since the border is near and it is not hard to find a Teutonic Knight. I know that there are strong knights among the Germans, I know that iron will not simply bounce off his skin. But, I think, not just anyone will be able to deal with him, for that rascal is quite skilled in combat. Look at how he overthrew Cztan of Rogow and Wolf of Birchwood in no time, although they are valiant lads and strong as bears. He will bring his peacock crests, but he won't bring Jurand's daughter, for I also spoke with Jurand, and I know how it is. Well, and then what? Then he will come back here—where else?"

"But when will he come back?"

"Hey, no one will blame you if you can't hold out. But meanwhile repeat to the abbot and to Zych what I've told you. Then they may be a little less severe in their anger against Zbyszko."

"What am I to say? Papa is more sad than angry, but it is dangerous to speak of Zbyszko in the abbot's presence. He was enraged both with me and with papa for that servant I sent to Zbyszko."

"What servant?"

"You know, there was a Czech here with us, whom papa took at Boleslawiec, a good and loyal servant. His name is Hlawa. Papa gave him to me to attend on me, for he was a nobleman over there. I gave him a worthy suit of armor, and sent him to Zbyszko to serve him and protect him in case of danger, and to let me know if, God forbid, something happened to Zbyszko. . . . I gave him a purse for the way, and he vowed to me on his soul's salvation that he would serve Zbyszko faithfully till death."

"My dear girl! God will reward you! And Zych wasn't opposed to this?"

"How could he be opposed to it! At first papa absolutely forbade it, yet when I began to embrace his knees, he came over to my side. There's never any trouble with him. But when the abbot found out about this from his attendants, he filled the whole room with curses, and there was such an uproar that papa ran away to the barn. In the evening the abbot took pity on my tears. But I was only too happy to suffer for Zbyszko and his safety."

"As God is dear to me, I don't know whether I love Zbyszko more or you. But he should be safe. He took a good-sized troop with him—and I also gave him money, though he did not want to take it. . . . Well, Mazovia is not overseas, after all. . . ."

Further talk was interrupted by the barking of dogs, shouts, and the sound of brass trumpets before the house. When she heard this, Jagienka said:

"Papa and the abbot have returned from their hunting. Let us go out on the terrace. It will be better for the abbot to see you first from a distance than to come upon you unexpectedly inside the house."

She took Macko out onto the terrace, from which they saw a number of men, horses, and dogs in the yard, and the carcasses of elks and wolves, pierced with spears or shot with crossbow arrows, lying on the snow. The abbot, seeing Macko before he had yet dismounted from his horse, threw his hunting-spear at him, not indeed with the intention of hitting him but to manifest his hatred against the owners of Bogdaniec. Macko, however, took off his cap to him from a distance as if he had noticed nothing. Jagienka really had noticed nothing, for she was amazed to see that her two suitors were in the abbot's train.

"Cztan and Wolf are there!" she exclaimed. "They must have met papa in the forest."

Macko's old wound pricked him at the sight of them. The thought flashed through his head that one of them might get Jagienka—and, with her, Moczydoly and the abbot's lands, forests, and money. Grief and anger possessed him, especially when a moment later he noticed something new. Wolf of Birchwood, although the abbot had not long ago wanted to engage in combat with his father, now ran up to him to help him dismount; and the abbot, dismounting, leaned intimately on the young nobleman's shoulder.

"The abbot will be reconciled with old Wolf," thought Macko, "and give his forests and lands with the girl."

But his bitter thoughts were interrupted by the voice of Jagienka:

"They have recovered from the beating Zbyszko gave them, but even if they came here every day, they would never get me."

Macko looked at her. The girl's face was red from both anger and the cold, and her blue eyes flashed, though she knew very well that Wolf and Cztan had taken her part at the inn and that it was for her sake that they had been beaten.

"Bah! you will do what the abbot tells you," said Macko.

But she instantly replied:

"The abbot will do what I want."

"Dear God!" thought Macko. "And that stupid Zbyszko ran away from such a girl!"

CHAPTER XIX

MEANWHILE the "stupid Zbyszko" had ridden away from Bog-daniec with a heavy heart. Firstly, he felt somewhat strange without his uncle, from whom he had not parted for many years, and to whom he was so accustomed that he himself did not know how to get on without him, whether on a journey or in war. Secondly, he was grieved for Jagienka, for although he told himself that he was going to Danusia, whom he loved with his whole heart, the time he had spent with Jagienka had been so pleasurable that only now did he realize what joy he had had with her and what sorrow he might have without her. He was surprised at his own grief and even somewhat perturbed. Had he longed for Jagienka as a brother longs for a sister, there would have been no problem. But he perceived that he longed to take her by the waist and set her on her horse or lift her from her saddle; he longed to carry her across rivers, squeeze the water out of the plaits of her hair, go with her through the forest and look at her and talk with her. He had become so accustomed to all that and had come to like it so much that now, when he began to think of it, he immediately became so absorbed that he completely forgot he was on a long journey to Mazovia, whereas he clearly recalled the moment when Jagienka had come to his aid in the forest as he was struggling with the bear. And it seemed to him that this had happened only yesterday, just as it was only yesterday that they had gone after beaver to Odstajan Lake. He had not seen her when she went swimming for the beaver, but now he could see her, and the same shiver began to run through him as a few weeks ago when the wind had been too free with

Jagienka's skirt. Then he recalled how she had ridden to church at Krzesnia, splendidly dressed, and how he had been surprised that so simple a girl had seemed like a young lady of a high family. All this caused his heart to become confused with a mixture of bliss and sorrow and desire. And when he thought that he might have done with her what he wanted, and how she also was drawn to him, how she looked in his eyes and how she sought his presence, he could scarcely sit on his horse. "If I had only dropped in and taken leave of her and embraced her before the journey," he said to himself, "maybe this feeling would have left me." But he soon sensed that this was not true and that "this feeling" would not have left him, for his skin seemed to burn at the mere thought of such a leave-taking, although the world was white with frost.

At length he became frightened of these memories, too similar to lusts, and he shook them from his mind like dry snow from his cloak.

"I am riding to Danusia, to my dearest love!" he told himself.

And then he understood that it was another kind of love, more devout, less unsettling. Gradually, as his feet began to freeze in the stirrups, and the cool wind chilled his blood, all his thoughts turned to Danusia, Jurand's daughter. It was to her that he really was indebted. If it had not been for her, his head would have fallen long ago on the marketplace at Cracow. She had called out in front of all the knights and burghers: "He's mine!" And by doing so, she had saved him from the hands of the executioner. From that time he belonged to her as a slave to a master. It was not he who had taken her, but she who had taken him. No opposition of Jurand's could alter that. She alone could dismiss him, as a mistress may dismiss a servant, although even in that case he would not have gone far, for his own vow would have bound him. He thought, however, that she would not dismiss him, that she would rather leave the Mazovian court and follow him, even to the end of the world. And when he thought that, he began to praise her in his heart and blame Jagienka, as if it had been solely her fault that he was tempted and that his heart was divided. He did not think about how Jagienka had cured old Macko, nor how without her help the bear might have torn his skin from his head that night. He was indignant with Jagienka purposely, trying thus to do Danusia a service and justify himself in his own eyes.

Suddenly, Hlawa, the Czech sent by Jagienka, rode up, leading a pack-horse with him.

"May the Lord be praised!" he said, bowing low.

Though Zbyszko had seen him once or twice at Zgorzelice, he did not recognize him, so he called out:

"For ever and ever! Who are you?"

"Your servant, famous lord."

"My servant? Those are my servants," he said, pointing to the two Turks who had been given him by Zawisza, and at two sturdy farm-hands riding palfreys and leading their master's stallions. "Those are mine; but who sent you?"

"The Lady Jagienka of Zgorzelice."

"The Lady Jagienka?"

Zbyszko had just been indignant with her, and his heart was still filled with animosity, so he said:

"Go back home and thank the lady for her favor. I don't want you."

But the Czech shook his head.

"I will not go back, lord. She gave me to you. Besides, I vowed to serve you till death."

"If she gave you to me then you are my servant."

"Yes, lord."

"Then I order you to go back."

"I vowed, and though I am a prisoner of war from Boleslawice and just a poor servant, still I am of noble birth."

Zbyszko grew angry.

"Be off! What is this? Will you serve me against my will? Be off, or I will order the crossbows to be ready."

The Czech calmly unstrapped a cloth cloak, lined with wolfskin, and gave it to Zbyszko, saying:

"The Lady Jagienka sent you this too, lord."

"Do you want me to break your bones?" asked Zbyszko, taking a lance from his attendant.

"And there's also a purse for your use," replied the Czech.

Zbyszko levelled his spear at him, but he remembered that the servant, though a prisoner of war, was a noble by birth and had evidently only remained with Zych because he had nothing to ransom himself with. So he lowered his weapon.

The Czech bowed again.

"Do not be angry, lord," he said. "If you bid me not to ride with you, I will ride a furlong or two behind you, but I will ride, for I vowed it on my soul's salvation."

"And if I have you slain or bound?"

"If you have me slain, the sin will not be mine; and if you have bound here, I shall remain until good people unbind me or wolves eat me."

Zbyszko did not answer. He merely rode on, his men behind him. The Czech, his crossbow on his back and his axe on his shoulder, fell to the rear and wrapped himself up in a shaggy bison-skin, for a sharp wind was beginning to blow, bringing with it a smother of sleet.

The snowstorm increased with every moment. The Turks, even in their hoods, became numb, while Zbyszko's attendants began to swing their arms to warm their blood. Zbyszko, being none-too-thickly dressed, glanced once or twice at the wolfskin cape brought by Hlawa and presently told a Turk to give it to him.

He wrapped himself snugly in it, and soon felt its warmth penetrating his whole body. The hood was particularly comfortable, for it protected his eyes and a considerable part of his face, so that the wind almost ceased to trouble him. Then, despite himself, he thought that Jagienka was, after all, a most kind girl—and he checked his horse a little, for he felt a desire to question the Czech about her and about everything that had happened at Zgorzelice.

So he beckoned to the servant and said:

"Does old Zych know that the young lady has sent you to me?"

"Yes," answered Hlawa.

"And he did not object?"

"He did object."

"Tell me what happened."

"The lord walked up and down the room, and the young lady followed him. He shouted, and the young lady said nothing. When he turned to her, she fell at his knees. And not a word from her. Finally the lord said: 'Are you deaf that you say nothing? Speak, or in the end I shall agree to send the Czech, and if I agree, the abbot will tear off my head!' Only then did the young lady feel sure that she would get what she wanted, and the next moment she was thanking him with tears in her eyes. Her father complained she had bewitched him and that she always had to have her own way in everything. But then he said: 'Promise me that you won't run out secretly to say good-bye to Zbyszko, and then I will agree, but not otherwise.' The young lady was troubled, but she promised, and the lord was glad, for both he and the abbot had been terribly afraid that she would want to see your grace again. . . . Well, that was not the end of it, for afterwards the young lady wanted to send two horses, and the lord opposed her; the young lady wanted to send a wolfskin and a purse, and the lord opposed her. But what was the good of such attempts? If she had conceived the idea of burning the house down, in the end the lord would have consented! So I have brought the two horses; I have brought the wolfskin and the purse."

"Kind girl!" thought Zbyszko in his heart.

Then he asked aloud:

"And there was no trouble with the abbot?"

The Czech smiled, like a shrewd servant who understands all that goes on around him, and replied:

"They both did it in secret without telling the abbot, and I don't know what happened when he found out, for I was gone by then. The abbot is the abbot. He sometimes roars at the young lady, but afterwards he follows her with his eyes to see whether he has hurt her too much. I myself once saw how he shouted at her and then went to a chest and took out a beautiful chain. You could not have found a more exquisite one even in Cracow. And he said to her: 'Take it!' She will be able to deal with the abbot, for her own father does not love her more than he does."

"I am sure it is so."

"As God is in heaven."

They fell silent and rode on through the wind and the driving sleet. Suddenly Zbyszko checked his horse. A piteous voice was heard in the forest at the side of the road, partially drowned out by the noise of the storm:

"Christians, save a servant of God in distress!"

At the same time a man ran out onto the road dressed in half-clerical and half-worldly garb, and, stopping in front of Zbyszko, exclaimed:

"Whoever you are, lord, give help to a human being and a neighbor in dire trouble."

"What has happened to you, and who are you?" asked the young knight.

"I am a servant of God, though not ordained. This morning my horse ran away, carrying boxes of sacred relics. I was left alone, without any weapons. Evening is coming on, and a wild beast may appear at any moment in the forest. I shall perish if you do not save me."

"If you were to perish because of me," replied Zbyszko, "I should have to answer for your sins. But how am I to know that you are speaking the truth, and that you are not a vagabond or a highway robber, of whom there are many to be found on the roads?"

"You may know by my boxes, lord. Many a man would give a purse full of ducats to possess what is in them, but I will give you something from them for nothing if you will take me and them."

"You say you are a servant of God, yet you do not know that help must be paid for, not with earthly but with heavenly rewards. How did you save your boxes if the horse carrying them ran away?"

"Before I could find him, the horse was devoured by wolves in a clearing in the forest, but the boxes were left. I dragged them up to the road to wait for pity and help from kindly folk."

To prove that he was speaking the truth, he pointed to two wooden boxes lying under a pine tree. Zbyszko looked at him distrustfully, for the fellow did not seem to him to be too honest, and his speech, though clear, betrayed that he came from far away. Still, he was unwilling to refuse him help, and allowed him to sit, together with his boxes, which seemed surprisingly light, on the spare horse the Czech had brought.

"May God multiply your victories, valiant knight!" said the stranger. Then seeing Zbyszko's boyish face, he added in a whisper: "And likewise the hairs on your chin."

Soon he was riding alongside the Czech. For some time they could not talk, for a strong wind was roaring in the trees of the forest. But when it grew a little quieter Zbyszko heard the following conversation behind him:

"I won't deny that you were in Rome, but you look like a beer-drinker," said the Czech.

"Beware of everlasting damnation," replied the stranger, "for you are speaking to a man who last Easter ate hard-boiled eggs with the Holy Father. Don't talk to me of beer when it is so cold, unless it be warm beer; but if you have a flask of wine about you, let me take a swig or two, and I will excuse you a month in purgatory."

"You are not ordained, for I heard you say so yourself, so how can you let me off a month of purgatory?"

"I was not ordained, but I have a shaven head, since I obtained permission; besides, I carry indulgences and relics."

"In those boxes?" asked the Czech.

"Yes. If you were to see everything I have, you would prostrate yourself, and not only you, but all the pines and wild animals in the forest."

But the Czech, who was shrewd and experienced, looked suspiciously at the peddler of indulgences, and asked:

"So the wolves ate your horse?"

"They ate it, since they are related to devils, but their stomachs burst afterwards. I saw one in that state with my own eyes. If you have any wine, give me some. Though the wind has fallen, I'm still frozen from sitting by the wayside."

The Czech, however, gave him no wine, and they rode on in silence until the peddler of relics continued:

"Where are you going?"

"Far. But first to Sieradz. Will you come with us?"

"I must. I will sleep in a stable, and tomorrow perhaps this pious knight will give me a horse. Then I shall go on."

"Where are you from?"

"From the vicinity of Malbork, under the authority of the Prussian lords."

Hearing that, Zbyszko turned his head and beckoned to the stranger to come nearer.

"You're from around Malbork?" he said. "Are you riding from there?"

"Yes."

"I suppose you're not a German, for you speak our language well. What is your name?"

"I am a German, and my name is Sanderus. I speak your language because I was born at Torun, where everyone speaks it. Later I lived at Malbork, but it's the same there. Why, even the brothers of the Order understand your language!"

"Did you leave Malbork a long time ago?"

"I have been, lord, in the Holy Land and then in Constantinople and Rome, from where I returned to Malbork through France, and from Malbork I travelled to Mazovia, carrying holy relics, which pious Christians are glad to buy for their soul's salvation."

"Have you been at Plock or Warsaw?"

"I've been in both places. May God grant good health to both duchesses! It is not without reason that even the Prussian lords love Duchess Alexandra, for she is a holy lady—although Duchess Anna, Janusz's wife, is no worse."

"Have you seen the court at Warsaw?"

"I did not find it at Warsaw, but at Ciechanow, where the duke and duchess received me hospitably as a servant of God and provided me generously with gifts for the road. In return, I left them relics, which must bring them divine blessing."

Zbyszko wanted to ask about Danusia, but he felt a certain shyness and a certain shame, for he understood that he would be confiding the story of his love to an unknown man of lowly origin, who, moreover, looked suspicious and might be common swindler. So, after a moment's silence, he asked:

"What sort of relics do you carry with you through the world?"

"I carry indulgences and relics, and the indulgences are of different kinds. I have plenary indulgences, and indulgences for five hundred years, for three hundred, for two hundred, and for less, cheaper ones, so that even poor people can buy them and thus shorten the pains of purgatory for themselves. I have indulgences for past sins and for future ones. But don't think, lord, that I keep for myself the money I receive. A piece of black bread and a drink of water—that's enough for me, and the remainder of what I collect I carry to Rome, so that in time they may have enough for a new crusade. It is true that many fakers are travelling about, with everything forged: indulgences and relics and seals and testimonials. The Holy Father very properly pursues them with letters, but the Prior of Sieradz has done me wrong and injustice, for my seals are genuine. Look, lord, at the wax and tell me yourself."

"And what has the Prior of Sieradz done?"

"Ah, lord! He unjustly thought that I was infected with the heretical teaching of Wycliffe. But if, as your squire told me, you are going to Sieradz, then I would rather not show myself to him, so as not to lead him into sin and blasphemy against holy objects."

"That means, in short, that he took you for a swindler and a highway robber?"

"If it were only me, lord, I would excuse him for love of my neighbor, as indeed I have already done. But he blasphemed against my sacred wares, and for that I greatly fear he will be eternally damned."

"What holy wares have you got?"

"Such that it is not fitting even to talk of them with one's head covered. But this time, as I have indulgences ready, I will give you permission, lord, not to throw off your hood, since the wind is blowing again. So buy a little indulgence when we stop next and the sin will not be counted against you. What have I not got! I have a shoe of the ass ridden on the flight into Egypt. It was found near the pyramids. The King of Aragon offered me fifty ducats of pure gold for it. I have a feather from the wing of the archangel Gabriel, which he lost during the Annunciation; I have two heads of quails sent to the Israelites in the desert; I have some of the oil in which the pagans wanted to boil St. John, and a rung of Jacob's ladder—and some tears of St. Mary of Egypt and a little rust off the keys of St. Peter. . . . But I cannot tell you all, because I am chilled to the bone, and your squire, lord, refused to give me wine. And besides, if I told you everything I have, I wouldn't be through even by nightfall."

"Your relics are great—if they are genuine!" said Zbyszko.

"If they are genuine? Take the pike from the hand of your attendant, lord, and level it, for the devil is near; it is he that gives you such thoughts. Keep him at lance-length, lord. And if you don't wish to bring misfortune upon yourself, then buy an indulgence from me for that sin, or else in three weeks one whom you love most in the world will die."

Zbyszko was afraid of the threat, thinking of Danusia, and replied:

"But it is not I who disbelieve, it is the Prior of the Dominicans at Sieradz."

"Look at the wax of the seals yourself, lord. As for the prior, God knows whether he still lives, for divine justice is quick."

However, when they arrived at Sieradz, it appeared that the prior was alive. Zbyszko even went to him to pay for two Masses, one for Macko, the other for those peacock crests that he had promised.

The prior, like many in Poland at that time, was a foreigner, in this case a native of Cylia, but in forty years spent at Sieradz he had learned Polish and had become a great enemy of the Teutonic Knights. So when he found out about Zbyszko's quest, he said:

"Greater divine punishment will find them yet, but I will not dissuade you from your design, firstly because you made a vow and secondly because Polish hands can never pound them enough for what they did here at Sieradz."

"What did they do?" asked Zbyszko, glad to know of all the misdeeds of the Teutonic Knights.

The old prior spread out his hands, and first began to repeat a requiem aloud. Then he sat down on a stool and kept his eyes shut for a while, as if trying to gather together ancient memories. Finally, he spoke:

"It was Vincent of Szamotuly who introduced them here. I was then twelve years old and had just come here from Cylia, from where my uncle Petzoldt, the custodian, had fetched me. The Teutonic Knights attacked the town by night and immediately set it on fire. We saw from our walls how they cut down men, women, and children in the marketplace with their swords and how they threw infants into the fire. . . . I saw even priests slain, for in their fury they did not spare anyone. It just so happened that Prior Nicholas, who came of a family living at Elbing, knew Commander Hermann, who was leading the army. So he went out with the older brethren to that wild knight and, kneeling before him, implored him in German to have pity on Christian blood. But Hermann said, 'I don't understand,' and ordered the massacre to continue. Then they cut down even the monks, and among them my uncle Petzoldt, while Nicholas was bound to a horse's tail. The next morning there was not a living soul in the town except the Teutonic Knights and me, for I had hidden myself in the church tower on a beam supporting the bell. God punished them for Sieradz at Plowce, but they always aimed at the destruction of this Christian kingdom and will aim at it until the hand of God wipes them out completely."

"It was at Plowce," replied Zbyszko, "that almost all the men of my family fell. But I don't grieve for them, since God gave King Wladyslaw the Short so great a victory, and twenty thousand Germans were slain."

"You will yet live to see a greater war and greater victories," said the prior.

"Amen!" replied Zbyszko.

And they began to talk of something else. The young knight asked a few questions about the peddler of relics he had met on the way and learned that many swindlers were tramping the roads and cheating the credulous. The prior also said that there were papal bulls ordering the bishops to prosecute similar peddlers, and if they had not genuine letters and seals, to pass immediate sentence on them. Because the testimonials produced by this vagabond had seemed suspicious to the prior, he wanted to send him at once to the bishop's court. If it had turned out that he was a real emissary with indulgences, then no harm would have come to him. But he preferred to flee. Maybe he was concerned about being delayed in his journey. But his flight exposed him to still greater suspicion.

At the end of the visit, the prior invited Zbyszko to rest and stay the night in the monastery, but the young knight could not accept his generosity, for he wanted to hang a card in front of his quarters with a challenge to combat on foot or on horseback to all knights who should deny that the Lady Danuta, Jurand's daughter, was the most beautiful and virtuous maiden in the kingdom—and, of course, he could not hang out such a challenge on the gates of a monastery. Neither the prior nor any other priest would even write him such a card, and this placed Zbyszko in a predicament. Only when he got back to his quarters did he think of asking the peddler of indulgences for help.

"The prior does not know whether you are a rogue or not," he told him. "He wondered why you should be afraid of the bishop's court if you have real testimonials."

"I am not afraid of the bishop," replied Sanderus, "only of the monks, who don't know seals when they see them. I do want to go to Cracow, but as I have no horse I must wait till some man gives me one. Meanwhile I will send a letter and attach my own seal to it."

"I also thought that if you were to show that you know how to write, it would be a sign that you are not a simpleton. But how will you send your letter?"

"By the hand of some pilgrim or of some wandering monk. Many people are going to Cracow to the grave of the queen."

"And can you write a card for me?"

"I will write anything you bid me, lord, in a fair hand and to the point, even on a board."

"It would be better on a board," said Zbyszko joyfully. "A board won't get torn, and I can use it again later."

So, after a certain time had passed, his attendants found and brought him a clean board, and Sanderus began to write. What he wrote Zbyszko could not read, but he ordered the challenge to be hung up immediately on the gate, his shield placed underneath, with the Turks guarding it in turn. Whosoever should strike it with his lance would thereby signify that he took up the challenge. At Sieradz, however, there were apparently few volunteers for undertakings of this sort. Neither that day nor the next before noon did the shield resound once from a blow, and in the afternoon the youth, rather troubled, continued on his journey.

Before that, however, Sanderus had gone to Zbyszko.

"Lord, if you hung up your shield in the countries of the Prussian lords, your squire would assuredly have had to help you buckle on your armor before now."

"How is that possible? A Teutonic Knight is, after all, a monk. He cannot have a lady-love. It is forbidden."

"I don't know if it is forbidden; but I do know they have them. It is true that a Teutonic Knight may not engage in single combat without sinning, for he has vowed that he will only combat singly for the faith. But besides the monks, there are a number of lay knights from distant parts who come to aid the Prussian lords. They are always looking for someone to engage, particularly the French knights."

"Bah! I have seen them at Wilno, and God grant I shall see them again at Malbork. I need peacock crests, for I have made a vow—do you understand?"

"Lord, buy from me two or three drops of the sweat which St. George shed when he was fighting the dragon. No relic is more useful for a knight. If you give me the horse I sat on for that, I will also add an indulgence for the Christian blood you will spill in combat."

"Be quiet, or I shall be angry. I will not take your wares until I know whether they are good."

"You are riding, lord, as you said, to Duke Janusz at the Mazovian court. Ask there how many relics they have bought of me—both the duchess herself and the knights and the young ladies at the weddings I attended."

"What weddings?" asked Zbyszko.

"The usual ones that take place before Advent. The knights married one after another, for it is said there will be war between the Polish king and the Prussian lords for the Land of Dobrzyn. Therefore, this one and that one says to himself, 'God knows whether I shall live'—and wants to find happiness with a woman first."

Zbyszko was greatly affected by the news of the war, but still more by what Sanderus said about the weddings, so he asked:

"What girls were given in marriage?"

"Court ladies of the duchess. I don't know whether one was left, for I heard how the duchess said that she would have to look for new women to wait on her."

Zbyszko was silent for a time. Then he asked in a somewhat changed voice:

"And the Lady Danuta, Jurand's daughter, whose name is on the board, was she also given in marriage?"

Sanderus hesitated with his answer, firstly because he himself did not know the whole story, and secondly because he thought that if he kept the knight in suspense he would gain a certain advantage over him and be able to manipulate him better. He had already formed the idea that it would be well to latch onto this knight, who had a worthy retinue and ample supplies. Sanderus knew men and things. Zbyszko's youth led him to think that he would be a generous master and scatter his money carelessly and easily. He had already noticed the costly Milan hauberk and the enormous stallions, which not everyone could possess, and he told himself that with such a master he would be certain to receive hospitality at the courts and would have frequent opportunity to sell his indulgences with profit, while at the same time he would be safe on the road. Most importantly, he would have plenty to eat and drink.

Therefore, hearing Zbyszko's question, he frowned, turned his eyes upwards as if straining his memory, and replied:

"The Lady Danuta, Jurand's daughter. . . . Where is she from?"

"Jurand's daughter, Danuta of Spychow."

"I saw them all, but what any particular one's name was, I don't remember very well."

"She's still quite young, and plays the lute, and rejoices the duchess by her singing."

"Aha . . . quite young . . . plays on the lute . . . . Even quite young girls married. She's not dark-complexioned like an agate?"

Zbyszko breathed out a sigh of relief.

"No! She is white as snow, though her cheeks are rosy, and she is fair-haired."

To which Sanderus replied:

"For one girl, dark like an agate, remained with the duchess, and almost all the others married."

"You say 'almost all,' that means 'not everyone.' Dear God, if you want a gift from me, try and remember!"

"In three or four days I might remember—but I should really like to have a horse to carry my sacred wares."

"You will get one if you speak the truth."

Then the Czech, who had been listening to the conversation from the beginning, and smiling to himself, exclaimed:

"We will find out the truth at the Mazovian court!"

Sanderus looked at him for a moment and then said:

"Do you think that I'm afraid of the Mazovian court?"

"I do not say that you are afraid of the Mazovian court but only that you won't ride away on a horse now, nor in three days' time, and that if it turns out that you have lied, you won't go away even on your own legs, for his lordship will have them broken for you."

"I swear I will!" said Zbyszko.

Sanderus consider that in view of such a promise it would be better to be cautious.

"If I wanted to lie," he replied to the Czech, "I should have said at once that she had married or that she had not married, but I said: I don't remember. If you had any intelligence, you would have immediately recognized my virtue by this answer."

"My intelligence is not brother to your virtue, for your virtue may be a dog's sister."

"My virtue doesn't bark like your intelligence. And he who barks in his lifetime will howl for certain after death."

"Ha! Surely your virtue will not howl after death but gnash its teeth, unless it lose them first in the service of the devil."

They began to quarrel, for the Czech had a quick tongue and found two words for every one uttered by the German. Meanwhile Zbyszko gave the order to ride on, and soon they proceeded, after making inquiries of people familiar with the road to Leczyca. Not long after leaving Sieradz, they entered a huge forest which covered the greater part of the country. However, a highway ran through the middle of it, at some places with ditches on either side, and elsewhere, in miry parts, paved with round logs, the work of King Kazimierz's administration. Although after his death, in the war-like disturbances kindled by the Nalecz and Grzymala clans, the roads had fallen out of repair somewhat, in the reign of Jadwiga, after the pacification of the kingdom, people again began to work eagerly with spades in the marshes and with axes in the forests, and toward the end of her life merchants could drive their heavy-laden wagons between the more important towns without fearing that they would break their axles in holes or sink in the mud. Wild beasts or robbers might indeed trouble the roads, but for wild beasts there were torches at night and crossbows by day, while there were fewer robbers and highwaymen than in the adjoining coun-tries. In any case, whoever rode with a troop and armed need have no fear.

Likewise, Zbyszko was not afraid of robbers or of armed knights. He did not even think of them, so overcome was he with anxiety, for his whole heart was at the Mazovian court. Whether he would find his own Danusia still in waiting on the duchess or the wife of some Mazovian knight, he himself did not know. He wrestled with the question from morning till night. At times it seemed impossible that she should have forgotten him, but at other instances he thought that perhaps Jurand had come to the court from Spychow and had given his girl in marriage to some neighbor or friend. He had indeed said at Cracow that Danusia was not fated to be Zbyszko's and that he could not give her to him—so evidently he had promised her to another; evidently he was bound by an oath, and now had kept his oath. When Zbyszko thought of that, he regarded it as certain that he would never again see Danusia as a maiden. So he called Sanderus over and questioned him once more, but his answers were becoming less and less clear. Often he would just about recall the lady-in-waiting, Jurand's daughter, and her marriage—but then would suddenly put his finger in his mouth, think for a time, and reply: "No, I don't think it was she." Over wine, which ought to have made his head clear, he could not recall her either. Thus the German continually kept the young knight between mortal fear and hope.

So Zbyszko rode in anxiety, sadness, and uncertainty. He thought no more of Bogdaniec, nor of Zgorzelice, but only of what he had to do. Above all, he had to ride to the Mazovian court and learn the truth; therefore, he went on in haste, stopping for short nights' rests at manor-houses, inns, and towns, so as not to wear out his horses. At Leczyca he again hung up the board with his challenge before the gate, telling himself that whether Danusia were still a maiden or whether she had taken a husband, she was always the lady of his heart and he ought to fight for her. But at Leczyca scarcely anyone could read the challenge, and those knights for whom clerics, versed in writing, read it aloud, shrugged their shoulders in ignorance of the foreign custom, saying, "This must be some fool, for how can anyone affirm or deny it when he's never set eyes on the girl?" So Zbyszko rode onward in increasing distress and with increasing haste. He had never ceased to love his Danusia, although at Bogdaniec and Zgorzelice, when talking almost every day with Jagienka and looking at her charms, he had not thought of Danusia so often. But now she never left his sight, or his memory, or his thoughts, day or night. He even saw her before him in his dreams, golden-haired, lute in hand, in red shoes, and with a chaplet on her head. She would stretch out her hands to him, but Jurand would draw her away. In the morning, when these dreams faded, their place was immediately taken by a longing more intense than before—and Zbyszko had never loved the girl so much at Bogdaniec as he began to love her now, when he was uncertain whether she had been taken from him.

He began to reflect that she must certainly have been given in marriage against her will, so he did not accuse her in his heart, particularly since she was a child and could not yet have had a will of her own. On the other hand, he was indignant with Jurand and with the duchess, Janusz's wife; and when he thought of Danusia's husband, his heart immediately rose to his throat, and he looked threateningly on his attendants who were carrying his weapons under their cloaks. He determined that he would not cease to serve her. Even if he found her another's wife, he would lay the peacock crests at her feet. But this thought caused him more grief than joy, for he did not know what he would do after that.

Only the thought of a great war cheered him. Although he did not want to live without Danusia, he had not made a promise to die. Instead, he felt that somehow his heart and memory would fade during the war, that he would get rid of all anxieties and cares. And a great war seemed to be in the air. It was not clear from where these reports originated, for there was peace between the king and the Order—and yet, everywhere that Zbyszko went, the talk was of nothing else. People seemed to have a foreboding that it must come, and some said openly: "Why did we unite with Lithuania if not to join with them against those Teutonic wolves? We must finish with them once and for all, so that they'll stop tearing out our entrails." Others said: "Raving monks! Was not Plowce enough for them? Death is over them, and yet they have taken the Land of Dobrzyn, which they will have to vomit out with blood." And preparations were made throughout the kingdom, seriously, without boasting, as is usual for a life-and-death struggle, and with the grim determination of a powerful people who had borne wrongs for too long and who at last were preparing to exact terrible vengeance. At all the manor-houses he passed, Zbyszko found men convinced that any day they might have to mount their horses, and he was surprised, for though he, like the others, thought that war must come, he had not heard that it would begin so quickly. However, it did not come into his head that in this case men's desires were outrunning events. He believed others and not himself and rejoiced at heart to see all the preparations that met him at every step. Everywhere all activities gave way to the care of horses and armor; everywhere lances, swords, axes, spears, helmets, breast-plates, straps, and rump-armor were earnestly being inspected. Smiths hammered night and day at iron plates, forging thick and heavy suits of armor, which the proud knights of the West could scarcely even lift, but which the sturdy squires of Great and Little Poland wore with ease. The older men took out moldy bags of money from chests in alcoves to outfit their sons for war. Once Zbyszko spent the night at the house of a well-to-do nobleman, Bartosz of Bielawy, who had twenty-two stout sons and pledged broad lands to the monastery at Lowicz to buy twenty-two breast-plates, the same number of helmets, and other equipment for war.

So Zbyszko, though he had heard nothing of war at Bogdaniec, thought that he would soon have to go to Prussia, and he thanked God that he was so splendidly equipped. In fact, his armor roused general admiration. He was taken for a voivode's son, and when he told people that he was only a simple nobleman and that such armor might be bought from the Germans if one only paid well with the axe, hearts were filled with the desire for war. But at the sight of that armor, more than one man could not restrain his greed and, catching up to Zbyszko on the high road, said: "Will you fight for it?" But he, travelling as he was on urgent business, declined to fight, and the Czech drew his crossbow. Zbyszko even ceased to hang out the board with the challenge before his quarters, for he noticed that the deeper he went into the country, the less people understood it, and the more inclined they were to regard him as a fool.

In Mazovia, people talked less about war. They also believed that it would come, but they did not know when. At Warsaw there was peace, all the more since the court was away, amusing itself at Ciechanow, which Duke Janusz had rebuilt after an old Lithuanian attack, or rather had erected anew, since of the former group of buildings only the castle was left. At the castle at Warsaw, Zbyszko was received by the constable, Jasko Socha, the son of Voivode Abraham, who had fallen at the Worskla. Jasko knew Zbyszko, for he had been with the duchess at Cracow, so he gladly entertained him. But before Zbyszko sat down to eat and drink, he began to question the constable about Danusia and whether she had not been given in marriage along with the duchess's other ladies-in-waiting.

But Socha was unable to give him an answer. The duke and duchess had been staying at the castle of Ciechanow since early autumn. At Warsaw only a handful of archers had been left under his command. He had heard that there had been various entertainments and weddings at Ciechanow, as was usual just before Advent, but which of the ladies-in-waiting had married and which were left, he, as a married man, had not inquired.

"I think, however," he said, "that Jurand's daughter was not married, since she could not be married without Jurand's presence, and I did not hear of his arrival. There are also two brothers of the Order, commanders, staying with the duke and duchess as guests, one from Jansbork, the other from Ortelsburg, and with them, it is said, some foreign guests. In that case Jurand will never come, for the sight of a white cloak immediately infuriates him. So if there was no Jurand, there was no marriage! But if you wish I will send a messenger to ask and will tell him to return quickly, although I assume that you will find Jurand's daughter still a maiden."

"I will go myself tomorrow, but God reward you for the consolation. As soon as my horse has rested, I will go on my way, for I shall have no peace until I know the truth. God reward you, however, for I feel already relieved by what you have said."

Socha, however, was not content to let the matter rest, and he made inquiries among the gentry staying in the castle and among the soldiers, as to whether anyone had heard of the marriage of Jurand's daughter. But no one had done so, although there were some who had been at Ciechanow and even at certain weddings. "Unless someone has taken her in the last few weeks, or in the last few days." And that might have happened, for in those times people lost no time in reflection. Meanwhile Zbyszko went to bed greatly cheered. When he had already lain down, he considered whether he ought not to dismiss Sanderus the next day; however, he thought the rogue might be useful to him with his knowledge of German when he went to challenge Lichtenstein. He considered also that Sanderus had not lied to him, and though he was a costly acquisition, since he ate and drank for four, he was, none the less, of service to him and showed his new master a certain attachment. Further, he knew the art of writing, and thereby had an advantage over the Czech squire and over Zbyszko himself.

All this led the young knight to allow Sanderus to ride with him to Ciechanow. This made the German very glad, not only because of the victuals he would get but also because he noticed that in honorable company he was met with greater trust and was able to sell his wares more easily. After one more night's rest at Nasielsk, travelling not too quickly and not too slowly, they saw the walls of the castle of Ciechanow before them the following evening. Zbyszko stopped at an inn in order to put on his armor and ride into the castle, helmet on head and lance in hand, according to the knightly custom—and then mounted an enormous stallion, part of his booty, made the sign of the cross in the air, and went forward.

But he had not gone ten paces when the Czech caught up to him.

"Your lordship," he said, "some knights are galloping behind us—Teutonic Knights, or what?"

Zbyszko turned his horse and no more than a half a furlong away he saw an imposing troop, at the head of which rode two knights on stout Pomeranian horses, in full armor, each wearing a white cloak with a black cross, and a helmet with a tall plume of peacock-feathers.

"Great heavens! Teutonic Knights!" said Zbyszko.

And involuntarily he leaned forward in his saddle and lowered his lance to the height of his horse's ear, seeing which the Czech spat on his hands so that his axe-helve might not slip.

Zbyszko's attendants, experienced men with a knowledge of the customs of war, also stood ready—not to fight, for servants took no part in knightly conflicts, but to measure out the space for a combat on horseback or to tread down the snowy ground for a fight on foot. Only the Czech, being a nobleman, made ready for business, but he, too, expected that Zbyszko would speak before he struck and was greatly surprised that his young lord levelled his lance before shouting a challenge.

Zbyszko came to his senses in time, however. He remembered his mad action near Cracow, when he had wanted to fight Lichtenstein without provocation, and all the misfortunes which had come of it; so he raised his lance, gave it to the Czech, and rode towards the knight-monks without drawing his sword. When he drew near he saw that, aside from the two of them, there was a third, also with a plume of feathers on his head, and a fourth, unarmed, with long hair, who seemed to him to be a Mazovian.

So he said to himself:

"While in prison I vowed to my lady not three crests but as many as I had fingers. I may get three now, however—if only they are not envoys."

Nevertheless, he thought that they must surely be some kind of envoys to the Duke of Mazovia, so he sighed and called out:

"May the Lord be praised!"

"For ever and ever," answered the unarmed, long-haired rider.

"God speed you!"

"And you, lord!"

"Glory be to St. George!"

"He is our patron. Greetings, lord, on your journey!"

They then began to bow to one another, and Zbyszko mentioned who he was, what escutcheon he bore, his motto and the place from which he was coming to the Mazovian court, while the long-haired knight said that his name was Andrew of Kropiwnica, and that he was conducting guests of the duke: brother Godfrey, brother Roger, and Sieur Fulk de Lorche of Lorraine, who was staying with the Teutonic Knights and wanted to see with his own eyes the Duke of Mazovia and particularly Duchess Anna, the daughter of the famous Kiejstut, Grand Duke of Lithuania.

While they were telling their names, the foreign knights, sitting erect on their horses, bowed their iron-helmeted heads from time to time, for, judging by Zbyszko's splendid armor, they thought that the duke had sent some honorable representative, perhaps a relative or a son, to meet them.

Andrew of Kropiwnica continued:

"The Commander, or as we would say Starost, of Jansbork, is staying with the duke as a guest and told him of these three knights, how eager they were to come, but did not dare. Most eager was the knight of Lorraine, for he, being from a distant country, thought that just beyond the Teutonic Knights' border lived Saracens, with whom war never ceases. So the duke, being a kind man, sent me to the border to conduct them safely past the castles."

"Do you mean they could not pass without your help?"

"Our nation is filled with much hatred against the Teutonic Knights, not so much because of their inroads—for we look in on them from time to time ourselves—but because of their great treachery. If a Teutonic Knight embraces you and kisses you on the face, he will be ready at the same time to stab you in the back, a custom that is truly base and against our Mazovian principles. Of course, everyone receives even a German under his roof and does no wrong to him when he is a guest, but on the road he gladly fights him. Indeed, there are some who do nothing else, for the sake of vengeance or for the sake of glory, which may God give to everyone."

"Who is the most famous among your people?"

"It would be better for a German to look upon death than upon him—Jurand of Spychow."

The young knight's heart leapt when he heard that name—and he immediately determined to find out more from Andrew of Kropiwnica.

"I know!" he said. "I have heard that his daughter, Danuta, was a lady-in-waiting of the duchess before she married."

Holding his breath, he studied the eyes of the Mazovian knight; however, the latter replied with great surprise:

"Who told you that? Why, she's quite young. It does sometimes happen that a girl so young marries, but Jurand's daughter has not married. It is but six days since I left Ciechanow, and I saw her in attendance on the duchess. And how could she marry during Advent?"

Zbyszko had to exert the entire strength of his will to refrain from embracing the Mazovian and shouting, "God reward you for your news!" So he checked himself and said:

"I heard that Jurand had given her to someone."

"The duchess wished to give her, not Jurand, but she could not go against Jurand's will. She wanted to give her to a knight at Cracow who made a vow to the girl and who is loved by her."

"She loves him?" cried out Zbyszko.

Andrew looked keenly at him, smiled, and said:

"You know, you're asking an awful lot of questions about that girl."

"I'm asking questions about acquaintances, to whom I'm going."

Little of Zbyszko's face was visible under his helmet, hardly more than his eyes and nose and a little of his cheeks, but his nose and cheeks were so red that the jesting, quick-witted Mazovian said:

"No doubt it is from the cold that your face has got as red as a beet!"

Zbyszko became still more confused.

"No doubt," he replied.

They moved forward and rode on for some time in silence, except for the snorting of their horses, who breathed out columns of steam from their nostrils, and the jargon of the foreign knights, conversing among themselves. Finally Andrew of Kropiwnica asked:

"What is your name? I did not hear very well."

"Zbyszko of Bogdaniec."

"Dear me! the one who vowed to Jurand's daughter had a name like that."

"Do you think I will deny it?" answered Zbyszko quickly with pride.

"There is no reason why you should. Dear God, then you are that Zbyszko whose head the girl covered with her veil! On their return from Cracow, all the girls at the court could talk of nothing else but you, and more than one wept a flood of tears while listening. So it is you! Hey! There will be joy at court, for the duchess likes you too."

"God bless her and you also for the good news. When they told me that she had married I couldn't bear it."

"How could she marry! She's a coveted thing, a girl like that, for the whole of Spychow stands behind her. But though there are plenty of handsome youths at court, none has looked into her eyes, for everyone respects her deed and your vow. Nor would the duchess have permitted it. Hey! There will be joy. It is true they sometimes tease the girl. Someone would say to her: 'Your knight will not come back.' And she would stamp her foot: 'He will! He will!' And more than once, when someone told her that you had married another, she burst into tears."

Zbyszko was moved by these words, but at the same time he was seized with anger at people's talk, so he said:

"I will challenge whoever said such things about me."

Andrew of Kropiwnica began to laugh.

"It was women who talked that way from spite! Will you challenge women? The sword is not much good against distaff."

Zbyszko, glad that God had sent him so merry and good-natured a companion, questioned him about Danusia, then about the customs of the Mazovian court and again about Danusia, then about Duke Janusz and the duchess, and again about Danusia; but, at last, remembering his vows, he told Andrew what he had heard on the way about war—how people were preparing for it and waiting for it from day to day. Then he asked whether the same thing was happening in the Mazovian duchy.

The Master of Kropiwnica did not think that war was so near. People said that it was inevitable, but he had heard how the duke himself once said to Nicholas of Longwood that the Teutonic

Knights had drawn in their horns and that if the king insisted, they would even give back the Land of Dobrzyn, for they feared his power—or at least they would protract the matter until they were well-prepared.

"Anyway," he said, "the duke not long ago rode to Malbork, where the grand marshal entertained him in the absence of the master and held tournaments for him, and now these commanders are staying with the duke—and fresh guests are still coming."

He reflected for a while, then added:

"People say that these Teutonic Knights are not staying with us and with Duke Ziemowit at Plock without reason. In case of war, they don't want our duke to help the Polish king, but only them. If they cannot bring this about, then at least they want him to stand quietly aside. But that won't happen. . . ."

"God grant that it won't! How could you sit at home? Your dukes are bound in duty to the Polish kingdom. I don't think that you'll sit this out."

"We shall not," replied Andrew of Kropiwnica.

Zbyszko looked again at the foreign knights and their peacock plumes.

"So that is why they are here?"

"The brothers of the Order, maybe. Who knows?"

"And that third one?"

"He is coming along because he is curious."

"He must be some important knight."

"Yes, three iron-bound wagons are going with him, with fine equipment, and he has nine men in his retinue. How wonderful it would be to fight with such a knight! It makes one's mouth water."

"But you cannot?"

"How could I? The duke ordered me to protect them! A hair will not fall from their heads before they reach Ciechanow."

"But supposing I challenged them? Supposing they were willing to fight with me?"

"In that case you would have to fight first with me. As long as I am alive, I must protect them."

Zbyszko looked amicably at the young nobleman.

"You understand knightly honor," he said. "I will not fight with you, for I am your friend, but God grant that at Ciechanow I may find some pretext against the Germans!"

"At Ciechanow you can do what you like. I am sure there will be jousting and, if the duke and the commanders give permission, fights with naked weapons."

"I have a board on which is a challenge to anyone who will not admit that the lady Danuta, Jurand's daughter, is the most virtuous and beautiful girl in the world. But, you know, everywhere people only shrug their shoulders and laugh."

"Because it is a strange custom and, to tell the truth, a stupid one, which our people do not know, save for a few on the borders. That Lorrainer there stopped a nobleman along the way and had him praise his own lady above all others. But no one understood him, and I did not allow them to fight."

"What? He had him praise his own lady? Great heavens! He must have no shame."

And he glanced at the foreign knight as if to convince himself how a man looks who has no shame. But he had to admit that Fulk de Lorche did not look at all like a common highwayman. On the contrary, from under his raised visor there looked out a pair of gentle eyes and a face young and full of a certain melancholy.

"Sanderus!" called Zbyszko suddenly.

"At your service," replied the German, approaching.

"Ask that knight who is the most virtuous and beautiful girl in the world."

Sanderus repeated the question in German to the French knight.

"Ulricha von Elner," replied Fulk de Lorche. And looking upwards, he began to sigh again and again.

Zbyszko, when he heard such blasphemy, was so indignant that he could scarcely breathe and was overcome by such anger that he reined in his stallion on the spot. Yet before he could speak, Andrew of Kropiwnica rode in between him and the foreigner.

"You shall not quarrel here," he stated.

Zbyszko turned again to the peddler of relics.

"Tell him from me that he loves an owl."

"My master says, noble knight, that you love an owl," said Sanderus in German.

At that Fulk de Lorche let go of his reins and with his right hand began to unfasten and then to pull off his iron glove. He then flung it in the snow before Zbyszko, who beckoned to his Czech to pick it up on the point of his lance.

Andrew of Kropiwnica turned to Zbyszko with a threatening expression.

"You will not meet, I tell you," he said, "until my guardianship ends. I will not permit either him or you."

"Why? It was not I who challenged him, but he who challenged me."

"But you called his lady an owl. Enough of this, and whoever disagrees—beware! I also know how to pull my belt around."

"I don't wish to fight with you."

"But you would have to fight with me, for I swore to defend that knight."

"Then what is to happen?" asked Zbyszko obstinately.

"It is not far to Ciechanow."

"But what will the Frenchman think?"

"Your attendant can tell him that you cannot meet here and that the duke must first give permission to you, and the commanders to him."

"And suppose they won't give permission?"

"Then you will find each other somewhere. Enough talking."

Zbyszko, seeing that nothing could be done, and understanding that Andrew of Kropiwnica really could not permit a combat, called Sanderus again to explain to the Lorrainer that they would fight only when they had arrived at their journey's end. De Lorche, hearing the German's words, nodded his head as a sign that he understood, and then, extending his hand to Zbyszko, he squeezed Zbyszko's fingers three times, which according to knightly custom signified that they must fight somewhere and at some time. Afterwards they went on towards the castle of Ciechanow in seeming harmony and soon saw its stumpy towers against the red evening sky.

They arrived while it was still light, but before they had declared themselves at the castle gates and the drawbridge was let down, deep night had fallen. They were received and entertained by Zbyszko's acquaintance, Nicholas of Longwood, who commanded a garrison composed of a handful of knights and three hundred first-class archers selected from the forest folk. As soon as he entered, Zbyszko learned to his great disappointment that the court was not there. The duke, wishing to honor the commanders from Ortelsburg and Jansbork, had arranged a great hunting party in the forest, to which the duchess also had gone with her ladies-in-waiting to make the spectacle more imposing. Of the women whom he knew, Zbyszko found only Ofka, widow of Krzych of Jarzabkowo and now chatelaine of the castle. She was very glad to see him. Since she had come back from Cracow, she had told everyone, whether they wanted to listen or not, of his love for Danusia and his adventure with Lichtenstein. These stories brought her a great reputation among the younger courtiers and ladies, so she was grateful to Zbyszko and now tried to console the youth in his sorrow at Danusia's absence.

"You will not recognize her," she said. "Time passes, and the seams in the girl's dresses are beginning to burst over her chest, for everything in her is budding. She is not a child anymore, and she loves you in a different way than before. Now, if anyone shouts in her ear 'Zbyszko!' she jumps as if she had been pricked with a needle. That is the way with all of us women, and there's no help for it, since it is the divine command. . . . And your uncle, tell me, is he well? Why did he not come? . . . Yes, such is our lot. It's terrible being a woman alone in the world. . . . Thank God that the girl hasn't broken her leg, for she goes up to the tower everyday to look at the road. . . . All of us women need friendship. . . ."

"I will feed my horses and ride to meet her, even if I have to go by night," replied Zbyszko.

"Do this, but take a guide from the castle, else you will lose you way in the forest."

At the supper which Nicholas of Longwood arranged for his guests, Zbyszko declared that he would ride to meet the duke and asked for a guide. After the meal the fatigued brothers of the Order decided to rest and not ride until the morrow, and they drew up to the enormous fireplaces where huge pine-logs were burning. But de Lorche, after making inquiries about what was happening, declared his readiness to ride with Zbyszko, saying that otherwise they might be late for the hunt, which he wished to see without fail.

Then he drew near to Zbyszko and, extending his hand to him, squeezed his fingers three times.

CHAPTER XX

BUT they were not destined to fight this time either, for when Nicholas of Longwood found out from Andrew of Kropiwnica what was in the air, he made them both promise on their word of honor that they would not meet without the knowledge of the duke and the commanders; and, in case they refused, he threatened to shut the gates against them. Zbyszko was anxious to see Danusia as soon as possible, so he did not dare object, while de Lorche, who gladly fought when there was occasion but was not at all blood-thirsty, swore on his knightly honor that he would wait for the duke's permission, especially because, if he did not, he might offend him. Also the Lorrainer, who had heard songs about tourneys and loved splendid gatherings and imposing ceremonies, desired to fight in front of the court, the dignitaries, and the ladies, thinking that thus the fame of his victory would spread more widely and that he would the more easily win golden spurs. Besides, he was interested in the country and its people, so the delay was quite opportune—particularly since Nicholas of Longwood, who had spent years as a prisoner among the Germans and could easily talk with foreigners, told marvellous tales about the ducal hunts of various beasts unknown in Western countries. So at midnight he started with Zbyszko for Przasnysz, taking with him his armed troop as well as men carrying torches for defence against wolves, which gathered in countless numbers in winter and might be dangerous even for a dozen or more well-armed riders. On this side of Ciechanow there was no lack of woodland, which not far beyond Przasnysz passed into the huge virgin forest of Kurpie, and that, in turn, united in the east with the impenetrable forests of Podlasie and Lithuania. Not too long ago, Lithuanian savages had been in the habit of making their way through these forests to Mazovia, avoiding the dangerous local settlers, and in 1337 they had penetrated as far as Ciechanow and had destroyed the town. De Lorche listened with the greatest interest to the stories about them related by the old guide, Macko of Turoboje, for his heart burned with desire to measure himself with the Lithuanians, whom he, like other Western knights, believed to be Saracens. The reason why he had come to these parts was to share in a crusade where he could win fame and salvation for his soul, and he had believed that war even with the Mazovians, whom he took for a half-pagan nation, would likewise assure the complete remission of his sins. So he scarcely believed his eyes when he arrived in Mazovia and saw churches in the towns, crosses on the towers, clergy, knights with sacred emblems on their armor, and a people turbulent indeed and hot-headed, ready to pick a quarrel and engage in a fight, but Christian and by no means more predatory than the Germans through whose country he had passed. So when he was told that this nation had acknowledged Christ for centuries, he did not know what to think of the Teutonic Knights. And when he learned that the deceased queen of Cracow had baptized Lithuania, his amazement and his anxiety knew no bounds.

So he began to question Macko of Turoboje whether the forests through which they were riding did not contain at least dragons to whom virgins had to be sacrificed and with whom one might fight. But Macko's answer was a complete disappointment in this respect also.

"In the forests there are various wild beasts, such as wolves, aurochs, bison, and bears, which give enough trouble," replied the Mazovian. "It may be also that there are evil spirits in the marshes, but I never heard of dragons, and if there were any, we would certainly not sacrifice virgins to them but gather in a large band and attack them. Bah, if there were any, the settlers in the wilderness would long since have been wearing dragon-skin belts!"

"What sort of people are they, and is it possible to fight with them?" asked de Lorche.

"One may fight with them, but it is not healthy to do so,"

answered Macko. "Besides, it is not befitting a knight, for they are a peasant people."

"The Swiss are also peasants. Do these here recognize Christ?"

"There are only Christians in Mazovia, and these are our people and the duke's. You saw the archers in the castle. They are all Kurps. There are no better archers in the world."

"The English and the Scots, whom I have seen at the Burgundian court—"

"I have seen them at Malbork," interrupted the Mazovian. "Sturdy lads, but God help them if they have to stand against the Kurps! Their seven-year-old boys get no food until they've shot it down from atop a pine tree."

"What are you talking about?" asked Zbyszko suddenly, for the repetition of the word "Kurps" had struck his ear.

"About Kurp and English bowmen. The knight says that the English and the Scots shoot better than all others."

"I have seen them at Wilno. Oh, how their arrows whizzed past my ears! There were knights from all countries who had sworn that they would eat us up without salt, but when they had tried once or twice, they lost their appetite."

Macko burst out laughing and repeated Zbyszko's words to Sieur de Lorche.

"They spoke of that at various courts," replied the Lorrainer. "They praised the tough spirit of your knights, but blamed them for defending pagans against the Cross."

"We defended against inroads and injustice a people who wanted to be baptized. The Germans wish to leave them in their paganism so as to have an excuse for war."

"God will judge this," said de Lorche.

"Perhaps soon," replied Macko of Turoboje.

The Lorrainer, hearing that Zbyszko had been at Wilno, questioned him about it, for the news of the fights and single combats of the knights there had already spread far and wide. The imagination of Western warriors had been particularly excited by the combat between four Polish knights and four French knights. So de Lorche began to look on Zbyszko with greater respect since he had taken part in such famous battles—and his heart rejoiced that he was to fight with one who was so distinguished.

So they rode on in peace, showing one another politeness at the places where they halted and toasting one another with wine, of which de Lorche had considerable store in his wagons. But when it came out from the conversation between him and Macko of Turoboje that Ulricha von Elner was not a maiden at all but a forty-year-old married woman with six children, Zbyszko got angry that the strange foreigner should dare not only to compare such an "old woman" with Danusia but to actually claim the prize of beauty for her. However, he thought that perhaps the Frenchman was not quite in his right mind and that a dark room and a lashing would suit him better than travelling through the world—and this idea restrained an outburst of sudden wrath.

"Do you not think," he said to Macko, "that an evil spirit has confused his mind? Maybe a devil is sitting in his head like a maggot in a nut and is ready to leap out on one of us at night. We must be on our guard. . . ."

Macko of Turoboje disputed this; nevertheless, he began to look at the Lorrainer with a certain unease, and finally said:

"There are times when more than a hundred of these evil spirits reside in a possessed man, and if there is too little room, they gladly seek a lodging in some other person. The worst devil of all is one sent by an old woman."

Then he turned suddenly to the French knight.

"Jesus Christ be praised!"

"I praise Him too," answered de Lorche with a certain surprise.

Macko of Turoboje was satisfied.

"You see," he said, "if an evil spirit had been sitting in him, he would immediately have foamed at the mouth, or the spirit would have thrown him to the ground because I addressed him so suddenly. We may ride on."

Calmed, they proceeded on their journey. It was not very far from Ciechanow to Przasnysz, and in the summer a messenger on a good horse could cover the distance between the two towns in a couple of hours. But they were riding much more slowly because of the night, their pauses, and the snowdrifts in the forest, and as they had set out considerably after midnight, they arrived at the duke's hunting-lodge at Przasnysz, at the edge of the woodland, only at dawn.

The house appeared to be leaning against the forest. It was large, low, built of wood, but with panes of glass balls for windows. In front of the house were well-sweeps and two sheds for horses, while the grounds teemed with numerous booths woven of pine branches, and leather tents. In the grey dawn the fires in front of the tents burned brightly. Surrounding the fires were beaters in sheepskin coats with the wool outside, and draped with capes of fox-, wolf-, or bear-skin. These people looked to Sieur de Lorche like wild beasts standing on their hind legs, for the majority of them wore caps made of animal heads. Some were leaning on their spears, others on their crossbows; some were rolling up enormous nets of rope, and others again were turning huge quarters of bison and elk over hot coals in preparation for the morning meal. The light of the flames fell on the snow and lit up these wild figures, who were partly veiled by the smoke of the fires, the mist of men's breath, and the steam rising from the roasting meat. Behind them, the russet trunks of gigantic pines were to be seen and other gatherings of men, whose number amazed the Lorrainer, unaccustomed as he was to the sight of such a great hunting-party.

"Your dukes," he said, "go to the chase as if to war."

"You are right," replied Macko of Turoboje. "They are not short either of hunting-gear or of men. These are the duke's beaters, but there are also others who come from the secluded forest glades to trade."

"What shall we do?" interrupted Zbyszko. "In the lodge they are still asleep."

"Well, we will wait until they get up," replied Macko. "We cannot knock at the door and wake the duke, our lord."

He led them to a fire. The beaters spread bison- and bear-skins for them and offered them plenty of smoking meat. Hearing a strange language, more and more of the Kurps gathered round to look at a German. Zbyszko's attendants soon spread the word that the knight came from "beyond the sea"—and then the throng became so dense that the Lord of Turoboje had to use his authority to protect the foreigner from their excessive curiosity. De Lorche also noticed women in the crowd, most of them dressed likewise in skins, but rosy-cheeked like apples and unusually pretty, so he asked whether they also took part in the chase.

Macko of Turoboje explained to him that they did not belong to the hunt but had come with the beaters out of feminine curiosity or as if to a fair, to buy wares from town and sell forest products.

And so it was in reality. The lodge was the focus towards which the two elements, town and forest, converged, even when the duke himself was not present. The beaters did not like to leave the virgin forest, for they did not feel at home without the soughing of the trees over their heads, so the inhabitants of Przasnysz transported their famous beer to the edge of the woods, as well as flour ground in the town windmills or in the water-mills on the Wegierka River, salt, which was a rare and eagerly sought-for commodity in the wilderness, iron-ware, straps, and similar fruits of human industry. In exchange, they took hides, costly furs, dried mushrooms, nuts, medicinal herbs, or pieces of amber, which it was not too difficult to find among the Kurps. For this reason, there was the bustle of an everlasting fair around the lodge, and there was still more activity at the time of the ducal hunts, when both duty and curiosity lured the inhabitants from the depths of the woods.

De Lorche listened to Macko's stories, looking eagerly at the figures of the beaters, who—living as they did in a healthy, invigorating climate and feeding, like the majority of peasants in those time, mainly on meat—amazed foreign travellers by their physique and their strength. Meanwhile Zbyszko, sitting by the fire, looked unceasingly at the door and windows of the house, and could barely remain in his place. Only one window was lit up, evidently a kitchen window, since smoke found its way out through the cracks caused by ill-fitting panes. The other windows were still dark, glittering only with the light of dawn, which grew brighter every moment and silvered the snowy wilderness behind the house. From a small side-door, servants dressed in the duke's colors emerged from time to time, going for water to the well with a pair of pails or wooden buckets on a yoke. When asked whether everyone was still asleep, they answered that the court, fatigued with yesterday's hunt, was still resting, but that food was already cooking for the morning meal.

Through the kitchen window came the smell of fats and saffron, spreading far among the camp fires. At last the front door creaked and opened, revealing a brightly-lit hall, and a man came out onto the veranda whom Zbyszko recognized at first sight as one of the minstrels he had seen among the duke's servants at Cracow. Without waiting for either Macko of Turoboje or de Lorche, Zbyszko ran to the house so swiftly that the surprised Lorrainer asked:

"Whatever has happened to that young knight?"

"Nothing," replied Macko of Turoboje. "He is merely in love with one of the duchess's ladies-in-waiting and wants to see her as soon as he can."

"Ah!" replied de Lorche, pressing both hands to his heart.

And looking upwards, he began to sigh again and again with such sorrow that Macko shrugged his shoulders, saying to himself, "Is he sighing like that for his old woman? Maybe in truth he's not quite in his right mind."

But he conducted him into the lodge, and they both found themselves in a spacious hall ornamented with the horns of aurochs, bison, elk, and stags, and lighted by dry logs burning on an enormous hearth. In the middle was a table covered with a kilim and laden with dishes. There were only a few courtiers present, and Zbyszko was conversing with them. Macko of Turoboje introduced Sieur de Lorche, but as the courtiers did not understand German, he had to keep him company himself. More and more courtiers arrived every moment, for the most part stalwart fellows, rough still, but well-grown, broad-shouldered, and fair-haired, and dressed for the forest. Those who knew Zbyszko and had heard of his Cracow adventures greeted him like an old friend, and it was obvious that he was held in high esteem among them. Others looked at him with that amazement with which one usually looks at a man over whose neck the executioner's axe has been raised. All around voices could be heard: "Yes, the duchess is here!" "Jurand's daughter is here!" "You will see her in a moment, poor fellow, and then you'll go hunting with us."

Suddenly two Teutonic Knights came in, the guests of the duke: brother Hugo von Danveld, Constable of Ortelsburg, a kinsman of whose had been marshal in his time, and Siegfried von Lowe, Governor of Jansbork, who also came of a family which had served the Order. The former was still comparatively young, but fat, with a sly beer-drinker's face and thick, moist lips; while the latter was tall, with stern but noble features. It seemed to Zbyszko that he had seen Danveld once at Duke Witold's and that Henry, bishop of Plock, had unhorsed him in a tournament, but these memories were disrupted by the entrance of Duke Janusz, towards whom both the Teutonic Knights and the courtiers turned and bowed. De Lorche and the commanders went up to him, as well as Zbyszko, and he greeted them courteously but with dignity in his smooth, countryman's face, framed in hair cut in a straight line over his brow and falling down on both sides to his shoulders. Presently trumpets sounded outside the windows, signifying that the duke was sitting down to table. They sounded once, twice, three times, and after the third time the large door on the right side of the hall opened and Duchess Anna appeared in the doorway, accompanied by a beautiful fair-haired girl with a lute hanging over her shoulder.

Seeing her, Zbyszko went forward and, putting his hands together as if in prayer, knelt on both knees in an attitude of great respect and adoration.

At this sight a murmur passed through the room, for the Mazovians were surprised at Zbyszko's behavior, and some of them were even indignant. "Well, I never!" said the older ones. "It's certain he has learned that custom from foreign knights or maybe directly from the pagans, for it does not exist even among the Germans." But the younger ones thought: "It's not surprising, since he owes his life to the girl." The duchess and Jurand's daughter did not immediately recognize Zbyszko, as he was kneeling with his back to the fire and had his face in shadow. The duchess thought at first that it was one of the courtiers who had offended the duke in some way and was begging for her intervention, but Danusia, whose sight was keener, took a step forward and, bending her fair head, cried out in a high, penetrating voice:

"Zbyszko!"

Then, without thinking that the whole court and the foreign visitors were looking at her, she sprang like a fawn to the young knight and, throwing her arms around him, began to kiss his eyes and mouth and cheeks, nestling against him and uttering joyful exclamations, until all the Mazovians burst into thunderous laughter, and the duchess pulled her away by the collar.

At that moment she looked around, and being struck with terrible embarrassment, she sprang behind the duchess and hid herself in the folds of her skirt, so that hardly more than the top of her head was to be seen.

Zbyszko embraced the lady's knees, and she made him get up, greeted him, and immediately began to question him about his uncle Macko: whether he was dead or still alive, and if he was alive, whether he had not also come to Mazovia. Zbyszko answered her questions somewhat absentmindedly, for he was leaning to one side and the other, trying to catch sight of Danusia, who peeped out from the duchess's skirt and then dived into its folds again. The Mazovians shook with laughter at this sight, and the duke himself laughed. Finally, when the hot dishes had been brought in, the duchess turned joyously to Zbyszko and said:

"Wait upon us, dear servant, and God grant not only at dinner but for always!" Then she said to Danusia: "And you, troublesome fly, come out at once from behind my dress, or you will tear it."

So Danusia emerged from behind the dress, blushing, confused, raising her anxious, ashamed, yet curious eyes every moment to Zbyszko—and so beautiful was she that not just Zbyszko was effected. The Teutonic Constable of Ortelsburg began to wipe his thick, moist lips again and again with his hand, while de Lorche was simply amazed; he held up both his hands and asked:

"By St. James of Compostella, who is that maiden?"

The Constable of Ortelsburg, who besides being short was fat, stood on his tiptoes and said in the Lorrainer's ear:

"The devil's daughter."

De Lorche looked at him. He blinked his eyes and then frowned.

"No true knight barks against beauty," he said through his nose.

"I wear golden spurs—and am a monk," replied Hugo von Danveld haughtily.

So great was the honor in which belted knights were held that the Lorrainer bowed his head, but he replied after a moment:

"And I am kinsman of the dukes of Brabant."

"Pax! Pax!" replied the Teutonic Knight. "Honor to the powerful dukes and friends of the Order, from whose hands, lord, you will shortly receive golden spurs. I do not deny the beauty of the girl, but listen while I tell you who her father is."

However, he was unable to tell his story, for at that moment Duke Janusz sat down to breakfast, and having learned beforehand from the Governor of Jansbork of the distinguished kinsmen of Sieur de Lorche, he gave him a sign to sit down beside him. Opposite the duke, the duchess took her place with Danusia, while Zbyszko stood behind their chairs to wait upon them as he had done before at Cracow. Danusia bent her head as low as she could over her plate, for she was ashamed, yet she tilted her head slightly so that Zbyszko might see her face. For his part, he looked eagerly and with delight at her small, fair head, her rosy cheeks, and her arms, covered by a close-fitting garment and which had already ceased to be the arms of a child; and he felt, as it were, a river of fresh love rising up in him and flooding his whole breast. He also felt the freshness of her kisses on his eyes, lips, and face. She had formerly appeared to him like a sister, and he had accepted kisses from her as if from a dear child. But now, at their fresh memory, the same thing happened to him as had happened sometimes with Jagienka: he was seized with the shivers and overcome with weakness, under which glowed a fire as on an ash-strewn hearth. Danusia seemed to him a completely grown-up young lady—and indeed she had grown up and blossomed. Besides, so much had been said, and so often, in her presence of love that, just as a flower-bud warmed by the sun gains color and opens ever wider, so her eyes had opened to love. Consequently, there was something in her now which had not been there before—some charm which was no longer that of a child and some powerful intoxicating attraction radiating from her as warmth radiates from a flame or perfume from a rose.

Zbyszko felt it, but he did not recognize it for what it was, because he was in another world. He even forgot that he had to wait at table. He did not see that the courtiers were looking at him, nudging one another with their elbows, pointing to Danusia and himself, and laughing. Nor did he notice the face of Sieur de Lorche, frozen, as it were, in astonishment, nor the bulging eyes of the Teutonic Constable of Ortelsburg, which, fixed on Danusia and reflecting the flame from the hearth, seemed red and shining like the eyes of a wolf. Zbyszko came to himself only when the trumpets sounded again, signifying that it was time to start for the forest—and when Duchess Anna Danuta turned to him, saying:

"You will ride with us, for I want you to enjoy yourself and speak to the girl of love; and I shall listen gladly to your talk."

She left with Danusia to get properly dressed for the hunt. Zbyszko ran into the yard, where all the horses were standing, already covered with frost and snorting. The area was not as full of people as it had been before, for the beaters had gone out with their axes into the wilderness. Their fires had died down and the day had dawned, bright and cold; the snow creaked underfoot, and from the trees, moved by a slight breeze, dry and glittering frost-flakes sprinkled down. Presently the duke came out and mounted his horse. Accompanying him was an attendant with a crossbow and a hunting-spear so long and heavy that few could wield it; the duke, however, did so with ease, for he was unusually strong, like others of the Mazovian Piasts. There were even women in the family who, when they married foreign dukes, bent broad iron choppers with their hands at their wedding banquets. Near the duke there were also two men ready to come to his aid in case of sudden need, picked from among the gentry in all the districts of Warsaw and Ciechanow, terrible to behold, with shoulders like forest trees— and at whom Sieur de Lorche, who had come from a far country, looked in amazement.

Meanwhile the duchess and Danusia came out, wearing hoods of white weasel-skin. Anna Danuta, being as she was the only daughter of Kiejstut, could shoot better with the bow than sew with the needle, and so a crossbow was carried behind her, richly ornamented and somewhat lighter than other crossbows. Zbyszko knelt in the snow and stretched out his hand, on which the lady placed her foot when mounting her horse. Then he lifted Danusia as he had lifted Jagienka at Bogdaniec, and they set out. The retinue stretched out like a long serpent. It turned to the right from the lodge, changing and twinkling along the edge of the forest like a colored hem on the edge of a dark garment, and slowly it entered the wilderness.

They were already deep in the woods when the duchess turned to Zbyszko and said:

"Why do you not talk? Go on, speak to her."

Though thus encouraged, Zbyszko was still silent for a while, for he was overcome with a peculiar shyness. Only after the time for one or two Aves had passed did he exclaim:

"Danusia!"

"What, Zbyszko?"

"I love you so much that—"

He stopped, in search of words, which came with difficulty; for though he had knelt before the girl like a foreign knight, though he showed her honor in every way and strove to avoid common-place turns of speech, he sought in vain for courteous phrases. He had a rustic soul, after all, and could speak only simply and sincerely.

So after a while, he said:

"I love you so much that my breath fails me!"

She raised her blue eyes to him from under her hood and a face pinched and rosed by the cold forest breeze.

"And I you, Zbyszko!" she answered, as if in haste.

Then she veiled her eyes with her long lashes, for she knew already what love was.

"Hey! my treasure! Hey! my girl!" exclaimed Zbyszko. "Hey!"

He fell silent again, this time from happiness and emotion, until the good but also curious duchess came to his aid once more.

"Tell her," she said, "how dreary it was without her. If you find a thicket and kiss her on the lips behind it, I shall not be angry, for thus you will best declare your love."

So he began to tell her "how dreary" it had been without her at Bogdaniec, nursing Macko and among "the neighbors." But the cunning fox said nothing about Jagienka. For the rest, he spoke sincerely, since at the present moment he so loved the beautiful Danusia that he wanted to seize her, seat her on his horse, hold her before him, and press her to his breast.

He did not dare to do that, however. But when the first thicket separated them from the courtiers and guests who were riding behind, he bent towards her, put his arms around her, and hid his face in her hood, thereby declaring his love.

But because in winter there are no leaves on the bushes in the forest, Hugo von Danveld and Sieur de Lorche saw him, and the courtiers likewise saw him and began to say among themselves:

"He has kissed her in the duchess's presence! For sure the lady will soon arrange a marriage for them."

"He's a valiant lad, but she is of Jurand's fiery blood!"

"Flint and steel, though the girl is quiet as a mouse. But sparks will fly from them, never fear. He clings to her like a tick on live skin!"

Thus they talked, laughing. But the Teutonic Constable of Ortelsburg turned his goatish, evil, and lustful face to Sieur de Lorche, and asked:

"Would you not like, lord, some Merlin to change you by black magic into that knight?"

"And you, lord?" asked de Lorche.

Evidently burning with jealousy and lust, the Teutonic Knight checked his horse impatiently and exclaimed:

"On my soul! . . ."

However, he recollected himself, and bending his head, continued:

"I am a monk who has vowed chastity."

And he looked keenly at the Lorrainer, fearing lest he might observe a smile on his face, for in this respect the Order had a bad reputation, and among all the monks Hugo von Danveld had the worst. A few years before he had been deputy governor of Sambia, and the complaints against him there had become so loud that despite the complaisance with which such things were regarded at Malbork, it was necessary to transfer him to Ortelsburg, where he was made captain of the castle garrison. He had arrived at the duke's court a few days ago with secret instructions, and having seen the beautiful daughter of Jurand, he burned in lust for her. Danusia's age was not any check on him, for in those times even younger girls than she used to marry; yet Danveld knew at the same time from what family the girl came, and since the name of Jurand was bound up with terrible recollections in his mind, his lust grew on the basis of savage hate.

De Lorche questioned him on precisely that issue.

"You called that beautiful girl the devil's daughter? Why did you call her that?"

Danveld now began to tell the story of Zlotorya. How when the castle was being rebuilt they successfully carried off the duke along with his court, and how on that occasion the mother of Jurand's daughter lost her life, and how since that time Jurand had taken terrible vengeance on all the Knights of the Teutonic Order. And, as he was telling the story, the knight became inflamed with hatred, for which he had personal cause. He himself had encountered Jurand two years before, when, at the sight of the terrible "Wild Man of Spychow," for the first time in his life his heart had failed him so disgracefully that he had abandoned two of his kinsmen, his men, and his plunder, and had fled like a madman the whole day to Ortelsburg, where he lay for a long time in a state of shock. When he regained his health, the grand marshal of the Order handed him over to a court of knightly justice, which acquitted him, since he swore on the Cross and his honor as a knight that a runaway horse had carried him from the field of battle, but debarred him from advancement to the higher offices of the Order. The knight, it is true, said nothing now of these events in the presence of Sieur de Lorche, but on the other hand he made so many complaints of the cruelty of Jurand and the ruthlessness of the whole Polish nation that there was scarcely room for them in the head of the Lorrainer.

"But surely," he said after a while, "we are among the Mazovians and not among the Poles."

"It's a separate duchy, but one nation," replied the constable. "Their wickedness and their hatred of the Order are the same. God grant that the German sword may exterminate the entire lot!"

"You speak justly, sir. The duke, who outwardly appears an honorable man, dared to build a castle against you on your own soil! Even among the pagans I never heard of such a lawless act."

"He built a castle against us, but Zlotorya lies on his soil, not on ours."

"Then glory to Christ for giving you victory over him! How did the war end?"

"There was no war at that time."

"But your victory at Zlotorya?"

"God blessed us in that the duke was without an army, but was only with his court and womenfolk."

De Lorche looked at the Teutonic Knight in amazement.

"What? In time of peace you fell upon womenfolk and a duke who was building a castle on his own soil?"

"For the glory of the Order and of Christianity there are no dishonorable deeds."

"And that terrible knight is only seeking vengeance for his young wife, slain by you in time of peace?"

"He who raises his hand against a Teutonic Knight is a son of darkness."

Sieur de Lorche was amazed at what he had heard, but he had no time to answer Danveld, for they had come out upon a wide clearing, overgrown with snow-clad bents, where the duke dismounted from his horse, and everyone else began to dismount after him.

CHAPTER XXI

SKILLED foresters, under the leadership of the chief huntsman, began to post the hunters in a long line across the clearing in such a way that, being themselves hidden, they had an empty space in front of them over which they could the more easily shoot. The two shorter sides of the clearing were lined with nets, behind which the "turners" concealed themselves. Their business was to turn the wild animals to the archers, or if they could not be driven, but became entangled in the nets, to kill them with their spears. Innumerable hosts of Kurps, skillfully posted in a semicircle, had to drive every living creature from the depths of the forest onto the clearing. Behind the archers and crossbow men there was another net spread to catch such animals as might penetrate their line.

The duke took up his position in the middle of the line in a slight depression that ran the whole breadth of the clearing. The chief huntsman, Mrokota of Mocarzewo, had chosen that spot for him, knowing that the largest beast in the forest would retreat before the beaters along that depression. The duke himself had a crossbow in his hand, and close beside him his heavy spear was leaning against a tree, while a little to the rear stood his two "protectors," huge men like the trunks of forest trees, with axes on their shoulders and crossbows bent and ready to be handed to the duke in case of need. The duchess and Jurand's daughter did not dismount, for the duke would not allow it because of the danger from aurochs and bison, from whose rage it was easier to escape on horseback than on foot. De Lorche, although summoned by the duke to stand at his right side, begged to be allowed to remain on horseback to defend the ladies, and he took up a position near them, looking like a long spike with his upright lance, which the Mazovians mocked quietly under their breath, considering it a weapon ill-suited for hunting. Zbyszko, on the other hand, planted his spear in the snow, swung his crossbow onto his back, and stood by Danusia on her horse. Sometimes he whispered to her and sometimes he put his arms around her legs and kissed her knees, for he was not in the least ashamed of his love, nor did he endeavor to conceal it from anyone. He quieted down only when Mrokota of Mocarzewo, who ventured into the forest to rebuke even the duke himself, ordered him to keep silent.

Meanwhile, far and far away in the depths of the forest were heard the Kurp horns, answered from the clearing by the brief, loud sound of the huntsman's horn, and followed by perfect silence. From time to time a jay called harshly in the tops of the pines, and from time to time the beaters in the semicircle croaked like ravens. The hunters strained their eyes, looking over the white empty space, on which the wind shook the reeds, white with frost, and the leafless osier bushes. Everyone waited impatiently to see the first beast appear on the snow. A rich and splendid hunt was anticipated, since the forest was full of bison, aurochs, and wild boar. The Kurps had smoked out a few bears from their dens. Rudely waked, they trudged through the thickets, angry, hungry, and watchful, guessing that soon they would have to fight, not for their quiet winter's sleep, but for their lives.

However, it was a long wait, since the men who were driving the wild beasts into the mouth of the semicircle and onto the clearing had occupied an enormous stretch of forest and were coming from so far away that even the barking of the dogs, which had been released immediately after the sounding of the trumpets, did not reach the ears of the hunters. One dog, evidently released too early, or perhaps wandering loose on his own, appeared on the clearing, ran right across it with his nose to the ground, and passed between the hunters. And again all was empty and quiet—only the turners croaked continually like ravens to signify that the work would shortly begin. At length, after the time for a few paternosters had passed, there appeared on the edge of the forest some wolves, which, being the wariest animals, had been the first to try and avoid danger. However, when they came out on the clearing and scented the people about, they plunged again into the forest, evidently seeking another way of escape. Then wild boars, rushing out of the depths of the forest, began to run in a long black chain across the snowy space, looking from the distance like a herd of tame pigs that at the call of the housewife make their way to the hut with shaking ears. But the chain stopped, listened, scented, turned around, and again listened. It made towards the hunters, snorting, approaching with more and more caution, yet coming nearer and nearer, until at last the sound of the iron hooks on the crossbows and the whiz of arrows were heard, and the first blood stained the pale, snowy ground.

Then a shout rang out, and the herd scattered as if struck by lightning. Some went blindly on, others threw themselves against the nets, others began to run singly or in groups, mingling with other beasts, of which the clearing had in the meantime come to be full. Now the sound of the horns came distinctly to the ear, as well as the baying of dogs and the distant calling of men advancing in line from the depths of the forest. The wild animals of the woods, driven in from the sides by the widely cast wings of this line, filled the forest meadow more and more densely. Nothing similar could be seen in foreign countries, or even in other Polish districts, for nowhere were there such virgin forests as in Mazovia. The Teutonic Knights, although they were frequently in Lithuania, where it happened at times that bison charged an army and threw it into confusion, were not a little astonished at the countless number of animals. But perhaps most astonished of all was Sieur de Lorche. Standing by the duchess and the court ladies like a crane on guard, but unable to talk with any of them, freezing in his iron armor, he had already been getting bored and was beginning to think the hunt a failure. When lo!—he saw before him a whole flock of light-footed fawns, sandy-colored deer, and elks with heavy heads crowned with antlers, all mingled together, dashing like a whirlwind over the clearing, blind with fear and seeking an outlet in vain. The duchess, in whom the blood of her father, Kiejstut, flowed hotly at the sight, released arrow after arrow against the varicolored throng, crying out with joy every time that a hit stag or elk reared up, fell heavily to the ground, and kicked the snow. Her damsels also frequently bent their faces to their bows, for all were seized with ardor for the hunt. Only Zbyszko did not think of it. Supporting his elbows on Danusia's knees and his head on his hands, he gazed into her eyes, while she, half laughing and half shamefaced, tried to close his eyelids with her fingers, as if unable to endure his stare.

The attention of Sieur de Lorche, however, was drawn by an enormous bear, with grey neck and shoulder-blades, which came suddenly out of the bents, close to the archers. The duke shot at it with his crossbow and then advanced upon it with his spear, and when the beast rose on its hind feet, roaring dreadfully, he pierced it before the eyes of the whole court so skillfully and quickly that neither of his two "protectors" needed to use an axe. Then the young Lorrainer thought that not many lords at the courts he had visited on his travels would have ventured on such an amusement and that the Order must have now, and would have in the future, a hard time with such dukes and such a people. Later he observed fierce, white-tusked boars pierced in the same way by other hunters—enormous beasts, far bigger and more savage than those chased in the woodlands of Lower Lorraine or in the German forest wilderness. Sieur de Lorche had never seen such skilled hunters before and such thrusts with the spear. As an experienced man, he explained their proficiency by the fact that all these men, living in the midst of boundless forests, were accustomed from childhood to the crossbow and the spear.

The clearing was soon densely covered with bodies of all kinds of animals, but the hunters had by no means finished yet. On the contrary, the most interesting and at the same time the most dangerous moment was still to come, since the semicircle of Kurp beaters was just driving a dozen or more aurochs and bison onto the clearing. Although in the forests these beasts usually kept apart, they now were all mingled together, but were not at all blinded by fear. They were rather threatening than terrified. They did not advance too quickly, seeming confident that with their enormous strength they would break all obstacles and pass through.

The ground rumbled with their weight. Bearded bulls, advancing first with their heads close to the earth, stopped at times as if considering in which direction to charge. From their powerful lungs came a dull roar like subterranean thunder, their nostrils breathed forth steam, and digging the snow with their forefeet, they seemed to seek with their bloodshot eyes the hidden foe.

Meanwhile the turners raised a mighty shout, which was answered from the main line and from the wings by hundreds of thunderous voice; horns and whistles blew; the forest re-echoed to its remotest depths, and at the same time the Kurp dogs burst onto the clearing with a terrible uproar, following the trail. The sight of them instantly enraged the female beasts leading their young. The herd, which had hitherto advanced slowly, scattered madly over the clearing. One of the aurochs, a sandy-haired, gigantic, almost monstrous bull, surpassing the bison in size, advanced with heavy leaps towards the line of archers, turned towards the right side of the clearing, and then, seeing the horses among the trees, fifty or sixty paces away, stopped and began to plough the earth with its horns, as if urging itself on to charge and fight.

At this terrible sight the turners raised a still louder shout, and shrill cries were heard among the hunters: "The duchess! the duchess! Save the lady!" Zbyszko seized the spear which he had stuck in the snow and rushed to the edge of the forest with a few Lithuanians behind him who were ready to perish in defence of Kiejstut's daughter. Meanwhile the crossbow twanged in the lady's hands, and an arrow whizzed and, passing over the bent head of the beast, pierced the back of its neck.

"It's hit!" cried the duchess. "It will come no closer. . . ."

But her words were drowned by a roar so dreadful that the horses sat back on their haunches. The aurochs threw itself like a storm straight on the lady, but suddenly, with an equal impetus, the valiant Sieur de Lorche rushed from among the trees and—leaning forward, lance couched as if at a knightly tournament—charged straight at the beast.

In a flash those present saw his lance sticking in the bull's neck and then bend like a bow and brake into small pieces, while the enormous horned head almost vanished under the belly of Sieur de Lorche's horse; and before anyone could utter a cry, both steed and rider were catapulted through the air.

The horse, falling on its side, began to kick in death agony, entangling its feet in its own entrails, while Sieur de Lorche lay motionless nearby, like an iron wedge on the snow. The aurochs seemed to hesitate for a time whether to leave them and charge the other horses. But having these first victims close before him, he turned again to them and began to take vengeance on the unhappy steed, crushing it with its head and savagely goring its open belly.

Men were rushing from the forest to rescue the foreign knight. Zbyszko, concerned with the protection of the duchess and of Danusia, was the first to run up and thrust the point of his spear under the beast's shoulder-blade. He struck so violently, however, that the spear broke in his hand on a sudden turn of the aurochs, while he himself fell on his face in the snow. "He's done for! He's done for!" shouted the Mazovians running to his aid. Meanwhile the bull's head covered Zbyszko and pressed him to the ground. The two powerful "protectors" had already rushed up from the duke's side. They would have arrived too late had they not fortunately been anticipated by the Czech, Hlawa, whom Jagienka had given to Zbyszko. He dashed up before them and, raising his broad axe in both hands, struck the aurochs's bent neck, right behind the horns.

The blow was so terrible that the animal fell as if struck by lightning, its backbone broken and its head almost half cut through. But in its fall it crushed Zbyszko. The two "protectors" dragged off the monstrous carcass in the twinkling of an eye, and meanwhile the duchess and Danusia, speechless with fear, leapt from their horses and ran to the wounded youth.

Pale as he was and covered with the blood of the aurochs and his own, he raised himself a little and tried to stand. But he staggered, fell on his knees and, supporting himself on one hand, managed to utter a single word:

"Danusia!"

Then blood stained his lips and darkness came over his eyes. Danusia took hold of him by the shoulders from behind, but being unable to support him, cried out for help. They were soon surrounded by men on all sides who rubbed him with snow and poured wine into his mouth. Finally the huntsman Mrokota of Mocarzewo gave orders to lay him on a cloak and stop the flow of blood by the aid of soft touchwood from the forest.

"He will live if it is only his ribs that are broken and not his spine," he said, turning to the duchess.

Meanwhile other damsels, assisted by the hunters, occupied themselves in attending to Sieur de Lorche. They turned him around, looking for holes or dints made in his armor by the bull's horns, but found nothing but flakes of snow which had made their way between the joints of the plates. The aurochs had avenged itself mainly on the horse, which lay nearby, all its entrails under its belly, while Sieur de Lorche was untouched. He had only fainted as a result of the fall, and, as was found later, his right arm had been put out. Now, when they took off his helmet and poured wine into his mouth, he opened his eyes and regained consciousness, and seeing the anxious faces of two young and fair damsels bent over him, he said in German:

"Surely I am in heaven and angels are over me?"

The damsels did not understand what he said, but they were glad that he had come to life and could speak, and they began to smile at him and lifted him up with the help of the hunters. Feeling the pain in his right arm, he groaned and supported himself with his left arm on the shoulders of one of the "angels." He stood for a while motionless, fearing to take a step, since he did not feel secure on his feet. Then he passed a tired glance over the field of battle. He saw the sandy carcass of the aurochs, which, close by, seemed monstrously large; he saw Danusia wringing her hands over Zbyszko, and Zbyszko himself lying on the cloak.

"Did that knight come to my aid?" he asked. "Is he alive?"

"He is gravely injured," answered one of the courtiers who understood German.

"Henceforth I will not fight with him, but for him!" said the Lorrainer.

At that moment the duke, who had been standing over Zbyszko, came up to him and began to praise him, saying that by his bold action he had protected from grave danger the duchess and other women and perhaps had saved their lives; for which, besides knightly awards, he would gain fame among men now living and their descendants. "In these effeminate times," he said, "there are ever fewer true knights riding through the world, so be my guest as long as you can, or stay in Mazovia altogether, for you have won my favor, and you will just as easily win the love of my people by your honorable deeds."

Sieur de Lorche's heart, eager for glory, melted at these words, and when he thought that he had done such an important knightly deed and had won such fame in those distant Polish lands of which only marvels were related in the West, he scarcely felt the pain in his dislocated arm, so great was his joy. He understood that a knight who could say at the Brabant or Burgundy court that he had saved the life of the Duchess of Mazovia at a hunt would walk in glory as in the sun. Under the influence of these thoughts he even wished to go straight to the duchess and vow her faithful service on his knees, but both the lady herself and Danusia were occupied with Zbyszko. The latter regained consciousness for a moment, but only smiled to Danusia, raised his hand to his brow, covered with cold sweat, and immediately fainted again. Experienced huntsmen, seeing how he closed his hands and how his mouth stayed open, told one another that he would not live; but the still more experienced Kurps, more than one of whom bore scars left by bear claws, boar tusks, or bison horns, had better hopes, asserting that the aurochs's horn had slipped between the knight's ribs, causing maybe one or two to be broken, but that his backbone was whole, otherwise the young lord would not have been able to raise himself even for a second. They also pointed out that the place where Zbyszko had fallen was covered with a snowdrift, which had saved his life; for the beast, pressing him with its forehead, had not been able to crush his chest or his back.

Unfortunately, the duke's physician, Father Wyszoniek of Dziewanna, was not at the hunt, although he usually attended, for he was occupied this time with baking sacred wafers in the house. The Czech, learning this, ran to fetch him, but in the meantime the Kurps carried Zbyszko on the cloak to the ducal lodge. Danusia wanted to go with him on foot, but the duchess opposed this, for it was a long way and the snow lay deep in the ravines of the forest, and it was important to hurry. So the Teutonic constable, Hugo von Danveld, helped the girl to mount her horse and then, riding by her side, just behind the men who were carrying Zbyszko, said in Polish in a low voice so as to be heard only by her:

"At Ortelsburg I have a miraculous healing balsam, which I got from a certain hermit in the Hercynian Forest. I could send it to you in three days."

"God will reward you!" answered Danusia.

"God will record every work of mercy, but may I expect payment from you too?"

"How can I repay you?"

The Teutonic Knight drew nearer and evidently was about to say something but hesitated, and spoke only after a while:

"In our Order, besides brothers, there are also sisters. . . . One of them will bring the healing balsam, and then I will speak of payment."

CHAPTER XXII

FATHER Wyszoniek attended to Zbyszko's wounds and found that only one rib was broken; yet on the first day he did not guarantee his recovery, for he did not know, he said, "whether the patient's heart was not twisted, and whether his liver was not dislocated." Meanwhile Sieur de Lorche was overcome with such weakness towards evening that he had to lie down, and the next day he could move neither arm nor leg without great pain in all his bones. The duchess and Danusia and the other damsels of the court tended the sick men and mixed various ointments and balsams for them according to Father Wyszoniek's prescription. Zbyszko, however, was seriously hurt, and from time to time blood dripped from his lips, to the priest's great dismay. But he was conscious, and on the following day, although still very weak, having learned from Danusia to whom he owed his life, he summoned his Czech to thank and reward him. He could not help remembering that he had got him from Jagienka and that if it had not been for her kind heart, he would have perished. This thought was painful to him, for he felt he would never repay the kind girl with good for good; indeed, he would be for her the cause of nothing but trouble and cruel sorrow. He did say to himself, "I cannot tear myself in two," but deep inside him there was, as it were, a guilty conscience, which the Czech inflamed still more.

"I swore to my lady," Hlawa said, "on my honor as a nobleman that I would protect you—and I will, without reward. You owe your safety to her, lord, not to me."

Zbyszko did not answer; he only began to sigh deeply. The Czech was silent for a while, and then began to speak again:

"If you bid me hasten back to Bogdaniec, I will. Perhaps you would be glad to see the old lord, for God knows what will happen to you."

"And what does Father Wyszoniek say?" asked Zbyszko.

"Father Wyszoniek says that he will know by the new moon, but that is four days away!"

"Then you need not go to Bogdaniec! I shall either die before my uncle comes, or I shall get well."

"You might send a letter to Bogdaniec. Sanderus will write it out clearly. Then they will at least know what's happened to you and can give something for a Mass."

"Leave me in peace now, for I am weak. If I die, you will go back to Zgorzelice and tell them what happened—and then they will pay for a Mass. I'll be buried here or at Ciechanow."

"I hope at Ciechanow or at Przasnysz. In the forest only Kurps are buried, and the wolves howl over the graves. I heard from the servants that the duke is going to Ciechanow with his court in two days' time, and after that he is going back to Warsaw."

"Surely they will not leave me here alone," replied Zbyszko.

He had guessed right. The duchess went that same day to the duke requesting permission to stay at the lodge with Danusia, the young ladies-in-waiting and Father Wyszoniek, who advised against taking Zbyszko to Przasnysz too soon. Sieur de Lorche felt considerably better after two days, and was able to get up, but when he learned that the dames were staying, he stayed also, so as to be able to accompany them on the way back and, in case of an attack by "Saracens," to defend them from mishap. Where those "Saracens" were to come from—that the valiant Lorrainer did not consider. The Lithuanians were called thus in the far West—but no possible danger from them could threaten the daughter of Kiejstut, sister of Witold and cousin of the powerful Cracow king, Jagiello. But Sieur de Lorche had been long enough among the Teutonic Knights to suppose that nothing good was to be expected from the Lithuanians—despite all he had heard in Mazovia of the baptizing of Lithuania and the union of the two crowns in the person of one ruler. The Teutonic Knights had told him stories, and he had not yet entirely lost faith in their words.

Meanwhile an incident occurred that threw a shadow between the Knights and Duke Janusz, their host. Brothers Godfrey and Roger, who had been staying at Ciechanow, arrived the day before the departure of the court, and with them came a certain Sieur de Fourcy, who brought bad news for the Knights: namely, that the foreign visitors who were staying with the Teutonic constable at Lubawa—that is to say, Sieur de Fourcy himself, and also de Bergow and Maineger, both of whom belonged to families which had served the Order in the past—having heard the stories about Jurand of Spychow, were so unawed by them that they had determined to draw the famous warrior into the field and convince themselves whether he was in reality as dreadful as he was made out to be. The constable had, it is true, attempted to deter them, pointing to the state of peace which existed between the Order and the Mazovian dukedoms. At length, however, perhaps in hopes of ridding himself of his dangerous neighbor, he had not only decided to look through his fingers at their incursion but had actually allowed his soldiers to take part in it. The knights then sent Jurand a challenge, which he readily accepted on the condition that they dismiss their men, and meet him and two companions on the border between Prussia and Spychow. However, they had refused either to dismiss their soldiers or to withdraw from the territory of Spychow, so he fell upon them, slew their men, transfixed Maineger ruthlessly with his lance, and took de Bergow prisoner, throwing him into the Spychow dungeon. De Fourcy alone escaped, and after wandering for three days in the Mazovian forests and learning from some pitch-burners that there were brothers of the Order staying at Ciechanow, he made his way there with the intention of enlisting their support for a complaint to the duke's majesty and asking for the punishment of Jurand and an order for the liberation of de Bergow.

This story immediately disrupted the good relations between the duke and his guests, since not only the two brothers who had arrived but also Hugo von Danveld and Siegfried von Lowe began to insist that the duke for once do justice to the Order and rid the border of a plunderer by finally punishing him for all his misdeeds. Hugo von Danveld in particular, having old scores of his own to settle against Jurand, the memory of which tormented him with bitterness and shame, demanded vengeance almost threateningly.

"The complaint will go to the grand master," he said, "and if we do not obtain justice from your Serene Highness, he will be able to do it himself, even if all of Mazovia stands behind the robber."

Though mild by nature, the duke became angry.

"What kind of justice is this you demand? If Jurand had attacked you first, burnt your villages, driven off your cattle and horses and killed your people, I should certainly have summoned him to judgment and dealt out punishment. But it was your people who attacked him. Your constable let his soldiers join them—and what did Jurand do? He accepted your challenge, demanding only that your men should withdraw. How can I punish him for that or summon him to judgment? You asked for trouble from a terrible man of whom everyone is afraid, and you brought disaster on your own heads—so what do you want? Have I to order him not to defend himself when it pleases you to attack him?"

"It was not the Order that assailed him but only their guests, the foreign knights," answered Hugo.

"The Order is responsible for its guests, and there were soldiers of the Lubawa garrison with them."

"Was the constable to give up his guests to be slaughtered?"

The duke turned to Siegfried.

"Look what justice turns to in your mouths," he said. "Are your subterfuges not an insult to God?"

But the stern Siegfried replied:

"De Bergow must be freed from captivity, for men of his family were elders in the Order and did great deeds in the Crusades."

"And Maineger's death must be avenged," added Hugo von Danveld.

Hearing this, the duke passed his hands through his hair and, rising from his seat, started towards the Germans with an expression on his face which boded them ill. But he evidently remembered that they were his guests. He checked himself once again and laid his hand on Siegfried's shoulder.

"Listen, constable!" he said. "You wear the Cross on your cloak, so answer on that Cross as your conscience tells you. Was Jurand justified or was he not?"

"De Bergow must be freed from captivity," answered Siegfried von Lowe.

There followed a moment of silence, and then the duke said:

"God give me patience!"

Siegfried, however, went on in a voice as sharp as the stroke of a sword:

"The injury which has been done to us in the persons of our guests is merely one more occasion for complaint. As long as the Order has been an Order, never, either in Palestine or in Transylvania, or in still pagan Lithuania, has one ordinary man done us so much evil as that robber of Spychow. Your Serene Highness! We demand justice and punishment not for one injury but for a thousand; not for one battle but for fifty; not for blood shed once but for whole years of such misdeeds as should have brought down fire from heaven on that godless nest of malice and cruelty. Whose groans call from it to God for vengeance? Ours. Whose tears? Ours. In vain we have made complaints, in vain have we called for judgment. Never have we been given satisfaction!"

Duke Janusz nodded and replied:

"Hah! Many a time the Teutonic Knights have been guests at Spychow, and Jurand was not your enemy until the woman he loved perished by your rope. But how many times have you assailed him yourselves in the hope of getting rid of him, as you did now, because he challenged and defeated your knights? How many times have you set murderers on his track? How many times have you shot at him with crossbows in the forest? He has attacked you, true, for he lusted for vengeance; but have not you, or the knights who occupy your lands, attacked peaceful folk in Mazovia, carried off flocks and herds, burnt villages and murdered men, women, and children? And when I complained to the master, he answered me from Malbork: 'Ordinary border licence!' Leave me alone! It does not become you to complain, you who once seized me when I was unarmed, in time of peace, on my own soil. Had you not feared the wrath of the king at Cracow, maybe I would still be groaning in your dungeons. Thus you repaid me, who come from the family of your benefactors. Leave me alone, for it is not for you to speak of justice!"

The knights looked at one another impatiently, being annoyed and ashamed to hear the duke recalling the events at Zlotorya before Sieur de Fourcy. So Hugo von Danveld, to put an end to further talk on the subject, said:

"In the case of your Serene Highness there was a mistake, which we put right not from fear of the king at Cracow but for justice's sake. But our master cannot be made answerable for border licence, for in all the kingdoms of the world, restless spirits disregard the law on their borders."

"You say that yourself and call for judgment on Jurand! What do you want?"

"Justice and punishment."

The duke clenched his bony fists.

"God give me patience!" he repeated.

"Your Serene Highness should also remember," continued Danveld, "that our acts of licence injure only laymen and people who do not belong to the German race, whereas your men raise their hands against the Teutonic Order and thereby affront the Redeemer himself. What torments and punishments are enough for those who defy the Cross?"

"Listen!" said the duke. "Do not fight with God, for you will not deceive Him!"

And putting his hands on the knight's shoulders, he shook him violently, whereupon the knight became immediately disconcerted and continued on in a milder tone:

"If it is true that our guests attacked Jurand first and did not dismiss their men, I do not praise them for it; but did Jurand actually accept their challenge?"

He looked at Sieur de Fourcy, blinking slightly as if to give him to understand he should deny it, but he, being unable or unwilling to do so, answered:

"He wanted us to dismiss our men and meet him, the three of us alone."

"Are you sure?"

"On my honor! De Bergow and I agreed, but Maineger refused."

The duke interrupted. "Constable of Ortelsburg! You know better than anybody that Jurand would not decline the challenge." Here he turned to them all: "I give permission to anyone of you to challenge him to combat on foot or on horseback. If Jurand is slain or taken, de Bergow will go free without ransom. Ask me for nothing more, for you will not get it."

After these words, deep silence fell.

Hugo von Danveld and Siegfried von Lowe, Brother Roger and Brother Godfrey, as valiant as they were, all knew the terrible Lord of Spychow too well to venture a life-and-death combat with him. A foreigner, coming from afar, like de Lorche or de Fourcy, might do it, but de Lorche was not present during this talk, and Sieur de Fourcy was still too full of fear.

"I saw him once," he muttered amid the silence, "and I do not want to see him again."

But Siegfried von Lowe said:

"Members of the Order are forbidden to meet in single combat without the express permission of the master and the grand marshal. Anyway, we are not asking for permission to engage in combat. We only demand that de Bergow should be freed from captivity and Jurand condemned to the block."

"It is not you who fix the laws on this earth."

"Hitherto we have borne with this troublesome neighbor in patience. But our master will be able to deal out justice."

"Your master and you have nothing to do with Mazovia!"

"Behind the master stands Germany and the Roman Emperor."

"And behind me, the King of Poland, lord of more land and nations."

"Does your Serene Highness want war with the Order?"

"If I wanted war, I would not wait for you in Mazovia but would march against you. But do not threaten me, for I am not afraid."

"What am I to tell the master?"

"Your master did not ask anything. Tell him what you like."

"Then we will deal out punishment and vengeance ourselves."

The duke stretched out his arm and began to wag his finger threateningly in the knight's face.

"Beware!" he said in a voice choked with anger. "Beware! I permit you to challenge Jurand, but if you invade my country with the Order's army, I will strike, and you will stay here as a prisoner and not as a guest!"

Evidently his patience was exhausted, for he flung his cap violently on the table and went out of the room, slamming the door. The knights paled with rage, while Sieur de Fourcy looked at them in bewilderment.

"So what will happen?" Brother Roger asked.

But Hugo von Danveld almost leapt on Sieur de Fourcy with his fists.

"Why did you say that you attacked Jurand first?"

"Because it was true!"

"You ought to have lied."

"I came here to fight, not to lie."

"You fought well indeed, I must say!"

"And did not you flee before Jurand to Ortelsburg?"

"*Pax!*" said von Lowe. "This knight is a guest of the Order."

"It doesn't matter what he said," put in Brother Godfrey. "Without a trial you could not punish Jurand, while at a trial the whole affair would come to light."

"So what will happen?" asked Brother Roger again.

A moment of silence followed, and then the stern and stubborn Siegfried von Lowe spoke:

"Once and for all we must be done with this bloody dog! De Bergow must be freed from his bonds. I will collect the garrisons from Ortelsburg, Insburk, and Lubawa; I will summon the Chelmno gentry and strike at Jurand. It is time to be done with him!"

But the cunning Danveld, who knew how to look at every proposition from both sides, clasped his hands behind his head, frowned and, after thinking a moment, said:

"Without the master's permission, we cannot do anything."

"If we succeed, the master will praise us!" cried out Brother Godfrey.

"And if we don't succeed? If the duke moves his lancers and strikes at us?"

"There is peace between him and the Order—he will not attack!"

"Bah! There is peace, but we shall be the first to break it. Our garrisons will not be enough against the Mazovians."

"Then the master will support us, and there will be war."

Danveld frowned again and sank in thought.

"No, no!" he said after a while. "If we succeed, the master's heart will be glad. Envoys will go to the duke, there will be solemn agreements, and we shall get off unpunished. But in case of disaster, the Order will not support us and will not declare war on the duke. Another kind of grand master would be needed for that. . . . Behind the duke stands the King of Poland, and the master will not quarrel with him."

"Yet we took the Land of Dobrzyn—which shows we were not afraid of Cracow."

"For there were pretexts. . . . The Opolian. . . . We took it by way of pledge, and even so. . . ."

Here he looked around and went on in a lower tone:

"I heard from Malbork that if they were to threaten us with war, we would give back the pledge as soon as they repaid us the money."

"Ah!" said Brother Roger, "if we had Markwart Salzbach here with us, or Schomberg, who strangled Witold's brats, they would find a way to deal with Jurand. Who was Witold? Jagiello's deputy! A grand duke! Yet nothing happened to Schomberg. He strangled Witold's children, and nothing happened to him! . . . In truth, we lack men who can find a way to deal with everything."

Hugo von Danveld leaned his elbows on the table, rested his head in his hands, and for a long time remained engrossed in thought. Suddenly his eyes brightened, he wiped his moist, thick lips with the back of his hand, and said:

"Blessed be the moment, pious brother, in which you mentioned the name of the valiant Brother Schomberg!"

"Why so? Have you thought of something?" asked Siegfried von Lowe.

"Speak quickly!" called Brothers Roger and Godfrey.

"Listen," said Hugo. "Jurand has here a daughter, his only child, whom he loves as the apple of his eye."

"That's right! We know her. Duchess Anna Danuta loves her too."

"Yes. Now listen. If you were to kidnap the girl, Jurand would give up for her not only Bergow but all his prisoners and in addition surrender himself and Spychow!"

"By the blood that Saint Boniface shed at Dochum!" cried out Brother Godfrey. "It would be as you say!"

After that they were silent, as if daunted by the boldness and difficulties of the enterprise. Only after a while did Brother Roger turn to Siegfried von Lowe:

"Your intelligence and experience," he said, "are equal to your courage. What then do you think of this?"

"I think the matter deserves consideration."

"For," went on Roger, "the girl is the duchess's lady-in-waiting.

Indeed she is more, almost her favorite daughter. Think, pious brothers, what an outcry will be raised."

Hugo von Danveld began to laugh:

"You said yourself that Schomberg poisoned or strangled Witold's brats, and what happened to him in consequence? They will raise an outcry over anything! But if we send Jurand in chains to the master, we are more likely to be rewarded than punished."

"There is an opportunity for an attack," said von Lowe. "The duke is going away, and Anna Danuta will be left here with only the damsels of the court. Yet a raid on the ducal court in time of peace would not be prudent. The ducal court is not Spychow. The same thing would happen that happened at Zlotorya. There would again be complaints to all the kingdoms and to the pope against the violent deeds of the Order. Again the accursed Jagiello would utter his threats. While the master—you know him—will gladly take what can be taken, but war with Jagiello he does not want. . . . Yes, there will be commotion in all the lands of Mazovia and Poland!"

"And meanwhile Jurand's bones will be bleaching at the end of a rope," replied Brother Hugo. "Anyway, who said she should be kidnapped here from the court, from the side of the duchess?"

"Well, certainly not from Ciechanow, where there are three hundred bowmen in addition to the gentry."

"No. But what if Jurand were to fall sick and send men to bring home his daughter? In that case the duchess will not forbid her to go, and if the girl is lost on the way, who will be able to accuse you or me of kidnapping her?"

"Go ahead then!" replied von Lowe impatiently. "Have Jurand fall sick and send for the girl!"

Hugo smiled triumphantly.

"I have among my people," he replied, "a goldsmith who was expelled from Malbork for thievery and who now resides at Ortelsburg. He is able to make every kind of seal. I also have men who, though our subjects, are of Mazovian origin. Do you still not understand me? . . ."

"I understand!" called out Brother Godfrey excitedly.

Brother Roger raised his hands aloft.

"God bless you, pious brother," he said. "Neither Markwart Salzbach nor Schomberg would have found a better way." Then he closed his eyes. "I see Jurand standing with a rope around his neck at the Danzig gate at Malbork, and our soldiers are kicking him. . . ."

"And the girl will be made a servant of the Order," added Hugo.

Siegfried von Lowe glanced severely at Danveld, but the latter wiped his lips again with the back of his hand, and said: "And now to Ortelsburg as quickly as we can!"

CHAPTER XXIII

HOWEVER, before setting out for Ortelsburg, the four brethren and de Fourcy came to take leave of the duke and duchess. It was not too friendly a leave-taking, yet the duke, not wishing to break an old Polish custom and let his guests go empty-handed, presented each of the brothers with a beautiful marten-skin rug and a mark of silver. They received these gifts, assuring him at the same time that, being monks, vowed to poverty, they would not keep the money for themselves but would distribute it among the poor, whom they would ask to pray for the health, fame, and future salvation of the duke. The Mazovians smiled covertly at these assertions, for they well knew the avarice of the Order and still better the mendacity of the Teutonic Knights. It was a common saying in Mazovia that "a skunk stinks and a Teutonic Knight lies." So the duke merely dismissed their thanks with a wave of the hand and, after their departure, commented that the prayers of the Knights would more likely get him out of heaven than into it.

But before that, when they were taking leave of the duchess, as Siegfried von Lowe was kissing her hand, Hugo von Danveld approached Danusia and began to stroke her head, saying:

"We are bidden to repay good for evil and to love our enemies, so a sister of the Order will come here and bring you, young lady, the Hercynian healing balsam."

"How am I to thank you, lord?" answered Danusia.

"Be a friend of the Order and its members."

This talk, nor the girl's beauty, did not escape the notice of de

Fourcy, and when the knights were on the road to Ortelsburg, he asked:

"Who was that beautiful damsel with whom you were talking just before our departure?"

"Jurand's daughter," answered Danveld.

Sieur de Fourcy was surprised.

"The one you have to grab?"

"The same. And when I get her, Jurand will be ours."

"It seems that not everything is bad that comes from Jurand. It would be worth while to be guardian of such a prisoner."

"You think it would be easier to fight with her than with Jurand?"

"You mean, do I think the same as you? The father is an enemy of the Order, but to the daughter you spoke honeyed words and promised her balsam, as well."

Hugo von Danveld obviously felt the need to justify himself.

"I promised her the balsam for the young knight who was hurt by the aurochs and to whom, as you know, she is betrothed. If they make an outcry after we have caught the girl, we will say that not only did we mean her no harm but we sent her medicaments in Christian charity."

"Good," said von Lowe. "But you must send someone you can trust."

"I will send a pious woman who is completely devoted to the Order. I will tell her to watch and listen. When our men arrive, supposedly from Jurand, they will find the ground prepared."

"Such men will be hard to find."

"No. The common folk where we are speak the same language. There are also men in the town, nay, even among the garrison, who have left Mazovia in flight from the law—murderers and thieves, true, but knowing no fear and ready for anything. To them I will promise, if they succeed, great rewards, and if they don't succeed—a rope."

"And suppose they betray us?"

"They won't betray us, for in Mazovia every one of them deserves being put to the rack, and over everyone hangs a sentence. It is only necessary to give them clean garments for them to be taken for genuine retainers of Jurand, and the main thing—a letter with Jurand's seal."

"Everything must be foreseen," said Brother Roger. "Jurand, after this recent fight, may perhaps want to see the duke to complain against us and justify himself. When he is at Ciechanow, he will go to the hunting-lodge to see his daughter. In that case it may happen that our people, having come for Jurand's daughter, may find Jurand himself."

"The men I shall choose are the most cunning of rogues. They will know that if they come across Jurand, they are destined to swing at the end of a rope. Their lives will depend upon not meeting him."

"Yet they may be caught."

"In that case we will deny both them and the letter. Who will be able to prove that it was we who sent them? And if the girl is not carried away, there will be no kidnapping and hence no outcry; and if a few Mazovian gallows-birds are quartered, no harm will be done to the Order by that."

But Brother Godfrey, the youngest of the monks, said:

"I don't understand this policy of yours, nor this fear should it come out that the girl was kidnapped by our Order. Once we have her in our hands, we shall have to send someone to Jurand to tell him: 'Your daughter is with us. If you want her to regain her freedom, give up, in exchange, de Bergow and yourself.' How else will this be done? And then it will be known that it was we who had the girl kidnapped."

"True!" said Sieur de Fourcy, the whole affair being not much to his taste. "Why hide what must come out?"

Hugo von Danveld began to laugh and, turning to Brother Godfrey, asked:

"How long have you worn the white cloak?"

"It will be six years on the First Sunday after Trinity."

"When you have worn it six more, you will understand the affairs of the Order better. Jurand knows us better than you. He will be told: 'Your daughter is being looked after by Brother Schomberg, and if you let out a word—remember Witold's children.'"

"And afterwards?"

"Afterwards de Bergow will be free, and the Order will also be free of Jurand."

"Excellent!" called out Brother Roger. "Everything is so carefully thought out that God ought to bless our undertaking."

"God blesses all actions whose purpose is the good of the Order," said the gloomy Siegfried von Lowe.

They rode on in silence, and before them, two or three bowshots away, went their outriders to clear the way, which had been blocked by a heavy snowfall during the night. On the trees lay a thick covering of frost. The day was cloudy but warm, so that the horses steamed. From the forests flocks of crows flew towards human settlements, filling the air with their hoarse cawing.

Sieur de Fourcy rode a little behind the knights, sunk in deep thought. For several years he had been the guest of the Order. He had taken part in expeditions to Samogitia, where he distinguished himself by his courage, and had been entertained everywhere as only Teutonic Knights knew how to entertain knights from distant parts. He had become strongly attached to them and, having no fortune of his own, was intending to enter their ranks. Meanwhile he sometimes stayed at Malbork and sometimes visited other commanderies in search of amusement and adventure. Having recently arrived at Lubawa with the rich de Bergow, and having heard of Jurand, he began to burn with desire to measure himself with a man who inspired such general dread. The arrival of Maineger, who had come off victorious from every combat in which he had been engaged, hastened the undertaking. The commander at Lubawa furnished the three knights with men, but told them so much, not only of Jurand's cruelty but also of his deceits and his treachery, that when Jurand demanded that they dismiss their soldiers, they were unwilling to agree, fearing that when they had done so, he would surround and butcher them or cast them into the subterranean cells of Spychow. And Jurand, supposing that they cared for plunder rather than for knightly combat, fell upon them as soon as they appeared, defeating them completely. De Fourcy saw de Bergow overthrown, together with his horse; he saw Maineger with a fragment of spear in his belly, and his men begging in vain for mercy. He himself with difficulty succeeded in fighting his way through. For several days he wandered along the roads and in the forests, and he would have died of hunger or become the prey of some wild beast had he not come upon Ciechanow, where he found Brothers Godfrey and Roger. The whole expedition left him with a feeling of humiliation, shame, hate, lust for vengeance, and sorrow for de Bergow, who was his close friend. Accordingly, he whole-heartedly supported the complaints of the Teutonic Knights when they demanded the punishment of Jurand and the liberation of his unfortunate companion, and when that complaint remained fruit-less he was at first ready to agree to any and every means that would lead to vengeance. Now, however, he began suddenly to feel scru-ples. When listening to the talk of the monks, and in particular to what was said by Hugo von Danveld, he was repeatedly unable to refrain from astonishment. In the course of several years he had come to know the Teutonic Knights from close quarters and was well aware that they were not what they were represented to be in Germany and the Western world. Still, at Malbork he had become acquainted with several stern and upright knights, who themselves frequently complained of the demoralization of the brethren and their licence and lack of discipline. De Fourcy felt that they were right, but being himself licentious and undisciplined, he did not take those faults too seriously in others, particularly as all the knight-monks made up for them by their courage. He had seen them at Wilno, clashing breast to breast with the Polish knights, and at the storming of castles, defended with superhuman tenacity by garrisons of Polish auxiliaries; he had seen them struck down by the blows of axes or swords in general battles or in single combats. They were relentless and cruel to Lithuania, but at the same time they were like lions—and sunned themselves in glory. Now, how-ever it seemed to Sieur de Fourcy that Hugo von Danveld sug-gested such things and such methods as ought to cause every true knight to shudder—yet the other brethren not only did not rise up against him in wrath but actually assented to his every word. So astonishment possessed him more and more, and at last he was consumed with doubt as to whether it befitted him to take part in such an enterprise.

If it had only been a question of kidnapping the girl and then of exchanging her for de Bergow, perhaps he would have agreed to it, although he was taken by Danusia's charm. If it had fallen to him to be her jailer, he would likewise have had nothing against it, and even would not have been certain whether she would pass out of his hands in the same state in which she came into them. But the knights were evidently planning something more than this. They intended through her to get hold of de Bergow and of Jurand himself by promising him that they would let her go if he would give himself up for her. Then they would murder him, and with him, to cover up their deceit and crime, doubtless the girl also. Indeed, they were already threatening her with the fate of Witold's children should Jurand dare complain. "They don't intend to keep a single promise, but to deceive and rid themselves of both," said de Fourcy to himself; "and yet they wear the Cross and ought to regard their honor even more than other knights." And his soul revolted ever more within him at the thought of such flagrant lack of honor. Determining to find out how far his suspicions were justified, he rode up to Danveld again and asked him:

"And if Jurand gives himself up to you, will you let the girl go?"

"If we were to let her go, the whole world would soon know that it was we who had grabbed both of them," replied Danveld.

"So what will you do with her?"

Danveld leaned towards the speaker and smiled, exposing his rotten teeth from behind his thick lips.

"What are you asking about? What we shall do with her before, or what we shall do after?"

Knowing already what he wanted to know, de Fourcy kept silent. For a time he seemed to be still struggling with himself; but then he raised himself slightly in his stirrups and said so loud that all the four brethren heard him:

"The pious brother Ulrich von Jungingen, who is a model and an ornament of chivalry, once said to me: 'Among the old Knights at Malbork you will still find some who are worthy of the Cross, but those who are posted in the border commanderies bring only shame upon the Order.'"

"We are all sinners, but we serve our Lord," replied Hugo.

"Where is your knightly honor? It is not by shameful deeds that the Lord is served—unless perhaps it is not the Redeemer whom you serve. Who is your Lord? Know this: I will not only not go along with your undertaking, but I will not permit you to do so."

"What will you not permit?"

"Deceit, treachery, and shame."

"And how can you prevent us? In the battle with Jurand you lost your troops and your wagons. You have to live by favor of the Order, and you will die of hunger if we do not throw you a piece of bread. Moreover, you are one, and we are four. How will you not permit us?"

"How will I not permit you?" repeated de Fourcy. "I may return to the court and warn the duke, or I may proclaim your designs to the whole world."

The brethren looked at one another, and their faces changed in a flash. Hugo von Danveld in particular looked long and questioningly into the eyes of Siegfried von Lowe; then he turned again to Sieur de Fourcy:

"Your forebears served with the Order, and you want to enter it, but we do not receive traitors."

"And I do not want to serve with traitors."

"Bah! You will not carry out your threat. Know that the Order is able to punish not only its members."

Enraged by these words, de Fourcy drew his sword, grasped the blade in his left hand, laid his right hand on the hilt, and said:

"On this symbol, shaped like a cross, on the head of Saint Dionysius, my patron, and on my knightly honor, I will warn the Duke of Mazovia and the grand master!"

Hugo von Danveld again looked questioningly at Siegfried von Lowe, who half-closed his eyelids, as if to signify that he agreed to something.

Then Danveld called out in a strangely dull and altered voice:

"Saint Dionysius may have carried his severed head under his arm, but once your head has fallen—"

"Are you threatening me?" interrupted de Fourcy.

"No, I'm killing you!" answered Danveld.

And he thrust his knife into de Fourcy's side with such force that the blade became buried in his body up to the hilt. De Fourcy uttered a dreadful cry and tried to grasp with his right hand the sword he was holding in his left, but it slipped to the ground, and at the same time the remaining three brethren began to stab him unmercifully in the neck, the back, and the stomach, until he fell from his horse.

Silence followed. De Fourcy, bleeding frightfully from a dozen wounds, quivered on the snow and clutched it with convulsively twisted fingers. From the leaden sky came only the cawing of crows, flying from the gloomy forests to the dwelling-places of man. A hasty interchange began between the murderers.

"The men saw nothing?" asked Danveld, panting.

"Nothing," replied von Lowe. "The outriders are in front and out of sight."

"Listen. There will be cause for fresh complaint. I will proclaim that Mazovian knights fell upon us and slew our comrade. I will raise such an outcry that it will be heard at Malbork. I'll say the duke sets murderers even on his guests. Listen! We must say that Janusz not only refused to hear our complaints against Jurand, but he had the complainant murdered."

Meanwhile de Fourcy turned in a last convulsion on his back and lay motionless, with a bloody foam on his lips and fear in his already glazed, wide-open eyes. Brother Roger looked at him and said:

"Observe, pious brothers, how God punishes the mere intention of treachery."

"What we have done, we have done for the good of the Order," replied Godfrey. "Glory be to those—"

But he broke off, for at that very moment a rider appeared at the turn of the snowy road behind them, galloping as hard as his horse could go. Seeing him, Hugo von Danveld called out quickly:

"Whoever this man is, he must die."

But von Lowe, who, although the eldest of the brethren, had extraordinarily keen sight, said:

"I recognize him. It's the squire who killed the aurochs with his axe. Yes—it is he!"

"Hide your knives so as not to alert him," said Danveld. "I will strike first again, and you after me."

Meanwhile the Czech rode up and stopped his horse eight or ten feet away in the snow. He saw a corpse in a pool of blood and a horse without a rider, and amazement was reflected in his face, but only for the twinkling of an eye. After a moment he turned to the brethren as if he had seen nothing.

"Greetings, valiant knights!" he said.

"We recognized you," answered Danveld, slowly approaching him. "Have you any message for us?"

"I am sent by Sir Zbyszko of Bogdaniec, whose lance I carry, since he could not come himself, having been hurt by an aurochs while hunting."

"What does your lord want of us?"

"Because you unjustifiably accused Jurand of Spychow, aspersing his reputation for knightly honor, my lord bade me tell you that you have not acted like true knights but have barked like dogs; and if any of you take offence at these words, he challenges him to combat, on foot or on horse, to the death, and will appear whenever you bid him as soon as his present weakness shall leave him by the grace and mercy of God."

"Tell your lord that Knights of the Order bear insults patiently in the name of the Redeemer and may not engage in single combat without special permission of the master or the grand marshal, for which, however, we will write to Malbork."

The Czech again looked at the corpse of Sieur de Fourcy, for it was to him in the first place that he had been sent. Zbyszko, of course, knew that members of a monastic Order may not fight duels, but he had heard that there was a lay knight among them, and wished to challenge him in particular, thinking that thus he would win the favor of Jurand and befriend him. Meanwhile that knight was lying there butchered like an ox amid the four Teutonic Knights.

The Czech did not understand, it is true, what had happened, but because he had been accustomed to all kinds of danger since he was a child, he perceived danger here. He was also surprised that Danveld, while speaking to him, came nearer and nearer, and the others began to move to the side, as if imperceptibly to surround him. For these reasons he began to be on his guard, particularly since he had no weapon, having been unable to catch one up in his haste.

Danveld, meanwhile, got close to him and continued:

"I promised your lord a healing balsam, and he repays me with evil. That is usual, however, among the Poles. . . . But since he is grievously hurt, and may soon stand before God, tell him—"

Here he put his left hand on the Czech's arm.

"Tell him that—this is my answer!"

In the same moment he flashed his knife at the squire's throat, but before he could thrust, the Czech, who had been following his movements, seized his right hand in his iron hands, bent and twisted it till the joints and bones cracked—and only when he heard a horrid scream of pain did he put spurs to his horse and shoot off like an arrow before the others could block his way.

Brothers Godfrey and Roger began to pursue him, but they soon came back, alarmed by a dreadful cry from Danveld. Von Lowe held his shoulders, but he, pale and faint, cried out so loud that the outriders, accompanying the wagons some distance ahead, reined in their horses.

"What is the matter with you?" asked the brothers.

But von Lowe ordered them to ride hard and bring a wagon, for Danveld obviously could not maintain himself in the saddle; presently a cold sweat covered his brow, and he swooned.

When the wagon had been brought, they laid him on straw and moved off towards the border. Von Lowe urged them on, for he understood that after what had happened no time must be lost, even in attending to Danveld. Seated beside him in the wagon, he wiped Danveld's face from time to time with snow but could not bring him back to consciousness.

Not until they were near the border did Danveld open his eyes. He looked about him as if in surprise.

"How are you?" asked Lowe.

"I do not feel pain, but neither do I feel my hand," replied Danveld.

"It has already stiffened; therefore, the pain has passed. In a warm room the pain will come back. Meanwhile thank God for this period of relief."

Roger and Godfrey immediately approached the wagon.

"A misfortune has happened," said the former. "What shall we do now?"

"We will say," replied Danveld in a weak voice, "that the squire murdered de Fourcy."

"A fresh crime of theirs, and the culprit is known!" added Roger.

CHAPTER XXIV

MEANWHILE the Czech rode at full gallop straight to the hunting-lodge, where he found the duke and told him first what had happened. Fortunately there were courtiers who had seen that the squire had gone without arms. One of them had even shouted to him on the way, half in jest, to take some iron weapon, for otherwise the Germans would injure him; but he, fearing that the knights might in the meantime cross the border, had leapt on his horse just as he stood, with only his sheepskin coat, and ridden after them. This evidence dispelled all the duke's doubts as to who might have been the murderer of de Fourcy, yet it filled him with such great turmoil and anger that in the first moment he wanted to pursue the Teutonic Knights and send them in chains to the grand master for punishment. Presently, however, he recognized that he would be unable to overtake them before they crossed the border, so he said:

"I will send a letter to the master so that he may know what they are doing here. All is not well with the Order. Their obedience used to be strict, but now every commander does what he will. God permits, but punishment will follow."

Then he took thought, and after a while he spoke again to his courtiers:

"One thing I cannot understand: why they slew their guest. If it had not been that this lad had ridden without arms, I should certainly have suspected him."

"Nay!" said Father Wyszoniek, "why should the lad have killed him when he had never seen him before? Furthermore, even if he had had a weapon, how could he alone have attacked five knights who had their armed troop behind them?"

"True," said the duke. "Their guest must have opposed them in something, or maybe he did not want to lie as they required, for I saw here how they winked at him to say that Jurand was the first to attack."

And Mrokota of Mocarzewo said:

"The lad is a sturdy fellow if he crushed that dog Danveld's hand."

"He says he heard the German's bones crack," replied the duke; "and considering how he displayed himself in the forest, that may very well be. One can see that both servant and master are fierce fellows. If it had not been for Zbyszko, the aurochs would have attacked the horses. And the Lorrainer also contributed much to the safety of the duchess."

"Certainly Zbyszko is a fierce fellow," repeated Father Wyszoniek. "Why, even now, though he is barely breathing, he has taken Jurand's part and sent a challenge to the knights. . . . This is a son-in-law for Jurand!"

"Jurand spoke differently at Cracow, but now I think he will not oppose the marriage," said the duke.

"The Lord Jesus will bring it about," exclaimed the duchess, who had just come in and heard the end of the conversation. "Jurand cannot not oppose it, if only God give Zbyszko back his health. But there must be some reward from us too."

"The best reward for him will be Danusia. I also think he will get her, for if women set their minds on something, even a Jurand will not be able to do anything against them."

"Did I not set my mind on what was just?" asked the duchess. "I wouldn't say this if Zbyszko were fickle, but I suppose there is no more faithful knight in the world. The girl is like that too. She doesn't leave his side now, and strokes his face, while he laughs to her through his pain. Why, sometimes tears come to my eyes! I speak the truth! It is worthwhile helping such love, for even the Virgin Mary is glad to look at human happiness."

"If it be God's will," said the duke, "then happiness will come to them. But he nearly lost his head because of that girl, and now the aurochs has injured him."

"Don't say 'because of that girl'!" exclaimed the duchess quickly, "for no one else but Danusia saved him at Cracow."

"True. But were it not for her, he would not have attacked Lichtenstein in order to pluck the feathers from his head, and he would not have risked his neck so readily for de Lorche. As for his reward, I have said already that they both deserve one, and at Ciechanow I will think of one for them."

"Zbyszko would be pleased by nothing so much as a knight's belt and golden spurs."

The duke smile good-naturedly at that and replied:

"Then let the girl bring them to him, and when the sickness leaves him, I will make sure that everything is done according to the usual custom. Let her bring them to him soon, for sudden joy is best!"

The duchess embraced her lord in front of the courtiers and then kissed his hands several times, while he smiled continually, and at last said:

"You see! A good idea came into your head! The Holy Ghost has given women at least a little sense. Call the girl now."

"Danusia! Danusia!" called the duchess.

And presently Danusia appeared in the doorway of a side room, red-eyed through lack of sleep, with a double-pot full of steaming kasha in her hand, which Father Wyszoniek used as a poultice on Zbyszko's crushed bones, and which an old lady-in-waiting had just given to her.

"Come to me, little orphan!" said Duke Janusz. "Put down the pot and come here."

And when she approached him with a certain shyness, for "the lord" always roused a certain fear in her, he drew her kindly to him and began to stroke her face, saying:

"Well, my child, trouble has come to you, has it not?"

"Yes, indeed!" replied Danusia.

And, with sorrow in her heart and tears ready to flow, she began to weep, but quietly, so as not to offend the duke.

"Why are you weeping?" he asked her.

"Because Zbyszko is sick," she replied, pressing her little fists into her eyes.

"Never fear, he will be all right. That's true, isn't it, Father Wyszoniek?"

"Sure! With God's help he's nearer to his wedding than his funeral," replied the good Father Wyszoniek.

"Wait!" said the duke. "I will give you a medicine for him which will give him relief or perhaps completely cure him."

"Have the Teutonic Knights sent the balsam?" exclaimed Danusia quickly, taking her hands from her eyes.

"Better smear a dog with what the Teutonic Knights send than a knight whom you love. I will give you something else."

Then he turned to his courtiers and called:

"Someone go for spurs and a belt!"

And presently, when they had been brought, he said to Danusia:

"Take these to Zbyszko, and tell him that from this moment he is belted. If he dies, he will stand before God as a *miles cinctus*, and if he lives, we will complete the ceremony at Ciechanow or at Warsaw."

Danusia first embraced the lord's knees, and then seized the emblems of knighthood in one hand and the double-pot in the other, and ran to the room where Zbyszko was lying. The duchess followed, not wishing to lose sight of their joy.

Zbyszko was gravely sick, but when he saw Danusia he turned his pale face to her:

"The Czech, my little berry, has he come back?"

"Never mind the Czech!" replied the girl. "I'm bringing you better news. The duke has dubbed you knight, and see what he has sent you!"

She laid the belt and golden spurs by his side. Zbyszko's pale cheeks flamed with joy and amazement; he looked at Danusia and then at the emblems, closed his eyes and began to repeat:

"How could he dub me knight?"

When the duchess came in at that moment, he raised himself a little on his arm, and began to thank her and beg the gracious lady's pardon that he could not fall at her feet, for he had guessed at once that it was through her intervention that this happiness had come to him. But she bade him keep quiet, and with her own hands helped Danusia to place his head again on the pillow. Meanwhile the duke arrived, and after him Father Wyszoniek, Mrokota, and some other courtiers. Duke Janusz motioned to Zbyszko to remain still, and then, sitting down by his bedside, spoke to him as follows:

"You know, it's not surprising that valiant and honorable deeds should be requited, for if virtue had to remain without reward, then human injustice would go through the world without punishment. Therefore, because you risked your life and defended us from grave sorrow at the loss of your health, we bid you gird yourself with this knight's belt, and walk in honor and glory from now on."

"Worshipful lord," replied Zbyszko, "I don't envy anyone now."

But he could say no more, because of his emotion and because the duchess laid her hands on his lips, since Father Wyszoniek did not allow him to talk. The duke, however, continued:

"I think you know the duties of a knight, and you will wear these ornaments worthily. You have to serve our Redeemer as is due, and war against the powers of hell. You are to be faithful to the Lord's anointed on earth, avoid unjust wars and defend innocence in oppression, to which may God and His Sacred Passion aid you!"

"Amen!" said Father Wyszoniek.

The duke rose, took leave of Zbyszko, and as he was departing added:

"And when you recover, ride straight to Ciechanow, where I will summon Jurand to meet you."

CHAPTER XXV

THREE days later the woman with the promised Hercynian balsam arrived, and with her came the captain of archers from Ortelsburg, bearing a letter signed by the brethren and sealed with Danveld's seal, in which the Teutonic Knights took heaven and earth to witness of the injuries they had received in Mazovia, and under threat of divine vengeance called for punishment for the murder of their "beloved companion and guest." Danveld had dictated the letter and added a complaint on his own account, demanding, in words at the same time humble and threatening, payment for his serious injury and a sentence of death on the Czech. The duke tore up the letter before the eyes of the captain, threw it at his feet and said:

"The master sent these Teutonic dogs here to win me to his side, but they have only roused my anger. Tell them from me that they themselves killed their guest, and they wanted to kill the Czech. I will write to the master about it and will add that he should choose better envoys if he wants me to be neutral in case of war with the King of Cracow."

"Worshipful lord," replied the captain, "am I to take back such an answer to the powerful and pious brethren?"

"If it is not enough for you, tell them that I regard them as curs, not as true knights."

With that the audience ended. The captain departed, for the duke also departed the same day for Ciechanow. The "sister" remained with the balsam, which the mistrustful Father Wyszoniek was unwilling to use, particularly as the sick man had slept well during the night and had awakened in the morning without a fever, though still very weak. The sister, after the duke's departure, immediately sent back one of her attendants, ostensibly for a new medicine, "basilisk's eggs," which, she asserted, had the power to restore strength even to the dying. She herself went about the house humbly, without the use of one arm, wearing a dress, lay, it is true, but resembling a nun's, with a rosary and a small pilgrim's bowl at her belt. She spoke Polish well and questioned the servants very anxiously about both Zbyszko and Danusia, to whom she gave a rose of Jericho at the first opportunity. The next day, while Zbyszko was asleep and Danusia was sitting in the dining-hall, she sat down next to her.

"God bless you, young lady!" she said. "Last night after prayers I dreamt that two knights came to you through falling snow, but one went first and wrapped you in a white cloak, while the second said, 'I see only snow; she is not here,' and turned back."

Danusia, who had been feeling sleepy, immediately opened her blue eyes with curiosity.

"What does it mean?" she asked.

"It means that the one who loves you the most will get you."

"That is Zbyszko!" replied the girl.

"I do not know, for I did not see his face. I saw only his white cloak, and then I woke up at once, since the Lord Jesus sends me pain in my legs every night and has taken away the use of my arm."

"So your balsam has been of no help to you?"

"Even the balsam does not help me, young lady, because of my grave sin. If you would like to know what sin, I will tell you."

Danusia bent her head to signify that she wished to know, so the sister went on:

"There are in the Order servants, women, who although they take no vows and may even be married, are yet obliged to fulfill duties to the Order, according to the commands of the brethren. And if such a favor and honor befalls anyone, she receives a pious kiss from a brother-knight as a sign that henceforth she has to serve the Order in deed and in speech. Ah, young lady, this great favor was to befall me, but I, in my sinful obstinacy, instead of receiving it gratefully, committed a grievous sin and drew down punishment on myself."

"What did you do?"

"Brother Danveld came to me and gave me a monkly kiss, but I, thinking that he did it out of licence, raised my godless hand against him. . . ."

She began to beat her breast and repeated several times: "God be merciful to me a sinner!"

"And what happened?" asked Danusia.

"The use of my hand was taken from me at once, and from that moment I have been crippled. I was young and foolish then; I did not know, and yet punishment fell on me. For even if it seems to a woman that a brother of the Order wants to do evil, she should leave judgment to God and offer no opposition herself, since whoever opposes the Order or a brother of the Cross will know the wrath of God."

Danusia heard these words with distress and apprehension. The sister sighed and continued to tell more of her troubles.

"I am not old, even today," she said. "I am barely thirty. But God, together with my arm, took from me my youth and beauty."

"If it were not for the arm," replied Danusia, "you would not need to complain. . . ."

Silence followed. Suddenly the sister, as if remembering something, said:

"I dreamt that a knight wrapped you in a white cloak on the snow. Maybe it was a Teutonic Knight! They also wear white cloaks."

"I don't want either Teutonic Knights or their cloaks," replied the girl.

Further talk was interrupted by Father Wyszoniek, who came into the room, nodded to Danusia, and said:

"Praise God and go to Zbyszko! He has awoke and wants to eat. He is considerably better."

So it was in fact. Zbyszko's condition had improved, and Father Wyszoniek was now almost certain that he would get well. But a sudden and unexpected event threw all calculations and hopes into confusion. Messengers from Jurand arrived with a letter to the duchess, containing nothing but horrible news. At Spychow a part of Jurand's fortalice had been burnt, and he himself had been crushed by a burning beam while fighting the fire. Father Caleb, who had written the letter in his name, reported that Jurand might indeed still get well, but that sparks and coals had so burned his one remaining eye that but little sight was left in it, and he was threatened with certain blindness.

For this reason Jurand summoned his daughter to come in haste to Spychow. He wanted to see her once again before darkness overwhelmed him. He said also that henceforth she was to stay with him, for if even blindmen who go about begging for bread have someone to lead them by the hand and show them the way, why should he be deprived of a similar consolation and die among strangers? There were also humble thanks for the duchess, who had brought up the girl as if she had been her own daughter. In conclusion, Jurand promised that, though blind, he would come once more to Warsaw to fall at the lady's feet and beg her favor for Danusia in the future.

When Father Wyszoniek had read her this letter, the duchess became nearly speechless. She had hoped that when Jurand, accustomed to visit his daughter five or six times a year, came for the approaching Christmas feast, her own influence and that of Duke Janusz would have reconciled him with Zbyszko and won his assent to the marriage in the near future. But this letter not only upset her designs, it also deprived her of Danusia, whom she loved like one of her own children. It came into her head that Jurand might immediately give the girl in marriage to one of his neighbors, so as to spend the rest of his days among his own people. There was no possibility of Zbyszko's going to Spychow, since his rib was only just beginning to heal, and, anyway, who could tell how he would be received? The lady knew that Jurand had unconditionally refused him Danusia, and he had told her that for secret reasons he could never permit their union. So in her heavy grief she sent for the oldest messenger to question him about the trouble at Spychow and at the same time to learn something of Jurand's designs.

She was greatly surprised when, in answer to her summons, a man completely unknown to her showed up, instead of old Tolima, who bore Jurand's shield behind him and usually rode with him to battle. This person told her that Tolima had been seriously injured in a recent fight with the Germans and was wrestling with death at Spychow, while the stricken Jurand begged for the quick return of his daughter, since his sight was growing weaker and weaker, and in only a few days complete blindness might set in. The messenger even begged most pressingly that he might be allowed to take the girl immediately, as soon as the horses had had a breathing-space. But, since it was evening, the lady opposed this firmly—especially since she did not wish to break Zbyszko's and Danusia's hearts and her own by separating them so suddenly.

Zbyszko, however, already knew everything, and lay in his room as if hit over the head with an axe. When the lady came in wringing her hands and called from the doorway, "Nothing can be done, for it's her father!" he repeated after her, like an echo, "Nothing can be done," and closed his eyes like a man who expects immediate death.

But death did not come, although grief grew ever stronger in his heart, and ever darker thoughts passed through his mind like storm-driven clouds that veil the sun and quench all joy on earth. Zbyszko understood, as well as the duchess, that once Danusia went to Spychow she would be lost to him forever. Here all were well-disposed to him, but there Jurand might even refuse to receive him or give him audience, particularly since he was bound by a vow or some other unknown cause as valid as a vow. Anyway, how could he go to Spychow when he was sick and barely able to move in his bed? A few days before, when the golden spurs and the knight's belt had fallen upon him by favor of the duke, he had thought that his joy would overpower his sickness and had prayed with his whole heart that he might soon rise and measure himself with the Teutonic Knights; but now he lost all hope again, for he felt that when Danusia was no longer by his bedside, he would lose—together with her—his desire for life and the strength to fight with death. Tomorrow and tomorrow would come, finally Christmas Eve and the holidays would arrive, and his bones would hurt as they did now, and he would be overpowered by the same faintness. And there would be no brightness radiating through the room from Danusia, nor delight in looking on her. What consolation and sweetness it was to ask several times a day, "Do you love me?" and then to see how she laughed and covered her shamefaced eyes with her hand, or bent down and answered, "Whom else?" Now, only the sickness would remain, and the pain, and the longing, while happiness would go—and never return.

Tears glistened in Zbyszko's eyes and rolled slowly down his cheeks. He turned to the duchess:

"Gracious lady, I think I shall never see Danusia again in this life."

The lady, anxious and troubled herself, replied:

"It would not be strange if you died of grief. But the Lord Jesus is merciful." Then, wishing to comfort him, if only a little, she added: "Should Jurand die, the guardianship of Danusia would pass to the duke and me, and we would give her to you at once."

"He die!" replied Zbyszko. "Not likely!"

Suddenly some new thought arose in his mind, for he lifted himself up, sat on the bed, and said in a changed voice:

"Gracious lady!"

But Danusia interrupted him, running in weeping and calling from the doorway:

"You've heard, Zbyszko! Oh, I am so sad for daddy, but I am sad for you too, poor thing!"

When she drew near him, Zbyszko put his sound arm around his love.

"How can I live without you, girl?" he said. "I did not ride through rivers and forests, I did not make my vow and serve you, to lose you again. Hey! Grief will not help, weeping will not help—nay, not even death, for though the grass were to grow over me, my soul would not forget you, even in the house of the Lord, even in the chambers of God the Father. . . . I say there is no hope, yet there must be hope, for without it one is nothing. I feel pain and sharp pangs in my bones. But do you fall at the lady's feet, for I cannot, and beg her to have compassion on us."

Danusia, quickly ran to the duchess and embraced her knees, hiding her bright face in the folds of her heavy garment, while the lady turned her eyes, full of pity, but at the same time of surprise, on Zbyszko.

"How can I show you compassion?" she asked. "If I do not let the girl go to her sick father, I shall draw down the wrath of God upon myself."

Zbyszko, who before had raised himself on the bed, now slid down again on the pillow, and for some time made no answer, as he was short of breath. However, he slowly moved one hand to the other on his breast until at last he joined them in an attitude of prayer.

"Rest," said the duchess, "and then tell me what you want; and you, Danusia, rise from my knees."

"Don't squeeze them, but don't rise," said Zbyszko. "Beg her with me." Then he went on in a weak and broken voice: "Worshipful lady . . . Jurand was against me at Cracow . . . and he will be against me now. But if Father Wyszoniek were to marry me to Danusia, then, even if she went afterwards to Spychow, no human power could take her from me. . . ."

These words took Duchess Anna so much by surprise that she sprang up from her seat and then sat down again, and said, as if not understanding correctly:

"Great heavens! Father Wyszoniek!"

"Gracious lady! . . . Gracious lady!" begged Zbyszko.

"Gracious lady!" Danusia repeated after him, embracing the duchess's knees again.

"How can that be, without you father's consent?"

"The divine command is more powerful," answered Zbyszko.

"God forbid!"

"Who is her father, if not the duke? . . . Who is her mother, if not you, gracious lady?"

And Danusia added: "Dear, gracious mother!"

"It is true that I have been, and am, like a mother to her," said the duchess, "and it was from my hand that Jurand received his wife. True! And if the marriage took place, then the affair would be settled. Maybe Jurand would be angry, but he owns allegiance to the duke as his lord. Besides, it would not be necessary to tell him at once, but only when he wished to give the girl to another or to make a nun of her. . . . And even if he has made some vow, it will not be his fault. No one can do anything against the will of God. . . . Great heavens, perhaps it is the will of God!"

"It cannot be otherwise!" exclaimed Zbyszko.

Overcome with emotion, the duchess said:

"Wait! I must think. If the duke were here I should go to him at once and ask him, 'Am I to give Danusia or not?' But without him I am afraid. . . . I'm all out of breath, and there's no time for anything, for the girl must go tomorrow. . . . Oh, dear Jesus! If she were to go as a married woman, I should feel at peace. But I cannot collect my thoughts, and I am afraid of something. Are you not afraid, Danusia? Speak!"

"I shall die if I do not marry her!" interrupted Zbyszko.

Danusia rose from the duchess's knees, and because she was not only allowed familiarity but also was in the habit of being caressed by the good lady, she threw her arms around her neck and began to hug her.

"Without Father Wyszoniek I cannot tell you anything," the duchess said. "Run and fetch him as fast as you can!"

Danusia ran to get Father Wyszoniek, while Zbyszko turned his pale face to the duchess and said:

"What the Lord Jesus has ordained for me will be, but may God reward you for this consolation, gracious lady."

"Do not bless me yet," replied the duchess, "for we do not know what will happen. And you must swear to me on you honor that if the marriage takes place you will not forbid the girl to go immediately to her father, else—God forbid!—you would draw down His curse upon both yourself and her."

"On my honor!" said Zbyszko.

"Don't forget! And the girl should not tell Jurand anything when she gets there. It's better that the news should not scorch him like fire. We will send for him from Ciechanow to come with Danusia, and then I myself will tell him, or ask the duke to do so. When he sees that nothing can be done about it, he will agree. He was never ill-disposed to you?"

"No," said Zbyszko, "he was not ill-disposed to me, so perhaps he will really be glad at the bottom of his heart at the marriage. If he has made a vow, it will then not be his fault if he does not keep it."

The entrance of Father Wyszoniek with Danusia interrupted further conversation. The duchess immediately called him to give advice and began excitedly to tell him of Zbyszko's designs, but he had no sooner heard what was in question than he crossed himself in amazement and said:

"In the name of the Father and of the Son and of the Holy Ghost! How can I do that? Why, it is Advent!"

"Heavens! That is true!" exclaimed the duchess.

Silence followed. Their distressed faces showed what a blow Father Wyszoniek's words had been to all of them.

After a while he went on:

"If I had a dispensation, I would not oppose you, because I am sorry for you. I should not necessarily ask for Jurand's permission, for as long as you, gracious lady, permitted and answered for the assent of the duke our lord—well!—you are father and mother for our Mazovia. But without a bishop's dispensation, I cannot. If only Bishop James of Kurdwanow were with us, maybe he would not refuse a dispensation—although, he is a strict priest and not like his predecessor, Bishop Mamphiolus, who used to answer everything with *'Bene! bene!'"*

"Bishop James of Kurdwanow is very fond of the duke and me," said the lady.

"That is why I say that he would not refuse a dispensation when there are reasons for it. . . . The girl must go, and the young man is sick and may die. . . . H'm! . . . *In articulo mortis.* . . . But without a dispensation it is impossible."

"I could ask Bishop James for a dispensation afterwards, and however strict he may be, he will not refuse me this favor. I guarantee that he will not refuse it."

Father Wyszoniek, who was a good and gentle man, replied:

"The word of God's anointed is a great word. I am afraid of the bishop, but it is a great word! . . . Maybe the young man could promise some gift to the cathedral at Plock. . . . I don't know. In any case, until the dispensation comes, it will be a sin, and no one else's but mine. . . . Yet the Lord Jesus is in truth merciful, and if anyone sins, not for his own advantage, but only out of pity for human misery, He will forgive it the more easily! Yet it will be a sin, and if the bishop were to be obstinate, who will give me absolution?"

"The bishop will not be obstinate!" exclaimed Duchess Anna.

And Zbyszko said:

"That fellow Sanderus who came here with me has indulgences for everything."

Perhaps Father Wyszoniek did not quite believe in Sanderus's indulgences, but he was glad to seize any pretext if he could only help Zbyszko and Danusia, for he had known the girl since she was small and loved her very much. Besides, he thought that at worst a penance would be laid upon him, so he turned to the duchess and said:

"I am a priest, but also a servant of the duke. What, gracious lady, do you command?"

"I do not wish to give commands; I prefer to ask," replied the lady. "But if Sanderus has indulgences. . . ."

"He has. It's merely a question of the bishop. He holds stern synods with the canons there at Plock."

"Never fear the bishop. I hear that he has forbidden priests to carry swords or crossbows, or to indulge in various kinds of licence, but he has not forbidden them to do good deeds."

Father Wyszoniek raised his eyes and his hands:

"Then let it be according to your will."

At these words the hearts of all his listeners were filled with joy. Zbyszko sat up again, and the duchess, Danusia, and Father Wyszoniek sat down near the bed and began to discuss how the business should be carried out. They determined to keep it such a secret that not a living soul in the house would know anything of what was to occur. They decided also that even Jurand must not know until the duchess herself explained everything to him at Ciechanow. Instead, Father Wyszoniek was to write a letter from the duchess to Jurand, asking him to come at once to Ciechanow, where he could find better medicines for his blindness and where he would be less tormented with loneliness. They decided finally that Zbyszko and Danusia should both go to confession, and that the marriage should take place at night, when everyone had gone to sleep.

Zbyszko thought of taking his Czech squire as a witness of the marriage, but he dismissed the idea, remembering that he had got him from Jagienka. For a moment she appeared in his mind as if really present, so that he seemed to see her flushed face and tearstained eyes and to hear her voice begging him, "Don't do this! Don't repay me with evil for good and with misery for love!"—and suddenly he was possessed with great pity for her, feeling that a grave wrong would be done to her, for which she would find no consolation either under the roof of Zgorzelice, or in the depths of the forest, or in the fields, or in the gifts of the abbot, or in the courtings of Cztan and Wolf. So he said to her in his heart: "God give you all the best, girl; I would gladly offer you even the moon, but I must go through with this." And in fact the conviction that it was not in his power to do anything else actually brought him relief and gave him back his peace of mind, so that he began to think only of Danusia and his marriage.

However, he could not do without the help of the Czech. So he summoned him but decided not to say anything about was to really happen. "I am going today to confession and to Holy Communion," he said. "Dress me in my cleanest clothes, as if I were going to the king's chambers."

The Czech became somewhat frightened and began to examine his face. Zbyszko, when he understood the reason, said:

"Don't be afraid; it is not just in preparation for death that men go to confession. The Christmas holidays are near. Since Father Wyszoniek is going to Ciechanow with the duchess, there will be no priest closer than at Przasnysz."

"And your grace is not going?" asked the squire.

"If I get well I will go, but that is in God's hands."

The Czech quickly went to the wooden chest and took out the white jacket embroidered with gold that the knight usually wore for great festivities, and also a beautiful rug to cover his feet and the bed. He raised Zbyszko with the help of the two Turks, washed him and combed his long hair, on which he put a scarlet band. Then he supported him with red pillows, and said, pleased with what he had done:

"If only your grace could dance, we could have a wedding-feast."

"It would have to be without the dancing," replied Zbyszko with a smile.

Meanwhile, in her own room, the duchess was considering how to dress Danusia. This was a very important matter in her feminine mind, as she would never have allowed her dear ward to be married in everyday apparel. The maidservants, who were told that the girl was dressing for confession in the colors of innocence, had no difficulty in finding a white dress in the chest, but it was difficult to choose a covering for her head. The thought of it filled the lady with strange sorrow, and she began to complain:

"If only I could find a wreath of rue for you, little orphan, in the forest! There's not a flower here, nor a leaf, save perhaps some green moss under the snow."

And Danusia, standing with her hair loose, was also troubled, for she cared about the wreath. After a while, however, she pointed to some bunches of everlastings, hanging on the walls of the room.

"Suppose we wind something out of them," she suggested, "for we shall find nothing else, and Zbyszko will take me even in such a wreath as that."

Fearing a bad omen, the duchess did not initially assent. But since there were no flowers in the lodge, to which the court came only for hunts, she finally took the everlastings. Meanwhile Father Wyszoniek arrived; he had just heard Zbyszko's confession and now it was the girl's turn. Then, silent night fell. After supper the duchess ordered the servants to bed. Jurand's messengers lay down, some in the servants' room, others with the horses in the stables. Soon the fires in the servants' quarters were covered with ashes and went out, and at last all was quiet in the hunting-lodge. Only the dogs barked from time to time at the wolves in the forest.

However, in the rooms of the duchess, of Father Wyszoniek, and of Zbyszko, the windows did not cease to shine, throwing red gleams on the snow outside. They silently kept vigil, listening to the beating of their own hearts, ill-at-ease and taken up with the solemnity of the moment soon to come. After midnight the duchess took Danusia by the hand and led her to Zbyszko's room, where Father Wyszoniek was already waiting for them with the Holy Sacrament. A large fire burned on the hearth, and by its bright but steady light Zbyszko caught sight of Danusia, looking rather pale from lack of sleep, the wreath of everlastings on her temples, and dressed in a stiff white gown that fell to her feet. Her eyes were nearly shut from emotion, her little hands hung down at her sides. She looked like a painting done on glass; indeed, there was something so church-like in her, that Zbyszko was surprised at the sight, thinking that he was to take to wife, not an earthly maiden, but some sprite from heaven. He thought so all the more when she knelt with folded hands to receive Communion, her head bent back, her eyes closed. At that moment she even seemed to him as if dead, and fear gripped him. This impression did not last long, however, for when he heard the priest say, *"Ecce Agnus Dei,"* he concentrated all his thoughts, which took flight towards God. In the room nothing was to be heard but the solemn voice of Father Wyszoniek— *"Domine, non sum dignus"*—and with it the crackling of the sparks on the hearth and the crickets chirping insistently, and somewhat sadly, in the crannies of the chimney. Outside the windows, the wind rose and soughed through the snowy forest, but soon all was quiet again.

Zbyszko and Danusia remained for some time in silence, while Father Wyszoniek took the chalice and went with it to the lodge chapel. After a while he returned, not alone, but with Sieur de Lorche, and seeing the surprise on the faces of those present, he laid his finger on his lips as if to warn them not to utter an unexpected cry.

"I thought," he said, "it would be better to have two witnesses of the marriage, but I first warned this knight, who has sworn to me on his honor and on the relics of Aix-la-Chapelle that he will keep the secret as long as is necessary."

Sieur de Lorche knelt first before the duchess and then before Danusia; then he rose and stood in silence, wearing his festal armor, the curves of which reflected red lights from the fire—a tall, motionless figure, who seemed to be filled with delight, for the white maiden with the wreath of everlastings on her temples also seemed to him like an angel in the window of a Gothic cathedral.

The priest made her stand by Zbyszko's bed, and wrapping his stole around their hands, he began the usual ceremony. Tear after tear flowed down the duchess's kindly face, and in her heart she did not at that moment feel disquiet, for she thought she was doing good in uniting these two handsome and innocent children. Sieur de Lorche knelt for the second time, and resting both his hands on the hilt of his sword, he looked exactly like a knight who has a vision. Zbyszko and Danusia repeated in turn the words of the priest: "I . . . take you . . ." And these soft, sweet words were accompanied by the renewed chirping of the crickets in the crannies of the chimney and the crackling of the fire on the hearth. At the conclusion of the ceremony, Danusia fell at the feet of the duchess, who blessed them both, giving them into the care of the heavenly powers.

"Rejoice, for now she is yours and you are hers," the duchess then said.

Zbyszko stretched out his sound arm to Danusia, and she put her small arms about his neck, and for a while nothing was to be heard but their whispered words:

"You are mine, Danusia."

"You are mine, Zbyszko."

But Zbyszko began to feel faint, for his emotions were too much for his strength, and he sank down on the pillows, breathing heavily. He did not, however, actually faint, and he did not cease to smile at Danusia, who wiped the cold sweat from his face, and he did not even cease to repeat, "You are mine, Danusia," on hearing which she bowed her fair head each time. The sight so moved Sieur de Lorche that he declared that never in any country had he seen hearts so tender, and he swore solemnly that he was ready to fight on foot or on horseback with any knight, wizard, or dragon who should dare to stand in the way of their happiness. And, in fact, he immediately took his oath on the cross-shaped hilt of his misericord, the dagger used by knights for dispatching the wounded. The duchess and Father Wyszoniek were called to witness this vow.

Yet the lady, unable to conceive of a wedding without some kind of rejoicing, brought wine, which they then drank. The hours of the night passed one after the other. Zbyszko, having overcome his weakness, embraced Danusia again and said:

"Since the Lord Jesus had given you to me, no one will take you from me, but I am grieved that you are going away, my darling little berry."

"I will come to Ciechanow with daddy," replied Danusia.

"If only some sickness does not attack you, or something. . . . God save you from any harm! You must go to Spychow, I know! . . . Well, thank Almighty God and the gracious lady that you are mine, for no human power can undo a marriage."

Because the marriage had taken place at night and in secret, and immediately after it there had to come a separation, a strange feeling of sorrow overcame not only Zbyszko at times, but all of them. Their talk ceased. Occasionally the fire on the hearth died down, and their heads were dimly visible in the near darkness. Father Wyszoniek then threw fresh logs on the coal. The wood squeaked plaintively, as sometimes happens when it is fresh.

"Souls in penance, what do you want?" Father Wyszoniek mused.

Only the crickets answered him. The flame grew bright and illuminated the sleepless faces of those present. The light was reflected off of de Lorche's armor, and it brightened Danusia's white dress and the everlastings in her hair.

The dogs outside began to bark again towards the forest, where they evidently scented wolves.

And as the hours of the night passed, silence fell more and more often, until at last the duchess said:

"Dear Jesus! If it is to be like this after a wedding, it would be better to go to sleep. But since we have to be up until morning, play for us something, little flower. Play on your lute for the last time before you go—for me and for Zbyszko."

Feeling tired and sleepy, Danusia was glad to refresh herself. She ran for her lute, soon returned with it, and sat down by Zbyszko's bed.

"What am I to play?" she asked.

"What?" said the duchess. "What, if not the song you sang at Tyniec, when Zbyszko saw you for the first time!"

"Hey! I remember—and I shall never forget," said Zbyszko. "When I heard it anywhere after that, tears came to my eyes."

"Then I will sing it," said Danusia.

And she began to strum her lute. Then, throwing her head back, as she usually did, she sang:

> *"Oh, if I but had*
> *Little wings like a dove,*
> *Away I would fly,*
> *Away, away to my love*
> *In Silesia.*
> *"Down I would light*
> *On the fence of his glade.*
> *Look, O my Jack,*
> *At a poor orphan maid*
> *In Silesia!"*

But her voice suddenly broke, her lips began to quiver, and from under her closed eyelashes a couple of tears forced their way down her cheeks. For a while she strove to keep more of them back, but she could not, and in the end she burst into tears, just as she had done before when singing that song to Zbyszko in the Cracow prison.

"Danusia! What is the matter, Danusia!" asked Zbyszko.

"Why are you crying? What kind of a wedding is this!" exclaimed the duchess. "Why?"

"I don't know," replied Danusia, sobbing. "I am so sad—such grief—for Zbyszko and you."

So all became anxious and tried to comfort her, and explained to her that she was not going for long, and certainly would come to Ciechanow with Jurand for the Christmas holidays. Zbyszko again put his arm around her, pressed her to his breast, and kissed the tears from her eyes. But a feeling of oppression remained in all their hearts, and in this oppression the night hours passed.

At last there was a noise in the yard, so sudden and shrill that it caused all of them to start. The duchess sprang up from her seat and exclaimed:

"Heavens! The well-sweeps! They are watering the horses."

Father Wyszoniek looked at the window, whose glass panes were turning grey, and said:

"The night is brightening, and the day is at hand. *Ave Maria, gratia plena.* . . ."

Then he went out of the room. He returned shortly.

"The day is dawning," he stated, "but it will be overcast. Jurand's men are watering their horses. It is time to take to the road, poor girl!"

At these words both the duchess and Danusia burst into loud weeping, and both of them together with Zbyszko began to complain as simple people do when they have to part; that is to say, there was in their complaint something conventional, something between a wail and a dirge, which flows from simple hearts as naturally as tears flow from the eyes.

> *"Heh! Further weeping is of no help,*
> *Now is the time we must part;*
> *Weeping is of no help,*
> *Now we must part, poor girl.*
>   *Farewell! Farewell!"*

But Zbyszko pressed Danusia for the last time to his breast and held her until his breath failed. Then the duchess took her from him to dress her for the road.

Meanwhile the morning became quite light. In the yard everyone was awake and busy. The Czech squire came to Zbyszko to ask about his health and wait for orders.

"Draw my bed up to the window," the knight said to him.

The Czech easily drew the bed to the window, but was surprised when Zbyszko told him to open it. He obeyed, however, and covered his master with his own sheepskin coat, since it was cold in the yard, though cloudy, and snow was falling soft and thick.

Zbyszko looked out. Through the falling snowflakes, a sleigh was to be seen in the yard, and around it Jurand's men, mounted on ruffled and steaming horses. All were armed, and some had metal plates on their goatskin coats, from which were reflected the pale and gloomy rays of daylight.

Danusia came into Zbyszko's room once again, already all wrapped up in her sheepskin coat and fox-skin hood. Once again she threw her arms around his neck, and once again she said to him on parting:

"Although I am going away, I am yours."

And he kissed her hands, cheeks, and eyes, which were barely to be seen under the fox-fur hood.

"God protect you!" he said. "God conduct you safely! You're mine now, mine till death!"

When they took her away from him again, he raised himself as much as he could, rested his head on the window, and through a veil of snowflakes watched Danusia getting into the sleigh, the duchess holding her long in her arms, the ladies-in-waiting kissing her, and Father Wyszoniek making the sign of the cross over her for the road. She turned towards him once more just before starting and stretched out her hands.

"God be with you, Zbyszko!"

"God grant that I shall see you at Ciechanow!"

But the snow was falling very thickly, as if it wanted to muffle and veil everything; therefore, these last words came so faintly to their ears that it seemed to both as if they were already calling to each other from far away.

CHAPTER XXVI

THICK snowfalls were followed by severe frosts and clear, dry days. In the daytime the forests sparkled in the rays of the sun, and ice bound the rivers and stiffened the marshes. Then came bright nights, in which the frost increased to such a degree that the trees cracked loudly in the forest. Birds drew near to houses; the roads became unsafe because of wolves, which began to gather in packs and attack not only single men but even villages. The population, however, sat contentedly by their fires in their smoky rooms, looking forward to good harvests after the hard winter and waiting cheerfully for the upcoming Christmas holidays. The hunting-lodge stood almost empty. The duchess and the court had gone to Ciechanow together with Father Wyszoniek. Zbyszko, now considerably better, but not yet quite strong enough to sit on horseback, remained at the lodge with his people, Sanderus, the Czech squire, and the local servants, over whom a stolid gentlewoman exercised the authority of housekeeper.

But the knight's heart longed for his young wife. It was, indeed, immeasurably sweet to think that Danusia was now his and that no human power could take her from him. But, on the other hand, this very thought increased his longing. He continually sighed for the moment in which he would be able to leave the lodge, and considered what he should do then, where he should go, and how he could reconcile Jurand. He also had moments of grave disquiet, but in general the future seemed joyous. To love Danusia and to pluck peacock feathers off helmets—that was to be his life. Frequently he was seized with a desire to talk about it with the Czech, whom he liked, but he observed that the latter, devoted as he was with his whole heart to Jagienka, was disinclined to talk of Danusia, while he himself, being bound by his secret, could not tell him all that had happened.

His health improved with each day. A week before Christmas Eve he mounted his horse for the first time, and although he felt that he could not have done it in armor, he was still greatly encouraged. Anyway, he did not expect any sudden need to put on his breastplate and helmet, and in the worst case hoped that he would shortly have strength enough even for that. In his room he tried to kill time by lifting his sword, and succeeded fairly well. Only his axe proved too heavy for him. He thought, however, that if he took the handle in both hands he would be able to swing it successfully.

Finally, two days before Christmas Eve, he ordered the wagons to be prepared and the horses saddled, and declared to the Czech that they were going to Ciechanow. The faithful squire was somewhat anxious, especially as the frost was crackling in the courtyard, but Zbyszko said to him:

"Don't trouble your head about that, Wisehead. (So he called him, translating his Czech name of Hlawa.) We have nothing to do in this lodge, and even were I to fall sick, I shall have no lack of care at Ciechanow. Besides, I am not going on horseback, but in a sleigh, wrapped up to my throat in hay and covered with skins, and I shall not mount my horse until I am close to Ciechanow."

And so it was. By now the Czech knew his young master and was aware that it was not good to oppose him and still worse not to carry out his orders quickly—so an hour later they started. At the moment of departure Zbyszko, seeing Sanderus climbing onto the sleigh with his boxes, said to him:

"Why do you cling to me like a bur to sheep's wool? You told me you wanted to go to Prussia."

"I told you I wanted to go to Prussia," said Sanderus, "but how am I to go there alone in such snow? The wolves will eat me before the first star comes out. There's nothing for me here, anyway. I prefer to be in town, to edify folk with my piety and present them with my sacred wares and save them from the wiles of the devil, as I swore to the Father of the whole of Christendom at Rome that I would do. Besides, I am very fond of your grace, and will not leave you till I depart for Rome, for perhaps I shall be able to do you some service."

"He is always ready to eat and drink for you, lord," said the Czech, "and that's the service he would like most. But if too great a pack of wolves falls upon us in the Przasnysz forest, we will throw him to them, for he is not good for anything else."

"Beware that your sinful words do not freeze to your moustache," replied Sanderus. "Such icicles can melt only in hellfire."

"Bah!" said Hlawa, wiping his scarcely sprouting moustache with his glove. "I will try first to warm some beer at the next stop, but I will not give you any."

"Yet the commandment tells us to give drink to the thirsty. Another sin!"

"Then I will give you a pail of water. Meanwhile here is something for you."

He took two great handfuls of snow and threw them at Sanderus's beard, but the German ducked and then said:

"Indeed there's nothing for you to do at Ciechanow. They already have a tame bear which throws snow."

Thus they teased one another, even though they liked one another pretty well. Zbyszko did not forbid Sanderus to ride with him, for the strange fellow entertained him and at the same time seemed to be really attached to him. So they started from the lodge early in the morning in such hard frost that they had to cover the horses. The entire countryside was covered with thick snow. The roofs of cottages were scarcely visible from under it, and in places columns of smoke, rosy in the light of dawn, seemed to rise straight from white snowdrifts. Spreading at the top into tufts, they resembled knights' plumes.

Zbyszko rode in the sleigh, firstly to save his strength and secondly because of the severe cold, against which it was easier to protect himself in a sleigh lined with hay and skins. He had Hlawa sit by his side with his crossbow ready in case of wolves, and meanwhile talked merrily with him.

"At Przasnysz," he said, "we will just feed our horses and warm ourselves, then continue on."

"To Ciechanow?"

"First to Ciechanow, to pay my respects to the duke and duchess, and attend Mass."

"And then?" asked Wisehead.

Zbyszko smiled and replied:

"Then who knows whether I shall not go to Bogdaniec?"

The Czech looked at him in surprise. The thought suddenly occurred to him that perhaps the young lord had given up on Danusia, and this seemed to him the more probable since she had gone away, and the news had reached the Czech's ears at the hunting-lodge that the Lord of Spychow was opposed to the young knight. So the honest squire rejoiced, for though he loved Jagienka, he looked upon her as on a star in heaven and would gladly have bought her happiness even with his own blood. He also loved Zbyszko, and desired with his whole heart to serve them both till death.

"Then your grace will stay at home?" he said joyously.

"How can I stay home," replied Zbyszko, "when I have challenged those Teutonic Knights, and before that, Lichtenstein? De Lorche said that the grand master will probably invite the king to be his guest at Torun. I will join the royal retinue, and I think that at Torun either Lord Zawisza of Garbowo or Lord Powala of Taczewo will obtain permission for me from our lord to meet those monks in single combat. Presumably they will enter the lists with their squires, so you also will have to fight."

"I would become a monk myself if it had to be otherwise," said the Czech.

Zbyszko looked at him with satisfaction.

"I pity the man who comes under you sword. The Lord Jesus gave you unusual strength, but it would be wrong of you to boast of it too much, for humility befits a true squire."

The Czech bent his head to signify that he would not boast too much of his strength but would also not be sparing of it against the Germans. Zbyszko continued to smile, no longer at his squire, but at his own thoughts.

"The old lord will be glad when we come back," said Hlawa after a while. "And they will be glad at Zgorzelice too."

Zbyszko suddenly saw Jagienka as clearly as if she were sitting in the sleigh by his side. It was always so: whenever he chanced to think of her, he saw her with extraordinary distinctness. . . .

"No!" he said to himself, "she will not be glad, for if I return to Bogdaniec it will be with Danusia, and she will have to take another." Here Wolf of Birchwood and young Cztan of Rogow flashed before his eyes, and he was suddenly pained by the thought that the girl might pass into the hands of one of them. "I should prefer her to find someone better," he said to himself in his heart, "for they are drinkers and gamblers, while the girl has a heart of gold." Then he thought how his uncle would be terribly grieved when he learned what had happened, but he also comforted himself with the thought that Macko always cared most for the interests of the family and the wealth which might increase the family's importance. Jagienka was nearer, it is true, just across the balk between their fields, but Jurand was a larger landowner than Zych of Zgorzelice. It was easy to foresee that Macko would not oppose such a union for long, especially since he knew of his nephew's love and his debt to Danusia. He would frown, but afterwards he would be glad and begin to love Danusia as if she were his own child.

And suddenly Zbyszko's heart was touched with devotion and longing for his uncle, who, though a hard man, loved him like the apple of his eye. In battles he defended him more than himself. He took booty for him, he strove to acquire property for him. They were two men alone in the world! They had not even kinsmen, save distant ones like the abbot. So whenever a separation occurred, the one did not know what to do without the other, and especially the old man, who now desired nothing in life for himself.

"Hey! he will be glad, he will be glad!" Zbyszko repeated to himself. "I only wish Jurand would receive me as he will receive me."

And he tried to imagine what Jurand would say and do when he learned of the marriage. He was somewhat disquieted by the thought, but not too much, particularly because the die was already cast. It wouldn't be proper for Jurand to challenge him to combat, and if he opposed him too much, Zbyszko might answer him: "Stop! I beg you, for your right to Danusia is human, but mine is divine—and she is not yours now, but mine." He had heard something at one time or another from a certain cleric versed in the Scriptures, that a woman ought to leave father and mother and follow her husband, so he felt that the greater right was with him. However, he did not expect that there would be a really violent quarrel between himself and Jurand, for he counted on the great effect of Danusia's own prayers, and as much, if not more, on the intervention of the duke, whose vassal Jurand was, and of the duchess, whom Jurand loved as the guardian of his child.

At Przasnysz they were advised to stay the night and were warned against wolves, which because of the cold had gathered in such great packs that they attacked even wayfarers travelling in large parties. Zbyszko did not take this advice, for at the inn he had met some Mazovian knights with their retinues who were also going to the duke's at Ciechanow and several armed merchants of Ciechanow who were bringing laden sleighs from Prussia. In so large a group there was no danger, so they started in the night, even though the wind had risen suddenly in the evening, bringing clouds and then a blizzard. They rode close, one behind the other, but so slowly that Zbyszko began to think they would not arrive before Christmas Eve. In some places they had to dig their way through the snowdrifts where the horses were quite unable to pass. Fortunately the forest road was straight. None the less, it was already dusk when they caught sight of Ciechanow in the distance.

In the drifting snow and whistling wind, they might even have passed the town without any idea that they were so near, had it not been for the fires burning on the eminence on which the castle had been built. No one knew for certain whether these fires were lit on Christmas Eve to guide travellers, or whether it was an ancient custom; in any case, none of Zbyszko's companions now thought of that; everyone merely wanted to find shelter in the town at the earliest possible moment.

Meanwhile the blizzard increased in intensity. The freezing wind drove immeasurable clouds of snow. It pulled at trees, it howled and went mad; it caught up entire snowdrifts, raising and twisting them, then scattering them in a fine powder that covered the sleighs and horses. The wind whipped the travellers' faces as if with sharp sand; it choked the breath in their lungs and stifled speech. The sound of the rattles fixed on the thills could no longer be heard at all, while in the howling and whistling wind plaintive voices seemed to be heard, sounding like the howling of wolves or the distant neighing of horses or sometimes men calling desperately for help. The exhausted horses leaned against one another, and moved ever more slowly forward.

"What a snowstorm!" exclaimed the Czech, choking. "It is

lucky, lord, that we are near the town and that those fires are burning, else it would go badly for us."

"If anyone is in the field, he will die," replied Zbyszko. "But, look, I don't see the fires anymore."

"That's because the snow is so thick that even a fire does not shine through it. And perhaps the wind has scattered the wood and coals."

In the other sleighs the merchants and knights also told one another that if any man was caught by the blizzard far from human habitations, he would not have the pleasure of hearing the church bells ringing tomorrow. Zbyszko became suddenly troubled and said:

"God forbid that Jurand should be somewhere on the way!"

Although fully occupied with looking out for the fires, the Czech heard Zbyszko's words.

"Then the Lord of Spychow was to come?" he asked, turning his head toward the young knight.

"Yes."

"With the young lady?"

"The fires are indeed hidden," replied Zbyszko.

The flames had, in fact, gone out, but a number of riders appeared before them, close to the horses and sleighs.

"Why are you blocking the way?" shouted the watchful Czech, grasping his crossbow. "Who are you?"

"The duke's people, sent out to help travellers."

"Jesus Christ be praised!"

"For ever and ever."

"Show the way to the town!" called out Zbyszko.

"Has none of you been left behind?"

"None."

"Where do you come from?"

"Przasnysz."

"And you saw no other travellers on the road?"

"No. But perhaps there are some on other highways."

"Our people are looking along all of them. Follow us. You came off the road! To the right! To the right!"

They turned their horses. For some time only the roar of the wind was to be heard.

"Are there many guests in the old castle?" asked Zbyszko presently.

The nearest horseman, not having heard well what he said, bent towards him:

"What did you say, lord?"

"I asked whether there were many guests with the duke and duchess?"

"As always, enough!"

"Is Jurand, the Lord of Spychow, there?"

"No, but he is expected. Men have ridden to meet him."

"With torches?"

"As if the wind would allow that!"

But they could not talk anymore, for the roaring of the blizzard increased.

"A real devil's wedding!" called out the Czech.

But Zbyszko bade him be silent and not call out the name of such a foul being.

"Don't you know," he said, "that at Christmas time a devil's power is lost, and that devils hide in holes cut in the ice? Once at Sandomierz, before Christmas Eve, the fishermen found one in their net. He was holding a pike in his mouth, but when he heard the sound of bells, he fainted at once, and they beat him with sticks until the evening. . . . The wind is indeed strong, but it is by the Lord Jesus' permission. He evidently wishes tomorrow to be all the more joyous by contrast."

"We were close to the town, yet, had it not been for these men, we might have gone on till midnight, for we had indeed gotten off the road," replied Wisehead.

"Because the fires had died down."

Now, however, they actually did reach the town. Snowdrifts lay in the streets, still bigger than outside. These drifts were so big, in fact, that in many places they almost covered the windows, and that's why the wayfarers, lost outside the town, had been unable to see any lights. The wind, however, was less audible here. Most of the inhabitants were already sitting at their Christmas Eve suppers. In front of some of the houses, boys with cribs and a goat were singing carols, heedless of the storm. On the marketplace folk were to be seen wrapped up in pea-straw, pretending to be bears. But in general the streets were empty. The merchants, who had accompanied Zbyszko, remained in the town, while Zbyszko and his retinue rode on to the old castle where lived the duke. Having glass panes in its windows, it shone cheerfully before them despite the storm.

The drawbridge over the moat was down, for the old days of Lithuanian inroads had passed, and the Teutonic Knights, foreseeing war with the Polish king, were anxious to obtain the friendship of the Mazovian duke. One of the duke's men blew a horn, and the gate was soon opened. It was guarded by fifteen or twenty archers, but on the walls and battlements there was not a living soul, since the duke had allowed the watchmen to go inside. The guests were met by old Mrokota, who had arrived two days before. He greeted them in the name of the duke and took them to rooms where they might change their clothes for supper.

Zbyszko immediately began to question him about Jurand of Spychow. He replied that Jurand was not there yet, but that they were expecting him, since he had promised to come, and if he had fallen seriously ill he would have let them know. They had sent a dozen or more horsemen to meet him and his daughter, for even the oldest people did not remember such a blizzard.

"Then perhaps they will be here before long."

"Verily, before long. The duchess has ordered plates to be set for them at the common table."

Although he was still somewhat afraid of Jurand, Zbyszko rejoiced in his heart, and said to himself, "Though he were to do I know not what, he cannot undo the fact that it is my wife who will arrive with him, my woman, my dearest Danusia." And when he repeated that to himself he could scarcely believe his own happiness. Then he thought that perhaps she had already confessed all to her father; perhaps she had reconciled him and begged him to freely give her up. "In truth, what else can he do? Jurand is a wise man and knows that even if he denied her to me, I should take her all the same, for my right is the stronger."

While dressing, he talked with Mrokota, asking him about the health of the duke, and particularly of the duchess, whom since his stay at Cracow he loved like a mother. So he was glad when he heard that all in the castle were well and cheerful, although the duchess greatly longed for her dear little songstress. It was Jagienka

who now played on the lute for her, and the duchess liked her
greatly, but not as she had loved Danusia.

"What Jagienka?" asked Zbyszko in surprise.

"Jagienka of Longwood, granddaughter of the old lord. A beautiful girl, with whom the Lorrainer has fallen in love."

"Then Sieur de Lorche is here?"

"Where else should he be? He came directly form the hunting-lodge, and he stays here because he is comfortable. Our duke never lacks guests."

"I shall be glad to see him, for he is a knight without reproach."

"And he loves you. But let us go now. The duke and duchess will take their seats at table very soon."

So they went. Large fires were burning in the two fireplaces in the dining-hall, attended by pages, while numbers of guests and courtiers were filling the empty space. The duke came in first, accompanied by the voivode and several esquires. Zbyszko bowed and kissed his hand.

The duke laid his hand on Zbyszko and then, taking him a little apart, said:

"I already know everything. I was displeased at first that you had done it without my permission, but in truth there was no time, for I was then in Warsaw, where I had wished to spend Christmas. Anyway, it is well known that if a woman sets her mind on something it is no good opposing her; one will get nothing by it. The lady duchess is as kind to you as a mother, and I would always rather agree with her than oppose her, to save her sorrow and weeping."

Zbyszko bowed for the second time.

"May God grant me to repay your ducal grace!"

"Praise be to His name that you are already well! Tell the duchess how kindly I received you, and the woman will rejoice. By heaven, her joy is my joy. I will also speak a good word for you to Jurand, and I think he will give permission, for he also loves the duchess."

"Even if he were unwilling to give Danusia, my right is first."

"Your right is first, and he must agree, but he may refuse you his blessing. No one can wrest it from him by force, and without a father's blessing, there is no divine blessing."

Zbyszko was troubled when he heard those words, for hitherto he had not thought of that. At that moment, however, the duchess entered with Jagienka of Longwood and other ladies-in-waiting. Zbyszko hastened to pay his respects to the duchess, and she greeted him even more graciously than the duke, and immediately began to speak of Jurand's expected arrival. Plates were already set for Jurand and Danusia, and men sent out to conduct them through the storm. It was impossible to wait any longer with the Christmas Eve supper, for that would displease the duke, but the Lord of Spychow and his daughter were sure to arrive before supper was finished.

"As for Jurand," said the duchess, "it will be according to God's inspiration. Either I will tell him everything today or tomorrow after the Shepherd's Mass. The duke has also promised to add a word of his own. Jurand is always obstinate, but not with those whom he loves and not with those to whom he owes an obligation."

Then she began to tell Zbyszko how to behave towards his father-in-law so as not to—God forbid!—offend him, and how not to rouse his obstinacy. She was in general cheerful about the prospect, but anyone with more experience of the world and keener insight than Zbyszko would have observed a certain apprehension in her words. Perhaps it was because the Lord of Spychow was not at all an easy person, or perhaps the duchess was beginning to be somewhat anxious about the delay in his arrival. The storm outside was still growing in violence, and all said that any man who was caught in the open field would never move again. The duchess, however, conceived of another idea: namely, that Danusia had already confessed to her father that she was united in marriage with Zbyszko, and that Jurand, offended, had determined not to come to Ciechanow at all. The lady did not wish to confide this thought to Zbyszko, nor was there time, since the pages were beginning to bring in the food and set it on the table. Zbyszko once again embraced her knees.

"If they come," he asked, "what will the sleeping arrangements be like? Mrokota told me that there was a special room for Jurand, with hay for bedding for his squires. But what about. . . ."

The duchess began to laugh, and striking him lightly in the face with her glove, she said:

"Be quiet! What do you want? Look at him!"

And she went to the duke. The servants were already drawing

back his chair so that he could sit down. Before that, however, one of them had given him a shallow dish, full of wafers and finely-cut pieces of flat-cake, which the duke was to divide with the guests, the courtiers, and the servants. A second similar dish was held for the duchess by a handsome youth, son of the castellan of Sochaczew. On the other side of the table stood Father Wyszoniek, who was to bless the supper laid out on sweet-smelling hay. But suddenly a man, covered with snow, appeared in the doorway, and he began to call out:

"Worshipful lord! Worshipful lord!"

"What?" said the duke, displeased at the Christmas ceremony being interrupted.

"There are some travellers on the Radzanow highway entirely buried in snow. We need more men to dig them out."

All were struck with fear when they heard that. The duke also was alarmed and, turning to the castellan of Sochaczew, shouted:

"Horsemen and spades, quickly!" Then he addressed the man who had brought the news: "Are there many buried?"

"We could not tell. The wind is blowing hard. There are horses and sleighs. A considerable retinue."

"You don't know whose it is?"

"They say it is the Lord of Spychow's."

CHAPTER XXVII

ZBYSZKO, hearing the terrible news, did not wait for the duke's permission but rushed to the stables and ordered the horses saddled. The Czech, who as a squire of good birth had been with him in the hall, had barely enough time to go back to his room and bring the warm fox-skin coat. He did not try to restrain his young master, for his innate intelligence told him that it would be useless and that delay might be fatal. So he mounted a second horse, snatched up several torches offered him by the gatekeeper, and set out with the duke's people, whom the old castellan had speedily provided. Outside the gate they were surrounded by impenetrable darkness, but the wind seemed to be falling. They might very possibly have lost their way beyond the town had it not been for the man who had given first notice of the accident, and who now led them quickly and accurately with the aid of a dog familiar with the route. In the open field the wind again cut their faces sharply, particularly as they were riding at a gallop. The highway was full of snow, in places so deep that the horses sank in it up to their bellies. The duke's people lit their torches and rode on in the midst of smoke and flames, which the wind blew so strongly that it seemed as if it would tear them from the tarry sticks of wood and carry them far into the fields and forests. The way was long. They passed the settlements nearest to Ciechanow, and then Niedzborz, after which they turned in the direction of Radzanow. Beyond Niedzborz the storm began to abate. The blasts of wind became weaker and no longer drove such clouds of snow before them. The sky grew brighter. Some snow still fell, but soon that also stopped.

Then here and there a star twinkled through a rift in the clouds. The horses began to snort; the riders breathed more freely. More stars came out every moment, and the frost intensified. After a few paternosters, all was quiet.

Sieur de Lorche, riding by Zbyszko's side, tried to cheer him, saying that most certainly Jurand, at the moment of danger, would think first of all of saving his daughter, and that even though they dug out all the other dead, they would most certainly find her alive, perhaps asleep under furs. But Zbyszko understood little of what he said, and actually had not much time to listen to him, since presently their guide, riding in front, turned off the highway.

The young knight pushed forward and asked him: "Why are we turning aside?"

"Because they were buried not on the highway but over there. Do you see that alder clump, lord?"

He pointed to a dark thicket some distance off, which stood out clearly against the white surface of the snow, for the clouds had rolled away from the face of the moon, and the night had become clear.

"I see that they went off the highway."

"Yes, and they went around in circles along the river. In the wind and snow such a thing easily happens. They rode and rode till their horses could go no more."

"How did you find them?"

"The dog led the way."

"Are there no peasants' huts nearby?"

"There are, but on the other side of the river. The Wkra is just here."

"Forward!" called out Zbyszko.

But it was easier to give the order than to carry it out. Although the frost had become sharp, unfrozen snow was still lying on the meadows, and the drifts were so deep that the horses sank in them to their knees; therefore, progress had to be slow. Suddenly they heard the barking of the dog, and right in front of them loomed up the thick and hunched trunk of a willow, over which a crown of leafless twigs glistened in the moonlight.

"The others are farther on," said the guide, "near the alder clump. But there must be something here too."

"There is a drift under the willow. Give a light!"

Several of the duke's men dismounted and held their torches so as to illuminate the spot, and one of them shouted:

"There's a man under the snow! I can see his head—right there!"

"And there's a horse too!" called another.

"Dig them out!"

Their spades began to plunge into the snow and throw it on either side.

After a while they saw the figure of a man sitting under the tree, his head bent on his breast and his cap pushed down over his face. With one hand he held the reins of his horse, lying beside him with its nostrils pressed to the snow. Evidently the man had left his company, perhaps in an effort to reach some human habitation and bring help, and when his horse had fallen he had taken shelter under the willow on the side away from the wind, and there had frozen.

"A light!" called Zbyszko.

An attendant held a torch close to the face of the frozen man, but it was difficult to recognize the features. It was only when a second attendant raised the man's head, that they all cried out at once: "The Lord of Spychow!"

Zbyszko ordered two men to take him to the nearest cottage and try to bring him to life. Without losing a moment, he himself rushed to save the remainder of the company with the aid of his other servants and the guide. On the way he thought he would find Danusia, his wife, perhaps already dead—and he pressed his horse to the utmost, though it sank in the snow up to its chest. Fortunately they did not have far to go, at most a few furlongs. Voices were heard in the dark, "Over here! over here!" from the men who had been digging out the victims from the snow. Zbyszko came up and leapt from his horse. "To the spades!"

Two sleighs had already been dug out by the men who had been left on guard. The horses and men in them were frozen beyond hope of recovery. The places where other teams were buried could be recognized by hillocks of snow, although not all the sleighs were entirely covered. By some of them horses were to be seen, their bellies resting on the snowdrifts, their legs extended as if in a gallop and frozen at the moment of their last effort. By one pair stood a man with a spear in his hand, deep in snow up to his belt, as immovable as a post; in other areas men had frozen by their horses' sides, holding them by their heads. Death had evidently overtaken them at the moment when they were trying to drag their horses out of the mounds of snow. One team at the very end of the line was not snowed up at all. The driver sat bent forward with his hands covering his ears, and behind him lay two men; long strips of snow, blown across their breasts, joined the drift at their side and covered them like sheets, under which they seemed to be sleeping quietly and peacefully. Others had perished, struggling with the blizzard to the last, frozen in attitudes of great physical effort. Some sleighs were overturned; others were broken down. Every moment the spades uncovered horses' backs, bent like bows, or heads biting the snow, men in sleighs and by the side of sleighs—but nowhere could they find any women. At times Zbyszko dug in the snow until the sweat poured from his brow; at other times he turned a light into the eyes of the corpses, his heart beating in fearful anticipation of finding Danusia's beloved face—but all in vain! The flame illuminated only the fierce, moustached faces of the Spychow warriors. There was no Danusia or other woman anywhere.

"What does this mean?" the young knight asked himself in amazement.

And he shouted to the men working not far away, asking them whether they had uncovered anyone; but they had uncovered only men. Finally the work was finished. The servants harnessed their own horses to the sleighs, and sitting on the seats, they moved off with the corpses in the direction of Niedzborz, where they intended to try once more in a warm house to bring back some of the frozen figures to life. Zbyszko stayed behind with the Czech and two men. He had begun to think that perhaps Danusia's sleigh had become separated from the company, that perhaps Jurand had ordered it to drive ahead—if, as was to be expected, her sleigh had the best horses—or perhaps he had left it somewhere by a peasant's hut on the way. Zbyszko himself did not know what to do. In any case he determined to examine closely all the snowdrifts and the alder clump, and then to turn back and search along the highway.

They found nothing in the snowdrifts. In the alder clump wolves' eyes gleamed at them sometimes like candles, but they found no trace of men or horses. The meadow between the alder clump and the highway was now shining in the moonlight, and on its white, melancholic surface there were indeed visible from a distance here and there a few darker spots, but these also were only wolves, which quickly disappeared at the approach of men.

"Your grace," said the Czech at last, "it is no use looking here, for the young lady of Spychow was not in the company."

"To the highway!" answered Zbyszko.

"We shall not find them on the highway either. I looked carefully to see whether there was any women's baggage on any of the sleighs. There was nothing. The young lady has remained at Spychow."

Zbyszko was struck by the wisdom of this remark, so he replied: "God grant it was as you say!"

The Czech thought still more deeply.

"If she had been anywhere in the sleighs, the old lord would not have left her, or if he had left the sleighs, he would have taken her in front of him on his horse, and we should have found her with him."

"Let us go there once more," said Zbyszko in alarm.

For he had begun to think that it might be as the Czech had said. Perhaps they had not searched carefully enough. Perhaps Jurand had taken Danusia in front of him on his horse, and when the horse fell, Danusia had left her father in order to try and get help. In that case she might be somewhere under the snow nearby.

But Wisehead, as if guessing his master's thoughts, repeated:

"In that case we should have found women's dresses in the sleigh, for she would not have been travelling to the court with only the clothes she was wearing."

Despite the logic of what he said, they went back to the willow, but found nothing either under it or for a furlong around it. The duke's men had already taken Jurand to Niedzborz, and all about was complete emptiness. The Czech further observed that the dog which had accompanied the guide and had found Jurand would have found the young lady also. Then Zbyszko breathed more freely, for he now felt almost certain that Danusia had remained at home. He even felt that he knew why: evidently Danusia had confessed all to her father, and he, not agreeing to the marriage, had purposely left her at home while he went to discuss the matter with the duke and ask his intervention with the bishop. At this thought Zbyszko could not refrain from a certain feeling of relief and even joy, for he considered that with the death of Jurand all obstacles had been removed. Jurand did not wish it, but the Lord Jesus wished it, said the young knight to himself, and the will of God was always stronger. Now all he had to do was to ride to Spychow and take Danusia as his own, and then fulfill his vow, which was easier to do on the actual border than at distant Bog-daniec. "The will of God! the will of God!" he said to himself. But suddenly he was ashamed of this swift joy, and turning to the Czech, he said:

"I do indeed grieve for him, and I declare it openly."

"People said that the Germans feared him like death," replied the squire. After a while, however, he asked: "Are we now going back to the castle?"

"Through Niedzborz," replied Zbyszko.

They presently arrived there and rode up before the manor, where they were received by the old landowner, Zelech. They did not find Jurand there, but Zelech gave them good news.

"They rubbed him with snow almost to the bones," he said, "and poured wine down his throat, and then steamed him in a hot bath, where at last he began to breathe again."

"He is alive?" asked Zbyszko joyfully, forgetting his own affairs at the news.

"He is alive, but whether he will live God knows, for the spirit does not like to return from the half-way point."

"Why did you send him away?"

"Because messengers came from the duke. They covered him with all the feathered quilts in the house and took him away."

"Did he say nothing of his daughter?"

"He scarcely breathed; he could not yet speak."

"And the others?"

"The others are with God. They will not attend the Shepherd's Mass, poor fellows, unless the one which the Lord Jesus celebrates himself in heaven."

"None of them was alive?"

"None. Come into the room instead of talking here in the hallway. And if you want to see them, they are lying near the fire in the servants' quarters. Come into the room."

But they were in haste and would not come in, though old Zelech urged them, for he liked to find people to chat with. It was still a considerable way from Niedzborz to Ciechanow, and

Zbyszko burned with eagerness to see Jurand as soon as possible and learn something from him.

So they rode as fast as they could along the windswept highway. When they arrived, it was already after midnight, and the Shepherd's Mass was just ending in the chapel. Zbyszko heard the lowing of oxen and the bleating of goats, for the pious imitated those sounds according to ancient custom in memory of the fact that the Lord Jesus was born in a stable. After Mass, the duchess came to Zbyszko with a distressed expression on her face, full of alarm, and questioned him:

"Danusia?"

"She is not there. Did Jurand say nothing? I hear he is alive."

"Merciful Jesus! This is divine punishment. Woe to us! Jurand has not yet spoken. He's lying like a log of wood now."

"Never fear, gracious lady, Danusia has remained at Spychow."

"How do you know?"

"Because there was not a trace of a woman's garment in any of the sleighs. He would not have brought her in nothing but a sheepskin coat."

"True, as God is dear to me!"

And her eyes immediately began to flash with joy, and after a while she exclaimed:

"Hey, little Jesus, who was born today, plainly Thy blessing is over us, not Thy wrath!"

Nevertheless she was surprised by Jurand's arrival without his daughter, so she asked: "Why should he leave her at home?"

Zbyszko explained to her his surmises. They seemed to her very just, but did not alarm her too much.

"Jurand will now owe us his life," she said, "and in truth will owe it to you, for you went to dig him out. He would have to have a heart of stone to resist any longer. This is God's warning to him not to fight again the Holy Sacrament. As soon as he regains consciousness and is able to speak, I will tell him."

"He must first regain consciousness, for we do not yet know why he did not bring Danusia with him. What if she is sick?"

"Don't say so! I am grieved enough that she is not here. But if she were sick, he would not have left her!"

"True!"

And they went to Jurand. In his room it was as hot as in a bath and quite light, for enormous pine-logs were burning on the hearth. Father Wyszoniek was attending to the sick man, who was lying on the bed covered with bearskins, his face pale, his hair stuck together with sweat, and his eyes closed. His mouth was open, and he seemed to breathe with difficulty, but so strongly that the skins with which he was covered rose and fell with his breaths.

"How is he?" asked the duchess.

"I poured a jug of heated wine down his throat," replied Father Wyszoniek, "and he began to sweat."

"Is he asleep?"

"Maybe not, for he's breathing terribly hard."

"Have you tried to talk to him?"

"I have tried, but he doesn't answer, and I think he will not speak before dawn."

"We will wait for the dawn," said the duchess.

Father Wyszoniek tried to persuade her to go to her chambers to sleep, but she would not listen to him. She always and in everything endeavored to equal the deceased Queen Jadwiga in the Christian virtues and, therefore, in nursing the sick, in order to redeem her father's soul by her own services. She never lost an opportunity in this country, which had been Christian for so many centuries, to show herself more zealous than others, and thereby to wipe out the memory that she had been born in paganism.

Besides, she was burning with desire to learn something from Jurand's lips of Danusia, for she was still concerned about her. So she sat down by his bed and began to repeat the rosary; then she dozed. Zbyszko, not yet completely well, and over-tired by his night-drive, soon followed her example, and after an hour they were both so sound asleep that maybe they would have slept until broad day, had they not been waked at dawn by the sound of the castle chapel bell.

The same sound awakened Jurand, who opened his eyes, sat up suddenly in bed, and looked around, blinking.

"Jesus Christ be praised! How are you?" said the duchess.

But he was evidently not yet fully conscious, for he looked at her as if he did not recognize her, and presently exclaimed:

"Over here! over here! Dig out the drift!"

"In God's name, you're now at Ciechanow," said the lady.

But Jurand frowned like a man collecting his thoughts with difficulty.

"At Ciechanow?" he replied. "The child is waiting with . . . the duke and duchess. . . . Danusia! Danusia! . . ."

And suddenly, closing his eyes, he fell back on the pillows. Zbyszko and the duchess feared that he was dead, but his breast began to heave with deep breathing, as in a man who has fallen soundly asleep.

Father Wyszoniek laid his finger to his lips and signaled with his hand not to wake Jurand, and then whispered:

"Maybe he will sleep like that the whole day."

"Yes, but what did he say?" asked the duchess.

"He said that his girl was waiting at Ciechanow," replied Zbyszko.

"He has not yet come to his senses," explained the priest.

CHAPTER XXVIII

FATHER Wyszoniek was even afraid that if Jurand were awakened a second time he might be seized with fever and lose consciousness for a long period. He promised, though, to let the duchess and Zbyszko know if the old knight spoke, and when they had gone he himself lay down to rest. Jurand did not awake until noon on the day following Christmas, but when he did he was quite conscious. The duchess and Zbyszko were present, so he sat up in bed, looked at her, recognized her, and said:

"Worshipful lady. . . . Heavens, then I am at Ciechanow?"

"Yes, and you have slept right through Christmas Day," replied the lady.

"I was buried in snow. Who rescued me?"

"This knight, Zbyszko of Bogdaniec. You remember, at Cracow. . . ."

Jurand examined the young man with his sound eye.

"I remember," he said. "But where is Danusia?"

"Why, surely she was coming with you?" asked the duchess.

"How could she come with me when I was coming to her?"

Zbyszko and the duchess looked at one another, supposing that he was still delirious, and the lady said:

"Wake up, in heaven's name! Was the girl not with you?"

"The girl? With me?" asked Jurand in amazement.

"Your men were all lost, but we did not find her among them. Why did you leave her at Spychow?"

But he answered in an alarmed tone:

"At Spychow? Why, she is with you, worshipful lady, not with me!"

"But you sent men with a letter to the hunting-lodge for her."

"In the name of the Father and of the Son!" replied Jurand. "I never sent for her!"

The duchess suddenly turned pale.

"What is that?" she said. "Are you sure that you have all your senses about you?"

"By God's mercy, where is my child?" exclaimed Jurand, springing up.

Hearing that, Father Wyszoniek left the room quickly, while the duchess went on:

"Listen! An armed troop came to the hunting-lodge to fetch Danusia with a letter from you, in which it was said that beams had injured you during a fire—that you were half-blind—that you wanted to see the child. . . . They took Danusia and went. . . ."

"Woe!" exclaimed Jurand. "As God is in heaven, there was never any fire at Spychow, and I never sent for her!"

Meanwhile Father Wyszoniek had returned with the letter, which he handed to Jurand, asking him:

"Is not that the handwriting of your priest?"

"I don't know."

"And the seal?"

"The seal is mine. What is in the letter?"

Father Wyszoniek read the letter. Jurand listened, pulling out his hair. Then he said:

"The letter is forged! The seal is false! Woe to me! They have seized my child and will do away with her!"

"Who?"

"The Teutonic Knights!"

"Great heavens! We must tell the duke! He must send envoys to the grand master!" exclaimed the lady. "Merciful Jesus, save her, help her! . . ."

Then she rushed from the room with a cry. Jurand leapt from the bed and began feverishly to dress his huge frame. Zbyszko sat as if petrified, but after a while his set teeth began to grind ominously.

"How do you know that the Teutonic Knights have carried her off?" asked Father Wyszoniek.

"I will swear it on the Divine Passion!"

"Wait! You may be right! They came to the hunting-lodge to

make a complaint against you. They desired vengeance against you."

"And it was they who carried her off!" exclaimed Zbyszko suddenly.

With these words he rushed from the room to the stables, where he ordered the horses to be harnessed and the stallions saddled, not knowing exactly what he was doing. He only grasped that it was necessary to go and rescue Danusia—immediately—and as far as Prussia—and once there tear her from hostile hands or perish.

Then he returned to the chamber to tell Jurand that the horses and men would be ready immediately. He was certain that Jurand would go with him. His heart was overflowing with wrath, pain, and grief, but at the same time he did not lose hope, for it seemed to him that the both of them, together, could accomplish anything, and might face the whole power of the Teutonic Order.

In the room—besides Jurand, Father Wyszoniek, and the lady—he found the duke and Sieur de Lorche, as well as the old lord of Longwood, Nicholas, whom the duke had called to counsel, as soon as he had heard the matter, because of his intelligence and his intimate knowledge of the Teutonic Knights, among whom he had spent long years as a prisoner.

"One must begin prudently, so as not to do wrong in one's excitement and lose the girl," said the Lord of Longwood. "One must make a complaint to the master at once, and if Your Serene Highness gives me a letter to him, I myself will take it."

"I will give you a letter, and you will deliver it," said the duke. "We will not allow the child to perish, so help me God and the Holy Cross. The master is afraid of war with the Polish king, and he is anxious to win my brother Ziemowit and myself to his side. I am sure it is not by his command she has been kidnapped. He will order her to be given back."

"But if it was by his command?" asked Father Wyszoniek.

"Although he is a Teutonic Knight, there is more honesty in him than in the others," replied the duke. "And as I have told you, he wants more to win me over than to rouse my anger. The power of the Jagiellos is not to be laughed at. . . . Yes! The knights have poured boiling fat on our skins as long as they could, but now they see that if we Mazovians help Jagiello, it will go badly for them."

"True!" said the Lord of Longwood. "The Teutonic Knights do

nothing without a purpose. I am certain that if they kidnapped the girl it was only to strike the sword from Jurand's hand, and either take a ransom for her or exchange her."

Here he turned to the Lord of Spychow.

"Whom have you now as a prisoner?"

"De Bergow," answered Jurand.

"Is he someone of importance?"

"It would appear so."

Sieur de Lorche, hearing the name of de Bergow, began to ask questions about him, and when he learned who he was, he said:

"Why, he is a relative of the Count of Guelders, a great benefactor of the Order, and comes from a family which has served it well in the past."

"Yes," said the Lord of Longwood, after translating his words to those present. "The de Bergows held high positions in the Order."

"And von Danveld and von Lowe were very insistent about him," said the duke. "Every time one of them opened his mouth, he said that de Bergow must be released. As God is in heaven, they must have carried off the child in order to get him back."

"They will give her back for him," said the priest.

"It would be good to know where she is," said the Lord of Longwood. "For suppose the master asks, 'Whom have I to order to give her back?' what shall we say?"

"Where she is?" asked Jurand dully. "There are certainly not keeping her on the border, for fear I should recover her, but somewhere far away on the sandbars of the Vistula or of the sea-coast."

But Zbyszko said:

"We will find her and get her back."

The duke burst out in sudden, stifled rage.

"Those curs kidnapped her from my court, thereby bringing shame on me! I will not forgive them for that as long as I live. I have had enough of their treacheries! Enough of their lawless attacks! Everyone would rather have werewolves for neighbors. But now the master must punish these commanders and give back the girl and send envoys to me with apologies. Else I will summon my vassals to war!"

He struck the table with his fist, adding:

"My brother of Plock will follow me, and Witold, and the power of King Jagiello is behind us. Enough restraint! A saint would lose patience over this. I've had enough!"

They were all silent, waiting with their advice until his anger would calm down. But Anna Danuta rejoiced that the duke took Danusia's cause so much to heart, for she knew that he was patient, but also resolute, and that once he undertook something he would not stop until he got his own way.

When the duke quieted down, Father Wyszoniek spoke:

"Once upon a time there was discipline in the Order. No commander dared to do anything on his own account without the permission of the chapter and of the grand master. Therefore God gave into their hands important countries and raised them almost above every other power on earth. But now there is neither discipline, nor truth, nor honesty, nor faith among them. Nothing but greed, as if they were wolves, not men. Why should they obey the commands of the master or of the chapter when they do not obey the commands of God? Each one sits in his own castle like an independent prince, and one helps the other to do evil. We will lodge a complaint to the master—they will deny everything. The master will order them to give back the girl—they will not give her back, saying: 'She is not here with us; we did not kidnap her.' He will order them to swear on an oath that they do not have her— they will swear. What will we do then?"

"What are we to do?" said the Lord of Longwood. "Let Jurand go to Spychow. If they kidnapped her for the sake of ransom, or to exchange her for de Bergow, they must let someone know, and they will let no one else know but Jurand."

"It was those who came to the hunting-lodge who kidnapped her," said the priest.

"Then the master will give them up to judgment or will bid them face Jurand in combat."

"They must face me in combat!" exclaimed Zbyszko. "I challenged them first!"

Jurand took his hands from his face and asked:

"Who were the men at the hunting-lodge?"

"There was Danveld and old von Lowe and two brethren, Godfrey and Roger," replied the priest. "They made complaints and desired the duke to order you to release do Bergow. But the duke, learning from de Fourcy that the Germans had attacked you first, thundered at them and sent them away with nothing."

The duke turned to Jurand.

"Go to Spychow," he said, "for they will go there. They have not gone there yet because this knight's squire crushed Danveld's arm when he brought them his challenge. Go to Spychow, and when they arrive, let me know. They will send you back your child in exchange for de Bergow. Yet I will not renounce my vengeance, for they have brought shame on me by taking her from my court."

Here he was seized afresh with rage, for the Teutonic Knights had really exhausted all his patience. After a while, he added:

"Hah! They have blown and blown the flames, but at last they will burn their ugly faces."

"They will deny it!" repeated Father Wyszoniek.

"As soon as they tell Jurand that his daughter is with them, they will not be able to deny it," answered Nicholas of Longwood somewhat impatiently. "I believe that they are not keeping her on the border, and that, as Jurand supposed, they have carried her off to some distant castle or to the sandbars of the coast. But when there is evidence that it is they who have done it, they will not be able to deny it before the grand master."

Jurand began to repeat in a strange and terrible voice:

"Danveld, Lowe, Godfrey, and Roger. . . ."

Nicholas of Longwood recommended that travelled and experienced men should be sent to Prussia to inquire at Ortelsburg and Insbork whether Jurand's daughter was there and, if she wasn't there, where she had been taken. The duke went out to give the necessary orders, while the duchess turned to Jurand, wishing to cheer him with a good word.

"How do you feel?" she asked.

He made no answer for a time, as if he had not heard her, and then suddenly said:

"As if someone had opened up my old wound."

"Trust in God's mercy. Danusia will come back if you give them de Bergow."

"I would not begrudge them even my own blood."

The duchess hesitated whether or not to tell him immediately about the marriage, but when she had thought it over, she was unwilling to add a new pain to Jurand's already grave misfortunes.

At the same time she was overcome with a certain fear. "He will look for her with Zbyszko, so Zbyszko may find an opportunity to tell him," she said to herself. "If he found out now, he might completely go mad." So she preferred to speak of something else.

"Do not blame us," she said. "Men came in your livery colors, with a letter bearing your seal, relating that you were sick, that you were losing your sight, and that you wanted to see your child once again. How could we refuse to fulfill a father's commands?"

Jurand embraced her knees.

"I blame no one, worshipful lady."

"Know also that God will bring her back to you, for His eye is on her. He will send help to her, as He did at the last hunt, when the wild aurochs attacked us and the Lord Jesus inspired Zbyszko to defend us. Zbyszko nearly lost his life and lay sick for a long time afterwards, but he saved Danusia and me, for which the duke gave him a knight's belt and spurs. So you see! The hand of God is over her. I thought she would come with you, I thought I should see my dearest child again, but meanwhile. . . ."

Her voice quivered and her eyes filled with tears, while Jurand's despair, which till now had been held in check, broke out, sudden and terrible as a whirlwind. He seized his long hair and began to beat his head against the beams of the wall, groaning and repeating hoarsely:

"Jesus! Jesus! Jesus!"

But Zbyszko sprang to him and, shaking him by the shoulders with all his strength, called out:

"We must be off! Off to Spychow!"

CHAPTER XXIX

"WHOSE troop is this?" asked Jurand suddenly, beyond Radzanow, rousing himself from his thoughts, as if from a dream.

"Mine," replied Zbyszko.

"All of my people died?"

"I saw them dead at Niedzborz."

"My old companions gone!"

Zbyszko did not reply. They rode on in silence and quickly, for they wished to be at Spychow as soon as possible, expecting to find envoys there from the Teutonic Knights. Fortunately for them the frosts returned and the road was beaten down, so they were able to hasten. Towards evening Jurand spoke again, asking questions about those brethren of the Order who had been at the hunting-lodge, and Zbyszko told him everything: about their complaints and departure, and the death of Sieur de Fourcy, and the action of his own squire who had crushed Danveld's arm so terribly. While he was relating all this, he remembered and was struck by one circumstance: the presence at the lodge of the woman who had brought healing balsams from Danveld. At the next stopping place, he therefore questioned both the Czech and Sanderus about her, but neither of them knew what had actually happened to her. They thought that she had gone either with the men who had come to Danusia or soon after them. Zbyszko now conceived the idea that she might have been sent in advance to warn the men, should Jurand himself have been at the lodge. In that case they would not have pretended to be men from Spychow, but might even have had some other letter ready which they would have given to the duchess instead of the forged writing from Jurand. It had all been planned with diabolic skill, and the young knight, who had hitherto known the Teutonic Knights only in the field, for the first time began to realize that in dealing with them the fist was not enough—they must be overcome with the help of the brain. This thought was bitter to him, for his great grief and pain had changed almost entirely into a lust for battle and blood. Even the rescue of Danusia appeared to him as a series of battles, either *en masse* or in single combat. Now he perceived that he must put his lust of vengeance on a chain like a bear, and search for entirely fresh means of saving and recovering the girl. Thinking thus, he regretted that Macko was not with him, for Macko was as cunning as he was valiant. However, he decided to send Sanderus from Spychow to Ortelsburg, to look for the aforementioned woman and endeavor to find out from her what had happened to Danusia. He told himself that even if Sanderus were to betray him, it would not do much harm, and that, in the opposite case, he might do him considerable service, as his trade opened the way for him everywhere.

Zbyszko chose, however, to talk to Jurand, but he put this off until they reached Spychow, particularly as night had fallen and Jurand, sitting in his high knight's saddle, seemed to have fallen asleep from fatigue and grave anxiety. But Jurand was only riding with his head bent because of the misfortunes which weighed upon him. It was evident that he was constantly thinking of these misfortunes and that he was in a very distraught mood, for he said at last:

"I would have preferred to have frozen to death at Niedzborz! Was it you who dug me out?"

"Yes, I and others."

"And at the hunt it was you who save my child?"

"What else was I to do?"

"And you are going to help me now?"

Suddenly Zbyszko was so overcome with both a feeling of love for Danusia and hatred for those Teutonic Knights who had wronged him, that he stood up in his stirrups and said tensely through set teeth:

"Listen to what I say: Even if I have to bite the Prussian castles with my teeth, I will bite them, and I will get her."

A moment of silence followed. Jurand's vengeful and unrestrained nature expressed itself forcibly under the influence of Zbyszko's words, for he began to grind his teeth in the darkness, and presently to repeat again the names:

"Danveld, Lowe, Godfrey, and Roger! . . ."

And in his heart he thought that if they demanded the release of de Bergow he would release him; if they bade him pay a ransom in addition, he would pay it, even though he had to throw in the whole of Spychow to make it up. But afterwards, woe to those who had raised their hands against his only child!

Throughout the night sleep did not close their eyes even for a second. Towards morning they scarcely recognized each other, so changed were their faces by that one night. Jurand at last was struck by Zbyszko's grief and resolution, and said:

"She covered you with her veil and saved you from death—that I know. But do you return her love?"

Zbyszko looked him almost insolently straight in the face, and replied:

"She is my wife."

Jurand reined in his horse and looked at him, blinking in amazement.

"What's that?"

"She is my woman and I am her husband."

The knight of Spychow covered his one eye with his glove as if dazzled by a sudden flash of lightning, but made no answer. After a while he spurred his horse forward, pushed up to the head of the troop, and rode on in silence.

CHAPTER XXX

BUT Zbyszko, riding behind him, could not restrain himself for long, and thought, "I would rather Jurand burst out in anger than clench his teeth in silence." So he rode up beside him and, touching his stirrup with his own, began to explain:

"Listen to how it happened. What Danusia did for me at Cracow you know, but you do not know that at Bogdaniec they wanted to give me Jagienka, the daughter of Zych of Zgorzelice. My uncle Macko wanted it; her father, Zych, wanted it; and so did the abbot, her kinsman, a rich man. . . . Why make a long story of it? She is a decent, good-looking girl, and her dowry is also considerable. But it could not be. I was grieved for Jagienka, but I was still more grieved for Danusia—and I went to her in Mazovia, for, frankly speaking, I could not live without her any longer. Remember how you fell in love yourself. Remember, and you will not wonder."

Here Zbyszko stopped, waiting for some answer from Jurand, but as the latter remained silent, he went on:

"At the hunting-lodge God granted me to save the duchess and Danusia from an aurochs. And the duchess said, 'Now Jurand will not oppose a marriage, for how could he not repay you for such a deed?' But even then I did not think of taking her without your paternal permission. Ha! I could not have done so, for the fierce beast had injured me so that it almost crushed the life out of me. Afterwards, you know, those men came for Danusia to supposedly take her to Spychow, and I still could not rise from my bed. I thought I should never see her again. I thought you would take her to Spychow and give her to another. At Cracow you had been against me, after all. . . . I thought I was on the point of death. Great God, what a night that was! Nothing but anxiety, nothing but grief! I thought that when she had gone the sun would never rise again. You understand human love and human pain. . . ."

Zbyszko's voice trembled with emotion, but as he had a strong heart he mastered himself and continued:

"The men came for her in the evening and wanted to take her at once, but the duchess had them wait till morning. Meanwhile the Lord Jesus sent me an idea to bow down before the duchess and beg her for Danusia. I thought that if I died I should have at least one consolation. Remember that the girl was to go and I was to stay, sick and near death. There was no time to ask your permission. The duke had already left the hunting-lodge, and the duchess was at a loss, not having anyone to ask for advice. But at last she and Father Wyszoniek had pity on me, and Father Wyszoniek married us. . . . Divine power, divine law—"

"And divine punishment," interrupted Jurand dully.

"Why has there to be punishment?" asked Zbyszko. "Remember that they sent for her before the marriage, and would have taken her away just the same whether it had been celebrated or not."

But Jurand again said nothing and rode on, shut up in himself, frozen, with such a stony face that Zbyszko, although he felt at first relieved, as one always does after confessing things which have long been kept secret, became afraid and began to tell himself with increasing disquiet that the old knight had shut himself up in anger and that from henceforth they would be like strangers to one another.

And he was overcome with dejection. Never since he left Bog-daniec had he felt so downcast. It seemed to him now that there was no hope of reconciling Jurand, nor, what was worse, of rescuing Danusia, that all was in vain, and that in the future ever more misfortunes would fall upon him, and ever greater misery. But his dejection lasted only a short time, or rather, in accordance with his nature, soon turned into anger, into a desire for quarrelling and for fighting. "He does not want harmony," he said to himself, thinking of Jurand. "Very well, let there be discord between us; let there be what he wants!" And Zbyszko was ready to spring right at Jurand. He was also seized with lust for combat with anybody, about anything, as long as he could do something, give some expression to his grief, bitterness, and wrath, as long as he could find some relief.

Meanwhile they reached an inn at the crossroads, called The Lantern, where Jurand usually rested his men and horses on his way from the ducal court to Spychow. Despite himself, he did so now. Presently he and Zbyszko found themselves alone in a room. Suddenly Jurand stopped before the young knight and, fixing his glance upon him, asked:

"Then it was for her that you came here?"

And he answered, almost roughly:

"Do you think I will deny it?"

And he began to look straight at Jurand, ready to answer his anger with an outburst of his own. But the face of the old warrior did not express stubbornness or hatred, but only boundless sorrow.

"And you saved my child?" he asked presently. "And you dug me out?"

Zbyszko looked at him with surprise and alarm, wondering whether he was confused in mind, since he now repeated exactly the same questions as he had put once before.

"Sit down," he said, "for it seems to me that you are still weak."

But Jurand lifted his hands and laid them on Zbyszko's shoulders—and suddenly drew him to his breast with his entire strength. Zbyszko, recovering from his amazement, caught him by the waist; and they held one another thus for a long time, bound together by common suffering and common misfortune.

When at last they let each other go, Zbyszko embraced the knees of the old knight and kissed his hand with tears in his eyes.

"You will not be against me?" he asked.

And Jurand replied:

"I was against you, for I had offered her in my heart to God."

"You offered her to God, and God offered her to me. It was His will!"

"His will!" repeated Jurand. "But now we need His compassion."

"Whom will God help, if not a father looking for his child, or a husband looking for his wife? He will not help robbers."

"Yet they carried her off," replied Jurand.

"You will give them back de Bergow."

"I will give them everything they ask for."

But at the thought of the Teutonic Knights, his old hatred soon awoke in him and took hold of him like a fire, so that presently he added through set teeth:

"And I will give them something they don't want."

"I also have sworn the same," replied Zbyszko, "but now we must go to Spychow."

And he began to hasten the men to saddle their horses. So when the horses had eaten their fodder, and the men had warmed themselves a little indoors, they went on, although it was already dusk in the yard. Because the road was long and a sharp frost had fallen with the night, Jurand and Zbyszko, who had not yet recovered their full strength, rode in a sleigh. Zbyszko told of his uncle Macko, for whom he longed with all his heart, and he regretted that the veteran warrior was not present, since they had need both of his valor and of his cunning, which was even more necessary in facing such enemies than valor. So he turned to Jurand and asked:

"Are you cunning? Because I cannot manage to be at all."

"Neither can I," replied Jurand. "I did not fight them with cunning but with this hand and the grief which has remained in me."

"Now I understand," said the young knight. "I understand because I love Danusia, and they have carried her off. If, God forbid. . . ."

He did not finish, for at the very thought he felt that he did not have a man's heart, but a wolf's. For some time they rode in silence along the white moonlit road, and then Jurand began to speak as if to himself:

"If they had a just reason for vengeance on me, I would not say anything! But, dear God, they had none. . . . I fought with them in the field when I went as an envoy from our duke to Witold, but here I was like a neighbor to them. Bartosz Nalecz seized forty knights who were going to Malbork, fettered them, and shut them up in the dungeons of Kozmin. The Teutonic Knights had to send him half a wagon-load of money to ransom them. But I, if a German came my way desiring to join the Teutonic Knights, entertained him as a knight and gave him gifts. Sometimes the Teutonic Knights rode against me through the marshes. I was not harsh to them even then, and yet they have done to me what I would not do to my worst enemy even today. . . ."

Terrible memories began to tear at his heart; his voice broke for a while, and then he said, half groaning:

"I had one beloved, a gentle, loving woman. We were like one heart in two breasts. They took her on a rope like a dog, and she died on the rope . . . and now my child—Jesus, Jesus!"

Silence fell again. Zbyszko raised his young face to the moon with an expression of wonder. Then he looked at Jurand.

"Father! It would be better for them to earn the love of men rather than their vengeance. Why do they do injury to every nation and to all people?"

Jurand spread out his hands in despair and answered dully: "I do not know. . . ."

Zbyszko thought for some time over the answer to his own question, but presently his mind turned to Jurand again.

"Men say that you took worthy revenge," he said.

Jurand meanwhile mastered his pain and collected himself.

"I took an oath," he replied. "I took an oath to God that if He would let me fulfill my vengeance I would give Him the child which was left me. That was why I was against you. But now I do not know whether it was His will or whether you have roused His wrath by your doings."

"No," said Zbyszko. "I told you just now that even if there had been no marriage, the curs would have seized her just the same. God heard your wish, but gave Danusia to me, for without His will all would have come to naught."

"Every sin is against the will of God."

"Sin is, but not a sacrament. A sacrament is something divine."

"For that reason there is no help."

"God be praised, there is none! Make no complaint about that, for no one would help you against those robbers as I will help you. Look! I will repay them for Danusia, but if a single one of those who carried off your wife is alive, give him to me and you will see!"

Jurand shook his head.

"No," he answered gloomily. "None of them is still alive. . . ."

For a time nothing was to be heard save the snorting of the horses and the dull sound of their hoofs beating on the hard road.

"Once in the night," continued Jurand, "I heard a voice which seemed to come from the wall, saying to me, 'Enough vengeance!' But I did not listen to it, for it was not the voice of my dead wife."

"Whose voice was it?" asked Zbyszko uneasily.

"I don't know. Often at Spychow something speaks and sometimes groans in the walls, for many men have died in chains in the dungeon."

"What does the priest say?"

"The priest blessed the fortalice and also said that I should give up further vengeance, but it could not be. I had become too powerful, and afterwards they themselves wanted to take vengeance on me. They laid ambushes and challenged me to combat. It was so now. Maineger and de Bergow challenged me first."

"Did you ever take ransom?"

"Never. Of those whom I took, de Bergow will be the first to come out alive."

Their talk ceased. They had turned from the broad highway onto a narrower road, which they now followed for some time, as it was winding and in places became a mere wooded defile, full of snowdrifts hard to breach. In spring or summer during the rains it must have been almost impassable.

"Are we near to Spychow yet?" asked Zbyszko.

"Yes," said Jurand. "There is still a considerable stretch of forest and then the warm swamps begin; in their midst is the fortalice. Behind the swamps are meadows and dry fields, but the fort can be reached only by a causeway. More than once the Germans have wanted to get me, but they could not, and many of their bones are rotting along the edges of the forest."

"It is not easy to find the way," said Zbyszko. "If the Teutonic Knights have sent men with letters, how will they get to you?"

"They've sent letters before and have men who know the way."

"God grant we may find them at Spychow," said Zbyszko.

This wish was to be realized sooner than the young knight expected. When they had ridden out of the forest onto the open plain, where Spychow lay among the marshes, they saw in front of them two riders and a low sleigh in which three dark figures were sitting.

The night was very bright, and so the whole group was clearly visible against the white background of the snow. The hearts of Jurand and Zbyszko beat more rapidly at the sight, for who could be riding to Spychow in the middle of the night if not envoys from the Order?

Zbyszko had his driver go more quickly, and they were soon near enough to be heard. The two horsemen, who were evidently guarding the sleigh, turned to them and, taking their crossbows from their shoulders, shouted:

"*Wer da?*"

"Germans!" whispered Jurand.

Then he raised his voice and said:

"It is my right to ask and yours to answer. Who are you?"

"Travellers."

"What sort of travellers?"

"Pilgrims."

"Where from?"

"From Ortelsburg."

"It is they!" whispered Jurand again.

Meanwhile the sleighs drew up to each other, and at the same time six riders appeared in front. These were the Spychow guard, which watched the causeway leading to the fortalice night and day. Alongside their horses ran huge and terrible dogs, looking very much like wolves.

The guard, recognizing Jurand, began to shout a greeting to him, with some surprise in their tone that their master was returning so soon and unexpectedly. But Jurand was completely engrossed with the envoys and addressed them again:

"Where are you going?"

"To Spychow."

"What do you want there?"

"That we can tell only the lord himself."

Jurand was on the point of saying, "I am the Lord of Spychow," but checked himself, understanding that they could not talk in front of his men. On the other hand, he asked whether they had any letters, and hearing that they had been bidden to talk with him only orally, he bade them drive as fast as their horses could go. Zbyszko also was so eager to learn news of Danusia that he could pay attention to nothing else. He was impatient when the guards stopped them twice more on the causeway; he was impatient when the drawbridge was being let down over the moat, behind which, on the ramparts, was an enormous palisade; and although he had frequently felt curious to know the look of that notorious fortalice, at the mere remembrance of which the Germans used to cross themselves, now he saw nothing save envoys from the Teutonic Knights, from whom he might hear where Danusia was and when she could be given back her freedom. He did not foresee that grievous disappointment was awaiting him.

Besides the escorting horsemen and the sleigh driver, the embassy from Ortelsburg was composed of two persons: one of them the same woman who had previously brought the healing balsam to the hunting-lodge in the forest, and the other a young pilgrim. Zbyszko did not recognize the woman, for he had not seen her at the lodge, but the pilgrim seemed to him to be a distinguished esquire. After they stopped, Jurand led both of them into a corner chamber of his fortalice, and stood before them huge and terrible in the light of the flames, which fell on him from the fire burning on the hearth.

"Where is my child?" he asked.

They were alarmed, finding themselves thus face to face with the dangerous man. The pilgrim, though he had an insolent face, trembled like a leaf, and the woman's legs shook under her. Her glance passed from the face of Jurand to that of Zbyszko, and then to the shining bald head of Father Caleb, who was also in the room, and then returned to Jurand as if asking what those two were doing there.

"Lord," she said finally, "we do not know what you are asking about, but we have been sent to you on important matters, and he who sent us ordered us expressly not to speak with you in the presence of witnesses."

"I have not secrets before these men!" said Jurand.

"But we have, noble lord," answered the woman; "and if you bid them stay, then we shall ask you for nothing but permission to depart tomorrow."

Anger was reflected in Jurand's face, unaccustomed as he was to opposition. For a while his sandy moustache began to more ominously; but he remembered that it was a question of Danusia and restrained himself. Zbyszko, who was anxious above all that the conversation should take place as quickly as possible, and was certain that Jurand would repeat it to him, said, "Since it has to be so, remain alone," and went out with Father Caleb. He barely had reached the main room, hung with captured shields and weapons, when Wisehead approached him.

"Lord," he said, "that is the same woman."

"What woman?"

"From the Teutonic Knights—the one who brought the Hercynian balsam. I recognized her at once, and so did Sanderus. She obviously came as a spy, and now certainly she knows where the young lady is."

"We shall also know," said Zbyszko. "And do you recognize the pilgrim?"

"No," replied Sanderus. "But do not buy indulgences from him, lord, for he's a false pilgrim. If he were put to the torture, he could tell us much."

"Wait!" said Zbyszko.

Meanwhile, in the corner room, scarcely had the door shut behind Zbyszko and Father Caleb when the sister of the Order approached Jurand quickly and whispered:

"Your daughter was carried off by robbers."

"With crosses on their cloaks?"

"No. But God blessed the pious brethren, so that they rescued her, and now she is with them."

"Where is she?"

"Under the protection of the pious Brother Schomberg," she replied, crossing her hands on her breast and bowing humbly.

Jurand, hearing the terrible name of the executioner of Witold's children, turned white as a sheet. He sat down on a bench, lowered his eyelids, and began to wipe off the cold sweat that stood in beads on his forehead.

Seeing this, the previously trembling pilgrim now put his hands on his hips, sat down in a sprawling position on another bench, stretched out his legs, and looked at Jurand with an expression of arrogance and contempt.

A long silence followed.

"And Brother Markwart is helping Brother Schomberg to watch over her," said the woman. "They are taking good care of her, and no harm will be done to the young lady."

"What have I to do to get her back from them?" asked Jurand.

"Humble yourself before the Order," said the pilgrim proudly.

Jurand got up, went to him, and, leaning over him, said in a choked and terrible voice:

"Be silent!"

And the pilgrim became terrified again. He knew that he might threaten and might say something which would restrain and break Jurand, but he was afraid that before he uttered a word something dreadful might happen to him. So he held his tongue. His eyes, round and petrified with fright, fixed on the Lord of Spychow's threatening face, and he sat motionless. Only his chin began to quiver violently.

Jurand turned to the sister of the Order:

"Have you a letter?"

"No, lord, we have no letter. What we have to say we were bidden to say by word of mouth."

"Then speak!"

But she repeated again, as if wishing to plant it firmly in his mind:

"Brother Schomberg and Brother Markwart are watching over the young lady, so, lord, restrain your anger. But nothing evil will happen to her, for though you have done serious injuries to the Order for many years, the brethren wish to repay you good for evil, if you will satisfy their just demands."

"What do they want?"

"They want you to release Lord de Bergow."

Jurand took a deep breath.

"I will give them de Bergow," he said.

"And the other prisoners whom you have at Spychow."

"There are Maineger's and de Bergow's two esquires, and also their attendants.

"You have to release them, lord, and recompense them for their imprisonment."

"God forbid I should bargain for my child."

"That was what the pious monks expected of you," said the woman, "but that is not all that I was bidden to tell you. Your daughter, lord, was carried off by some men, doubtless robbers, and doubtless in order to get a rich ransom from you. God permitted the brethren to rescue her, and now they demand no more than that you should release their companion and guest. But the brethren know, and you know, lord, what hatred there is towards them in this country, and how unjustly all their deeds, even the most pious, are judged. For that reason the brethren are certain that if it were known here that your daughter was with them, it would immediately be supposed that they had carried her off, and thus their virtue would be exposed to accusations and false suspicions. Oh, yes! evil and malicious men hereabouts have more than once repaid them thus, and the reputation of the pious Order has suffered greatly. The brethren must care for their good name, and therefore, they add only this condition, that you yourself declare to the duke of this land, and to the whole fierce knighthood, what the truth is—that not the brethren of the Cross but robbers carried off your daughter, and that you had to ransom her from robbers."

"It is true," said Jurand. "Robbers carried off my daughter, and I must ransom her from robbers. . . ."

"You are not to tell anyone otherwise. If but a single man were to learn that you had come to an agreement with the brethren—if but a single living soul—or if but a single complaint were to be made either to the grand master or to the chapter, then grave difficulties would arise."

Disquiet was reflected in Jurand's face. At first it seemed to him natural enough that the commanders should demand secrecy out of fear of the consequences and the infamy which would fall upon them, but now the suspicion was born in him that there might be some other reason. Since he could not figure out what the reason could be, he was seized with fear, such as overcomes the boldest of men when they are threatened with danger, not to themselves but to those who are near and dear. He determined, however, to learn more from the servant of the Order.

"The commanders wish for secrecy," he said, "but what secrecy can be preserved when I release de Bergow and the others in exchange for my child?"

"You will say that you took a ransom from the Lord de Bergow so as to be able to pay the robbers."

"Men will not believe it, for I have never taken a ransom," replied Jurand gloomily.

"It has never been a question of your child," hissed the woman.

And again silence fell, after which the pilgrim, who in the meantime had plucked up courage, thinking that Jurand must now restrain himself more, said:

"Such is the will of Brother Schomberg and Brother Markwart."

The woman continued:

"You will say that the pilgrim who has come with me brought

you a ransom, and we will go away from here with the noble de Bergow and the other prisoners."

"What?" asked Jurand, frowning. "Do you think I shall give you back my prisoners before getting my child?"

"Then do something else, lord. You may come yourself for your daughter to Ortelsburg, where the brethren will bring her to meet you."

"I? To Ortelsburg?"

"For if robbers were to kidnap her again on the way, again your suspicions and those of the people hereabouts would fall on the pious knights, and therefore they prefer to give her into your own hands."

"And who will guarantee me that I shall return, if I put my head in the wolf's mouth?"

"The virtue of the brethren, their justice and piety."

Jurand began to walk up and down in the room. He began now to foresee treachery and he feared it. But he felt at the same time that the Knights might lay such conditions on him as they liked, and that he was powerless in their hands.

However, some plan evidently entered his head, for he suddenly stopped in front of the pilgrim and looked at him sharply, and then turned to the woman and said:

"Good, I will come to Ortelsburg. You and this man who is wearing the dress of a pilgrim will stay here until my return, and then you will go with de Bergow and the prisoners."

"You do not wish, lord, to trust the monks," said the pilgrim, "so how can they trust you to let us and de Bergow go after your return?"

Jurand's face turned pale with indignation. There followed a threatening moment, in which it seemed that he was on the point of seizing the pilgrim by the throat and crushing him on the floor—but he restrained his wrath, breathed deeply, and said slowly and clearly:

"Whoever you are, do not strain my patience too far or it will break."

The pilgrim turned to the sister.

"Tell him."

"Lord," she said, "we should never dare to disbelieve your oath on your sword and on your knightly honor, but it would not befit

you to take an oath in front of simple people like us, and we were
not sent for your oath."

"What were you sent for?"

"The brethren told us that, without saying a word to anyone,
you have to present yourself at Ortelsburg with Lord de Bergow
and the prisoners."

At that Jurand's shoulders began to straighten, and his fingers to
spread like the talons of a bird of prey. Finally, standing in front of
the woman, he bent down as if to speak in her ear.

"Did they not tell you," he said, "that I would have you and de
Bergow put to the rack at Spychow?"

"Your daughter is in the power of the brethren and under the
care of Schomberg and Markwart," said the sister with emphasis.

"Robbers! Poisoners! Hangmen!" burst out Jurand.

"Who are able to avenge us, and who said to us at parting: 'If he
does not fulfill all our commands, it would be better for his girl to
die as Witold's children died.' Choose!"

"And understand that you are in the power of the commanders,"
said the pilgrim. "They do not wish to do you injury, and the
Constable of Ortelsburg sent you word by us that you will go free
from his castle. But in return for what you have done to them in
the past, they wish that you should come and bow down before the
cloak of the Order, and beg them, as conquerors, to show mercy.
They are willing to forgive you, but first they wish to bend your
proud neck. You have declared them to be traitors and perjurers, so
they wish you to put your trust in them. They will give you and
your daughter back your freedom, but you must beg for it. You
have trampled on them, so you must swear that you hand will never
again be raised against the white cloak."

"Such is the wish of the commanders," added the woman, "and
also of Markwart and Schomberg."

A moment of deadly silence followed. It seemed as if among the
beams of the roof a muffled echo repeated in alarm: "Markwart . . .
Schomberg. . . ." From outside the window came the calls of
Jurand's archers, watching on the ramparts by the palisade.

The pilgrim and the sister looked for some time, now at one
another and now at Jurand, who sat with his back against the wall,
motionless, his face in the shadow of the bundle of skins hung up
in the window. There was only one thought left in his head, that if

he did not do what the Teutonic Knights demanded, they would strangle his child. Yet he realized that even if he did what they wanted, he might not be able to save either Danusia or himself. He saw no hope, no way out. He felt an unmerciful power over him, throttling him. In his mind he already saw the iron hands of the Teutonic Knights at Danusia's throat; for knowing them as he did, he doubted not for a moment that they would murder her, bury her in the moat of a castle, and then deny it—deny it on oath—and who would be able to prove that it was they who had carried her off? Jurand had, it is true, their messengers in his hands. He could send them to the duke; he could force confessions from them by torture. But the Teutonic Knights had Danusia, and they could torture her as well. And for a while it seemed to him that his child was stretching out her hands to him from afar, begging for rescue. If he only knew for certain that she was at Ortelsburg, he might move that same night to the border, fall upon the unsuspecting Germans, take the castle, cut down the garrison, and liberate his child. But she might not be—indeed, certainly was not—there. It further flashed through his mind that, if he were to seize the woman and the pilgrim and send them straight to the grand master, perhaps the master would force confessions from them and order Danveld to give back his daughter. But that thought disappeared as quickly as it had arrived. For they could tell the grand master that they had come to ransom de Bergow and that they knew nothing about any girl. No! that road led nowhere. But what road did lead to something? He reflected that, if he were to go to Ortelsburg, they would fetter him and cast him into a dungeon, and even then they would not let Danusia go, if only to prevent it becoming known that they had kidnapped her. And meanwhile death hung over his only child, over the last head that was dear to him! . . . And at last his thoughts became muddled, and his pain became so great that his feelings were numbed. He sat motionless, as if carved out of stone, because his body had become insensible. If he wanted to rise at that moment, he could not have done so.

Meanwhile the other two were annoyed by the long wait, so the sister stood up and said:

"The dawn is not far off, so let us go, lord, for we need rest."

"And food after the long road," added the pilgrim.

Then they both bowed to Jurand and went out.

But he continued to sit immovable, as if asleep or dead.

After a while the door gently opened and Zbyszko appeared, with Father Caleb behind him.

"Well? What do they want?" asked the young knight, approaching Jurand.

Jurand shivered but made no answer. Then he began to blink like a man awakened from deep sleep.

"Lord, are you sick?" asked Father Caleb, who knew Jurand better and perceived that something strange was happening to him.

"No," replied Jurand.

"And Danusia?" asked Zbyszko further. "Where is she, and what did they say to you? What proposal have they come with?"

"With—a—ransom," replied Jurand hesitatingly.

"With a ransom for Bergow?"

"For Bergow. . . ."

"How for Bergow? What is the matter with you?"

"Nothing."

But his tone was so strange and helpless that the two men were seized with sudden fear, particularly because Jurand spoke of ransom and not of the exchange of Bergow for Danusia.

"Dear God!" exclaimed Zbyszko. "Where is Danusia?"

"She is not with the Teu-to-nic Knights—no!" replied Jurand in a sleepy voice, and suddenly rolled like a dead man off the bench onto the floor.

CHAPTER XXXI

ON the following day at noon the messengers had an interview with Jurand, and departed a little later, taking with them de Bergow, two esquires, and a dozen or more other prisoners. Then Jurand summoned Father Caleb and dictated a letter to the duke, stating that Danusia had not been kidnapped by the Knights of the Order, but that he had been able to find out where she was concealed, and hoped that in a few days he would get her back again. He repeated the same thing to Zbyszko, who since the previous night had been overcome with amazement and fear. The old knight had refused to answer any of his questions, telling him that he must wait patiently and do nothing himself to rescue Danusia, since it was unnecessary. Towards evening he shut himself up again with Father Caleb, whom he first bade write out his last will, and to whom he then made his confession. After receiving Communion he summoned Zbyszko and the old, ever-silent Tolima, who had been his comrade in all his expeditions and fights, and who in time of peace was administrator at Spychow.

"Here," he said, turning to the old warrior, while raising his voice as if speaking to someone who was hard of hearing, "here is the husband of my daughter, whom he married at the ducal court. He had my consent to do this. Accordingly, he is to be lord here after my death and owner of the fortalice, the lands, the forests, the meadows, the men, and all the goods which are to be found at Spychow."

Tolima was greatly amazed and turned his square head now towards Zbyszko, now towards Jurand. But he did not say a word, for by nature he was taciturn; he merely bowed to Zbyszko and lightly clasped his knees.

Jurand then continued:

"My will has been written down by Father Caleb, and under the writing is my seal in wax. You are a witness that you heard it from me, and that I ordered the same obedience to be given to this young knight as to me. Whatever booty and money there is in the treasury, you will show him, and you will serve him faithfully in peace and in war until death. Have you heard?"

Tolima raised his hands to his ears and bent his head, and then at a sign from Jurand bowed and went out. Jurand turned to Zbyszko and said meaningly:

"With what is in the treasury you may tempt even the greatest avarice and may ransom, not one, but a hundred captives. Don't forget!"

"Why are you giving me Spychow already?" asked Zbyszko.

"I am giving you more than Spychow, I am giving you my child."

"And the hour of death is unknown," said Father Caleb.

"Yes, it is unknown," said Jurand sorrowfully. "Not long ago the snow covered me, and although God saved my life, my strength has abandoned me."

"Dear God!" exclaimed Zbyszko. "Something has changed in you since yesterday. You speak of death rather than of Danusia. Dear God!"

"Danusia will return; she will return," replied Jurand. "Over her is God's protection. But when she returns—listen—take her to Bogdaniec and give Spychow to Tolima's care. He is a trusty man and our neighbors here are hard to deal with. At Bogdaniec they will not take her on a rope. It is safer there."

"Heh!" exclaimed Zbyszko. "You speak as if from the other world. What is the matter?"

"A part of me has already been in the other world, and now it seems to me that some sickness has got hold of me. And I am concerned for my child. She is all I have. And you, too, for I know that you love her."

He broke off, and drawing his short misericord from its sheath, he held out the hilt to Zbyszko:

"Swear to me on this small cross that you will never hurt her and will always love her."

Suddenly tears came to Zbyszko's eyes. He threw himself on his knees and placing his finger on the hilt, said aloud:

"I swear on the Holy Passion that I will never hurt her and that I will always love her!"

"Amen!" said Father Caleb.

Jurand replaced the misericord in its sheath and opened his arms:

"Then you, too, are my child!"

They parted after that, for deep night had already fallen and they had had no proper rest for several days. None the less, Zbyszko rose at dawn. Since yesterday he had been concerned that some illness had come over Jurand, and now he wanted to know how the old knight had spent the intervening hours.

Before the door of Jurand's room he met Tolima, just coming out.

"How is the lord? Is he well?" he asked.

Tolima bowed, put his hand behind his ear, and said:

"What are your grace's commands?"

"I ask you: how is the lord?" repeated Zbyszko louder.

"The lord is gone."

"Where to?"

"I do not know. He was dressed in his armor. . . ."

CHAPTER XXXII

THE dawn was just beginning to whiten the trees, the bushes, and the limestone blocks scattered here and there over the fields, when the hired guide walking beside Jurand's horse stopped and said:

"Let me rest, Sir Knight, for I am out of breath. There is thaw and fog, but it is not far now."

"You will lead me to the highway and then go back," replied Jurand.

"The highway will be on the right beyond the wood, and from the knoll you will immediately catch sight of the castle."

The peasant began to swing his arms to warm himself, for he was chilled with the early morning damp, and then he sat down on a rock, for the exercise had made him still more out of breath.

"You do not know whether the commander is in the castle?" asked Jurand.

"Where else should he be, since he is sick?"

"What is the matter with him?"

"People say that Polish knights gave him a thrashing," replied the old peasant.

And in his tone there was a certain satisfaction. He was a subject of the Teutonic Knights, but his Mazovian heart rejoiced that the Polish knights had had the advantage.

So he presently added:

"Hey! Our lords are strong, but they find it hard to deal with the Poles."

He looked sharply at the knight and said, as if to assure himself that he would not suffer for the words which had slipped out unawares:

"You, sir, speak our language; you are not a German?"

"No," replied Jurand; "but lead on."

The fellow got up and began to walk again by the horse's side. As he went he put his hand from time to time into a leather pouch and brought out a handful of unground rye which he pushed into his mouth. When he had satisfied his first hunger, he began to explain why he ate raw grain, though Jurand, too much occupied with his own misfortune and his own thoughts, had not noticed his actions.

"Praise God even for this!" he said. "Life is hard under our German lords. They have laid such a tax on milling that a poor man must eat his grain together with the husks like an animal, and if they find a hand-mill in a hut they beat the owner brutally and take his livestock. Ha! they don't even spare children and women. They fear neither God nor the priest, for when the provost of Wielbork blamed them, they dragged him away on a chain. Oh, it's a hard life under the Germans! If a man grinds a little corn between two stones, he saves the handful of flour for Sunday, but on a Friday he has to eat like a bird. . . . But praise God even for this, for when the end of winter comes, before next year's harvests are ripe, there will be not be even this. Fishing is forbidden—hunting also. It's not like in Mazovia."

Thus the Teutonic Knights' peasant complained, speaking half to himself and half to Jurand, while they passed through the wilderness, covered with blocks of limestone hidden by the snow, and entered the forest, which seemed grey in the early morning light, and from which there came a harsh, damp chill. Thankfully, full day now broke; otherwise it would have been difficult for Jurand to pass along the forest track, which went uphill and was so narrow that in places his huge war-horse could barely squeeze between the trunks. But the forest soon ended, and after a few paternosters they found themselves on the top of a white knoll, across which ran a beaten highway.

"Here's the road," said the peasant. "Now you will be able to find the way yourself."

"I will," replied Jurand. "Go home, my man."

And putting his hand in the leather bag fastened to the front of his saddle, he took out a silver coin and gave it to the guide. The fellow, accustomed rather to blows than gifts from the hands of the local Teutonic Knights, scarcely believed his eyes, and when he had snatched the coin, he bowed his head to Jurand's stirrup and took it in his hands.

"Oh, Jesus!" he exclaimed. "God reward you, worshipful Lord!"

"God be with you."

"May God's power guide you! Ortelsburg is before you."

The peasant bowed once again to the stirrup and then vanished. Jurand remained alone on the hill and looked in the direction pointed out to him by the peasant and saw the grey, damp screen of mist which veiled the world in front. Beyond the mist was hidden that ill-omened castle to which armed might and misery were driving him. It was near now, near! And then whatever was to happen would happen. At this thought there arose in Jurand's heart—besides his fear and anxiety for Danusia, besides his readiness to ransom her from hostile hands even at the price of his own blood—an incredibly bitter and hitherto unknown feeling of humiliation. Here he was, Jurand, at the mention of whose name the border commanders had shivered, now riding at their behest with humbled head. He, who had vanquished and trampled on so many of them, now felt himself vanquished and trampled on by them. They had not indeed vanquished him in the field, by courage or knightly strength, but nevertheless he felt himself vanquished. And that was for him something so unheard of, so impossible, that it seemed the whole order of the world was overthrown and turned to naught. He was riding to humiliate himself before the Teutonic Knights; he who, if it had not been for Danusia, would have preferred to face the entire power of the Order alone. Had it not happened before that a single knight, making his choice between shame and death, had charged an entire army? But he felt that shame might befall him too, and at the thought of that his heart seemed to howl with pain like a wolf when it feels the spear-point in its side.

But he was a man who had not only an iron body but also an iron soul. He knew how to break others, and he knew how to break himself.

"I will not move," he said to himself, "until I can control my temper, with which I might ruin, rather than save, my child."

And he immediately wrestled with his proud heart, his bitter hatred, and his lust for battle. Whoever might have seen him on that eminence, in full armor, motionless, on his huge horse, would have said that he was a giant cast in iron, and would not have suspected the motionless knight was at the moment fighting the hardest of all battles that he had ever fought in his life. He struggled with himself until he felt that his will would not fail.

Meanwhile the fog thinned, and although it did not entirely disperse, something dark loomed up at last. Jurand guessed that it was the walls of Ortelsburg Castle. At the sight he did not yet move from his spot, but began to pray, as warmly and ardently as a man prays when nothing is left to him on earth but God's compassion.

And when finally he rode forward, he felt that his spirits were beginning to be revived. He was ready to endure anything that might befall him. He recalled St. George, a descendant of the greatest family in Cappadocia, who endured various shameful tortures and yet did not lose his honor, but is seated at the right hand of God and is the appointed patron of all knights. Jurand had more than once heard stories of his adventures from pilgrims who had come from far countries, and now he bolstered his heart by remembering them.

Slowly even hope began to awaken in him. The Teutonic Knights were known indeed for their vengefulness, and so he did not doubt that they would take vengeance on him for all the defeats he had inflicted on them, for the disgrace which had fallen on them at every meeting, and for the fear in which they had lived for so many years.

But it was precisely that which raised his spirits. He thought that they had kidnapped Danusia only to get him, and when they had got him, what would they want of her? Yes! They would undoubtedly fetter him, and would not keep him in the neighborhood of Mazovia but send him to some distant castle, where perhaps he would have to groan in a dungeon for the rest of his life. But they would be willing to let Danusia go. Even if it came to light that they had got hold of him by fraud and were tormenting him, neither the grand master nor the chapter would take it too ill of them; for he, Jurand, had indeed been a dire enemy of the Teutonic Order and had shed more of their blood than any other knight in the world. On the other hand, the grand master might punish them for imprisoning an innocent child, a ward of the duke, whose favor he had been endeavoring to gain in view of the threatening war with the Polish king.

Hope therefore grew stronger in him as he rode along. At times it seemed to him almost a certainty that Danusia would return to Spychow, under Zbyszko's powerful protection. "And he's a tough lad," he thought. "He won't let her be wronged by anyone." He began to recall with a certain emotion everything he knew of Zbyszko: how he had fought the Germans at Wilno, how he had engaged in single combat with them, how he and his uncle had defeated the Frisians, and how he had also attacked Lichtenstein and had defended Danusia from the aurochs and had challenged those four knights, whom he certainly would not forgive. So Jurand raised his eyes and said:

"I gave her to Thee, O God, and Thou gave her to Zbyszko."

And he felt still lighter at heart, for he considered that since God had given her to the young man He would not allow the Germans to mock Him, and He would tear her from their hands even if the whole power of the Teutonic Order refused to let her go. Then he began to think again of Zbyszko. "Yes! he's not only a tough lad but also as pure as gold. He will guard her, he will love her, and grant, Jesus, to my child, the best that Thou canst, but it seems to me that by his side she will not regret either the ducal court or her father's love." At this thought Jurand's cheeks were suddenly wet with tears, and in his heart awoke an immense yearning. He longed to see his child once again in this life, and to die some day, any day, at Spychow with the two of them, and not in the dark dungeons of the Knights. But God's will be done! . . . Ortelsburg was already visible. The walls were outlined ever more clearly in the mist, the hour of sacrifice was at hand. He began to take comfort and say to himself as follows:

"Yes, God's will be done! But the evening of life is at hand. A few years more or less—it doesn't matter. I should like to look on both children again, but in truth I must admit that I have lived my life. What one had to go through, one has gone through; whom one had to avenge, one has avenged. And what now? Rather to God than to the world; but if one must suffer, one must. Danusia and Zbyszko will not forget me, however prosperous they are. Assuredly they will sometimes remember and say: 'Where is he? Is he alive or is he already in counsel with God?' They will ask, and perhaps they will find out. The Teutonic Knights are greedy for vengeance, but they are also greedy for ransom, and Zbyszko would not refuse to ransom even my bones. And they will assuredly sometimes pay Masses for my soul. They both have honest, loving hearts, for which bless them, O God, and Thou, most Holy Mother."

The highway not only widened but became filled with people. Wagons laden with wood and straw moved towards the town. Herdsmen were driving cattle. Frozen fish were being brought on sleighs from the lakes. At one point four archers were leading a peasant on a chain, evidently to be judged for some fault, since his hands were bound behind him and on his feet were fetters, which dragged in the snow and scarcely allowed him to move. The breath came out of his panting nostrils and mouth in clouds of steam, while the archers sang as they drove him along. Seeing Jurand, they looked at him with curiosity, evidently wondering at the gigantic size of rider and horse, but at the sight of his gold spurs and knight's belt they lowered their crossbows to the ground as a mark of greeting and honor. In the little town it was still noisier and more congested, but people quickly made way for the armed man, and he passed through the main street and turned towards the castle, which was wrapped in mist and seemed yet to be asleep.

But not everything around it was asleep. At least the crows and ravens were not sleeping. Whole flocks of them whirled over the rising ground which formed the approach to the castle, flapping their wings and cawing. Jurand, approaching, understood the cause for this birds' council. By the side of the road leading to the castle gate stood a large gallows, on which hung the bodies of four Mazovian peasants belonging to the Teutonic Knights. There was not a breath of wind, so the corpses, which seemed to be looking at their own feet, did not swing except when the black birds sat on their shoulders or heads, pushing one another, knocking against the ropes, and pecking the hanging heads. Some of the figures must have been hanging for a long time, for their skulls were completely exposed and their legs extraordinarily elongated. As Jurand approached, the flock scattered with a great fluttering but soon came back and began to settle on the front beam of the gallows. Making the sign of the cross, Jurand rode past the gallows and approached the moat. He came to a stop at the point where the drawbridge was raised before the gate, and loudly blew into a horn.

Then he blew it three more times, and waited. On the walls there was not a living soul, and not a voice came from behind the gate. After a while, however, a heavy shutter, visible behind an iron grating near the lock of the gate, opened with a grinding noise and showed the bearded head of a German soldier.

"*Wer da?*" asked a rough voice.

"Jurand of Spychow," answered the knight.

The shutter closed again, and a hollow silence ensued.

Time passed. No movement was to be heard behind the gate; only the croaking of the birds near the gallows could be heard.

Jurand stood for a long time before he grasped the horn and blew it again.

Once more he was answered by silence.

Then he understood that they were keeping him in front of the gate because of their Teutonic pride, unbounded in the presence of the vanquished, in order to humiliate him like a beggar. He guessed also that he would have to wait until nightfall or longer. At first his blood boiled within him. He was seized by a sudden desire to dismount from his horse, lift up one of the boulders lying before the moat, and hurl it at the grating. That is what he would have done in different circumstances—he and every other Mazovian or Polish knight—to make them come out from behind the gate and fight. But remembering why he had come, he controlled himself.

"Have I not sacrificed myself for my child?" he said to himself in his heart.

So he waited.

Meanwhile the crenels atop the wall began to darken. There appeared fur head-coverings, dark hoods, and even iron helmets, from beneath which curious eyes looked out at the knight. More of them came every moment, for the terrible Jurand, waiting alone at the castle gate, was a marvellous sight for the garrison. Whoever had faced him before had faced death, but now they could look at him in safety. Heads were raised higher and higher, until at last all the crenels near to the gate were filled with soldiers. Jurand thought that the elders must surely also be looking at him through the gratings of the windows in the gate tower, so he looked up, but the windows were cut deep in the walls, and it was impossible to see through them except from a distance. Meanwhile the crowd on the battlements, which at first had looked at him in silence, began to show signs of life. One man and another repeated his name; here and there laughter was heard; hoarse voices shouted as at a wolf, ever more loudly, ever more insolently, and, as evidently no one inside restrained them, they finally began to throw snow at the knight standing beneath them.

He moved forward, as if involuntarily, on his horse, and for a moment the lumps of snow ceased to fly, the voices fell silent, and some of the heads even vanished behind the walls. Terrible indeed must have been Jurand's name. However, soon the most cowardly remembered that they were separated from the Mazovian by a wall and a moat, so the rude soldiery began again to throw lumps not only of snow but of ice, and even rubble and stones, which rebounded noisily from his breastplate and from the armor of his horse.

"I have sacrificed myself for my child," Jurand repeated to himself.

And he waited. Afternoon came; the walls were mostly deserted, since the men had been called to dinner. The few who had to remain on guard ate on the walls, and afterwards amused themselves by throwing the gnawed bones at the hungry knight. Then they began to joke around with one another and ask each other who would undertake to go down and give him a blow on the back of the neck with his fist or his pikestaff. The others, when they returned from dinner, called out to him that if he was disgusted with waiting he might hang himself, as there was still a place available on the gallows. The afternoon hours passed amid such insults, outbursts of laughter, and cursing. The short winter day gradually drew to a close, but the drawbridge still hung in the air and the gate remained shut. Right before evening a wind arose, scattered the fog, cleared the sky, and revealed the sunset. The snow became blue and then violet. There was no frost and the night promised to be clear. Except for the guard, all the men vanished again from the walls. The ravens and crows flew away from the gallows to the forests, and at last the sky grew dark and complete silence fell.

"They will not open the gate before night," thought Jurand.

And for a moment the thought passed through his mind that he might return to the town, but he immediately dismissed it. "They want me to stand here," he said to himself. "If I turn back, they won't let me go home but will surround and take me, and will then say that they have no obligation to me, for they took me by force. And even if I overcame them, I must return. . . ."

The extraordinary endurance of cold, hunger, and fatigue which foreign chronicles mention with admiration in the Polish knights often enabled them to accomplish deeds beyond the power of the more effeminate people of the West. Jurand possessed that endurance in a still greater degree than others; so although hunger had long begun to gnaw his innards, and the evening frost had penetrated his sheepskin coat underneath his mail, he determined to wait, even if he had to die in front of the gate.

Suddenly, however, before night had completely fallen, he heard behind him the crunch of steps in the snow.

He looked around. Six men armed with spears and halberds were coming towards him from the direction of the town, and in their midst was a seventh man, who supported himself on a sword.

"Maybe the gate will be opened for them, and I can enter with them," thought Jurand. "They will not try to take me by force, or to kill me, for there are too few of them; and if they do attack me, it will be a sign that they do not wish to keep any faith with me, and then—woe to them!"

Thinking thus, he lifted the steel axe which hung at his saddle, an axe so heavy that it was too much for an ordinary man to wield even with both hands, and he rode towards them.

But they did not think of attacking him. The soldiers immediately stuck the butt ends of their spears and halberds in the snow, and, as the night was not yet quite dark, Jurand was able to see that the shafts trembled somewhat in their hands.

But the seventh man, who seemed to be in command, hastily extended his left hand and, turning the palm up, called out: "You, sir, are Jurand of Spychow?"

"I am."

"Do you wish to hear the message I have been sent with?"

"I am listening."

"The strong and pious commander von Danveld bids me say to you, lord, that as long as you do not dismount, the gates will not be opened to you."

Jurand remained for a while motionless. Then he dismounted from his horse, and one of the spearmen immediately sprang forward for it.

"And your weapons are to be given up to us," called out the man with the sword.

The Lord of Spychow hesitated. Would they afterwards fall upon him unarmed and pierce him like a wild beast? Or would they seize him and thrust him into a dungeon? But after a while he thought that if that had been their intention, more of them would have been sent. For if they were to throw themselves upon him, they would not immediately pierce his armor, and he would be able to snatch a weapon from the nearest man and slay them all before help could arrive. They knew him, after all.

"Even if," he said to himself, "they wished to shed my blood, I came here for nothing else."

So he threw down first his axe, then his sword, and then his misericord—and waited. They picked up all these, and then the man who had spoken to him withdrew a dozen paces, stopped, and said in a loud, insolent tone:

"For all the wrongs which you have done to the Knights, you must, by order of the commander, put on this coarse sack which I leave you, hang the scabbard of your sword from your neck by a rope, and wait in humility at the gate until the favor of the commander orders it to be opened."

Jurand was left alone in the darkness and the silence. The penitent's sack and the rope lay before him, starkly outlined against the snow, but he stood a long time, feeling that in his soul something was melting, something was breaking, something was dying, and that in a moment he would no longer be a knight, he would no longer be Jurand of Spychow, but a miserable slave without a name, or fame, or honor.

So a long time still passed before he approached the penitent's sack.

"How can I do otherwise?" he said. "Thou, Christ, knowest: they will strangle my innocent child unless I do what they command. And Thou also knowest that I would not do this for my own life. Disgrace is a bitter thing! A bitter thing! But they disgraced even Thee before Thy death. Well, in the name of the Father and the Son. . . ."

Then he bent down, put on the sack, which had openings cut in it for head and arms, hung the scabbard around his neck by the rope, and dragged himself to the gate. He did not find it open, but now it made no difference to him whether they opened it sooner of later. The castle rose up before him in the silence of the night; only the watch called out from time to time at the corners. In the gate tower one window alone, high up, showed a light; the others were dark.

The hours of the night passed one after another; a crescent moon rose in the sky and lighted the gloomy walls of the castle. The silence became such that Jurand could hear the beating of his own heart. But he grew numb and petrified, as if his soul had been taken from him, and he no longer cared what happened. Only one thought remained in him, that he had ceased to be Sir Jurand of Spychow, but what he was he did not know. . . . At times he saw Death walking quietly towards him from the gallows nearby. . . .

Suddenly he quivered and grew wide awake.

"Merciful Christ! What is that?"

From the high window in the gate tower there came, scarcely audible at first, the sound of a lute. Jurand, when riding to Ortelsburg, had been certain that Danusia was not in the castle, yet the sound of that lute in the night stirred his heart in an instant. It seemed to him that he knew those sounds and that no one else was playing, only she—his child, his beloved! So he fell on his knees, clasped his hands, as if to pray, and listened, shivering as if in a fever.

Meanwhile a half-childish and immeasurably longing voice began to sing:

> *"Oh, if I but had*
> *Little wings like a dove,*
> *Away I would fly,*
> *Away, away to my love*
> *In Silesia."*

Jurand wanted to call out, to shout her beloved name, but the words were choked in his throat as if by a vise. A sudden wave of pain, tears, longing, and misery passed through his breast, and he threw himself on his face in the snow and began to call eagerly to heaven in his spirit, as in a prayer of thanksgiving:

"O Jesus! I hear the voice of my child once again! O Jesus!"

And sobs began to shake his enormous body. Up above, the longing voice continued to sing in the undisturbed quiet of the night:

"Down I would light
On the fence of his glade.
Look, O my Jack,
At a poor orphan maid
In Silesia!"

In the morning a fat, bearded German soldier kicked the knight lying at the gate.

"To your feet, dog! The gate is open, and the commander orders you to stand before him."

Jurand awoke as if from sleep. He did not seize the man by the throat, he did not crush him in his iron hands; his face was calm and almost humble. He got up and, without saying a word, followed the soldier through the gate.

Scarcely had he passed it, when he heard behind him the grinding of chains. The drawbridge began to rise, while in the gateway the heavy iron portcullis fell. . . .

CHAPTER XXXIII

FINDING himself in the castle yard, Jurand did not at first know where to go, since the man who had led him through the gate left him and went towards the stables. It is true that soldiers were standing on the battlements, singly or in groups, but their faces were so insolent and their glances so mocking that it was easy for the knight to guess that they would not show him the way, or if they did answer his questions, would do so with insulting words.

Some laughed, pointing at him with their fingers; others began to throw snow at him as they had done the day before. But he, seeing a door larger than the rest, with a figure of Christ on the Cross carved in stone above, went towards it, supposing that if the commander and the elders were in another part of the castle or in other rooms someone would surely call him back and show him the right way.

And so it happened. The moment Jurand approached the door, its two halves opened suddenly, and there before him stood a youth with a shaven head, like a cleric's, but dressed in lay attire.

"Lord, are you Jurand of Spychow?" he asked.

"I am."

"The pious commander bade me conduct you. Follow me."

He led him through a large vaulted passage to a staircase, at the foot of which, however, he stopped for a second, and scanning Jurand from head to foot, he spoke again:

"You have no weapons whatever on you? They bade me search you."

Jurand raised both arms, so that his guide might get a good look at his entire figure.

"Yesterday I gave up everything," he answered.

The guide lowered his voice and said almost in a whisper:

"Beware of bursting into anger, for you are under force and excess of force."

"But also under God's will," replied Jurand.

Then he looked attentively at his guide. Seeing something like sympathy and pity in his face, he said:

"Honesty looks out of your eyes, my lad. Will you answer sincerely what I ask you?"

"Make haste, lord," said the guide.

"Will they give back my child in exchange for me?"

The youth raised his eyebrows in surprise.

"Your child is here?"

"My daughter."

"The damsel in the gate tower?"

"Yes. They promised to send her back if I would give myself up to them."

The guide threw out his hand in sign that he knew nothing, but his face expressed disquiet and doubt.

Jurand asked further:

"Is it true that she is guarded by Schomberg and Markwart?"

"Those brethren are not in the castle. Nevertheless, lord, take her away before Constable Danveld gets better."

Hearing that, Jurand quivered, but there was no time to ask more, for they had reached the room on the first floor in which Jurand was to stand before the Constable of Ortelsburg. The lad opened the door and then went back to the stairs.

The knight of Spychow entered and found himself in a spacious chamber, very dark, since the leaded glass panes let through but little light, and the sky was wintry and cloudy. At the far end of the chamber there was, it is true, a fire burning on a large hearth, but the damp logs gave little flame. It was only after some time, when Jurand had become accustomed to the half-light, that he made out a table at the other end of the room and knights sitting at it, and further on, behind their backs, a whole company of armed esquires and men, among whom the castle fool held a tame bear on a chain.

Jurand had once fought in single combat with Danveld, and

after that he had seen him twice as an envoy at the court of the Mazovian duke, but some years had passed since then. None the less, despite the dim light, he recognized him at once by both his fatness and his face, as well as by the fact that he was sitting at the middle of the table in an armchair, his arm bound in splints and supported by the armrest. At his right sat old Siegfried von Lowe of Insburk, the implacable foe of the Polish race in general and Jurand of Spychow in particular; at his left, the younger brethren Godfrey and Roger. Danveld had invited them purposely to see his triumph over his dangerous foe, and at the same time to enjoy the fruits of the treachery they had devised together and had helped to carry out. So they sat at their ease, dressed in soft garments of dark cloth, with light swords at their sides, joyful and sure of themselves, looking at Jurand with pride and with that boundless contempt which they always had in their hearts for the weak and the vanquished.

The silence lasted some time, for they wished to satiate themselves with the sight of the man whom they had formerly feared, but who now stood before them with bowed head, wearing the coarse penitent's sack, a rope around his neck, and the scabbard of his sword hanging from it.

They apparently wished the largest possible number of people to witness his humiliation. Anyone who wanted to come in through the side doors from other rooms was free to do so, and soon the chamber became almost half filled with armed men, all of whom looked with boundless curiosity at Jurand, talking aloud and making remarks about him. When he saw them, however, he took courage, for he thought, "If Danveld had not intended to keep his promise, he would not have called so many witnesses."

Meanwhile Danveld waved his hand for silence and then beckoned to one of his esquires, who went up to Jurand, took hold of the halter around his neck, and drew him several paces nearer the table.

Then Danveld looked triumphantly at the company and said:

"See how the power of the Order conquers malice and pride!"

"God grant it may always do so!" replied those present.

There followed another period of silence, after which Danveld turned to the prisoner:

"You bit the Order like a mad dog, and therefore God has caused you to stand before us like a dog, with a rope around your neck, begging for our mercy and favor."

"Do not compare me with a dog, commander," replied Jurand, "for if you do, you deprive of honor those who have fought with me and have perished by my hand."

At these words a murmur arose among the armed Germans. It was not known whether they were angered at the boldness of his answer or struck by its truth.

But the commander was not pleased at such a turn, so he said:

"See how even here he spits in our eyes in his pride and arrogance!"

Jurand raised his hands like a man who calls heaven to witness and answered, nodding his head:

"God knows my pride was left outside the gate. God knows and will judge whether in disgracing my knighthood you do not disgrace yourselves. There is a common knightly honor, which all who are belted ought to respect."

Danveld frowned, but at the moment the castle fool began to rattle the chain on which he was holding the bear, and called out:

"A sermon! A sermon! An eloquent preacher has come from Mazovia. Listen! A sermon!"

Then he turned to Danveld.

"Lord!" he said. "Count Rosenheim, when the ringer woke him too early by ringing for the sermon, had him eat the bell-cord from end to end. This preacher has a rope around his neck. Have him eat it before he finishes his sermon."

So saying, he looked at the commander somewhat uneasily, not being sure whether he would laugh or order him to be beaten for speaking out of turn. But the brethren of the Order, suave, courteous, and even humble when they did not feel themselves the stronger, knew no bounds in face of the vanquished. So Danveld not only nodded to the buffoon as a sign that he allowed his mockery, but himself broke out with a gibe so coarse that even the faces of some of the younger esquires expressed astonishment.

"Do not complain that you have been disgraced," he said, "for though I were to make a dog-keeper of you, it is better to be a dog-keeper of the Order than one of your knights."

The emboldened fool called out:

"Bring a comb and curry the bear, and then he will curry your shaggy hair with his paw."

Here and there laughter was heard among the Germans, and from behind the brethren's backs a voice called out:

"In the summer you will cut reeds by the lake!"

"And catch crayfish with carrion!" exclaimed another, while a third added:

"Now you will begin by driving away the crows from the gallows! There is no lack of work for you here."

Thus they mocked the once terrible Jurand. Gradually the company grew merry. Some of them got up from the table and approached the prisoner, looking at him closely and saying: "So this is the Wild Boar of Spychow, whose tusks our commander has knocked out; doubtless he has foam in his mouth; he would be glad to bite, but he cannot!" Danveld and the other brethren of the Order, who at first had intended to give the hearing the appearance of a solemn trial, now seeing that things had taken a different turn, got up from the bench themselves and mingled with those who had approached Jurand.

This did not please old Siegfried of Insburk, but the commander said to him: "Cease your frowning, there will be still more amusement!" And they also began to look closely at Jurand, availing themselves of the rare occasion, for when any knight or soldier had seen him so near in the past, he had usually closed his eyes forever afterwards. Some of them said: "He's broad-shouldered, though he has only a sheepskin under his sack; one might wrap him in pea-straw and exhibit him at fairs." Others called for beer to make the day still merrier.

Soon foaming tankards were clinking with one another, and the dark room was filled with the smell of the froth running over from under the lids. The joyous commander said: "It's a good thing; let him not think that his disgrace is any great matter!" So the Germans went up to him again, knocked his chin with their mugs, and said: "Your Mazovian snout would like a little taste, eh?" Some of them poured beer into their palms and splashed it in his eyes, as he stood in their midst bullied and mocked. Finally, feeling that he could not hold out longer, he went towards old Siegfried and shouted so loud as to drown out the noise in the room:

"By the Passion of the Redeemer and everlasting salvation, give me back my child as you promised!"

And he tried to seize the hand of the old commander, who quickly stepped back and said:

"Away, slave! What do you want?"

"I have released Bergow from captivity, and I have come myself, because you promised that you would give me back my child who is here."

"Who promised you?" asked Danveld.

"On my conscience and my faith—you, commander!"

"You will not find any witnesses, but witnesses are of no account when a word of honor is in question."

"By your honor! By the honor of the Order!" exclaimed Jurand.

"Then your daughter will be given back to you," replied Danveld.

And he turned to the company, saying:

"All that has happened to him here is an innocent game and has nothing to do with his faults and crimes. But since we promised to give him back his daughter if he would appear and humble himself before us, then know that the word of a Teutonic Knight must be as sacred as the word of God, and that we will now set free the girl whom we rescued from the robbers, and will allow him also to return home, after he has done exemplary penance for his sins against the Order."

This speech astonished some of those present, for they knew Danveld and his hatred of Jurand, and had not expected of him such honesty. So old Siegfried, and with him brother Roger and brother Godfrey, looked at him, lifting their eyebrows in amazement and then frowning. He pretended, however, not to see these questioning glances, and went on:

"I will send back your daughter under a guard, but you will stay here until our guard returns safely and until you pay the ransom."

Jurand himself was somewhat amazed. He had already lost hope that his sacrifice would be of any avail, even for Danusia, so now he looked at Danveld in near gratitude and replied:

"God reward you, commander!"

"Recognize the Knights of Christ," said Danveld.

To which Jurand replied:

"All compassion is from Him. But since I have not seen my child for a long time, let me look upon my daughter and bless her."

"In front of all of us, of course, so that there may be witnesses of our faith and our mercy."

And he ordered one of the esquires to bring Danusia, while he himself went up to von Lowe, Roger, and Godfrey, and began to talk quickly and animatedly with them.

"I shall not object, even though this was not your previous intention," said old Siegfried.

But the hot-tempered Roger, famed for his valor and his cruelty, said:

"What's this? Will you let go not only the girl but also this hound of hell so that he can bite us anew?"

"He will do more than just bite us!" exclaimed Godfrey.

"Bah! He will pay the ransom!" replied Danveld nonchalantly.

"Even if he were to give everything he has, in a year he will have taken twice as much booty."

"I do not object as far as the girl is concerned," repeated Siegfried, "but that wolf will make our flock suffer again and again."

"What about our word?" asked Danveld, smiling.

"You spoke differently before. . . ."

Danveld shrugged his shoulders.

"You did not have enough amusement?" he asked. "You want more?"

Men had surrounded Jurand once more, and feeling the glory which had fallen on all members of the Order from Danveld's honorable action, they began to boast in front of him.

"Well, bone-breaker!" said the captain of the castle archers, "your pagan brothers would not have treated our Christian knights like this."

"You were fond of drinking our blood."

"And we are giving you bread for a stone."

But Jurand no longer noticed either the pride or the scorn in their words; his heart was moved and his eyelids were wet with tears. He thought that presently he would see Danusia, and that he would see her indeed by their favor, so he looked at the speakers almost with repentance and finally replied:

"True! True! I was hard on you, but I was never treacherous."

Suddenly, at the other end of the chamber, a voice cried out:

"They are bringing the girl!" Silence immediately fell over the whole room. The soldiers made way on either side. Although none of them had yet seen Jurand's daughter, and the majority, owing to the mystery with which Danveld surrounded his actions, did not even know of her presence in the castle, those who did know whispered to the others of her rumored beauty and her charm. So all eyes were turned with extraordinary curiosity to the door through which she was to come.

First an esquire apppeared, and behind him a woman-servant of the Order whom all knew, the same one who had gone to the hunting-lodge, and behind her a girl dressed all in white, with flowing hair bound with a ribbon on her forehead.

And then an enormous burst of laughter, like the roaring of thunder, filled the chamber. Jurand, who at first had sprung to meet his daughter, suddenly drew back and stood white as a sheet, looking in amazement at the pointed head, blue lips, and vacant eyes of the idiot girl whom they were giving him instead of Danusia.

"This is not my daughter!" he said in a voice full of fear.

"Not your daughter?" exclaimed Danveld. "By St. Liborius of Paderborn! Then either it was not your daughter whom we rescued from the robbers or some enchanter has changed her, for there's no other girl at Ortelsburg."

Old Siegfried, Roger, and Godfrey exchanged quick glances, full of the greatest admiration for the cunning of Danveld, but none of them had time to speak before Jurand began to shout in a terrible voice:

"There is! She is at Ortelsburg! I heard her singing. I heard my child's voice!"

Danveld turned to the company and said calmly but emphatically:

"I take those of you present here to witness, and particularly you, Siegfried of Insburk, and you, pious brothers Roger and Godfrey, that, according to my word and my promise, I am giving back the girl whom the robbers, defeated by us, said was the daughter of Jurand of Spychow. If, however, she is not his daughter, it is no fault of ours, but rather it is the will of our Lord, who thus has deigned to give Jurand into our hands."

Siegfried and the two younger brethren bowed their heads as a sign that they heard, and would bear witness in case of need. Then they again exchanged quick glances, for this was more than even they had expected: to catch Jurand, and not give him back his daughter, and yet outwardly to keep the promise—what other man could have done that?

Jurand threw himself on his knees and began to implore Danveld by all the relics of Malbork, and then by the dust and heads of his parents, to give him back his real child, and not to behave like a liar and a traitor, breaking his oaths and his promises. In his voice there was so much despair and sincerity that some began to suspect treachery, while others conceived the idea that perhaps some enchanter had really changed the girl.

"God looks upon your treachery!" cried out Jurand. "By the wounds of the Redeemer! By the hour of your death, give me back my child!"

And, rising from his knees, he went, bent double, towards Danveld, as if he were about to embrace his legs. His eyes flashed almost with madness, and his voice broke in turn with pain, fear, despair, and menace. Danveld, however, hearing himself accused of treachery and deceit in front of the company, began to snort. Wrath flushed his face like a flame, and he determined to trample on the unfortunate man yet more. So he moved towards him, and bending to his ear, hissed through set teeth:

"If I give her back to you—it will be with a bastard of mine."

Almost at the same moment Jurand roared like a bull, seized Danveld with both his hands, and lifted him into the air. A piercing cry filled the room: "Spare me!" Then the body of the commander was hurled to the stone floor with such frightful force that his brains spattered over Siegfried and Roger, who were standing nearby.

Jurand sprang to the wall where the weapons were grouped, seized a great two-handed sword, and rushed like a storm on the petrified Germans.

They were men accustomed to fights, massacres, and blood; yet their hearts sank to such an extent that even when their numbness passed they began to draw back and flee like a flock of sheep before a wolf that kills with a single bite. The chamber rang with shouts of fear, the trampling of men's feet, the clatter of overturned vessels, the howling of the pages, and the roaring of the bear—

which had broken away from the buffoon and begun to climb to the high window—and with despairing cries for weapons, shields, swords, and crossbows. Weapons flashed at last, and scores of blades were turned against Jurand. But he cared for nothing, half-mad as he was, and rushed upon them. A wild, unheard-of fight began, more like a massacre than an armed combat. The young and fiery Brother Godfrey was the first to stand in Jurand's way, but the Mazovian knight severed his head, shoulder-blade and arm with a lightning flash of his sword; after him, the captain of the archers and steward of the castle, von Bracht, fell by his hand; and next an Englishman, Hugh, who, though he did not understand very well what it was all about, and had pitied Jurand and his torment, seized a weapon after Danveld had been killed. The others, seeing the frightful strength and fury of the man, gathered in a group to oppose him. But this led only to their still worse defeat. With his hair standing on end and his one eye wild, covered with blood and thirsting for blood, abandoned to fury and beside himself with rage, he broke, tore, and cut into the closely-packed crowd with vicious slashes, overthrowing men onto the blood-splashed floor as a storm overthrows bushes and trees. A moment of horror followed, in which it seemed that the terrible Mazovian would cut down and kill them all, and that as a noisy pack of hounds cannot without the help of archers overcome a fierce wild boar, so those armed Germans would be unable to face his power and fury, and the fight with him would end only in their destruction and death.

"Scatter! Surround him! Strike him from the rear!" called out old Siegfried von Lowe.

So they spread through the hall as a flock of starlings scatters in the field when a crook-beaked hawk swoops on them from above, but they could not surround him. In his fury, instead of seeking a place to defend himself, he began to drive them about the walls, and whosoever was overtaken died as if by lightning. Humiliation, despair, and disappointed hope were all transformed into a single lust for blood that seemed to multiply his enormous natural strength tenfold. The sword which required two hands of even the mightiest of the Teutonic Knights, he wielded like a feather with one. He did not seek life, he did not seek safety, he did not even seek victory. He sought vengeance. And as a fire, or as a river which bursts its dam, blindly destroys all that obstructs its way, so he, a terrible, blind-with-rage destroyer, cut up, broke, trampled, slaughtered, and annihilated the living.

They could not strike him in the back, since from the start they could not reach him; besides, the common soldiery feared to approach him even from the rear, knowing full well that if he were to turn around, no human power could save them from death. Others were seized with terror at the thought that no ordinary man could cause such disaster and that they had to deal with someone aided by superhuman powers.

Old Siegfried, and with him Brother Roger, rushed to the gallery which ran above the large windows of the chamber, and called to the others to follow, which they promptly did, so that the narrow stairway was blocked with men trying to get up with the greatest speed and to strike from there the mighty opponent with whom every fight at close quarters had proved disastrous. Finally the last man slammed the door leading to the gallery, and Jurand was left alone below. The gallery began to ring with shouts of joy and triumph, and heavy oak stools, benches, and iron torch-sockets were hurled down at the knight. One of these missiles struck him on the forehead and covered his face with blood. At the same time the great entrance doors burst open, and a crowd of soldiers, summoned from the upper windows, broke into the hall, armed with pikes, halberds, axes, crossbows, pointed stakes, poles, ropes, and every kind of weapon which they could snatch up in their haste.

The maddened Jurand wiped the blood from his face with his left hand, lest it should blind him, gathered himself together, and threw himself on the whole crowd. The hall again rang with groans, the clank of iron, the grinding of teeth, and the shrill cries of slaughtered men.

CHAPTER XXXIV

IN the evening, in that very hall, old Siegfried was sitting at the table. He had temporarily taken over the administration of Ortelsburg after Constable Danveld's death. With him now were Brother Roger, Sir de Bergow—Jurand's former prisoner—and two young men of noble birth, novices who would soon wear the white cloak. The winter gale howled outside the windows and shook their lead cames; it wavered the torchlights burning in iron sockets, and from time to time blew clouds of smoke into the hall from the chimney. Although they had gathered for counsel, silence reigned among the brethren. They were waiting for Siegfried to speak, but he sat gloomily, his elbows leaning on the table, his hands clasped over his grey, bent head. His face was in shadow and dark thoughts filled his soul.

"On what are we taking counsel?" asked Brother Roger at last.

Siegfried raised his head, looked at the speaker and, rousing himself from his thoughts, said:

"On the disaster that befell us, on what the master and the chapter will say, and on the means of preventing our actions from resulting in harm to the Order."

Then he was silent again. Presently he looked around and twitched his nostrils:

"There is still a smell of blood here."

"No, commander," replied Roger. "I ordered the floor to be washed and censed with sulphur. It is sulphur that you smell here."

Siegfried looked strangely at the company and said:

"Have mercy, Spirit of Light, on the souls of Brother Danveld and Brother Godfrey!"

They understood that he was calling for divine mercy on those souls, because the mention of sulphur had brought to his mind an image of hell; so a shiver went through their bones, and they all answered together:

"Amen! amen! amen!"

For a while again nothing was to be heard but the howling of the wind and the rattling of the window-cames.

"Where are the bodies of the commander and Brother Godfrey?" asked the old man.

"In the chapel. The priests are chanting litanies over them."

"Are they already in their coffins?"

"Yes. The commander's head is covered, however, for his skull and face are smashed."

"Where are the other corpses? And the wounded?"

"The corpses are in the snow so that they can stiffen before their coffins are made, and the wounded are already being attended to in the hospital."

Siegfried again clasped his head:

"And one man did this! Spirit of Light, take the Order under Thy protection when it comes to a great war with this wolf's race!"

Roger looked up, as if remembering something, and said:

"I heard at Wilno how the Governor of Sambia said to his brother, the grand master: 'If you do not wage a great war and wipe them out so that their very name perishes, then woe to us and our nation.'"

"God give us such a war where one can engage them!" said one of the noble-born novices.

Siegfried looked at him meaningly, as if to say, "You could have engaged one of them today," but seeing the slender, youthful figure of the novice, and perhaps remembering that he himself, though famed for his courage, had been unwilling to face certain death, he refrained from reproach.

"Which of you has seen Jurand?" he asked instead.

"I," replied de Bergow.

"Is he alive?"

"He is alive, lying in the same net in which we entangled him.

When he came to, the soldiers wanted to finish him off, but the chaplain would not allow it."

"One may not finish him off," replied Siegfried. "He is a man of importance among his own people, and there would be a mighty outcry. It will also be impossible to hide what has happened, for there were too many witnesses."

"What then are we to say and do?" asked Roger.

Siegfried thought for a time, and at length said:

"You, noble Count de Bergow, go to the master at Malbork. You have groaned in captivity at Jurand's place, and you are a guest of the Order, so they will the more readily believe you as a guest who is not necessarily forced to speak in favor of the brethren. Therefore, tell what you saw. Say that Danveld rescued some girl from border robbers and, thinking her to be Jurand's daughter, let Jurand know; so Jurand came to Ortelsburg and—what happened afterwards you know yourself. . . ."

"Pardon, pious commander," said de Bergow. "I endured harsh captivity at Spychow, and as your guest I should always be ready to bear witness for you, but for my own peace of mind tell me: Was Jurand's real daughter not at Ortelsburg, and was it not Danveld's treachery that brought her terrible father to madness?"

Siegfried von Lowe hesitated a while before answering. By nature he had a deep hatred for the Polish race; cruelty was not foreign to him—indeed he even surpassed Danveld in it—nor ferocity when the Order was in question, nor pride, nor greed of plunder. But he did not have the temperament for ignoble subterfuges. The greatest bitterness and vexation of his life was that in recent times indiscipline and licence had become widespread in the Order, and deception had become one of its commonest and most indispensable instruments. Accordingly, de Bergow's question touched the most painful chord of his soul, and it was only after a long silence that he replied:

"Danveld stands before God, and God will judge him. Count, if they ask you what you think, say what pleases you; but if they ask what you have seen with your eyes, then say that we entangled a madman in a net, and that you saw nine corpses, besides wounded men, on the floor; and among them the bodies of Danveld, Brother Godfrey, von Bracht, and Hugh, and two noble youths—God grant them everlasting rest! Amen!"

"Amen! amen!" repeated the novices.

"And say also," added Siegfried, "that although Danveld wanted to subdue an enemy of the Order, yet none here was the first to draw sword against Jurand."

"I shall tell only that which my eyes have seen," replied de Bergow.

"Before midnight be in the chapel, where we also shall come to pray for the souls of the dead," answered Siegfried, and he extended his hand to him as a sign both of gratitude and of dismissal, since he wished to remain alone for further counsel with Brother Roger, whom he loved like the apple of his eye, as a father might love his only son. This boundless love even gave rise to various suppositions among the Order, but no one knew the truth, particularly since the knight whom Roger regarded as his father still lived in his castelet in Germany and had never disowned his son.

So after Bergow's departure Siegfried sent away the two novices also, under pretext of wanting them to supervise the work of making coffins for the soldiers slain by Jurand, and when the door had closed behind them, he turned animatedly to Roger:

"Listen to what I am going to say. There is only one way out, and that is that no living soul may ever learn that the real daughter of Jurand was among us."

"That will not be difficult," replied Roger, "since no one knew that she was here save Danveld, Godfrey, us two, and the woman-servant of the Order who is attending her. Danveld gave command to intoxicate the men who brought her from the hunting-lodge, and then he had them hanged. There were some among the garrison who suspected something, but the appearance of that idiot girl has confused them, and now they do not know whether there was not a mistake on our part or whether some enchanter did not really change Jurand's daughter."

"Good!" said Siegfried.

"But I thought, noble commander, that perhaps, since Danveld is dead, the whole blame might be laid on him."

"And admit before the whole world that in time of peace and agreement with the Duke of Mazovia we kidnapped from his court a ward of the duchess and her favorite court damsel? No, that cannot be! We have been seen with Danveld at the court, and the grand hospitaller, his kinsman, knows that we always undertook everything together. If we accuse Danveld, he will want to avenge his memory."

"Let us think this through," said Roger.

"Let us think it through and find good counsel, else woe to us! If Jurand's daughter is given back, she will say herself that we did not rescue her from robbers, but that the men who seized her brought her straight to Ortelsburg."

"True."

"And it is not a question only of responsibility. The duke will complain to the King of Poland, and their emissaries will not fail to shout aloud at every court against our violence, our treachery, and our crime. How much harm that may bring to the Order! The master himself, if he knew the truth, ought to command the girl to be concealed."

"But if she disappears will they not accuse us nevertheless?" asked Roger.

"No! Brother Danveld was a cunning man. Do not forget the conditions he imposed on Jurand. Not only did Jurand have to appear at Ortelsburg alone, but he first had to declare and write the duke that he was going to ransom his daughter from robbers, and that he knew she was not with us."

"True, but how in that case shall we explain what has happened at Ortelsburg?"

"We will say that, knowing Jurand was looking for his daughter, and having rescued from robbers a girl who could not say who she was, we told him, thinking that it might be his daughter. However, when he arrived, he went mad at the sight of the girl and, possessed by an evil spirit, shed so much innocent blood that many a skirmish with the enemy costs less."

"In truth," said Roger, "the intelligence and experience of age speaks through your mouth. The evil deeds of Danveld, even if the whole blame were laid only upon him, would always be reckoned to the Order's account, which means to the account of all of us, the chapter and the grand master himself. But in this way our innocence will be shown, and all will fall upon Jurand, upon the malice of the Poles, and their union with the powers of hell."

"And then let judge us who will: the pope or the Roman emperor!"

"Yes!"

A moment of silence followed, after which Brother Roger asked:
"So what shall we do with Jurand's daughter?"

"Let us take counsel."

"Give her to me."

Siegfried looked at him and said:

"No! Listen, young brother! If the Order is in question, spare neither man nor woman, but also spare not yourself. Danveld was reached by the hand of God, for he desired not only to avenge the wrongs of the Order but also to satisfy his own lusts."

"You judge me wrongly!" said Roger.

"Spare not yourself," Siegfried interrupted, "or you will make effeminate both your body and your soul, and some day the knee of that hard race will crush your chest, and you will never rise again."

And for the third time he rested his gloomy head on his hands, but evidently he was communing only with his own conscience and thinking only of himself, for after a while he said:

"A heavy burden of human blood and grief weighs on me too. . . . When the Order was in question, and I knew that I could not succeed by force alone, I, too, did not hesitate to seek other ways. But when I stand before the Lord, whom I honor and love, I shall say to Him: 'I did it for the Order; for myself I chose only suffering.'"

Then he pressed his temples with his hands, raised his head, and looked up, saying:

"Renounce voluptuous pleasure and debauchery, harden your bodies and your hearts, for I see the Polish eagle's feathers in the air, and its talons red with Teutonic blood."

His further words were interrupted by a blast of wind so strong that a window in the upper gallery burst open with a crash, and the whole hall was filled with the howling and whistling of the blizzard and with flakes of snow.

"In the name of the Spirit of Light! 'Tis an evil night," said old Siegfried.

"A night of the unholy powers," replied Roger. "But why, instead of 'in the name of God' do you say 'in the name of the Spirit of Light'?"

"The Spirit of Light is God," replied the old man; and then, as if wishing to turn the conversation, he asked:

"Are the priests by Danveld's body?"

"Yes. . . ."

"God be merciful to him!"

Both were silent, and then Roger called the pages, whom he ordered to shut the window and trim the torches. When they had gone, he asked:

"What will you do with Jurand's daughter? Will you take her from here to Insburk?"

"I shall take her to Insburk and do with her as the good of the Order may require."

"And what am I to do?"

"Is your heart courageous?"

"Have I done anything that you should doubt it?"

"I do not doubt it, for I know you, and for your valor I love you more than anyone in the world. Go then to the court of the Mazovian duke and tell him all that has happened here as we have agreed upon."

"Am I to expose myself to certain death?"

"If your death results in the glory of the Order, you ought to do so. But no! Death does not await you. They do no wrong to guests—unless one wanted to challenge you, as that young knight did who challenged all of us; either he, or someone else, but that would not be a horrible thing. . . ."

"God grant it! But they may seize me and thrust me into a dungeon."

"They will not do that. Remember that there is Jurand's letter to the duke, and you will go, besides, to complain of Jurand. You will tell with sincerity what he did at Ortelsburg, and they must believe you. It was we who first let him know that a girl was here; it was we who first invited him to come and look at her; he came, went mad, and slew the commander and many of our men. That is what you will say, and what can they do? Danveld's death will soon be known throughout Mazovia. Confronted with his, they will have to give up on any potential grievance. They will of course look for Jurand's daughter, but since Jurand himself has written that she is not with us, their suspicion will not fall on us. We must make up with courage for what has occurred, and must shut their jaws. They will think that none of us would have the courage to come to them if we were guilty."

"True! After Danveld's funeral I will immediately take to the road."

"God bless you, my boy! If we do all as we should, not only will they not detain you, but they will have to renounce Jurand, that we may not say: 'See how they behave towards us!'"

"And thus we should complain at every foreign court."

"The grand hospitaller will take care of that, both for the good of the Order and as Danveld's kinsman."

"Yes, but what if that devil from Spychow comes to life once more and regains his freedom?"

Siegfried looked somberly straight ahead and answered slowly and emphatically:

"Even if he were to regain his freedom, he will never utter a word against the Order."

Then he began to instruct Roger further as to what he had to say, and what demands he had to make, at the Mazovian court.

CHAPTER XXXV

THE news of the events at Ortelsburg reached Warsaw before the arrival of Brother Roger, and roused amazement and alarm. Neither the duke nor anyone at the court could understand what had happened. Not too long ago, just when Nicholas of Longwood was about to go to Malbork with a letter from the duke, in which he complained bitterly of the kidnapping of Danusia by unruly border commanders, and even demanded her immediate return with half-threats, there had come a letter from the Master of Spychow declaring that his daughter had been seized, not by the Teutonic Knights, but by common border robbers, and that she would shortly be ransomed. Consequently the emissary had not gone, for it passed through no one's head that the Teutonic Knights might have forced Jurand to write the letter under threat of killing his child. In any case it was difficult to understand what had happened, since the freebooters of the border, whether they were subjects of the duke or of the Order, made their mutual attacks in the summer, and not in the winter when their tracks would remain in the snow. Moreover, they usually attacked merchants or robbed villages, seizing people and driving off their flocks and herds. But that they should dare to offend the duke himself and carry off his ward, who was at the same time the daughter of a powerful knight, widely feared, seemed to pass the limits of human belief. None the less, this and other doubts seemed to be answered by Jurand's letter, sealed with his own seal, and brought, this time, by a man who was known to belong to Spychow. In face of it all, suspicions became impossible. But the duke fell into such wrath as he had rarely displayed, and ordered a punitive expedition to be sent out against the highway robbers along the whole border of his duchy, calling upon the Duke of Plock to do the same, and not to spare any of the insolent evildoers.

And then, just at that time, came the news of what had happened at Ortelsburg.

It passed from mouth to mouth and was exaggerated tenfold. It was said that Jurand had arrived with five other men at the castle, had burst in through the open gate, and made such a slaughter that but few of the garrison remained alive; help from neighboring castles had to be sent for, and the knights and units of armed footmen summoned. Only after a two days' siege were the Germans able to force their way into the castle and dispose of Jurand and his companions. It was also said that the army thus assembled would probably now move to the frontier, and that a great war was inevitable. The duke, who knew how anxious the grand master was that, in case of war with the Polish king, the armies of both the Mazovian duchies should stand aside, did not believe these reports. It was no secret to him that if the Teutonic Knights began war with him, or with Ziemowit of Plock, no human power could restrain the Poles of the kingdom, and the master was afraid of such a war. He knew that it must come, but he desired to put it off, firstly because he was of a peaceful nature, and secondly because, if he was to measure himself with the power of Jagiello, he must prepare such forces as the Order had never yet placed in the field, and must at the same time assure himself of the aid of the dukes and the knighthood, not only in Germany but in the whole of the West.

So the duke was not afraid of war, but he wanted to know what had happened and what really to think of the events at Ortelsburg, the disappearance of Danusia, and all the reports which had come from over the border. So, although he could not endure the Teutonic Knights, he was glad when one evening the captain of his archers reported that a Knight of the Order had arrived and was asking for an audience.

He received him, however, haughtily, and although he recognized at once that he was one of the brethren who had been at the hunting-lodge, he pretended as if he had forgotten, asking who he was, from where he had come, and what had brought him to Warsaw.

"I am Brother Roger," replied the Teutonic Knight, "and not long ago I had the honor of bowing before your ducal grace."

"Why, then, if you are a brother, have you not any emblems of the Order on your dress?"

The knight explained that he had not put on the white cloak with the Cross because, if he had done so, he would have been inevitably taken prisoner or slain by the Mazovian knighthood; everywhere in the whole world, in all kingdoms and duchies, the sign of the Cross of the cloak protected and assured goodwill and hospitality; in the duchy of Mazovia alone the Cross exposed its wearer to certain death.

The duke interrupted him angrily.

"Not the Cross," he said, "for we, too, kiss the Cross, but only your depravity. And if you are better received elsewhere, it is because they know you less." Then, seeing that the knight was greatly taken aback by these words, he asked: "Have you been at Ortelsburg, or do you know what has happened there?"

"I have been at Ortelsburg and I know what has happened there," replied Roger, "and I have come here, not as emissary from anyone, but simply because the experienced and holy commander of Insburk said to me, 'Our master loves the pious duke and has confidence in his justice, so while I hasten to Malbork do you go to Mazovia and present to him the wrong done us, how we have been disgraced, and the misery inflicted on us. The just lord will not praise the violator of peace and the fierce assailant who has shed as much Christian blood as if he were the servant, not of Christ, but of Satan.'"

Then he began to tell all that had happened at Ortelsburg: how Jurand, invited by the knights themselves to see whether the girl whom they had rescued from robbers was his daughter, instead of repaying them with gratitude, fell into a mad rage; how he slew Danveld, Brother Godfrey, the Englishman Hugh, von Bracht, and two noble esquires, not counting the soldiers; how they, mindful of the divine command, were unwilling to slay him, and had to eventually entangle in a net the terrible man, who then raised his weapon against himself and wounded himself cruelly; and finally how, not only in the castle but also in the town, were men who had heard in the wintry gale during the night after the battle horrible laughter and voices calling in the air: "Our Jurand! The enemy of the Cross! The shedder of innocent blood! Our Jurand!"

The whole story, and particularly the Teutonic Knight's last words, made a great impression on all present. They began to fear that Jurand might really have called upon the unholy powers to his aid, and a dull silence fell on them. But the duchess, who was present, and who, loving Danusia, was deeply grieved at heart for her loss, turned to Roger with an unexpected question:

"You say, sir," she said, "that when you had rescued the idiot girl you thought she was Jurand's daughter, and therefore you summoned him to Ortelsburg?"

"Yes, worshipful lady," replied Roger.

"How could you think that when you had seen the real daughter of Jurand with me at the hunting-lodge?"

Unprepared for the question, Brother Roger became confused. The duke rose and fixed him with a stern glance, while Nicholas of Longwood, Mrokota of Mocarzewo, Jasko of Jagielnica, and other Mazovian knights sprang forward at once to the monk, asking in threatening tones:

"How could you think that? Speak, German! How could that be?"

But Brother Roger recovered himself and said:

"We monks do not raise our eyes to women. There were quite a few court damsels at the hunting-lodge with the gracious duchess, but which among them was Jurand's daughter, none of us knew."

"Danveld knew," said Nicholas of Longwood. "He talked with her even at the hunt."

"Danveld stands before God," replied Roger, "but I will say of him only this, that on the next morning they found roses in bloom on his coffin, which could not in winter have been put there by human hand."

Silence followed again.

"How did you know of the kidnapping of Jurand's daughter?" asked the duke.

"The godlessness and audacity of the deed made it notorious here and among us. So when we learned of it we celebrated a Mass of thanksgiving that it was only an ordinary court damsel, and not one of your grace's own children, who had been kidnapped from the hunting-lodge."

"But it is still a wonder to me that you could take an idiot girl for Jurand's daughter."

Brother Roger replied:

"Danveld said this: 'Satan often betrays his servants, so perhaps he changed Jurand's daughter.'"

"But simple robbers could not imitate Caleb's writing and Jurand's seal. Who could do that?"

"An evil spirit."

And again no one could find an answer.

Roger looked straight in the duke's eyes and said:

"In truth, these questions are like swords in my breast, for accusation and suspicion are concealed behind them. But I, trusting in the justice of God and in the power of truth, ask your ducal grace: Did Jurand himself accuse us of this deed, and if he did, why before we called him to Ortelsburg did he hunt for robbers all along the border, to ransom his daughter from them?"

"Yes—true," said the duke. "Although one may hide a thing from men, it will not be hidden from God. Jurand suspected you at first, but then . . . then had other thoughts."

"See how the light of truth vanquishes darkness!" said Roger, and he looked triumphantly around the hall, for he thought that in the heads of the Teutonic Knights there was more cleverness and intelligence than in those of the Poles, and that the Polish race would always be the plunder and the sustenance of the Order, as a fly is the plunder and sustenance of the spider.

So casting off his former politeness, he went up to the duke and said in a loud, harsh voice:

"Requite us, lord, for our losses, our wrongs, our tears, and our blood! That son of hell was your subject, so in the name of God, from whom flows the power of kings and princes, in the name of justice and of the Cross, requite us for our wrongs and our blood!"

The duke looked at him in amazement.

"By the dear God!" he said, "what do you want? If Jurand shed your blood in madness, have I to be answerable for his deed?"

"He was your vassal, lord," said the knight. "In your duchy lie his lands, his villages, and his fort, in which he imprisoned servants of the Order; let at least that domain, let at least those lands and that godless castelet become from now on the property of the Order. 'Tis true, it will not be fitting payment for the noble blood which has been shed; 'tis true, it will not bring to life again the dead; but perhaps it will in part appease divine anger, and wipe out the disgrace which otherwise would fall on the whole of this duchy. Lord! Everywhere the Order possesses lands and castles which the favor and piety of Christian dukes have bestowed upon it; only here there is not a handbreadth of land in its hold. May our wrong, which calls to God for vengeance, be requited us, if only to enable us to say that here, too, live men who have the fear of God in their hearts."

Hearing all this, the duke was amazed still more, and only after a long silence replied:

"Great heavens! By whose favor is your Order established in this region, if not by that of my ancestors? Are the lands, districts, and towns which once belonged to us and to our nation, but today are yours, not enough for you? Why, Jurand's daughter is still alive; no one has told you of her death. Yet you wish to rob an orphan of her dowry and requite yourselves with orphan's bread?"

"Lord, you admit the wrong," said Roger, "so recompense us as your ducal conscience and your spirit of justice bid you."

And again he rejoiced at heart, for he thought: "Now not only will they make no accusation, but they will take counsel how to wash their own hands and extricate themselves from this affair. No one will now reproach us, and our face will be like the white cloak of the Order—without a spot."

But the voice of old Nicholas of Longwood was unexpectedly heard:

"People accuse you of greed, and God knows whether not justly, for even in this affair you care more for profit than for the honor of the Order."

"True!" replied the Mazovian knights in chorus.

The Teutonic Knight advanced several paces, raised his head proudly and, measuring them with a haughty glance, said:

"I have not come here as an envoy, but only as a witness to the truth and as a Knight of the Order, ready to defend the honor of the Order with my blood to my last breath! If anyone, therefore, despite what Jurand himself said, dares to suspect the Order of having had a part in the kidnapping of his daughter, let him take up this knightly gage, and let him venture on the wager of battle, where God will judge and punish!"

And he threw down his gauntlet to the floor. But they stood in dull silence, for though many of them would have been glad to notch their swords on the necks of the Teutonic Knights, they yet feared the wager of battle. It was no secret to any that Jurand had expressly declared it was not the Knights who had kidnapped his child, and so each one thought in his heart that it must be true, and that therefore victory would be with Roger.

So he grew all the more insolent and, putting his hands on his hips, asked:

"Is there anyone who will take up the gauntlet?"

And then a knight, whose entrance had not been noticed, but who had been listening for some time by the door, advanced to the middle of the room, took up the gauntlet, and said:

"I will!"

And having spoken, he threw his own glove straight at Roger's face, and then said in tones which reverberated like thunder throughout the silent hall:

"In the face of God, in the face of the noble duke, and all the honorable knighthood of this land, I tell you, Teutonic Knight, that you are barking like a dog against justice and truth, and I challenge you to the lists, to battle on horseback or on foot, with lance or axe, with short or long sword—and not to captivity, but to the last breath, to the death!"

In the hall a fly might have been heard on the wing. All eyes turned to Roger and the challenging knight, whom no one knew, for on his head he had a helmet, visorless, it is true, but with a circular flap coming down below his ears, completely covering the upper part of his face and throwing a deep shadow over the lower part. The Teutonic Knight was not less amazed than all the rest. Confusion, pallor, and frightful rage passed over his face like lightning in the night sky. He took hold of the elk-skin glove, which had caught on his shoulder-piece when it had fallen down from his face, and asked:

"Who are you who challenge the justice of God?"

The other undid a buckle beneath his chin, took off his helmet, from under which appeared a fair, young head, and said:

"Zbyszko of Bogdaniec, the husband of Jurand's daughter."

They were all astonished, and Roger with the rest, for none of them—save the duke and duchess, Father Wyszoniek and de Lorche—knew of Danusia's marriage, while the Teutonic Knights were certain that besides her father, Danusia had no other natural defender. But Sieur de Lorche stepped forward and said:

"On my knightly honor I testify to the truth of his words; if any dare to doubt it, there is my gage!"

Roger, who did not know the meaning of fear, and whose heart was raging at that moment, might have picked up the glove, but remembering that the man who had thrown it was a rich lord on his own account, and, furthermore, a kinsman of the Count of Guelders, he restrained himself, particularly since the duke himself stood up and said, frowning:

"You may not take up that gage, for I also testify that the knight has spoken the truth."

The Teutonic Knight, hearing that, bowed, and then said to Zbyszko:

"If you will, on foot, in enclosed lists, with axes."

"As it is, I already challenged you once before," replied Zbyszko.

"God grant victory to justice!" exclaimed the Mazovian knights.

CHAPTER XXXVI

THERE was great concern for Zbyszko's sake in the whole court, both among the knights and the women, for he was liked by all, and in face of Jurand's letter none doubted that justice was on the side of the Teutonic Knight. Moreover, it was known that Roger was one of the most famous brothers of the Order. His squire, van Krist, spread the story among the Mazovian gentry, perhaps purposely, that his lord, before he became an armed monk, had once sat at the table of honor of the Knights, to which were admitted only knights famous in the world—such as had made an expedition to the Holy Land, or had fought victoriously with giants, dragons, or powerful enchanters. Hearing such tales of van Krist's, and at the same time his boastful assertion that his lord had more than once fought five opponents with misericord in one hand and axe or sword in the other, the Mazovians became anxious, and some said: "If but Jurand had been here, he could have dealt with two Rogers. Woe to the youth! His opponent surpasses him in strength, in years, and in practice." Others regretted they had not picked up the gauntlet, asserting that had it not been for that statement of Jurand's they would unfailingly have done so. "But trial by battle, under God's watchful eye, is to be feared." They also took occasion to mention, for their own encouragement, the names of the Mazovian and Polish knights who had won numerous victories over knights from the West at court tournaments or in combats with sharp weapons. The name most frequently mentioned was Zawisza of Garbowo, known also as Zawisza the Black, with whom no knight in the whole of Christendom could measure himself. But there were some who had reason to hope for Zbyszko's success. "He is no young sprig," they said, "and as you have heard he has already once split the heads of Germans on levelled ground." But their hearts were particularly cheered by the action of Zbyszko's squire, the Czech, Hlawa, who on the evening before the meeting, hearing van Krist telling of the incredible victories of Roger, and being an impulsive youth, seized van Krist by the beard, pulled his head back, and said, "If you're not ashamed to tell lies before men, look up, so that God may hear you!" And he kept him in that position for as long as it would take to say a paternoster. When he was let go, van Krist immediately began to ask him of his parentage, and learning that the Czech came of a noble line, he challenged him to a fight with axes.

The Mazovians were gladdened by Hlawa's action, and more than one said: "Such men will not restrain themselves in a fight, and if truth and God are on their side, these Teutonic dogs will not get out alive." But Roger was able to throw dust in the eyes of all, so that many were unsure on which side lay the truth, and the duke himself shared this uncertainty.

So, on the evening before the combat, he summoned Zbyszko to a talk at which only the duchess was present, and asked him:

"Are you certain that God will be with you? How do you know that they seized Danusia? Did Jurand tell you anything? For here, as you see, is Jurand's letter—the handwriting of Father Caleb and Jurand's seal—and in it Jurand says he knows that it was not the Teutonic Knights. What did he tell you?"

"He said that it was not the Teutonic Knights."

"How then can you risk your life and face the trial by battle?"

Zbyszko was silent. For a time his jaws quivered, and tears gathered in his eyes.

"I know nothing, worshipful lord," he said. "I left here with Jurand, and on the way I confessed to him about the marriage. Then he began to reproach me, saying it might be a wrong done to God, but when I told him it was God's will, he grew calmer and forgave me. The entire way he said that no one else had kidnapped Danusia, only the Teutonic Knights. What happened then, I don't know! The same woman who had brought medicine to the hunting-lodge came to Spychow, and with her was another messenger. They shut themselves up with Jurand and held counsel together.

What they said I do not know; I only know that after that talk his own servants could not recognize Jurand, for he looked as if he had been taken out of a coffin. He told us: 'Not the Teutonic Knights.' And he released de Bergow and all the prisoners he had from the dungeon, God knows why, and himself rode off without any squire or attendant. He said he was going to the robbers, to ransom Danusia, and he bade me wait. Well! I waited. And then came news from Ortelsburg that Jurand had slaughtered Germans and was killed himself! Oh, worshipful lord! The ground of Spychow burned under by feet, and I almost went mad. I mounted my men to avenge Jurand's death, but Father Caleb told me: 'You will not take the castle, so do not begin war. Go to the duke; perhaps they know something about Danusia there.' So I came, and arrived right at the moment when that dog was barking about the wrong done to the Knights and Jurand's madness. I, lord, took up his gauntlet, for I had challenged him before, and although I know nothing, one thing I know, that they are hellish liars—without shame, without honor, and without faith. Look, gracious lord and lady! They stabbed de Fourcy and tried to put the blame on my squire. By heaven! They stabbed him like an ox, and then they came to you, lord, for vengeance and requital! Who then will swear that they did not lie to Jurand before, and are not now lying to you? . . . I do not know where Danusia is! I do not know! But I challenged him, for though I should lose my life, I would prefer death than life without my love, without the one who is dearest to me in the whole world!"

In his emotion, he took off the net from his head, so that his hair fell down on his shoulders, and, clutching it, began to sob grievously. Duchess Anna Danuta, herself deeply afflicted by the loss of Danusia and pitying his sorrow, laid her hands on his head and said:

"God aid, comfort, and bless you!"

CHAPTER XXXVII

THE duke did not forbid the combat, for according to the customs of the times it was not in his power to do so. He only had Roger write a letter to the master and to Siegfried von Lowe, saying that he had been the first to throw down the gauntlet to the Mazovian knights, as a result of which he was about to engage in combat with the husband of Jurand's daughter, who, besides, had already challenged him once before. The Teutonic Knight also explained to the grand master that if he fought without permission it was because the honor of the Order was at stake, and the foul suspicions which might bring shame upon it had to be rebutted, suspicions which he, Roger, was ready to wipe out with his own blood. This letter was sent immediately to the border by one of the knight's pages, and beyond that it was to go to Malbork by the post which the Teutonic Knights had invented many years before other people and introduced into their territories.

Meanwhile in the castle yard the snow was beaten down and covered with ashes so that the feet of the combatants might not stick or slip on its smooth surface. There was an extraordinary flutter of activity throughout the entire castle. The knights and the court damsels were so overcome with emotion that the night before the combat no one slept. They said to one another that a fight on horseback with lances or even with swords often ended with wounds, whereas a fight on foot, particularly with the terrible axes, was always mortal. All hearts were on the side of Zbyszko. The more friendly anyone was to him or to Danusia, the greater was the alarm with which he or she remembered what had been said about the fame and skill of Teutonic Knight. Many women spent the night in the church, where Zbyszko also knelt in penance after confessing himself to Father Wyszoniek. One girl said to another, looking at his truly boyish face: "Why, he is still a child! Why must such a young head be given to the German axe?" And they prayed the more eagerly for him. But when he rose at dawn and went through the chapel to put on his armor in the chamber, they took heart again somewhat, for, though Zbyszko's head and face were indeed boyish, his body was extraordinarily sturdy and strong, so that he seemed to them a valiant fellow who could deal with even the toughest man.

The combat was to take place in the castle yard, around which was a cloister.

When day had fully dawned, the duke and duchess came with their children and sat down in the middle between posts, with the best view of the whole yard. Beside them the leading courtiers, noblewomen, and knights took their places. Every corner of the cloister was filled; the attendants took up positions behind the bank of snow swept from the center, and some clung to oriels, and even to the roof. The commoners said to one another: "God grant that our men may not fail!"

The day was cold, damp, but clear. The air was full of crows which usually inhabited the roofs and tops of the bastions, but which now, disturbed by the unusual movement, circled over the castle with a great flapping of wings. Despite the cool, men sweated with emotion, and when the trumpets sounded, announcing the entrance of the champions, all hearts began to beat like hammers.

They came in from opposite sides of the lists and stopped at the barriers. Every onlooker then held his breath, everyone thought that before long two souls would haste before the judgment seat of God and two corpses would be lying on the snow—and the lips and cheeks of the women grew pale and blue at this thought, while the eyes of the men were fixed on the antagonists as if on a rainbow, for each desired to forecast from their figures and their weapons on which side victory would fall.

The Teutonic Knight wore a blue cast-iron breastplate and cuisses, and a similar helmet with raised visor and a splendid plume of peacock feathers on the crest. Zbyszko's chest, sides, and back were covered by the magnificent Milanese armor he had won from the Frisians. On his head he had a helmet with a hood, unclosed, without a plume, and on his legs ox-leather thigh-guards. On their left arms the warriors bore shields painted with their escutcheons: the Teutonic Knight's a checker pattern above and three lions rampant below, and Zbyszko's a Blunt Horseshoe. In their right hands they held terrible broad axes, fitted with blackened oak handles longer than the arm of a grown man. They were accompanied by their squires: Hlawa, whom Zbyszko called Wisehead, and van Krist, both wearing dark iron plates and both also carrying shields and axes. Van Krist had a sprig of Genista as his escutcheon, while that of the Czech was like the *Pomiano*, with this difference, that instead of an axe stuck in the bull's head, a short sword was plunged half-way in the eye.

The trumpets sounded for the second time; the third signal would begin the match. The combatants were now separated only by a small space sprinkled with grey ashes; over that place hovered, like a bird of ill-omen, the spirit of death. But before the third signal was given Roger approached the posts between which the duke and duchess were sitting, raised his steel-clad head, and shouted in a voice which carried into the far corners of the cloister:

"I take to witness God, and you, distinguished lord, and the whole knighthood of this land, that I am innocent of this blood which will be shed."

At these words the hearts of the spectators were again oppressed; the Teutonic Knight was so sure of himself and his victory. Zbyszko, who had a simple soul, turned to his Czech:

"This boasting is noisome to me; it would be more in place after my death, but not while I live. Moreover, that boaster has a plume of peacock feathers on his helmet, and I vowed at first three such, and afterwards as many as I have fingers on my hands. God has given him to me!"

"Lord," asked Hlawa, bending down and taking up a little of the ashes and snow to rub on his hands so that the axe-handle should not slip through them, "perhaps Christ will grant me to finish quickly with this Prussian knave; in that case may I, if not strike the Teutonic Knight, at least thrust the axe handle between his knees and tumble him to the ground?"

"God forbid!" exclaimed Zbyszko quickly. "You would cover yourself and me with shame."

Then the trumpets sounded from the third time. Hearing them, the squires rushed together quickly and eagerly, while the knights moved more slowly and carefully, as their dignity required until they actually met.

Few of the spectators paid attention to the squires, but those experienced men and servants who did so realized at once what an enormous advantage there was on the side of Hlawa. The axe seemed heavier in the hand of the German, and the movements of his shield were also slower. Under his shield could be seen his long legs, weak and less resilient than the powerful tight-clad legs of the Czech. Furthermore, Hlawa attacked with such ardor that van Krist had to retreat almost from the first moment. It could be seen at once that one of these antagonists rushed upon the other like a storm, and pushed and pressed and struck like lightning, while the other, feeling that death was over him, defended himself only to defer the frightful moment to the utmost. So indeed it was. The boaster, who in general was accustomed to fight only when he could not avoid it, realized that his insolent and careless words had brought him to battle with a man of fearful strength, whom he ought to have avoided like the plague. So when he now felt that every one of those blows might fell an ox, his heart sank in his breast. He almost forgot that it was not enough to parry blows with his shield, but that he must deal them in turn. He saw the flashing axe above him and thought each flash the last. He held up his shield and blinked involuntarily with a felling of fear and doubt whether he would ever open his eyes again. It was seldom that he dealt a blow, and then it was without hope of reaching his antago-nist; he merely raised his shield higher and higher above his head to defend it again and again.

At last he began to tire, while the Czech struck at him more and more powerfully. As from a tall pine-tree enormous chips fly off under a peasant's axe, so under the Czech's blows began to crumble and fly off metal plates from the armor of the German squire. The upper edge of his shield bent and split. His right shoulder-piece fell to the ground, its strap cut off and covered with blood. Van Krist's hair stood on end, and he was seized with mortal fear. He struck once and again with all the strength in his arm at the Czech's shield, but finally seeing that, in view of the frightful power of his oppo-nent, there was no hope for him of safety, and that he could escape only by some exceptional effort, he threw himself with the whole weight of his armor and his body at Hlawa's legs.

They both fell to the ground and struggled together, rolling and turning in the snow. But the Czech soon got on top. For a while he pinned down his desperate antagonist, and at last knelt on the iron ring-mail covering his stomach. Then he drew from his belt his short three-edged misericord.

"Spare me!" whispered van Krist, raising his eyes to the eyes of the Czech.

But he, instead of replying, stretched himself out on him to reach his throat more easily and, cutting through the strap which fastened his helmet under his chin, stabbed the unfortunate man twice in the throat, directing the point downwards to the middle of his chest.

Then van Krist's eyeballs rolled up in their sockets, and his hands and feet began to rub the snow as if to clear it of ashes. Soon he lay still, his lips puffing out red foam and torrents of blood.

The Czech stood up and wiped his misericord on the German's garment. Then he took his axe and, leaning on it, began to watch the harder and more stubborn fight between his knight and Brother Roger.

The knights of the West were accustomed to comfort and luxury, whereas the landowners of Little and Great Poland and Mazovia led hard, stern lives, as a result of which even strangers were compelled to admire the sturdiness of their bodies and their endurance of all fatigue, whether constant or temporary. It appeared on the present occasion that Zbyszko surpassed the Teutonic Knight in the strength of his arms and legs no less than his squire had surpassed van Krist; but it also appeared that, being younger, he was inferior in the skills of knightly combat.

It was to some extent favorable for Zbyszko that Roger had chosen to fight with axes, for any kind of fencing with such weapons was impossible. With short or long swords it was necessary to know how to cut and thrust and parry, and the German would have had a notable advantage. Even as it was, however, both Zbyszko and the spectators perceived from Roger's movements and the way he wielded his shield that they had before them an experienced and dangerous man, who was not fighting this type of battle for the first time. At every swing of the axe by Zbyszko, Roger held up his shield, and at the moment when the axe struck, withdrew it slightly, so that even the greatest blow lost its force and could neither cut through nor crumble the smooth surface. Sometimes he moved back, sometimes he pressed forward, slowly or so quickly that his movements could scarce be followed by the eye. The duke was afraid for Zbyszko, and the faces of the onlookers darkened, for they thought that the German was purposely playing with his antagonist. At times Roger did not even hold up his shield, but made a half turn to one side when Zbyszko struck, so that the axe blade cut through empty air. This was most frightening because Zbyszko might lose his balance and fall, and then his death would be inevitable. Seeing that, the Czech, standing over the slaughtered Krist, became most anxious, and said to himself: "Oh, God! If my lord falls, I will strike the German between the shoulders with the head of my axe, so that he will tumble down also."

But Zbyszko did not fall, for, having enormous strength in his legs and planting them widely, he could support on each the whole weight of his body and the impetus of the attack.

Roger noticed this at once, and the spectators were wrong in thinking that he regarded his antagonist lightly. On the contrary, after the first blows, when despite all his skill in withdrawing his shield, his arm was almost numbed under it, he understood that he would have great difficulty with this youth, and that if he did not overthrow him by some sleight, the struggle might be long and dangerous. He had counted on Zbyszko falling in the snow after cutting the empty air, and when this did not happen he began to feel real alarm. Under the steel hood he saw the distended nostrils and set lips of his antagonist, and sometimes his flashing eyes, and he reassured himself with the belief that in his fiery eagerness Zbyszko would forget himself, lose his head, and blindly think more of dealing blows than self-defence. But in this, too, he was mistaken. Zbyszko was not able to avoid blows by making a half turn, but he did not forget his shield, and when he swung his axe he did not expose himself more than was necessary. Evidently his attention was redoubled, and realizing the experience and skill of his antagonist, he not only did not forget himself, but became focused, more watchful, and put into his blows a calculation which only cold fury could have enabled him to display.

Roger, who had seen not a little of war and had fought no few

battles, in groups or single-handed, knew from experience that
there are men like birds of prey, created for battle and peculiarly
gifted by nature, who seem to divine all that others attain by years
of practice, and he soon saw that he had to do with such a person.
From the first blow he perceived that in this youth there was
something of the hawk, which sees in its antagonist nothing but its
prey, and thinks of nothing else except of reaching it with its
talons. Despite his own strength, he also perceived that he was not
equal to Zbyszko, and that if he exhausted himself before he was
able to give the decisive blow, the fight with this terrible, though
less experienced youth might end disastrously for him. Thinking
this, he determined to fight with the least possible expenditure of
effort. He drew his shield nearer to his body, he did not advance or
withdraw too far, he limited his movements, concentrated the will
of his mind and the strength of his arm for one decisive blow, and
waited for his opportunity.

The fierce battle lasted longer than usual. Deathly silence fell
over the spectators in the cloister. Nothing was to be heard save the
sharp clash or dull pounding of axe blades and heads on shields.
Neither the duke and duchess, nor the knights, nor the courtiers
were unaccustomed to such sights, yet a feeling akin to fear gripped
the hearts of all. They understood that here was not merely a
question of displaying strength and skill and valor, but that in this
fight there was immense rage, immense despair, immense and
implacable hatred, and a deep desire for vengeance. On the one
hand, terrible wrongs, love, and grief unfathomable; on the other,
the honor of a whole Order and profound hatred. Such were the
passions which inspired the combatants in this trial before the
judgment seat of God.

Meanwhile the pale winter morning grew brighter, the grey
curtain of mist cleared, and the rays of the sun illuminated the blue
breastplate of the Teutonic Knight and the silvery Milanese armor
of Zbyszko. The chapel bell rang for Terce, and flocks of jackdaws
rose from the castle roofs, flapping their wings and cawing noisily,
as if with joy at the sight of the blood and the corpse which now
lay motionless on the snow. Roger cast his eyes on it once or twice
during the fight and suddenly felt dreadfully alone. All the eyes
which were looking at him were the eyes of enemies. All the
prayers, wishes, and silent vows which the women were making

were in favor of Zbyszko. Moreover, although the Teutonic Knight was sure that Zbyszko's squire would not throw himself upon him from the rear and strike him treacherously, none the less the presence and nearness of this dangerous figure filled him with the same kind of involuntary alarm felt by a man at the sight of a wolf, a bear, or a bison from which he is not separated by bars. And he could not help this feeling, particularly as the Czech, following the course of the fight, moved and changed his place, standing now at one side of the combatants, now behind them, and now in front. At the same time, he was bending his head and looking at Roger ominously through the slits in his iron visor, and sometimes lifting his bloody axe a little, as if unconsciously.

Fatigue began at last to lay hold of the Teutonic Knight. One after another, he dealt two short but terrible blows directed at Zbyszko's right shoulder, but his antagonist parried them with his shield with such strength that the axe handle quivered in Roger's hand, and he himself had to step back quickly so as not to fall. From that moment he retreated continually. Not merely his strength was exhausted, but his cool blood and his patience. A few shouts as if of triumph escaped from the breasts of the spectators at the sight of his retreat, and this roused his anger and despair. The axe-blows became ever more frequent. Sweat flowed over the brows of both combatants, and their breath came panting through set teeth. The spectators ceased to bear themselves calmly; every moment there were shouts of men or women: "Strike! At him! The judgment of God! Divine punishment! God aid you!" The duke waved his hand several times for silence but could not restrain the spectators. The noise increased; children began to cry here and there in the cloisters—and at last, close by the duchess's side, a young and tearful woman's voice called out:

"For Danusia, Zbyszko! For Danusia!"

Zbyszko knew very well that he was fighting for Danusia. He was certain that the knight had had a hand in her kidnapping, and fighting with him he was fighting to redress her wrong. But, being young and eager for battle, during the fight he thought of nothing but the fight. That sudden cry reminded him of her loss and her misery. Love, grief, and vengeance poured fire into his veins. His heart leapt within him in fresh pain, and he was quite simply seized by a fighting frenzy. The Teutonic Knight could no longer parry the frightful weight of his blows, which were like thunderbolts, nor could he now avoid them. Zbyszko smashed his own shield against his with such superhuman strength that the German's arm suddenly grew numb and fell to his side. He retreated in fear and terror, and leaned back. Suddenly the flash of the axe blinded his eyes, and the edge struck like lightning his right shoulder.

The spectators heard only a shrill cry: "Jesus!" And then Roger withdrew another step and fell backwards on the ground.

In the cloisters there was an uproar and a rush, as in a beehive when it is warmed by the sun. The knights ran in crowds down the stairs, and the servants overleapt the bank of snow; all wanted to look at the corpses. Everywhere shouts were heard: "You see the judgment of God! Jurand has an heir! Glory and thanks be to God! What an axeman!" And others shouted: "Look and wonder! Jurand himself could not have cut him down better!" A group of curious spectators gathered around the corpse of Roger as he lay on his back, his face pale as snow, his mouth wide open, and his bloody shoulder almost severed from neck to armpit, and hanging only by a few sinews. So they exclaimed: "He was alive and walked the earth in pride, but now he does not move even a finger!" Some marvelled at his size, for he had taken up a large space on the field of combat and seemed even larger after his death; while others admired his peacock-feather crest, changing its colors wonderfully on the snow; still others were impressed by his armor, which they valued at the price of a good village. Hlawa came up with two of Zbyszko's pages to strip it from the dead warrior. So the curious surrounded Zbyszko, praising him and exalting him to the skies, for it rightly seemed to them that the splendor of his fame would fall on the whole of the Mazovian and Polish knighthood. Meanwhile he was relieved of his shield and axe, and Mrokota of Mocarzewo unbuckled his helmet and covered his sweaty hair with a cap of scarlet cloth. Zbyszko stood as if but half-conscious, breathing heavily, the fire not yet quenched in his eyes, his face pale with effort, quivering a little with emotion and fatigue. They took him by the hand and led him to the duke and duchess, who were waiting for him by the chimney in their warm chamber. There Zbyszko knelt before them, and after Father Wyszoniek had made the sign of the cross over him, and repeated a requiem for the souls of the dead, the duke embraced the young knight and said:

"The Most High God has judged between the two of you and has guided your hand, for which His name be blessed, amen!"

Then, turning to Sieur de Lorche and the others, he added:

"I take you, foreign knight, and all of you present here, as witness to what I testify: that they met in combat according to law and custom, and as trials by battle are practised everywhere, so this one also was practised in a knightly and proper manner."

The local warriors shouted their assent in chorus. When the duke's words were interpreted to Sieur de Lorche, he rose and declared that not only would he testify that everything had been done in a knightly and proper fashion, but if anyone in Malbork or in any other ducal court were actually to dare to question it, he, de Lorche, would immediately challenge him to the lists, to fight on horseback or on foot, even if this person were not a common knight, but a giant or an enchanter surpassing Merlin himself in magical powers.

Meanwhile Duchess Anna Danuta, at the moment when Zbyszko was embracing her knees in turn, said, bending down to him:

"Why do you not rejoice? Rejoice and thank God, for if God in His mercy has aided you now, He will not leave you hereafter, but will lead you to happiness."

But Zbyszko replied:

"How am I to rejoice, worshipful lady? God has granted me victory and vengeance over this Teutonic Knight, but as Danusia has not been found, she is no nearer to me now than before."

"The most inveterate enemies, Danveld, Godfrey, and Roger, are dead," answered the duchess. "And of Siegfried they say that he is juster than they, though cruel. Praise be to merciful God for that. And Sieur de Lorche said that if the Teutonic Knight fell, he would go straight to Malbork and ask the grand master himself for Danusia. They will not dare to disobey the grand master."

"God grant health to Sieur de Lorche," said Zbyszko. "I will go with him to Malbork."

The duchess was terrified at these words. It was as if Zbyszko had said that he would go unarmed among the wolves which gathered in winter in packs in the deep forests of Mazovia.

"What for?" she exclaimed. "For certain death? Immediately after such a combat neither de Lorche can help you, nor the letter which Roger wrote before the battle. You will rescue no one, and you will ruin yourself."

But he stood up and put his hands in the form of a cross.

"Help me, God," he said, "to go to Malbork and even farther for her. Dear Lord, bless me in my undertaking. I will keep on looking for her until my final breath! It is easier for me to fight Germans and meet then in armor than for her, poor orphan, to groan in a dungeon. Oh, easier! Far easier!"

And he said this with such grief and such pain—as always when he mentioned Danusia—that sometimes his words seemed to follow one another with difficulty, as if someone were clutching at his throat. The duchess perceived that it would be vain to try to dissuade him. Whoever would want to hold him back would have to manacle him and throw him into a dungeon.

Zbyszko, however, could not depart immediately. The knights of those times might disregard all obstacles, but not the knightly custom which required that the victor in single combat should spend the whole day till midnight on the field of battle, both to show that he was master of it, and to prove his readiness to fight again, if any of the kinsmen or friends of the defeated should wish to challenge him anew. This custom was observed even by whole armies, who sometimes lost the advantage which haste in following up their victory might have brought them. Zbyszko, therefore, made no attempt to evade the inexorable law, but after a light meal put on his armor and stood till midnight in the castle yard, under the gloomy winter sky, waiting for the enemy who could not come from anywhere.

At midnight the heralds announced by trumpet his victory for the last time. It was only then that Nicholas of Longwood called him to supper and also to confer with the duke.

CHAPTER XXXVIII

THE duke was the first to speak at the conference:

"It is a pity that we have no writing and no evidence against the commanders. For though our suspicion seems justified, and I myself think that it was they who kidnapped Jurand's daughter, what of it? They will deny everything. And when the grand master asks for some proof, what shall we show him? Why, even Jurand's letter is evidence in their favor."

Then he turned to Zbyszko:

"You say that they forced the letter from him by threats. That may be true; indeed, it seems certain, for if justice had been on their side, God would not have helped you against Roger. But if they forced one letter from him, they may have forced two. Perhaps they also have a testimony from Jurand saying that they are innocent of the kidnapping of the hapless girl. And in that case they would show it to the master, and what then?"

"But they themselves admitted, worshipful lord, that they rescued Danusia from robbers and have her with them."

"I know. But now they say that they made a mistake, and that it was another girl, and the best proof is that Jurand himself denied her."

"He denied her, for they showed him another girl, and that was what infuriated him."

"Certainly it was, but they may say that these are only suppositions on our part."

"Their lies," said Nicholas of Longwood, "are like a forest; at the edge something may still be seen, but the deeper one goes, the thicker is the undergrowth, until at last one loses one's way and wanders about helplessly."

Then he repeated his words in German to Sieur de Lorche, who said:

"The grand master himself is better than they, and his brother, though he has an arrogant heart, is sensitive to knightly honor."

"Yes," replied Nicholas, "the master has human feelings. He cannot restrain the commanders or the chapter, and cannot help the fact that everything the Order does is based on wrongs to others, but he is not pleased. Go, go, Sieur de Lorche, and tell him what has happened here. They are more ashamed before strangers than before us, for they do not want foreign courts to be told of their treacheries and their dishonorable dealings. And when the master asks you for proofs, say to him: 'To know the truth is a divine thing, but to seek it is human; so if you wish for proofs, lord, seek for them. Order the castles to be searched, inquire of men, and let us look also, for it is a silly fairy-tale to say that the orphan was kidnapped by outlaws of the forest.'"

"A silly fairy-tale," repeated de Lorche.

"For outlaws would not have lifted their hands against a ducal court or against Jurand's child. And even if they had kidnapped her, it would have been for ransom, and they themselves would have let us know that they had her."

"I will tell him everything," said the Lorrainer, "and I will also look for de Bergow. We are from the same country, and although I do not know him, they say that he is a kinsman of the Count of Guelders. He was at Ortelsburg, so he can tell the master what he saw."

Zbyszko understood something of what was said, and what he did not understand was interpreted to him by Nicholas, so he embraced Sieur de Lorche, and pressed him to his breast until the knight groaned.

The duke addressed Zbyszko:

"Do you feel you must also go?"

"I must, gracious lord. What else can I do? I wanted to capture Ortelsburg, even if I had to gnaw the walls with my teeth, but how can I begin war without permission?"

"Whoever would begin war without permission would kneel under the headsman's sword," said the duke.

"The law is the law," replied Zbyszko. "So then I wanted to challenge everyone who was at Ortelsburg, but it was said that Jurand slaughtered many people there, as if they were oxen, and I did not know who was alive and who dead. . . . So help me God and the Holy Cross, I will never forsake Jurand!"

"You speak nobly and you please me," said Nicholas of Longwood. "And you've shown some sense, for you did not rush off to Ortelsburg. They would never have kept Jurand or his daughter there, and must have carried them off to other castles. Because you came here, God rewarded you with Roger."

"Well!" said the duke, "according to Roger, of those four only old Siegfried is still alive; the others God has already punished by Jurand's hand or yours. As for Siegfried, he is less of a scoundrel than the others, but maybe he is the cruellest of them all. It is bad that Jurand and Danusia are in his hands, and we must rescue them swiftly. I will give you a letter to the grand master, so that misfortune may not befall you. Listen carefully, and understand that you are not going as an envoy, but only as a messenger. I have written to the master the following: 'Since they had at one time laid hands on our person, though we are the descendant of their benefactors, it is probable that they seized Jurand's daughter, particularly since they were inflamed with hatred for Jurand. I therefore request the master to have a diligent search made for her, and if he wants my friendship, to give her back at once into your hands.'"

Hearing that, Zbyszko threw himself at the duke's feet and embraced his knees.

"And Jurand, gracious lord!" he said. "What about Jurand? Intercede for him also! If he has mortal wounds, let him at least die in his own house and among his children."

"There is mention of Jurand also," said the duke graciously. "The master is to send two arbitrators, and I two others, who will judge the actions of the commanders and of Jurand according to the laws of chivalry. And they are to choose a fifth who will be their head, and as they all decide, so it will be."

The conference then ended, and Zbyszko took leave of the duke, since he was soon to take the road. But before he departed, Nicholas of Longwood, who was a man of experience and knew the Teutonic Knights, took Zbyszko aside and asked him:

"Are you going to take that Czech attendant with you to the Germans?"

"He will not leave me, for sure. Why do you ask?"

"Because I feel sorry for him. He is a valiant lad, but note what I say: You will bring your head back safe from Malbork, unless you fight in single combat against a man better than yourself, but his death is certain."

"Why?"

"Because the curs accused him of having caused de Fourcy's death. They must have written to the master about his death, and they must undoubtedly have written that the Czech shed his blood. They will not forgive him that at Malbork. Judgment and vengeance await him, for how will you convince the master of his innocence? Besides, it was he who crushed Danveld's arm, and Danveld was a kinsman of the grand hospitaller. I pity him, and I repeat to you that if he goes, it will be to his death."

"He will not go to his death, for I shall leave him at Spychow."

But it happened otherwise, as there were reasons why the Czech did not remain at Spychow. Zbyszko and de Lorche set out with their retinues the following morning. De Lorche, whom Father Wyszoniek had absolved of his vows regarding Ulricha von Elner, rode happily and in silence, his thoughts full of the charms of Jagienka of Longwood; while Zbyszko, not being able to talk with him about Danusia because they did not understand one another's language very well, talked with Hlawa, who still knew nothing about the intended expedition to the country of the Teutonic Knights.

"I am going to Malbork," he said. "God alone knows when I shall return. Maybe soon, maybe in the spring, maybe in a year, or maybe never. Do you understand?"

"I understand. Your grace is doubtless going to challenge those knights. And God be praised that each one of them has a squire."

"No," replied Zbyszko, "I am not going there to challenge them, unless it happens by itself, and you are not going at all, but will remain at Spychow."

Hearing that, the Czech was at first greatly saddened, and he began to complain bitterly and then to beg his young lord not to leave him behind.

"I have sworn not to part with your grace; I swore it on the Cross and on my honor. And if some misfortune befell your grace, how could I show myself before the eyes of my lady at Zgorzelice? I swore to her, lord. So have compassion on me, that I may not be shamed before her."

"And did you not swear to her that you would obey me?" asked Zbyszko.

"Certainly! In everything, but only not in that, to go away. If your grace dismisses me, I shall follow at a distance, so as to be at hand in case of need."

"I do not and will not dismiss you," replied Zbyszko, "but I should truly feel constrained if I could not send you away somewhere, even on the longest journey, nor get rid of you for a single day. You will not stand over me unceasingly like a hangman over a good soul! And how would you help me in battle? I am not speaking of war, for in war men fight in groups; but in single combat you will not fight for me. If Roger had been more powerful than I, his armor would not have been on our wagon, but mine on his. Besides, you should know that it would be worse for me there with you. You might expose me to danger."

"How so, your grace?"

Zbyszko began to tell him what he had heard from Nicholas of Longwood, that the commanders, rather than admit the murder of de Fourcy, had accused him of it and would pursue him for vengeance.

"And if they catch you," he said finally, "I cannot leave you in their dogs' jaws, and therefore I may expose my own head to danger."

The Czech became dejected when he heard those words, for he felt their truth. Nevertheless he tried once more to find a way out according to his desires.

"None of those who saw me are alive anymore. It is said that three were slain by the old Lord of Spychow, and Roger was slain by you."

"The attendants who were riding not far behind them saw you, and that old knight is still alive and doubtless is now at Malbork, or if he is not, he will come, for, God grant, the master will summon him."

To that there was not answer, so they rode on in silence to Spychow. There they found everything ready for war, for old

Tolima had expected that either the Teutonic Knights would attack the fortalice, or that Zbyszko, when he returned, would lead them to rescue the old lord. Sentinels were on guard everywhere, at the crossings through the marshes and in the fortalice itself. The men were armed. War was no novelty to them, and so they waited for the Germans with satisfaction, promising themselves considerable booty. In the fortalice Father Caleb received Zbyszko and de Lorche, and immediately after supper showed him the parchment with Jurand's seal, on which he had written with his own hand the Lord of Spychow's last will.

"He dictated it to me," he said, "on the night he went to Ortelsburg. He did not expect to return."

"Why did you not say anything?"

"I did not say anything because he declared to me in the secrecy of the confessional what he was about to do. Lord, grant him everlasting rest, and may eternal light shine on his path!"

"Do not say a prayer for him. He is still alive. I know that from the words of Brother Roger, with whom I fought at the duke's court. There was a trial by battle between us and I slew him."

"All the more reason that Jurand will not be returning. Unless the divine power. . . ."

"I am going with this knight to tear him from their hands."

"Evidently you do not know the Teutonic Knights' hands. I know them, for before Jurand of Spychow received me, I was a priest in their country for fifteen years. Only God can save Jurand."

"And He can help us also."

"Amen!"

Then Father Caleb unrolled the document and began to read it. Jurand left all his lands and his whole estate to Danusia and her issue, and in case of her death without issue to her husband, Zbyszko of Bogdaniec. At the end he recommended his last will to the care of the duke: "In order that, if there is anything in it not according to law, the duke's grace may change it into law." This conclusion was added because Father Caleb knew only the canon law, while Jurand, occupied as he was exclusively with war, knew only the laws of chivalry. After reading the document to Zbyszko, the priest read it again to the older members of the Spychow garrison, who immediately recognized the young knight as the heir and promised him obedience.

They thought that Zbyszko would soon lead them to the rescue of the old lord, and they rejoiced, for in their breasts beat stern and warlike hearts, greatly attached to Jurand. So they were all overcome with great sorrow when they learned later that day that they were to stay at home, and that the lord was going to Malbork with only a small troop, not to wage war but to make a complaint. Their sorrow was shared by the Czech, Wisehead, although, on the other hand, he was happy that Zbyszko's property had been so notably increased.

"Hey! I know who would be glad," he said. "The old lord of Bogdaniec! And he would know how to run this place! What is Bogdaniec in comparison with such an inheritance!"

At that moment, Zbyszko was seized with a sudden longing for his uncle, such as came over him frequently, particularly in difficult and dangerous moments of his life, so he turned to his squire and said without thinking:

"Why should you sit idly here? Go to Bogdaniec and carry a letter."

"If I am not to go with your grace, I would prefer to go there," replied the attendant joyfully.

"Tell Father Caleb to come to me, and let him write everything which has happened. My uncle will have the letter read to him by the provost of Krzesnia, or by the abbot, if he is at Zgorzelice."

When he had said that, he passed his hand over his youthful moustache and added, as if to himself:

"Bah! The abbot. . . ."

And immediately Jagienka passed before his eyes—blue-eyed, dark-haired, pretty as a deer, with tears on her eyelashes. He felt troubled, and for a time rubbed his forehead with his hand, and then at last muttered, "You will be sad, girl, but not worse than I."

Meanwhile Father Caleb came and sat down at once to write. Zbyszko dictated to him in detail all that had happened from the moment he had arrived at the hunting-lodge. He concealed nothing, for he knew that old Macko, when he had considered the matter well, would in the end be glad. Bogdaniec was indeed not to be compared with Spychow, which was a wide and rich estate, and Zbyszko knew that Macko always cared very much about such things.

When finally, after laborious effort, the letter was written and sealed, Zbyszko called his squire again and handed it to him, saying:

"Maybe you will return here with my uncle. I would be very glad if that happened."

But the Czech looked as if he were troubled. He dallied, shifting from one foot to the other, and did not go. Finally the young knight said:

"If you have anything to say, say it."

"Your grace, I should like. . . ." replied the Czech. "I should like to ask one thing more. What am I to tell people there?"

"What people?"

"Not at Bogdaniec, but in the neighborhood, because they will certainly want to know."

Zbyszko, who had determined to hide nothing, looked at him keenly and said:

"You are not concerned about people, but only about Jagienka of Zgorzelice."

The Czech flushed and then paled somewhat, and replied:

"Yes, lord."

"And how do you know that she has not married Cztan of Rogow or Wolf of Birchwood?"

"The young lady has not married anyone," replied the squire firmly.

"The abbot may have commanded her."

"The abbot obeys the young lady; she does not obey him."

"Then what do you want? Tell the truth to her as to everyone else."

The Czech bowed and went away in a bad mood.

"God grant," he said to himself, thinking of Zbyszko, "that she has forgotten you! God grant her someone better than you! But if she has not forgotten you, I will tell her that you are married, but without a woman, and that God grant you may become a widower before you enter the marriage bed."

The squire had, indeed, become attached to Zbyszko, and also had compassion on Danusia, but he loved Jagienka above anything else in the world, and from the time when he had learned of

Zbyszko's marriage, just before the last fight at Warsaw, he had borne grief and bitterness in his heart.

"God grant you may become a widower first!" he repeated.

But then other, and evidently sweeter, thoughts passed through his head, for as he was going out to the horses, he said:

"Praise God that I shall at least embrace her knees!"

Meanwhile Zbyszko was anxious to take to the road, for he was consumed with feverish thoughts and images. In so far as he was not compelled to occupy himself with other things, he went through tortures, thinking unceasingly of Danusia and Jurand. Nevertheless, he had to stay at Spychow at least for one night, if only for the sake of Sieur de Lorche and the preparations required for such a long journey. He himself was greatly exhausted by his battle, the subsequent waiting in the castle yard, the journey, his sleeplessness, and his anxiety. So when it was already late at night he threw himself on Jurand's hard bed in the hope that he might get at least a short sleep. But before he fell asleep Sanderus knocked at his door, then came in and bowed.

"Lord," he said, "you saved me from death, and with you I was better off than I had been for a long time. God has now given you a large estate, so that you are richer than your ancestors, and the treasury of Spychow is not empty. Give me, lord, a sum of money, and I will go to Prussia, from castle to castle, and although I shall not be very safe there, maybe I can do you a service."

Zbyszko, who at first had wanted to throw him out of the room, reflected on these words, and presently took out of his travelling bag by the bedside a fat purse and threw it to him.

"There, go!" he said. "If you are a rogue, you will cheat me; if you are an honest man, you will do me a service."

"Lord, as a rogue, I will cheat," said Sanderus. "But not you. You—I will serve honestly."

CHAPTER XXXIX

SIEGFRIED von Lowe was on the point of departing for Malbork when a postrider unexpectedly brought him the letter from Roger with news from the Mazovian court.

This news touched the old knight to the quick. Above all, it was evident from the letter that Roger had presented and carried on the case against Jurand before Duke Janusz excellently. Siegfried smiled when he read that Roger had further demanded the surrender of Spychow into the hands of the Teutonic Knights in return for the wrongs done to the Order. On the other hand, the second part of the letter contained unexpected and less pleasant news. Roger reported how, for the better demonstration of the innocence of the Order as regards the kidnapping of Jurand's daughter, he had thrown down his gauntlet to the Mazovian knights, challenging anyone who doubted to the judgment of God, that is to say, to single combat in face of the whole court. "No one took it up," continued Roger, "for they all knew that Jurand's own letter was evidence for us, and they were afraid of divine justice. Meanwhile there appeared the youth whom we had seen at the hunting-lodge, and he took up the gage. For this reason do not wonder, pious and wise brother, that I am late in returning, for, as I made the challenge myself, I must fight. And since I am doing it for the glory of the Order, I hope that neither the grand master nor you will take it ill of me, for I honor you and love you with the heart of a son. My antagonist is almost a child, and battles are, as you know, nothing new to me, so I shall easily shed his blood for the glory of the Order, and particularly with the help of Jesus Christ, who certainly cares for those who wear His Cross more than for such a man as Jurand, or the wrong done to a miserable girl of the Mazovian nation."

Siegfried was most amazed by the news that Jurand's daughter was married. The old commander was even seized with a certain alarm at the thought that Spychow might be occupied by a fresh, dangerous, and vengeful enemy. "Obviously," he said to himself, "he will seek vengeance, particularly if he recovers the girl, and she tells him that it was we who kidnapped her from the hunting-lodge! Then it would become clear that we had brought Jurand here only to destroy him, and that no one thought of giving him back his daughter." Here it occurred to Siegfried that as a result of the duke's letters, the grand master would probably order a search to be made at Ortelsburg, if only to clear himself in the eyes of the duke. For the master and the chapter were most anxious that the Mazovian dukes should stand aside in case of war with the power-ful King of Poland. Considering the dukes' strength, which in view of multitude of the Mazovian gentry, was not small, and in view of their valor was not contemptible, it would be good not to treat them lightly. Peace with them would ensure the Teutonic Knights' borders throughout an enormous stretch of territory, and would allow the monks to concentrate their forces. The subject had been frequently spoken of in Siegfried's presence at Malbork, and the hope had been expressed that after victory over the king some pretext would be found to attack Mazovia. Then no force would be able again to wrest that country from the hands of the Knights. It was an important and a reliable plan, and so it was quite certain that the master would do everything he could in the meantime to avoid alienating Duke Janusz, particularly since the latter, being married to Kiejstut's daughter, was more difficult to win over than the other duke, Ziemowit of Plock, whose wife was, for some unknown reason, completely devoted to the Order.

As a result of these thoughts, old Siegfried—who, ready as he was for all kinds of crime, treachery, and cruelty, still loved the Order and its glory above everything else—began to reckon with his conscience. "Would it not be better to release Jurand and his daughter? Treachery and shame will burden the name of Danveld, but he is dead. And even," he thought, "were the master to punish me and Roger severely, since we shared in Danveld's deeds, would it not be better for the Order?" But his vengeful and cruel heart began to rage at the thought of Jurand.

Let him go! This oppressor and hangman of the Order's members, the victor in so many fights, the cause of so many defeats and so much disgrace, the victor over, and afterwards the slayer of, Danveld, the victor over de Bergow, the slayer of Maineger, the slayer of Godfrey and Hugh, the man who at Ortelsburg itself had shed more German blood than was shed by a good battle in time of war! "I cannot! I cannot!" Siegfried repeated in his heart, and at the very thought his predatory fingers clutched convulsively and his old dried-up breast took breath with difficulty. And yet, suppose it were to be for the greater glory and advantage of the Order! Suppose the punishment, which would then fall on the still-living authors of the crime, should win over the hitherto hostile Duke Janusz and facilitate an agreement or even an alliance with him? "These Mazovians are impetuous," the old commander reflected further; "but if one shows them a little kindness they easily forget their wrongs. Why, even the duke, though he was taken captive in his own country, did not take vengeance." He began to walk up and down the hall in great distress of mind, when suddenly he seemed to hear a voice speaking from on high: "Wait for Roger's return!" Yes, it would be better to wait. Roger would undoubtedly slay the youth, and then it would be necessary either to conceal Jurand and his daughter, or to give them up. In the first case the duke would not, indeed, forget about them, but having no certainty as to who had kidnapped the girl, he would search for her, he would send letters to the grand master, not making a complaint but asking for information—and the matter would be dragged out indefinitely. In the second case his joy at the return of Jurand's daughter would be greater than his desire for vengeance for her kidnapping. "And in any case we can always say that we found her after Jurand's attack." This last thought completely calmed Siegfried. As for Jurand himself, he and Roger had long since thought of a method of preventing him from taking vengeance on them or accusing them, if they should have to let him go. Siegfried rejoiced in his fierce heart at the thought of this method. He likewise rejoiced at the trial by battle which was to take place at the court of Warsaw. As to the result of the combat, he felt no concern. He remembered a certain tournament at Konigsberg, where Roger had defeated two famous knights, who in their native country of Anjou had been regarded as invincible champions. He remembered also a combat at Wilno with a certain Polish knight, a courtier of Spytko of Melsztyn, whom Roger had slain. And his face brightened, and his heart swelled with pride, for it was he himself who had first led Roger, already a famous knight, on an expedition into Lithuania and had taught him the best methods of warfare against that nation. And now this son of his would once again shed hated Polish blood and return covered with glory. Furthermore, it was a judgment of God, and so the Order would be at the same time cleared of suspicion. "Judgment of God!" For an instant his old heart was constricted with a feeling akin to fear. Roger was to engage in combat to the death in defence of the innocence of the Knights, while they were not innocent, and he would therefore fight for a lie. . . . Suppose some misfortune were to happen? But a moment later this seemed again impossible. Roger could not be vanquished.

Having calmed himself in this manner, the old knight considered further whether it would not be better in the meantime to send Danusia to some more distant castle, which could not under any circumstance be taken by the Mazovians. But after a moment's consideration he dismissed the idea. An attack could be planned and headed only by the husband of Jurand's daughter, but he would die at Roger's hand. . . . Then there would be only inquiries, letters, and complaints from the duke and duchess, but that would enable the affair to become stalled and obscured, and then indefinitely postponed. "Before they get at anything," Siegfried said to himself, "I shall die, and maybe Jurand's daughter will grow old in a Teutonic prison." Nevertheless, he had the castle readied for defence, and also made preparations for the road, since he did not know exactly where his conference with Roger might lead. Then he waited.

Two days passed after the time by which Roger had originally promised to return, and then three, and four; yet no company of armed men appeared before the gate of Ortelsburg. It was only on the fifth day, almost at dusk, that the sound of a horn was heard before the gatekeeper's tower. Siegfried, who had just finished his late-afternoon activities, immediately sent an attendant to find out who had arrived. The attendant presently returned with his face changed, but Siegfried did not perceive the change, for the fire in the chamber was burning in a deep-set hearth and illuminated the dusk but little.

"Have they come?" asked the old knight.

"Yes!" replied the servant.

But in his voice there was something which suddenly alarmed the knight, so he said:

"And Brother Roger?"

"They have brought Brother Roger."

Siegfried rose from his chair. For a long time he kept his hand on the armrest, as if fearing to fall, and then he said in a choked voice: "Give me my cloak."

The servant threw the cloak over his shoulders, but Siegfried had apparently already recovered his strength, for he put his hood on his head himself and went out of the chamber.

After a moment he found himself in the castle yard, where it was already fairly dark, and he went slowly through the crunching snow to the company, which had passed through the gate and stopped near it. There was already a dense crowd of men standing there, and some torches were burning, brought by the soldiers of the garrison. At the sight of the old knight the soldiers made way. By the light of the torches, however, alarmed faces could be seen, and voices were heard whispering in the twilight.

"Brother Roger. . . ."

"Brother Roger slain. . . ."

Siegfried went up to the sleigh, in which the cloak-covered body was lying on straw, and raised the corner of the cloak.

"Bring a light," he said, throwing off his hood.

One of the soldiers brought his torch forward, and by the light of it the old knight saw Roger's head and his face white as snow, frozen in death, wrapped in a dark kerchief, which had been tied around the chin with the evident purpose of preventing the mouth remaining open. The whole face was drawn and so changed that it might have been taken for another man's. The eyes were closed, and around them and on the temples were blue spots. On the cheeks there was a glaze of frost.

The commander looked for a long time, amid general silence. The others looked at him, for they knew that he had been like a father to the dead man and that he loved him. But not a single tear flowed from his eyes. His face merely grew sterner than usual and took on an expression of icy calm.

"They have sent him back like this!" he said at last. But immediately afterwards he turned to the castle steward: "Order a coffin made before midnight and put the body in the chapel."

"There is one coffin left of those which were made for Jurand's victims," replied the steward. "I will have it lined with cloth."

"And cover him with a cloak," said Siegfried, veiling Roger's face. "Not such a cloak as this, but the cloak of the Order." After a moment he added: "And do not close the lid."

The men approached the sleigh, and Siegfried pulled on his hood again, but he suddenly remembered something else before he went, and asked: "Where is van Krist?"

"Slain also," replied one of the attendants; "but they had to bury him at Warsaw, for he began to decay."

"Very well."

Then he went away with a slow step. Returning to his chamber, he sat down in the same chair where the news had found him. He sat with stony face, motionless, and for such a length of time that his attendant became alarmed and put his head through the doorway with greater frequency. Hour after hour passed; the usual movement in the castle ceased. From the direction of the chapel came the dull, indistinct knocking of a hammer, and then nothing more disturbed the quiet except the calls of the watchmen.

It was already nearly midnight when the old knight awoke as if from sleep. He called his attendant.

"Where is Brother Roger?" he asked him.

But the boy, unstrung by the quiet, the events of the night, and by lack of sleep, apparently did not understand him, for he looked at him in alarm and said in trembling tones: "I do not know, lord."

The old man smiled a slow, sad smile, and said gently: "I am asking you, child, is he already in the chapel?"

"Yes, lord."

"That is good. Tell Diederich to come with a lantern and wait until I return. Let him bring also a brazier with coals. Is there a light already in the chapel?"

"Candles are burning around the coffin."

Siegfried put on his cloak and went out.

When he reached the chapel he looked around from the doorway to see if there was anyone inside; then he shut the door carefully, approached the coffin, moved two candles out of the six which were burning by it in large bronze candlesticks, and knelt down beside it.

His lips did not move at all, so he was not praying. For some time he merely looked at Roger's stiff, but still handsome, face, as if he wished to find traces of life in it.

In the silence of the chapel, he whispered in a soft voice:

"My dear son! My dear son!"

And he became silent. It seemed that he was waiting for an answer.

Then, stretching out his hands, he put his lean, talon-like fingers under the cloak which covered Roger's breast and began to touch it with them. He felt about, in the middle and at the sides, below the ribs and along the collarbones, and at last felt through the clothing the gash which reached from the top of the right shoulder to the armpit, plunged his fingers, passed them along the whole length of the wound, and said in a voice in which there quivered something like a complaint:

"Oh! What a merciless blow! And you said that he was almost a child! . . . The whole arm! The whole arm! So many times you raised it against the pagans in defence of the Order. And now a Polish axe has hewn it off. . . . And this is your end! This is what your life has come to! God did not bless you, for perhaps He does not care for our Order. He has abandoned me also, although I have served Him for many, many years."

His lips began to tremble, and there was again dull silence in the chapel.

"My dear son! My dear son!" In Siegfried's voice there was now an entreaty, and he spoke still more softly, like a man asking about some important and terrible secret. "If you are here, if you hear me, give me a sign; move your hand, or open your eyes for a second— for my heart is torn in my old breast—give a sign. I loved you. Speak!"

And resting his hands on the edge of the coffin, he fixed his vulturine eyes on Roger's closed eyelids and waited.

"Bah! How can you speak?" he said at last. "A cold and deathly odor emanates from you. But since you are silent, I will tell you something, and let your spirit float between these burning candles and listen." So saying, he bent over the face of the corpse. "You remember how the chaplain would not let us do away with Jurand, and how we swore to him? Very well. I will keep my oath; but I will give you joy wherever you are."

He drew back from the coffin, put the candlesticks where they had been before, covered the face of the corpse again with the cloak, and went out of the chapel.

At the door of his chamber, his attendant was in a deep sleep, while, according to Siegfried's command, Diederich waited inside.

He was a short, stumpy man with bow legs and a square face, partly concealed by a dark, jagged hood which fell down to his shoulders. He was wearing a caftan of untanned buffalo hide, and around his waist he had a buffalo-hide belt, from which hung a bunch of keys and a short knife. In his right hand he held an iron lantern with membrane sides, and in his left a bronze brazier and a torch.

"Are you ready?" asked Siegfried.

Diederich bowed in silence.

"I told you to have coals in the brazier."

The stumpy man again did not answer, but only pointed to the logs burning on the hearth. He went over and took an iron shovel standing by the chimney, and began to throw coals into the brazier. Then he lit his lantern and waited.

"Now listen, dog," said Siegfried. "You once divulged something Commander Danveld had ordered you to do, and the commander had your tongue cut out. But you still can show the chaplain everything you like on your fingers. Therefore I warn you: If you show him with the slightest movement what you now will do by my command, I shall have you hanged."

Diederich again bowed in silence. But his face twitched ominously at the frightful memory, for his tongue had been torn out for a reason quite different from what Siegfried had said.

"Now go forward and lead me to Jurand's dungeon."

The executioner seized the handle of the brazier with his huge hand and lifted up his lantern, and they went out. Passing the sleeping page outside the door, they descended the stairs and proceeded, not to the main doorway, but to the rear of the stairway. Here a narrow corridor ran the whole breadth of the building, ending in a heavy door concealed in a recess of the wall. Diederich opened it, and they found themselves under the open sky, in a little yard, surrounded on four sides with stone chambers where grain was stored in case the castle should be besieged. Under one of these granaries, to the right, were the dungeons for the prisoners. No guard stood there, for even had a prisoner been able to break out of the dungeon, he would have found himself in the yard, and the only exit was through the small door.

"Wait!" said Siegfried.

And resting his hand on the wall, he stopped, for he felt not quite right. He was short of breath and his chest seemed constricted, as if by too tight a breastplate. All he had gone through had been too much for his declining strength. Realizing that his hood-covered forehead was sweaty, he decided to pause for a few breaths.

After a cloudy day, the night had become unusually fine. The moon shone in the sky, and the whole yard was flooded with its bright light, in which the snow glittered green. Siegfried eagerly drew into his lungs the fresh and rather frosty air. But he remembered at the same time that it was on a moonlit night like this that Roger had set out for Warsaw, from which he had returned a corpse.

"And now you are lying in the chapel," he muttered softly.

Thinking that the commander was speaking to him, Diederich raised his lantern. The light shone on Siegfried's terribly pale, almost corpse-like face. His head looked like the head of an old vulture.

"Lead on!" said Siegfried.

The yellow circle of light from the lantern swayed again on the snow, and they went on. In the thick wall of the granary was a recess, in which a few stairs led down to a great iron door. Diederich opened the door, and descended more stairs into a black abyss, lifting the lantern high to light the way for the commander. At the end of the stairs was a corridor, and to the right and the left of it the unusually low doors of the prison cells.

"To Jurand!" said Siegfried.

After a while the bolts creaked, and they went in. But in the cavern it was completely dark, so Siegfried, not seeing well by the faint light of the lantern, ordered a torch to be lit, and then in the bright glare of its flames he saw Jurand lying on the straw. The prisoner had fetters on his legs and a rather longer chain on his hands, permitting him to put food to his mouth. He was dressed in the same coarse sack in which he had stood before the commanders, but it was now covered with dark stains of blood, for on that day on which the battle had been ended only by the entanglement of the maddened knight in a net, the soldiers had wanted to dispatch him and had given him a dozen wounds with their halberds. The local chaplain of Ortelsburg had prevented them from killing him, and the thrusts had not turned out to be mortal, though Jurand had lost so much blood that they had carried him into the prison half-dead. It was generally supposed in the castle that he might die at any moment, but his huge strength overcame death, and he lived, though his wounds were not attended to, and he had been cast into a frightful dungeon, where the vaulted roof dripped during the thaw, and in time of frost the walls were covered with a thick coating of ice-crystals and rime.

So he was lying on straw, in chains, helpless, but so huge that, especially in that posture, he looked like a fragment of rock which had been chiselled into the shape of a man. Siegfried ordered the light to be thrown directly on his face, and for some time looked at him in silence. Then he turned to Diederich.

"You see that he has only one eye," he said. "Put it out."

In his voice there was something weak and decrepit, but for that very reason his terrible command seemed still more terrible. Therefore the torch trembled in the hand of the executioner, but he inclined it, and soon great burning drops of tar began to fall into Jurand's eye, and at last covered it completely from the eyebrow to the protruding cheekbone.

Jurand's face constricted, his sandy moustache moved up and uncovered his set teeth. But he did not say a word, and whether from exhaustion or from innate stubbornness, he did not even groan.

Then Siegfried spoke:

"You were promised that you would go free, and you will go free. But you will not be able to accuse the Order, for the tongue with which you blasphemed it will be torn out."

And again he gave a sign to Diederich, but the latter uttered a strange throaty sound and motioned that he needed both hands and wanted the commander to hold the light.

Then the old man took the torch and held it in his extended, trembling hand; however, when Diederich knelt on Jurand's chest, he turned his head away and looked at the frost-covered wall.

For a while the clatter of chains was to be heard, and after that the panting of human breasts, something like a dull, deep groan, and then silence.

At last the voice of Siegfried was heard anew:

"Jurand, the punishment which you have brought upon yourself had to befall you anyhow; but I also promised Brother Roger, slain by the husband of your daughter, to lay your right hand in his coffin."

Hearing these words, Diederich, who had already got up, bent over Jurand again.

Some time later the old commander and Diederich found themselves again in the moonlit yard. After passing through the narrow corridor, Siegfried took the lantern from the hand of the executioner and also a dark object wrapped up in a cloth, and said aloud to himself:

"Now back to the chapel, and then to the tower."

Diederich looked keenly at him, but the commander ordered him to go to bed, while he himself went slowly towards the lighted windows of the chapel, the lantern swaying by his side. On the way he thought of what had happened. He felt quite certain that his own end also was coming and that these were his last deeds on earth. Yet his Teutonic soul, although by nature cruel rather than deceitful, had become, under the influence of inexorable necessity, so accustomed to stratagems and ruses and to hiding the bloody actions of the Order that even now he reflected involuntarily whether he might not put the shame and responsibility for Jurand's torture on the shoulders of others rather than on his own and those of the Order. Diederich was dumb, after all, and would tell nothing; although he was able to explain himself to the chaplain, he would not do so for very fear. Then what? Who could prove that Jurand had not received all those wounds in the fight? He might easily have lost his tongue by a spear-thrust between his teeth; and he had only one eye—so would it be strange if it had been knocked out while he was madly throwing himself against the whole Ortelsburg garrison? Ah, Jurand! The heart of the old Teutonic Knight trembled with joy—the last joy still left to him. Yes, Jurand, if he lived ought to be set free! Here Siegfried remembered how he had once conferred with Roger on the subject, and how the young brother had said, laughing: "Let him go where his eyes lead him, and if he cannot find the way to Spychow, let him ask." For what had happened had been in part determined upon between them. And now, when Siegfried went into the chapel again and, kneeling by the coffin, laid Jurand's bloody hand at Roger's feet, the joy which had thrilled him a short while before was reflected also in his face for the last time.

"You see," he said, "I have done more than we agreed upon; for King John of Luxembourg, though blind, still went to battle and perished gloriously. Jurand, however, will not go to battle anymore but will die like a dog in the ditch."

Again he felt a shortness of breath as he had done before when going to Jurand's cell, and on his head a weight like that of an iron helmet, but it lasted only for a second. He breathed deeply and said:

"It is time for me too. I had you, and now I have no one. But if it is destined for me to live yet a while, I vow to you, son, that I will lay the hand which slew you on your grave, or perish myself. Your slayer is still alive—"

His teeth closed, and he was seized by so fierce a spasm that his words were cut short. It was only after some time that he began to speak again, this time in a broken voice:

"Yes—your slayer still lives, but I will get him—and before I get him I will make him suffer something worse than death itself."

And he fell silent.

After a while he rose and, approaching the coffin, began to speak calmly.

"So, I bid you farewell. . . . I will look on your face for the last time, and perhaps I shall see whether you are glad of my promise. For the last time!"

He uncovered Roger's face, and suddenly shrank back.

"You are laughing," he said, "but it is a dreadful laugh. . . ."

The body had thawed under the cloak, or perhaps from the heat of the candles, as a result of which it had begun to decompose with unusual quickness, and the face of the young commander had become indeed dreadful. The enormously swollen and blackened ears had something monstrous about them, and the puffed blue lips were twisted as if in a smile.

Siegfried quickly covered this frightful human mask.

Then he took the lantern and went out. On the way his breath failed him for the third time, so he returned to his chamber, threw himself on his hard monk's bed, and lay there for some time motionless. He had wanted to fall asleep, but he was suddenly seized by a strange feeling. It seemed to him that sleep would never visit him again, while, if he stayed in that chamber, death would come at once.

Siegfried was not afraid of death. He saw some type of eternal rest in a boundless fatigue where no hope of sleep existed. But he did not want to give himself up to it that night, so he sat up on the bed and said: "Give me time till tomorrow."

Then he distinctly heard a voice whispering in his ear:

"Go out of this room. Tomorrow it will be too late and you will not be able to fulfill what you promised. Go out of this room!"

The commander got up with difficulty and went out. On the battlements the watchmen called from the corners. Near the chapel a yellow gleam fell on the snow from the windows. In the middle, near a stone well-head, two black dogs were playing, pulling at some rag. Otherwise the yard was empty and silent.

"Must it be tonight?" asked Siegfried. "I am wearied beyond measure, but I am coming. . . . Everyone is asleep. Jurand, overcome by torment, perhaps sleeps also. I alone cannot sleep. I am coming, I am coming, for in my chamber is death, and I have promised you. . . . But then let death come when it will, since sleep is not to come. You are laughing there, but my strength fails me. You are laughing, so you are glad. But, you see, my fingers are numb; strength has left my hands, and I myself shall not be able to do this. . . . The servingwoman who sleeps with her shall do it. . . ."

He went with heavy step to the tower near the gate. Meanwhile the dogs, which had been playing by the stone well, ran to him and began to fawn upon him. In one of them Siegfried recognized the mastiff which was such an inseparable companion of Diederich that they said in the castle that the dog was his pillow at night.

After greeting the commander, it gave two low barks and then turned and bounded towards the gate as if it had guessed his human thoughts.

Siegfried presently found himself before the narrow door of the tower, which at night was bolted from the outside. After pushing back the bolts he felt for the handrail by the stairs, which began just inside the door. He started to ascend. In his distraction he had forgotten the lantern, and now felt his way upward, placing his foot carefully on each step.

After several steps he suddenly stopped, for he heard right above him something like the heavy breathing of a man or a beast.

"Who is there?"

There was no answer; the breathing became quicker.

Siegfried was a man who knew no fear. His was not afraid of death, but his courage and self-control already had been exhausted by this horrible night. The thought passed through his head that it was Roger blocking his way, and his hair stood on end, while his brow became covered with cold sweat.

He withdrew almost to the door.

"Who is there?" he asked in a choked voice.

At that moment something struck him on the breast with such terrible force that the old man fell unconscious on his back in the open doorway, without uttering even a groan.

Silence followed. A dark figure slipped from the tower, and it went stealthily toward the stable which lay beside the armory on the right side of the yard. Diederich's great mastiff followed this figure in silence. The second dog likewise sprang after them and vanished in the shadows of the wall, but soon it appeared again with its head lowered, running slowly back, as if following a scent. Thus it approached the motionless Siegfried, sniffed him carefully, and at last, sitting down by his head, raised its jaws and began to howl.

Its howling was heard for a long time, filling the gloomy night with fresh lamentation and terror. At last a door concealed at the side of the great gate creaked, and the gatekeeper appeared in the yard, halberd in hand.

"A plague on that dog!" he said. "I will teach it to howl at night."

And raising his weapon he was about to strike the dog when he saw someone lying next to it, near the open door of the tower.

"*Herr Jesus!* What is that? . . ."

Bending his head, he looked in the face of the prostrate man and began to shout:

"Help! Help! Here! Over here!"

Then he rushed to the gate and began to pull the bell-rope with all his might.

CHAPTER XL

ALTHOUGH Wisehead was in a hurry to get to Zgorzelice, he could not ride as quickly as he wished, for the roads had become immeasurably difficult. The hard winter, the severe frosts, and the copious snowfalls which had covered whole villages had been followed by a great thaw. February, despite it being one of the harshest of months, had not shown itself to be at all severe. At first there had been thick, impenetrable fogs, and then near torrential rains, under which the white snowdrifts melted before one's eyes; while in the intervals between the rainstorms there was such a wind as usually blows in March. Fitful and sudden, it drove and scattered the heavy clouds through the sky. On the ground it howled through the bushes, shrieked through the forests, and devoured the snow, under which not long before the bushes and branches had slept their quiet wintry sleep.

The forests likewise soon darkened. In the meadows the flood waters rippled far and wide; rivers and streams overflowed. Only the fishers rejoiced in this excess of the water element, while all the rest of the population, held as on a leash, remained in the shelter of their houses and cottages. In many places it was only possible to go from village to village by boat. It is true there was no lack of dikes or highways through the marshes and forests, made of trunks and round logs laid side by side, but now the dikes were weakened and the trunks in the low-lying places had sunk so deep into the sloughs that it was dangerous or quite impossible to pass. The Czech found it particularly difficult to make his way through the lake country of Great Poland, where the floods every spring were

greater than in other parts, and the going, particularly for horsemen, was more difficult.

So he frequently had to stop and wait for entire weeks, sometimes in small towns, sometimes in villages with the landowners,
who, anyway, received him and his men hospitably according to
custom and gladly listened to his stories of the Teutonic Knights,
paying with bread and salt for news. Accordingly, the spring had
already made itself felt on the earth, and the greater part of March
had already passed, before the he found himself in the neighborhood of Zgorzelice and Bogdaniec.

His heart beat rapidly at the thought that he would soon see his
lady. Though he knew that he would never get her, just as one
would never get a star from heaven, he nevertheless worshipped
and loved her with his whole heart. However, he decided to go first
to Macko, because, for one thing, he had been sent to him, and,
for another, he was bringing with him men who had to remain at
Bogdaniec. Zbyszko, after slaying Roger, had taken his troop,
which numbered, according to the regulations of the Order, ten
horses and ten men. Two of the latter had gone back with the body
of the slain man to Ortelsburg, but Zbyszko had sent the rest with
Wisehead as a gift to his uncle, for he knew how eagerly the old
warrior sought settlers.

On his arrival at Bogdaniec, the Czech did not find Macko at
home. He was told that the old knight had gone to the forest with
his dogs and his crossbow. But Macko returned before nightfall
and, learning that a considerable troop had arrived at his house,
hastened his steps in order to greet the newcomers and offer them
hospitality. He did not recognize Wisehead at first, and when the
latter told him his name he was at first greatly alarmed, and
throwing his crossbow and his cap on the ground, he cried out:

"Great God! They have killed him! Tell me what you know!"

"He is not dead but in good health!" replied the Czech.

Hearing that, Macko was somewhat ashamed and began to pant;
finally he caught his breath.

"Praise to Christ the Lord!" he said. "Where is he?"

"He has gone to Malbork, and has sent me here with news."

"And why has he gone to Malbork?"

"To fetch his wife."

"By the wounds of Christ, fellow! To fetch what wife?"

"To fetch Jurand's daughter. I will tell you about it all night if need be, but, honorable lord, allow me a little rest now, for I have had a hard journey and have been travelling constantly since midnight."

So Macko ceased to question him for a while, mainly because he was speechless from amazement. When he had grown calmer, he shouted to a page to throw wood on the fire and to bring the Czech some food, and then he began to walk up and down the chamber, waving his hands and speaking to himself:

"It's unbelievable—Jurand's daughter—Zbyszko married. . . ."

"Married and not married," said the Czech.

Then, taking his time, he began to relate what had happened and how it happened, while Macko listened eagerly, interrupting once in a while with a question or two, for not everything in the Czech's story was clear. For example, Wisehead did not know exactly when Zbyszko had married, since there had been no wedding ceremony, yet he asserted firmly that there had been a marriage and that it had come about through the efforts of the duchess herself, Anna Danuta, though it had been proclaimed openly only after the arrival of the Teutonic Knight, Roger, whom Zbyszko had challenged to a trial by battle, and with whom he had fought in the presence of the whole Mazovian court.

"Aha! He fought with him?" exclaimed Macko with flashing eyes and intense curiosity. "Well, what happened?"

"He split the German in two, and God gave me good luck also with his squire."

Macko began anew to pant, this time from satisfaction.

"Well!" he said, "he's not a lad to be laughed at. He is the last of the Hailstones, but, so help me God, not the worst. And that time with the Frisians! He was a mere stripling at that point. . . ."

Then he looked attentively once or twice at the Czech.

"But you also please me," he said. "One can see that you are not lying. I can recognize a liar even through a board. Not that I think much of that squire, for you say yourself that you didn't have much trouble with him. But you crushed the arm of the cur, and before that you slew the aurochs. Those are worthy deeds!" Then he asked suddenly: "And the booty? Is that also good?"

"We took arms, horses, and ten men, eight of whom the young lord has sent to you."

"What did he do with the other two?"

"He sent them back with the body."

"Could not the duke have sent his own men? We shall never get those people back."

The Czech smiled at Macko's greed, which was often displayed.

"The young lord does not need to care about that now," he said. "Spychow is a large inheritance."

"Large, yes, but not yet his."

"Then whose is it?"

Macko go up:

"Tell me! It is Jurand's—no?"

"Jurand is in a dungeon among the Teutonic Knights, and death is over him. God knows whether he will live, and if he lives whether he will return. But even if he were to live and return, Father Caleb has read his last will and declared to everyone that the young lord is to be the heir."

This news evidently made an enormous impression on Macko. It was to such an extent favorable and unfavorable that he could not collect himself nor bring his feelings to order. The news that Zbyszko had married pained him at first, for he loved Jagienka like a father, and desired with all his strength to unite Zbyszko with her. But, on the other hand, he had already accustomed himself to regard that matter as lost. Besides, Jurand's daughter had brought that which Jagienka could not bring, namely, the favor of the duke and a much greater dowry as an only child. Macko already pictured Zbyszko as a *comes* of the duke, Lord of Bogdaniec and Spychow, and in the future even a castellan. This was not impossible, for in those days they used to say of a poor nobleman: "He had twelve sons, six fell in battle, and six became castellans." So both the nation and its families were on their way to greatness. A considerable fortune could only help Zbyszko on that road, so Macko's greed and family pride had something to feed on. Nevertheless, the old man had reasons for concern. He himself had once gone to the Teutonic Knights to rescue Zbyszko and had brought back an iron splinter under his rib; and now Zbyszko was going to Malbork, as if to the wolves' den. Would he find his wife there, or death? "They will not be happy to see him," thought Macko. "He has just slain one of their important knights, and before that he attacked Lichtenstein, and those dogs love vengeance." This thought caused the old knight much anxiety. He also reflected that the visit could hardly go off without Zbyszko's meeting one or another German in single combat, for he was an impetuous fellow. But that was the lesser danger. He was most afraid that they would seize him. "They seized old Jurand and his daughter. They did not hesitate on another occasion to seize even the duke at Zlotorya. So why should they be more gentle with Zbyszko?"

Then the question suggested itself to him: What would happen if the young man, escaping from the hands of the Teutonic Knights, failed to find his wife? For a moment Macko was consoled by the thought that Zbyszko would inherit Spychow from her, but that was a short-lived joy. Macko cared much about property, but he cared not less about the family, about Zbyszko's children. "If Danusia vanishes like a stone in water, and no one knows whether she is alive or dead, Zbyszko will not be able to marry another— and then there will be no more Hailstones of Bogdaniec in the world. Hey, it would be different with Jagienka! Moczydoly is no small piece of land, and such a girl could bear fruit every year, like an apple-tree in the orchard." So Macko grief became greater than his joy at the new inheritance—and in his grief and alarm he began again to question the Czech as to how the marriage had taken place and when.

"Honorable lord, I already told you," replied the Czech. "I do not know when it occurred, and I cannot swear to what I only suppose."

"What do you suppose?"

"I did not leave the young lord in his sickness, and I slept with him in the chamber. Once, though, they had me go away in the evening; yet I saw who entered my lord's chamber. The worshipful duchess herself and with her the young lady, Jurand's daughter, Sieur de Lorche, and Father Wyszoniek. I was surprised, for the young lady had a wreath on her head, but I thought they were going to administer the Holy Sacrament to him. Maybe it happened then. I remember that my master bade me dress him nicely, as if for a wedding, but I thought that it was for the reception of the Body of Christ."

"And then what? Did Zbyszko and Danusia remain alone?"

"Ah! They did not remain alone, and even if they had, the lord had no strength at that time even to eat. And men had already come for the young lady, supposedly from Jurand, and in the morning she went away."

"Has Zbyszko seen her since then?"

"No one has seen her."

A moment of silence followed.

"What do you think?" asked Macko after a while. "Will the Teutonic Knights give her back?"

The Czech shook his head and then waved his hand discouragingly.

"In my opinion," he said slowly, "she is lost forever."

"Why?" asked Macko, almost with fear.

"Because if they said they had her, there would be some hope. It would be possible to make a complaint, or to pay a ransom, or to recover her by force. But they say: We did rescue some girl and let Jurand know, but he refused to acknowledge her, and did us so much harm in return for our kindness that a good battle would not have cost more."

"Then they did show some girl to Jurand?"

"They say they did. God only knows. Maybe it's not true, or maybe they showed him another. This only is true, that he slew their men, and that they are ready to swear that they never kidnapped his daughter. It is a terribly difficult matter. Even should the grand master give an order, they would reply that they do not have her—and who will prove otherwise? What's more, the courtiers at Ciechanow spoke of a letter from Jurand, in which he said she was not with the Teutonic Knights."

"Maybe she is not?"

"Your grace, please! If it were robbers who had kidnapped her, it would have been only for ransom. And robbers would not have been able to write the letter, or imitate the Lord of Spychow's seal, or send a considerable retinue of men with it."

"True, but what do the Teutonic Knights want of her?"

"What about vengeance on Jurand's own flesh and blood? They prefer vengeance to mead and wine, and as for reasons, they have them. The Lord of Spychow was terrible to them, and what he did at the end has enraged them to the limit. My master, so I heard, raised his hand against Lichtenstein, and he slew Roger. I, with God's help, crushed the cur's arm. Hey! don't forget. Four of those dogs there were, and now only one of them is alive, and he is old. We also have teeth, your grace."

There followed another moment of silence.

"You are an intelligent squire," said Macko finally. "What do you think they will do with her?"

"Duke Witold—he's a powerful duke. They say that even the German emperor bowed low before him. But what did the Teutonic Knights do with his children? Do they have less castles now? Dungeons? Wells? Ropes, halters?"

"By the living God!" exclaimed Macko.

"God grant that they may not bury my young lord, even though he went with a letter from the duke, and with Sieur de Lorche, who is a rich lord and kin to dukes! I didn't want to come here, for there would have been more opportunity for combat over there, but he commanded me. I once heard how he said to the old Lord of Spychow: 'Are you cunning? I can accomplish nothing by cunning, but against them one needs it. Oh! Uncle Macko, he would serve us well here.' That's why he sent me here. But even you, lord, will not find Jurand's daughter, for she may be already in the other world, and against death the greatest cunning is of no avail. . . ."

Macko reflected, and after a long silence said:

"Hah! Nothing can be done now! Against death cunning is of no avail. But if I were to go there and learn something, even if it were only that they had killed her, then Spychow would remain Zbyszko's, and he might come back here and take another girl."

Macko drew a deep breath as if he had cast a weight from his heart, and Wisehead asked in a sly, soft voice:

"The young lady of Zgorzelice?"

"Yes!" replied Macko. "Particularly as she is an orphan, and Cztan of Rogow and Wolf of Birchwood pursue her with more fervor than before."

The Czech sprang to his feet:

"The young lady an orphan? And what of Zych?"

"Then you don't know?"

"Great God! What has happened?"

"Ah, true, how could you know, for you have only just arrived, and we have been talking only of Zbyszko. Yes, she is an orphan. Zych of Zgorzelice, it is true, never stayed much at home unless he had guests. Otherwise Zgorzelice bored him. The abbot wrote to him one day that he was going on a visit to Duke Przemko of Oswiecim, and asked him to go along. And Zych was very glad, for he knew the duke and had spent some good times with him. So Zych came to me and said: 'I am going to Oswiecim and afterwards to Gliwice; keep on eye on Zgorzelice for me.' Something immediately troubled me, and I said: 'Don't go! Look after your estate and Jagienka, for I know that Cztan and Wolf are plotting something bad.' You ought to know that the abbot, when he was angry with Zbyszko, wanted to give the girl to Wolf or to Cztan, but later, knowing them better, he thrashed both of them with his stick and threw them out of Zgorzelice. It was a good thing too; but not entirely, for they've become quite determined. Now we have a little peace; they wounded each other and are laid up, but until then we had not a moment's rest. Everything depended on me: the defence of Zgorzelice and the care of Jagienka. And now Zbyszko wants me to go. How Jagienka will manage, I don't know. But I will tell you about Zych. He did not attend to my warning, but rode off. Well, they banqueted and made merry! From Gliwice they went to old Nosak, father of Duke Przemko, who rules at Cieszyn. Then Jasko, Duke of Racibor, out of hatred to Duke Przemko, sent robbers against them under the leadership of Chrzan, a Czech. And Duke Przemko was slain and with him Zych of Zgorzelice, who was struck by an arrow in the windpipe. The abbot was stunned with an iron flail so that his head still shakes, and he knows nothing of the world and has lost his speech, perhaps forever. Well, old Duke Nosak bought Chrzan from the Lord of Zampach and tortured him so that the oldest people had never heard of such torments—but all this did not diminish his grief for his son, nor did it bring Zych to life again, or dry Jagienka's tears. So those were their good times. . . . Six weeks ago they brought Zych here and buried him."

"He was such a strong man!" said the Czech sadly. "At Boleslawiec I was no stripling, but he dealt with me in less than a paternoster and took me captive. But it was such captivity as I would not have exchanged for freedom. He was a good, honorable lord! God grant him everlasting peace. Oh, it is sad, sad! But worst of all for the young lady, poor thing."

"She is indeed a poor thing. Many a girl does not love her mother as she loved her father. Furthermore, it is dangerous for her to live at Zgorzelice. After the funeral, the snow had not yet covered Zych's grave-mound when Cztan and Wolf made an attack on the manor-house at Zgorzelice. Luckily, my men learned of it beforehand, so I galloped to help them with my farm-hands, and God permitted us to give them a good beating. After the fight the girl embraced my knees and said: 'I cannot be Zbyszko's, but I will not be anyone else's. Save me from these awful men, for I would prefer death rather than them.' I tell you, you would not now recognize Zgorzelice. I have made a real castle out of it. They made two further attacks afterwards, but they could not deal with us. Now we have peace for a while, for as I told you, they have fought one another so that neither of them can move hand or foot."

Wisehead made no answer to that. At the mention of Cztan and Wolf he began to grind his teeth so loudly that it sounded as if someone were opening and closing a creaking door, and then he rubbed his powerful hands on his thighs, for they obviously itched. Finally one word escaped his tight-set lips:

"Villains!"

At that moment voices were heard in the passage, the door opened suddenly, and into the room burst Jagienka, and with her the eldest of her brothers, the fourteen-year-old Jasko, who resembled her so much that they could have been twins.

She had learned from the Zgorzelice peasants that some men under the leadership of the Czech, Hlawa, were riding along the road to Bogdaniec, and she had become as alarmed as Macko. Indeed, when she learned that Zbyszko was not among them, she felt almost certain that some misfortune had happened, so she rushed straight off to Bogdaniec to learn the truth.

"What has happened? Dear God!" she called out from the threshold.

"What should have happened?" replied Macko. "Zbyszko is alive and well."

The Czech sprang towards the young lady and, kneeling on one knee, began to kiss the hem of her garment. However, she paid no attention to him at all, for when she had heard the old knight's answer she had turned her head to the shadows, away from the fire. It was only after a while that she seemed to remember that it was necessary to greet him, so she said:

"Jesus Christ be praised!"

"For ever and ever," replied Macko.

Then, noticing the Czech at her knees, she bent over him:

"I am glad to see you, Hlawa, from the bottom of my heart, but why did you leave your master?"

"He sent me, gracious young lady."

"What did he command?"

"He commanded me to go to Bogdaniec."

"To Bogdaniec? And what else?"

"He sent me for advice—and with greetings."

"To Bogdaniec? And that is all? Well, good. And he himself, where is he?"

"He went to the Teutonic Knights at Malbork."

Jagienka's face again reflected alarm.

"Does he not love life? Why did he go there?"

"To seek, gracious young lady, that which he will not find."

"Indeed he will not find it!" interrupted Macko. "As you cannot drive a nail without a hammer, so you cannot drive the human will without the divine."

"What are you talking about?" asked Jagienka.

But Macko answered her question with another:

"Did Zbyszko ever tell you of Jurand's daughter? I heard that he did."

Jagienka at first did not answer, and only after a while did she reply, stifling a sigh:

"Yes, he told me! What harm was it to tell me?"

"Good, it will be easier for me to speak," said the old man.

And he began to relate what he had heard from the Czech, wondering himself that sometimes his narration was difficult for him, and his story disconnected. However, being indeed a cunning man, and not wishing to scare Jagienka, he laid great emphasis on what, in fact, he himself believed, namely, that Zbyszko had never been Danusia's husband in reality, and that she was lost forever.

The Czech confirmed his statements from time to time, nodding his head or repeating: "By the living God!" or "So it was and not otherwise!" And the girl listened with lowered eyelashes, asking no questions and so quiet that her silence concerned Macko.

"Well, and what do you say?" he asked, when his story was finished.

But she made no answer; only two tears glistened under her lowered eyelashes and rolled down her cheeks.

In the next moment, however, she approached Macko, kissed his hand, and said:

"Jesus Christ be praised!"

"For ever and ever," replied the old man. "Are you in such haste to go home? Stay with us."

But she would not stay, explaining that she had not given out the food for supper at home. Although Macko knew that at Zgorzelice there was an old gentlewoman, Sieciechowa, who could have taken her place, he did not urge her to stay, understanding that sorrow does not like to show its tears, and that a human being is like a fish, which when on the hook takes refuge in the deepest water it can find.

So he just stroked the girl's head and then went out with her and the Czech into the yard. The Czech brought his own horse from the stable, mounted it, and rode after the young lady.

Returning inside, Macko sighed and shook his head, muttering:

"That Zbyszko is an idiot! She has left such a sweet smell in this room!"

And he gave himself up to his grief. He thought that if Zbyszko had taken her immediately after his return, there might have been joy and pleasure by now. But what was there in actuality? "Whenever she remembers him, tears fall from her eyes, while the lad goes about the world and will beat his head somewhere against the spikes of Malbork until he breaks it. But at home it is empty; only the armor grins from the walls. No profit from farming. One's efforts are for nothing. Spychow and Bogdaniec are for nothing, since there will be no one to leave them to." And anger began to rage in Macko's heart.

"Wait, vagabond!" he said aloud. "I will not go after you. Do what you like!"

But at the same moment he was seized, as if in spite, by so cruel a longing for Zbyszko that he said: "Well, suppose I do not go— shall I be able to sit quietly at home? No! A plague on it! Not to be around that good-for-nothing at least once in my life—oh, that cannot be! Again he has split the head of one of those curs and again has taken booty. . . . Others grow grey before they get their knight's belt, but the duke has already given him his—and rightly so, for there are plenty of valiant lads among the gentry, but another such as he is not likely to be found."

And giving way to his emotion, he first looked over the armor, swords, and axes which had blackened in the smoke, as if considering what to take with him and what to leave. Then he went out of the room, firstly because he could not endure it, and secondly to order the wagons to be greased and a double feed to be given to the horses.

In the yard, where it was already dusk, he remembered Jagienka, who had mounted her horse there a short time before, and he suddenly became concerned again.

"Go! One can go," he said to himself, "but who will defend the girl against Cztan and Wolf? May lightning strike them!"

Meanwhile Jagienka and little Jasko were riding along the forest road to Zgorzelice, the Czech following them in silence, his heart full of love and grief. He had seen the girl's tears and now looked at her dark form, scarcely visible in the dusk of the forest, and divined her sorrow and pain. It also seemed to him that any moment the clutching hands of Wolf or Cztan might stretch out for her from the twilight and the thickets—and at that thought he was seized with a wild craving to fight. This craving became at times so powerful that he was seized with a desire to swing his axe or sword and strike the pine-trees by the roadside. He felt that if he were to exhaust himself in this activity it would give him relief. He would gladly have set his horse to a gallop, but the two riders in front of him were moving slowly, side by side, barely speaking, since little Jasko, talkative though he usually was, had perceived after several attempts that his sister did not want to talk, and so he also kept silent.

But when they were near Zgorzelice the grief in the Czech's heart outweighed his anger against Cztan and Wolf: "I would not begrudge even my blood," he said to himself, "to gladden your heart. But what, unhappy girl, can I do? What am I to tell you? Maybe I will tell you that he asked me to give you his best wishes. God grant that this should suffice to comfort you." With these thoughts, he pushed up his horse alongside of Jagienka's.

"Gracious young lady. . . ."

"You are riding with us?" asked the girl, rousing herself as if from sleep. "What have you to say?"

"I forgot what my master bade me tell you. As I was departing from Spychow, he called me and said: 'Embrace the knees of the young lady of Zgorzelice, for I shall never forget her, no matter what. And may God reward her and keep her in health for that which she did for my uncle and for me."

"God reward him also for the good word," replied Jagienka. Then she added in so strange a tone that the Czech's heart was melted: "And you, Hlawa."

They were silent for a time, but the squire was pleased with himself and with what he had told the young lady. "At least she will not think that she has been rewarded with ingratitude," he thought. Then he began to rack his honest brains as to what more he could tell her, and presently he began again:

"Young lady. . . ."

"What?"

"Well—I—I wanted to say, as I did to the old Lord of Bog-daniec, that she is lost forever and that he will never find her, even if the grand master himself were to help."

"She is his wife," replied Jagienka.

But the Czech shook his head.

"Yes and no. . . ."

Jagienka did not answer that, but at home after supper, when Jasko and her younger brothers had gone to bed, she sent for a tankard of mead and, turning to the Czech, asked him:

"Maybe you would rather sleep, but I should like to talk with you a little."

The Czech, travel-worn as he was, was yet ready to talk till morning if she wished, so they began, or rather he related again in detail all the adventures of Zbyszko, Jurand, Danusia, and himself.

CHAPTER XLI

MACKO made ready for the road, and Jagienka did not show herself at Bogdaniec for two days, which she spent in conferring with the Czech. The old knight met her only on the third day, a Sunday, on the way to church. She was riding to Krzesnia with her brother Jasko and a considerable troop of armed men, for she was not certain whether Cztan and Wolf were still laid up or whether they might not make some attack upon her.

"I wanted to come to Bogdaniec after Mass anyway," she said, greeting Macko, "for I have an urgent matter to speak of with you, but we can talk now."

She pushed up to the front of the procession, evidently not wanting the men to hear their conversation, and when Macko was by her side, she asked him:

"Are you going for certain?"

"God grant tomorrow, not later!"

"To Malbork?"

"To Malbork or any other place. Wherever I must."

"Then listen to me. I have been thinking long on what I ought to do, and now I want to ask you for your advice. Formerly, you know, as long as papa was alive and the abbot strong, it was different. Furthermore, Cztan and Wolf thought that I would take one of them, so they restrained each other. But now I shall be left without any defence, and I shall either remain behind the palisade at Zgorzelice, as if in prison, or some wrong will most certainly be done to me by them. Tell me yourself whether it is not so?"

"Yes," said Macko, "I thought of that myself."

"And what help did you devise?"

"I did not devise anything, but I must say this one thing, that we are a Polish country and there are cruel punishments in the statutes for violence against a girl."

"Good, but it is not difficult to escape over the border. I know that Silesia also is a Polish country, yet the dukes there constantly quarrel and attack one another. Were it not so, my dear papa would still be alive. The Germans have been filtering in, and they ferment trouble and do wrong, so whoever wants to hide among them can easily do so. It is true that I would not easily give myself either to Cztan or to Wolf, but I am also concerned about my brothers. If I am not here, there will be peace, but if I stay at Zgorzelice, God knows what will happen. There may be attacks and fights, and Jasko is already fourteen, and no power, least of all mine, will restrain him. The last time, that time you arrived to our aid, he was already rushing to the front of the fray, and when Cztan hurled his club against the crowd he narrowly missed his head. Hey! Jasko has already told the servants that he will challenge them to combat on trodden ground. There will not be a single day of peace, I tell you, for some ill may befall even my younger brothers."

"Truly both Cztan and Wolf are curs," said Macko vehemently. "Yet they will not raise their hands against children. Faugh! Only a Teutonic Knight would do a thing like that."

"They will not raise their hands against children, but in the confusion—or, which God forbid, in case of fire—an accident might easily happen. What is the good of talking? Old Sieciechowa loves my brothers as if they were her own children, and they will not lack care and protection with her. But it will be safer for them without me than with me."

"Maybe," replied Macko.

Then he looked keenly at the girl:

"What do you want?"

She replied softly:

"Take me with you."

Though it had not been difficult for him to guess the outcome of this conversation, Macko was nevertheless amazed, and he reined in his horse, exclaiming:

"Dear God, Jagienka!"

She lowered her head and replied shyly—and sadly:

"Well! As for me, I prefer to speak sincerely rather than to conceal my thoughts. Both Hlawa and you say that Zbyszko will never find her again, and the Czech expects something even worse. God is my witness that I wish her no harm. May the Mother of God guard and protect her, poor thing! She was dearer than I to Zbyszko. Well, that cannot be helped—such is my fate. But, you see, until Zbyszko finds her—or if, as you believe, he never finds her—then, then. . . ."

"Then what?" asked Macko, seeing that the girl became more and more confused.

"Then I don't wish to be either Cztan's or Wolf's or anyone's."

Macko took a deep breath of satisfaction.

"I thought you had already forgotten him," he said.

She answered him still more sadly:

"Hey! you know the way it is. . . ."

"Then what do you want? How can I take you among the Teutonic Knights?"

"You don't have to take me necessarily among the Teutonic Knights. Now I should like to go to the abbot, who is lying sick at Sieradz. He has not a single kindly soul with him, for his gleemen care more for the tankard than for him. And he is my godfather and benefactor, after all. And even if he were well, I should seek his protection, for people fear him."

"I shall not argue with you," said Macko—who at the bottom of his heart was glad of Jagienka's decision, for, knowing the Teutonic Knights as he did, he firmly believed that Danusia would never leave their hands alive. "I will tell you one thing, though: there's always trouble on the road with a girl."

"Maybe with another girl, but not with me. I have never fought, but I know how to handle a crossbow and I can endure hardships when hunting. Never fear—I can do whatever must be done. I will wear Jasko's garments, I will take his net on my hair, gird his short-sword to my side, and ride with you. Jasko, though younger, is not a hair shorter than I, and is so like me in the face that when we disguised ourselves for carnival even papa could not tell us apart. You will see, not even the abbot will recognize me, nor will anyone else."

"Not even Zbyszko?"

"If I see him. . . ."

Macko reflected for a while, and then smiled suddenly.

"Wolf of Birchwood and Cztan of Rogow will be angry," he commented.

"Let them be angry. What's worse is that they may follow us."

"Well, don't worry! I am old, but it's best not to come under my fist. Or that of any of the Hailstones! They already tried once with Zbyszko."

Conversing thus, they reached Krzesnia. Old Wolf of Birchwood was in the church, and from time to time threw dark glances at Macko, but Macko took no notice of that, and after Mass he returned home in good spirits with Jagienka. But when they had taken leave of one another at the crossroads, and he found himself alone at Bogdaniec, less cheerful thoughts began to pass through his head. He understood that in point of fact nothing threatened either Zgorzelice or Jagienka's family in case of her departure. "They would try to get hold of the girl," he said to himself. "That's a different matter. But they will not raise their hands against orphans or against their property, for they would cover themselves with dreadful shame, and every living man would hunt them down like wolves. But Bogdaniec will remain dependent on God's favor alone! They will move the landmarks, they will drive away the herds and entice away the yeomen. God grant when I return I may get it back, send them a challenge, and call them to judgment, for not merely the fist but the law rules among us. But shall I return? And when? They are terribly bitter against me because I prevent them from approaching the girl, and if she goes away with me they will be still more bitter."

And he was overcome with sorrow, for he had finally gotten Bogdaniec into some kind of order, and now he was certain that when he returned he would find it again laid to waste and desolate.

"Well, one must find a way out of this!" he reflected.

So after dinner he had his horse saddled, and he mounted it and rode straight to Birchwood.

He arrived at dusk. Old Wolf was sitting in the front room over a tankard of mead, while the young man, wounded as he had been by Cztan, was lying on a bench covered with skins, and drinking also. Macko entered the room unexpectedly and stood in the doorway, stern-faced, tall, bony, unarmed but for a stout broad-sword at his side. They recognized him immediately, for the bright

light of a fire fell on his face, and in the first moment both father
and son sprang to their feet like lightning, rushed to the wall, and
seized the first weapon that came to hand.

But old Macko, who had had much experience, and knew men
and their customs through and through, was not in the least bit
perturbed, and did not reach for his sword, but merely put his hand
on his hip and said in a quiet voice with hint of mockery in it:

"What? Is this your noble hospitality at Birchwood?"

At these words they dropped their hands, and the old man
presently let his sword fall clattering on the floor, the young man
let go of his pike, and they stood with their necks stretched out to
Macko, their faces still ominous, but now expressing amazement
and shame.

Then he smiled and said:

"Jesus Christ be praised!"

"For ever and ever."

"And St. George!"

"We serve him."

"I've come as a neighbor—with goodwill."

"We greet you with goodwill. A guest is sacred here."

Then old Wolf hastened to Macko, and the young man after
him, and both began to squeeze his right hand, after which they
made him sit in the place of honor at the table. In no time fresh
wood had been thrown on the fire, the table had been covered with
a woven kilim, and dishes of food served, flagons of beer and a
tankard of mead brought over—and they began to eat and drink.
Once in a while young Wolf threw a peculiar glance at Macko in
which respect for a guest strove to overcome hatred for the man,
but he waited on him so assiduously that he grew pale with fatigue,
since he was still not well and did not possess his usual strength.
Both father and son burned with curiosity to know why Macko had
come, but neither of them asked him, waiting until he should
begin to speak himself.

But Macko, knowing the customs, praised the food and drink
and hospitality, and only when they had eaten their fill did he look
gravely ahead and say:

"Sometimes it happens that men quarrel—and, yes, even fight
in single combat—but peace among neighbors is above everything!"

"There is no more worthy thing than peace," replied old Wolf with equal gravity.

"It is also the case," continued Macko, "that when a man has to go on a long journey, even if he has lived in enmity with someone, he is still sorry to leave him and does not like to go without saying good-bye."

"God reward you for the kind thought."

"Not thought but deed, for I have come."

"We are glad from the bottom of our hearts. Come every day if you like."

"Would that I could entertain you at Bogdaniec as befits men who know knightly honor, but I am in haste to take to the road."

"Are you going to war or to some holy place?"

"Either one or the other would be better than where I am going—among the Teutonic Knights."

"Among the Teutonic Knights?" cried out father and son together.

"Yes!" replied Macko. "And whoever goes among them when he is not their friend had better reconcile himself with God and man, lest he lose not only his life but also his everlasting salvation."

"It is strange," said old Wolf. "I have never yet seen a man who met them without experiencing wrong and oppression."

"Like the whole of our kingdom!" added Macko. "Neither Lithuania before it received Holy Baptism nor the Tartars were more serious enemies to our kingdom than these diabolical monks."

"That's the honest truth, but you know, they have gathered and gathered until their measure is full, and now it is time to be finished with them."

So saying, the old man spat a little into both his hands, and his son added: "It cannot be otherwise."

"The moment will surely come, but when? It is not our heads which will decide, but only the king's. Maybe soon, maybe not so soon. God knows, but meanwhile I must ride to them."

"Not with a ransom for Zbyszko?"

At this mention by his father of Zbyszko, young Wolf's face instantly grew pale with hatred and turned ominous.

But Macko replied calmly, "Maybe with a ransom, but not for Zbyszko."

These words increased still more the curiosity of both the owners of Birchwood, so the old man could not help saying:

"It is for you to say or not to say why you are going there."

"I will tell you! I will tell you!" said Macko, nodding. "But first
I will tell you something else. Consider this: After my departure
Bogdaniec will be left to the protection of God. Formerly when
Zbyszko and I fought under Duke Witold, the abbot kept an eye
on our flocks and herds—and, yes, Zych of Zgorzelice helped a
little too. But now neither of them can do it. It is terribly painful
to a man to think that he has toiled and labored in vain. . . . You
understand what will happen. They will entice away my men, they
will plough over my boundary, and everyone will steal such cattle
as he can. Even if the Lord Jesus were to let me return, I should
find only a desert. . . . There's only one way and only one salvation
in this case: a good neighbor. That is why I have come to ask you
in neighborly fashion to take Bogdaniec under your protection and
not allow me to suffer wrong."

When they heard this request old Wolf looked at young Wolf,
and young Wolf looked at old Wolf, and both were extremely
surprised. There followed a moment of silence, since neither of
them knew what to say. Macko raised a mug of mead to his lips and
drained it, and then went on as calmly and intimately as if both of
them had been his best friends for many years:

"Now I will tell you frankly from whom I fear most injury. From
no one else but Cztan of Rogow. I would not fear anything from
you, even if we were to separate in enmity. You are knightly people,
who will stand before your enemy face to face, but will not take
vengeance on him behind his back. Yes, with you it's quite different. A knight is a knight! But Cztan is a peasant, and from a
peasant anything may be expected; particularly because, as you
know, he is terribly bitter against me because I stood between him
and Jagienka, Zych's daughter."

"Whom you are saving for your nephew!" burst out young Wolf.

Macko fixed him for a moment with a cold glance. Then he
turned again to the old man and said calmly:

"You know, of course, that my nephew has married a Mazovian
heiress and has received a considerable dowry."

There followed a deeper silence than before. Father and son

looked at Macko for some time, open-mouthed, and at length the old man exclaimed:

"Ho! What is that? People said something. . . . Will you tell us about it?"

But Macko, as if taking no notice of the question, went on:

"That is the reason why I have to go, and therefore I ask you to look in at Bogdaniec from time to time, and don't let me be wronged by anyone. And particularly protect me from the attacks of Cztan, like good and honest neighbors!"

Meanwhile young Wolf, who had a keen enough intelligence, perceived that, since Zbyszko had married, it would be better to have Macko for a friend, since Jagienka trusted him and was ready to follow his advice in all things. Suddenly entirely new horizons opened before the eyes of the young hothead. "It is not enough not to oppose Macko, one must win his favor," he said to himself. So, though he was a little drunk, he quickly stretched his hand under the table, grasped his father's knee, and squeezed it as a sign to him not to say anything unnecessary, while he himself spoke:

"Don't worry about Cztan! Ha! let him only try! He hurt me a little—that's true!—but I damaged his hairy face so much that his own mother did not recognize him. Don't worry about a thing! Go on your journey in peace. Not a single crow from Bogdaniec shall be lost to you!"

"I see that you are honorable people. Do you promise?"

"We promise," exclaimed both.

"On your knightly honor?"

"On our knightly honor."

"And on your coat-of-arms?"

"And on our coat-of-arms! Bah! And on the Cross! So help us God!"

Macko smiled with satisfaction.

"Well," he said, "that is what I expected of you. And since it is so, I will tell you something else. Zych, as you know, made me guardian of his children. That was why I stood in your way, young man, and in Cztan's, when you wanted to break into Zgorzelice. But now, when I am at Malbork, or God knows where, what sort of guardianship can I exercise? . . . It is true that orphans are under the care of God, and that a man who wrongs them is not only beheaded with the axe but is also declared to have lost his honor.

However, it is painful for me to be going. Terribly painful. Promise me that you will not do any wrong to Zych's orphans nor let anyone else wrong them."

"We swear! We swear!"

"On your knightly honor and your coat-of-arms?"

"On our knightly honor and our coat-of-arms!"

"And on the Cross also?"

"And on the Cross!"

"God has heard—amen!" concluded Macko.

And he drew a deep breath of relief, for he knew that they would keep such an oath even if each of them should have to gnaw his fist in rage and vexation.

Then he began to take his leave, but they kept him almost by force. He had to drink and be sociable with old Wolf, while the young one, though he usually looked for quarrels when he was drunk, this time only threatened Cztan, and waited on Macko as assiduously as if he were to get Jagienka from him first thing the next day. Before midnight, however, he fainted from exhaustion; and after they had brought him around, he fell into a deep sleep. The old man soon followed his example, so Macko left them both as if dead at the table.

He himself, however, having an unusually strong head, was not drunk but only a little cheery, and on his way home he thought almost with joy of what he had accomplished.

"Well!" he said to himself. "Bogdaniec safe and Zgorzelice safe. They will be enraged because of Jagienka's going, but they will protect my property and hers, because they must. . . . The Lord Jesus gave man wits. What one cannot do by the fist, one must do by one's intelligence. . . . If I return, the old man will certainly challenge me to the field, but never mind. . . . God grant that I may trap the Teutonic Knights like that! But it is harder with them. Though there are Polish curs, a Pole, when he has sworn on his knightly honor and coat-of-arms, will keep his oath; but for the Teutonic Knights an oath is like spitting on water. But perhaps the Mother of Christ will help me to be of some use to Zbyszko, as I have now been of use to Zych's children and to Bogdaniec."

Then it came into his head that the girl did not have to go, for the two Wolfs would guard her like the apple of their eye. He presently rejected this idea, however. "The Wolfs will guard her, but on the other hand Cztan will attack her all the more. God knows who will prove stronger, and it is certain that there will be fights and assaults, in which Zgorzelice, Zych's orphans, and even the girl herself may suffer. It will be easier for the Wolfs to protect Bogdaniec alone, and it will be better in any case for the girl to be far from these ruffians and, at the same time, near to the rich abbot." Macko did not believe that Danusia could escape alive from the hands of the Teutonic Knights, so he had not yet abandoned hope that if in time Zbyszko should return as a widower, he would inevitably feel drawn towards Jagienka.

"Oh, mighty God!" he said to himself. "If, having Spychow, he were afterwards to take Jagienka with Moczydoly—and with what the abbot will leave her—I should not begrudge even a bit of wax for holy candles!"

With such thoughts the road from Birchwood seemed short enough; yet it was late at night when he reached Bogdaniec, and he was surprised to see the windowpanes brightly lit up. The farmhands also were not asleep, for scarcely had he ridden into the yard when the stableman ran towards him.

"Some guests?" asked Macko, dismounting.

"The young lord of Zgorzelice is present, and the Czech," replied the stableman.

Macko was surprised by the visit. Jagienka had promised to come early in the morning, and they were to start at once. So why was Jasko here at such a late hour? The old knight thought that perhaps something had happened at Zgorzelice, and so he entered the house with an anxious mind.

But in the room, in the great clay chimney—which in a manorhouse took the place of the usual stone hearth in the middle of the floor—pine chips burned bright and merry, and on the table two torches flamed in iron sockets, by the light of which Macko saw Jasko, Hlawa, and another young page with cheeks as red as an apple.

"How are you, Jasko? And what is the matter with Jagienka?" asked the old nobleman.

"Jagienka bade me tell you," said the boy, kissing his hand, "that she has changed her mind and prefers to stay at home?"

"Great heavens! What is this? How? What has come into her head?"

The boy raised his blue eyes to him and began to laugh.

"What is so funny?"

But at that moment the Czech and the other youth also burst into merry laughter.

"You see!" said the supposed boy. "Who will recognize me if you did not?"

Only then did Macko look more closely at the graceful figure.

"In the name of the Father and the Son!" he exclaimed. "A regular carnival! Why are you here, you imp?"

"Why? Whoever has to take the road must value his time."

"But you were to come tomorrow at dawn."

"Indeed! Tomorrow at dawn, so that everyone can see me! Tomorrow they will think at Zgorzelice that I am visiting you, and they won't look for me until the following day. Sieciechowa and Jasko know, but Jasko promised me on his knightly honor that he will not tell until they begin to worry. But you did not recognize me, did you?"

Then Macko began to laugh in his turn.

"Let me look at you again. . . . Hey! You're a terribly graceful youth! And a peculiar one, for from such a youth posterity may be expected. I speak the truth! If I were not so old—well! I will tell you this: Beware, girl, of passing before my eyes! Beware!"

And he threatened her with his finger, laughing, but he looked at her with great pleasure, for such a page he had never seen in his life before. On her head she had a red silk net; she was wearing a green cloth jacket, hose puffed out at the hips but tight-fitting lower down, one leg being the color of the net, and the other with long stripes. And with a richly ornamented dagger at her side, and a face smiling and bright as the dawn, she looked so beautiful that one could barely take one's eyes off her.

"Heavens!" said Macko merrily. "Are you some wonderful young lord, or are you a flower, or what?"

Then he turned to the second page and asked:

"And this one here? Doubtless he also is a changeling?"

"Why, that's Sieciechowa's daughter," replied Jagienka. "It would have been unbecoming for me to venture alone among you; how could I? So I took Anulka with me. It's easier if there are two of us, and I have help and service. No one will recognize her either."

"What a party! One was not enough, so there will be two."

"Don't tease me."

"I will not tease you, but in the daytime everyone will recognize her, and you too."

"Will they? How?"

"Because your knees press together—and hers too."

"Leave me in peace!"

"I will, for my time is past, but whether Cztan and Wolf will, God knows. Do you know, girl, where I have come from? Birch-wood."

"Dear God! What are you saying?"

"It is true, as it is also true that the Wolfs will defend both Bogdaniec and Zgorzelice from Cztan. Well, to challenge one's enemies and fight with them is easy, but to make one's enemies guardians of one's own property, no regular fellow can do that."

Then Macko began to tell about his visit to the Wolfs, how he had won them over and led them on a hook. Jagienka listened in great amazement, and when he had at last finished, she said:

"The Lord Jesus was not sparing of cunning with you, and I see that everything will always be as you wish."

But Macko shook his head sorrowfully.

"Eh, girl, if everything were as I wish, you would long since have been mistress of Bogdaniec!"

Jagienka looked at him for some time with her blue eyes and then went up and kissed his hand.

"Why do you kiss me?" asked the old man.

"For no reason. I'm only saying good-night, for it is late, and tomorrow we must start at dawn."

She took Anulka and went out. Macko led the Czech to the bed-alcove, where they lay down on bison-skins and slept deeply and refreshingly.

CHAPTER XLII

ALTHOUGH Kazimierz the Great had rebuilt Sieradz after the destruction, fire, and slaughter wreaked on it by the Teutonic Knights in 1331, the town was not too splendid and could not be compared with other fortified posts in the kingdom. But Jagienka, whose life so far had passed between Zgorzelice and Krzesnia, could not contain herself at the sight of the walls, towers, town hall, and particularly the churches, of which the wooden church at Krzesnia had failed to give her the least idea. She lost her usual composure to such an extent that she did not dare to speak aloud, and only questioned Macko in a whisper about all the marvels which dazzled her eyes. When the old knight assured her that Sieradz was to Cracow like a torch to the sun, she could not believe her ears, for it seemed to her impossible that there should be another such splendid town in the world.

At the monastery they were received by the same decrepit prior who remembered the slaughter by the Teutonic Knights in his childhood and who had received Zbyszko before. The news about the abbot caused them anxiety and trouble. He had stayed long in the monastery, but two weeks before he had gone to his friend, the Bishop of Plock. He was still sick. He had been in possession of his faculties in the mornings, but in the evenings his mind wandered, and he would spring up, call for his breastplate, and challenge Duke John of Raciborz to single combat. His clerics had to keep him in bed by force, which was done with great difficulty, and even danger. Two weeks ago he had come to his senses, and though still very weak, he had ordered himself to be taken at once to Plock.

"He said that he trusted no one like the Bishop of Plock," concluded the prior, "and that he wanted to receive the Sacrament from his hand and to leave his will with him. We opposed the journey as much as we could, for he was very faint, and we were afraid that he would not live for more than a mile. But it was not easy to oppose him. So his gleemen prepared a wagon and took him, God grant happily."

"If he had died when he was still near Sieradz, you would surely have heard," said Macko.

"We should have heard," replied the old man, "so I think he did not die, and that he did not breathe his last at least until he reached Leczyca. But what happened after that we do not know. If you follow him, you will learn on the road."

Macko became alarmed when he heard all this and went for advice to Jagienka, who had already learned from the Czech where the abbot had gone.

"What should I do?" he asked her. "And what will you do with yourself?"

"You will ride to Plock and I will go with you," she answered shortly.

"To Plock!" repeated Anulka in her thin voice.

"See how they rule here! Do you think that going to Plock is as simple as a sweep of a sickle?"

"How could I go back alone with Anulka? If I am not to go on with you, it would have been better not to start at all. Don't you think that those men will be more angry and bitter against me now?"

"The Wolfs will defend you against Cztan."

"I am just as much afraid of Wolf's defence as of Cztan's attack. I see that you are only arguing with me for the sake of arguing and not because you are serious."

In truth Macko was not serious in his opposition. On the contrary, he preferred that Jagienka should go with him rather than return, so when he heard her words he smiled and said:

"She's thrown away her skirt and now claims to be wise."

"Wisdom is nowhere else but in the head."

"It is out of my way to go through Plock."

"The Czech said that it is not out of the way. He claims it is even nearer to Malbork that way."

"Then you have already been conferring with the Czech?"

"Yes, and he also said, 'If the young lord has got into difficulties at Malbork, we might do much with the help of Duchess Alexandra of Plock, for she is of the royal family; besides, being a particular friend of the Teutonic Knights, she enjoys great respect among them.'"

"True, as I love God!" exclaimed Macko. "Everyone knows about that, and if she were to give us a letter to the grand master, we should travel safely through all the lands of the Teutonic Knights. They like her, for she likes them. . . . This is good advice; he's not a stupid lad—that Czech!"

"He certainly is not!" exclaimed Anulka eagerly, raising her blue eyes.

Macko suddenly turned to her. "What are you doing here?"

The girl became terribly embarrassed and, dropping her long eyelashes, flushed like a rose.

Macko saw that he would have to take both girls with him, and in his heart he wanted to do so. Therefore the next morning he took leave of the old prior and they continued on their journey. Because of the melting of the snows and the spread of floodwater, they travelled with more difficulty than before. On the way they kept asking about the abbot and found many manor-houses, parsonages, and, where there were none of these, even inns where he had stayed the night. It was easy to follow his tracks, for he had distributed generous alms, had paid for Masses, and given money for bells and the rebuilding of ruined churches, so that more than one beggar on the tramp, more than one sacristan, nay, more than one parson, remembered him with gratitude. It was generally said that he "rode like an angel," and prayers were offered for his health, though here and there fears were expressed that he was already nearer to everlasting salvation than to temporal health. In some places he had stopped two or three days because of his great weakness, so it seemed likely to Macko that they might overtake him.

However, he was mistaken in this, for they were detained by the swollen waters of the Ner and the Bzura. Before reaching Leczyca they were compelled to wait four days in an empty inn which the innkeeper had deserted, evidently from fear of floods. The road from the inn to the town, although covered with transverse logs, had sunk, and for a considerable distance had become nothing more than a muddy slough. Macko's page, Vit, who was born in these parts, had heard something about a passage through the woods, but he was unwilling to serve as guide, for he knew also that unholy powers had their abode in the Leczyca fens; that is to say, the powerful Boruta, who gladly led people astray into the bottomless quagmires and then saved them only at the price of their souls. The inn itself also had a bad name, and although in those days travellers took provisions with them and so were not afraid of hunger, even old Macko was filled with disquiet at the idea of staying in such a place.

At night noises were heard on the roof, and sometimes there was a knock at the door. Jagienka and Anulka, sleeping in the alcove next to the large chamber, also heard the rustle of little feet on the floor and even on the walls. They were not greatly afraid, for they had both been accustomed at Zgorzelice to goblins, which old Zych used to feed, and which, according to the general belief in those times, were not malicious if only broken bits of food were left for them. But one night a dull and ominous roar was heard in the neighboring brakes, and the next morning tracks of huge hooves were found in the mud. It might have been a bison or an aurochs, but Vit maintained that it could also have been Boruta. Though he had human form—even that of a nobleman—he had cloven feet, and in the fens he used to take off the boots which he wore among men. Macko, having heard that he might be appeased by a drink-offering, reflected the whole day long whether it would be a sin to make a friend of an evil spirit and even consulted Jagienka on the point.

"I might hang up an ox-bladder of wine or mead on the fence at night," he said, "and if it were drunk in the night, then we would at least know that he is wandering about."

"If only the heavenly powers are not offended!" replied the girl. "We need their blessing if we are to rescue Zbyszko successfully."

"I am afraid of that too; but I think that, after all, mead is not the same as one's soul. I shall not give my soul, and what is one bladder of mead to the heavenly powers?"

Then he lowered his voice and added:

"It is the usual thing for a nobleman to entertain another

nobleman, even if he be the greatest highway robber; and men say that he is a noble."

"Who?" asked Jagienka.

"I don't wish to mention his unholy name."

None the less, that same evening Macko hung a large ox-bladder on the fence; such a bladder was commonly used for carrying drink—and next morning it was quite empty.

It is true that the Czech smiled somewhat strangely when they spoke of it, but no one paid any attention to him, and Macko was glad at heart, for he hoped that when they had to pass through the mire they would not find any unexpected obstacles nor have any unpleasant adventures.

"Unless it is a lie that he knows what honor is," he said to himself.

It was first necessary to find out whether there was a passage through the woods. There might be, for where the soil is held together by the roots of trees and plants it does not easily soften from the rains. However, Vit, who, being a local man, might easily have gone to find out, at the very mention of it shouted: "Kill me instead, lord! I will not go!" It was vain to explain to him that unholy spirits have no power in the day. Macko offered to go himself, but in the end Hlawa, who was a fearless lad, glad to show his courage, especially in front of the girls, took an axe in his belt and a staff in his hand and went.

He started at dawn, and it was expected that he would return about noon. But when he didn't come back by that time, they began to worry. It was in vain that the servants listened for any sound in the forest, even in the afternoon. Vit wrung his hands: "He will not return, or if he does, it will be woe to us, for God knows whether he will not be changed into a werewolf with wolf's jaws." Hearing that, they were all afraid; even Macko was not his usual self, and Jagienka turned toward the forest and made the sign of the cross. Meanwhile Anulka felt in vain for her apron, her knees being now covered with hose, and not finding anything with which to wipe her eyes, covered them with her fingers, which soon became wet with trickling tears.

However, at the time of the evening milking, when the sun was just about to set, the Czech returned—and not alone, but with some human figure, which he drove before him on a rope. They all ran to meet him with shouts of joy, but fell silent at the sight of that figure, which was small, bow-legged, shaggy, black, and dressed in wolfskins.

"In the name of the Father and the Son, what sort of a creature have you brought?" exclaimed Macko, mastering his initial excitement.

"What does it matter?" replied the Czech. "He says he is a man and a pitch-burner; but whether it is true, I do not know."

"Oh, that is no man; that is no human!" exclaimed Vit.

Macko ordered him to be silent, then looked attentively at the captive, and suddenly said:

"Cross yourself! Cross yourself instantly!"

"Jesus Christ be praised!" exclaimed the captive, and crossing himself as quickly as he could, he took a deep breath of relief and looked with more confidence at the company.

"Jesus Christ be praised!" he repeated. "For I, too, did not know whether I was in the hands of Christians or devils. Oh, Jesus. . . ."

"Don't be afraid. You are among Christians who are glad to hear Holy Mass. What are you?"

"A pitch-burner, lord. There are seven of us in huts with our women and children."

"How far are you from here?"

"Not quite ten furlongs."

"How do you go to the town?"

"We have our own way through a ravine called the Devil's Ditch."

"The Devil's Ditch? Cross yourself again!"

"In the name of the Father and of the Son and Holy Ghost, Amen!"

"Good. Can a wagon pass that way?"

"Now there is mud everywhere; though there is not so much there as on the highway, for the wind blows in the ravine and dries it up. It's difficult as far as Budy, but even to Budy a man who knows the forest can guide you slowly."

"Will you guide us for a *skojca*, or maybe for two?"

The pitch-burner gladly undertook to guide them, asking, however, for half a loaf of bread as well, for in the forest, though his people did not suffer hunger, they had not seen bread for a long time. It was agreed that they should start the next morning, since "it wouldn't be good" to go in the evening. As for Boruta, the pitch-burner said that he sometimes stormed terribly in the forest but did no harm to simple folk; he was jealous of the duchy of Leczyca and therefore chased all other devils through the brushwood. It was only bad to meet him at night, particularly if one had been drinking. In the daytime, and if one was sober, there was no cause for fear.

"And yet you were afraid," said Macko.

"Because that knight seized me unexpectedly with such strength that I thought he could not be a man."

Jagienka laughed, because they all had taken the pitch-burner for something "unholy," and the pitch-burner had thought the same of them. Anulka, Sieciechowa's daughter, laughed with her, till Macko said:

"Your eyes are not yet dry from weeping for Hlawa, and now you are grinning again?"

So the Czech looked at her rosy face, and seeing that her eyelashes were still wet, he asked her: "Were you weeping for me?"

"Oh no!" replied the girl. "I was only afraid, that was all."

"But you are a gentlewoman, and a gentlewoman should be ashamed of fear. Your mistress is not so timid. What would happen to you in the daytime and among people?"

"Not to me, but to you."

"But you said that you were not weeping for me?"

"No, because I wasn't."

"Why were you weeping?"

"Because I was afraid."

"And now you are not afraid?"

"No."

"Why not?"

"Because you've come back."

The Czech looked at her with gratitude, smiled, and said: "We could talk like this till morning. You are very cunning."

But she might have been charged with anything other than cunning, and Hlawa, himself a sharp youth, understood that very well. He understood also that the girl was becoming more attracted to him with every day. He himself loved Jagienka, but as a subject loves a daughter of a king; that is to say, in all humility and honor, but without hope. Meanwhile the journey was bringing him closer to Anulka. While they were on the road, old Macko usually rode first with Jagienka and he with Anulka, and since he was a lad like an aurochs, and his blood was hot like boiling water, when he looked at her bright eyes, at her golden curls which would not stay under the net, at her whole slender and graceful figure, and particularly at her shapely, well-turned legs, clasping her black horse as she rode, he shivered from head to foot. He could not refrain from looking ever more frequently and more greedily at all these splendors, and he thought involuntarily that if the devil were to turn into such a page he might easily lead him into temptation. Besides, she was a page that was as sweet as honey, and so obedient that she only looked into her lord's eyes, and as merry as a sparrow on a roof. At times strange thoughts came into the Czech's head, and once, when he and Anulka had fallen a little to the rear, near the pack-horses, he suddenly turned to her and said:

"Do you know, I'm riding by your side like a wolf by a lamb?"

Her white teeth flashed in frank laughter.

"Would you like to eat me?" she asked.

"Yes, bones and all!"

And he looked at her with such a look that she flushed under it, and then silence fell between them, and only their hearts beat strongly, his with desire, and hers with some sweet, intoxicating fear.

At first desire had the upper hand over affection in the Czech, and when he said that he looked at Anulka like a wolf at a lamb, he was speaking the truth. It was only that evening, when he saw her cheeks and eyelashes wet with tears, that his heart softened. She seemed to him good and in some way near to him and in some way his; and since he himself had an honest and at the same time knightly nature, he not only did not grow proud and haughty at the sight of those sweet tears but became shyer and more attentive to her. His former heedlessness of speech left him, and although at supper he made some fun of the timid girl, it was in a different way, and at the same time he waited on her as a knightly squire should wait on a noblewoman. Old Macko, although he was thinking chiefly of the next day's passage through the forest and of their further journey, noticed this, but only praised him for his good manners, which, as he said, he must have learned with Zbyszko at the Mazovian court.

Then he turned to Jagienka and added: "Hey! Zbyszko! He
would be at home even with a king!"

After supper, when they had separated for the night, Hlawa,
having kissed Jagienka's hand, raised Anulka's in turn to his lips and
said:

"Not only have no fear for me, but have no fear with me, for I
will not give you to anyone."

Then the men lay down in the front room, and Jagienka and
Anulka in the alcove, on a single but broad and well-covered
plank-bed. Neither of them could fall asleep right away, and
Anulka in particular tossed on her coarse sheet; so after some time
Jagienka pushed her head to her and whispered:

"Anulka?"

"What?"

"Well . . . it seems to me that you're terribly fond of that Czech. . . .
Are you?"

But the question remained unanswered, so Jagienka whispered
again: "I understand, after all. . . . Tell me."

Anulka did not answer even now, but only pressed her lips to her
mistress's cheek and kissed her again and again.

And poor Jagienka's maiden breast also began to heave again and
again with sighs.

"Oh, I do understand, I do understand!" she whispered, so softly
that Anulka could scarcely catch the words.

CHAPTER XLIII

ON the morrow, after a misty, mild night, there came a windy day, now clear, now overcast with clouds which sped in wind-driven flocks over the sky. Macko ordered the company to start as soon as it was light. The pitch-burner who had undertaken to guide them to Budy said that the horses would be able to pass everywhere, but that the wagons in places would have to be taken apart and carried across in pieces, together with the boxes of clothing and stores of food. This would mean effort and delay, but the men, who were hardened and accustomed to fatigue, preferred the greatest fatigue to just idly sitting about in the empty inn, and so they gladly set off. Even the timid Vit, encouraged by the words and presence of the pitch-burner, showed no fear.

Immediately after leaving the inn they entered a forest of lofty trees with no undergrowth, in which, with skillful driving, it was possible to make way between the tree-trunks even without taking the wagons to pieces. At times the wind ceased, at others it rose again with unheard-of violence, beating the tops of tall pines as if with huge wings, bending and twisting them, whirling them like the sails of a windmill, and snapping them; the whole forest yielded under its violent blast, and even in the intervals between one gust and the next it did not cease to roar and thunder, as if in anger at the wind's attack and its superior force. From time to time the daylight was entirely cut off by clouds; then a slashing rain mingled with snowflakes, and it became as dark as dusk at evenfall. Then Vit would again lose his courage and cry out that the Evil One was angry and was hindering them, but no one listened to him; even the timid Anulka did not take his words to heart, especially since the Czech was so near that she could touch his stirrup with her own, and he looked ahead as boldly as if he wished to challenge the devil himself to a fight.

The lofty forest was followed by undergrowth, and then by thickets through which it was impossible to drive. The wagons had to be taken apart, but that was done skillfully in the twinkling of an eye. Wheels, poles, and forecarriages were carried by the sturdy attendants on their shoulders, and likewise the packs and stores of provisions. There were just three furlongs of this bad road, yet they reached Budy only at evening, where the pitch-burners received them hospitably and assured them that it would be possible to reach the town through the Devil's Ditch, or, more strictly speaking, along the sides of it. These men, who had lived long in the wilderness, seldom saw bread or flour, but they did not starve, for they had an abundance of all kinds of cured meats and especially smoked weatherfishes, with which all the fens were swarming. They offered a large quantity of them, stretching out eager hands for flat cakes in return. There were women and children among them, all black from tarry smoke, and there was also one old fellow, more than a hundred years old, who remembered the massacre of Leczyca in 1331 and the complete destruction of that town by the Teutonic Knights. Macko, the Czech, and the two girls, although they had heard almost the same story from the prior at Sieradz, listened with curiosity to the gaffer, who sat by the fire and raked the coals, seeming at the same time to rake up the terrible memories of his youth. Yes! at Leczyca, just as at Sieradz, neither churches nor priests had been spared, and the blood of old men, women, and children had flowed under the knives of the victors. The Teutonic Knights, always the Teutonic Knights! Macko's and Jagienka's thoughts flew constantly to Zbyszko, who had gone, as it were, into the wolf's jaws, into the midst of a hostile race which knew neither mercy nor the laws of hospitality. Anulka's heart also sank, for she was not certain whether in their pursuit of the abbot they would not have to go even among those cruel knights.

But the old man then began to tell about the battle of Plowce, which put an end to the Teutonic Knights' invasion, and in which he had taken part, armed with an iron flail, as a foot-soldier in the contingent furnished by the yeomanry of the commune. In that battle almost the whole line of the Hailstones had perished, so Macko knew very well every detail of it, and yet he listened now attentively to the stories of the frightful defeat of the Germans, when they were beaten down under the swords of the Polish knighthood and the power of King Wladyslaw like cornfields under hail.

"Ha! I do remember," the old man was saying. "They invaded the land and set fire to towns and castles—why, they murdered children in their cradles, but it came to a dark end for them. That was indeed a splendid battle. Yes! Every time I close my eyes, I see the field. . . ."

He closed his eyes and fell silent, only poking the coals gently in the fireplace, until Jagienka impatiently asked him: "What happened?"

"What happened?" repeated the old man. "I remember the battlefield as if I were looking at it now; there were thickets, and on the right a wet meadow and a stretch of rough stubble, like a small field. But after the battle neither thickets nor meadow nor stubble was to be seen, but everywhere iron weapons—swords, axes, pikes, and beautiful breastplates—one on top of the other, as if the whole world had been covered with them. Never have I seen so many slain men in one place, nor so much human blood flowing."

Macko's heart was cheered again by this memory, so he said:

"True! The Lord Jesus was merciful! They overran the kingdom at that time like a fire or a pestilence. They destroyed not only Sieradz and Leczyca, but many other towns as well. And what of it? Our nation is extraordinarily vigorous and has inexhaustible strength. Although you seize it by the throat, you Teutonic dogs, you will not be able to strangle it; it will knock out your teeth. Just look! King Kazimierz rebuilt both Sieradz and Leczyca so splendidly that they are finer than they were before, and diets are held in them as they used to be, and the Teutonic Knights who were defeated at Plowce lie there and rot. God grant always such an end."

The old fellow, when he heard these words, nodded at first in assent, but finally said:

"No, they are not lying and rotting. The king ordered us foot-soldiers to dig trenches after the battle, and the peasants from the neighborhood also came to help, so that there was a great clanking of spades. Then we laid the Germans in the trenches and covered them with earth so that no pestilence might spread from them, but they did not stay there."

"What do you mean? What happened to them?"

"I myself did not see it. I'm only telling you what people have said. After the battle there came a great gale which lasted for twelve weeks, but only at night. In the daytime the sun shone as usual, but at night the wind was almost enough to tear the hair from one's head. It was the devils blustering in great swarms in the whirlwind, each one with a pitchfork, and when one flew over the graves, whoop! down to the ground with his pitchfork, and up comes a Teutonic Knight and off with him to hell! The folk at Plowce heard a noise as if packs of dogs were howling, but they could not tell whether it was the Germans howling for fear and grief, or the devils howling for joy. It went on until the priests exorcized the trenches, and until the ground froze so hard at New Year that pitchforks could not pierce it."

He was silent for a while, then added: "But God grant, Sir Knight, such an end as you spoke of, for though I myself shall not live to see it, such pages as those two will, and they will not have to go through the terrible things that I've had to go through."

Then he gazed at Jagienka and at Anulka, wondering at their beautiful faces, and shook his head.

"Like poppies among the corn," he said. "Such pages I have never yet seen."

In talk like this they passed part of the night. Then they lay down to sleep in the huts on moss as soft as down, covered with warm skins, and after deep sleep had rested their limbs, they started the next morning when it was already full daylight. The road along the ravine was certainly not too easy, but it was also not so difficult as to prevent them reaching the castle of Leczyca before sunset. The town had risen again from its ashes, partly in red brick and partly even in stone. It had high walls, defended with towers, and churches still more splendid than those at Sieradz. At the monastery of the Dominican friars they easily obtained news of the abbot. He had stayed with them; he was better, they said, and was cherishing the hope of complete recovery; indeed, he had gone on a few days before. Macko was not too anxious to overtake him on the road, as he had now determined to take the two girls to Plock, where the abbot would have taken them in any case; but since he was anxious to find Zbyszko, he was greatly troubled by another piece of news: that immediately after the abbot's departure the rivers had swollen up so much as to make it impossible to proceed. The Dominicans, seeing a knight accompanied by a considerable troop, and learning that he and his people were on the way to Duke Ziemowit, received them and entertained them hospitably. They even gave Macko a tablet of olive-wood to take with him, on which was written in Latin a prayer to the angel Raphael, the patron of travellers.

The forced stay at Leczyca lasted two weeks. One of the constable's squires discovered that the pages of the knight who was passing through were girls, and fell passionately in love with Jagienka on the spot. The Czech wanted to challenge him immediately to single combat on trodden ground, but since this happened the evening before their departure, Macko dissuaded him from doing so.

By the time they continued their journey to Plock, the wind had somewhat dried the highways. Although the rains were frequent, yet—as usual in spring—they did not last long. The rain-showers were also warm and heavy, for spring had finally arrived. In the fresh-ploughed fields bright strips of water shone in the furrows, and from the interjacent lands the breeze brought the strong smell of damp earth. On the marshes appeared a golden cover of marigolds, and in the forests wild anemones burst into blossom and songbirds twittered merrily among the branches. The hearts of the travellers were filled with new joy and hope, particularly because they made good progress on the road. After sixteen days' journey they reached the gates of Plock.

But they arrived at night, when the gates of the town were already shut, so they had to pass the night at a weaver's, outside the walls. The girls went to sleep late, but after the fatigue and discomforts of the long journey they slept like logs. Macko, who could not be overcome by any type of fatigue, was unwilling to wake them. He went alone into the town as soon as the gates were open, and easily found the cathedral and the house of the bishop, where the first news he heard was that the abbot had died a week before.

He had died a week before, but according to the custom of the times, Masses were celebrated by his coffin and funeral repasts were held for six days; the funeral was to occur that very day, and, after it, services and the last repast to celebrate the memory of the deceased.

Macko was so upset that he did not even look about the town, which in any case he knew from the days when he had ridden with a letter from Duchess Alexandra to the grand master. He hastened as quickly as possible to the weaver's house outside the walls, and on the way said to himself:

"He is dead! God give him everlasting rest! I can't do anything at all about that, but what am I to do now with these girls?"

He began to reflect whether it would be better to leave them with Duchess Alexandra or with Duchess Anna Danuta, or whether perhaps to take them to Spychow. For it had frequently entered his mind during the journey that if it turned out that Danusia was dead, there would be no harm in Jagienka's being near Zbyszko. He did not doubt that Zbyszko would long mourn and weep for Danusia, his dearly beloved; but he also did not doubt that such a girl as Jagienka, if she were close to his side, would have her effect. He remembered how the youth, although his heart drew him far over the forests and pinewoods to Mazovia, was seized with shivers when he was near Jagienka. For these reasons, and in the deep belief that Danusia was lost, he sometimes had thought that in case of the abbot's death he would not let Jagienka go. But since he was rather greedy for landed estates, he was interested also in the property which the abbot had left. The abbot had indeed been angry with them and threatened to leave them nothing, but what if he had repented before his death? It was certain that he had left Jagienka something, for he had often mentioned it at Zgorzelice, so Zbyszko might come into possession of it through Jagienka. At times Macko was seized with a desire to stay at Plock, to find out more and to attend to the matter, but he soon rejected the idea. "Am I to run after property here," he thought, "while my boy is perhaps stretching out his hands to me from some Teutonic dungeon and waiting for me to rescue him?" There was, it was true, one way out: to leave Jagienka under the care of the duchess and the bishop, and beg them not to allow her to be wronged if the abbot had left her anything. But this solution did not quite please Macko. "The girl has a considerable dowry in any case," he said to himself, "and if she inherits more from the abbot, some Mazovian will try to get her, as God is in heaven, and she will not hold out very long, for Zych used to say before he died that even then she seemed to be walking on hot coals." And the old knight was afraid, thinking that in such a case Zbyszko might lose both Danusia and Jagienka. This he didn't want for anything in the world.

"Let him have the one whom God has intended for him, but one he must have."

So he finally determined to go first to Zbyszko's rescue, and to leave Jagienka, if he had to part from her, either at Spychow or with Duchess Danuta, but not here at Plock, where the court was incomparably more splendid and where there were plenty of handsome knights.

Troubled with these thoughts, he walked quickly to the house of the weaver to inform Jagienka of the abbot's death, but he proposed not to tell her at once, for unexpected bad news might easily take her breath away and afterwards make the girl barren. When he reached the house he found them both dressed, even handsomely, and as merry as warblers, so he sat down on a wooden stool, called to the weaver's apprentices to bring him a bowl of warm beer, and then, looking even more grave and stern than was his wont, he said:

"Do you hear how the bells are ringing in the town? Guess why they are ringing, for it is not Sunday, and you have slept past Matins. Would you like to see the abbot?"

"Of course I would," said Jagienka.

"Well, you will not."

"Has he gone away?"

"He has indeed. Do you not hear the bells?"

"He has died?" cried out Jagienka.

"Say a prayer for his everlasting rest."

She and Anulka immediately knelt down and began to say a requiem with voices as clear as a bell. Then the tears began to course in streams down Jagienka's face, for she had loved the abbot greatly, and although he was hot-tempered, he never wronged anyone and did much good; and he loved her, his godchild, as if she were his own daughter. Macko, remembering that he had been his own and Zbyszko's kinsman, was also moved, and wept a little, and only after part of their pain had flowed away with their tears did he take the Czech and the two girls to church for the funeral.

It was a splendid funeral. The procession was headed by the bishop himself, James of Kurdwanow; all the priests and all the monks of the convents at Plock were present; all the bells were rung, speeches were made which none but the clergy understood, for they were made in Latin, and then the clergy and laymen together went to the bishop's residence for a splendid repast.

Macko went to it, taking with him his two pages, since as a kinsman of the deceased abbot and an acquaintance of the bishop he had every right. The bishop received him gladly and with distinction as a kinsman of the deceased, and said to him right after greeting him:

"There are some forests here left to you Hailstones of Bogdaniec, and what is left and does not go to the monasteries or the abbey is pass to a goddaughter of his, a certain Jagienka of Zgorzelice."

Macko, who had not expected much, was pleased with the forests, and the bishop did not notice that one of the old knight's pages at mention of Jagienka of Zgorzelice raised dewy eyes of cornflower blue, saying, "God reward him, but I would rather that he were alive."

Macko turned around and said crossly, "Be quiet, or you will bring shame on yourself."

But he suddenly broke off and his eyes flashed with surprise while his face grew stern and wolf-like, for not far away, by the door through which Duchess Alexandra was just entering he saw, bowed forward in courteous salutation, the figure of Kuno Lichtenstein—the same person through whom Zbyszko had almost lost his life at Cracow.

Jagienka had never seen Macko like that in her life: his face cramped like the muzzle of a dog, his teeth flashing from under his moustache. Suddenly he pulled around his belt and went towards the hated Teutonic Knight.

But he stopped half-way and passed his broad hand through his hair. He had remembered in time that Lichtenstein could be only either a guest at the court of Plock or, more probably, an envoy, and that if he were to strike him without asking any question he would be doing exactly the same as Zbyszko on the road from Tyniec.

So, having more sense and experience than Zbyszko, he stopped, pushed his belt back again, relaxed his face, and waited; and then, when the duchess, after greeting Lichtenstein, began to talk with Bishop James of Kurdwanow, he approached her and, bowing low, told her who he was and that he regarded her as his benefactress because of the letter which she had once given him.

The duchess scarcely remembered him but easily recalled the letter and the whole affair. She also knew what had happened at the neighboring court of Mazovia; she had heard of Jurand, of the imprisonment of his daughter, the marriage of Zbyszko, and his mortal combat with Roger. It all interested her immeasurably, like some tale of chivalry or one of the songs which the minstrels used to sing in Germany and the local bards in Mazovia. The Teutonic Knights were not, indeed, as hateful to her as to Anna Danuta, Janusz's wife, especially since, wishing to win her to their side, they paid her excessive homage and flattery and heaped her generously with gifts; but this time her heart was on the side of the lovers. She was ready to help—and, besides, she was glad that she had someone before her who could tell her in detail the course of events.

Macko, however, who had determined already to make the best use he could of the influential duchess's protection, seeing with what eagerness she listened, readily told her of the unhappy fates of Danusia and Zbyszko, and moved her almost to tears, especially because he himself felt his nephew's misery deeply and grieved over it with his whole heart.

"I have never in my life heard anything more touching," said the duchess in the end. "And most of all I grieve for the reason that he married the girl—she was already his—and yet he did not experience any joy with her. You are certain of this, no?"

"Hey! Almighty God," replied Macko, "if he only had had some joy with her! But he married her in the evening when he was bedridden, and at dawn they took her away."

"And you suspect the Teutonic Knights? For we were told of robbers who deceived the Knights, giving them another girl. We were also told of a letter of Jurand's. . . ."

"No human judgment has decided these things, but God's. Roger was a great knight, they say, who overcame the strongest, and yet he fell at the hands of a child."

"Such a child," said the duchess smiling, "that it would be better not to get in his way. Wrong has been done—true! And you are justified in complaining. Yet of those four, three are already dead, and the old knight who is left scarcely escaped death, as I heard."

"And Danusia? And Jurand?" replied Macko. "Where are they? And God knows whether some ill has not befallen Zbyszko since he went to Malbork."

"I know, but the Knights are not quite such curs as you think. At Malbork, at the side of the grand master and of his brother Ulrich, who is a knightly figure, nothing ill could have befallen your nephew, who, I am sure, had letters from Duke Janusz. Unless he challenged some knight there and was killed, for at Malbork there are always a number of famous knights from all over the world."

"Eh, I am not too afraid of that," said the old knight. "As long as they have not shut him up in a dungeon or killed him through treacherous means, as long as he had some iron in his hand, I am not too concerned. Only once did he find someone stronger than himself, who overthrew him in the lists, and that was Henry, Duke of Mazovia—the same duke who was bishop here and who fell in love with the fair Ryngalla. But Zbyszko was a mere stripling at that time. Besides, there is only one knight whom he would definitely challenge, and that is the one I vowed to challenge also, who is here."

So saying he indicated by a glance Lichtenstein, who was talking with the Voivode of Plock.

The duchess frowned.

"You may have vowed or not," she said in the stern, dry tone which she always used when anger started to rise within her, "but remember this, that he is our guest here; and if you wish to be our guest you must observe our customs."

"I know, worshipful lady," replied Macko. "I already pulled around my belt and was going towards him, but I stopped, remembering that he might be an envoy."

"He is an envoy. And he is a man of importance among his own people, on whose advice the master himself relies, and whom he would not deny a favor. Maybe it was God's doing that he was not at Malbork during your nephew's visit, for they say that Lichtenstein, though of an honorable family, is obstinate and vindictive. Did he recognize you?"

"He could hardly recognize me, since he has seen me but little.

On the road from Tyniec we were wearing helmets, and after that I was once in front of him, to speak of Zbyszko's case, but it was in the evening, for the matter was urgent; and once we saw one another at court. Since then I have changed in appearance, and my beard has grown much greyer. I observed now that he looked at me rather long, but evidently only because I am speaking with you, gracious lady, for he turned quite calmly in another direction. Zbyszko he would have recognized, but me he has forgotten, and perhaps he has not heard of my vow, having better things to think of."

"What better things?"

"They say that Zawisza of Garbowo has made a vow to challenge him also, and Powala of Taczewo, and Martin of Wrocimowice, and Paszko the Thief, and Lis of Fair-Ground. Each of them, gracious lady, could deal with ten such as he, and what when there are so many! It would have been better for him not to be born than to have even one such sword over his head. But not only shall I not remind him of my vow, but I shall try to enter into his confidence."

"Why will you do that?"

Macko's face became cunning, like the face of an old fox.

"So that he may give me a letter, with which I can pass safely through the country of the Teutonic Knights and rescue Zbyszko in case of need."

"Is that worthy of your knightly honor?" asked the duchess with a smile.

"It is worthy," replied Macko firmly. "If, for example, I were to attack him in battle from the rear and not call out to him to defend himself, I should bring shame upon myself; but to outwit an enemy in time of peace, no true knight would be ashamed of that."

"I will introduce you," replied the duchess.

And greeting Lichtenstein, she introduced Macko to him, thinking that, even should Lichtenstein recognize him, no great matter would come of it.

But Lichtenstein did not recognize him, for he had seen him only in his helmet on the Tyniec road, and afterwards he had spoken with him only once, in the evening when Macko had come to ask him to forgive Zbyszko's fault.

However, he bowed proudly enough, and it was only when he saw behind the knight two beautiful, richly dressed pages that he thought that not everyone could have such attendants, and his face brightened somewhat, although he did not cease to pout his lips proudly as he always did when he was speaking to anyone but a ruling duke.

The duchess said, pointing to Macko:

"This knight is going to Malbork, and I myself recommend him to the favor of the grand master, but he has heard of the respect which you enjoy in the Order and would like to have a letter from you too."

Then she went over to the bishop, while Lichtenstein fixed his cold, steely eyes on Macko.

"What reason leads you, sir, to visit our pious and modest capital?" he asked.

"An honest reason and a pious reason," replied Macko, raising his eyes. "If it were otherwise, the gracious duchess would not have spoken for me. But besides my pious vows I should like also to meet your master, who brings peace on earth and is the most famous knight in the world."

"The man for whom the worshipful duchess, our lady and benefactress, speaks will not have to complain of our poor hospitality. However, it will be difficult for you to see the master, since he went a month ago to Danzig, and from there was intending to go to Konigsberg and still farther towards the border; for though he is a lover of peace, he must defend the inheritance of the Order against the treacherous attacks of Witold."

Hearing that, Macko became so visibly worried that Lichtenstein, from whose eyes nothing could be concealed, said:

"I see that you were just as anxious to become acquainted with the grand master as to perform your pious vows."

"I was, indeed I was!" replied Macko quickly. "So war with Witold over Samogitia is already certain?"

"He began it himself, by furnishing aid to the insurgents in breach of his oath."

A moment of silence followed.

"May God grant the Order the success which it deserves!" said Macko. "I shall not be able to make the acquaintance of the master, but I will fulfill my vows."

However, notwithstanding these words, he himself did not know what to do for the time being, and it was with a feeling of great distress that he asked himself: "Where am I to look for Zbyszko now, and where shall I find him?"

It was easy to foresee that if the master had left Malbork to go to the war, there was no use looking for Zbyszko at Malbork—and in any case it was necessary to get more accurate information about him. Old Macko was very anxious, but since he was quick and resourceful, he determined to lose no time and to continue his journey the very next morning. It was easy for him to obtain a letter from Lichtenstein with the support of Duchess Alexandra, in whom the commander had unlimited confidence. At the same time he obtained a recommendation to the constable at Brodnica and to the grand hospitaller at Malbork, in return for which, however, he presented Lichtenstein with a large silver cup of Breslau workmanship; such a cup as the knights were accustomed to put, full of wine, by their bedside for the night, so as to have both a sleeping-draught and a source of pleasure in case of insomnia. This generosity of Macko's somewhat surprised the Czech, who knew that the old knight was not very inclined to load anyone with gifts, and least of all a German; but Macko said:

"I did it because I had made my vow and shall have to fight with him, and it would be unworthy to have designs on a man's life when he has done me a favor. It is not our custom to strike a benefactor."

"But it is a pity to lose so valuable a cup," replied the Czech a little obstinately.

Macko answered: "I am not doing this without some fore-thought, never fear! For if the Lord Jesus in His mercy permits me to overthrow the German, I shall get back the cup and shall take many other valuable things as booty with it."

Then they both began to confer with each other, and Jagienka with them, on what to do next. It seemed reasonable to Macko to leave her and Anulka at Plock under the care of Duchess Alexandra because of the abbot's will, which was deposited with the bishop. But the girl opposed this with the entire strength of her unbreakable will. It is true that it would have been quicker to travel without the two girls, for it would not have been necessary to look for separate rooms at the night quarters, nor to regard the rules of polite behavior, nor to care for their safety, and there were various other reasons of a similar kind. But, as Jagienka stated, they had not come from Zgorzelice merely to remain at Plock. The abbot's will, being deposited with the bishop, would not be lost, and as for them, if it were to turn out that they had to stay somewhere on the road, it would be better for them to stay under the protection of Duchess Anna than of Alexandra, for at Anna's court there was less love for the Teutonic Knights, and therefore more for Zbyszko. Macko, indeed, declared that intelligence was not a feminine quality and that a girl ought not to draw conclusions as if she really possessed it—but he did not oppose too much, and he soon gave way altogether when Jagienka drew him aside and said with tears in her eyes:

"God looks at my heart and is aware that every morning and evening I pray for Danusia and also for Zbyszko's happiness. God in heaven knows best! But both Hlawa and you say that she is already lost, that she will never leave the hands of the Knights alive—and if it is to be so, then I. . . ." She hesitated a little, tears rolled slowly down her cheeks, and she finished softly, "Then I want to be near Zbyszko."

Macko was touched by these tears and her words, but he replied:

"If Danusia is lost, Zbyszko will be so grieved that he will not look at you."

"I do not want him to look at me, I only want to be near him."

"You know, of course, that I should like the same thing as you; but in his first grief he may even make reproaches against you."

"Let him reproach me," she replied with a melancholy smile. "But he will not do it, for he will not know that it is I."

"He will recognize you."

"He will not. You did not recognize me. Tell him that it is not I but Jasko; Jasko is quite like me in the face. Tell him that he has grown, and that is all. It will not even occur to him that it is not Jasko."

The old knight remembered something about knees pressed together, but since boys, too, sometimes press their knees together, that would be no obstacle—particularly since Jasko really had almost the same face as his sister, and his hair had grown long since it had been cut, and he wore it in a net like other noble pages and the knights themselves. For these reasons Macko gave way and began to speak of the journey. They were to start in the morning. Macko determined to enter the lands of the Teutonic Knights and reach Brodnica where he would make inquiries, and if the grand master, contrary to Lichtenstein's report, was still at Malbork, he would go there; while in the opposite case he would follow the Teutonic border in the direction of Spychow, asking on the way for news of a young Polish knight and his retinue. The old knight even thought that it might be easier to learn something of Zbyszko at Spychow or at the court of Duke Janusz of Warsaw than anywhere else.

They started next morning. It was already full spring, and the floods, particularly of the rivers Skrwa and Drweca, hindered their progress, so that it was only on the tenth day after leaving Plock that they crossed the border and found themselves at Brodnica. It was a clean and tidy little town, but at the very entrance there was evidence of the harsh government of the Germans, for a huge stone gallows, erected outside on the road to Gorczenica, was decked with hanging bodies, one of which was a woman's. Atop both the watchtower and the castle was a flag with a red hand on a white field. The travellers did not, however, find the commander himself in the place, for he had marched out with a portion of the garrison and at the head of the local gentry to Malbork. Macko obtained this information from an old knight, blind in both eyes, who had once been commander of Brodnica himself, and now, being attached to the place and the castle, was spending his last days there. When the local chaplain had read him Lichtenstein's letter, he received Macko hospitably, and since he had lived among a Polish population and knew Polish well it was easy to talk with him. It had also happened that six weeks before he had gone to Malbork, being summoned as an experienced knight to the council of war, so he knew what was happening in the capital.

When he was questioned about a young Polish knight, he said that he did not remember names but that he had heard of someone who had been admired, firstly, because despite his youthful years he was already a belted knight, and secondly, because he had jousted successfully at a tournament held by the grand master according to custom for his foreign guests, before starting out on his expedition. He gradually recalled that the young knight had been liked and had been taken into special protection by the valiant and noble brother of the grand master, Ulrich von Jungingen, and that Ulrich had given him "iron letters," with which the young knight had later, so it was said, departed for the east. Macko was immensely pleased with this news, for he had not the least doubt that the young knight was Zbyszko. Accordingly, there was for the time being no reason why he should go to Malbork, for although the grand hospitaller or other officials and knights of the Order who had remained there might perhaps give him still more accurate information, they would certainly not be able to tell him exactly where Zbyszko was. Besides, Macko himself knew best where to find him. It was not difficult to suppose that he was making for Ortelsburg or, if he had failed to find Danusia there, that he was looking for her in the further eastern castles and commanderies.

So losing no time, they went into the country of the Teutonic Knights, towards the east and Ortelsburg. They travelled quickly, for the frequent towns, large and small, were united by highways which the Teutonic Knights, or rather the merchants settled in the towns, maintained in good condition—hardly worse than the Polish roads which had been built under the prosperous and energetic rule of King Kazimierz the Great. Besides, the weather had become beautiful. The nights were starlit and the days bright, while at the time of the midday milking there was a warm dry breeze which filled men's breasts with freshness and health. The corn in the fields was turning green, the meadows were covered richly with flowers, and the pine-woods were beginning to drop their resinous perfume. The whole way to Lidzbark, and from there to Dzialdowo and on to Niedzborz, the travellers never saw a cloud in the sky. It was only at Niedzborz that there was torrential rain in the night, accompanied by thunder, the first that had been heard that spring; but it lasted only a short time, and the next day the morning dawned in streams of light, clear, rosy, golden, and so translucent that as far as eye could see the earth glistened as though besprinkled with diamonds and pearls, while the whole countryside seemed to smile at the sky and rejoice in abundant life.

On such a morning they left Niedzborz for Ortelsburg. The Mazovian border was not far away, and it would have been easy for them to turn aside to Spychow. There was even a moment when Macko wanted to do so, but all things considered he preferred to go first to the terrible nest of the Teutonic Knights, in which a portion of Zbyszko's fate had been so gloomily decided. So he took a peasant as guide and bade him show the way to Ortelsburg, although a guide was not really necessary, for there was a straight highway from Niedzborz, on which the German miles were marked with white stones.

The guide rode fifty or sixty paces ahead, and behind him Macko and Jagienka on horseback, and then, at some distance, the Czech with the fair Anulka; and finally the wagons, surrounded by armed attendants. It was early in the morning. The rosy color had not yet passed from the eastern sky, although the sun had already risen, changing the drops of dew on the trees and on the grass into opals.

"Are you not afraid to go to Ortelsburg?" asked Macko.

"I am not afraid," replied Jagienka. "God is over me, for I am an orphan."

"They do not keep faith there at all. The worst dog was indeed that Danveld whom Jurand slew along with Godfrey. So the Czech said. The second worst was Roger, who fell by Zbyszko's axe. But the old man also is cruel; he has sold himself to the devil. Nothing is known for certain, but I think that if Danusia has perished, it was by his hand. They say that some misfortune befell him, but the duchess told me at Plock that he managed to wriggle out of it. We shall have to deal with him at Ortelsburg. It's good that we have a letter from Lichtenstein, for the curs apparently fear him more than the grand master himself. They say he has great influence and enjoys great respect, but is also vindictive. He never forgives the least wrong. Without this letter I would not be going to Ortelsburg so calmly."

"And what is the name of the old man?"

"Siegfried von Lowe."

"God grant that we may be able to deal with him!"

"God grant it!"

Then Macko laughed and presently said:

"The duchess at Plock told me: 'You complain, you complain, like sheep against wolves, and here three of those wolves are already dead, for the innocent sheep have strangled them.' And, to tell the truth, so it is."

"What about Danusia? And her father?"

"I said the same thing to the duchess. But my heart rejoices that it has been shown how dangerous it is to wrong us. We know how to grasp an axe in our hands and swing it worthily! But as for Danusia and Jurand, that is true. I think, as does the Czech, that they are no longer in this world, but in actual fact no one really knows. . . . I am grieved for Jurand, though. In his lifetime he was worn out with trouble for his daughter, and if he is dead, he died a painful death."

"Every time anyone mentions him to me, I immediately think of my father, who also is no longer in this world," replied Jagienka.

And she raised her wet eyes to the sky. Macko nodded and said:

"He is doubtless sitting at the divine council and in everlasting light, for there never was a better man than he in the whole of our kingdom."

"Oh, there never was indeed!" sighed Jagienka.

Further talk was interrupted by the peasant guide who suddenly reined in his colt and then turned and galloped back to Macko, exclaiming in a strange, alarmed voice:

"Great God! Look, Sir Knight! Someone is coming towards us from the knoll."

"Who? Where?" exclaimed Macko.

"Over there! He must be a giant, or what. . . ."

Macko and Jagienka checked their palfreys, looking in the direction pointed out by the guide, and they did actually see on the knoll, half a furlong or more away, a figure whose dimensions seemed considerably more than human.

"He is right, the fellow is big," muttered Macko.

Then he frowned, suddenly spat to the side, and said:

"May the spell be broken!"

"Why do you say that?" asked Jagienka.

"Because I remember how on a similar morning Zbyszko and I saw perhaps the same giant on the road from Tyniec to Cracow. They said it was Walgierz the Charming. Well, it turned out to be the Lord of Taczewo, but no good came of it anyway. May the spell be broken!"

"That is no knight, for he is going on foot," said Jagienka, straining her eyes. "I even see that he has no weapon, only a staff in his left hand."

"And he is feeling with it in front of him, as if it were night," added Macko.

"And he scarcely moves. Yes! He must be blind, or what?"

"He is blind, blind, as I live!"

They moved their horses forward and after a while stopped opposite an old man who was coming down from the knoll very slowly, feeling his way with a staff.

It was a really enormous old man, although seen from close at hand he no longer appeared to be a giant. They saw that he was completely blind. Instead of eyes he had two red cavities. He also lacked his right hand, in place of which he had a dirty rag tied up in a knot. His white hair fell down to his shoulders, and his beard reached his belt.

"The poor man has neither attendant nor dog and has to grope his way alone," said Jagienka. "Heavens, we cannot leave him without help. I do not know whether he will understand me, but I will speak to him in our language."

She leapt quickly from her horse and, stopping in front of the old man, began to feel for money in a leather pouch which hung from her belt.

The old man, hearing the clattering of horses' hooves and human voices in front of him, stretched out his staff and lifted his head as blind men do.

"Jesus Christ be praised!" said the girl. "Do you understand Christian language, old man?"

But he, when he heard her sweet, young voice, trembled, and over his face passed a strange light as if of emotion and tender feeling; he covered his empty eye-sockets with his eyelids, and suddenly dropped his staff and fell on his knees before her with outstretched arms.

"Please get up! I shall help you in any case. What is the matter with you?" asked Jagienka in surprise.

He did not answer, only two tears flowed down his cheeks, and from his mouth there came a groan-like sound:

"Aa! Aa!"

"By God's mercy! Are you dumb, or what?"

"Aa! Aa!"

He then raised his hand; first he made the sign of the cross, and then he passed his left hand over his mouth.

Jagienka, not understanding, looked at Macko, who said:

"Perhaps he's trying to show you that they have torn out his tongue."

"Have they torn out your tongue?" asked the girl.

"Aa! Aa! Aa! Aa!" repeated the old man several times, nodding his head.

Next he pointed to his eyes and then stretched out his right arm without a hand, while with his left he made a motion like cutting.

Now they both understood him.

"Who did that to you?" asked Jagienka.

The old man again made the sign of the cross several times in the air.

"The Teutonic Knights!" cried out Macko.

The old man sank his head on his breast in sign of assent.

A moment of silence followed. Macko and Jagienka looked at one another uneasily, for they had before them clear evidence of that lack of mercy and lack of measure in punishment for which the Knights of the Teutonic Order were known.

"Their rule is harsh!" said Macko at last. "They have punished him severely, and God knows whether justifiably. We shall get no answer concerning that. If we only knew where to take him, as he must be a man of this neighborhood. He understands our speech, for the common folk are the same here as in Mazovia."

"You understand, don't you, what we say?" asked Jagienka.

The old man nodded.

"Are you from here?"

"No," replied the old man by signs.

"Perhaps you are from Mazovia?"

"Yes."

"From Duke Janusz's domain?"

"Yes."

"And what were you doing among the Teutonic Knights?"

The old man could not answer, but his face took on an expression of such immeasurable pain that the tender heart of Jagienka quivered in yet greater sympathy, and even Macko, although he was not easily moved, said:

"Assuredly the curs have wronged him, perhaps without his fault."

Jagienka pressed a few small coins into the beggar's hand.

"Listen," she said. "We will not leave you. You will come with us to Mazovia, and at every village we will ask you whether it is yours. Perhaps we shall find the right one. Get up now, for we are not saints."

But he did not get up; on the contrary, he bent and embraced her legs, as if giving himself to her protection and thanking her, but at the same time a certain surprise, even disappointment, flashed over his face. It may be that he had thought from her voice that he was standing before a girl, while his hand now felt untanned leather boots, such as knights and squires wore when travelling.

She continued:

"So it shall be. Our wagons will come in a moment, so you will be able to rest and eat. But you will not get to Mazovia very soon, for we first have to go to Ortelsburg."

At that word the old man sprang to his feet. Horror and amazement were reflected in his face. He extended his arm as if to block the way, and strange sounds, which seemed full of alarm, began to come from his throat.

"What is the matter?" exclaimed Jagienka, frightened.

But the Czech, who had ridden up shortly before and had been looking intently at the old man, suddenly turned to Macko with a changed face and said in a strange tone:

"By the wounds of Christ, lord! Permit me to speak to him, for you have no idea who he may be!"

Then without waiting for permission, he hastened to the old man, laid his hands on his shoulders, and asked:

"Do you come from Ortelsburg?"

The old man calmed down, as if struck by the sound of his voice, and nodded.

"Were you not seeking your child there?"

A dull groan was the only answer to the question.

Then Hlawa grew somewhat pale, looked keenly at the old man's features for a moment, and then said slowly and emphatically:

"Then you are Jurand of Spychow!"

"Jurand!" cried out Macko.

But Jurand at that moment staggered and fainted. The torments he had undergone, the lack of food, the fatigues of the road, had deprived him of strength. It was now the tenth day that he had been thus groping his way, wandering and feeling with his stick, hungry, worn out, and uncertain of where he was going. Not being able to ask, he guided himself in the daytime by the warm rays of the sun, while the nights he spent in ditches by the wayside. When he happened to pass through a village or settlement, or meet people, he begged alms with hand and groans, but rarely was he met with pity, for he was generally regarded as a criminal on whom the law had taken just revenge. For two days he had been living on bark and leaves, and had already begun to doubt whether he would ever reach Mazovia—when suddenly he found himself surrounded by tender hearts and the voices of his own people, one of which reminded him of the sweet voice of his own daughter; and when at last his own name was mentioned, his emotions became too much for him, his heart constricted in his breast, his thoughts rushed through his head in a whirl, and he would have fallen on his face in the dust of the highway if he had not been held up by the sturdy arms of the Czech.

Macko leapt from his horse, and the two of them lifted him up and carried him to the wagon train, where they placed him in a cart lined with hay. Jagienka and Anulka brought him around and gave him food and wine, and Jagienka, seeing that he could not hold a mug, gave him the drink herself. Immediately after, he was overcome by an overpowering, sound sleep, from which he was to wake only on the third day.

Meanwhile they held a swift consultation on the spot.

"I'll be brief," exclaimed Jagienka. "Do not go to Ortelsburg now but to Spychow, so that Jurand may be taken care of among his own people."

"See how you take command!" replied Macko. "We must send him to Spychow, but it is not essential for all of us to go; one wagon will be enough."

"I do not take command. I merely think that we might learn much from Jurand about Zbyszko and Danusia."

"And how will you talk with him when he has no tongue?"

"And who, if not he, showed you that he had none? You see that even without talking we have learned all that we needed, and how will it be when we have become accustomed to the signs he makes with his head and hand? Ask him for example, whether Zbyszko returned from Malbork to Ortelsburg, and he will either nod or shake his head. And the same with other things."

"True!" exclaimed the Czech.

"I do not deny that this is true," said Macko, "and I myself had the same idea, only I am accustomed to think first and speak afterwards."

He had the wagons turn back towards the Mazovian border. During the journey Jagienka repeatedly rode up to the wagon in which Jurand was lying, fearing that he might have died in his sleep.

"I did not recognize him," said Macko, "but that is not very strange. He used to be like an aurochs. The Mazovians said that he was the only one among them who could fight with Zawisza himself, and now he's a mere skeleton."

"There were reports," said the Czech, "that he had died under torture, but some people refused to believe that Christians could so treat a belted knight who also had St. George for his patron."

"God granted Zbyszko to avenge him, if only partially. Look what a difference there is between them and us! It is true that of the four curs three have already fallen; but they fell in battle, and no one tore out their tongues in captivity or put out their eyes."

"God will punish them," said Jagienka.

Macko turned to the Czech: "How did you recognize him?"

"I did not recognize him at once either, although I had seen him more recently than you, lord. But something passed through my head, and the more I looked at him the more it continued to do so. He had no beard, his hair was not white, he was a rich and powerful lord; how could one recognize him in an old beggar like this? But when the young lady said that we would go to Ortelsburg and he began to howl, my eyes opened up at once."

Macko reflected.

"From Spychow we ought to take him to the duke, who certainly cannot let such a wrong done to a distinguished man go unpunished."

"They will deny it, lord. They kidnapped his child and denied it, and they will say that the lord of Spychow lost his tongue and hand and eye in the fight with them."

"True," said Macko. "They carried off the duke himself on one occasion. He cannot wage war against them, for his strength is not sufficient, unless our king would help him. People talk and talk about a great war, and there is not even a small one."

"There is with Duke Witold."

"Praise God that at least he despises them. . . . Hey! Duke

Witold, that is a duke! They will not get the better of him even by cunning, for he alone is more cunning than all of them. There were times when the curs pressed him so hard that death was hanging like a sword over his head, but he would wriggle out like a snake and immediately bite them. Beware of him when he fights you, but beware of him still more when he caresses you."

"Is he like that with everyone?"

"Not with everyone, only with the Teutonic Knights. With others he is a good and generous duke!"

Macko began to reflect, as if trying to recall Witold better.

"He's a man quite different from the dukes here," he said at last. "Zbyszko ought to go to him, for under him and through him one can do most against the Knights."

Presently he added:

"Who knows whether he and I shall not meet there, since the best chance of getting vengeance is there."

Then they talked of Jurand again, of his unhappy fate, and the indescribable wrongs he had suffered from the Knights, who first murdered his beloved wife for no reason and then, paying vengeance with vengeance, carried off his child—and tortured him with such cruel tortures as even the Tartars could not have improved upon. Macko and the Czech ground their teeth at the thought that even his release was a new and refined form of cruelty. The old knight promised himself in his heart that he would endeavor to find out everything that had happened and then to repay with interest.

Amid such talk and thoughts the road to Spychow passed quickly. After a fine day the night was calm and starry, so they did not stop to take lodging but only to feed the horses abundantly three times. They crossed the border in darkness, and next morning, under the guidance of a paid guide, they reached the domain of Spychow. Old Tolima evidently ruled there with an iron hand, for scarcely had they entered the forest when two armed men rode to meet them; however, seeing that they were not an army but only a small troop, they not only let them pass without asking questions but conducted them through the swamps and marshes, which were impenetrable for any who did not know the terrain.

At the fortalice the guests were received by Tolima and Father Caleb. The news that the lord had arrived, brought home by pious people, spread like lightning through the garrison. But when they saw in what state he had come from Teutonic hands, such a storm of threats and curses broke out that if there had still been a Teutonic Knight in the Spychow dungeons, no human power could have saved him from a terrible death.

The horsemen wanted to mount at once, ride to the border, catch the first Germans they saw, and throw their heads at the lord's feet; but Macko restrained them, knowing that the Germans stayed within their small towns and forts, while the rural population was of the same blood as at Spychow, only it was kept down by force. Neither the talk, nor the shouts, nor the creaking of the sweeps by the wells waked Jurand, who had been carried to the bed in his room on a bearskin. Father Caleb, his old friend who loved him like a brother, stayed with him and began to pray and implore the Redeemer of the world to give back to the unfortunate man his sight and tongue and hand.

The travellers, worn out by their journeying, also went to rest after the morning meal, and it was late afternoon before Macko awoke and bade a page summon Tolima.

Knowing beforehand from the Czech that Jurand previous to his departure had commanded everyone to obey Zbyszko and had made him heir of Spychow by the mouth of the priest, he said to the old man in the tone of a superior:

"I am the uncle of your young lord, and until he returns I will give the orders here."

Tolima bent his grey head, similar to the head of a wolf, and putting his hand to his ear, asked:

"Then you, lord, are the noble knight of Bogdaniec?"

"Yes," replied Macko. "How do you know about me?"

"Because the young lord, Zbyszko, expected you and asked about you."

Hearing that, Macko sprang to his feet and, forgetting his dignity, cried out: "Zbyszko at Spychow?"

"He was, lord; two days ago he went away."

"Dear God! Where did he come from and where has he gone?"

"He came from Malbork, and along the way he was at Ortelsburg; but where he was going he did not say."

"He did not say?"

"Perhaps he told Father Caleb."

"Heh, mighty God! Then we passed one another!" said Macko, slapping his thigh.

Tolima cupped his other ear: "What do you say, lord?"

"Where is Father Caleb?"

"With the old lord, at his bedside."

"Bring him here! Or no, I will go to him myself."

"I will bring him," said the old man, and went out. But before he had brought the priest, Jagienka came in.

"Come here! Do you know what has happened? Two days ago Zbyszko was here."

Her face changed in a moment, and her legs, in their close-fitting striped hose, trembled visibly under her.

"He has been here and has gone?" she asked with a racing heart. "Where to?"

"Two days ago, and the priest may know where he has gone."

"We must go after him!" she said firmly.

Presently Father Caleb came in, and thinking that Macko had summoned him to ask about Jurand, he said, anticipating the question: "He is still asleep."

"I have heard that Zbyszko was here!" exclaimed Macko.

"He was. He went away two days ago."

"Where to?"

"He did not know himself. To search. He went towards the Samogitian border, where there is war now."

"By the dear God, tell me, father, what you know about him!"

"I know only what I heard from him. He was at Malbork and gained powerful protection there—that of the grand master's brother, who is the first knight among them. By his command Zbyszko was allowed to search in all the castles."

"For Jurand and Danusia?"

"Yes, but he did not search for Jurand, for they told him he was dead."

"Start from the beginning."

"I will, only let me get my breath and come to my senses, for I am returning from the other world."

"How from the other world?"

"From that world to which a man does not ride on horseback but on a prayer; and from the feet of Christ, our Lord, where I prayed for mercy for Jurand."

"You prayed for a miracle? Have you such powers?" asked Macko with great curiosity.

"Power I have none, but the Redeemer has, and if He wishes He will give Jurand back his sight and tongue and hand."

"If He wished, He could do it," replied Macko, "but it is no small thing for which you have prayed."

Father Caleb did not answer; perhaps he had not heard, for his eyes still seemed vacant, and it was evident that he had indeed lost himself in prayer.

So now he covered his face with his hands and sat for some time in silence. At length he shook himself, rubbed his eyes, and said: "Now ask me."

"In what way did Zbyszko win over the Governor of Sambia?

"He is not Governor of Sambia anymore."

"No matter. Note what I ask and tell what you know."

"He won his favor at a tournament. Ulrich is fond of jousting in the lists, so he jousted with Zbyszko, for there was a large number of knightly guests at Malbork, and the master arranged a tourney. Ulrich's saddle-girth burst, and Zbyszko might easily have unhorsed him, but seeing what had happened he stuck his lance in the ground and held up the tottering knight."

"Well, you see!" exclaimed Macko, turning to Jagienka. "So that is why Ulrich became fond of him?"

"Yes, he would not meet him with sharp lances or with blunt, and became fond of him. Zbyszko, for his part, told him his troubles, and Ulrich, since he cares for knightly honor, was filled with rage and took Zbyszko to his brother, the grand master, to lodge his complaint. God will give him salvation for that, for there are not many among them who love justice. Zbyszko also told me that Sieur de Lorche had helped him much, for they respect him on account of his noble birth and his wealth, and he supported Zbyszko in everything with his testimony."

"And what came of the complaint and the testimony?"

"This: The grand master sternly ordered the commander of Ortelsburg to immediately send all prisoners and captives at Ortelsburg to Malbork, including Jurand. As regards Jurand, the commander wrote back that he had died of his wounds and was buried there near the church. The other prisoners he sent, and among them was the idiot girl, but no trace of our Danusia."

"I know from the squire Hlawa," said Macko, "that Roger, the knight slain by Zbyszko, made some mention of such an idiot girl at the court of Duke Janusz. He said that they had taken her for Jurand's daughter, and when the duchess replied that they knew the real Jurand's daughter and that she was not an idiot, he rejoined: 'You speak the truth, but we thought she had been changed by enchantment.'"

"The commander wrote the same thing in a letter to the grand master—that they had not been keeping that girl in prison but under their care, having rescued her from robbers, who swore that she was Jurand's daughter, transformed."

"And the grand master believed this?"

"He did not know himself whether to believe it or not, but Ulrich burst into yet greater wrath, and induced his brother to send an official of the Order with Zbyszko to Ortelsburg. When these two arrived, they did not find the old commander, who had gone to the eastern castles to take part in the war against Witold, but only a sub-warden, whom the official commanded to open all the vaults and dungeons. Then they searched and searched but found nothing. They also cross-examined the people, one of whom told Zbyszko that he might learn much from the chaplain, since he was able to understand the executioner of the place, a man who is dumb. But the old commander had taken the executioner with him, and the chaplain had gone to some ecclesiastical *congressus* at Konigsberg. They often meet there and send complaints to the pope concerning the doings of the Teutonic Knights, for even the poor chaplains have a hard life under them."

"I am surprised that they did not find Jurand," observed Macko.

"The old commander had evidently released him before that. There was more malice in this release than if they had simply cut his throat. They wanted him, before he would die, to suffer all—nay more—than a man of his condition could endure. Blind, dumb, and without his right hand. Great God! Unable to find his way home or even to beg for bread along the way. They thought he would die of hunger under a fence or get drowned in some lake or river. What have they left him? Nothing but the memory of who he was and the realization of his misery. That is indeed torment upon torment! Perhaps he was sitting somewhere near a church, or by the roadside, and Zbyszko rode by without recognizing him.

Perhaps he heard Zbyszko's voice and could not call out to him. Oh, I cannot refrain from tears! God performed a miracle in causing you to meet him, and therefore I think He will perform a yet greater one, although it is my unworthy and sinful lips which pray to Him for it."

"And what else did Zbyszko say? Where has he gone?" asked Macko.

"He said: 'I know that Danusia was at Ortelsburg, but they have either starved her or carried her off elsewhere. It was old von Lowe who did it, and so help me God, I will not rest until I get him.'"

"He said that? Then he has certainly gone to the eastern commanderies, but there is war there now."

"He knew there was war, and that's why he went to join Duke Witold. He said he would accomplish something against the Teutonic Knights quicker by his aid than by that of the king himself."

"To Duke Witold then!" exclaimed Macko, springing up. And he turned to Jagienka: "Now you see what intelligence is! Did I not say the same? I foretold, as I live, that we should have to go to Witold."

"Zbyszko hoped," said Father Caleb, "that Witold would penetrate into Prussia and storm the castles there."

"If he has time, he will not fail to do so," replied Macko. "Well, praise be to God, we know at least where to look for Zbyszko!"

"We must start at once!" said Jagienka.

"Be quiet!" exclaimed Macko. "It does not befit a page to break in with advice."

And he gave her a meaningful glance, as if to remind her that she was a page, and she controlled herself and was silent.

Macko reflected a while and finally said:

"We shall surely find Zbyszko now, for he can be nowhere else but at Duke Witold's side. But we ought to know whether he has anything else to seek in the world besides those Teutonic Knights' heads which he vowed to get."

"And how can we find that out?" asked Father Caleb.

"If I knew that that priest of Ortelsburg had returned from the synod, I should like to see him," replied Macko. "I have letters from Lichtenstein and can go to Ortelsburg in safety."

"It was not a synod but merely a *congressus*," replied Father Caleb, "and the chaplain must have returned long ago."

"Good! Leave the rest to me. I will take Hlawa with me and two attendants with war-horses—and go."

"And then to Zbyszko?" Jagienka inquired.

"And then to Zbyszko. But in the meantime you will stay here and wait till I return from Ortelsburg. I think I shall not be more than three, or at most four, days. My bones are hard, and fatigue is nothing new to me. But first I will ask you, Father Caleb, for a letter to the Ortelsburg chaplain. He will believe me more readily if I show him a letter from you, for priests always have more confidence in priests."

"People speak well of that priest," said Father Caleb. "And if anyone knows anything, it is he."

Father Caleb prepared the letter towards evening, and the next day, before the sun rose, old Macko was already gone.

CHAPTER XLIV

JURAND awoke from his long sleep in the presence of Father Caleb, and having forgotten in his sleep what had happened, and not knowing where he was, he began to feel the bed and the wall by which it stood. But Father Caleb caught him in his arms and said, weeping tenderly:

"It is I! You are at Spychow! Brother Jurand! God has tested you, but you are among your own people at last. Pious people have brought you. Brother Jurand! Brother!"

And pressing him to his breast, he began to kiss his brow and his empty eyes, and again to press him to his breast, and again to kiss him, and Jurand was at first stunned and seemed not to understand; but at last he passed his left hand over his brow and his head, as if trying to push aside and scatter the heavy clouds of sleep and stupor.

"Do you hear and understand me?" asked Father Caleb.

Jurand signified by a nod of the head that he heard and then reached for a silver crucifix which he had once captured from a rich German knight, took it from the wall, pressed it to his lips and to his breast, and gave it to Father Caleb, who said:

"I understand you, brother! He is left to you, and just as He brought you out of the land of captivity, so can He give you back all that you have lost."

Jurand pointed upwards, to indicate that only in heaven would all be given back to him, while his eye-sockets filled with tears, and boundless pain was reflected on his tortured face.

Father Caleb, seeing that movement and that pain, took it to mean that Danusia was no longer alive, and he knelt by the bed.

"Lord Jesus, grant her everlasting rest," he said, "and may eternal light shine upon her; may she rest in everlasting peace, amen."

But the blind man rose, and sitting on the bed, began to shake his head and wave his hand, as if to contradict and to restrain Father Caleb, but they could not reach an understanding, for at that moment old Tolima came in, and after him the garrison of the castle, the foremen, the foremost and the oldest Spychow yeomen, foresters, and fishers; for the news of the lord's return had already spread throughout the place. They embraced his knees, they kissed his hand, and burst into bitter tears at the sight of that maimed old man, who in no way recalled the former threatening Jurand, defeater of the Teutonic Knights and victor in every encounter. But some, who had gone with him on expeditions, were swept away by a tempest of wrath; their faces paled and took on an expression of fierce resolve. Presently they gathered in groups, whispering, nudging one another, and pushing, until at last one of the fortalice guards stood forth—the blacksmith of Spychow, Sucharz by name—approached Jurand, embraced his legs, and said:

"When they brought you here, lord, we wished to start for Ortelsburg at once, but the knight who brought you forbade us. Permit us now, lord, for without vengeance we cannot remain. Let it be as it was before. They never put shame upon us unpunished, nor shall they now. We used to march against them under your command, and we will march now under Tolima's, or without him. We must take Ortelsburg and let that dog-blood flow—so help us God!"

"So help us God!" a dozen voices repeated.

"To Ortelsburg!"

"We must have blood!"

The flame of wrath immediately laid hold of their ardent Mazovian hearts, their brows began to frown, their eyes to flash, and here and there was heard the gnashing of teeth; but presently their voices and the gnashing of their teeth were heard no more, and the eyes of all were fixed upon Jurand.

His cheeks at first glowed as if the old hate and lust for battle were flaming in them. He rose and again began to feel along the wall. The men thought he was looking for his sword, but his fingers found the cross which Father Caleb had hung up again in its old place.

So he took it for the second time from the wall; his face grew pale. He turned to his men, raised his empty eye-sockets, and held up the crucifix in front of him.

Silence followed. Outside, evening was coming on. Through the open window there came the chirping of birds, which were going to sleep under the eaves of the building and in the lime trees growing in the yard. The last red rays of the sun fell into the room, illuminating the raised cross and Jurand's white hairs.

The smith, Sucharz, looked at Jurand, and then around at his companions, and then at Jurand a second time, and finally crossed himself, and went out of the room on tiptoe. He was followed by the others in like silence, and it was only when they reached the yard that they stopped and began to whisper among themselves:

"Well, what now?"

"Are we not going, or what?"

"He forbade us!"

"He leaves vengeance to God. One can see that his heart has also changed."

And so it was indeed.

Meanwhile in the chamber with Jurand there remained only Father Caleb and old Tolima, and with them Jagienka and Anulka, who had observed a number of armed men passing through the yard, and so had come in to see what was happening.

Jagienka, more daring and certain of herself than Anulka, now went up to Jurand.

"May God help you, Sir Jurand!" she said. "It is we, we who brought you here from Prussia."

At the sound of her young voice his face brightened. Evidently, also, he remembered more clearly all that had happened on the Ortelsburg highway, for he began to thank her, nodding his head and laying his hand several times on his heart. She told him how they had met him and how Hlawa, Sir Zbyszko's squire, had recognized him, and how they had finally brought him to Spychow. She told also of herself, how she and her companion carried sword, helmet, and shield for Sir Macko of Bogdaniec, Zbyszko's uncle, who had left Bogdaniec to seek his nephew and had now gone to

Ortelsburg, but who in three or four days would return again to Spychow.

At the mention of Ortelsburg Jurand did not indeed grow so excited as that first time on the highway, but great alarm was reflected on his face. However, Jagienka assured him that Sir Macko was as cunning as he was valiant and would not be tricked by anyone, and, besides, he carried letters from Lichtenstein, with which he could travel everywhere in safety. These words calmed him considerably. It was also noticeable that he desired to ask about many other things, and not being able to do it, suffered in spirit. Observing this, the keen-witted girl said to him:

"After we have talked together more often, we shall be able to tell each other everything."

He smiled again, extended his hand to her and, laying it on her head, kept it there for some time as though blessing her. He did in fact owe her much, but in addition to that his heart was apparently warmed by her youth and her chatter, which reminded him of the chirping of birds.

From that moment, whenever he was not praying—which he did almost the entire day—or was not sunk in sleep, he desired to have her near him, and when she was not, he yearned for her voice and endeavored in every way to convey to Father Caleb and Tolima that he wanted to have that pleasant page by his side.

She came, since her kind heart took sincere compassion on him, and further, the time passed quicker for her by his side while she waited for Macko, whose stay at Ortelsburg was strangely prolonged.

He was to have returned in three days, and now the fourth and the fifth day had passed. On the sixth, towards evening, the worried girl was on the point of asking Tolima to send men out to reconnoitre, when suddenly a sign was given from a watch-post on an oak tree that horsemen were approaching Spychow.

Presently horse-hooves rang on the drawbridge, and the squire Hlawa, with another attendant from the troop, rode into the yard. Jagienka, who had already come down from the upper room to wait outside, sprang to meet him before he could dismount.

"Where is Macko?" she asked, her heart throbbing with fear.

"He has gone to Duke Witold and bids you remain here," replied the squire.

CHAPTER XLV

JAGIENKA, hearing that she was to stay at Spychow by Macko's command, could not speak for a while in her surprise, grief, and anger; she only looked at the Czech with wide-open eyes, and he, understanding very well what unpleasant news he had brought, said:

"I should like to give you an account of what we heard at Ortelsburg, for there is plenty of important news."

"Is there news of Zbyszko?"

"No, only Ortelsburg news—you know. . . ."

"I understand! Let the attendant unsaddle the horses; you will follow me." Having given the order to the servant, she took the Czech upstairs. "Why has Macko left us? Why must we stay at Spychow, and why have you come back?" she asked all in one breath.

"I have come back," replied Hlawa, "because Sir Macko ordered me. I wanted to go to the war, but a command is a command. Sir Macko said to me: 'You will return, you will attend upon the young lady of Zgorzelice, and wait for news from me. Maybe you will have to take her back to Zgorzelice, as she cannot go alone.'"

"Dear God! What has happened! Has Jurand's daughter been found? Has Macko gone, not to join Zbyszko, but to get him? Have you seen her? Have you talked to her? Why did you not bring her, and where is she now?"

Hearing this avalanche of questions, he bowed low and said:

"May your grace not be angry with me if I do not answer

everything at once, for it is impossible; I will answer one thing after
another in turn, if I find nothing to prevent me."

"Good! Has she been found?"

"No, but there is certain news that she was at Ortelsburg and
that they have taken her away, supposedly to the eastern castles."

"And why must we stay at Spychow?"

"Well, suppose she is found? Then, your grace sees . . . there
would be no reason. . . ."

Jagienka was silent, but her cheeks were flushed.

The Czech continued:

"I thought, and I still think, that we shall not get her alive from
the talons of these accursed knights, but all is in God's hands. I
must begin at the beginning. We arrived at Ortelsburg—and all
was well. Sir Macko showed Lichtenstein's letter to the sub-warden, and the latter, who in his youth had been Kuno's sword-bearer,
kissed the seal before our eyes, received us hospitably and suspected
nothing. If only we had had a few men nearby, we could have taken
the castle, so much did he trust us. . . . We had no difficulty, either,
in seeing the priest, and we talked with him for two nights and
learned strange things, which he knew from the executioner, Diederich."

"The executioner is dumb."

"He is dumb, but he knows how to show everything to the priest
on his fingers, and the priest understands as well as if he were
actually speaking to him. This is a strange and wonderful thing,
and God must have something to do with it. The executioner cut
off Jurand's hand, tore out his tongue, and put out his eye. He is
such a person that when it is a question of a man, he will not
shudder at any torture, and even were he ordered to tear him with
his teeth he would do it. But he will not raise his hand against any
unripe girl—not even if he himself were to be mercilessly tortured.
And the reason is that he once had an only girl, whom he loved very
much and whom the Teutonic Knights—"

Hlawa broke off and did not know how to go on, seeing which
Jagienka said:

"What do I care about a hangman's daughter?"

"But it has to do with the matter," replied the Czech. "When our
young lord slew Sir Roger, the old commander, Siegfried, almost
went mad with rage. At Ortelsburg they said that Roger was his

son, and the priest declared that never had a father loved his son more. And to get his revenge he sold his soul to the devil. The executioner saw this! Siegfried talked with the dead man like I am talking to you, and the corpse laughed from the coffin, ground its teeth, and licked its lips with its black tongue for joy that the old commander promised it Zbyszko's head. But since he could not get Lord Zbyszko, he ordered Jurand to be tortured in the meantime, and then put his tongue and his hand in the coffin that held Roger, who ate them raw. . . ."

"What a terrible story!" Jagienka exclaimed. "In the name of the Father and of the Son and of the Holy Ghost, amen!" And getting up she threw some bits of wood on the fire, for evening had now completely fallen.

"Yes, indeed!" continued Hlawa. "I do not know how it will be at the Last Judgment, for what was Jurand's must go back to him. But this is beyond human reason. The executioner saw it all. When he had fed the vampire with human flesh, the old commander went to bring it Jurand's child, for it must have whispered to him that it wanted to wash it down with innocent blood. But the executioner, who, as I said, will do anything except endure a wrong being done to a girl, had taken up his seat on the stairs beforehand. The priest said that he is not quiet sane, and in point of fact is like a beast, but he understands that one thing, and when there is need, no one can equal him in cunning. So he sat down on the stairs and waited until the commander should come. When the latter heard his breathing and saw his gleaming eyes he was afraid, for he took him for a phantom. Then the executioner struck him with his fist on the neck, thinking that he would break his spine and leave no mark; but he did not kill him. The commander fainted and fell ill with fear, and when he recovered was afraid to lift his hand against Jurand's daughter."

"But he took her away."

"He took her away, and the executioner with her. He did not know that it was the executioner who had defended her; he thought it was some supernatural power, bad or good. But he did not want to leave the executioner at Ortelsburg. He was afraid of his testimony, I suppose. He is dumb, but if there were a hearing in court he might tell through the priest what he eventually did tell. . . . So the priest finally said to Sir Macko: 'Old Siegfried will not kill Jurand's daughter, for he is afraid, and even if he were to order someone else to do it, as long as Diederich lives he will not give her up; particularly as he has already defended her once.'"

"Did the priest know where they had taken her?"

"Not really, but he heard them say something about Ragneta, which is a castle not far from the Lithuanian or the Samogitian border."

"And what did Macko say to that?"

"Sir Macko, hearing that, said to me next day: 'If it is so, maybe we shall find her, but I must hasten to Zbyszko with the greatest speed to prevent them from trapping him with Jurand's daughter as they trapped Jurand himself. Should they tell him that they will give her up if he comes himself to her, he will go, and then old Siegfried will take such a vengeance on him for Roger as human eye has never seen.'"

"True! true!" exclaimed Jagienka in alarm. "If that is why he was in such haste, it is good."

After a moment she turned to Hlawa again.

"He did one thing wrong. He sent you back here. Why should you have to guard us at Spychow? Old Tolima will guard us, and there you might be of use to Zbyszko, for you are both strong and prudent."

"And who, lady, will take you back to Zgorzelice in case of need?"

"In that case, you will come here before them. If they have to send news by anyone, they will send it by you—and you will take us back to Zgorzelice."

The Czech kissed her hand and asked with emotion:

"And in the meantime you will remain here?"

"God is over orphans. I will remain here."

"And will you not find it tiresome? What will you do?"

"Pray to the Lord Jesus to give back Zbyszko his happiness and preserve all of you in health."

Then she burst into tears.

The squire again bowed low before her.

"Such as you," he said, "are like the angels in heaven."

CHAPTER XLVI

BUT she dried her tears and, taking the squire, went with him to Jurand to tell him the news. She found him in the large chamber, with a tame she-wolf at his feet, sitting with Father Caleb, Anulka, and old Tolima. The local sacristan, who was at the same time a minstrel, was singing to them, accompanied by the lute, a song of one of Jurand's old battles with the "obscene Teuton Knights," while they leaned their heads on their hands and listened in deep thought and sorrow. Moonlight filled the room. After a truly sultry day, the night was quiet and extraordinarily warm. The windows were open, and in the moonlight dorbeetles were visible flying through the room and swarming in the linden trees in the yard. On the hearth there still glowed a few brands, by which an attendant was warming a mead mixed with strengthening wine and sweet-smelling herbs.

When Jagienka came in, the minstrel, or rather Father Caleb's sacristan and attendant, was just beginning a new song, "The Fortunate Meeting":

"Jurand is riding, is riding
Bestriding his yew-black steed—"

"Jesus Christ be praised!" interrupted Jagienka.

"For ever and ever," replied Father Caleb.

Jurand was sitting in an armchair, his elbows resting on the armrests, but when he heard her voice he immediately turned towards her and greeted her with his milk-white head.

"Zbyszko's squire has come from Ortelsburg," said the girl,

"with news from the priest. Macko is not returning here but has gone to Duke Witold."

"How not returning?" asked Father Caleb.

She began to tell all that she had learned from the Czech. About Siegfried, and how he had taken vengeance for the death of Roger; about Danusia, how the old commander wanted to bring her to Roger for him to drink her innocent blood, and how the executioner unexpectedly defended her. She did not conceal the fact that Macko hoped he and Zbyszko would find Danusia, would rescue her, and bring her to Spychow, for which reason he himself had gone straight to Zbyszko, while ordering them to remain here.

Her voice trembled at the end, as if with sorrow or grief, and when she had finished there was human silence in the chamber. In the linden trees outside the song of nightingales resounded and seemed to pour through the open window, filling the whole room. The eyes of all turned to Jurand, who had lowered his eyelids and thrown his head back, and gave not the slightest sign of life.

"Did you hear?" Father Caleb asked him at last.

He threw his head still further back, raised his left arm, and pointed to heaven.

The moonlight fell directly on his face, on his white hair, and his blinded eyes, and there was in that face so much suffering and, at the same time, such boundless surrender to the will of God, that it seemed to all of them that they were looking at a spirit released from its bodily fetters; a spirit which, separated once and for all from its earthly life, expected and looked for nothing more from it.

So silence fell again, and again nothing was to be heard but the song of the nightingales, flooding the courtyard and the chamber with waves of sound.

But Jagienka was suddenly seized with limitless pity and a kind of childish love for the unhappy old man; so following her impulse, she went up to him and, taking his hand, kissed it and wet it with her tears.

"I, too, am an orphan!" she cried from the depths of her full heart. "I am not a page at all, but Jagienka of Zgorzelice. Macko took me to protect me from evil men, but now I will stay with you until God gives you back Danusia."

Jurand did not show surprise; it seemed as if he had known

before that she was a girl. He only embraced her and pressed her to his breast, while she, continually kissing his hand, went on in a broken, tearful voice:

"I will stay with you, and Danusia will return. Then I will go back to Zgorzelice. God is over orphans! The Germans slew my father also, but your loved one is alive and will return. Grant that, merciful God, grant it, most compassionate Holy Mother."

Father Caleb knelt down and said in a solemn tone:

"*Kyrie eleison!*"

"*Christe eleison!*" answered the Czech and Tolima together.

They all knelt down, for they understood that it was a litany repeated not only in the hour of death but for the rescue from mortal peril of persons near and dear. Jagienka knelt, Jurand dropped from his chair onto his knees, and they repeated in chorus:

"*Kyrie eleison! Christe eleison!* O God, Father in heaven, have mercy upon us! Oh, Son, Redeemer of the world, have mercy upon us!"

The human voices and the supplication "Have mercy upon us!" mingled with the song of nightingales.

Suddenly the she-wolf got up from the bearskin by Jurand's chair, went to the open window, put its paws on the frame and, raising its triangular muzzle to the moon, began to howl low and plaintively.

Although the Czech adored Jagienka, and his heart was drawing more and more to the fair Anulka, his young, bold spirit impelled him, above all, to war. It is true he had returned to Spychow by Macko's command, for he was obedient, and at the same time he found a certain sweetness in the thought that he would be a guardian and protector to the two young ladies; but when Jagienka herself told him, what was indeed the truth, that there was no danger to them at Spychow and that his duty was to be at Zbyszko's side, he gladly agreed. Macko was not his direct superior, so he could easily justify himself for not having stayed at Spychow by pleading the orders of his rightful mistress, who had bidden him go to Zbyszko.

Jagienka had done it, thinking that a squire of his strength and skill might always be useful and rescue his lord from more than one danger. He had proved this, after all, during the ducal hunt, when

Zbyszko had almost lost his life in dealing with the aurochs. He might be all the more useful in war, particularly such a war as was being waged on the Samogitian border. Wisehead was so anxious to take the field that when he and Jagienka left Jurand's room, he embraced her knees, saying:

"I wish to bow before your grace and beg a good word for the journey."

"What?" asked Jagienka. "Do you want to go this very day?"

"Tomorrow at dawn, when the horses have had a night's rest. It is a terribly long way to Samogitia."

"Then go, for you will the more easily overtake Sir Macko."

"It will be difficult. The old lord is hardened to all kinds of fatigue and started a few days before me. Besides, he will go through Prussia to shorten the way, whereas I must go through the wild forest. He has letters from Lichtenstein which he can show on the way, whereas the only thing I can show to open a free passage for myself is this—"

He laid his hand on the hilt of the short sword at his side, seeing which Jagienka exclaimed:

"But be careful! As long as you are going, you must reach the end of your journey and not lie in some Teutonic dungeon. Even in the forests you must be on your guard, for various evil demons live there now, which were worshipped by the people thereabouts before they accepted Christianity. I remember how Sir Macko and Zbyszko spoke of them at Zgorzelice."

"I remember, but I have no fear, for they are poor creatures, not divinities, and they have no strength. I shall be able to deal both with them and with the Germans, whom I shall also meet, if only war breaks out in earnest."

"Has it not already broken out? Tell me what you heard of it among the Germans."

The prudent youth frowned, reflected a moment, and then said:

"It has broken out, and it has not broken out. We inquired diligently of everything, and particularly Sir Macko, who is cunning and knows how to get around every German. He pretends to ask about something else, he feigns friendship, he never gives himself away, but hits the mark and draws out news from everyone as if he were getting fish on a hook. If your grace will listen patiently, I will tell you. Some years ago Duke Witold, having designs against the Tartars and wishing to assure peace on the German side, yielded Samogitia to the Germans. There was great friendship and accord between them. He allowed them to build castles; nay, he even helped them. He used to meet the grand master on an island, where they ate and drank and vowed friendship. Even hunting in those forests was not forbidden to the Teutonic Knights, and whenever the unhappy Samogitians rose in revolt against the Order, Duke Witold helped the Germans and sent his armies to their aid, for which reason it was muttered throughout Lithuania that he was betraying his own blood. All this was told us by the sub-warden of Ortelsburg, who also praised the Order's rule in Samogitia, saying that they had sent the Samogitians priests to christen them and grain in time of famine. So, indeed, they did, for the grand master, who has more fear of God than the others, ordered them to do so. But in return they carried off the Samogitians' children to Prussia and dishonored their women before the eyes of their husbands and brothers; and if any man opposed them, they hanged him. And for that reason, young lady, there is war."

"And Duke Witold?"

"For a long time the duke shut his eyes to the wrongs done in Samogitia and favored the Teutonic Knights. It wasn't too long ago that the duchess, his wife, went on a visit to Prussia—indeed, to very Malbork. There she was received as if she had been the Queen of Poland herself. This happened not too long ago, not too long ago! She was loaded down with gifts, and no one could count the number of tournaments, banquets, and various wonders in every town. People thought that the friendship between the Teutonic Knights and Duke Witold would last forever, but suddenly he had a change of heart."

"Judging from what my father and Macko used to say, his heart changes often."

"Not against virtuous men, but against the Teutonic Knights, for this reason, that they themselves never keep faith in anything. Now they wanted him to hand over runaways. He told them he would hand over men of base condition, but he would not think of handing over a freeman, since freemen have the right to live where they wish. Then their relations grew sour, and they began to write letters of complaint and to threaten each other. Hearing that, the Samogitians fell upon the Germans. They cut down garrisons, they stormed small castles, and now they are falling upon Prussia itself, while Duke Witold not only does not check them but even laughs at the concerns of the Germans and secretly sends aid to the Samogitians."

"I understand," said Jagienka. "But if he aids them in secret, there is as yet no war."

"There is with the Samogitians, and even with Witold there is, in fact. The Germans are going in all directions to defend their border castles. They would gladly make a great raid on Samogitia, but for that they must wait long, till winter, for the country is marshy, and knights are unable to fight in it. Where a Samogitian can pass, a German will sink. So winter is a friend of the Germans. When the frosts set in, the whole power of the Order will move, and Duke Witold will go to the aid of the Samogitians—and he will go with the permission of the Polish king, who is sovereign lord both of the grand duke and the whole of Lithuania."

"Then perhaps there will be war with the king too?"

"People say so, both here among us and over there among the Germans. Apparently the Teutonic Knights are already begging for aid in all the courts, and their heads are hot under their hoods, as usual with thieves, for the power of the king is no joke, after all; and the Polish knighthood, if anyone speaks of a Teutonic Knight, immediately spit into their hands and make ready for action."

Jagienka sighed on hearing all this.

"A man always has a merrier life in this world than a girl," she said. "For example, you will go to the war, as Zbyszko and Macko did, while we shall stay here at Spychow."

"How can it be otherwise, young lady? You will stay, but in complete safety. Even now the name of Jurand is terrible to the Germans, as I saw myself at Ortelsburg, for when they learned that he was at Spychow, they were immediately seized with fear."

"We know that they will not come here. The marsh protects us, as does old Tolima. But it will be hard to sit still without any news."

"If anything happens, I will let you know. Even before our departure for Ortelsburg, two good servants here were preparing to go to the war of their own will, and Tolima could not forbid them, for they are nobles from Lekawica. Now they will go with me, and if anything happens, I will straightaway send one of them here with the news."

"God reward you! I always knew that you had good sense in every enterprise. For your kindness to me and for your goodwill, I shall be grateful to you until death."

The Czech knelt on one knee.

"I have only had benefits from you," he said. "Sir Zych took me captive at Boleslawiec when I was a lad and gave me my freedom without ransom, but service with you has been dearer to me than freedom. God grant me to shed my blood for you, my lady!"

"God conduct you and bring you back again!" replied Jagienka, extending her hand to him.

But he preferred to bend down and kiss her feet in order to pay her the greater honor; then he lifted his head and, without rising from his knees, said shyly and with humility:

"I am a simple youth, but a noble and your faithful servant. Give me some keepsake for the road. Do not refuse me! The time of war is at hand, and, as St. George is my witness, I shall be found in the front and not at the rear!"

"What kind of keepsake are you asking for?" inquired Jagienka with some surprise.

"Give me a strip of something, for if I come to die, it will be easier if I'm wearing a headband of yours."

And again he bent to her feet and then placed his hands together and implored her, looking in her eyes. But Jagienka's face reflected grave sorrow—and presently she replied, as if with an outburst of involuntary bitterness:

"Ah, my dear! Do not ask me for that, for my ribbon will do you no good. Let someone who is happy herself give you something; that will bring you good fortune. But, in truth, what is there within me? Nothing but sorrow! And what's before me? Nothing but misery! Oh, I shall not be able to give you, nor anyone else, good fortune, for I cannot bestow what I do not have. Oh, Hlawa, I feel so wretched that, that—"

She stopped suddenly, feeling that if she said another word she would burst into tears; even as it was a cloud seemed to come over her eyes. The Czech was greatly moved. He understood that it would be bad for her to return to Zgorzelice, within reach of the clutching hands of Cztan and Wolf, and equally bad to stay at

Spychow, where sooner or later Zbyszko might come with Danusia.
Hlawa understood perfectly all that was happening in her heart,
but as he saw no help for her unhappiness, he only embraced her
feet again, repeating:

"Oh! To die for you! To die for you!"

"Rise," she said, "and let Anulka give you a ribbon to take to the
war, or some other keepsake, for she has looked on you joyfully for
some time."

And she called her, and Anulka came out quickly from the
adjoining chamber. Listening as she had been behind the door, she
had not showed herself sooner through shyness, although she was
burning with desire to take leave of the handsome squire. Hence
she came out embarrassed, with beating heart, her eyes shining
both with tears and sleepiness; and dropping her eyelids, she stood
before him like an apple blossom, unable to utter a word.

Hlawa felt for Jagienka not only the most profound attachment
but also honor and reverence, so he did not dare to reach out for
her even in thought. On the other hand, he often did reach out for
Anulka; feeling the blood running swiftly through his veins, he
could never resist her charm. He was possessed by it all the more
now, particularly because of her confusion and tears, through
which love appeared like a golden bed of a stream through clear
water.

So he turned to her and said:

"You know I am going to war; maybe I shall perish. Do you not
feel sorry for me?"

"Yes!" she replied in her high girlish voice.

And she began to shed tears, for she always had them ready. The
Czech was moved to the utmost and kissed her hands, stifling in
the presence of Jagienka his desire for more intimate kisses.

"Tie a ribbon around him, or give him some keepsake for the
road, so that he may fight under your sign," said Jagienka.

But it was not easy for Anulka to give him anything, wearing
man's attire as she was. She began to look. No headband, no
ribbon! And since their women's clothes were still inside boxes,
untouched since they had left Zgorzelice, she fell into no small
perplexity, from which Jagienka saved her again, advising her to
give him the net she was wearing on her head.

"Dear God, let it be the net then!" exclaimed Hlawa with some amusement. "I will hang it on my helmet, and unhappy will be the mother of that German who tries to get it."

So Anulka put both hands to her head, and presently bright rays of hair fell down on her back and shoulders. Seeing her so golden-haired and lovely, Hlawa trembled. His cheeks flushed, then immediately paled. He took the net, kissed it, and stowed it in his pocket; he embraced Jagienka's knees once again and then Anulka's, somewhat more strongly than was necessary, and he said: "Let it be so!" Then, without another word, he went out of the chamber.

Though he was travel-weary and had had no rest, he did not go to bed. He drank deeply the whole night with the two young nobles from Lekawica, who were to go to Samogitia with him. Yet he did not get drunk—at the first light of dawn he was already in the yard, where the horses were waiting, ready for the road.

In the wall over the wagon-house a membrane window opened slightly, and blues eyes looked out through the crack into the yard. The Czech saw them and wanted to move towards them to show the net fastened to his helmet, and to take leave once again, but he was prevented by Father Caleb and old Tolima, who came out to give him advice for the road.

"Go to the court of Duke Janusz," said Father Caleb. "Maybe Sir Macko has gone there also. In any case you will find sure tidings, for you do not lack acquaintances there. The roads from there to Lithuania are known, and you will easily find a guide through the forests. You wish, doubtless, to go to Lord Zbyszko, but do not go straight to Samogitia, for there is a strip of Prussian territory in the way; go through Lithuania. Beware lest the Samogitians slay you before you shout out who you are; it will be different if you come from the direction of Duke Witold. God bless you and both those knights! May you return in health and bring back the child, in which intention I will lie crosswise every day from vespers until first star-rise!"

"Thank you, father, for your blessing," replied Hlawa. "It will be no easy task to rescue the victim alive from those devils' hands, but all is in the hands of our Lord Jesus, and hope is better than sorrow."

"Indeed it is better, so do not lose it. Yes, I cherish hope, although my heart is not without fear. The worst is that Jurand himself, if her name is mentioned, straightaway points to heaven, as if he already saw her there."

"How can he see her if he has lost his eyes?"

The priest began to speak, half to the Czech and half to himself:

"It frequently happens that if a man has lost his earthly eyes, he sees things which others cannot perceive. It is so; it is! And it seems impossible that God should let such a little lamb be wronged. What harm has she done to the Teutonic Knights? None! She was innocent as a lily of God, and good to people, and sang like a bird of the field! God loves children and has compassion on human suffering. . . . Nay! Even if they have killed her, He may raise her from the dead, as He did Piotrowin, who rose from the grave and was active for many years afterwards. Go in health, and may the hand of God guard you all and her!"

After having said that, he returned to the chapel to celebrate morning Mass, while the Czech mounted his horse, bowed once again before the half-open membrane window, and rode away, for day had fully arrived.

CHAPTER XLVII

DUKE Janusz and the duchess had gone with a part of their court to Czersk for the spring fishing, since they were extraordinarily fond of the sight and found in it the greatest of pleasures. However, the Czech learned from Nicholas of Longwood many important things touching private affairs, as well as the war. In the first place he learned that Sir Macko had evidently given up the idea of going to Samogitia straight through "the Prussian strip," since he had been in Warsaw a few days ago, where he had found the duke and duchess before their departure. Old Nicholas confirmed all the reports of the war which Hlawa had heard at Ortelsburg. The whole of Samogitia had risen like one man against the Germans, and Duke Witold not only ceased helping the Order but aided Samogitia with money and men, with horses and grain, though he had not yet declared war and was still deluding the Knights with negotiations. In the meantime both he and the Knights were sending envoys to the pope, the emperor, and other Christian lords, with mutual accusations of breach of faith, deception, and treachery. The grand duke had sent his letters with the wise Nicholas of Rzeniewo, who knew how to unravel the threads tangled by German cunning by showing proofs of the measureless wrongs inflicted on the lands of Lithuania and Samogitia.

Meanwhile, as the bonds between Lithuania and Poland had been further strengthened at the diet of Wilno, the hearts of the Teutonic Knights were troubled, for it was easy to foresee that Jagiello, as the suzerain of all the lands owing allegiance to Duke Witold, would be on his side in case of war. Count John Sayn,

commander of Grudziadz, and Count Schwartzburg, commander
of Danzig, had gone to the king by command of the grand master,
to ask what they were to expect from him. The king gave no answer,
although they brought him gifts: swift hunting-hawks and costly
vessels. So they threatened war, but not sincerely, for they knew
well that the master and chapter were afraid in their hearts of the
terrible power of Jagiello and desired to put off the day of wrath
and downfall.

So all negotiations broke down time and again, like threads of
gossamer, and particularly the negotiations with Witold. In the
evening after Hlawa's arrival, fresh news reached the Warsaw castle.
Bronisz of Ciasnoc arrived, a courtier of Duke Janusz, whom he
had sent once before to Lithuania for tidings, and with him came
two important Lithuanian dukes with letters from Witold and the
Samogitians. The news was threatening. The Order was preparing
for war, strengthening its castles, grinding gunpowder, shaping
stone cannonballs, and marching knights and soldiers to the border; indeed, light forces of horse and foot had already burst across
the frontiers of Lithuania and Samogitia from the direction of
Ragneta, from Gotteswerder, and other border castles. Already in
thickets, fields, and villages warlike shouts were heard, and in the
evenings over the dark sea of forests the glow of fires filled the sky.
Witold at last openly took Samogitia under his protection; he had
sent out his governors and had appointed Skirwoillo, a man famed
for his valor, as leader of the armed populace. Skirwoillo had burst
into Prussia, burning, destroying, and ravaging. The duke himself
had pushed his army towards Samogitia; some castles he had pro-
visioned; others, like Kowno, he had destroyed so that they should
not be used as bases by the Knights; and it was no secret to anyone
that when winter set in and frost bound the quagmires and the
bogs, or even earlier, if the summer should prove dry, a great war
would begin, embracing all the lands of Lithuania, Samogitia, and
Prussia; and that if the king came to the aid of Witold, a day must
come on which the German wave would either overflow half the
world or retreat for long ages into its former bed.

But this was not about to happen just yet. In the meantime
groans and calls for justice spread through the world. A letter from
the unhappy Samogitian nation was read at Cracow and at Prague,
and at the papal court and in the kingdoms of the West. It was

brought to Duke Janusz by the boyars who accompanied Bronisz of Ciasnoc. So more than one of the Mazovians involuntarily laid hand to the sword by his side and considered whether he should not join Witold of his own free will. They knew that the grand duke liked the hardened Lechitic nobles, who were as ardent and courageous in war as the Lithuanian and Samogitian boyars, but better trained and better armed. Some were urged on by hatred to the old enemies of the Lechitic race, and others by compassion. "Listen! listen!" the Samogitians called to the kings and dukes of all nations. "We were a free people, of noble blood, but the Order wants to make us into slaves. They do not seek our souls but our lands and cattle. Our poverty is already such that we must beg or rob. How can they wash us with the water of baptism when they themselves do not have clean hands? We want baptism, but not in blood, nor by the sword. We want the faith, but only that which the honorable rulers Jagiello and Witold teach us. Hear and save us, for we are being exterminated! The Order wishes to baptize us in order to put the yoke on us more easily; it does not send us priests but hangmen. Already our beehives, our flocks and herds, and all the products of the soil have been taken from us; already we are forbidden to catch fish or hunt wild beasts in the forests. We implore you. Hear us! For they have bent our once free necks to night labor in their castles; they have carried off our children as hostages; and they dishonor our wives and daughters before the eyes of their husbands and fathers. We ought rather to groan than speak! Our families they have burned with fire; our lords they have carried off to Prussia; great people like Korkuc, Wassygin, Swolko, and Sagajlo they have slaughtered, and like wolves they drink our blood. O hear us! For we are men and not beasts. So we call to the Holy Father to have us baptized by Polish bishops, for we desire baptism with our whole hearts, but baptism in the water of grace and not in the living blood of destruction."

In such and similar terms did the Samogitians tell their wrongs; so when their complaints were heard at the Mazovian court, some knights and courtiers determined to immediately go to their aid, understanding that they need not even ask Duke Janusz for permission, if only because the duchess was Duke Witold's own sister. Hearts in general burned with wrath when it was learned from Bronisz and the boyars that many noble Samogitian youths, carried hostage to Prussia and unable to endure the shames and cruelties which the Teutonic Knights laid upon them, had taken their own lives.

Hlawa rejoiced at this eagerness on the part of the Mazovian knighthood, for he thought that the more men went from Poland to join Duke Witold, the greater would be the war which would break out, and the more certainly might one accomplish something against the Order. He also rejoiced that he would see Zbyszko, to whom he had grown attached, and the old Sir Macko, whom he thought it would be worthwhile to watch in action; and that he would see not only them but new, wild countries, unknown towns, knights and armies he had never seen before, and, finally, Duke Witold himself, whose fame at that time resounded widely through the world.

Thinking thus, he determined to go "by great and urgent marches," never stopping longer than necessary to rest his horses. The boyars who had come with Bronisz of Ciasnoc and several other Lithuanians who were at the duke's court, knowing as they did all the roads and passages, were to conduct him and the Mazovian volunteers from settlement to settlement, from fort to fort, through the pathless, immeasurable forests that covered the greater part of Mazovia and Lithuania and Samogitia.

CHAPTER XLVIII

IN the forest, five miles to the east of Kowno, which Witold himself had destroyed, stood the main forces of Skirwoillo. In case of necessity these forces could move with lightning speed from place to place, making sudden raids either on the Prussian border or on the castles, large and small, which were still in the hands of the Knights, and spreading the flames of war throughout the whole region. There the trusty squire found Zbyszko, and with him Macko also, who had arrived only two days before. After greeting Zbyszko, the Czech slept the whole night like a log, and it was only in the evening of the second day that he went to greet the old knight. Macko, being tired and cross, received him in a bad mood, asking why he had not obeyed his commands and remained at Spychow; and it was only when Hlawa found a suitable moment, in which Zbyszko was not in the tent, and pleaded Jagienka's express command as his excuse, that Macko's sourness was dispelled.

He told him also that, besides her command and besides his inborn love of war, he had been brought in this direction by the desire to send a messenger with news to Spychow, should it be necessary. "The young lady," he said, "who has a spirit like an angel, prays herself for Jurand's daughter, though it is not in her own interest to do so. But to everything, there must be an end. If Jurand's daughter is dead, may God grant her everlasting light, for she was as innocent as a lamb; but if she is found, then we must let my young lady know as soon as possible, so that she may leave

Spychow at once and not after the return of Jurand's daughter, when she would seem to be driven out with shame."

Macko listened with reluctance, repeating form time to time: "That has nothing to do with you." But Hlawa, determined to speak frankly, was not deterred, and finally said:

"It would have been better for the lady to remain at Zgorzelice; the journey was in vain. We persuaded the unhappy girl that Jurand's daughter was dead, but perhaps it will turn out differently."

"And who said that she was dead, if not you?" asked Macko angrily. "You ought to have kept your mouth shut. I took her with me because she was afraid of Cztan and Wolf."

"That was just an excuse," replied the squire. "She could have remained safely at Zgorzelice, for each of them would have hindered the other. But you were afraid, lord, that in case of Danusia's death Zbyszko might lose my young lady also, and therefore you took her with you."

"Why have you become so insolent? Are you already a belted knight and not a servant?"

"A servant I am, but a servant of the young lady, and therefore I am anxious that she should not be shamed."

Macko reflected gloomily, for he was not pleased with himself. More than once he had reproached himself for having taken Jagienka from Zgorzelice. He felt that there was something humiliating for her to be thus taken to Zbyszko, and if Danusia should be found, there would be more humiliation. He felt also that in the Czech's bold words there was truth, for though he had taken Jagienka to bring her to the abbot, he might have, when he learned of the abbot's death, left her at Plock; but he had brought her all the way to Spychow in order that, in case of certain developments, she might be near to Zbyszko.

None the less, wanting to convince the Czech and himself, he said: "Why, it never came into my head; she insisted herself on coming."

"Of course, she insisted, because we had persuaded her that the Lady Danusia was dead and that her brothers would be safer without her than with her; so she came."

"It was you who persuaded her!" shouted Macko.

"It was I, and the fault is mine. But now the truth must come out. We have to get results, lord, or else it would be better to perish."

"What will you get," asked Macko impatiently, "with such an army, in such a war? If things improve, it will be only in July, for the Germans have two campaigning seasons—winter and a dry summer. There's no fire here, only smouldering. Duke Witold is said to have gone to Cracow to talk with the king and obtain his permission and his aid."

"But there are castles of the Teutonic Knights in this neighborhood. If we were to capture only two of them we might find Jurand's daughter, or we might get news of her death."

"Or we might get nothing."

"But Siegfried carried her off in this direction. They told us so at Ortelsburg and everywhere else, and we thought so ourselves."

"Have you seen this army? Go out of this tent and take a look. Some of them have only clubs, and some have bronze swords from their great-grandfathers."

"Bah! I heard they are good fighters!"

"But they cannot take castles, particularly those of the Teutonic Knights, with nothing but naked bellies."

Further talk was interrupted by the arrival of Zbyszko and Skirwoillo, the leader of the Samogitians. The latter was a man of short stature, but sturdy and broad-shouldered. His chest was so convex that it almost looked like a hump, and his extraordinarily long arms nearly reached his knees. In general he recalled Zyndram of Maszkowice, the famous knight whom Macko and Zbyszko had met at Cracow, for he had the same enormous head and the same bowlegs. It was said that he was skilled in waging war. His life had been spent in the field of battle, fighting the Tartars for long years in Ruthenia, and the Germans, whom he hated like the plague. In those wars he had learned Ruthenian and, afterwards, at the court of Witold, a little Polish. Of German he knew, or at least used, only three words—fire, blood, and death. His enormous head was always full of military schemes and ruses, which the Teutonic Knights could neither foresee nor prevent—and that's why they were afraid of him in the border commanderies.

"We were speaking of a raid," Zbyszko said to Macko with unusual animation, "and therefore we have come to you for your experienced opinion."

Macko had Skirwoillo sit down on a pine-stump covered with bearskin, and then he ordered an attendant to bring a keg of mead, from which the knights drew with pewter mugs and drank. When they had sufficiently refreshed themselves, he asked:

"So you want to make a raid?"

"I want to destroy German castles."

"Which?"

"Ragneta or New Kowno."

"Ragneta," said Zbyszko. "Four days ago we were at New Kowno, and they defeated us."

"That is so," said Skirwoillo.

"How did they do it?"

"Very well."

"Wait," said Macko, "I do not know this country. Where is New Kowno, and where is Ragneta?"

"From here to Old Kowno is not quite a league," replied Zbyszko, "and from Old to New Kowno is another league. The castle is on an island. We wanted to cross to it, but they defeated us as we were making the attempt. They pursued us for half a day, until we concealed ourselves in the forest, and our army was so scattered that some of our men were not found until this morning."

"And Ragneta?"

Skirwoillo extended his long arm to the northward and said: "Far! Far!"

"That's why we should attack it!" replied Zbyszko. "There is peace in that region, for all the armed men from that side of the border have been sent towards us. The Germans there do not expect any attack now, so we shall fall upon them unawares."

"That makes sense," said Skirwoillo.

But Macko asked:

"Do you think it will be possible to take the castle?"

Skirwoillo shook his head in sign of negation, and Zbyszko said:

"The castle is strong, so the only chance would be by surprise. But we will devastate the country, burn villages and towns, destroy foodstuffs, and above all take prisoners, among whom may be people of importance, and these the Teutonic Knights will gladly ransom or exchange."

Here he turned to Skirwoillo:

"You yourself, duke, admitted that I make sense, and now consider this: New Kowno is on an island. We shall not destroy any villages there, nor carry off any flocks, nor take any prisoners; and, besides, they have only just defeated us. Let us rather go where we are not expected."

"Those who have defeated others are the least likely to expect an attack," muttered Skirwoillo.

Now Macko began to speak, and he supported Zbyszko's opinion. He thought that the young man would have a better chance of learning something at Ragneta than at New Kowno, and that at Ragneta it would be easier to take at least one important captive, who might be exchanged. He also thought that it was better to go farther and fall unawares upon a less well-guarded region than to attack an island defended by nature and guarded, in addition, by a strong castle and a victorious garrison.

He therefore spoke clearly, like a man experienced in war, and cited such strong reasons as might have convinced anyone. The others listened attentively. Skirwoillo from time to time raised his eyebrows, as if in sign of assent, and sometimes he muttered: "That makes sense." At length he sank his huge head between his broad shoulders, so that he looked exactly like a hunchback, and plunged deep into thought.

After a certain time he got up and, without saying anything, began to take his leave.

"Well, duke, how will it be?" asked Macko. "In which direction shall we go?"

He answered: "To New Kowno." And he went out of the tent.

Macko and the Czech looked at Zbyszko for some time in surprise, and then the old knight slapped his thigh and exclaimed:

"Ha! What a stump! He appears to listen and listen, and then sticks to his own opinion. What a waste of words. . . ."

"I've heard that he was like that," replied Zbyszko. "Indeed, the whole nation here is obstinate like few others. They listen to a man's opinion and then act as if the wind had carried away his words."

"Then why does he ask?"

"Because we are belted knights, and because he wants to consider everything from both sides. But he is not stupid."

"It may be that they are expecting us least of all at New Kowno," observed the Czech, "for the very reason that they have just defeated you. In that he was right."

"Let us go and look at the men whom I am to lead," said Zbyszko, who felt cramped in the tent. "We must tell them to be ready."

They went out. Over the camp, night had now fallen, cloudy and dark, lit up only by the fires around which the Samogitians were sitting.

CHAPTER XLIX

FOR Macko and Zbyszko, who had served with Witold before and had seen enough of the Lithuanian and Samogitian warriors, the sight of the encampment was nothing new; but the Czech looked at it with interest, considering in his mind what might be expected of such men in battle and comparing them with the Polish and German knighthood. The camp was pitched on a plain, surrounded by forest and marsh, and therefore completely safe from attack, for no other army would have been able to make its way through those treacherous quagmires. The plain itself on which the huts stood was also slushy and muddy, but the Samogitians had cut pine and fir branches and thrown them down so thickly that their men rested as well as if the place had been quite dry. For Duke Skirwoillo they had quickly constructed a *numa*, a Lithuanian hut made of earth and rough wooden logs. For the more important men, fifty or sixty huts had been woven of branches, while the common warriors sat around their fires under the open sky, protected from changes of weather and from rain only by the sheepskins and hides they wore on their naked bodies. No one in the camp was yet asleep, for the men, having had nothing to do after their recent defeat, had slept in the daytime. Some were sitting or lying around the bright fires, fed with dry twigs and juniper branches; others raked in the embers, already extinguished and covered with ash, from which spread the smell of baked turnips, the usual food of the Lithuanians, and the steam of roasted meat. Between the fires were to be seen heaps of weapons, piled near at hand so that in case of need it would be easy for each man to grasp his own. Hlawa looked with curiosity at the spears, with their long, narrow points made of hardened iron; at the clubs made of young oak-trees, studded with nails or stones; at the short-handled axes, similar to Polish hatchets, used by the horsemen, and at the axes with handles almost as long as those of halberds, swung by the footmen. Among them were some even of bronze, which had come down from earlier times when iron was still little used in these remote parts. Some swords were likewise made of bronze, but the majority were of good steel from Novgorod. The Czech handled the spears, swords, and axes, and the tarry bows, tempered in fire, and looked at their excellence by the light of the flames. There were not many horses near the campfires, since the herds were feeding in the forests and on the meadows not far away, under the care of watchful grooms; but, since the more important boyars wanted to have their steeds within call, there were some fifty or sixty of them within the camp; their lords' thralls fed them by hand as they stood. Hlawa was amazed by the shaggy bodies of these horses, which were unusually small, with powerful shoulders, and in general were so strange that the knights of the West took them for some entirely different kind of forest beast, resembling unicorns more than real horses.

"Large war stallions would be of no use here," said the experienced Macko, recalling his former service with Witold, "for a large horse would sink at once in the bogs, while these horses can pass everywhere almost as easily as a man."

"But in the field they would be unable to face the large German steeds," replied the Czech.

"True. But, on the other hand, a German cannot escape if he is fleeing from a Samogitian, nor can he catch a Samogitian who is fleeing before him, for these horses are as swift as, or even swifter than, the Tartar breed."

"That's surprising. When I saw the Tartar prisoners whom Sir Zych brought back to Zgorzelice, they were not tall, and any horse might have carried them, whereas these people are quite big."

The Samogitians were, indeed, impressively built. In the light of the campfires their broad chests and powerful arms could be seen under their sheepskins. Man for man they were on the lean side, but sturdy and tall. In general they surpassed in physique the inhabitants of the other Lithuanian districts, for they were settled in the better and richer lands, where famine, which visited Lithuania from time to time, made itself rarely felt. Yet they were wilder than even the Lithuanians. At Wilno was the grand duke's court; to Wilno came priests from the East and from the West. Embassies visited it and foreign merchants came to it in large numbers; consequently the inhabitants of the town and neighborhood were somewhat accustomed to foreigners. But here a stranger appeared only in the figure of a Teutonic Knight or a Brother of the Sword, bringing fire, captivity, and baptism in blood to the remote forest settlements; so everything here was coarser, rawer, and more akin to ancient times, and more opposed to anything new. Customs and methods of waging war were older, and paganism more stubborn, because the religion of the Cross had been taught, not by gentle messengers of good news, with an apostle's love, but by armed German monks who had the souls of hangmen.

Skirwoillo and the more important dukes and boyars were already Christians, for they had followed the example of Jagiello and Witold. The others, even the simplest and wildest warriors, had a deep-seated feeling in their hearts that the passing of the old world, and of their old faith, was at hand. And they were ready to bend their heads before the Cross, if only it was not borne by hated German hands. "We ask for baptism," they called to all dukes and nations, "but remember that we are men and not beasts to be given, bought, and sold." Meanwhile, when the old faith was dying, like a fire on which no one throws any wood, and their hearts were turning away likewise from the new faith because it was forced upon them by German power, a void was left in their souls, disquiet and grief for the past, and deep sorrow. The Czech, who had grown up from childhood amidst the merry babble of soldiers, amidst songs and noisy music, now for the first time in his life saw a camp so overcome by quiet and gloom. It was only here and there, by the fires which were further from Skirwoillo's *numa*, that the sound of pipes or whistles was to be heard, or the words of some soft song, sung by a *burtinikas*. The warriors listened with lowered heads, their eyes fixed on the glow of their fires. Some, wrapped in hides like forest beasts of prey, were squatting around the coals, their elbows resting on their knees, their faces hidden by their hands. But when they raised their heads as the knights approached, the light of the flames shone on gentle faces and blue eyes, not at all stern or predatory, but having the look of children who are sad and have been wronged. At the outskirts of the camp the wounded from the last battle lay on moss. Soothsayers muttered incantations over them or tended their wounds, laying on them healing herbs, while the men lay in silence, patiently enduring their pain and torment. From the depths of the forest, from the direction of the clearings and meadows, came the whistling of the grooms; from time to time a breeze rose, covering the camp with smoke and filling the dark forest with the soughing of branches. The night advanced; the fires began to die down and go out, and silence fell yet deeper, strengthening the feeling of sadness and depression.

Zbyszko gave orders to the men whom he was leading, and with whom he could easily talk, for there were among them a handful from Plock; then he turned to his squire and said:

"You have looked around long enough; now it is time to go back to the tent."

"I have looked around," replied the squire, "but I am not very pleased with what I have seen. It is immediately evident that these are beaten men."

"Twice beaten: four days ago at the castle and, before that, at the crossing. And now Skirwoillo wants to go there a third time, to suffer a third defeat."

"How is it he does not know that nothing can be accomplished against the Germans with such an army? Sir Macko told me, and now I see myself, that these lads must be no good in battle."

"Yet in that you are mistaken, for they are bold people, like few others in the world. Only they fight in a disorderly crowd, and the Germans in serried ranks. If one can break their ranks, then a Samogitian will more frequently slay a German than a German a Samogitian. The Germans know that and close their ranks, standing like a wall."

"But as for taking castles, it is certainly not to be thought of," said the Czech.

"Because we have no equipment for such work," replied Zbyszko. "Duke Witold has the equipment; and until he comes to join us, we shall not be able to take any castle, unless by surprise or treachery."

Amid this talk they reached their tent, in front of which was burning a great fire, kept up by the attendants, with meat roasting over it. In the tent it was cool and damp, so the two knights and Hlawa lay down on skins before the fire.

Then they took some food and tried to sleep, but could not. Macko turned from side to side. Seeing that Zbyszko was sitting before the flames embracing his knees, he asked him:

"Listen! Why did you advise going so far, to Ragneta, instead of to New Kowno, which is nearby? What was your intention?"

"Something tells me that Danusia is at Ragneta, and there they are less watchful than here."

"We haven't had time to talk the matter over, for I myself was weary, and you were collecting men in the forest after the defeat. But now tell me: Do you want to go on looking for that girl forever?"

"She is not a girl, she is my wife," Zbyszko replied.

Silence followed. Macko understood very well that there was no answer to that. If Danusia had been still Jurand's young daughter, the old knight would undoubtedly have tried to persuade his nephew to renounce her, but in view of the sanctity of the Sacrament the search for her became a plain duty. Macko would not even have put such a question but for the fact that he had not been present either at the marriage or at the wedding feast, so that he unconsciously still regarded Jurand's daughter as a maiden.

"Well!" he said presently. "What I had time to ask during these two days I asked, and you've told me that you know nothing."

"I do know nothing, except that I think the wrath of God is over me."

Meanwhile Hlawa sat up on his bearskin and, pricking his ears, began to listen intently and eagerly.

"As long as sleep does not overcome you, speak," Macko stated to Zbyszko. "What did you see, what did you do, and what did you accomplish at Malbork?"

Zbyszko pushed back his hair, which had not been cut in front for some time and fell down to his eyebrows, sat awhile in silence, and then said:

"If only I knew as much about my Danusia as I know about Malbork! You ask what I saw there. I saw the measureless power of the Teutonic Knights, supported by all kings and all nations, with which I know not whether any other in the world can measure itself. I saw a castle such as I suppose even the Roman emperor does not possess. I saw unending treasures; I saw weapons of war; I saw hosts of armed monks, knights, and soldiers, and relics such as the Holy Father has at Rome—and I tell you that my heart trembled within me, for I thought: How can anyone attack them? Who can overpower them? Who can stand against them? Who?"

"We can and will!" exclaimed Hlawa, unable to contain himself.

Zbyszko's words seemed odd to Macko, so, though he wished to learn all the young man's adventures, he nevertheless interrupted him:

"Have you forgotten Wilno? And have we not fought with them quite a few times shield to shield and face to face? Have you forgotten what ill-fortune they had with us, and how they complained of our obstinacy: that it was not enough to sweat horses and break lances, but that they had to cut our throats or give us their own? There were guests among them who challenged us—and all went away disgraced. Why are you so soft?"

"I am not soft, for I fought at Malbork, where they jousted with sharp lances. But you do not realize the immensity of their power."

The old man grew angry.

"Do you know the extent of Polish power? Have you seen all our banners assembled together? You have not. Their power rests on human wrong and treachery; they do not possess a handbreadth of land which is rightfully theirs. Our dukes received them as one receives a poor man into one's house and loaded them down with gifts; but they, when they had grown in strength, bit the hand which fed them, as shameless mad dogs are wont to do. They seized lands; they took towns by treachery—that is their power! But even if all the kings of the earth came to their aid, the day of judgment and vengeance is at hand!"

"Since you told me to tell you what I had seen, and now you are angry, I prefer to be silent," said Zbyszko.

Macko snorted for a time in anger, but soon calmed himself and continued:

"Let me put it another way. A fir tree stands in the forest like a stern tower. You would think that it would stand for ever and ever, but if you give it a good blow with the head of your axe it will sound hollow, and dust will fly from it. Such is the power of the Teutonic Knights! But I bade you tell me what you had done, and what you had accomplished. You jousted with sharp weapons, you say?"

"I did. They received me at first with arrogance and ingratitude, for they already knew that I had fought with Roger. Perhaps something bad would have befallen me had I not travelled with a letter from the duke and had not Sieur de Lorche, whom they respect, defended me from their malice. But afterwards there were banquets and tournaments, at which the Lord Jesus blessed me. You have heard how Ulrich, the brother of the grand master, showed me affection and gave me a written order from the master himself that Danusia should be delivered to me?"

"People told us," said Macko, "that his saddle-girth burst and that, seeing this, you refrained from striking him."

"I raised my lance, and from that moment he began to hold me dear. Heh, dear God! He gave me some potent letters, with which I could go from castle to castle and search. I thought that the end of my trouble and misery was at hand—and now I am sitting here, in this wild region, without any recourse, in sadness and grief, and every day I feel my yearning worse and worse."

He was silent for a while, and then threw a piece of wood into the fire with all his might, so that sparks flew from the burning brands.

"If that unhappy girl," he said, "is groaning in some castle hereabouts and thinks that I have forgotten her, may sudden death not pass me by!"

And so hotly did he burn with impatience and grief that again he threw a piece of wood into the fire, as if carried away by sudden, blind pain, while the others were amazed, not having supposed that he loved Danusia so much.

"Control yourself!" exclaimed Macko. "How was it with that safe-conduct? Do you mean that the commanders refused to obey the orders of the grand master?"

"Control yourself, lord," said the Czech. "God will comfort you—perhaps shortly."

Tears glistened in Zbyszko's eyes, but he calmed himself somewhat and said:

"These villains opened castles and prisons for me. I went everywhere, I searched everywhere! Then war broke out—and at Gierdawe the constable von Heideck told me that wartime law is different and that safe-conducts given in time of peace have no validity. I challenged him at once, but he would not meet me and gave orders to put me out of the castle."

"And in the other castles?" asked Macko.

"Everywhere it was the same. At Konigsberg the commander, who is the superior of the constable of Gierdawe, refused even to read the master's letter, saying that war is war—and he told me to begone while my head was still whole. I asked at other places—with the same result."

"Now I understand," said the old knight. "Seeing that you would accomplish nothing, you preferred to come here, where at least vengeance may be obtained."

"That is so," replied Zbyszko. "I thought also that I might take captives and perhaps a few castles, but these men do not know how to storm castles."

"Hey! Duke Witold is coming, and then it will be different."

"God grant it!"

"He is coming. I heard at the Mazovian court that he is coming, and perhaps the king will be with him, with the whole of the Polish power."

Further speech was interrupted by the arrival of Skirwoillo, who came unexpectedly out of the shadows and said:

"We are marching."

Hearing that, the knights sprang to their feet, while Skirwoillo put his huge head close to their faces.

"We have news," he said in a low voice. "Reinforcements are on the way to New Kowno. Two knights are bringing soldiers, cattle, and foodstuffs. We shall surprise them."

"Then shall we cross the Niemen?" asked Zbyszko.

"Yes. We know a ford."

"Do they know about these reinforcements in the castle?"

"Yes, and they will come out to meet them, but on the way they will be attacked by you."

Then he began to explain where they had to lie in ambush so as unexpectedly to strike at those who sallied forth from the castle. He planned to fight two battles at the same time and avenge his recent defeats, which might be done the more easily since, after their recent victory, the enemy felt perfectly safe. So he pointed out to them the place and the time when they had to go; he left the rest to their valor and foresight. For their part, they were glad at heart, since they recognized at once that an experienced and skilled warrior was speaking to them. When he had finished he bade them follow him, and returned to his *numa*, in which dukes and boyar captains were already waiting for him. There he repeated his commands and issued new ones, and finally, raising to his lips a whistle made of wolf-bone, he blew a shrill, penetrating call, which was heard from one end of the camp to the other.

At that sound new life began to seethe by the dying fires; here and there sparks began to fly; then small flames gleamed, grew, and increased in number every moment—and by their light could be seen the wild figures of warriors gathering around the piles of weapons. The forest quivered and awoke. Presently the calls of the grooms were heard from its depths as they drove their animals towards the camp.

CHAPTER L

THEY reached the Niewiaza in the early morning and crossed it: some on horseback, some holding on to their horses' tails, some on bundles of osiers. This was done so quickly that Macko, Zbyszko, Hlawa, and those Mazovians who had come as volunteers, marvelled at the skill of the people and understood now for the first time why neither forests nor swamps nor rivers could stop the Lithuanian raids. After leaving the water, not one of them put off his garments or cast aside his sheepskin or wolfskin; they dried themselves standing with their backs to the sun until they were smoking like a pitch-burner's kiln—and, after a short rest, they moved swiftly northwards. It was already dusk when they reached the Niemen. The crossing here was not easy, since it was over a great river, swollen with the waters of spring. The ford of which Skirwoillo knew had changed in places into a hole, so that the horses had to swim more than a quarter of a furlong. The current carried away two men near Zbyszko and the Czech, who tried in vain to rescue them; but in the dark and the rushing water they soon lost sight of them, while the drowning men did not dare to call for help, because their leader had ordered that the crossing should be made in deepest silence. All the rest of the men reached the other shore successfully and remained there without a fire until the morning.

At daybreak the whole army was divided into two sections. With one, Skirwoillo went inland to meet those knights who were bringing reinforcements to New Kowno, while Zbyszko led the second force straight towards the island to surprise the castle soldiers as they came to meet the reinforcements. The day overhead had become bright and calm, but down below, the forest, meadows, and bushes were covered with a thick, whitish fog, which prevented anything being seen at any good distance. This was a favorable circumstance for Zbyszko and his men, as the Germans marching from the castle would not be able to see them and withdraw in time. The young knight was extremely glad and said to Macko, who was riding beside him:

"We will attack first, before they can see us in such a fog. God grant that it may not disperse—at least not until midday."

He hastened forward to give commands to the captains riding at the head of the company, but soon returned.

"Before long," he said, "we shall come to the highway leading from the island ferry into the interior of the country. There we shall take up our position in the thickets and wait for them."

"How do you know about the highway?" asked Macko.

"From local peasants, of whom I have a dozen or more among my men. They are our guides everywhere."

"And how far from the castle and the island will you fall upon them?"

"About a German mile."

"Good; if it were nearer, soldiers might push out from the castle to their assistance; but as it is, not only will they not do so, but they will not hear any shouts."

"Yes, I have thought of that."

"You have thought of one thing; now think of another. If these peasants are trusty men, send forward two or three to let us know when the Germans are coming."

"I have done that."

"Then I will tell you something else. Order a hundred or two hundred men to take no part in the battle, but to slip away as soon as it has begun and cut the road from the island."

"That's the first thing that will be done!" replied Zbyszko. "I have given the order already. The Germans will fall into a trap."

Macko looked at his nephew with satisfaction, glad that, despite his young years, he understood war so well; so he smiled and muttered:

"Our true blood!"

And the squire, Hlawa, was even more glad at heart than Macko, for there was no greater delight for him than battle.

"I do not know," he said, "how these men of ours will fight, but they are advancing quietly and skillfully, and their willingness is obviously great. If Skirwoillo has thought out everything thoroughly, then not one of the enemy should escape alive."

"God grant it!" said Zbyszko. "But I have ordered that as many prisoners as possible be taken, and if a Knight or a Brother of the Order should be found among them, he is not to be killed."

"Why is that, lord?" asked the Czech.

"Take care yourself that it be so. A knight, if he is one of their guests, goes about in cities and castles, sees numbers of people and hears a lot of news, and, if he is one of the Order, then still more than others. As God lives, this is true: I have come here to capture someone of importance and exchange him. This is the only hope that I have left—if it is left."

He put spurs to his horse and pushed forward again to the head of the company, to give his last directions and also escape from melancholic thoughts, for which indeed there was no time, since the place selected for the ambush was not far distant.

"Why does my young lord think that his wife is still living and is to be found in these parts?" asked the Czech.

"Because if Siegfried did not murder her when she was at Ortelsburg," replied Macko, "he may justifiably hope that she is still alive. And if he had murdered her, that Ortelsburg priest would not have told us such things as Zbyszko also heard. It is hard even for the greatest villain to lift his hand against a defenseless woman—nay, against an innocent child!"

"Yes, but not for a Teutonic Knight. Remember Duke Witold's children."

"It is true that they have wolves' hearts, but it is also true that Siegfried did not slay her at Ortelsburg and that he came himself to these parts; so perhaps he has hidden her in some castle."

"If we could only get this island and this castle!"

"Just look at those men," said Macko.

"Yes, yes! But I have an idea which I will tell my young master."

"If you had ten ideas, you could not overthrow walls with spears."

Macko pointed to a row of spears, with which the majority of the warriors were armed, and then asked:

"Did you ever see such an army?"

The Czech had indeed never seen anything like it. Before them advanced a dense mass of warriors, and they advanced without order, for in the forest and among the bushes it would have been difficult to keep ranks. Besides, footmen were mingled with horsemen and, in order to keep up with the horses, held on to their manes, saddles, or tails. The shoulders of the warriors were covered with the skins of wolves, wild cats, and bears, and their heads were stuck with wild boar tusks, stag horns, or shaggy animal ears; so that, had it not been for their upright weapons, their tarry bows, and their quivers full of arrows on their backs, anyone looking at them from behind, particularly in the fog, might have thought that whole herds of wild forest beasts were issuing from their secret lairs and moving forward, driven on by a lust for blood or hunger. There was in this sight something terrible and at the same time as unusual as if one had been watching that miracle called *gomon*, when, as the simple folk believe, wild beasts, and even bushes and stones, leap up and rush forward.

So one of those small landowners from Lekawica, who had come with the Czech, approached him, made the sign of the cross and said:

"In the name of the Father and of the Son! Why, we are going with a pack of wolves and not with men."

Though it was the first time that he had ever seen such an army, Hlawa replied like an experienced man who has learned to know all kinds of things and is surprised at nothing:

"Wolves run in packs in the winter, but the Teutonic dogs' blood tastes good even in the spring."

And, in truth, it was already spring—it was May! The hazelgrowth of the forest was covered with bright green. From the downy, soft mosses, over which the feet of the warriors stepped without noise, peeped out white and blue anemones, young berry bushes, and dentate ferns. The trees, moistened with abundant rains, gave forth the odor of damp bark, and from the ground beneath came the strong smell of fallen pine needles and decaying wood. The sun played in rainbow colors on the drops of water hanging from the leaves, and the birds above sang joyously.

They went forward ever more quickly, Zbyszko urging them on. Presently he rode back to the rear, where Macko and the Czech were with the Mazovian volunteers. The hope of a good battle had evidently animated him greatly, for in his face there was no longer the usual anxiety, and his eyes flashed as they did of old.

"We must march in front now, not in the rear!" he cried out.

And he led them to the head of the company.

"Listen," he said. "Maybe we shall take the Germans by surprise, but if they notice us and are able to form their ranks, then we must the first of our company to attack them, for we have the armor, and our swords are better."

"So it shall be!" exclaimed Macko.

The others sat more firmly in their saddles as if about to charge straightaway. One and another drew a deep breath and felt whether his sword would draw easily from its scabbard.

Zbyszko repeated to them once again that if among the footmen they should find Knights or Brothers with white mantles over their armor, they should not kill them but take them captive; and then he hastened once more to the leaders and soon halted the company.

They had come to the highway that ran from the landing-stage opposite the castle into the interior of the country. In point of fact, it was not yet a real highway, but rather a trail made through the wilderness not long before and levelled only so far as to enable armies and wagons to pass. On both sides rose lofty forest trees, and on both sides lay trunks of old pines cut down to open the road. The hazel undergrowth was in places so dense as to entirely hide the rest of the forest. Accordingly, Zbyszko chose a place by a bend in the road, where those approaching might not be able to see him from a distance, nor have time to withdraw or form their ranks for battle. There he occupied both sides of the track and gave command to await the enemy.

The Samogitians, accustomed as they were to forest life and warfare, dropped down so skillfully behind tree-trunks, mounds of earth, hazel bushes, and tufts of young firs, that it seemed as if the earth had swallowed them up. Not a man spoke, not a horse snorted. From time to time a small or large beast of the forest passed near the concealed men, to dash aside, panting with terror, when it almost touched them. At times a breeze rose and filled the forest with a solemn and majestic sound; at times all was still, and only the distant calling of the cuckoos and the nearby hammering of the woodpeckers were to be heard.

The Samogitians listened to these sounds with joy, for they regarded woodpeckers as heralds of good tidings. The forest was full of them, and their hammering came from all sides, strong and insistent, like the work of men's hands. You would have said that they all had their forges in the forests and had begun their busy labor early in the morning. To Macko and the Mazovians it seemed as if they were listening to carpenters nailing rafters on a new house, and it reminded them of their native homes.

But time passed, and still nothing was to be heard but the soughing of the wind in the trees and the calls of the birds. The fog lying below had thinned; the sun had risen considerably and began to give warmth; and they were still lying on the ground. At last Hlawa, who was irked by the waiting and the silence, bent to Zbyszko's ear and whispered:

"Lord! If God grant that none of the curs escape alive, might we not advance by night to the castle, cross over, and take it unawares?"

"And do you think that boats are not on guard there, and that they have no password?"

"They are on guard, and they have a password," whispered back the Czech, "but captives under the knife will tell us the word, nay, will even call it out themselves to them in German. If we could reach the island, then the castle itself—"

Here he stopped, for Zbyszko suddenly placed his hand over his mouth. From the highway came the croaking of a raven.

"Quiet!" he said. "That is the signal!"

About two paternosters later, a Samogitian on a shaggy pony appeared on the road; the horse's hooves were wrapped in sheepskin, so as to make no clattering and leave no tracks in the mud.

The rider, looking sharply from side to side, and suddenly hearing an answer to his croaking from the thickets, plunged into the forest and was quickly at Zbyszko's side.

"They're coming!" he said.

CHAPTER LI

ZBYSZKO quickly asked how they were coming, how many there were, how many foot, and, above all, how far away they were still. From the answers of the Samogitian, he learned that the detachment did not amount to more than one hundred and fifty warriors, of whom fifty were horsemen, under the command, not of a Teutonic Knight, but of some lay knight; that they were marching in column, bringing empty wagons with spare wheels; that in front of the detachment, at two bow-shots' distance, was an advance guard composed of eight men, which frequently left the highway and examined the forest and the thickets, and, finally, that the force was about a quarter of a German mile away.

Zbyszko was not too glad to hear they were marching in column. He knew from experience how difficult it was to break a disciplined band of Germans in such case and how such a group could defend itself while retreating and fight like a wild boar at bay. On the other hand, he was pleased at the news that they were not more than a quarter of a mile away, for he concluded that the detachment which he had sent out first must already be in the rear of the Germans, and that, should the Germans be defeated, not a living soul would escape. As for the advance guard, he was not too concerned about it. In the expectation that they would come, he had already given his Samogitians orders either to let them pass quietly or, if some of them tried to examine the interior of the forest, to catch them noiselessly to the last man.

But this last command turned out to be unnecessary. The patrol soon appeared. Concealed as they were behind mounds near the highway, the Samogitians saw these men perfectly, as they halted at the bend and began to talk to one another. Their leader, a sturdy, red-bearded German, signalled to them to be silent. It was apparent that he was hesitating whether to go into the forest, but finally, hearing only the hammering of the woodpeckers, he evidently concluded that the birds would not have worked so freely if anyone had been concealed in the forest; so he waved his hand and led his patrol farther.

Zbyszko waited until they had disappeared around the next turning; then he moved quietly to the highway at the head of the heavier-armed men, among whom were Macko, the Czech, the two small landowners from Lekawica, three young knights from Ciechanow, and a dozen or more of the more important, better-armed Samogitian boyars. Further concealment was not too necessary, so Zbyszko proposed, as soon as the Germans should appear, to advance into the middle of the track, rush upon them, strike, and scatter them. If that succeeded, and if the general battle were turned into a series of single combats, he might be sure that the Samogitians would be able to deal with the Germans.

Again a moment of silence followed, disturbed only by the usual sounds of the forest. But soon there came to the ears of the warriors, from the eastern side of the highway, human voices as well. At first confused and distant, they grew by degrees nearer and more distinct.

Zbyszko led his detachment into the middle of the road and drew it up in the form of a wedge. He himself stood at the head, with Macko and the Czech immediately behind him. In the next rank stood three men and in the one after that, four. They were all well armed; they had not, it is true, the powerful "trees" or lances which knights were wont to use, but which would have been a great hindrance on forest marches; instead, they held in their hands short, light Samogitian spears for the first attack, and had swords and axes at their saddle-bows for fighting in a melee.

Hlawa eagerly pricked his ears, listened, and then whispered to Macko: "Those accursed dogs are singing!"

"But it is strange that the forest is closed before us and that we still cannot see them from here," replied Macko.

Zbyszko, who now considered further concealment and even talking in low tones unnecessary, turned and said:

"It is because the highway follows the stream and turns frequently. We shall meet unexpectedly, but so much the better."

"They are singing something merry!" said the Czech.

And indeed the Germans were singing a song which was certainly not religious, as could be easily recognized from its notes. The listener might also distinguish that only a dozen men or so were singing and that all of them were repeating only one refrain, which resounded through the forest like thunder.

And so they advanced towards death, merry and full of good spirits.

"We shall see them shortly," said Macko.

His face suddenly darkened and took on a wolfish expression, for his soul was unbending and fierce. Besides, he had not yet paid the Germans for that crossbow shot which he had received when he was going to rescue Zbyszko with a letter from Witold's sister to the master. Hence his heart began to storm in his breast and a lust for vengeance to boil over in him.

"I pity the man who engages him first," thought Hlawa, glancing at the old knight.

Meanwhile the breeze carried clearly the refrain which all were repeating in chorus: *"Tandaradei! Tandaradei!"* And straightaway the Czech heard the words of a song which he knew well:

> *"Bin den rosen er wol mac,*
> *Tandaradei!*
> *Merken wo mir's houbet lac . . ."*

Suddenly the song was broken off, for on both sides of the track there came a croaking as noisy and frequent as if there had been a parliament of ravens meeting in that corner of the forest. The Germans wondered where so many could have come from and why all their croaks came from the ground and not from the treetops. The first rank of soldiers rounded the bend and stood thunderstruck at the sight of unknown horsemen facing them.

At that instant Zbyszko bent to his saddle-bow, put spurs to his horse, and dashed forward: "At them!"

Behind him rushed the others. From both sides of the forest rose the terrible cry of the Samogitian warriors. About two hundred paces divided Zbyszko's men from the Germans, who in the twinkling of an eye lowered a forest of pikes against the riders, while the farther ranks turned with equal speed to face both flanks and defend themselves. The Polish knights would have admired their skill if they had found time and if their horses had not borne them at full speed against the glittering, levelled points.

Luckily for Zbyszko, the German horse was in the rear of the detachment, by the wagons. They moved at once, it is true, towards their footmen, but could neither pass through them nor go around them, and consequently could not defend them from the first attack. Meanwhile hosts of Samogitians rushed out of the thickets, like an angry swarm of wasps whose nest a careless traveller has disturbed with his foot. At the same time Zbyszko and his men charged the footmen.

But they charged without success. The Germans thrust the butt ends of their heavy pikes and halberds into the ground and held them so evenly and firmly that the light Samogitian horses could not break the wall. Macko's horse, struck by a halberd on the cannon-bone, reared up on its hind legs and then dug its nostrils in the ground. For a moment death hung over the old knight, but he, experienced as he was in every kind of battle and adventure, withdrew his feet from the stirrups and grasped with his powerful hands the point of German pike, which, instead of entering his breast, served him as a support; then he broke loose, sprang between the horses and, drawing his sword, began to strike at the pikes and halberds, as a fierce hawk falls savagely upon a flock of long-billed cranes.

Zbyszko also drew his sword, for, when his horse was checked in mid-career and sat down almost on its haunches, the young knight had leaned on his spear, breaking it in the process. The Czech, who believed in the axe most of all, threw his at a group of Germans and was momentarily left defenseless. One of the Lekawica landowners fell, and the second one was seized with such mad rage at that sight that he began to howl like a wolf and, after holding back his bloody horse until it reared, drove blindly into the enemy. The Samogitian boyars hewed with their sword-blades at the pike-points and shafts, from behind which looked out the faces of the soldiers, faces paralyzed with amazement and drawn by stubborn determination. But the line did not break. Likewise, the Samogitians who had attacked from the flanks sprang back from the Germans as if from a porcupine. They returned soon, it is true, with still greater impetuosity, but could accomplish nothing.

Some climbed in a flash into the trees by the roadside and began to shoot into the midst of the soldiers, whose leader, seeing this, gave command to withdraw towards their horsemen. The German crossbowmen began to shoot back; so from time to time a Samogitian, concealed in the branches of a pine, fell to earth like a ripe cone and, dying, tore the moss of the forest with his hand or writhed like a fish out of water. Surrounded as they were on all sides, the Germans could not, it is true, count on victory; but seeing the success of their defence, they thought that at least a handful might succeed in escaping from the straits they were in and getting back to the river.

No one thought of yielding, for, as they themselves gave no quarter, they knew that they could count on no pity from a people brought to revolt and despair. Hence they retreated in silence, man beside man, shoulder to shoulder, raising and lowering their pikes and halberds, cutting, thrusting, shooting with their crossbows, as far as the confusion of battle permitted, and drawing nearer all the time to their horsemen, who themselves were engaged in a life-and-death struggle with other detachments of the enemy.

Meanwhile something unexpected happened, which had a decisive effect on the fate of the desperate struggle. The landowner from Lekawica, who had been seized with mad rage at the death of his brother, bent down, without dismounting, and lifted the body from the earth, apparently wishing to secure it from loss and put it in some quiet place where he might more easily find it after the battle. But at the same moment a new wave of frenzy rushed to his head and deprived him of all consciousness of what he was doing; instead of leaving the road, he dashed at the soldiers and threw the body on the points of their pikes, which stuck into its chest, belly, and thighs, and sank under the weight; and before the soldiers could draw them out, he rushed like a madman through the gap thus made into their ranks, overthrowing them like a whirlwind.

Dozens of hands stretched out immediately to pull him down, dozens of pikes pierced the flanks of his horse, but in the meantime the ranks were broken, and before they could be restored, the nearest Samogitian boyar rushed in, and after him Zbyszko, and after him the Czech, and the terrible confusion increased with

every moment. Other boyars likewise caught up bodies of the
fallen and threw them on the pike-points; the Samogitians from
the flanks attacked again. The entire German detachment, which
up to that time had stood firm, wavered, shook like a house whose
walls are bursting, split like a log under a wedge, and finally broke.

The battle instantly changed into a slaughter. The long pikes
and halberds of the Germans were useless in such a melee. On the
other hand, the horsemen's sword-blades bit into skulls and necks.
The horses reared up in the crowd of men, overthrowing and
trampling the unfortunate soldiers. It was easy for the horsemen to
strike from above, as they did without taking breath or rest. From
the sides of the road rushed forth ever new hosts of wild warriors
in wolfskins, with a wolfish lust for blood in their hearts. Their
howls smothered the voices of those begging for mercy and
drowned the groans of the dying. The vanquished threw away their
weapons; some tried to slip into the forest; others fell on the
ground, feigning death; others stood upright, their faces pale as
snow, their eyes half-shut; others prayed; one soldier, apparently
beside himself with terror, began to play on a pipe, and then
smiled, looking upwards, until a Samogitian sword split his skull.
The forest ceased to sough in the wind, as if terrified at death.

Finally the handful of Teutonic warriors dwindled away. Occasionally the noise of a short fight was still heard in the thickets or
a shrill cry of despair. Zbyszko and Macko, followed by all the
horsemen, now charged against the German horse.

These latter still defended themselves, drawn up in a dense
circle, for the Germans always made this maneuver when the
enemy succeeded in surrounding them in superior force. The riders, mounted on good horses and in better armor than the footmen, fought valiantly and with a stubbornness worthy of
admiration. There was no white mantle among them. Most were
Prussian nobles of middle and lower rank, whose duty it was to
present themselves for war at the command of the Order. Their
horses were also armored for the most part, some with rump plates,
and all with iron frontlets around a centered steel horn. The leader
of these horsemen was a tall, slender knight in a dark-blue breastplate and a helmet of the same color with closed visor.

A shower of arrows fell upon them from the forest, but the
points beat harmlessly on their frontlets, breastplates, and tem-

pered shoulder-pieces. A wave of Samogitians on horse and on foot surrounded them closely, but they defended themselves, cutting and thrusting with their long swords so fiercely that a circle of bodies lay before their horses' hooves. The first ranks of the attackers tried to withdraw, but, pushed on from behind, could not. All around was press and confusion. Eyes were dazed by the glitter of spears and the flashing of swords. Horses began to neigh, bite, and rear. The Samogitian boyars attacked, as did Zbyszko and the Czech and the Mazovians. Under their heavy blows, the "clump" began to rock and sway like a forest in a storm, as they, like woodmen chopping brushwood, pushed slowly forward with great toil and sweat.

Macko ordered the long German halberds on the battlefield collected, and arming about thirty wild warriors with them, he began to press through the crowd towards the Germans. Reaching them, he shouted: "Strike the horses' legs!" The result was devastating. The German knights could not reach these men with their swords, while the halberds cut the horses horribly. The blue knight perceived that the battle was lost and that only two options remained: an attempt to break through the detachment that cut off his retreat, or death.

He chose the first, and, at his command, a compact mass of knights turned immediately in the direction from whence it had come. The Samogitians were on their backs at once, but the Germans put their shields behind them and, cutting in front and at the flanks, broke the ring which surrounded them, gave rein to their horses, and rushed like a hurricane to the east. They were met by a detachment just coming up to the battle, but this force, crushed by superior armor and horses, fell flat in one moment, like a field of wheat in a storm. The road to the castle was open, but rescue was distant and uncertain, for the Samogitian horses were swifter than the German. The blue knight understood this well.

"Woe!" he said to himself. "Not a single man will be saved, unless I buy their safety with my blood."

With this thought in mind, he shouted to the nearest to hold in their horses, while he himself turned around and, without caring whether anyone obeyed his call, faced the enemy.

Zbyszko raced up first, so the German struck at the hood of his helmet which served as visor, but did not split it or injure his face.

Meanwhile Zbyszko, instead of answering blow with blow, seized the knight by the waist, grasped him tightly and, wishing to take him alive at all costs, strove to drag him from the saddle. But his own stirrup broke under the pressure, and both men fell to earth. For a while they struggled, fighting with hands and feet, but soon the unusually sturdy youth got the better of his opponent and, kneeling on his stomach, held him down as a wolf holds a dog that has dared to face him in the thickets.

He held him unnecessarily, for the German had fainted. Meanwhile Macko and the Czech rushed up. When he saw them, Zbyszko shouted: "Come and bind him! He is some important knight—and belted!"

The Czech leapt from his horse. Seeing the helplessness of the knight, he did not bind him, but disarmed him, unfastened his shoulder-pieces, took off his belt with the misericord which hung from it, cut the strap which held his helmet, and finally came to the screws that closed his visor.

Scarcely had he seen the knight's face, when he sprang up, shouting:

"Lord! Lord! Just look here!"

"De Lorche!" Zbyszko exclaimed.

De Lorche lay with pale, sweaty face and closed eyes, motionless as a corpse.

CHAPTER LII

ZBYSZKO ordered him to be put on one of the captured wagons, laden with new wheels and axles for the expedition bringing aid to the castle. He himself mounted another horse and started with Macko to continue the pursuit of the fleeing Germans. It was not very difficult, for the German horses were not good for flight, especially as the track was extremely soft after the spring rains. Macko in particular, riding a light, swift mare which had belonged to one of the dead landowners from Lekawica, passed almost all the Samogitians in the course of a few furlongs and soon came up with the nearest German rider. He summoned him, it is true, according to the knightly custom, to surrender or to turn and fight, but when the German pretended to be deaf, and even threw away his shield to lighten his horse, leaning forward, setting spurs to its sides, the old knight struck him a terrible blow with his broad axe between the shoulders and overthrew him.

Thus he avenged himself on the fugitives for the arrow, so treacherously shot at him in the forest when he was riding to Malbork; and the Germans fled before him like a herd of deer, with unbearable fear in their hearts, and no thought of fighting or defending themselves but only of escaping from the terrible warrior. Some got away into the forest, but one got stuck in the mud as he was trying to cross a stream, and he was strangled with a rope by the Samogitians. The remainder were followed by whole bands into the thickets, which soon became the scene of wild hunts, ringing with cries, shouts, and calls. The depths of the forest long resounded with them, until the last German was finally caught.

Then the old knight of Bogdaniec, accompanied by Zbyszko and the Czech, returned to the first battlefield, where lay the bodies of the slain soldiers, already stripped naked by the victors and some savagely mutilated. The victory was an important one, and the Samogitians were intoxicated with joy. After Skirwoillo's last defeat at New Kowno, their hearts had begun to fail them, particularly since the reinforcements promised by Witold had not arrived as quickly as they had expected; but now their hopes were renewed, and their ardor broke out again like a flame when fresh wood is thrown on the coals.

Too many, both of the Samogitians and of the Germans, had fallen for it to be possible to bury them, but Zbyszko ordered graves to be dug with spears for the two landowners from Lekawica, who had contributed greatly to the victory. They were laid in them at the foot of two pine-trees, in the bark of which he cut crosses with his sword. Then, bidding the Czech to look after Sieur de Lorche, who was still unconscious, he moved off with his men in haste to join Skirwoillo and bring him aid should it prove necessary.

However, after a long ride he found the battlefield empty of the living and strewn, like the other, with bodies of Samogitians and Germans. Zbyszko understood at once that the terrible Skirwoillo must also have won an important victory, for if he had been beaten, he himself would have met the Germans marching to the castle. None the less, the victory must have been bloody; even beyond the actual field of battle, the ground was covered with corpses. The experienced Macko concluded that a portion of the Germans had even succeeded in withdrawing.

Whether Skirwoillo had pursued them or not it was difficult to say, since the tracks were confused and half-obliterated. Yet Macko felt justified in concluding that the battle had taken place some time ago, perhaps even before Zbyszko's, for the bodies were blackened and swollen and some already partly eaten by wolves, which had fled into the forest at the approach of armed men.

Accordingly, Zbyszko decided not to wait for Skirwoillo, but to return to his old, safe camp. Arriving late at night, he found the Samogitian leader already there. He had reached the spot not long before, and his usually gloomy face was this time lit up with sinister joy. He immediately began to ask about the battle; and when he was told of the victory, he said in a hoarse voice, resembling the croak of a raven:

"I am pleased with myself and pleased with you. Aid will not come quickly, and if the grand duke arrives, he also will be pleased, for the castle will be ours."

"Whom have you taken captive?" asked Zbyszko.

"Only roaches, no pike. There were one or two, but they escaped. Sharp-toothed pike they were. They cut through our men and escaped."

"God granted me one," replied the youth. "A wealthy knight and distinguished, although not a monk, but a guest of the Order."

The terrible Samogitian put his hands about his neck and then made a gesture with his right hand, indicating a rope going upwards.

"This is what's going to happen to him!" he said. "Just like the others."

Zbyszko frowned.

"That's not going to happen to him, for he is my captive and my friend. Duke Janusz dubbed us knights together, and I won't let a hair on his head be touched."

"You won't give him over?"

"I won't."

They looked one another in the eye, frowning. It seemed that both would burst into rage, but Zbyszko, not wishing to quarrel with the old leader, whom he valued and respected, and being, besides, much moved by the events of the day, suddenly threw his arms around his neck, pressed him to his breast, and exclaimed:

"Do you want to tear him from me, and my last hope with him? Why wrong me so?"

Skirwoillo did not resist his embrace. Finally, he lifted his head from Zbyszko's shoulder and began to look at him from underneath his eyebrows, breathing deeply.

"Well," he said, after a few moments' silence, "tomorrow I will have my captives hanged, but if you need any one of them, I will give him to you."

Then they embraced a second time and parted in good humor, to the great satisfaction of Macko, who said:

"One will get nothing from him by quarrelling, but with kindness one may mold him like wax."

"Such is the whole nation," Zbyszko replied. "Only the Germans do not know it."

Then he sent for Sieur de Lorche, who was resting in a hut woven of branches; and presently the Czech brought him to the fire, unarmed, without his helmet, and wearing only a leather jacket dented by his coat of mail, and a red cap on his head. De Lorche had learned already from the squire whose captive he was, but for that very reason he bore himself with cold pride, and in the light of the flames one could see in his face stubbornness and contempt.

"Thank God," said Zbyszko to him, "that He has delivered you into my hands, for no evil will befall you from me."

And he extended his hand to him in friendship, but de Lorche did not move.

"I will not give my hand to knights who have shamed their knightly honor by fighting along with Saracens against Christians."

One of the Mazovians present translated his words, the meaning of which Zbyszko had anyhow guessed. At first his blood boiled in his veins.

"Fool!" he cried, clutching involuntarily the hilt of his misericord.

De Lorche raised his head.

"Kill me!" he said. "I know that you do not spare your captives."

"And do you spare yours?" exclaimed the Mazovian, unable to bear such words in silence. "Did you not hang on the shore of the island all the captives whom you took in the last battle? That is why Skirwoillo is now hanging his."

"It was done as you say," replied de Lorche, "but that was because they were pagans."

Nevertheless, his answer betrayed a certain feeling of shame, and it was not difficult to guess that in his heart he did not approve of the action.

Meanwhile Zbyszko had calmed down, and now spoke with quiet dignity:

"De Lorche! We received our belts and spurs from the same hand; you know me, and you know that knightly honor is dearer to me than life and happiness. So listen to what I tell you on my oath by St. George. Many of these men received baptism long ago, and those who are not yet Christians stretch out their hands to the Cross in hopes of salvation. But do you know who puts obstacles in their way, denies them salvation, and refuses them baptism?"

The Mazovian translated Zbyszko's words as he spoke, so de Lorche looked questioningly in the young man's face.

Then Zbyszko said: "The Germans!"

"Impossible!" cried the knight of Guelders.

"By the lance and the spurs of St. George, it is the Germans! For if the Cross were to rule here, they would lose the pretext for their inroads, for their domination of this land, and for their oppression of its unhappy population. You know them, de Lorche, and you know best whether their deeds are just."

"I thought they were wiping out their sins by fighting against pagans and urging them to baptism."

"They baptize them with the sword and with blood, not with the water of redemption. Just read this letter, and you will see at once that you are serving evildoers, beasts of prey, and constables of hell against Christian faith and love."

He handed him the Samogitians' letter to kings and princes, which had been published abroad everywhere, and de Lorche took it and cast his eyes over it by the light of the fire. He looked through it quickly, for the difficult art of reading was not strange to him; and he was amazed beyond measure.

"Is all this true?" he asked.

"So help me God; He knows best that I am here not just to serve my own interests but also to serve the cause of justice."

De Lorche was silent for a while and then said:

"I am your captive."

"Give me your hand," replied Zbyszko. "You are my brother, not my captive."

So they grasped each other's hands and sat down to a common supper which the Czech had bidden the attendants prepare. During the meal de Lorche learned with no little surprise that Zbyszko, notwithstanding his possession of the letters of safe-conduct, had not recovered Danusia and that the commanders had denied the validity of the documents in view of the outbreak of war.

"Now I understand why you are here," he said to Zbyszko, "and I thank God for giving me to you as your captive. I think that the Knights of the Order will surrender whom you want in exchange for me, else there would be a great outcry in the West, since I come from a powerful family. . . ." Suddenly he slapped his own head and exclaimed: "By all the relics of Aix-la-Chapelle! The forces that were marching to the relief of New Kowno were headed by Arnold von Baden and old Siegfried von Lowe. I know that from letters which came to the castle. Were they not taken captive?"

"No!" said Zbyszko, springing up. "No one of high-rank was taken! But, by God, you tell me important news! By God, there are other captives, from whom I will learn, before they are hanged, whether there was not any girl with Siegfried."

He called to the attendants to light his way with a torch and ran towards the place where the captives taken by Skirwoillo were confined. De Lorche, Macko, and the Czech accompanied him.

"Listen!" said the knight of Guelders to him along the way. "If you release me on my word of honor, I myself will seek her throughout all Prussia; and when I find her, I will return to you, and then you will exchange me for her."

"If she is alive! If she is alive!" replied Zbyszko.

They had reached the band of Skirwoillo's captives. Some of them were lying on their backs; others were standing by trees, to which they were mercilessly tied with bonds of bast. The torch threw a bright light on Zbyszko's head, so the eyes of all the unhappy prisoners turned to him.

At that moment a loud voice, full of fear, cried out from amidst them:

"My lord and defender! Save me!"

Zbyszko snatched a few burning brands from the hand of a page, rushed with them to the tree from whence came the voice and, holding them aloft, exclaimed:

"Sanderus!"

"Sanderus!" repeated the Czech in amazement.

And Sanderus, unable to move his bound hands, stretched out his neck and called again:

"Mercy! I know where Jurand's daughter is! Save me!"

CHAPTER LIII

THE attendants unbound him at once, but his limbs were numb and he fell down; when they lifted him up, he swooned again and again, for he had been indeed cruelly handled. By Zbyszko's orders, he was brought to the fire, given food and drink, rubbed with bear's grease, and covered with warm skins—all to no avail. Sanderus could not come to himself, but at length fell so soundly asleep that it was only on the following day at noon that the Czech was able to wake him.

Zbyszko, burning with impatience, came to him at once. At first, however, he could not get any information from him, for, whether from fear after his terrible experiences or from the relief which usually overcomes weak spirits when threatening danger has passed, Sanderus burst out weeping so unrestrainedly that all attempts to get him to answer questions were futile. His throat was constricted by sobs, his lips trembled, and from his eyes poured an abundant rain of tears.

At last he regained some measure of self-control, and after being refreshed with mare's milk, a drink which Lithuania had learned to use from the Tartars, he began to complain that the "sons of Belial" had beaten him black and blue with spears, and had taken from him his horse, on which he was carrying relics of exceptional power and value, and that, finally, when he had been bound to the tree, ants had bitten his legs and whole body so fiercely that he would certainly die on the morrow.

But Zbyszko became enraged and sprang up, saying:

"Answer my questions, vagabond, and take care that nothing worse happens to you!"

"There is a red anthill not far away," said the Czech. "Have him put on it, lord, and his tongue will loosen."

Hlawa did not really mean what he said; he even smiled, for he was well disposed to Sanderus at heart. But the latter was terrified and cried out:

"Mercy! Mercy! Give me some more of that pagan drink and I will tell you everything I have seen and not seen!"

"If you lie just once, I will drive a wedge between your ribs," replied the Czech.

But he put the skin of mare's milk to his lips again, and Sanderus took hold of it and sucked, as a child its mother's breast, opening and shutting his eyes in the process. When he had drawn two quarts or more he shook himself, put the skin on his knees, and said, as if resigning himself to the inevitable:

"Vile stuff!" And then to Zbyszko: "Now ask me, saviour?"

"Was my wife in the detachment with which you marched?"

Sanderus's face reflected a certain surprise. He had heard, it is true, that Danusia was Zbyszko's wife, but also that the marriage was secret and that she had been kidnapped immediately afterwards, so he had always thought of her in his heart as Jurand's daughter. However, he replied hastily:

"Yes, voivode, she was! But Siegfried von Lowe and Arnold von Baden broke through the enemy."

"Did you see her?" asked the young man, with racing heart.

"I did not see her face, lord, but I saw between two horses a wicker litter, completely closed, in which someone was being carried, and attended by the same lizard, that woman-servant of the Order, who came from Danveld to the hunting-lodge. And I heard, also, the sound of mournful singing coming from the litter."

Zbyszko paled with emotion, sat down on a stump, and for some time did not know what more to ask. Macko and the Czech were also greatly moved, for this was important and serious news. The Czech thought perhaps of his own beloved lady who had remained at Spychow and for whom this news would be like a sentence of misery.

A short silence followed.

Finally the cunning Macko, who did not know Sanderus and

had heard hardly anything of him before, looked at him suspiciously and asked:

"Who are you and what were you doing among the Teutonic Knights?"

"Let these here tell you who I am, gentle knight," replied the vagabond; "this valiant duke," pointing at Zbyszko, "and that brave Czech count, who have known me for a long time."

The mare's milk now began evidently to take effect on him, for he grew lively and, turning to Zbyszko, began to speak in a loud voice that did not betray a trace of his former weakness.

"Lord, you twice saved my life. If it were not for you, the wolves would have devoured me, or I should have been punished by the bishops, who were led into error by my enemies—oh, how evil is this world!—and issued an order for my prosecution for selling relics, the genuineness of which they doubted. But you, lord, took me under your protection. Thanks to you the wolves did not digest me, and the prosecution failed to reach me, for I was taken for one of your men. With you I never wanted for food and drink—better than this mare's milk, which disgusts me, but of which I will drink some more, just to show that a poor, pious pilgrim shrinks from no mortification."

"Tell us quickly, rogue, what you know and make no foolish jests!" exclaimed Macko.

But Sanderus, as if he had not heard Macko's words, put the milk-skin again to his lips and emptied it completely, before turning to Zbyszko:

"So on that account I came to love you, lord. The saints, say the Scriptures, sinned nine times an hour, so it may happen even to Sanderus to sin sometimes, but Sanderus never was and never will be an ingrate. So remember, lord, what I said to you when misfortune came upon you: 'I will go from castle to castle and, teaching folk by the way, will seek what you have lost.' Whom have I not asked! Where have I not been! It would take a long time to tell you everything. Suffice to say that I found her and from that moment have stuck to old Siegfried as a bur sticks to a cloak. I made myself his servant and followed him unceasingly from castle to castle, from commandery to commandery, from town to town, until this last battle."

Zbyszko meanwhile had controlled his emotion.

"I am grateful to you," he said, "and you shall not miss your reward. But now answer me. Will you swear on your soul's salvation that she is alive?"

"I swear on my soul's salvation," replied Sanderus gravely.

"Why did Siegfried leave Ortelsburg?"

"I do not know, lord, but I can guess. He was never constable of Ortelsburg, and he left it perhaps because he feared the grand master's orders, which were, they say, that he should give back his hostage to the duchess of Mazovia. Perhaps he fled before that letter, for his soul was tormented by pain and lust of vengeance for Roger. They say now that he was his son. I don't know how it was; I know only that something went wrong in his head from rage and that as long as he lives he will not let Jurand's daughter—I mean the young married lady—out of his hands."

"All this sounds odd to me," interrupted Macko suddenly, "for if that old dog were so enraged against the whole house of Jurand, he would have killed Danusia."

"Yes, he wanted to," replied Sanderus, "but something so dreadful befell him that afterwards he was seriously ill and almost breathed his last. His men whisper much about it. Some relate that when he went at night to the tower to murder the young lady, he met the Evil One, while others say it was an angel. In any case he was found lying unconscious on the snow before the tower. Even now when he remembers it, his hair stands on end, and that is why he is afraid himself to lift a hand against her and fears to order others to do so. He carries with him a dumb man, a former executioner at Ortelsburg, but no one knows why, since he, too, is afraid, like everyone else."

These words made a great impression. Zbyszko, Macko, and the Czech came nearer to Sanderus, who crossed himself and went on:

"It is not good to be among them there. More than once I saw and heard things that made my flesh creep. I have already told your graces that something went wrong in the old commander's head. How, indeed, could it be otherwise, when spirits visit him from the other world? If he is alone, something near him begins to pant, as if from lack of breath. That is Danveld, who was slain by the terrible Lord of Spychow. Then Siegfried says to him: 'What do you want? Masses are no good to you. What have you come for?' But the other only gnashes his teeth and pants again. But more frequently it is Roger who comes, leaving a smell of sulphur in the room, and with him the commander talks still more: 'I cannot!'— he says—'I cannot! When I come by myself, then I will, but now I cannot.' I heard also how he asked him: 'Will that bring you relief, my dear son?' And so it goes on. Sometimes he does not say a word to anyone for two or three days, while his face shows signs of bitter pain. Both he and the woman-servant of the Order guard the litter so that no one can ever get sight of the young lady."

"Do they torture her?" asked Zbyszko dully.

"I will tell your grace the pure truth: I have not heard the sound of any beating or any cries, but I have heard the sound of mournful singing and, at times, what seemed like the alarmed calling of a bird."

"Woe!" muttered Zbyszko through his teeth.

But Macko put an end to further questions.

"Enough of this!" he said. "Tell us now of the battle. Did you see it? How did they get away, and what happened to them?"

"I saw it," answered Sanderus, "and I will relate faithfully what took place. At first they fought fiercely enough, but when they perceived that they were hemmed in on all sides, they began to think only of how to break out. Sir Arnold, who is a real giant, burst through the circle and made such a path that the old commander escaped with a few men and the litter, which was tied between two horses."

"Was there no pursuit? How did it happen that they were not overtaken?"

"There was a pursuit, but it was of no avail, for when they drew too close, Sir Arnold turned and fought with all of them. God save anyone from meeting him. He is a man of such frightful strength that it's nothing for him to fight a hundred men. Three times he turned thus; three times he checked the pursuit. The men who were with him perished, every one. He, I believe, was wounded, as was his horse; but he saved himself and gave the old commander time to escape."

Macko listened to this story and concluded that Sanderus was telling the truth. He remembered how the road from the place where Skirwoillo had given battle was covered for some distance back with the bodies of Samogitians, terribly cut up, as if by a giant's hand.

"Nevertheless, how is it that you were able to see all this?" he asked Sanderus.

"I saw it," replied the vagabond, "because I took hold of the tail of one of the horses carrying the litter and fled with it until I got kicked in the stomach. Then I fainted, and that is why I fell into the hands of your grace's men."

"This might have happened," said Hlawa, "but beware of lying, for you'll regret it!"

"The mark is still there," replied Sanderus. "Whoever wants to, may see it. But it is better to believe my word than be damned for disbelief."

"Even though you have sometimes unwillingly told the truth, you will howl in hell for trafficking in sacred things."

And they began to chafe one another, as had been their custom before, but Zbyszko interrupted:

"You have travelled through this country, so you know it. What castles are there in the neighborhood, and where do you think Siegfried and Arnold can find shelter?"

"There are no castles in the neighborhood, for it is all wild forest, through which the highway was only recently made. Nor are there any villages or settlements. The Germans themselves burnt whatever there was, because when this war began, the population, which comes of the same stock as these warriors here, rose likewise against Teutonic rule. I think, lord, that Siegfried and Arnold are now wandering in the forest, and will try either to return from whence they came or to reach in secrecy the castle for which they were bound."

"Doubtless it is so!" exclaimed Zbyszko.

And he plunged deep into thought. From his frowning brows and concentrated gaze, it was easy to see with what effort he was thinking, but it was not for long. Soon he raised his head.

"Hlawa!" he said. "Get the horses and men ready, for we will start at once."

The squire, who never asked the reason for any command, got up and ran to the horses without a word; but Macko glanced at his nephew and asked in amazement:

"But, Zbyszko? Heh! Where are you going? Well?"

Zbyszko, however, answered likewise with a question: "And you, what do you think? That I shouldn't go?"

The old knight fell silent. His amazement gradually disappeared from his face; he shook his head once, twice, and finally drew a deep breath and said, as if to himself:

"Well! I suppose there's no help for it!"

And he went also towards the horses. Zbyszko turned to Sieur de Lorche and, with the aid of the Mazovian who knew German, said to him:

"I cannot ask you to help me against men with whom you have served under one banner, so you are free to go where you will."

"My knightly honor prevents me now from helping you with my sword," replied de Lorche. "As to my freedom, I cannot accept it. I will remain your captive on my word of honor to present myself at your summons wherever you bid me. And you, if anything happens to you, remember that the Order will exchange for me any captive, for I come of a family which is not only wealthy, but has done good service to the Teutonic Knights."

So they took leave of one another, putting their hands according to custom on each other's shoulders and kissing each other's cheeks, and de Lorche said:

"I shall go to Malbork or to the Mazovian court, so be assured that you will find me at one or the other. Let your messenger say only two words to me: Lorraine Guelders!"

"Good!" replied Zbyszko. "I will first go to Skirwoillo and get him to give you a pass which the Samogitians will respect."

He then betook himself to Skirwoillo, and the old leader gave him a pass and put no difficulties in the way of his departure, for he knew what was at stake, and he liked Zbyszko and was grateful to him for his services in the last battle. Moreover he had no right to detain a knight who belonged to another country and had come of his own free will. So he thanked him for all he had done, provided him with food, which might be very useful in a devastated country, and took leave of him with the wish that they might meet again at some great and decisive battle with the Teutonic Knights.

For his part, Zbyszko was in haste, almost seeming feverish with impatience. When he reached his troop, he found everything ready and, among his men, his uncle Macko, already mounted, in hauberk and helmet. So he approached him and said:

"So you are coming with me?"

"What else am I to do?" Macko asked, rather gruffly.

Zbyszko made no answer to that, but kissed his uncle's mailed right hand, and then mounted and moved off.

Sanderus went with them. The road to the battlefield they knew well, but farther on he was to be their guide. They also hoped to come upon local peasants in the forests, who, out of hatred of their Teutonic masters, would be ready to aid them in tracking the old commander and that Arnold von Baden of whose superhuman strength and fortitude Sanderus had told so much.

CHAPTER LIV

THE road to the battlefield on which Skirwoillo had so mauled the Germans was easy, being familiar. So they quickly reached the place, but passed it hastily because of the intolerable stench emanating from the unburied bodies. As they passed, they disturbed not only wolves but huge flocks of crows, ravens, and jackdaws; then they began to look for tracks on the ground. Although a whole detachment had gone that way earlier, the experienced Macko had no difficulty in finding the marks of enormous hoofs pointing in the opposite direction on the trampled ground, and he explained his scoutcraft thus to the young men, who were less skilled in the arts of war:

"It is fortunate that there has been no rain since the battle. Now pay attention: Arnold's horse, bearing as it did an unusually big man, must also have been enormous. It is easy to understand that when galloping away in flight, his horse struck the ground harder than when advancing slowly in the other direction and, consequently, left deeper tracks. See, for you have eyes, how clearly defined are the hoofprints on damp ground. God grant we may track the curs successfully, if they have not found shelter somewhere behind walls first."

"Sanderus said," replied Zbyszko, "that there are no castles in this neighborhood, and so it is, for the district was but lately occupied by the Teutonic Knights, and they have not been able to fortify posts in it. Where then can they find shelter? The peasants who live here are in camp with Skirwoillo, because they are of the same stock as the Samogitians. The villages, as Sanderus says, have been burnt by the Germans, and the women and children are concealed in the depths of the forest. If we do not spare our horses, we shall catch up to them."

"But we must spare our horses, for even if we succeed in overtaking the enemy we shall need them afterwards for our own salvation," said Macko.

"Sir Arnold," Sanderus interrupted, "was struck in the back with a club during the course of battle. He paid no attention to it, he fought and slew, but later he must have felt it, for it is always so; at first it is nothing, but afterwards there is pain. So it will not be too easy for him to escape quickly, and perhaps he will need to rest."

"He has no men with him, you say?" asked Macko.

"There are two who are carrying the litter between their horses and, besides them, Sir Arnold and the old commander. There was a large party of other men, but the Samogitians caught and slew them."

"This is my plan," said Zbyszko. "The men with the litter will be bound by our attendants; you, uncle, will go at old Siegfried, while I shall attack Arnold."

"Well!" replied Macko. "I will deal with Siegfried, for by the grace of our Lord Jesus there is still strength in my bones. But, you, don't be over-confident, for Arnold is said to be a giant."

"Pooh! We shall see!" replied Zbyszko.

"You are a stout fellow, I do not deny, but there are stronger men even than you. Have you forgotten those knights of ours whom we saw at Cracow? Would you be able to deal with Powala of Taczewo? or Paszko the Thief of Biskupice? And what about Zawisza the Black? Eh? So do not take your task too lightly, and be watchful."

"Roger was no weakling," Zbyszko muttered.

"And will there be work for me?" asked the Czech.

But he got no answer, since Macko's thoughts were elsewhere.

"If God blesses us," the old knight said, "all we have to do afterwards is to get to the Mazovian forest. There we shall be safe, and finally all will be over."

But presently he sighed, doubtless thinking that even then all would not be over, for they would have to do something with the unhappy Jagienka.

"Heh!" he muttered. "Strange are the decrees of Providence. I have wondered more than once why it did not fall to your lot to marry peacefully and to mine to settle peacefully with you. For that is how it most frequently is. Of all the nobility in our kingdom, we alone have to wander through various lands and along rough paths, instead of keeping house in godly fashion at home."

"True! true! But it is God's will," Zbyszko replied.

For some time they rode on in silence, and then the old knight turned again to his nephew:

"Do you trust that vagabond? Who is he?"

"A light-minded fellow and perhaps a good-for-nothing, but well-disposed to me, and I am not afraid of treachery from him."

"If that is so, let him ride ahead, for if he catches up to them, they will not scatter. He shall tell them that he has escaped from captivity, which they will readily believe. It will be better that way. If they caught sight of us from afar, they would either be able to conceal themselves or prepare their defence."

"He will not ride ahead alone at night, for he is a coward," replied Zbyszko. "But in the daytime it is certain that it will be better that way. I will tell him to stop three times in the day and wait for us; and if we do not find him at the halting-place, it will be a sign that he is with them, and then we shall follow in his tracks and fall upon them unexpectedly."

"And he will not warn them?"

"No. He is better disposed to me than to them. I will also tell him that when we have overcome them, we shall bind him also, so that he need not fear their vengeance afterwards. He should not admit that he knows us at all."

"Then you are thinking of leaving them alive?"

"How can it be otherwise?" answered Zbyszko, somewhat mournfully. "You see. . . . If we were in Mazovia, or somewhere among us, we would challenge them, as I did Roger, and fight with them to the death, but here in their country that cannot be. Here we have to think of Danusia and of haste. We must act quickly and quietly, so as not to draw down trouble on ourselves, and then, as you said, we must make for the Mazovian forest with all possible speed. If we fall upon them unexpectedly, perhaps we shall surprise them without armor, nay, even without swords. And, in that case, how could we slay them? I fear disgrace. Both of us are belted knights, and so are they."

"Yes," said Macko. "Yet perhaps it may come to a fight."

Zbyszko frowned. In his face was reflected the stubborn determination that was apparently inborn in all the men of Bogdaniec, for in that moment he became, particularly in the expression of his eyes, so similar to Macko that it seemed as if he were his son.

"What I should like," he said dully, "would be to throw that bloody dog, Siegfried, at Jurand's feet. God grant I may!"

"Grant it! grant it!" repeated Macko at once.

Thus talking, they had ridden a good piece of the way. Night fell, clear but moonless. They had to stop to rest the horses and refresh the men with food and sleep. At that point, Zbyszko warned Sanderus that on the morrow he had to ride ahead alone, to which he readily agreed, making only the condition that he could turn back in case of danger from wild beasts or the natives of those parts. He also asked to halt four times instead of three, since he always felt uneasy when alone, even in Christian lands, and much more in such a wild and uncanny forest as they now found themselves in.

Then they made ready for the night, and after refreshing themselves with food, they lay down on skins by a small fire, kindled in a hollow, half a furlong from the road. The servants took turns watching the horses, which, after rolling and eating their fodder, slept with their heads on one another's necks. Scarcely had the first light of dawn silvered the trees, when Zbyszko sprang up and awoke the others. And at daybreak they continued on their way. The enormous hoofprints of Arnold's stallion were again found without difficulty, for they had dried in the low and mostly muddy ground and thus were preserved. Sanderus rode ahead and vanished from their sight, but between sunrise and noon they found him at the halting-place. He told them that he had not seen a living thing save a great aurochs, from which, however, he had not fled, since the beast had gone out of his way first. At noon, however, at the first meal, he declared that he had seen a man, a beekeeper with a ladder, and that he had not detained him simply because he feared there might be more men in the depths of the forest. He had tried to question him about this and that, but they could not understand one another.

During the following march, Zbyszko began to feel uneasy. What would happen if they came to a higher and drier part, where

the tracks visible hitherto should cease on the hard ground? Or if
the pursuit should last too long and bring them to a more populous
region, where the inhabitants had long since accustomed themselves to obey the Teutonic Knights, and where it would be almost
impossible to attack Danusia's captors and rescue her? For, even
though Siegfried and Arnold were not protected by the walls of any
castle or fortalice, the local population would assuredly take their
side.

Fortunately these fears proved groundless. At the next halting-
place they did not find Sanderus at the appointed time, but observed a great cut in the form of a cross on a pine-tree close by the
roadside, evidently freshly made. Then they exchanged glances and
their faces grew grave, while their hearts began to beat more eagerly
than before. Macko and Zbyszko immediately leapt from their
saddles and examined the tracks on the ground, though not for
long, since they were obvious enough.

Sanderus had evidently left the road and gone into the forest,
following the great hoofprints, which were not as deep as on the
highway, but were clear enough, for the ground here was peaty and
the heavy horse had pressed the pine-needles into it with its calks
at every step, leaving holes black on the edges.

Zbyszko's keen eyes did not miss certain other imprints. He
mounted his horse, as did Macko after him, and they began to take
counsel together, with the Czech, in low tones, as if the enemy were
close at hand.

The Czech advised going at once on foot, but they were unwilling to do that, not knowing how far they might have to penetrate
the forest. They decided to send the unmounted men forward as a
scouting party.

Soon they advanced into the forest. A second cut on a pine-tree
assured them that they had not lost touch with Sanderus. They
quickly perceived, also, that they were on a path, or at least on a
forest track which had frequently been trodden by human feet.
This made them certain that they would find some forest huts,
containing those whom they sought.

The sun was already rather low and shone gold among the trees.
The evening promised to be clear. The forest was still, for beasts
and birds had gone to rest. Only here and there, among the
branches shining in the sun, squirrels flashed by, red in the evening

rays. Zbyszko, Macko, the Czech, and the men rode one after the other in single file. Knowing that the unmounted men were considerably in front and would warn them in time, the old knight talked to his nephew without lowering his voice too much.

"Let us count by the sun," he said. "From the last halting-place to where we saw the cross cut on the tree was a good long way. By the Cracow clock it would be about three hours. So Sanderus has been among them for a considerable while and has had time to tell them his adventures. If only he did not betray us."

"He will not betray us," answered Zbyszko.

"And if only they believe him," concluded Macko, "for if they do not, it will be bad for him."

"Why should they not believe him? Do they know about us? But they know him. It frequently happens that a captive escapes."

"What I fear is that if he has told them that he escaped from captivity, they may think he will be pursued, and they'll move on at once."

"No. He will be able to throw dust in their eyes. And they know the pursuit could not continue so far."

For a while they were silent, but presently Macko thought that Zbyszko was whispering something to him, so he turned and asked:

"What are you saying?"

But Zbyszko had his eyes upturned and was not whispering to Macko, but recommending Danusia and his bold undertaking to God.

Macko began also to cross himself, but he had scarcely made the first sign when one of the men who had been sent ahead suddenly came towards him out of the hazel thickets:

"Pitch-burners' huts!" he said. "They are there!"

"Halt!" whispered Zbyszko, and in the same moment he leapt from his horse.

He was followed by Macko, the Czech, and the attendants, of whom three received orders to stay with the horses, holding them ready and taking care that none of them—God forbid!—should neigh. To the five remaining, Macko said:

"There will be the two grooms and Sanderus, whom you have to bind in the twinkling of an eye, and if anyone should be armed and try to defend himself, then go for him."

They advanced. Along the way, Zbyszko whispered again to his uncle:

"You take Siegfried, and I will take Arnold."

"But be careful!" answered the old man. And he winked at the Czech, giving him to understand that he had to be ready at any moment to help his young lord.

Hlawa nodded assent, drew a deep breath, and felt whether his sword drew easily out of its scabbard.

Zbyszko noticed this, and said:

"No! I order you to rush immediately to the litter and not move an inch from it during the struggle."

They advanced swiftly and silently through the hazel thickets, but they did not go far, for after two furlongs at most the undergrowth suddenly ceased, giving way to a small clearing, on which they could see the pitch-burners' extinguished kilns and two *numas*, in which the pitch-burners had doubtless lived until they were expelled by the war. The bright light of the setting sun fell on the meadow, the kilns, and the two *numas*, standing far apart. Before one of them, the two knights were sitting on a log; and before the other, a broad-shouldered, red-haired lout and Sanderus. The latter two were engaged in wiping breastplates with cloths, and at Sanderus's feet lay also two swords, which he was evidently intending to clean later.

"Look!" said Macko, squeezing Zbyszko's arm with all his strength, to hold him back a moment or two longer. "He has taken their swords and breastplates on purpose. Good! The one with the grey head must be—"

"Forward!" shouted Zbyszko suddenly.

They rushed like a whirlwind onto the clearing. The two Teutonic Knights sprang up, but before they could reach Sanderus, the terrible Macko seized old Siegfried by the chest, bent him backwards, and in a moment was on top of him. Zbyszko and Arnold engaged like two hawks, gripping one another and wrestling fiercely. The broad-shouldered German who had been sitting near Sanderus reached for a sword, but before he could wield it, Macko's attendant, Vit, struck him on his red head with the head of his axe, instantly laying him flat. They then threw themselves on Sanderus to bind him, as the old lord had commanded, while Sanderus, though he knew that it had been so arranged, began to howl with fear like a calf whose throat is to be cut.

Zbyszko, though he was so strong that he could squeeze a branch until the sap dripped out, felt as if he had got into the embrace of a bear rather than of a mere man. He even felt that had it not been for his breastplate—which he was wearing because he had not known whether he would have to fight the huge German blade to blade—his ribs would have been crushed or his spine broken. He did, indeed, lift Arnold a little, but the latter lifted him still higher and put forth all his strength in an effort to hurl him to the ground with such force that he would never rise again.

But Zbyszko gripped him with such enormous power that the German's eyes were filmed with blood; then he put his leg between his knees, kicked him in the hamstring muscle, and threw him to the ground.

Or rather, both of them fell together, the young man underneath; but at that moment the watchful Macko threw the half-crushed Siegfried into his men's arms and rushed to the wrestlers. In a split second he had fettered Arnold's legs with his belt, after which he bestrode him as if he were a slaughtered boar and put the edge of his misericord to his neck.

Arnold cried out shrilly, his hands slipped weakly from Zbyszko's sides, and he began to moan, not so much from the pricking as from the sharp and indescribable pain he suddenly felt in his back, where he had been struck by the club in the course of the battle with Skirwoillo.

Macko gripped him with both hands by the collar and pulled him away from Zbyszko. The young knight rose a little from the ground and sat down. He tried to stand up, but could not; so he sat down again and remained still for some time. His face was pale and covered with sweat, his eyes bloodshot, and his lips blue, and he looked straight ahead, as if not fully conscious.

"What is the matter with you?" asked Macko anxiously.

"Nothing, I'm just very exhausted. Help me to stand on my feet."

Macko put his hands under his arms and lifted him up immediately.

"Can you stand?"

"Yes."

"Are you in pain?"

"No. I'm just short of breath."

Meanwhile the Czech, evidently realizing that the fight was already over, appeared before the *numa*, holding the woman-servant of the Order by the scruff of the neck. At that sight, Zbyszko forgot his exhaustion, his strength came back to him at once, and he rushed to the *numa* as if he had never wrestled with the terrible Arnold.

"Danusia! Danusia!"

But no voice answered his call.

"Danusia! Danusia" he cried again.

Then he was silent. It was dark inside, so that at first he could make out nothing. However, from beyond the stones paving the hearth, there came to his ears the sound of quick, loud breathing, like that of a frightened animal.

"Danusia! For God's sake! It is I! Zbyszko!"

And suddenly he saw in the darkness her eyes, wide open, terrified, wild. So he sprang to her and caught her in his arms, but she did not recognize him at all, and tearing herself from his embrace, she began to repeat in a panting whisper:

"I'm afraid! I'm afraid! I'm afraid!"

CHAPTER LV

NEITHER soft words, nor caresses, nor entreaties were of any avail. Danusia recognized no one and did not regain her senses. The one feeling that dominated her whole being was fear, a fear similar to that timid fear which is shown by captured birds. When food was brought her, she was unwilling to eat in the presence of others, although from the greedy glances she threw at it, it was easy to see that she was hungry and perhaps had been for a long time. When she was left alone, she threw herself on the food like some eager little animal, yet when Zbyszko entered the hut she straightaway ran into the corner and hid herself behind a bundle of dry hops. In vain Zbyszko opened his arms, in vain he stretched out his hands, in vain he implored, keeping back his tears. She would not come out of hiding even when they had kindled a fire inside and she might easily have recognized Zbyszko's features by its light. It seemed that she had lost her memory together with her senses. So he looked at her and her emaciated face with its frozen expression of fear, at her sunken eyes, at the torn rags of clothing in which she was clad, and his heart whined in pain and rage at the thought of the hands in which she had been and the treatment she had received. Finally he was carried away by a wave of anger so terrible that he grasped his sword and ran with it towards Siegfried, and he would undoubtedly have killed him had not Macko caught him by the arm.

Then they began to wrestle with one another, almost like enemies, but the young man was so weakened by his previous struggle with the gigantic Arnold that the old knight overpowered him and, twisting his arm, exclaimed:

"Are you mad or what?"

"Let me go!" replied Zbyszko, grinding his teeth, "for my heart will break within me."

"Let it break! I will not let you go! Better to dash your head against a tree than to bring shame upon yourself and your whole line."

And squeezing Zbyszko's hand as if in iron pincers, he said threateningly:

"Beware! Vengeance will not escape you, and you are a belted knight. What? Would you stab a bound captive? You would not help Danusia, and what will you gain? Nothing but shame. You say that kings and princes have frequently murdered their captives? Bah! Not among us! And what will pass in their case will not in yours. They have kingdoms, towns, and castles, and what have you? Your knightly honor. The man who would not blame them would spit in your eyes. Control yourself, for God's sake!"

A moment of silence followed.

"Let me go," Zbyszko said gloomily. "I will not stab him."

"Come to the fire; we will take counsel together."

And he led him by the hand to the fire, which the servants had kindled near the kilns. Sitting there, Macko reflected for a while, and then said:

"Remember also that you have promised him to old Jurand. He will most certainly take vengeance on him for his sufferings and Danusia's! He will repay him, never fear! And you ought to satisfy Jurand in this. It is his right. And what is forbidden for you will not be forbidden for Jurand, because he did not take him captive but will receive him as a present from you. Without shame and without reproach he can even flay him alive—do you understand me?"

"Yes, I understand," replied Zbyszko. "You are right."

"I see your wits are returning. If the devil tempts you again, remember this too: You have challenged Lichtenstein and other Teutonic Knights, but if you slay an unarmed captive, and it becomes known through the talk of the servants, no knight will be willing to face you, and rightly so. God forbid! Misfortunes are not lacking, but shame must not be added to them. But let us talk of what we must do now and where we must turn."

"Advise me," said the young man.

"My advice is that that snake who was with Danusia should be killed, but since it does not befit knights to stain their hands with women's blood, we will give her up to Duke Janusz. She plotted treachery already at the duke and duchess's hunting-lodge, so let the Mazovian courts judge her, and if they do not break her on the rack for that, they will surely outrage divine justice. But until we find some other woman to attend on Danusia, she will be needed; afterwards, I will tie her to a horse's tail. Now we must make our way as speedily as possible to the Mazovian forests."

"Not just now, for it is night. Perhaps also God will grant Danusia more self-control tomorrow."

"Let the horses have a good rest. At daybreak we will move."

Further talk was interrupted by the voice of Arnold von Baden, who was lying on his back not far off, trussed to his own sword, and now called out something in German. Old Macko got up and went over to him, but not being able to understand exactly what he was saying, he looked about for the Czech.

But Hlawa could not come at once, for he was busy with something else. During their talk by the fire, he had gone to the woman-servant of whom they had just spoken, and had put his hand on the scruff of her neck. Shaking her, he said:

"Listen, bitch! You will go to the hut and make a bed of skins for the lady. But before that you will put your decent garments on her and dress yourself in the rags which you have made her wear, you accursed wretch!"

And, unable any more than Zbyszko to control his sudden rage, he shook her so powerfully that her eyes started out. Maybe he would have twisted her neck, but since she seemed to be still needed, he let her go at last, saying:

"And then we will choose a branch for you."

Terrified, she caught him by the knees. But when he kicked her for an answer, she ran to the hut and threw herself at Danusia's feet, screaming:

"Defend me! Don't give me up!"

Danusia merely closed her eyes, and from her lips came the usual panting whisper:

"I'm afraid! I'm afraid! I'm afraid!"

And then she went quite numb, for every contact with the woman-servant of the Order always had this effect. She let herself be undressed and clad in the new garments. The servant made the bed and placed her on it, as if she were a figure of wood or wax, and then sat down by the fire, afraid to go out of the hut.

But soon the Czech entered and, turning first to Danusia, said:

"You are among friends, lady, so in the name of the Father, the Son, and the Holy Ghost, sleep calmly."

He made the sign of the cross over her, and then, not raising his voice for fear of frightening Danusia, he said to the servant:

"You will lie bound right outside, but if you cry out and frighten her, I will strangle you at once. Get up."

When he had taken her out of the hut, he tied her up tightly as he had promised; then he went to Zbyszko.

"I had that lizard clothe the lady in the garments she had on herself," he said. "The bed is made and the lady is asleep. It will be better not to go there at present, lord, lest she be alarmed. God grant that tomorrow, when she wakes up, she may come to herself! Now you must also think of food and rest."

"I will lie down in front of her hut," replied Zbyszko.

"Then I will drag that bitch aside to the corpse with shaggy red hair. But now you must eat. You have a long road and much toil before you."

He went to fetch from the saddlebags some smoked meat and smoked turnips they had been provided with at the Samogitian camp, but scarcely had he set a quantity before Zbyszko, when Macko called him away to Arnold.

"Find out," he said, "exactly what this giant wants. Though I know a few words, I cannot understand him at all."

"I will bring him to the fire, lord, and you can talk there," replied the Czech.

He took off his belt, passed it under Arnold's arms, and hoisted him on his back. He staggered under the giant's weight, but, being a sturdy fellow, carried him to the fire and threw him down beside Zbyszko like a sack of peas.

"Take off my fetters," said the Teutonic Knight.

"I might," old Macko answered through the Czech, "if you swore on your knightly honor that you will regard yourself as a prisoner. However, even without that, I will have the sword with-drawn from under your knees and your hands freed, so that you may sit by us, but I will not take off the cords on your legs until we have had a talk."

And he beckoned to the Czech, who cut the bonds on the German's wrists and helped him into a sitting position. Arnold looked arrogantly at Macko and at Zbyszko, and asked:

"Who are you?"

"How do you dare to ask? What is that to you? Find out for yourself."

"I ask because I can swear on my knightly honor only to other knights."

"Then look."

Macko drew aside his cloak, revealing the knight's belt around his waist.

The Teutonic Knight was quite amazed, and it was only after a little while that he said:

"How can this be? And you go plundering through the wilds? And you aid pagans against Christians?"

"You lie!" exclaimed Macko.

Thus began a conversation hostile and arrogant, more often resembling a quarrel. But when Macko shouted excitedly that it was the Teutonic Order which had refused baptism to Lithuania, and when he cited all the proofs, Arnold was amazed again and made no reply, for the truth was so evident that it was impossible not to see it or to deny it. The German was particularly struck by the words which Macko said, making the sign of the cross: "Who knows whom you really serve? If not all of you, at least some!" And these words struck him because even in the Order itself there was a suspicion that some of the commanders worshipped Satan. No formal charge or accusation was made against them, for fear of bringing shame on the whole community, but Arnold was well aware that such things were whispered among the brethren and that such rumors were current. Meanwhile Macko, knowing of Siegfried's unbelievable behavior from Sanderus, disquieted the simple-hearted giant to the bottom of his soul.

"And that Siegfried," he said, "with whom you marched to war: does he serve God and Christ? Have you never heard that he spoke with evil spirits, that he whispered and laughed with them, or gnashed his teeth along with them?"

"It is true!" Arnold muttered.

But Zbyszko, whose heart had overflowed with a fresh wave of sorrow and grief, suddenly shouted:

"How dare you speak of knightly honor? Shame upon you! for you aided a hangman and a hell-hound. Shame upon you! for you looked calmly on the sufferings of a defenseless girl and a knight's daughter—and perhaps tormented her yourself. Shame upon you!"

Arnold stared at him and, making the sign of the cross, said:

"In the name of the Father and the Son and the Holy Ghost! What, that mad girl, in whose head dwell twenty-seven devils? I?"

"Woe! Woe!" Zbyszko interrupted hoarsely.

And grasping the hilt of his misericord, he began again to cast wild glances in the direction of Siegfried, who was lying not far away in the darkness.

Macko laid his hand calmly on his arm and squeezed it with all his might to bring him back to his right senses, while he himself turned to Arnold and said:

"That woman is the daughter of Jurand of Spychow and the wife of this young knight. Now you understand why we tracked you, and why you have become our prisoner."

"By God!" said Arnold. "Whence? How? She is out of her mind. . . ."

"Because the Teutonic Knights carried her off like an innocent lamb and brought her to this state by torment."

At the words "innocent lamb," Zbyszko put his fist in his mouth and bit on his knuckle, while great tears of unrestrained grief began to fall one by one from his eyes. Arnold sat deep in thought, while the Czech told him in a few words the story of Danveld's treachery, the kidnapping of Danusia, the sufferings of Jurand, and the single combat with Roger. When he had finished, silence followed, which was disturbed only by the soughing of the wind in the trees and the crackling of the brands in the fire.

They sat thus for some time. Finally Arnold raised his head and said:

"I swear to you, not only on my knightly honor, but on the Cross of Christ, that I scarcely saw that girl, that I did not know who she was, and that I never at any time had any share in her tormenting."

"Then swear further that you will come with us of your own free will and that you will not attempt to escape—and I shall have you completely unbound," said Macko.

"Let it be as you say. I swear! Where will you take me?"

"To Mazovia, to Jurand of Spychow."

So Macko cut the cords on his legs and then offered him meat and turnips. After some time Zbyszko got up and went to rest in front the hut. There he failed to find the woman-servant of the Order, as the men had taken her among the horses. He lay down on a skin brought him by Hlawa, determined to lie awake until daybreak or until some happy change in Danusia's state.

The Czech went back to the fire, for such a load oppressed his spirit that he wanted to talk of it with the old knight of Bogdaniec. He found him also plunged in thought and paying no attention to the snoring of the fatigued Arnold, who, after consuming an immeasurable quantity of smoked turnips and meat, was sleeping like a log.

"Will you not rest, lord?" asked the squire.

"Sleep flees from my eyelids," Macko replied. "God grant a good morrow!" And he looked up at the stars. "The Wain is already visible in the sky, and I am wondering all the time how this will end."

"I, too, cannot sleep, for my head is full of the young lady of Zgorzelice."

"Eh! True! Fresh trouble. She is at Spychow."

"Yes, at Spychow. We brought her from Zgorzelice, God knows why."

"She herself wanted to go to the abbot, and when there was no abbot, what was I to do?" Macko replied impatiently, for he did not like to speak of it, since he really felt at fault.

"Yes, but what now?"

"Ha! What now? I will take her back home, and let God's will be done." After a while, he continued: "Yes, God's will be done; but if only she, Danusia, were well and normal, one would at least know what to do. As it stands, one is left in the dark. Supposing she does not get well—and does not die! May the Lord Jesus grant one thing or the other!"

But the Czech at that moment was thinking of Jagienka.

"You see, your grace," he said, "the young lady, when I was

taking leave of her at Spychow, said to me: 'If anything should happen, come here before Zbyszko and before Macko; if they will have to send news by someone, they will send it by you, and you shall take me back to Zgorzelice.'"

"Yes," Macko replied. "It is certain that it would be unfitting to leave her at Spychow till Danusia came. It is certain that she must now go to Zgorzelice. I am grieved for the little orphan, sincerely grieved, but as it was not the will of God, what is to be done? But how is this to be arranged? Wait! You say that she bade you return before us with the news and then conduct her back to Zgorzelice?"

"She did, as I have faithfully repeated to you."

"Well, then you can start before us! Old Jurand must also be informed that his daughter has been found, else the sudden joy might kill him. As I love God, there is nothing better we can do. Go back! Tell them that we have rescued Danusia and shall soon be coming with her, and then take the poor girl and conduct her home."

The old knight sighed, for he was really grieved for Jagienka and for the plans that he had cherished in his heart.

"I know that you are a prudent and strong fellow," he said, after a while, "but can you protect her from all injury and misadventure? One thing or another may easily happen on the road."

"I can, even if I have to give up my life! I will take a few good men, whom the Lord of Spychow will not begrudge me, and will conduct her safely to the end of the world if need be."

"Well, be not over-confident. Remember also that once you get to Zgorzelice, you must again keep an eye on Wolf of Birchwood and Cztan of Rogow. . . . Ah! I see I'm talking nonsense. Now the situation is different, of course. Before, there was a reason to be on guard against them. But now I cherish no hope; let come what may."

"Nevertheless I shall guard the young lady even from those knights, for the other, Lord Zbyszko's unfortunate wife, is worn and thin and barely alive. Supposing she died. . . ."

"True, as I love God: she is worn and thin and barely alive. Supposing she died. . . ."

"We must leave that to God. Now let us think only of the young lady of Zgorzelice."

"By rights, I ought to conduct her back to her father's house," said Macko. "But it is difficult to manage. For various reasons, I cannot leave Zbyszko now. You saw how he gnashed his teeth and rushed at the commander to stab him like a pig. If, as you say, the girl dies on the road, I don't know whether I shall be able to restrain him. But if I am not there, nothing will check him, for sure, and everlasting shame will fall on him and on his whole line—which God forbid, amen!"

"There's a simple way out of this," replied the Czech. "Give me that hangman, and I will not let go of him until I throw him down at Lord Jurand's feet."

"God give you health! Oh, you are clever!" exclaimed Macko joyfully. "It's a simple thing. A simple thing. Take him with you, and once you get him to Spychow, do with him what you like."

"Then give me also that bitch from Ortelsburg! If she doesn't cause trouble on the road, I will bring her there too; but if she does, I will hang her from a tree!"

"Danusia may lose her fear and come to herself sooner if she does not see those two about her anymore. But if you take the woman-servant, how will Danusia manage without female help?"

"In the forests you should come across some local peasants, or refugees, with their women-folk. Take the first available woman; she will certainly be better than that lizard. In the meantime Lord Zbyszko's attendants will suffice."

"For some reason your words today are wiser than usual. You are right. Perhaps she will recover her senses sooner if she sees Zbyszko constantly about her. He can be like a father and a mother to her. Good! And when shall you start?"

"I shall not wait for daybreak, but I will lie down a little. I don't think it is midnight yet."

"The Wain, as I said, is already shining, but the Larger Bear has not yet risen."

"God be praised that we have thought of something, for I was terribly worried."

So saying, the Czech stretched himself out by the dying fire, covered himself with a shaggy skin, and in a moment was asleep. The sky had not yet paled, even a bit, when he awoke, crawled out from under the skin, and looked at the stars. After stretching his somewhat stiffened limbs, he woke up Macko.

"It is time for me to go," he said.

"Where to?" asked Macko half-consciously, rubbing his eyes.

"To Spychow."

"Ah, yes. Who is that snoring over there? He could wake the dead."

"Sir Arnold. I will throw some branches on the live coals and then go to my men."

So he went, but quickly returned, calling out in a low voice:

"Lord, there is news—bad news!"

"What has happened?" exclaimed Macko, springing up.

"The woman-servant has escaped. My men took her among the horses and unbound her legs, blast them! And when they had gone to sleep, she crawled away like a snake and escaped. Come, lord."

The troubled Macko hastened with Hlawa to the horses, but they found only one attendant with them. The rest had scattered in pursuit of the fugitive. However, it was a foolish task, looking for her in the darkness and the thickets, so they soon returned with lowered heads. Macko belabored them with his fists in silence, and then, since there was nothing else to do, he returned to the fire.

Soon Zbyszko joined him. Unable to sleep, he had been on guard before the hut and had heard the tramping. Macko told him what he and the Czech had devised together, and then informed him of the escape of the woman-servant.

"It is no great misfortune," Macko said, "for she will either perish of hunger in the woods or she will be found by peasants, who will put an end to her if the wolves do not find her first. I regret only that she will escape punishment at Spychow."

Zbyszko also regretted the same thing, but otherwise received the news calmly. He raised no objections to the departure of the Czech with Siegfried, because he was indifferent to anything that did not directly concern Danusia. In fact, he began immediately to speak of her.

"I will take her in front of me on my horse tomorrow, and we will ride like that," he said.

"And how is she? Is she asleep?" asked Macko.

"Sometimes she chirps a little; but whether she is dreaming or awake, I do not know, and I don't want to go in for fear of frightening her."

Further talk was interrupted by the Czech, who saw Zbyszko and exclaimed:

"So your grace is already on your feet? Well, it is time for me to go! The horses are ready and the old devil is tied to a saddle. Day will soon break, for the nights are short now. God be with your graces!"

"Go with God, and farewell!"

But Hlawa drew Macko aside for a further moment:

"I wanted to ask you, lord, in case anything should happen— you know—some misfortune or something—to send a man immediately to Spychow. If we have already left Spychow, let him ride after us."

"Good!" said Macko. "And I forgot to tell you to take Jagienka to Plock, do you understand? Go to the bishop there and tell him who she is, that she is the abbot's god-daughter, mentioned in the will that is in the bishop's possession, and beg him to be her guardian, for that also is in the will."

"And if the bishop bids us stay at Plock?"

"Listen to him in everything and do as he advises."

"So it shall be, lord. May God be with you!"

"And with you too!"

CHAPTER LVI

WHEN he learned next morning of the woman-servant's escape, Sir Arnold smiled under his moustache but said the same thing as Macko: that she would either be eaten by wolves or killed by the Lithuanians. This was quite probable, for the local population, of Lithuanian origin, hated the Order and everything connected with it. Some of the peasants had fled to Skirwoillo, while others had revolted and, after murdering Germans here and there, had taken refuge with their families and cattle in the impenetrable depths of the forests. Nevertheless, search was made for the woman, but without success, for it was carried out none too diligently, since Macko and Zbyszko had their heads full of other things and had not given strict enough orders. They were anxious to get to Mazovia and wanted to start at sunrise, but they could not do that, as Danusia had fallen into a deep sleep at dawn, and Zbyszko would not let her be wakened. He had heard her "chirping" in the night and had supposed that she was awake, so now he hoped much good would come from this sleep. Twice he stole into the hut, and twice he saw by the light coming though the cracks between the rafters her closed eyes, open mouth, and deeply-flushed face, such as children have when sound asleep. Then his heart melted within him, and he said to her: "God grand you rest and health, sweet and gentle flower!" And he continued: "Your misery is ended, your weeping is ended, and may the merciful Lord Jesus grant that your happiness will be as inexhaustible as the ever-flowing waters of a river!" Then, having a simple and kind heart, he lifted it up to God and asked himself how he could express his gratitude, with what he could repay, what he could offer to some church of his cattle, his grain, his flocks, his wax, or other such things acceptable to the Lord. He might even have made a vow right then and there, and named each thing he would offer; but he preferred to wait, for, not knowing in what state of health Danusia would wake, or whether she would wake in her right senses, he was not yet certain whether there would be anything for which to be grateful.

Macko, although he knew that they would not be quite safe until they reached Duke Janusz's domains, was none the less of the opinion that Danusia's rest ought not to be disturbed, since it might be her salvation; so he kept the men and pack-horses ready, but waited.

However, when noon had passed and she still slept, they began to feel anxious. Zbyszko, who continually kept looking through the chinks and through the door, finally went into the hut for the third time and sat down on a block that the servingwoman had brought in the previous evening to use as a seat for Danusia while she was being dressed.

So he sat down and looked at her, but she did not open her eyes. Only after the lapse of so much time as would be needed for repeating a paternoster and an ave without haste did her lips quiver slightly, and she whispered, as if seeing through her closed eyelids:

"Zbyszko. . . ."

He instantly threw himself on his knees before her, took her thin hands in his, and kissed them ardently.

"Thank God!" he said in a broken voice. "Danusia! You recognize me!"

His voice woke her completely. She sat up on the bed and repeated, this time with open eyes:

"Zbyszko. . . ."

Then she blinked and looked about as if in surprise.

"You are no longer in captivity," said Zbyszko. "I have rescued you, and we are going to Spychow."

But she drew her hands out of his and said:

"All this happened because daddy's permission was lacking. Where is my lady?"

"Wake up, little berry! The duchess is far away, and we have got you back from the Germans."

She seemed not to have heard his words. Instead, as if remembering something, she said, "They took away my lute and broke it against the wall!"

"Dear God!" exclaimed Zbyszko.

Only then did he notice that her eyes were wild and flashing, and her cheeks burning. At that moment the thought came to him that perhaps she was seriously ill and that she had pronounced his name twice only because she was delirious and it was running in her head.

So his heart palpitated with fear, and cold sweat covered his forehead.

"Danusia!" he said. "Do you see me and understand me?"

But she replied in a tone of humble request:

"I'm thirsty! . . . Water!"

"Merciful Jesus!"

And he ran from the room. Before the door he bumped into old Macko, who was just coming in to see how she was. Uttering only the one word, "Water," he ran as fast as he could to the stream that flowed nearby among the bushes and mosses of the forest.

Soon he came back with a full vessel and gave it to Danusia, who drank thirstily. Before that, Macko had gone into the hut and looked at the sick girl, the sight of whom evidently troubled him.

"Is she feverish?" he asked.

"Yes," groaned Zbyszko.

"Does she understand what you say?"

"No."

The old man frowned. He raised his hand and began to scratch his neck and the back of his head.

"What to do?"

"I don't know."

"There is only one thing. . . ." began Macko.

But at that moment Danusia interrupted him. After finishing her drink, she fixed her wide-open, feverish eyes upon him and said:

"I did not do you any harm. Have compassion on me!"

"I have compassion on you, child, and want only what's good for you," the old knight replied with a certain emotion. And then to Zbyszko: "Listen! It makes no sense to keep her around here. When the wind blows upon her and the sun warms her, then perhaps she will be better. Don't lose your head, boy, but take her and put her in the same litter in which they carried her, or even on horseback, and set out. Do you understand?"

Then he went out of the hut to give the necessary final directions. But scarcely had he taken a step, when he suddenly stopped and stood still, as if rooted to the ground.

For a strong detachment of footmen, armed with pikes and halberds, surrounded the hut, the kilns, and the clearing on four sides, like a wall.

"Germans!" he thought.

Horror filled his heart. In a flash he grasped the hilt of his sword, set his teeth, and stood like a wild beast which has been unexpectedly surrounded by dogs and gets ready for desperate defence.

Meanwhile the gigantic Arnold came towards him from a kiln, accompanied by another knight. When he drew near, he said:

"Swift is the wheel of fortune. I was your prisoner, but now you are mine."

He looked arrogantly at the old knight, as if he were a creature on a lower scale than himself. He was not thoroughly bad, nor too cruel, but he had that fault common to all the Teutonic Knights, who, though humane and even polished in misfortune, were never able to conceal their contempt for the vanquished or their boundless pride when they felt greater force behind them.

"You are our prisoners!" he said with haughtiness.

The old knight looked around gloomily. In his breast beat a heart which was far from timid—nay, it was too audacious. If he had been in armor on his war-horse, if he had had Zbyszko beside him, and if they both had had in their hands swords or axes or those terrible clubs which the Lechitic gentry of those days wielded so well, maybe he would have tried to break through the wall of pikes and halberds that enclosed him. But here he was standing before Arnold on foot, alone, and without breastplate; so, seeing that his men had already thrown down their weapons, and considering that Zbyszko was quite unarmed in the hut with Danusia, he realized, as an experienced man versed in the arts of war, that there was no possible escape.

So he slowly drew his misericord from its sheath and threw it at the feet of the knight who stood beside Arnold. This knight, with no less arrogance than Arnold's, but with more grace, addressed him in good Polish.

"Your name, lord? If you will give your word of honor, I will not have you bound, for I see you are a belted knight and you treated my brother well."

"I give you my word," replied Macko.

And explaining who he was, he asked whether he might go into the hut and warn his nephew, "lest he do something rash." Then, having received permission, he vanished through the door and after some time reappeared with a misericord in his hand.

"My nephew has not even a sword with him," he said, "and begs that he may stay with his wife until you are ready to go."

"Let him stay," said Arnold's brother. "I will send him food and drink, for we are not starting at once, as our men are weary and we ourselves need sustenance and rest. I invite you also, lord, to our company."

He turned and went towards the same fire by which Macko had spent the night, but whether it were through pride or through ill manners—common enough among the Germans—he went first, leaving Macko to trail after him. But he, being a much-experienced man, who knew what custom should be observed in every event, asked him:

"Are you inviting me, lord, as a guest or as a prisoner?"

Then Arnold's brother was ashamed; he stopped and said:

"Pass, lord."

The old knight passed; but not wishing to wound the proper pride of a man on whom much might depend, he said:

"One can see, lord, that you not only know various languages but also have courtly manners."

Thereupon Arnold, who understood only a few words, addressed his brother:

"Wolfgang, what is he saying?"

"He speaks to the point," replied Wolfgang, who was evidently flattered by Macko's words.

Then they sat down by the fire, and food and drink were brought. The lesson given the Germans by Macko was not, however, wasted, for Wolfgang offered him food first. From the talk which followed, the old knight learned how they had fallen into the trap. Wolfgang, Arnold's younger brother, was bringing up footmen from Czluchowa to New Kowno against the revolting Samogitians, but, since they came from a distant commandery, they could not catch up with the horsemen. Arnold did not feel the need to wait for them, because he knew that on the road he would find other detachments of footmen from towns and castles nearer the Lithuanian border. For this reason Wolfgang was several days' march behind, and he happened to be on the trail near to the pitch-burners' settlement when the woman-servant of the Order, having escaped by night, informed him of the misadventure which had befallen his elder brother. Arnold, hearing this account translated for him into German, nodded with satisfaction and finally declared that he had expected things would turn out thus.

But the experienced Macko, who in every situation endeavored to find some way out, reflected that it would be useful to reconcile these Germans with himself; so after a moment he said:

"It is always a hard fate to fall into captivity, but I thank God that He has given me into your hands and not into the hands of others, for verily you are true knights and protect your honor."

Wolfgang closed his eyes and nodded his head, stiffly indeed, but with evident satisfaction.

And the old knight continued:

"And you know our language so well! I see that God has given you intelligence for everything!"

"I know your language because the people at Czluchowa speak Polish, and my brother and I have served for seven years under the commander there."

"And given time you will succeed to his office. It cannot be otherwise. However, your brother does not speak Polish as well as you."

"He understands a little, but he does not speak it. My brother has greater strength than I, although I myself am no weakling, but he has the blunter wit."

"Hey! he doesn't seem to me to be stupid!" exclaimed Macko.

"Wolfgang! What is he saying?" asked Arnold again.

"He is praising you," Wolfgang replied.

"Of course, I am praising him, for he is a true knight—and that is what matters. I will tell you frankly that today I was thinking of releasing him on his word of honor, to go where he would, so long as he presented himself within a year's time. Such is the custom among belted knights, after all."

And he looked attentively at Wolfgang's face, but the latter frowned and said:

"Maybe I, too, would have released you, if it were not that you helped these pagan dogs against us."

"That is not true," Macko replied.

And there began again the same sharp dispute as with Arnold on the preceding day. However, although the old knight had right on his side, he found he had a harder task this time, for Wolfgang was really of keener intelligence than his elder brother. Still, the dispute had this positive result, that the younger brother also heard of all the crimes, perjuries, and treacheries at Ortelsburg, and, at the same time, of the fate of the unfortunate Danusia. Indeed, he had no answer to that and to all the wickedness which Macko revealed, and was forced to admit that the vengeance taken by the Polish knights was justified and that they had a right to act as they had done. Finally he said:

"By the blessed bones of Liborius! I certainly shall not grieve for Danveld. They said of him that he practised black magic, but the power and the justice of God are stronger than black magic. As for Siegfried, I do not know whether he also served the devil, but I shall not go after him, for, in the first place, I have no horsemen and, in the second place, if he has tormented that girl as you say, he can go to hell for all I care." Here he crossed himself, then added: "God, be at hand to help me now and when I die!"

"And what is to happen to that unfortunate martyr?" asked Macko. "Will you not allow her to be conducted home? Is she to die in your dungeons? Think of the wrath of God."

"I have nothing to do with the girl," replied Wolfgang roughly. "One of you may conduct her to her father and then present himself to us again; but I will not let both of you go."

"Not if I swore on my honor and the lance of St. George?"

Wolfgang hesitated a little, for that was a great and powerful imploration, but at that moment Arnold asked for the third time:

"What is he saying?"

And when he heard what was at stake, he objected vehemently and rudely to releasing them both on parole. He had his own selfish motives. He had been defeated in the bigger battle by

Skirwoillo and in single combat by the Polish knights. As a soldier, too, he knew that his brother's footmen would now have to return to Malbork, for if they persisted in going on to New Kowno, after the destruction of the previous detachments, they would be merely offering themselves up for slaughter. So he knew that he would have to stand before the grand master and the marshal, and he concluded that he would be less shamed if he had at least one important captive to show. A living knight, who could be produced before the master's eyes, would weigh more than a story that he had taken two such captives.

So Macko, hearing Arnold's hoarse and noisy argument, perceived at once that he must take what they gave, since he would not get anything more. He therefore turned to Wolfgang and said:

"There is one other thing I would ask of you, lord. I am sure that my nephew will understand that it befits him to stay with his wife, and me to remain with you. But, should that not be the case, allow me to make it clear to him that there is nothing to be said about it, for such is your will."

"Very well; it makes no difference to me," replied Wolfgang. "Let us speak of the ransom which your nephew has to bring for himself and for you, as everything depends on that."

"Of the ransom?" asked Macko, who would have preferred to postpone the discussion of this topic. "Won't we have time for that later? When an affair concerns a belted knight, his word is as good as ready money, and as for the price, one may rely on his conscience. We, for example, took captive an important knight of yours at New Kowno, a certain Sieur de Lorche, and my nephew— for it was he who took him—released him on his word of honor without saying anything about the price."

"You took Sieur de Lorche?" asked Wolfgang with animation. "I know him. He is a wealthy knight. Why did we not meet him on the road?"

"Evidently he did not go that way, but either to New Kowno or in the direction of Ragneta," Macko replied.

"He is a wealthy knight and of distinguished family," repeated Wolfgang. "You will get a fine ransom for him! But it is good that you mentioned it, for now I shall not release you too cheaply."

Macko bit his moustache, but he raised his head proudly:

"We know our value without that."

"All the better," said the younger von Baden. But immediately afterwards he added: "All the better, not for us, who are humble monks, sworn to poverty, but for the Order, which will use your money for the glory of God."

Macko made no reply to that, but merely looked at Wolfgang, as much as to say: "Tell that to someone else!" In the next moment they began to bargain. This was a hard and vexatious proceeding for the old knight. On the one hand, he was sensitive to any loss; and on the other, he realized that it would not befit him to set too low a value on himself and Zbyszko. So he wriggled like a fish, the more that Wolfgang, suave as he might be in speech and manners, proved immeasurably avaricious and as hard as a rock. Macko's only comfort was the thought that de Lorche would pay for it all; but even so he grieved for his lost hopes of gain, since he did not count on any profit from the ransom of Siegfried, feeling sure that Jurand, and even Zbyszko, would not renounce their vengeance on him for any price.

After long bargaining, he finally agreed on the number of marks to be paid and the date for their delivery; and after arranging how many men and how many horses Zbyszko was to take, he went to let him know, advising him, at the same time, to start immediately, for he feared that the Germans might suddenly change their minds.

"This is what it's like being a knight," he said sighing. "One day you're holding him by the scruff of his neck, and the next day he's holding you! Well, well! God grant our turn may come again soon. But now lose no time. If you ride fast you will overtake Hlawa, and both of you will be safer together. Once you get out of the forest region and reach populated country in Mazovia, you will find hospitality and help and care at every nobleman's or small land-owner's house. Even to strangers such things are not refused among us, so how much more will they be given to our own folk. It may mean salvation for the poor girl."

While saying this, he looked at Danusia, who was sunk in a half-slumber, breathing rapidly and noisily. Her transparent hands, lying on the dark bearskin, trembled feverishly.

Macko made the sign of the cross over her and said:

"Heh, take her and go! May God change her fate, for it seems to me thin-spun!"

"Don't say that!" Zbyszko exclaimed with despairing emphasis.

"Everything is in God's hands. I will have your horse brought here, and then you must be off!"

He went out of the hut and arranged everything for their departure. The Turks given him by Zawisza brought up the horses with the litter lined with moss and skins. Zbyszko's attendant Vit led him his charger—and presently Zbyszko came out of the *numa*, holding Danusia in his arms. There was something so touching in their appearance that both the von Baden brothers, whom curiosity had brought to the hut, when they saw Danusia's still child-like figure, her face, resembling the faces of holy virgins in church pictures, and her great weakness, which prevented her from raising her head, supported as it was on the young knight's shoulder, began to look at one another in surprise and to be deeply indignant against the authors of her misery. "Indeed, Siegfried had the heart of a hangman, not of a knight," whispered Wolfgang to his brother. "And that snake, although it was by her doing that I am free, I will have beaten with rods." They were also moved by the fact that Zbyszko carried Danusia in his arms, as a mother carries a child, and they understood his love, for they both still had young blood in their veins.

Zbyszko hesitated a while as to whether he should take the sick girl on his saddle and hold her to his breast on the road, or whether he should put her in the litter. Finally he decided on the latter course, as he thought she would be more comfortable lying down. Then he went up to his uncle and bent over his hand to kiss it and take his leave. Macko, who loved him as the apple of his eye, was unwilling to show emotion before the Germans, yet he was unable to restrain himself and, clasping him close, pressed his lips to his thick golden hair.

"God conduct you!" he said. "And don't forget this old man, for captivity is always hard to bear."

"I shall not forget," Zbyszko replied.

"May the most Holy Mother give you comfort!"

"God reward you for that—and for everything!"

A moment later, Zbyszko was already mounted, but Macko remembered something else; he bent towards him and laid his hand on his knee, saying:

"Listen! If you overtake Hlawa, beware lest you bring shame on yourself and on my grey hairs. Jurand may take vengeance on

Siegfried, but not you. Swear to me on your sword and on your honor."

"I will even prevent Jurand from taking vengeance on Siegfried at your expense," Zbyszko replied.

"You care so much for me?"

The young man smiled sadly.

"You know I do."

"Off you go! Farewell!"

The horses moved off and were soon hidden from view in the bright hazel thickets. Macko suddenly felt terribly sad and lonely, and his heart yearned mightily for the beloved youth, who was the whole hope of his line. But he immediately shook off his grief, for he was a hard man and had control over himself.

"Thank God that I am the captive, and not Zbyszko!" And he turned to the Germans. "And you, lords, when will you move, and where to?"

"When we please," answered Wolfgang. "And we shall go to Malbork, where you, lord, must first stand before the grand master."

"Alas, the people there are ready to cut my throat for aiding the Samogitians," Macko said to himself.

But he was calmed by the thought that he had Sieur de Lorche in reserve and that the von Badens themselves would defend his life, if only in order not to lose his ransom.

"Of course, if I they do away with me," he said to himself, "Zbyszko would not need either to present himself or to pay for me."

And this thought gave him a certain satisfaction.

CHAPTER LVII

ZBYSZKO was unable to overtake his squire, for the latter rode day and night, resting only as much as was absolutely necessary for the sake of the horses. Fed as they were only on grass, they were weak and could not make such long rides as in districts where oats were easier to get. Hlawa did not spare himself, and he had no regard for Siegfried's age and weakness. The old Teutonic Knight suffered terribly because of this, particularly as the muscular Macko had previously dislocated his bones. But the worst thing for him was the mosquitoes, which swarmed in the damp wilderness and which he could not drive away since his hands were bound and his legs tied beneath his horse's belly. The squire did not indeed inflict any special tortures on him, but he had no mercy on him and freed his right hand only at the halts, so that he might take food. "Eat, you wolf-face, so that I may bring you alive to the lord at Spychow." Such were the words with which he encouraged him to take his meals. At the beginning of the journey, Siegfried had cherished the thought of starving himself to death; but when he heard Hlawa's threat to prize his teeth open with a knife and push his food down his throat by force, he preferred to yield rather than expose his monkly dignity and knightly honor to insult.

The Czech was extremely anxious to reach Spychow before his master, in order to shield his adored young lady from shame. Simple nobleman as he was, sensible and not without knightly feelings, he understood very well that there would be a certain humiliation for Jagienka in being at Spychow at the same time as Danusia. "I shall tell the bishop at Plock," he thought, "that the old Lord of Bogdaniec, as her guardian, had to take her with him; and then, once it becomes known that she is under episcopal protection and that, in addition to Zgorzelice, she will inherit property from the abbot, no voivode's son will be too good for her." And this thought lightened the fatigues of his journey, for he had been worried that the good news he was bringing to Spychow would be a sentence of misery for the young lady.

Often, also, he pictured the red-cheeked Anulka. At such times, if the road permitted, he would tickle the flanks of his horse with his spurs, so eager was he to get to Spychow.

They travelled along difficult roads, or rather along no roads at all, through the forest, straight as an arrow. The Czech knew only that if he travelled somewhat to the west and constantly to the south, he would in the end reach Mazovia, and then all would be well. He steered by the sun during the daytime and by the stars when the march was prolonged into the night. The wilderness before him seemed to have no limits and no end. Days and nights went by in its dim shadows. More than once Hlawa thought that the young knight would not bring his wife alive through that frightful, uninhabited region, where the horses had to be guarded at night against wolves and bears, and where in the daytime it was necessary to avoid herds of aurochs and bison; where terrible boars sharpened their curved tusks on the roots of pines; and where the man who did not shoot a spotted buck or boar pig with his crossbow, or stick it with his pike, had to go whole days without food.

"How will it be," Hlawa thought, "to ride with such a tormented, worn-out girl, who is about to breathe her last?"

Time and again he had to avoid extensive swamps or deep ravines, at the bottom of which roared torrents swollen by the spring rains. There were also lakes in the wilderness, in which were to be seen at sunset whole herds of elk or deer swimming in the reddened, smooth waters. The riders sometimes also caught sight of columns of smoke, proclaiming the presence of human beings. Hlawa frequently approached these forest settlements, but there poured out to meet him such wild folk, clad in skins on their naked bodies and armed with clubs and bows, and shooting such threatening looks from beneath their tangled hair, that it was well to take advantage of their first surprise at the sight of knights and ride off as fast as possible.

On two occasions arrows whistled past the Czech, and he was pursued by shouts of *"Wokili!"* (Germans!), but he preferred to withdraw rather than explain who he was. After several days, he began to think that he must have passed the border, but there was no one around to ask. Finally he learned from some beaters, whose native tongue was Polish, that he had reached Mazovian soil.

Now the going was easier, although the whole of eastern Mazovia was also one great primeval wilderness. Where there was a settlement, the inhabitants were less unfriendly, perhaps because they were not continually fed with hate, or perhaps because the Czech addressed them in a language they could understand. He had to suffer only from the measureless curiosity of these people, who surrounded him and his men in crowds and deluged them with questions. When they learned that he was bringing a captive Teutonic Knight, they would say: "Give him to us, lord! We will deal with him!" And they insisted so tenaciously that the Czech showed anger and made it clear that the captive was the duke's. Then they gave way. Later, in the inhabited districts, it was not so easy with the gentry and small landowners. They burned with hatred against the Teutonic Knights, for they vividly remembered everywhere all the treachery and wrong done to the duke when the Knights had kidnapped him at Zlotorya in time of profound peace and held him prisoner. They did not indeed want to "deal with" Siegfried, but one or another hardened nobleman would say: "Unbind him, and I will give him a weapon and challenge him to life-and-death combat." However, he hammered it into their heads that the unfortunate Lord of Spychow had the first right of vengeance and that he must not be deprived of it.

But, on the other hand, travelling was easier in the settled districts, for there were roads of one kind or another, and oats or barley everywhere for the horses. So the Czech rode fast, not stopping anywhere, and ten days before Corpus Christi he reached Spychow.

He arrived in the evening, as he had done that time when he had been sent by Macko from Ortelsburg with the news of his departure for Samogitia; and just as she had done that time, Jagienka caught sight of him from the window and ran down to meet him, and he fell at her feet, unable for some time to utter a word. But she lifted him up and took him upstairs as quickly as possible, since she did not want to question him in the presence of others.

"What news?" she asked, trembling with impatience and scarcely able to draw breath. "Are they alive? Are they well?"

"Alive and well!"

"And she has been found?"

"She has. They rescued her."

"Jesus Christ be praised!"

But despite her words her face froze, for all her hopes were scattered in an instant to the winds.

But her strength did not leave her, nor did she lose consciousness; and presently she came fully to herself and began again to question him:

"When will they be here?"

"In a few days. Travelling is difficult—with a sick woman."

"Is she sick?"

"Tormented. Her mind has given way under her sufferings."

"Merciful Jesus!"

A short silence followed; only Jagienka's white lips moved as if in prayer.

"Did she not recover with Zbyszko?" she said, resuming her questioning.

"Perhaps she did; I do not know, for I left at once to give you the news, lady, before they came."

"God reward you! Tell me what happened."

So the Czech told her in a few words how they had rescued Danusia and taken the gigantic Arnold captive together with Siegfried. He also informed her that he had brought Siegfried with him, since the young knight wished to give him to Jurand as a present and for vengeance.

"Now I must go to Jurand," said Jagienka when he had finished.

And she went out, but Hlawa was not left long alone, for Anulka ran out of the alcove to him, and—whether it was that he was not quite himself after the fatigues he had undergone, or that he longed for her and forgot himself at the sight of her—he caught her by the waist, pressed her to his chest, and began to kiss her eyes, cheeks, and lips, as if he had long since told her everything which one ought to tell a girl before such doings.

Indeed, perhaps he had already told her in spirit during his journey, for he kissed her and kissed her unceasingly, and hugged her so tightly that she could scarcely breathe; while she yielded, at first from surprise and then from a faintness so great that if less strong arms had been holding her, she would have slipped to the ground. Fortunately all this did not last too long, for steps were audible on the stairs, and presently Father Caleb hastened into the room.

So they sprang apart, and Father Caleb began in his turn to load Hlawa with questions, which he answered with difficulty, being out of breath. The priest supposed it was from fatigue. However, having heard confirmation of the news that Danusia was found and rescued, and her tormentor brought to Spychow, he threw himself on his knees to thank God. Meanwhile Hlawa's blood cooled somewhat; and when the priest rose, he was able to tell him more calmly how they had found and rescued Jurand's daughter.

"God has not liberated her," said the priest when he had heard it, "in order to leave her mind and spirit in darkness and under the control of unholy powers. Jurand will lay his sainted hands on her and with one prayer will restore her to her senses and to health."

"Jurand?" asked the Czech in surprise. "Has he such power? Has he become a saint in his lifetime?"

"Yes, before God; and when he dies, people will have one martyr and patron more in heaven."

"But you said, reverend father, that he would lay his hands on his daughter's head. Has his right hand grown again? I know you begged the Lord Jesus to make it grow."

"I said 'hands' as we usually do," replied the priest, "but, by God's grace, one alone will be enough."

"Certainly," answered Hlawa.

But his tone betrayed disillusion, for he had expected to see a miracle. Further talk was interrupted by the entrance of Jagienka.

"I told him the news cautiously," she said, "so that sudden joy should not kill him, and he immediately fell crosswise to the floor and began to pray."

"He often lies thus whole nights long, and this time he will assuredly not rise to his feet again until dawn," said Father Caleb.

And so it was. Several times they looked in at him, and each time they found him lying, not in sleep, but in prayer so ardent that he entirely forgot his own self.

It was not until next morning, when Jagienka went to look at him some considerable time after Matins, that he signified his desire to see Hlawa and the captive. So Siegfried was brought from the dungeon with his hands tied crosswise on his breast, and they all accompanied Tolima into the presence of the old man.

For the first few moments the Czech could not see anything clearly, for the membrane windowpanes let through but little light, and the day was dark because of the clouds, which entirely covered the sky and foreshadowed a serious storm. But when his keen eyes had become accustomed to the half-light, he scarcely recognized Jurand, so thin and emaciated had he become. The gigantic man had turned into a gigantic skeleton. His face was so white that it was not very different from the milky color of his hair and beard, and when he leaned back in his chair and closed his eyes, he seemed to Hlawa exactly like a corpse.

By his chair stood a table, on which was a crucifix, a jug of water, and a loaf of black bread, in which was stuck a misericord, the ugly knife used by knights to dispatch the wounded. Jurand had long been accustomed to take no other food but bread and water. His garment, which he wore over his bare flesh, was a thick hair-shirt, girted with a cord. Thus, since his return from captivity at Ortelsburg, lived the wealthy and once terrible knight of Spychow.

Hearing the steps of those who came in, he pushed away his tame she-wolf, which warmed his bare feet, and leaned back. Then he seemed to the Czech indeed like one dead. A moment of waiting followed, for he was expected to give some sign that one of them should speak, but he sat motionless, white and calm, with partly opened lips, as if indeed sunk in the everlasting sleep of death.

"Hlawa is here," said Jagienka finally in her sweet voice. "Would you like to question him?"

He nodded assent, so Hlawa began his story for the third time. He made short mention of the battles fought against the Germans at New Kowno and told of the fight with Arnold von Baden and the rescue of Danusia, but not wishing to give the old martyr pain after the good news, or rouse in him fresh anxiety, he concealed the fact that Danusia was out of her mind after long days of cruel misery.

On the other hand, embittered as he was against the Teutonic Knights, and desiring that Siegfried should be punished without mercy, he purposely revealed the fact that she had been found terror-struck, miserable, and sick. It was obvious, he declared, that she had been treated inhumanly and that, if she had remained longer in those terrible hands, she would have faded and died like a trampled flower. This gloomy story was accompanied by the no less gloomy mutterings of the approaching storm. Leaden masses of cloud gathered ever more heavily over Spychow.

Jurand listened to the story without a quiver or a movement, so that it might have been thought he was sunk in sleep. Yet he heard and understood everything, for when Hlawa began to speak of Danusia's misery, two great tears gathered in his empty eyes and rolled down his cheeks. Of all earthly feelings only one was still left to him: love for his child.

Then his blue lips began to move in prayer. In the fortalice yard reverberated the first distant claps of thunder, and flashes of lightning began to illuminate the window from time to time. He prayed long, and tears dropped anew on his white beard. Finally he stopped, and silence fell, extending beyond measure, until it became at last unbearable to the bystanders, who knew not what to do.

So old Tolima, Jurand's right hand, his companion in all his battles, and head of the Spychow guard, spoke up and said:

"There stands before you, lord, that hell-hound, that Teutonic werewolf, who tortured you and your child. Let me know what I am to do with him, and how I am to punish him."

At those words a sudden light seemed to pass over Jurand's face, and he beckoned to bring the prisoner up to him.

Two attendants seized him by the shoulders and brought him before the old man, who stretched out his hand and passed it over Siegfried's face, as if wishing to recall his features or to impress them on his memory for the last time; then he lowered his hand to the knight's breast, felt his crossed hands and touched the cords, and again closed his eye-sockets and lowered his head.

The bystanders thought he was considering what to do. But whatever it was, it did not take long. He roused himself and put out his hand towards the loaf of bread in which was stuck the ominous misericord.

Then Jagienka, the Czech, and even old Tolima and all the servants, held their breath. Punishment was a hundred times deserved; vengeance was justified—and yet the thought of that old man, half-alive, groping his way to butcher a bound captive made everyone shudder.

But he grasped the knife by the middle, put his forefinger on the end of the blade so as to know what it touched, and began to cut the cords on the Teutonic Knight's arms.

All were struck with amazement. They now understood what he wanted, yet were unwilling to believe their eyes. It was too much for them. Hlawa was the first to mutter something, then Tolima, and, after him, the men. Only Father Caleb asked in a voice broken by uncontrollable weeping:

"Brother Jurand, what do you want? Do you want to give the captive his freedom?"

"Yes," answered Jurand by nodding his head.

"Do you want him to go without vengeance and punishment?"

"Yes."

The mutterings of wrath and indignation increased, but Father Caleb, not wanting this unheard-of deed of mercy to be wasted, turned to the murmurers and called out:

"Who dares oppose a saint? On your knees!"

And, kneeling down himself, he repeated:

"Our Father, who art in heaven, hallowed be Thy name; Thy kingdom come. . ."

And he recited the Lord's Prayer to the end. At the words, "And forgive us our trespasses as we forgive those who trespass against us," his eyes turned involuntarily to Jurand, whose face was indeed lit up by some unearthly splendor.

And that sight, in conjunction with the words of the prayer, touched the hearts of those present, and old Tolima, heart-hardened as he was by incessant battles, made the sign of the Holy Cross and embraced Jurand's knees, saying:

"Lord, if your will is to be fulfilled, the captive must be conducted to the border."

"Yes," Jurand nodded.

Lightning more frequently illuminated the windows; the storm was getting closer and closer.

CHAPTER LVIII

TWO riders were making for the Spychow border through the gale and, at times, torrential rain: Siegfried and Tolima. The latter conducted the German, fearing lest he might be slain on the way by the peasant lookouts or by servants from Spychow, inflamed as they were with terrible hatred and a lust for vengeance. Siegfried rode unarmed but also unfettered. The storm, driven by the gale, was already upon them. From time to time, when there was an unexpected clap of thunder, the horses sat back on their haunches. The men rode in deep silence along a sunken ravine, sometimes so near together, owing to the narrowness of the road, that their stirrups touched. Tolima, accustomed for years to guard captives, looked at Siegfried even now with an occasional watchful eye, as if fearing he might unawares escape, and each time he involuntarily shuddered, for it seemed to him that the eyes of the Teutonic Knight shone in the twilight like the eyes of an evil spirit or a vampire. He even thought of making the sign of the cross over him, but at the thought that if he did Siegfried might howl in inhuman tones and, turning into some ghastly shape, snap at him with his teeth, he was seized with yet greater fear. The old warrior, who knew how to fight single-handed against whole groups of Germans, as a hawk swoops upon a flock of partridges, was yet afraid of unholy powers and wanted nothing to do with them. He would even have preferred simply to show the German the way and return, but he was ashamed of himself, so he conducted him right to the border.

There, when they had reached the edge of the Spychow forest, the rain stopped for a while and the clouds were brightened by a strange yellow gleam. It grew lighter and Siegfried's eyes lost their former uncanny luminance. But then Tolima was befallen by another temptation: "They ordered me to take that rabid dog safely to the border," he said to himself, "and I have done so. But is he to ride away with no vengeance taken on him and unpunished, tormentor of my lord and of his child? And would it not be a worthy deed and pleasing to God to kill him? Suppose I challenged him to life-and-death combat? He has no weapon, it is true, but a league from here, at the small manor of Lord Warcim, they will surely give him a sword or an axe—and I will fight him. God grant I may overthrow him, and then I will stab him as befits and bury his head in a dunghill!" So Tolima said to himself, and looking greedily at the German, he began to twitch his nostrils as if he already scented fresh blood. And he had to struggle hard against that lust and wrestle with himself, before he finally conquered it, reflecting that Jurand had not given his captive life and freedom only up to the border and that, if he slew him, his lord's saintly act would be for nothing and his reward in heaven would be diminished. So he said:

"Here is our border, and it is not far to yours. Ride in freedom. If your conscience does not choke you, and if no divine thunderbolt blasts you, nothing threatens you from men."

So saying, he turned back, while Siegfried rode on with a strange, stony expression on his face, saying not a single word and seeming not to have heard that he was spoken to.

And he rode on along the broad highway, lost, one would have said, in a dream.

The break in the storm was short, and the brightness did not last long. It became so dark again that one would have said evening was falling, and the clouds came down low, almost to the treetops. From above came an ominous rumble and, as it were, the impatient hiss and growl of thunderbolts, held up as yet by the angel of the storm. Every moment streaks of lightning vividly lit up the threatening heavens and the terrified earth, and then one could see, running between two black walls of forest, the broad road and, in the middle, a lone rider on his horse.

Siegfried rode half-conscious, devoured by feverish unrest. The despair which had racked his soul since the death of Roger, the crimes he had committed in his vengeance, the anxieties, the terrifying visions and inner conflicts of his spirit had long affected his mind to such a degree that it was only by the greatest effort that he kept himself from madness, and at times he did actually give way to it. And now the fresh fatigues of the journey under the hard hand of the Czech, and the night spent in the Spychow prison, and the uncertainty of his fate, and, above all, that unheard-of, almost superhuman act of mercy and grace, which had really frightened him—all these things shook him to the bottom of his soul. At times his mind grew so torpid and blunted that he entirely lost consciousness of what was happening; but afterwards fever wakened him again, and wakened in him at the same time some dull feeling of despair and loss and ruin—a feeling that all was now gone and extinguished, that an end had come, that about him was only night, black night, and nothingness, and some dreadful abyss filled with terror, towards which, nevertheless, he had to go.

"Go! Go!" whispered suddenly a voice in his ear.

He turned and saw Death. Death himself—a skeleton, sitting on a skeleton horse—was riding close at his side, white and rattling his bones.

"Is it you?" asked the Teutonic Knight.

"It is I. Go! Go!"

Then he noticed that he also had a companion at his other side: stirrup to stirrup with him rode a creature, in body like a man, but with an inhuman face, for its head, with erect ears, was a beast's—long, pointed, and covered with black, bristly hair.

"Who are you?" Siegfried cried out.

Instead of answering, the other showed its teeth and began to growl.

Siegfried closed his eyes, but immediately heard the rattling of bones, louder than before, and a voice speaking right at his ear:

"It is time! It is time! Hurry up! Go!"

And he answered:

"I am going! . . ."

The answer came from his breast as if someone else had given it.

Then, seemingly impelled by some irresistible internal force, he dismounted from his horse and took off it his high knight's saddle and then the bridle. His companions dismounted also, not leaving him even for a second, and led him from the middle of the road to the edge of the forest. There the black vampire bent a branch down for him and helped him to fasten his bridle-rein to it.

"Hurry!" whispered Death.

"Hurry!" murmured voices from the treetops.

As if sunk in sleep, Siegfried passed the second rein through the buckle, made a loop—and, standing on the saddle, which he had previously placed beneath the tree, put the rein around his neck.

"Kick away the saddle! Now! Aaa!"

The saddle rolled several feet away—and the body of the ill-fated Teutonic Knight hung heavily.

For a split second it seemed to him that he heard a hoarse, muffled growl and that the horrible vampire threw itself on him, rocking him and tearing at his breast with its teeth to bite into his heart. But then his fading vision caught yet another sight: Death was melting into a kind of whitish cloud, which slowly moved towards him, seized him, embraced him, encompassed him, and finally covered everything with a frightful, impenetrable veil.

At that moment the storm began to rage again with measureless violence. A thunderbolt fell into the middle of the road with such a terrible crash that it seemed the earth had been shaken to its core. The whole forest bent beneath the whirlwind. The soughing, whistling, howling, and creaking of the tree-trunks and the cracking of broken branches filled the depths of the woods. Waves of rain, driven by the wind, covered the world—and it was only during the short, blood-red lightning-flashes that the corpse of Siegfried could be seen, swinging wildly by the roadside.

Next morning a numerous company passed that way. At its head rode Jagienka with Anulka and the Czech, and they were followed by wagons, guarded by four men armed with crossbows and swords. Each of the wagoners had also at his side a pike and a small axe, not counting iron pitchforks and other implements that might prove useful on the way. These were needed for defence against wild beasts, as well as bands of robbers, who ranged continually on the Teutonic border and against whom bitter complaints were made by Jagiello to the grand master, both in letters and personally at conferences at Raciaz.

But if one had stout men and good weapons there was no need to fear them, and so the troop rode along, confident in itself and free from anxiety. After the storm of the preceding day, the morning was most beautiful: fresh, calm, and so bright that where there was no shade the eyes of the travellers were dazzled and forced to blink. Not a leaf moved on the trees, and from each one hung great drops of water, shot with rainbow colors in the sun. Among the pine needles glittered what looked like great diamonds. The torrential rain had left small rivulets on the highway, which flowed with a merry babble to the lower ground, where they formed shallow pools. The whole landscape was wet and bedewed, but smiling in the morning brightness. On such a day the human heart is also filled with joy, so the wagoners and grooms sang quietly to themselves, wondering at the silence which reigned among the riders up ahead.

These, however, were silent because Jagienka was burdened with grave anxiety. Something had finished, something had broken in her life, and the girl, though not too meditative of mind and unable to interpret clearly to herself what was going on within her, felt that all which she had lived for until now had disappointed her and had gone to waste, that all her hopes had dissolved like morning mists over the fields and that she would now have to renounce them all, cast them behind her, forget them, and begin life completely anew. She thought also that, even if by God's grace this new life might not prove entirely bad, it could not be other than melancholy, or at least not as good as what might have been.

And measureless grief for the past, now closed forever, constricted her heart and brought tears to her eyes. But she did not wish to weep, for, in addition to the entire burden crushing her spirit, she felt shame. She would have preferred never to have left Zgorzelice, rather than to return thus from Spychow. She knew that she had not come here merely because she did not know what to do after the abbot's death or because she wanted to deprive Cztan and Wolf of an excuse to make attacks on Zgorzelice. No! Macko also knew, for he, too, had brought her for another reason than those, and assuredly Zbyszko also would come to know. At that thought her cheeks began to burn and bitterness to flood her heart. "I was not prudent enough," she told herself, "and now I have what I deserve." And to her anxiety, her uncertainty of the morrow, her harassing sorrow, and her fathomless grief for the past was now added the feeling of humiliation.

But the further course of her grave thoughts was interrupted by the sight of a man hastening to meet her. The Czech, who had a watchful eye for everything, rode forward and concluded from the crossbow on the man's back, his badger-skin pouch, and the jay feathers in his cap that he was a forester.

"Hey! Who are you? Stop!" he called out, nevertheless, for certainty.

The other approached hastily and with an expression on his face such as people usually have when they bring unusual news.

"Up ahead there's a man hanging by the roadside!" he called out.

The Czech feared it might be the doing of robbers, so he began to ask questions quickly:

"Far from here?"

"A crossbow shot away. Close by the roadside."

"There's no one with him?"

"No one. I drove away a wolf, which was smelling him."

The mention of the wolf calmed Hlawa, for it showed that there were no men, nor any ambush, in the vicinity.

Meanwhile Jagienka said:

"See who it is."

Hlawa rode swiftly forward and soon returned with even more speed.

"It is Siegfried!" he shouted, reining in his horse before Jagienka.

"In the name of the Father and of the Son and of the Holy Ghost! Siegfried, the Teutonic Knight?"

"The Teutonic Knight! He hanged himself with his bridle-rein!"

"Himself?"

"Himself, as can be seen, for the saddle is lying nearby. If robbers had done it, they would simply have killed him and have taken his saddle, since it's a good one."

"How shall we pass?"

"Let us not go that way!" exclaimed the timid Anulka. "Something will cling to us!"

Jagienka also was rather afraid. She believed that a multitude of evil spirits gather around the body of a suicide; but Hlawa, who was bold and afraid of nothing, said:

"Pooh! I was near him and even prodded him with my spear, yet I do not feel any devil on my back."

"Don't blaspheme!" exclaimed Jagienka.

"I am not blaspheming," replied the Czech. "Only I trust in the power of God. Still, if you are afraid, we can ride around through the forest."

Anulka begged her to ride around, but Jagienka, after a moment of reflection, said:

"We cannot leave a dead man unburied! It is a Christian act to bury him, and one commanded by the Lord Jesus; after all, he is a human being."

"Bah, but a Teutonic Knight, a gallows-bird, and a torturer! The ravens and the wolves will look after him."

"Don't say such things! For his faults, God will judge him. Let us do our part. Besides, no evil spirit will cling to us if we fulfill the divine commandment."

"Very well; then let it be as you will," replied the Czech.

And he issued the required order to his men, who obeyed slowly and with disgust. Nevertheless, fearing Hlawa, they took pitch-forks and axes to dig a hole in the ground, as there were not enough spades, and went to bury the dead man. The Czech accompanied them for the sake of example and, after crossing himself, cut with his own hand the strap by which the corpse was hanging.

Siegfried's face had already turned blue in the air and he looked horrible enough, for his eyes were wide and showed an expression of terror, and his mouth was open as if to catch his last breath. So they quickly dug a hole nearby and pushed the body into it, face downward, with the handles of their forks; then, when they had covered it with earth, they looked for stones, since it was an immemorial custom to cover the graves of suicides with stones, so that they might not rise at night and bother travellers.

There were plenty on the road and among the moss in the woods. Soon, therefore, a large cairn was raised over the Teutonic Knight, and then Hlawa cut a cross with his axe on the trunk of a pine-tree—not for Siegfried's sake, but to discourage evil spirits from gathering at that spot—and returned to his company.

"His soul is in hell, and his body is already in the ground," he told Jagienka. "Now we can proceed."

So they started. However, as she rode by, Jagienka plucked a branch of pine and threw it on the stones, an example which was followed by all the others, for such was also the prescription of custom.

For a long time they rode deep in thought, reflecting on the ill-omened monkish knight and the penalty which had overtaken him, until at last Jagienka said:

"Divine justice does not make exceptions. And it is not fitting even to say a requiem for him, since for him there is no pity."

"In any case, you have a compassionate heart, in that you bid us bury him," replied the Czech.

And then he said with a certain hesitation:

"People say—or perhaps not people, but witches and wizards—that a cord or strap from a gallows-bird brings a happy outcome to all one's undertakings; but I did not take the strap from Siegfried, because I do not look for happiness for you from magic spells, but from the power of our Lord Jesus."

Jagienka did not immediately reply; only after sighing several times, did she say, as if to herself:

"Alas! My happiness is behind me, not before me!"

CHAPTER LIX

IT was not until nine days after Jagienka's departure that Zbyszko reached the Spychow border, but Danusia was now so near to death that he had lost all hope of bringing her alive to her father. Immediately on the second day, when she had begun to wander in her answers, he had observed that not only was her mind out of joint but that her body was in the grip of some illness, which the girl had not the strength to resist, worn out as she was by captivity, imprisonment, torment, and incessant fear. Maybe the echoes of the bitter struggle that Zbyszko and Macko had had with the Germans had filled her cup of terror to the brim and caused her then to fall thus ill. In any case the fever did not leave her from that time until almost the end of the journey. It was even in some sense a favorable circumstance, for she had been conveyed unconscious through all the fearful forest wilds and amidst measureless fatigues. After they had passed through the forest and reached "pious" country, with settlements of yeomen and gentry, the perils and fatigues were over. When people learned that they were bringing a child of their country, rescued from the Teutonic Knights, and that she was actually the daughter of the famous Jurand, of whom the minstrels already sang many songs at castles, manors, and huts, they hastened to give all the help and service that they could. They furnished supplies of food and horses. All doors were open. Zbyszko no longer had to carry Danusia in a litter slung between horses. Strong youths carried her on a stretcher from village to village as gently and carefully as if she had been some sacred relic. Women surrounded her with the most tender care. Men, when they heard the story of her wrongs, gnashed their teeth, and more than one straightaway put on his metal cuirass, caught up sword, or axe, or lance, and rode on with Zbyszko to take vengeance with interest, for it did not seem enough to that fierce generation simply to repay wrong with wrong.

But Zbyszko was not then thinking of vengeance, but only of Danusia. He lived between flashes of hope, when the sick girl was temporarily better, and dull despair, when her state was obviously worse. And as to that, he could no longer be under any delusion. More than once in the course of his journey the superstitious thought passed through his head that perhaps somewhere there in the trackless wilderness through which they had passed, Death was riding behind them step by step and only waiting for a suitable moment to throw himself upon Danusia and suck out the last of her life. This vision, or rather feeling, was so distinct, particularly on dark nights, that frequently he was seized by a desperate desire to turn around and challenge the tormenting figure, as one challenges a knight, and fight with Death to the last breath. But towards the end of the journey it was still worse. No longer did he sense Death behind the company, but in the midst of it, invisible, it is true, but so near that his cold breath blew around him. And he understood that against that foe neither valor would avail, nor a strong hand, nor any weapon, and that he would have to give up the dearest head in the world without a struggle.

And this was the most terrible feeling, for joined to it was grief, as uncontrollable as the storm, as bottomless as the sea. Zbyszko could not but writhe in anguish of heart when he looked at his beloved and said to her, as if in involuntary reproach: "Was it for this I loved you, was it for this I sought you and rescued you, to cover you with earth tomorrow and never see you more?" And so saying, he looked at her cheeks, red with fever, and at her tired, unseeing eyes, and asked her anew: "Will you leave me? Are you not grieved for me? Would you rather go from me than be with me?" And then he thought that perhaps he himself was mad, and his chest was oppressed with a grievous desire to sob. But he could not cry, because his tears were blocked by rage and anger against the merciless force which, blind and cold, had discharged itself against an innocent child. If the ill-omened Teutonic Knight had then been in his train, he would have torn him like a wild beast.

When they reached the ducal hunting-lodge, he wished to stop, but the place was deserted in the spring. From the watchmen he learned that the duke and duchess had gone to visit their brother, Ziemowit, at Plock, so he gave up his design of going to Warsaw, where the court physician might have attended the sick girl. He had to go on to Spychow, which was a dreadful thing, for it seemed to him that all was now over and that he would bring to Jurand only a corpse.

However, a few hours short of Spychow, a brighter ray of hope again fell on his heart. Danusia's cheeks began to pale, her eyes became less tired, her breath was not so loud and rapid. Zbyszko noticed this at once, and after a certain time ordered a halt so that she might breathe more calmly. They were perhaps a league from Spychow, far from human habitations, on a narrow track between field and meadow. But a wild pear-tree nearby gave welcome shade, so they stopped under its branches. The men slipped off their horses and unbridled them, allowing the horses to graze unchecked. Two women, who had been hired to attend Danusia, and the youths who carried her, being wearied by the road and the heat, lay down in the shade and slept. Zbyszko watched by the stretcher, sitting on the roots of the pear-tree, and never took his eyes off the sick girl.

She lay quietly in the noonday silence, her eyelids closed. Yet it seemed to Zbyszko that she was not asleep. When a peasant cutting hay at the far end of the wide meadow stopped and began to whet his scythe with a stone, she quivered slightly at the sound and opened her eyes, but immediately shut them again; her breast rose as if with a deep breath, and from her lips came a scarcely audible whisper:

"The flowers smell sweet. . . ."

They were the first sensible words she had spoken since the beginning of the journey, for the breeze did indeed bring from the sun-warmed meadow a strong scent, mingled of hay and honey and various sweet-smelling herbs. So Zbyszko's heart throbbed with joy at the thought that the sick girl was regaining consciousness. In his first excitement he wanted to throw himself at her feet, but he checked himself for fear of frightening her, and merely knelt by the stretcher and, leaning over it, said in a low tone:

"Danusia! Danusia!"

She opened her eyes again. For some time she looked at him, and then a smile brightened her face. And just as she had done at the pitch-burner's hut, but far more consciously, she uttered his name:

"Zbyszko! . . ."

And she tried to stretch out her hands to him, but found herself too weak, while he put his arms about her with a full heart, as if he were thanking her for some measureless boon.

"You have awoke!" he said. "Oh, praise God—praise God!"

Then his voice failed him, and for a time they looked at one another in silence. The stillness of the fields was disturbed only by the scented breeze rustling the leaves of the pear-tree, the chirping of the grasshoppers in the grass, and the distant, indistinct singing of the mower.

Danusia looked more and more conscious, and did not cease to smile, like a child which sees an angel in its sleep. Slowly, however, her eyes began to reflect a certain surprise:

"Where am I?" she asked.

Then a whole swarm of short answers, broken by joy, burst out of him.

"You are with me. Near Spychow. We are going to your father. Your misery is over. Oh, my Danusia! Oh, Danusia! I sought you and I rescued you. You are not in the power of the Germans now. Never fear! Presently we shall be at Spychow. You have been sick, but the Lord Jesus had compassion on you. How much anguish there was, and how much weeping! Danusia! But now all is well. There's nothing but happiness before you. How I looked for you! How I journeyed to find you! Almighty God!"

And he drew a deep breath, almost a groan, as if he had cast out the last burden of anguish from his breast.

Danusia lay quietly, recalling something, considering something, and finally she asked:

"Then you did not forget me?"

And two tears that had gathered in her eyes rolled down her face onto the pillow.

"How could I ever forget you, Danusia!" Zbyszko exclaimed.

More was conveyed by that stifled cry than by the greatest oaths and entreaties, for he had always loved her with his whole soul; and from the time when he had regained her, she had become dearer to him than the whole world.

Meanwhile silence fell again; in the distance the mower ceased to sing and began to whet his scythe a second time.

Danusia's lips began to move anew, but in a whisper so low that Zbyszko could not catch it; so he bent over her and asked:

"What is it you say, my little berry?"

And she repeated:

"The flowers smell sweet. . . ."

"Because we are by a meadow," he replied. "But soon we shall go on—to your father, who has also been redeemed from captivity. And you will be mine till death. Do you hear me well? Do you understand?"

Sudden anxiety took hold of him. He noticed that she was growing paler and paler, and that thick drops of sweat were coming out on her face.

"What's the matter?" he asked in dreadful fear. And he felt how his hair was standing on end and how his body was turning ice cold. "What's the matter?" he repeated. "Tell me!"

"It is dark!" she whispered.

"Dark? The sun is shining, and you find it dark?" he asked breathlessly. "Just a moment ago you were speaking sensibly! In God's name, say something!"

She moved her lips but could no longer even whisper. Zbyszko realized that she was mouthing his name and calling him. Soon after that, her emaciated hands began to tremble and flutter on the kilim rug covering her. This didn't last long. There was no more room for delusion. She was dying.

In his terror and despair, he began to implore her, as if his prayer could effect anything:

"Danusia! Oh, merciful Jesus! Wait at least until Spychow! Wait! wait! Oh, Jesus! Jesus! Jesus!"

As he was thus imploring, the women awoke, while the men, who had been with the horses not far away on the meadow, ran up. But understanding at the first glance what was happening, they all knelt down and began to recite the litany aloud.

The breeze dropped, the leaves of the pear-tree ceased to rustle. Amid the great silence of the fields, only the prayer could be heard.

Right before end of the litany, Danusia opened her eyes once more, as if to look for the last time on Zbyszko and on the sunlit world, and then she immediately fell into an everlasting sleep.

The women closed her eyes and went to the meadow for flowers. The men followed. And so they moved in the sunshine amid the thick grass, like spirits of the fields, bending down every moment and weeping out of pity and sadness. Zbyszko, motionless and speechless, and seemingly dead himself, knelt in the shade by the stretcher, his head on Danusia's knees; while they wandered near and far, plucking the golden marigold and bluebells, and the abundant red pimpernel and the white, honey-sweet thyme. They also found wild lilies in moist hollows and broom on the balks by the fallows. When their arms were full, they stood in a mournful circle around the stretcher and began to adorn it. The herbs and flowers nearly covered the body of the dead girl. Only her face was left unveiled, lily-pale amid the pimpernel and bluebells, a serene, angelic face, calmed in never-wakening sleep.

To Spychow was not even quite a league, so presently, when their first sorrow and grief had flowed out with their tears, they raised the stretcher and moved towards the forests that marked the border of Jurand's lands.

The men led the horses at the rear. Zbyszko himself carried the head of the stretcher, while, preceding him, the women, loaded with fresh bunches of herbs and flowers, sang hymns—and thus they slowly went on and on, between the green meadow and the level, grey fallows, like some solemn funeral train.

In the blue sky was not a single cloud, and the whole world basked in the golden radiance of the sun.

CHAPTER LX

FINALLY they arrived with the corpse of the girl to the Spychow forests, on the borders of which Jurand's men kept watch night and day. One of them hastened with the news to old Tolima and Father Caleb, while others conducted the train along a woodland road— at first, winding and sunken but, afterwards, broad—to the place where the forest ended and extensive sloughs and swamps began, and marshes swarming with water-birds, beyond which, on a dry eminence, lay the fortalice of Spychow itself. They perceived at once that the mournful news of them had already reached the place, for scarcely had they come out of the shade of the forest onto the bright meadows when the sound of the castle chapel-bell reached their ears. Soon they saw a numerous company, including men and women, coming out to meet them. When it had approached to within a couple of bowshots, it was possible to make out the persons in it. At the head went Jurand himself, supported by Tolima and feeling with his staff before him. It was easy to recognize him by his huge figure, the red cavities in place of his eyes, and the white hair falling to his shoulders. Beside him walked Father Caleb in a white surplice, holding a cross. Behind them was borne a banner with Jurand's coat-of-arms, followed by the Spychow warriors and then the married women with kerchiefs on their heads and the golden-haired maidens. At the rear of the company was a wagon, on which the corpse would be carried.

When Zbyszko saw Jurand, he had the stretcher set down, the pillow end of which he himself had been bearing until now, and went towards him, calling out in tones expressive of measureless anguish and despair:

"I sought her until I found her and rescued her, but she preferred to go to God rather than to Spychow!"

And his anguish overcame him completely; he fell on Jurand's breast, put his arms about his neck, and groaned:

"O Jesus! Jesus! Jesus!"

At that sight, the hearts of the Spychow armed retainers were roused, and they began to strike their spears against their shields, not knowing how else to give vent to their grief and desire for vengeance.

The women uttered a lament, and one after another raised their aprons to their eyes or completely covered their heads with them, calling out at the top of their voices: "Ah, woe! Ah, woe is me! For you is joy, but for us weeping. Death has mown you down; his icy hand has clutched you. Ay, me! alas!" And some, throwing their heads back and shutting their eyes, called out: "Was there no happiness for you here among us, little flower? Ah, woe! Ah, woe is me! Your father is left in deep mourning, while you already walk through the divine chambers. Ay, me! Alas!" Others, in turn, reproached the dead girl for not having compassion on her father's and husband's loneliness and tears.

And this lamenting and this mourning was half in song, for that folk knew not how else to express their grief.

Meanwhile Jurand, freeing himself from Zbyszko's arms, extended his staff in front of him to signify that he wanted to go to Danusia. Then Tolima and Zbyszko led him to the stretcher, where he knelt by the corpse, felt her with his hand from her forehead to her crossed hands and nodded his head several times, as if he wanted to say that it was she, his Danusia, none other, and that he recognized his child. Then he put one arm around her and raised the other, which had no hand, aloft, which the bystanders guessed to be a silent complaint to God, more eloquent than many words of grief. Zbyszko, whose face after his momentary outburst had frozen stiff again, knelt on the other side in silence, like a statue of stone, and it became so quiet that one could hear the chirr of the grasshoppers and the buzz of every passing fly. At last Father Caleb sprinkled Danusia, Zbyszko, and Jurand with holy water, and began to intone the requiem. On its conclusion, he prayed aloud for a long time. The people seemed to hear the voice of a prophet, for he begged that the torments of that innocent child might be the last drop filling the cup of injustice to the brim and that the day of judgment, punishment, wrath, and calamity might come.

Then they proceeded to Spychow, but they did not place Danusia on the wagon; they bore her at the head of the train on her flower-entwined stretcher. The chapel bell, tolling unceasingly, seemed to summon and invite them all to come, and they moved, singing, over the wide grassy area, under the expansive golden afterglow, as if the dead girl were conducting them to everlasting brightness and splendor. It was already evening and the cattle were returning from the fields when they arrived. The chapel, in which the body was laid, was bright with torches and lighted candles. By the order of Father Caleb, seven maidens recited the litany over the body in turn, until dawn. Likewise until dawn, Zbyszko did not leave Danusia, and at Matins he himself laid her in the coffin, which skilled craftsmen had cut out during the night from an oak trunk, fitting a pane of golden amber in the lid over her head.

Jurand was not there, for strange things were happening with him. Immediately after returning to the house, he lost the use of his legs; and when he was laid on his bed, he lost the power of movement and the consciousness of where he was and what was happening to him. In vain did Father Caleb speak to him, in vain did he ask what was wrong; he heard not, he answered not. Lying on his back, he only raised the lids of his empty eyes and smiled with a bright and happy face, and sometimes moved his lips as if talking with someone. The priest and Tolima supposed that he was talking with his blessed daughter and smiling to her. They supposed also that he was on the point of death and that he saw his own everlasting bliss with the pupils of his soul; but in this they erred, for he smiled thus, insensible and deaf to everything, for whole weeks, and when Zbyszko finally set out with the ransom for Macko, he left him still alive.

CHAPTER LXI

ZBYSZKO was not bedridden after Danusia's burial, but he lived in a kind of torpor. For the first few days he did not feel so bad. He walked about, talked of his dead wife, visited Jurand, and sat with him. He also told the priest of Macko's captivity, and they decided together to send Tolima to Prussia and Malbork to find out where Macko might be and to ransom him, paying at the same time as many marks for Zbyszko as should be agreed upon with Arnold von Baden and his brother. There was no lack of silver in the vaults of Spychow, either made as profit by Jurand from his estates, or captured, so the priest supposed that the Teutonic Knights, if they received money, would readily release the old knight and would not require the young one to present himself personally.

"Go the Plock," the priest said to Tolima at the outset of his journey, "and obtain a safe-conduct from the duke there. Otherwise the first commander whom you meet will take you captive, and you'll be a prisoner yourself."

"Bah! I know them," old Tolima replied. "They are quite prepared to take captive even those that travel with safe-conducts."

And he set out. But soon afterwards, Father Caleb regretted that he had not sent Zbyszko himself. He had been afraid, it is true, that in the first days of his grief the young man would not be able to do what was necessary, or that he might even burst into anger against the Teutonic Knights and expose himself to danger; and he knew likewise that, in his fresh sorrow and fresh loneliness, it would be difficult for him to leave his beloved's coffin so soon after his terrible and grievous journey all the way from New Kowno to

Spychow. Afterwards, however, he regretted that he had taken all this into account, for with every new day, Zbyszko became more depressed. Until Danusia died, he had lived in great effort, in cruel tension, wherein he had to put forth all his powers. He had travelled through many countries, fought single combats, rescued his wife, made his way through wild forests. Suddenly, all that had come to an end, as if cut off short by a stroke of the sword, and he was left only with the memory that everything had been in vain. His toils were finished, it is true, but with them a part of his life was finished; hope and goodness were gone, his love had perished, and nothing was left. Every man lives for tomorrow, every man forms some design and makes some plan for the future; but Zbyszko became indifferent about tomorrow, and as for the future, he had the same feeling as Jagienka when she said, on starting from Spychow: "My happiness is behind me, not before me." In addition to all this, the feelings of helplessness, emptiness, and misery grew in his heart, nourished by his deep grief and ever greater mourning for Danusia. This grief took hold of him, mastered him, and at the same time grew ever more tenacious in his heart, so that in the end there was no room left for any other feeling. He thought only of it, and cherished it, and lived with it alone, insensible to everything else, shut up within himself, sunk in a stupor, unconscious of what went on around him. All the powers of his soul and body, all his former quickness and valor had slackened and faded. In his glance and in his movements there was now a kind of senile sluggishness. Entire days and nights he spent sitting either in the vault by Danusia's coffin or on a bench in front of the house, warming himself in the sunshine during the afternoon hours. At times he was so lost in brooding that he did not answer when addressed. Father Caleb, who was fond of him, began to fear that his grief would consume him as rust consumes iron; and with regret he thought that perhaps it would have been better to send him away, even if it were to the Teutonic Knights with the ransom. "He needs," Father Caleb said to the local sacristan, with whom, in lack of other company, he used to talk of his troubles, "he needs some adventure to shake him as a windstorm shakes a tree, else he is likely to break down completely." And the sacristan agreed, wisely comparing him with a man who has swallowed a bone, for whom the best treatment is a slap on the back.

But no adventure befell him. Instead, a few weeks later, de Lorche unexpectedly arrived. The sight of him gave Zbyszko a shock, for it reminded him of the expedition to Samogitia and the rescue of Danusia. De Lorche himself had no hesitation in touching on those painful memories. In fact, when he learned of Zbyszko's sorrow, he went at once to pray with him by Danusia's coffin; he also spoke of her incessantly; and then, being no bad minstrel, he composed a song about her. Accompanying himself on a lute, he sang this song at night by the grating of the vault, and he sang it so tenderly and mournfully that, although Zbyszko did not understand the words, the music alone affected him to tears, and he remained weeping until the light of dawn.

Afterwards, however, worn out by his weeping and sorrow and fatigue, he fell into a sound sleep; and when he awoke his grief had evidently been assuaged by his tears, for he was fresher than on the preceding days, and his glances were brighter. He also took great pleasure in the company of Sieur de Lorche and thanked him for coming, and then asked him how he had learned of his misfortune.

De Lorche told him through the mouth of Father Caleb that he had learned of Danusia's death only at Lubawa from old Tolima, whom he had seen in fetters at the local commander's, but that he would have come to Spychow in any case to give himself up as Zbyszko's captive.

The news of Tolima's imprisonment made a great impression, both on Zbyszko and the priest. They concluded that the ransom money was lost, for there was nothing more difficult in the world than to wrest money from the Teutonic Knights once they had got it in their hands. It would, therefore, be necessary to go with the same sum a second time.

"This is most unfortunate!" exclaimed Zbyszko. "My poor uncle is waiting there and thinks that I have forgotten him. I must now go to him with all the speed I can."

Then he turned to Sieur de Lorche:

"Do you know what happened to my uncle? Do you know that he is in the hands of the Teutonic Knights?"

"I know," replied de Lorche, "for I saw him at Malbork. That is why I came here."

Meanwhile Father Caleb began to complain.

"We've proceeded badly," he said. "No one was thinking. But I expected more from Tolima's intelligence. Why did he not go to Plock, and why did he venture among those robbers without a safe-conduct?"

Sieur de Lorche shrugged his shoulders.

"What are safe-conducts to them? Did not the Duke of Plock himself, like your duke here, suffer wrongs enough at their hands? There's always trouble on the border—for your men, too, do not forgive. Every commander, nay, every chief, does what he will, and in rapacity one outdoes another."

"All the more reason for Tolima to have gone to Plock."

"So he intended to do, but they carried him off from his night quarters as he was on his way by the border. They would have killed him had he not lied to them by saying that he was bringing money for the commander of Lubawa. In this way, he saved his life, but the commander will now produce witnesses to what Tolima said."

"And how is my uncle Macko? Is he well? Do they have designs against his life?" asked Zbyszko.

"He is well," replied de Lorche. "Their hatred against 'King' Witold and those who are aiding the Samogitians is intense, and they would certainly have beheaded the old knight had it not been that they would have regretted the loss of his ransom. The brothers von Baden also protect him for the same reason. And, of course, the chapter cares for my head, for if it were sacrificed, the knighthood in Flanders and Guelders and Burgundy would blaze up against the Order. As you know, I am a kinsman of the Count of Guelders."

"Why should your head be at stake?" Zbyszko interrupted in surprise.

"I was taken captive by you. I told them at Malbork: 'If you put the old knight of Bogdaniec to death, then the young knight will do likewise.'"

"I will not! So help me God!"

"I know you will not, but they are afraid you will, and so Macko will be safe among them. They told me that you also are in captivity, for the Badens only released you on your word of honor as a knight, and that therefore I need not give myself up. But I replied that when you took me prisoner, you were free. So here I am! As long as I am in your hands, they will not do anything either to you or to Macko. Pay the ransom to the von Badens, and demand twice, or three times, as much for me. They must pay. I do not say so because I think I am worth more than you, but to punish their avarice, which I scorn. I had quite a different opinion of them formerly, but now I am disgusted with them and their hospitality. I will go to the Holy Land and seek adventures there, for I have no desire to serve them any longer."

"You could stay with us, lord," said Father Caleb. "I think you will, for it seems to me that they will refuse to pay a ransom for you."

"If they will not pay, I will pay myself," replied de Lorche. "I have come here with a considerable troop, and I have laden wagons, and what is on them will be enough."

Father Caleb repeated to Zbyszko these words, to which Macko would certainly not have been indifferent, but Zbyszko, being young and caring little for riches, replied:

"On my honor! It shall not be as you say. You have been a brother and a friend to me, and I will not take any ransom from you."

Then they embraced, feeling that a new bond had been made between them.

De Lorche smiled and said:

"Good! Only do not let the Germans know, else they will haggle over Macko. You see, they must pay. They will be afraid that otherwise I shall proclaim it abroad among the knights and at the courts that they gladly invite and receive foreign guests, but if one of them falls into captivity, they forget him. The Order is particularly eager to recruit such guests now, for they are afraid of Witold, and still more of the Poles and their king."

"Then this is what we will do," said Zbyszko. "You will stay here, or anywhere you like in Mazovia, and I will go to Malbork for my uncle and will simulate the most bitter hatred against you."

"By St. George, do so!" answered de Lorche. "But first listen to what I will tell you. At Malbork they say that the King of Poland is to arrive at Plock and meet the grand master either there or somewhere on the border. The Teutonic Knights are very anxious that he should come, for they want to find out whether he will help Witold if the latter declares open war on them for Samogitia. Ha! they are as cunning as snakes, but in Witold they have found their master. The Order is afraid of him, too, because they never know what he has in mind and what he will do. 'He gave up Samogitia to us,' they say in the chapter, 'but because of this, he holds a sword over our heads. All he has to do is say the word, and the uprising will begin!' So it is. I must go to his court one day. Maybe I shall be able to joust in the lists; besides, I hear that the women there are of angelic charm."

"You were speaking, lord, of the arrival of the Polish king to Plock?" Father Caleb interrupted.

"Yes. Let Zbyszko join the royal court. The grand master wishes to win the king over to his side and will refuse him nothing. You know that no one can be humbler than the Teutonic Knights when it is necessary. Let Zbyszko join his train, and let him claim his rights; let him cry as loud as possible against injustice. They will give him a different hearing in the presence of the king and in the presence of the Cracow knights, who are famed throughout the world and whose judgments are widely esteemed among all knights."

"Excellent advice! By the Holy Cross! Excellent!" exclaimed the priest.

"Yes!" de Lorche said. "And there will be no lack of opportunities. I heard at Malbork that there will be banquets and tournaments, for the foreign guests are most eager to meet the royal knights. By God! Why, even Sir John of Aragon is to come, the greatest knight in all Christendom. Haven't you heard? He is reported to have sent his gauntlet all the way from Aragon to your Zawisza, so that it may not be said at the courts that there is another like him in the world."

De Lorche's arrival, the sight of him, and his whole conversation, so roused Zbyszko from the grievous stupor in which he had previously been plunged that he listened to his news with keen interest. He had heard of John of Aragon, since it was the duty of every knight in those days to know and remember the names of all the most famous warriors, and the fame of the Aragonese nobility, and of John in particular, filled the world. No knight could ever stand against him in the lists, while the Moors fled at the mere sight of his armor; and the opinion was generally held that he was the first knight in the whole of Christendom.

So Zbyszko's martial, knightly soul was roused at this news, and he asked with the greatest interest:

"He challenged Zawisza the Black?"

"Apparently it's been a year since he sent his glove, and Zawisza sent back his."

"Then John of Aragon will certainly come."

"Whether it is so certain, they do not know, but there are such rumors. The Teutonic Knights sent him an invitation long ago."

"God grant I may see such things!"

"God grant it!" said de Lorche. "And even if Zawisza were to be defeated, which may easily happen, it is a great honor for him to have been challenged by a John of Aragon—yes, and an honor for the whole of your nation."

"Well, we shall see!" said Zbyszko. "I only say: God grant I may see it!"

"I say the same thing."

However, their wish was not to be fulfilled this time, for the old chronicles relate that the combat between Zawisza and the famous John of Aragon took place some ten or fifteen years later, at Perpignan, where Zawisza the Black, in the presence of Emperor Sigismund, Pope Benedict XIII, the King of Aragon, and many dukes and cardinals, overthrew his opponent on the first blow and won a glorious victory. In the meantime, however, both Zbyszko and de Lorche rejoiced at heart, thinking that, even if John of Aragon were unable to be present at these tournaments, they would yet witness distinguished knightly deeds; for there was no lack in Poland of champions but little inferior to Zawisza, and among the guests of the Teutonic Order there were always excellent swordsmen—French, English, Burgundian, and Italian—ready to measure themselves with anyone.

"Listen!" said Zbyszko to Sieur de Lorche. "I long for my uncle Macko, and I'm in a hurry to ransom him, so tomorrow at dawn I intend to start for Plock. But why should you stay here? You are supposed to be my captive, so ride with me and you will see the king and court."

"I was about to ask permission," replied de Lorche. "I have long wanted to see your knights; furthermore, I have heard that the ladies of the royal court are more like angels than inhabitants of this mortal vale."

"You just said the same thing about Witold's court," Zbyszko observed.

CHAPTER LXII

ZBYSZKO reproached himself for having forgotten his uncle in his grief, and since he was always accustomed to carry out quickly what he had determined, he set out for Plock with Sieur de Lorche on the very next day at dawn. The border roads were unsafe even in times of profound peace because of bandits who were supported and protected by the Teutonic Knights, a thing of which King Jagiello complained to them most bitterly. Despite his accusations, which were even supported by the prestige of Rome, despite his threats and stern measures of justice, the neighboring commanders frequently allowed their mercenaries to join the robbers, washing their hands, indeed, of those who were so unfortunate as to fall into Polish hands, but giving shelter to such as returned with booty and prisoners, not only in the Order's villages but also in its castles.

Travellers and dwellers on the border repeatedly fell into the hands of robbers such as these; children of rich people were particularly sought for ransom purposes. But the two young knights, accompanied as they were by considerable troops, each composed, besides wagoners, of a dozen or more armed retainers on foot or horseback, were not afraid of attack, and reached Plock without incident. Immediately on their arrival, they were met by a pleasant surprise.

At the inn they found Tolima, who had arrived a day before them. This was possible because the constable of Lubawa, hearing that the messenger had succeeded in concealing a portion of the ransom when he was attacked not far from Brodnica, sent him to that castle, with a recommendation to the commander that he

should be compelled to reveal where the money was hidden.
Tolima took advantage of the opportunity to escape. When the
knights expressed surprise that he had been able to do it so easily,
he explained as follows:

"It was all due to their greed. The constable of Lubawa was loath
to give me a strong guard, for he was loath to have the existence of
the money generally known. Possibly he had agreed to divide it
with the commander of Brodnica, and they were afraid that if all
this became known, they would have to send a considerable part of
the money to Malbork or give up the whole of it to the von Badens.
So I had only two guards: a trusty soldier who had to row with me
on the Drweca, and a clerk. And since it was important for them
that no one should see us, we went at night, and, as you know, the
border is quite near. Furthermore, they gave me an oaken oar. . . .
Well! God's grace was with me—for here I am at Plock."

"I know. And those two never returned!" exclaimed Zbyszko.

A smile brightened Tolima's stern face.

"The Drweca flows into the Vistula, you must remember. How
could they return against the current? I suppose the Teutonic
Knights will find them at Torun." Presently he turned to Zbyszko
and added: "The commander of Lubawa robbed me of part of the
money, but that which I concealed when attacked, I found again,
and now I have given it to your squire, lord, to keep, since he lives
in the castle with the duke, and there it is safer than with me at the
inn."

"Then my squire is here at Plock? What is he doing here?"
Zbyszko asked in surprise.

"After bringing Siegfried to Spychow, he went on with the young
lady who had been there, and who is now in waiting on the duchess
here. So he said yesterday."

But Zbyszko, who in his stupefaction after Danusia's death had
asked no questions at Spychow and knew nothing of what had
happened there, only now remembered that the Czech had been
sent on ahead with Siegfried—and at that memory his heart was
constricted with grief and a desire for vengeance.

"True!" he said. "Where is that hangman? What has happened to
him?"

"Did Father Caleb not tell you? Siegfried hanged himself, and
you, lord, passed by his grave." A moment of silence followed.

"Your squire said," Tolima continued, "that he was going to join you, and he would have done it before now, but that he had to attend the young lady, who fell sick here after her arrival from Spychow."

Zbyszko, shaking himself free of his mournful memories, asked as if in a dream:

"What young lady?"

"Why, that one," the old man replied, "your sister, or kinswoman, who came with Sir Macko to Spychow dressed in boy's garments, and on the way found our lord groping along blindly. Had it not been for her, neither Sir Macko nor your squire would have recognized him. After that, our lord grew very fond of her, for she cared for him like a daughter and, aside from Father Caleb, was the only person who understood him."

The young knight opened his eyes wide in surprise.

"Father Caleb did not tell me of any young lady, and I have no kinswoman."

"He did not tell you, lord, because you were dazed by grief and knew nothing of what was going on in the world around you."

"What was her name?"

"Jagienka."

It seemed to Zbyszko that he was dreaming. The thought that Jagienka could have come from far-off Zgorzelice to Spychow was one that he could scarcely entertain. What for? Why? It was, indeed, no secret to him that the girl had been attracted to him at Zgorzelice, but he had admitted to her that he was wived, so he could not suppose that old Macko had brought her to Spychow with the idea of bringing about their marriage. Besides, neither Macko nor even the Czech had said a word about her. All this seemed to him exceedingly strange and completely unintelligible, so he began anew to ply Tolima with questions, like a man who mistrusts his ears and wishes to have improbable news repeated.

Tolima, however, could add nothing to what he had already said, so he went to the castle to fetch the squire, and soon returned with him, shortly before sunset. The Czech greeted his young lord with joy, but also with sorrow, as he had already previously learned all that had befallen at Spychow. For his part, Zbyszko was equally rejoiced to see him, feeling that he had a friendly and faithful heart and was one of those persons who are most needed in misfortune.

He therefore gave free rein to his emotion and told him of Danusia's death, and he shared his pain and grief and tears with him as brother does with brother. All this took some time, particularly that at the end, at Zbyszko's request, Sieur de Lorche repeated for them the plaintive song he had composed for the dead girl, singing it by an open window, lute in hand and his eyes raised to the stars.

After their sorrow was considerably unburdened, they began to speak of what awaited them at Plock.

"I have come here on my way to Malbork," Zbyszko said. "You know that my uncle Macko is in captivity and that I am going to ransom him."

"I know," replied the Czech. "You have done well, lord. I wanted to come to Spychow myself and advise you to go to Plock. The king is to conduct negotiations with the grand master at Raciaz, and it will be easier to make your complaint before the king, inasmuch as the Teutonic Knights are not so arrogant in the presence of majesty, and they simulate Christian honesty."

"Tolima told me that you were about to come to me, but were detained by the sickness of Jagienka, Zych's daughter. I heard that my uncle Macko brought her to these parts and that she was even at Spychow. I was terribly surprised. Tell me, for what reason did my uncle Macko take her from Zgorzelice?"

"There were a number of reasons. Sir Macko was afraid that if he left her without any protection, the knights Wolf and Cztan might make raids on Zgorzelice, and the younger children also might be wronged. Without her they would be safer, for in Poland, as you know, it may happen that a nobleman takes a girl by force—if he cannot get her any other way—but against little orphans no one will raise a hand, since for that there is the executioner's axe and, worse than that, dishonor! There was also another reason. The abbot died and left the young lady heiress to his landed estates, over which the bishop here had the guardianship. So Sir Macko brought the young lady to Plock."

"But he also took her to Spychow?"

"Yes, while the bishop and the duke were away, and there was no one with whom to leave her. And it was indeed fortunate that he did. Had it not been for the young lady, the old lord and I should have ridden past Sir Jurand, taking him merely for a beggar. It was only when she had compassion on him that we recognized who he was. God arranged it all through her merciful heart."

He went on to tell how afterwards Jurand could not do without her and how he loved and blessed her; and Zbyszko, though he knew it already from Tolima, was greatly moved when he heard it again, and he felt deep gratitude to Jagienka.

"God grant her health!" he said at last. "I'm just surprised that you told me nothing about her."

The Czech, being somewhat embarrassed, and wanting to gain time for reflection before he answered, asked:

"Where, lord?"

"When we were with Skirwoillo in Samogitia."

"Did we not tell you? Surely we did, but your head must have been full of something else."

"You told me that Jurand had returned, but you said nothing of her."

"Eh! Have you forgotten? Well, God knows! Maybe Sir Macko thought that I had told you, while I thought that he had. It was no good telling you anything then, lord. No wonder! But now I have something else to say. It is lucky that the young lady is here, for she will be helpful to Sir Macko."

"What can she do?"

"Let her say but a word to the duchess here, who loves her immensely. The Teutonic Knights, in their turn, will refuse the duchess nothing, firstly because she is of royal birth, and secondly because she is a great friend of the Order. Now, as you may have heard, Duke Skirgiello, brother of the king, has revolted against Duke Witold. He has taken refuge with the Teutonic Knights, who want to aid him and put him in Witold's place. The king loves the duchess very much, and gladly, they say, lends her his ear, so the Teutonic Knights want her to incline him to Skirgiello's side against Witold. They know very well, the accursed dogs, that if they get rid of Witold, they will be left in peace. So the Teutonic envoys bow before the duchess from morning to night and try to divine her every wish."

"Jagienka loves my uncle Macko very much and will certainly use her influence for him," said Zbyszko.

"You may be sure she will. But go, lord, to the castle and tell her how and what to say."

"I was going to the castle with Sieur de Lorche anyway,"
Zbyszko replied. "That was what we came here for. But we must
first comb our hair and dress ourselves in our best garments." After
a while, he added: "I wanted to cut my hair short out of grief, but
I forgot."

"All the better!" said the Czech.

He went out to call the attendants and presently came back with
them. While the two young knights were arraying themselves
worthily for the evening banquet at the castle, he continued his
relation of what was going on at the courts of the king and the
duke.

"The Teutonic Knights," he said, "are doing their best to undermine Duke Witold. As long as he is alive and rules over a powerful
country as representative of the king, they will know no peace. Yes,
he is the only person they fear! They are digging and digging, like
moles. They have already stirred up both the duke and duchess here
against him, and it is rumored that they have even succeeded in
turning Duke Janusz against him, because of Wizna."

"Are Duke Janusz and Duchess Anna also here?" asked Zbyszko.
"I shall find a large number of acquaintances, for it is not the first
time I have been at Plock."

"Yes," replied the squire, "they are both here. They have no few
matters against the Teutonic Knights, which they wish to throw in
the master's face before the king."

"And the king? Whose side is he on? Is he not angry against the
Teutonic Knights, and does he not shake his sword over their
heads?"

"The king does not love them, and they say he has long been
threatening them with war. As for Duke Witold, the king prefers
him to his own brother Skirgiello, who is a drunkard and bad-tempered. That is why the knights in attendance on his majesty say
that the king will not declare against Witold or promise the Teutonic Knights not to help him. And this may be true, for Duchess
Alexandra has been making efforts to change the king's position for
some days, and looks despondent."

"Is Zawisza the Black here?"

"He is not here, but there are so many knights present that you
cannot look enough at them. If it come to something—hey! Al-

mighty God! Chips and splinters will fly from the Germans, that they will!"

"I shall not grieve for them."

A few paternosters later, dressed splendidly, they went to the castle. The evening's banquet was to take place that day, not at the duke's, but at the spacious house of the town warden, Andrew of Jasieniec, situated within the castle walls, near the Greater Bastion. Because it was a very beautiful, but rather too warm night, the warden, fearing lest the air might be too stifling for his guests within doors, had ordered the tables to be laid in the yard, where rowan and yew trees grew by the stone slabs of the pavement. Burning tar-barrels illuminated the space with bright yellow flames, but still brighter was the light of the moon, which shone in a cloudless sky, amid swarms of stars resembling a knight's silver shield. The crowned guests had not yet arrived, but the place was already full of local knights, churchmen, and courtiers, royal and ducal. Zbyszko knew many of them, particularly from the court of Duke Janusz. Of his former Cracow acquaintances, he saw Krzon of Goat's Head, Lis of Fair-Ground, Martin of Wrocimowice, Domarat of Kobylany, and Staszko of Charbimowice, as well as Powala of Taczewo, the sight of whom gave him especial pleasure, for he remembered the kindness shown him by the famous knight that time at Cracow.

But it was difficult to get near to them. Each was surrounded by a close circle of local Mazovian knights, asking questions about Cracow, the court, the entertainments, and various military achievements, while admiring their fine garments, the way their hair was combed, and their wonderful locks stiffened with white-of-egg, and regarding them as perfect models of fashion and manners.

However, Powala of Taczewo recognized Zbyszko and, pushing the Mazovians aside, went up to him.

"I recognized you, young man," he said, clasping his hand. "How are you, and where have you come from? Heavens, I see that you already wear a belt and spurs! Others wait for that until they are grey-haired, but you evidently serve St. George worthily."

"God bless you, noble lord!" Zbyszko replied. "If I had unhorsed the most distinguished German, I should not be as glad as I am to see you in good health."

"I also am glad. But where is your father?"

"Not my father; my uncle. In captivity among the Teutonic Knights, and I am going to ransom him."

"And that young girl who covered you with her veil?"

Zbyszko made no answer, but raised his eyes, which in a moment became filled with tears. Seeing this, the Lord of Taczewo said:

"This is a vale of tears—nothing but a real vale of tears! But come to the seat under the rowan tree, and you shall tell me your sad adventures."

He drew him to the corner of the yard, where Zbyszko sat down beside him and told him of Jurand's misery and Danusia's capture, of how he sought her, and how she died after the rescue. Powala listened attentively, while amazement, wrath, horror, and compassion in turn were reflected on his face. At length, when Zbyszko had finished, he said:

"I will tell the king, our lord! He already intends to complain to the grand master about little Jasko of Kretkowo and demand severe punishment for those who kidnapped him. They kidnapped him because he is of a rich family, and they want ransom. It is nothing to them to raise their hands against a child." He reflected for a moment and then continued, as if to himself: "An insatiable race, worse than Turks and Tartars. For they fear both the king and us in their hearts, and yet cannot refrain from robbery and murder. Those wolves fall upon villages, massacre yeomen, drown fishermen, and capture children. What would they be like if they did not fear us! The master sends letters against the king to foreign courts, but to his face he fawns, for he knows better than others of our power. But in the end the appointed measure will be passed."

Again he was silent for a moment. Then he laid his hand on Zbyszko's shoulder.

"I will tell the king," he repeated. "His blood has been boiling for a long time, and you may be certain that terrible punishment will not fail to overtake the authors of your misery."

"None of them, lord, is now alive," Zbyszko replied.

Powala looked at him with the friendliest of glances.

"God bless you! Evidently you do not forgive injuries. Lichtenstein alone you have not repaid, but I know that you could not. We also at Cracow vowed to challenge him, but for that we must wait for war—which God grant, since he cannot meet us without the permission of the grand master. The master needs Lichtenstein's wisdom and experience, on account of which he is continually sending him to various courts. That is why he will not easily give permission."

"First I must ransom my uncle."

"Yes. . . . I have been making inquiries about Lichtenstein. He is not here, nor will he be at Raciaz, since he has been sent to the King of England for archers. But do not trouble yourself too much about your uncle. If the king or the duchess here says a word, the master will not permit his people to haggle over the ransom."

"Particularly as I have a distinguished captive, Sieur de Lorche, who is a wealthy man and famous among them. He would certainly be glad to pay his respects to you and make your acquaintance, for no one worships famous knights more than he."

Zbyszko beckoned to Sieur de Lorche, who was standing nearby, and de Lorche, having asked previously with whom Zbyszko was speaking, came readily, for he really did burn with desire to know so famous a knight as Powala.

So when Zbyszko had made them acquainted, the elegant Guelders knight bowed most courteously and said:

"There would only be one honor greater, lord, than clasping your hand, and that would be to meet you in the lists or in battle."

The powerful knight of Taczewo smiled, since next to the small and slender Sieur de Lorche he looked like a mountain, and said:

"But I am glad that we shall meet only over full tankards and, God grant, not otherwise."

De Lorche hesitated somewhat and then declared with a certain shyness:

"If, however, noble lord, you should wish to assert that the damosel Jagienka of Longwood is not the fairest and most virtuous lady in the world—it would be a great honor for me—to contradict and—"

Here he broke off and looked Powala in the eyes with respect, nay, even with worship, yet keenly and attentively.

But Powala, either because he knew he could crack him between his fingers like a nut or because he had an extraordinarily good and merry nature, laughed aloud and said:

"Why, in my time I vowed my love to the Duchess of Burgundy, but she was then ten years older than I; so if you should wish, lord, to assert that my duchess is not older than your damosel, then we must mount our horses at once."

Hearing that, de Lorche looked at the Lord of Taczewo for a while in amazement. Then his face began to quiver, and finally he burst into wholehearted laughter.

But Powala bent down and put his arms around his waist, lifted him suddenly from the ground and began to rock him as easily as if he had been an infant.

"*Pax! pax!* as Bishop Sprinkler says," he said. "I like you, sir, and by God, we will not fight for any lady."

Then he embraced him and put him down, for trumpets suddenly sounded at the entrance to the yard—and Duke Ziemowit of Plock entered, together with his wife.

"The duke and duchess have arrived before the king and before Duke Janusz," said Powala to Zbyszko, "for although the banquet is at the warden's, they are always the hosts at Plock. Come with me to the lady. You know her from the time you were at Cracow, when she intervened with the king on your behalf."

And taking him by the arm, he led him across the yard. The duke and duchess were followed by the courtiers and ladies-in-waiting, all dressed quite magnificently because the king was to be present, so that soon the whole yard seemed bright with flowers. Zbyszko, approaching with Powala, looked at their faces from a distance, hoping to find some acquaintances among them—when suddenly he stopped in amazement.

For close beside the duchess, he did indeed catch sight of a well-known figure and a well-known face, but so serious, so beautiful, and so ladylike that he thought his eyes were deceiving him:

"Is it Jagienka or perhaps the daughter of the Duke and Duchess of Plock?"

But it was Jagienka of Zgorzelice. For when their eyes met, she smiled to him warmly and compassionately; then she paled somewhat and, lowering her eyelids, stood there, with a gold band over her dark hair, and in the measureless glory of her beauty, tall and lovely, a veritable princess.

CHAPTER LXIII

ZBYSZKO fell at the Lady of Plock's feet and offered her his service, but she did not recognize him at first, as it had been a long time since she had seen him. Only when he told her his name did she say:

"Of course! And I thought it was someone from the royal court. Zbyszko of Bogdaniec! Yes! Your uncle, the old knight of Bogdaniec, was a guest here with us, and I remember how I and my ladies shed floods of tears when he told us about you. Did you find your wife? Where is she now?"

"She died, your grace."

"O dear Jesus! Do not speak, else I shall be unable to keep back my tears. The one consolation is that she is in heaven, and you are young. Almighty God! Woman is but a weak creature. But in heaven there is reward for everything, and that is where you will find her. Is the old knight of Bogdaniec here with you?"

"No. He is in captivity with the Teutonic Knights, and I am on my way to ransom him."

"Then he, too, has had misfortune. He seemed to be a keen-witted man, knowing all the prescriptions of custom. But when you have ransomed him, come back to us. We shall be glad to entertain you, for I will tell you frankly, he has no equal in wit, nor you in good looks."

"I will, worshipful lady, particularly as I came here on purpose to ask your grace for a good word on his behalf."

"Good. Come tomorrow before the start for the hunt. I shall have time then."

Her further words were interrupted by the renewed sound of trumpets and drums, proclaiming the arrival of Duke Janusz of Warsaw and his duchess. Because Zbyszko and the Lady of Plock were standing close to the entrance, Duchess Anna Danuta saw him at once and immediately approached him, without acknowledging the bows of their host, the warden.

The young man's heart was torn again at the sight of her. He knelt down before her and, embracing her knees, remained silent. Bending over him, she stroked his temples and dropped tear after tear on his fair head, just like a mother weeping over the misfortune of her son.

And, to the great surprise of the courtiers and guests, she wept long, repeating: "O Jesus! O merciful Jesus!" Then, raising Zbyszko from his knees, she said:

"I am weeping for her, for my Danusia, and I am weeping over you. God, however, has so ordained it that your fatigues were for naught, and our tears now are for naught. But tell me of her and of her death; even if I were to listen until midnight, I should never have enough."

And she took him aside, as the Lord of Taczewo had previously done. Those of the guests who did not know Zbyszko began to ask about his adventures, and so for some time everyone was talking of him, of Danusia, and of Jurand. The Teutonic Order's envoys, Frederick von Wenden, commander of Torun, sent to meet the king, and Jan von Schonfeld, commander of Osteroda, also inquired about the young knight. The latter, a German born in Silesia, who knew Polish well, soon grasped the essence of the matter, and after hearing the account from the lips of Jasko of Zabierze, a courtier of Duke Janusz, he said:

"Danveld and von Lowe were suspected by the grand master himself of practising black magic." But he realized that the mere mention of such things might cast a shadow on the whole Order, such as had previously fallen on the Templars, so he quickly added: "At least gossips said so, but it is not true, for there are no men of that type among us."

But the Lord of Taczewo, standing nearby, answered:

"He who has hindered the baptism of Lithuania may also be disgusted by the Cross."

"We wear the Cross on our cloaks," replied Schonfeld proudly.

But Powala replied:

"You ought to wear it in your hearts."

Meanwhile the trumpets sounded still more loudly, and the king came in, followed by the Archbishop of Gniezno, the Bishop of Cracow, the Bishop of Plock, the Castellan of Cracow, and other dignitaries and courtiers, among whom were Zyndram of Maszkowice, with the sun for his escutcheon, and the young Duke Jamont, a royal page. The king had changed but little since Zbyszko had seen him last. He had the same deep flush on his cheeks, the same long hair, which he was continually pushing back behind his ears, and the same restlessly glancing eyes. But it seemed to Zbyszko that he had more dignity and more majesty now, as if he felt more secure on that throne which he had wanted to resign right after the death of the queen, not knowing whether he could maintain himself on it, and as if he was more conscious of his measureless power and strength. The two Mazovian dukes placed themselves immediately at the sides of their lord, while the German envoys made obeisance in front, and round about stood the dignitaries and leading courtiers. The walls surrounding the yard shook from the unceasing shouts, the fanfare of the trumpets, and the rolling of the drums.

When silence finally fell, the Teutonic envoy von Wenden began to speak of the business of the Order, but the king, realizing after a few words to what the exordium was leading, waved his hand impatiently and said in his deep, resonant voice:

"Please! We have come here for entertainment and would rather look at food and drink than at your parchments."

But he smiled good-naturedly at the same time, not wishing the Teutonic Knight to think that he was answering in anger, and added:

"There will be time to talk of business with the master at Raciaz." Then he turned to Duke Ziemowit: "And tomorrow we go hunting in the forest, do we not?"

This question was also a declaration that he did not wish to talk of anything else that evening but the chase, which he loved with his whole heart, and for which he always gladly came to Mazovia, since Little and Great Poland were less wooded and, in some districts, so thickly populated already that there were no forests at all.

So men's faces lit up, since it was known that when talking about hunts the king was merry and extraordinarily gracious. Duke Ziemowit immediately began to tell where they were going and what beast they would hunt, while Duke Janusz sent one of the courtiers to bring from the town his two "protectors," who dragged bison from their haunts by the horns and broke the bones of bears, for he wanted to show them to the king.

Zbyszko was very anxious to go and make obeisance to the lord, but he could not get near him. Only Duke Jamont, who had evidently forgotten the sharp answer which the young knight had previously given him at Cracow, nodded to him in friendly fashion from a distance, while signalling him to come as soon as he found a chance. But at that moment a hand touched the young knight's arm, and a sweet, sad voice spoke close by his side:

"Zbyszko!"

The young man turned and saw Jagienka before him. Occupied as he had been, first by greeting Duchess Alexandra and then by his talk with Duchess Anna Danuta, he had been unable hitherto to approach the girl, so she herself now took advantage of the confusion caused by the arrival of the king to come to him.

"Zbyszko!" she repeated. "May God and the Most Holy Virgin console you!"

"God reward you!" answered the knight, looking with gratitude into her blue eyes, which were momentarily veiled as if with dew. Then they stood face to face in silence. Though she had come to him like a kind, sad sister, she seemed to him, with her royal pose and her splendid court attire, so different from the Jagienka of old that at first he did not dare even to address her familiarly as he had used to at Zgorzelice and Bogdaniec; and she thought that after the words which she had spoken she had nothing more to say to him.

And embarrassment was reflected in their faces. At that moment, however, there was a general movement in the yard, for the king had taken his seat at the banquet. Duchess Anna approached Zbyszko again and said:

"It will be a melancholy banquet for both of us, but wait on me as you did before."

So the young knight had to leave Jagienka, and when the guests had taken their seats, he stood behind the duchess, changing her plates and pouring out her water and wine. While thus waiting on her, he could not help from time to time looking at Jagienka, who, being a lady-in-waiting of the Duchess of Plock, was seated next to her—and he could not help admiring her beauty. In the few years since he had seen her she had changed considerably, not so much, however, through having grown, as through an added gravity, of which she had shown not a trace before. Formerly, when she had galloped through the woods and forests in her sheepskin coat, with leaves in her hair, she might have been taken for a good-looking peasant girl, but now one could see immediately that she was a girl of distinguished family and good blood, such composure was there in her face. Zbyszko observed also that her former merriment had vanished, but he was not surprised at this, for he knew of the death of Zych. What did surprise him most was a certain dignity she had, and at first he thought it was her dress which gave it to her. So he looked in turn at the gold band encircling her snow-white forehead and dark hair, which fell in two large plaits down her back, and at the close-fitting blue dress, bordered with a purple stripe, under which was clearly outlined her slender figure and maiden breasts, and he said to himself: "She's a real princess!" But then he realized that not only her attire was the cause of the change in her, and that even were she now to put on a simple sheepskin, he could not take her so lightly and be so free with her as before.

Presently he observed that various younger, and even older, knights looked at her eagerly and greedily, and once, when he was changing the plate in front of the duchess, he noticed the intent and, as it were, transfigured face of Sieur de Lorche, and at the sight felt anger at him in his heart. The Guelders knight was not unobserved by Duchess Anna either, for she suddenly said:

"You see de Lorche! He must have fallen in love again, for he is quite dreamy." Then she leaned forward a little over the table and, looking sideways towards Jagienka, said: "Verily, other candles are dimmed by the light of that torch."

Zbyszko was drawn to Jagienka, however, because she seemed to him like a loving and beloved kinswoman, and he felt that he would never find a better partner of his grief, nor greater compassion in any heart. But that evening he could not speak with her any more, firstly because he was occupied with his table service, and secondly because throughout the banquet the minstrels sang songs or the trumpets made such noisy music that even those who were sitting side by side could scarcely hear one another speak. The two duchesses, followed by all the ladies, rose from table earlier than the king, the dukes, and knights, who were accustomed to amuse themselves over their cups until late into the night. It was impossible for Jagienka, who was carrying a cushion for the duchess, to stay, so she withdrew also; but on her way out, she smiled again to Zbyszko and nodded her head.

It was not until early the next morning that Zbyszko, Sieur de Lorche, and their two squires left the banquet to go back to their inn. For some time they walked along, lost in thought, but when they were not far from the house, de Lorche said something to his squire, a Pomeranian who knew Polish well, and the latter turned to Zbyszko:

"My lord would like to ask your grace something."

"Very well," Zbyszko replied.

Then de Lorche and his squire spoke together for a few moments, after which the Pomeranian said, smiling slightly:

"My lord would like to ask whether it is certain that the young lady with whom your grace was talking before the banquet is mortal or is she perhaps an angel or a saint?"

"Tell your lord," Zbyszko replied with a certain impatience, "that he has talked this way before, and that I can't believe what I'm hearing. Amazing! He told me at Spychow that he was heading to the court of Witold on account of the charm of the Lithuanian maidens, and then for the same reason he wanted to come to Plock, and today at Plock he wanted to challenge the knight of Taczewo for the sake of Jagienka of Longwood, and now he is pointing at someone else. Is this his dignity? Is this his knightly faith?"

Sieur de Lorche heard this answer from the lips of his Pomeranian, sighed deeply, looked for a moment at the paling night sky, and answered Zbyszko's reproaches thus:

"You are right. Neither dignity nor faith! For I am a sinful man and unworthy to wear a knight's spurs. As for the damosel Jagienka of Longwood—true, I vowed her my love, and God grant I may keep my vow, but observe how I shall move you when I tell how cruelly she behaved to me at the castle of Czersk."

Again he sighed, again he looked at the sky, on which an ever brighter strip was showing in the east, and after waiting for the Pomeranian to interpret his words, he presently continued:

"She told me that her enemy was a certain wizard, living in a tower amid the forests, who every year sent a dragon against her. This dragon, she said, came up to the walls of Czersk each spring to see whether it could not catch her. After I heard this, I straightaway declared that I would fight the dragon. Ah! Listen to what I shall tell you now. When I reached the appointed place I saw a dreadful monster waiting motionless for me, and joy overflowed my heart, for I thought that I should either fall or rescue the maiden from its filthy jaws and win immortal fame. But when I struck the creature at close quarters with my lance, what do you think I saw? A great sack of straw on wooden wheels, with a rope for its tail! And I won men's laughter instead of fame. I even had to challenge two Mazovian knights, from each of whom I got a heavy fall in the lists. Thus she behaved toward me, she whom I worshipped above all and whom alone I wished to love."

The Pomeranian, translating the knight's words, put his tongue in his cheek and sometimes bit it, to prevent himself from bursting into laughter. At any other time Zbyszko would have most certainly also laughed, but his grief and misery had cleansed him of all merriment, so he answered gravely:

"Maybe she did it only from folly and not from malice."

"Maybe, so I forgave her," replied de Lorche. "The best proof you have of this is the fact that I wanted to meet the knight of Taczewo in combat for her beauty and her virtue."

"Do not do that," said Zbyszko still more gravely.

"I know that it would mean death, but I would rather die than live in everlasting sorrow and anxiety."

"Lord Powala has other things in his head now. Better come with me to him tomorrow and make friends with him."

"So I will, for he embraced me warmly. Tomorrow, however, he is going hunting with the king."

"Then we will go to him early. The king loves the chase, but he does not scorn rest, and today he banqueted till late."

But this effort was in vain. The Czech, who had hastened to the castle even before them, to see his mistress, informed them that Powala was not sleeping in his own quarters that night, but in the royal apartments. Nevertheless, their disappointment was made good, for Duke Janusz met them and bade them join his train, thereby enabling them to take part in the chase. During the ride into the forest, Zbyszko also found opportunity to talk with Duke Jamont, who told him good news.

"While I was undressing the king for bed," he said, "I reminded him of you and your Cracow adventure. Sir Powala was present also, and he immediately added that the Teutonic Knights had seized your uncle, and begged the king to intervene on his behalf. The king, who is exceeding angry against them for their kidnapping of little Jasko of Kretkowo and other raids, was still more enraged. 'It is no good,' he said, 'going to them with good words, but with the pike, the pike, the pike!' And Powala purposely added wood to the fire. So in the morning, when the Teutonic envoys were waiting by the gate, the king did not look at them, though they made obeisance to the ground before him. Hey! now they will get no promise from him not to aid Duke Witold. And they will not know what to do. But you may be certain that the king will not fail to press the grand master himself for the release of your uncle."

Thus his heart was rejoiced by the young duke. Yet his heart was even more rejoiced by Jagienka, who had accompanied Duchess Alexandra to the forest and obtained permission from her to ride in the back with Zbyszko. There was usually great freedom during such hunts, and the company therefore usually returned in pairs; and since no pair particularly wanted to be near another, it was possible to talk freely. After having learned from the Czech of Macko's captivity, Jagienka had not wasted any time. At her request the duchess had written a letter to the master; the duchess also had induced von Wenden, the commander of Torun, to mention the matter in his report of the doings at Plock. Indeed, he even boasted before the duchess that he had added in his report: "Desiring, as we do, to humor the king, we must not make difficulties for him in this affair." At this time the grand master was most anxious to humor the powerful ruler as far as possible, so that he could freely direct all his forces against Witold, whom the Order had so far not been able to handle.

"And so what I could, I have done, taking care that there should be no delay," Jagienka concluded; "and I have the best hopes that the king, not wishing to yield to his sister in great matters, will assuredly endeavor to satisfy her in smaller ones."

"If the Knights were not so treacherous," Zbyszko answered, "I should simply have taken them the ransom money and the affair would have been over; but with them the same thing may happen that happened to Tolima. They will steal the money and not let the man who brought it go, unless that man has some power behind him."

"I understand," Jagienka replied.

"Now you understand everything," Zbyszko observed, "and as long as I live I shall be grateful to you, lady."

She raised her sad, kind eyes to him and asked: "Why do you not call me Jagienka, since you have known me since I was little?"

"I don't know," he answered truthfully. "I find it difficult somehow. . . . You are no longer the slip of a girl you used to be, but—as it were—something quite. . . ."

He could not find the right comparison, but she interrupted his effort and said:

"Some years have passed—and the Germans killed my father in Silesia."

"True!" Zbyszko replied. "God grant him everlasting light!"

For some time they rode side by side in silence, sunk in thought and listening to the evening soughing of the pines, and then she asked:

"And after ransoming Macko will you stay in these parts?"

Zbyszko looked at her in surprise, for hitherto he had been so completely taken up with grief and sorrow that it had never entered his head to think what he would do later. So he raised his eyes meditatively, and presently replied:

"I do not know. Merciful Christ! How can I know? I know only that wherever I wander, my misery will go with me. Alas! Deep misery! I will ransom my uncle, and then I suppose I will go to Witold to fulfill my vows against the Teutonic Knights—and perhaps perish."

At that the girl's eyes became misty, and leaning slightly towards the young man, she said softly, almost in a pleading tone:

"Don't perish! Don't perish!"

Again they ceased to talk, until, just before the walls of the town, Zbyszko shook off the thoughts which were troubling him.

"And you, Jagienka," he asked, "will you stay here with the court?"

"No," she replied. "It is dreary without my brothers and without

Zgorzelice. Cztan and Wolf must have married already, and even if they have not, I am no longer afraid of them."

"God grant that my uncle Macko may take you to Zgorzelice! He is such a friend to you that you may rely on him in everything. For your part, don't forget about him."

"I promise you faithfully that I will be to him like his own child."

And after these words she burst into tears, for her heart had grown unutterably sad.

Next morning Powala of Taczewo came to Zbyszko's inn and told him:

"Immediately after Corpus Christi the king is going to Raciaz to meet the grand master, and you are enrolled among the royal knights and will accompany us."

Zbyszko became overwhelmed with joy at these words. Not only did his enrollment among the royal knights secure him from treasons and stratagems on the part of the Teutonic Knights, but it covered him with measureless glory. For among the number of the knights were included such men as Zawisza the Black, and his brothers Farurej and Kruczek, and Powala himself, and Krzon of Goat's Head, and Staszko of Charbimowice, and Paszko the Thief of Biskupice, and Lis of Fair-Ground, and many other terrible and famous men, whose names were known at home and beyond the border. King Jagiello was not taking a large body of these knights with him, for some remained at home and others were seeking adventures in distant countries beyond the sea; but he knew that with them he might ride even to Malbork without fear of Teutonic treason, for in case of need they would smash the walls down and cut him a path through the Germans. Zbyszko's young heart might well swell with pride at the thought of having such companions.

So he immediately forgot his grief and, grasping Powala of Taczewo's hands, said to him with joy:

"I owe this to you and to no one else, lord! To you! Only to you!"

"In part to me," replied the knight, "and in part to the duchess here, but most of all to our gracious lord, whose legs you must straightaway go and embrace, else he will suspect you of ingratitude."

"So help me God, I am ready to die for him!" Zbyszko exclaimed.

CHAPTER LXIV

THE conference on the Vistulan island of Raciaz, to which the king went about the time of Corpus Christi, was held under unfavorable auspices and did not lead to such agreement and settlement of various matters as the second, held in the same place two years later, at which the king regained the land of Dobrzyn, with the town of Dobrzyn itself and Bobrowniki, which had been treacherously pledged by the Duke of Opole to the Teutonic Knights. Jagiello arrived greatly annoyed at the rumors spread about him by the Teutonic Knights at the Western courts and even in Rome, and at the same time enraged at the dishonesty of the Order. On purpose, the grand master was unwilling to negotiate about Dobrzyn; and both he himself and the other dignitaries of the Order repeated daily to the Poles: "We do not want war with you, nor with Lithuania, but Samogitia is ours, for Witold himself gave it to us. Promise that you will not aid him, and the war against him will be ended sooner. Then it will be time to talk about Dobrzyn, and we shall make you many concessions." But the king's counsellors, who had keen, experienced wits and knew the falsehood of the Teutonic Knights, were not to be led by the nose. "If you grow in power, you will be still more arrogant," they told the grand master in reply. "You say that you have no claims on Lithuania, yet you wish to put Skirgiello on the throne at Wilno. But, great God! that is Jagiello's inheritance, and he alone has the right to appoint whom he will as duke. So beware, lest our great king chastise you." To that the master replied that if the king was the real lord of Lithuania, he should order Witold to stop the war and give back

Samogitia to the Order, else the Order must strike at Witold where it could reach and wound him. And so the argument dragged on from morning to evening. The king, not wanting to pledge himself to anything, grew still more impatient and told the master that if Samogitia had been happy under Teutonic rule Witold would not have lifted a finger, for he would have found neither cause nor pretext. The master, who was a peaceable man and realized better than the other brethren the power of Jagiello, endeavored to appease the king and, paying no heed to the murmuring of some hot-headed and proud commanders, did not spare even flattery, and at times simulated humility. But since through this humility there sounded more than once veiled threats, it led to nothing. The negotiations about important matters quickly evaporated, and on the second day only minor matters were discussed. The king accused the Order sharply of maintaining bands of robbers, of raiding and plundering on the border, of kidnapping Jurand's daughter and little Jasko of Kretkowo, and of murdering yeomen and fishermen. The master denied it, made excuses, and vowed that it had been without his knowledge; and he complained, in his turn, that not only Witold but also Polish knights were helping the pagan Samogitians against the Cross—as proof of which he cited Macko of Bogdaniec. Fortunately the king already knew from Powala what the knights of Bogdaniec had been doing in Samogitia, and he was able to answer the reproach, the more easily that in his train was Zbyszko, and in the grand master's were the two von Badens, who had come in the hope that they might find a chance to joust with Poles in the lists.

But nothing came of that either. The Teutonic Knights had wished, in case things went well for them, to invite the great king to Torun and arrange several days of banquets and games in his honor; but in view of the abortive negotiations, which gave birth only to mutual dislike and anger, no one had any inclination for amusement. Only privately, in the morning hours, did the knights compete among themselves in strength and skill, but, as the merry Duke Jamont said, the Teutonic Knights felt vexed, like a cat stroked the wrong way, when Powala of Taczewo showed himself stronger in the arm than Arnold von Baden, or Dobko of Olesnica proved superior with the lance, or Lis of Fair-Ground overcame all comers at vaulting, heavy-armed, over horses. Zbyszko took the opportunity to come to an agreement with Arnold von Baden respecting the ransom. De Lorche, who, as a count and lord of great distinction, looked down on Arnold, objected to this, maintaining that he would take everything on himself. Zbyszko, however, thought that his honor as a knight required him to pay the number of marks he had pledged, and therefore, though Arnold was willing to lower the price, he refused to accept either this concession or the mediation of de Lorche.

Arnold von Baden was a simple fellow, chiefly distinguished for the gigantic strength of his arms, rather stupid, somewhat greedy of money, but almost honest. He had none of the Teutonic Knights' cunning, and therefore did not conceal from Zbyszko his real motive for being ready to lower the agreed price: "The negotiations," he said, "between the great king and the master will lead to nothing, but there will be an exchange of prisoners—so you may get your uncle back for nothing. I would rather get something than nothing, since my purse is usually empty and frequently contains hardly enough for three gallons of beer a day, whereas I feel short without five or six." But Zbyszko was angry with him for saying such things. "I will pay, for I have given my knightly word, and I do not wish to give less, so that you may know we are worth that much." Thereupon Arnold embraced him, and the knights, both Polish and German, praised him, saying: "It is right that he should wear belt and spurs although so young, for he is aware of what honor and dignity demand."

Meanwhile the king and the master did, in fact, agree upon an exchange of captives, and then strange things came to light, concerning which the bishops and dignitaries of the kingdom afterwards wrote letters to the pope and various courts; for there were indeed a goodly number of captives in Polish hands, but they were grown men in the prime of their life, taken by force of arms in border battles and combats. But the majority in the hands of the Teutonic Knights were women and children, seized in night raids and held to ransom. The pope in Rome himself turned his attention to it and, despite all the cunning of Jan von Felde, attorney of the Order at the Apostolic See, loudly expressed his wrath and indignation against the Order.

As for Macko, there were difficulties. The master did not make them seriously, but only as pretexts, to give weight to each concession. So he asserted that a Christian knight who fought alongside the Samogitians against the Order ought, in justice, to be put to death. In vain the royal counsellors cited afresh all that they knew of Jurand and his daughter and the terrible wrongs that the servants of the Order had committed against them both and against the knights of Bogdaniec. By an odd coincidence the master, in his answer, made use of almost the same words as Duchess Alexandra, Ziemowit's wife, had used to the old knight of Bogdaniec:

"You claim to be lambs, and that our men are wolves. Yet of the four wolves who took part in the kidnapping of Jurand's daughter, not one is alive, while the lambs go about in safety."

That was the truth, but the Lord of Taczewo, who was present at the discussions, answered it with the following questions:

"Yes, but was any one of them slain by treachery? And of those that fell, did they not fall sword in hand?"

To that the master had no reply, and when he observed that the king was beginning to frown, and his eyes to flash, he yielded, not wishing to provoke the terrible ruler to an outburst. It was afterwards agreed that each side should send envoys to receive the prisoners. Those nominated on the Polish side were Zyndram of Maszkowice, who desired to have a closer view of the Teutonic Knights' power, and Sir Powala, together with Zbyszko of Bogdaniec.

Zbyszko owed this favor to Duke Jamont. He spoke to the king on his behalf, stating that the young man would see his uncle sooner and would be more certain to bring him back if he went for him in the character of royal envoy. And the king did not refuse the young duke's request, for he was a favorite with the whole court because of his cheerfulness, good humor, and good looks; and, besides, he never asked anything for himself. So Zbyszko thanked him with his whole heart, since he was now quite sure that he would get back Macko from the hands of the Teutonic Knights.

"More than one person envies you," Zbyszko told him, "because you are near the king's majesty, but it is right that you should be, for you use your intimacy with the king only for men's good, and there cannot be a better heart than yours."

"It is good to be near the king," replied the young boyar, "but I should prefer to take the field against the Teutonic Knights, and I envy you that you have already fought with them." Presently, however, he added: "Von Wenden, the commander of Torun, arrived yesterday, and this evening you will go to him for the night, with the master and his train."

"And then to Malbork?"

"And then to Malbork."

Duke Jamont laughed.

"The road will not be long, but sour; for the Germans have not succeeded in getting anything out of the king, and with Witold they will have no satisfaction either. He is said to have gathered the whole power of Lithuania and to be marching into Samogitia."

"If the kings helps him there will be a great war."

"All our knights are praying for it. But even if the king is sorry to shed Christian blood and does not make war, he will help Witold with grain and money. Furthermore, it is certain that some of the Polish knights will join him as volunteers."

"Most certain," Zbyszko replied. "But perhaps the Order itself will declare war on the king?"

"Oh, no!" replied Jamont. "As long as the present master lives, they will not do that."

And he was right. Zbyszko knew the grand master before, but now, on the road to Malbork, with Zyndram of Maszkowice and Powala almost constantly at his side, he could study his face and get to know him better. That journey confirmed him in the conviction that the grand master, Conrad von Jungingen, was not a bad or corrupt man. He had often to proceed in an unjust manner, for the whole Teutonic Order rested on injustice. He had to do wrongs, for the whole Order was built on human wrongs. He had to lie, for he had inherited lying along with the insignia of his mastership and had been accustomed from his early years to regard it as merely political adroitness. But he was not cruel; he feared divine judgment, and he restrained as far as he could the pride and arrogance of those dignitaries of the Order who intentionally acted so as to bring on war with the power of Jagiello. He was, however, weak. The Order had been so accustomed for centuries to await its chance of robbing others and to acquire adjacent lands either by force or stratagem, that Conrad was not only unable to appease their predatory hunger, but involuntarily, by the force of momentum, he was driven to yield and attempt to satisfy it. The times of Winrich von Kniprode were already long past—the times of strict discipline, which made the Order the wonder of the world. Already under Jungingen's predecessor, Conrad Wallenrod, the Order had become drunk with its ever-increasing power, which temporary disasters were unable to weaken, and was intoxicated with fame and success and human blood to such an extent that the bonds which kept it strong and united were loosened. The master maintained law and justice as far he could; and as far as he could, he personally softened the iron hand of the Order that weighed down on the peasants, the burghers, and even on the clergy and the gentry, who by feudal right lived in its territories. And so it happened that in the neighborhood of Malbork one or another yeoman or burgher might boast not merely of a comfortable competence but of wealth, while in the more distant districts the arbitrary, stern, and unchecked will of the commanders trampled on law, spread oppression and extortion, squeezed out the last penny under pretext of taxation or without any pretext at all, squeezed out tears and often blood—all this to such an extent that in the whole of their wide territories there was nothing but lamentation, misery, and complaint. Even if the good of the Order required less harshness, as sometimes in Samogitia, its requirements were powerless to effect a change, in view of the indiscipline of the commanders and their innate cruelty. So Conrad von Jungingen felt like a charioteer in charge of wild horses, who lets go the reins and leaves his chariot to be the sport of fate. His spirit was, accordingly, often dominated by evil forebodings, and often there came into his mind the prophetic words of St. Bridget: "I appointed them to be bees of usefulness and established them on the edge of Christian lands, but lo! they rose against Me. For they have no care for the souls and no compassion for the bodies of a people who have turned from their error to the Catholic faith and to Me. They made thralls of them, and do not teach them the divine commandments, and by taking from them the Holy Sacraments, they condemn them to still greater pains in hell than if they had remained in paganism. And they wage wars for the satisfaction of their greed. Therefore the time will come when their teeth shall be broken, and their right hand cut off, and their right leg lamed, that they may acknowledge their sins."

The master knew that these reproaches, made against the Teutonic Knights by the mystical Voice in the vision of the saint, were justified. He understood that the edifice constructed on others' lands and at the price of others' wrongs, supported on falsehood, deceit and tyranny, could not last long; he feared lest, undermined for years by blood and tears, it should fall at one blow from the powerful Polish hand; he felt that the chariot drawn by wild horses must wind up in the abyss; but he endeavored at least to put off the day of judgment, wrath, disaster, and misery. For this reason, despite his weakness, in one thing only did he offer unswerving resistance to his proud and arrogant counsellors: he did not let things come to war with Poland. In vain he was reproached with timidity and incompetence; in vain the border commanders urged him with all their strength to war. Whenever the conflagration was just on the point of breaking out, he always withdrew at the last moment and then thanked God at Malbork that he had succeeded in holding off the sword raised over the Order's head.

But he knew that it must come to war in the end. And so the conviction that the Order was based, not on divine law, but on injustice and lies, and the foreboding of approaching doom made him one of the unhappiest men in the world. He would undoubtedly have given his life and blood that it might be otherwise, and that there might still be time to return to the right road, but he felt that time had run out. To return would have meant giving back to the rightful owners all the fertile, rich lands which the Order had seized God knows how long ago, and with them a number of towns as rich as Danzig. Nor would that have been enough! It would have meant renouncing Samogitia, renouncing attacks on Lithuania, sheathing the sword—indeed entirely withdrawing from these regions, in which the Order had now no one to baptize any more, and settling anew, either in Palestine or on one of the Greek islands, there to defend the Cross against true Saracens. But that was an impossibility, for it would have been equivalent to a sentence of death on the Order. Who would have agreed to that? And what grand master could demand anything of the kind? Conrad von Jungingen's soul and life were under shadow, but he himself would have been the first to condemn the author of any such proposal to the dark chamber. It was necessary to go on and on, until the day when God himself should set a limit.

So he went on, but in anguish and sorrow of heart. The hair of his beard and on his temples was already silvered, and his once keen

eyes were half covered by their heavy lids. Never once did Zbyszko
see a smile on his face. The countenance of the master was not
threatening, nor even clouded, but only weary with silent suffering. In his armor, with the cross on his breast and a black eagle
framed at its center, in his large white cloak, also adorned with the
cross, he produced an impression of majesty and melancholy. Conrad had once been merry and fond of jests, and even now he was
not averse to splendid banquets, spectacles, and tournaments—indeed, he arranged them himself. But neither in the throng of
famous knights who came as guests to Malbork, nor in the joyous
noise, amid the sound of trumpets and the clash of arms, nor over
the goblets filled with malmsey wine did he ever become cheerful.
At those times, when everything around him seemed to breathe
strength, splendor, limitless wealth, and invincible power, when
the envoys of the emperor and of the kings of the West shouted in
their enthusiasm that the Order alone sufficed for all kingdoms
and for the power of the whole world—he alone was not deluded,
he alone remembered the ominous words revealed to St. Bridget:
"The time will come when their teeth shall be broken, and their
right hand cut off, and their right leg lamed, that they may acknowledge their sins."

CHAPTER LXV

THEY went by land through the province of Chelmno to Grudziadz, where they stayed for a night and a day, since the master had
to judge a dispute about fishing rights between the Teutonic constable of the castle and the local gentry, whose lands bordered the
Vistula. The remainder of the journey to Malbork was made on
barges belonging to the Teutonic Knights. Zyndram of Maszkowice, Powala of Taczewo, and Zbyszko spent the entire time by
the grand master's side, and he was curious to see what impression
a close-up view of the Order's power would make upon them, and
more particularly upon Zyndram, who was not only a valiant
knight, terrible in single combat, but an unusually skilled warrior.
In the whole kingdom there was none who understood as he did
the leadership of large armies, the marshalling of troops for battle,
the building and storming of castles, the bridging of wide rivers,
the armaments of different nations, and all the methods and principles of war.

The master, knowing that at the royal council much depended
on the opinion of this man, thought that if he could impress him
with the greatness of the Teutonic wealth and armies, the war
might still be long deferred. Above all, the sight of Malbork might
fill the heart of every Pole with fear, for no other fortress in the
whole world could even distantly compare with this, made up, as
it was, of the High Castle, the Middle Castle, and the Lower
Castle. When they were still far distant, floating down the waters
of the Nogat, the knights caught sight of its tremendous bastions
outlined against the sky. The day was bright and clear, so they were

excellently visible, and after some time, when the boats drew nearer, the spires of the church in the High Castle and the huge walls towering one above another shone still more strikingly. These walls were partly brick-red, but mostly covered with the famous greyish-white plaster which only the stonemasons of the Order knew how to produce. Their size surpassed anything the Polish knights had seen in their lives. It seemed as if edifice grew upon edifice there, forming, in a previously level area, a mountain, whose summit was the Old Castle and whose flanks were the Middle and the extensive Lower Castle. This huge lair of armed monks reflected a might and a power so extraordinary that even the long and usually gloomy face of the master brightened somewhat at the sight.

"*Ex luto Marienburg!* Malbork from the mud!" he said, turning to Zyndram. "But no human power will crumble that mud."

Zyndram made no answer but scanned in silence all the bastions and the enormous mass of the walls, strengthened by monstrous buttresses.

Conrad von Jungingen added after a few moments' silence:

"You, lord, who understand fortresses, what do you say of this one?"

"It seems to me impregnable," replied the Polish knight, as if lost in thought; "but. . . ."

"But what? What fault do you find in it?"

"Any fortress may change its lords."

The master frowned.

"What do you mean by that?"

"I mean that the judgments and verdicts of God are concealed from human eyes."

And again he looked broodingly at the walls, while Zbyszko, to whom Powala had translated his answer, gazed at him with admiration and gratitude. He was struck at that moment by the likeness between Zyndram and the Samogitian leader, Skirwoillo. Both had similar huge heads, planted between broad shoulders; both had equally powerful chests and similar bowlegs.

Meanwhile the master, not wishing the last word to be left with the Polish knight, continued:

"It is said that our Malbork is six times larger than the Cracow Wawel."

"On a rock there is not so much space as on a plain," replied the Lord of Maszkowice, "but the heart in our Wawel is greater."

Conrad raised his eyebrows in surprise:

"I don't understand."

"What is the heart in every castle, if not the church? And our cathedral is equal to three like that."

He pointed to the castle church—indeed, not large—on which shone a huge mosaic picture of the Most Holy Virgin against a gold background.

The master was again displeased at such a turn in the conversation.

"You have ready answers, but they are strange, lord," he said.

Meanwhile they arrived at their journey's end. The excellent police of the Order had evidently notified the town and castle of the approach of the grand master, for a few brethren were already waiting at the landing-place, besides the town trumpeters, who usually played for him when he landed. Horses were waiting, mounting which the train passed through the town and through the Shoemakers' Gate, past the Sparrow Bastion, and into the Lower Castle. In the gateway, the master was welcomed by the grand commander, William von Helfenstein—whose office was indeed only titular, since for some months its duties had been performed by Kuno Lichtenstein, now on a mission to England— and then by the grand hospitaller Conrad Lichtenstein, a relative of Kuno; the grand keeper of the wardrobe, Rumpenheim; the grand treasurer, Burghard von Wobecke, and, lastly, by the petty commander, or bailiff, in charge of the workshops and administration of the castle. Besides these dignitaries, there were also a dozen or more ordained brethren who dealt with matters concerning the Church in Prussia, and who harshly oppressed other monasteries, as well as the parish clergy, whom they even forced to perform labor on the roads and break ice on the rivers; and behind them a group of lay brothers, that is to say, knights, who were not obliged to observe the canonical hours. Their tall and powerful figures (the Teutonic Order would not admit weaklings), their broad shoulders, their curly beards and stern glances made them look more like predatory German robber-knights than monks. Their eyes betrayed daring, arrogance, and pride. They did not like Conrad because of his fear of war with the powerful Jagiello; more than once at the

chapters they had openly reproached him with timidity; they had
caricatured him on the walls, and had persuaded jesters to ridicule
him before his face. However, at the sight of him, they now bowed
their heads in simulated humility, particularly because he was
accompanied by foreign knights, and they sprang forward in a
body to hold his horse's bridle and his stirrup.

The master, after dismounting, turned at once to Helfenstein
and asked him:

"Is there any news from Werner von Tettingen?"

Werner von Tettingen, being grand marshal, or leader of the
armed forces of the Order, was at that moment on an expedition
against the Samogitians and Witold.

"There is no important news," replied Helfenstein, "but damage
has been done. The barbarians have burnt the settlement at Ragneta and the market towns outside other castles."

"My hope is in God that one great battle will break their malice
and stubbornness," replied the master.

After these words, he raised his eyes heavenward, while his lips
moved in a moment of prayer for the success of the Order's armies.
Then he pointed to the Polish knights.

"These are envoys of the Polish king: the knight of Maszkowice,
he of Taczewo, and he of Bogdaniec, who have come with us to
exchange captives. Let the castle bailiff show them the guest apartments and receive them with fitting hospitality."

The knightly brethren looked with curiosity at the envoys, and
particularly at Powala of Taczewo, whose name was known already
to some as that of a famous champion. Those who had not heard
of his deeds at the Burgundian, Bohemian, and Cracovian courts
wondered at his huge stature and at his war stallion, which was so
big as to remind experienced men, who had visited the Holy Land
and Egypt in their youth, of camels and of elephants.

Some also recognized Zbyszko, who had previously fought in
the lists at Malbork, and greeted him with considerable courtesy,
remembering that the master's powerful brother, Ulrich von Jungingen, who enjoyed great esteem in the Order, had shown him
sincere friendship and goodwill. The least attention and admiration was given to the one who in the not-distant future was to be
the most terrible scourge of the Order, namely Zyndram of Maszkowice, for when he dismounted, his unusually dumpy figure and

high shoulders made him look almost hunchbacked. His overlong arms and bowlegs brought smiles to the faces of the younger brethren. One of them, well known for his jokes, even went up to him with the intention of making fun of him, but when he had caught the Lord of Maszkowice's eye, he somehow lost his desire to do so and withdrew in silence.

Meanwhile the bailiff collected the guests and took them with him. They first came to a small courtyard, on which, besides a school, an old granary and a saddler's shop, was the chapel of St. Nicholas, and then they crossed the Nicholas Bridge into the actual Lower Castle. The bailiff led them for some time amid powerful walls, strengthened here and there by larger or smaller bastions. Zyndram of Maszkowice looked attentively at everything, while their guide gladly pointed out to them the various buildings, even without being asked, as if he were particularly anxious that the guests should examine everything as closely as possible.

"The huge building which your graces see before you on the left," he said, "is our horse stable. We are but poor monks, yet people say that elsewhere even knights do not have such good quarters as these horses."

"People do not suspect you of poverty," replied Powala. "But there must be something here besides a stable, for the building is mighty high, and horses presumably do not go up stairs."

"Over the stable, which is at the bottom and has room for four hundred horses," said the bailiff, "are granaries, containing grain enough for ten years. This place will never be besieged, but if it were, it would not be taken by hunger."

So saying, he turned to the right and led them over another bridge between the St. Laurence and Armored bastions into a second courtyard, of enormous size, lying in the very center of the Lower Castle.

"Observe, your graces," said the German, "that all which you see to the north, though by the grace of God it cannot be taken, is but the *Vorburg*—and in fortification is not to be compared either with the Middle Castle, to which I am conducting you, or still less, with the High Castle."

A separate moat and a separate drawbridge divided the Middle Castle from the yard, and it was not until they came to the castle gateway, which lay considerably higher, that the knights, turning on the advice of the bailiff, could cast their eyes again over the whole huge square called the *Vorburg*. In it, building rose by the side of building, so that it seemed to Zyndram that he was looking at a whole town. There were measureless stocks of timber arranged in piles as big as houses, stores of stone balls sticking up like pyramids, cemeteries, hospitals, and storehouses. A little to one side, by the pond in the middle, rose the powerful red walls of the "temple," that is to say, of the great magazine and dining-room for the mercenaries and the servants. Under the northern rampart were to be seen more stables, for the horses of the knights and the master's picked chargers. Along the mill-stream rose barracks for the squires and mercenaries and, on the opposite side of the quadrangle, dwellings for the various functionaries and officials of the Order—and, once again, storehouses, granaries, bakeries, wardrobes, armorers' shops, the immense arsenal, or *Karwan*, prisons, and the old armory: each building so solid and defensible that it might be held like a separate fortress, and the entirety surrounded by a wall and a number of threatening bastions, and beyond the wall by a moat, and beyond the moat by a ring of enormous stakes, beyond which, finally, to the west rolled the yellow waves of the Nogat, to the north and east glittered the deep waters of a huge pond, and to the south rose the still more strongly fortified Middle and High Castles.

A terrible lair, expressive of inexorable power, and uniting the two greatest forces then known in the world: that of the Church and that of the sword. Whoever resisted the one was struck down by the other. Whoever raised his hand against them found an outcry made against him in every Christian country, because he had raised it against the Cross.

And soon knights would come from all sides to their aid. The lair was therefore continually swarming with craftsmen and soldiers, and there was a continual hum as in a hive of bees. In front of the buildings, in the passageways, by the gates, in the workshops—everywhere there was activity as at a fair. The place reverberated with the sound of hammers and chisels shaping stone balls, the creaking of mills and treadmills, the neighing of horses, the clash of armor and weapons, the sound of trumpets and fifes, shouts and commands. In those courtyards you heard all the languages of the world and might meet soldiers from every nation:

unerring English archers, who could hit a pigeon, tied to a mast, at a hundred paces, and whose arrows pierced breastplates as easily as if they were made of cloth; terrible Swiss footmen, who fought with two-handed swords; valiant Danes, immoderate in their love of food and drink; French knights, inclined to laugh as well as quarrel; reserved and proud Spanish nobles; famous Italian knights, the most skilled of fencers, clad in silk and samite and, for war, in impenetrable armor forged at Venice, Milan, or Florence; Burgundian knights, and Frisians; and finally Germans from every German land.

Among them moved the "white cloaks" as hosts and superiors. "A tower full of gold," or more accurately a special chamber built in the High Castle, next to the master's dwelling, and filled from floor to roof with coined money and bars of precious metal, enabled the Order to receive its guests worthily, as well as to hire mercenaries, who were sent out on expeditions and to all the castles, where they were at the disposal of the governors, constables, and commanders. Thus, by the power of the sword and the power of the Church, were gathered enormous riches, and at the same time an iron discipline was forged, which, although by this time weakened in the provinces by overconfidence and an intoxication with power, was yet maintained at Malbork by virtue of long custom. Monarchs came here not only to fight with pagans or to borrow money but also to learn the art of government, and knights to learn the art of war. For in the whole world none knew how to govern and to war like the Order. When it had first come to those parts, besides a small district and a few castles given it by a careless Polish duke, it did not possess an inch of earth; but now it ruled a vast region, larger than many kingdoms, full of fertile lands, powerful cities, and impregnable castles. It governed and watched, as a spider governs its outspread web, gathering all its threads under itself. Thence, from this High Castle, commands went out from the master and the white cloaks through the postriders in all directions: to the feudal nobility, to the town councils, to the burgomasters, to the governors, sub-governors, and captains of mercenaries; and what was conceived and determined upon by thought and will here, was quickly executed there by hundreds and thousands of iron hands. To this point flowed money from the whole country, grain, all kinds of foodstuffs, and donations from the secular clergy, groaning under a harsh yoke, and from other monasteries, at which the Order looked with disapproval; from this point predatory hands were stretched out towards all the neighboring lands and peoples.

Numerous Prussian tribes which spoke Lithuanian had already been wiped from the surface of the earth. Lithuania had until recently felt the iron heel of the Teutonic Knights pressing so terribly on its breast that with every breath blood was forced from its heart; Poland, though victorious in the terrible battle of Plowce, lost in the time of Wladyslaw the Short its lands on the left bank of the Vistula, together with Danzig, Tczew, Gniew, and Swiecie. The Livonian Order of Knights reached out for Ruthenian lands, and both orders together advanced like the first huge wave of a German sea, flooding ever-wider expanses of Slavonic soil.

But suddenly the sun of the Teutonic Knights' prosperity sank behind a cloud. Lithuania received baptism from Polish hands, and the throne of Cracow together with the hand of the beautiful princess was taken by Jagiello. The Order did not, indeed, thereby lose a single land or a single castle, but it felt that its force was confronted by another force, and it lost the reason for its existence in Prussia. After the christianization of Lithuania, the Order ought to have returned to Palestine and protected the pilgrims visiting the holy sites. But to return would have meant the renunciation of wealth, rule, power, domination, towns, lands, and whole kingdoms. So the Order began to writhe in fear and hatred, like some monstrous dragon whose side is pierced by a lance. Grand Master Conrad was afraid to stake all on one throw of the dice and trembled at the thought of war with the great king, ruler of the Polish and Lithuanian lands and of extensive demesnes in Ruthenia that Olgierd had snatched from the jaws of the Tartars; but the majority of the knights pressed for it, feeling that they must wage war for life and death while their forces were intact, while the spell of the Order had not yet faded, while the whole world was hastening to its aid, and while the papal thunderbolts had not yet fallen on their lair, whose life-and-death question was now, not the extension of Christianity, but actually the maintenance of paganism.

Meanwhile, before nations and at courts, they accused Jagiello and Lithuania of a false and simulated baptism, claiming that it was a thing impossible for that to have happened in the course of a year which the sword of the Order had been unable to bring about in centuries. They stirred up kings and knights against Poland and against its rulers, as against guardians and defenders of paganism; and these voices, which only in Rome were disbelieved, spread in a broad wave through the world and drew to Malbork dukes, counts, and knights from the south and the west. The Order gained confidence and felt itself powerful. Malbork, with its threatening castles and lower-castle, dazzled folk more than ever before by its power, its riches, and its apparent discipline; and the whole Order seemed to be more masterful and more eternally unconquerable than before. And none of the dukes, none of the knightly guests, no one—save the master alone—even among the Teutonic Knights, understood that from the moment of Lithuania's baptism something decisive had happened: as if the waves of the Nogat, which sheltered the terrible fortress on one side, had begun quietly and inexorably to undermine its walls. No one understood that in that huge body there was still strength, but no more soul. Whosoever arrived for the first time and gazed upon that Malbork raised *ex luto*, upon those walls and bastions, and the black crosses on the gates, the buildings and the robes, thought foremost that even the gates of hell could not prevail against that northern capital of the Cross.

Such thoughts filled the minds not only of Powala of Taczewo and Zbyszko, who had been here before, but even of Zyndram of Maszkowice, who was much keener-witted than they. Even his face grew dark when he looked at that moment upon this fortress, swarming ant-like with soldiers and framed in bastions and enormous towers, and there came involuntarily into his mind the proud words with which the Teutonic Knights of old had threatened King Kazimierz:

"Our power is the greater, and if you do not yield, we will chase you to Cracow itself with our swords."

But in the meantime the bailiff led the knights to the Middle Castle, the great chambers being in its eastern wing.

CHAPTER LXVI

MACKO and Zbyszko held each other in a lengthy embrace. They had always loved each other, but during the recent years their common adventures and misfortunes had made that love even stronger. Upon first seeing his nephew, the old knight had guessed that Danusia was no longer in this world. He asked no questions, therefore, but only pressed the young man to his breast, desiring to show him by the strength of his embrace that he was not left entirely alone and that he still had near him a living soul ready to share his misery.

At last, when their sorrow and pain had been considerably relieved by their tears, Macko asked after a long silence:

"Did they wrest her from you again, or did she die in your arms?"

"She died in my arms quite close to Spychow," replied the youth, and he began to tell him what had happened and how it had happened, interrupting his narration with weeping and sighs, while Macko listened attentively, sighed also, and at the end began to question him again:

"Is Jurand still alive?"

"He was alive when I left, but he was not long for this world, and certainly I shall never see him again."

"Then perhaps it would have been better not to leave him."

"How could I have left you here?"

"A few weeks earlier or later wouldn't have mattered."

But Zbyszko looked at him attentively and said:

"Surely you must have been sick here? You look like Piotrowin."

"Though the sun warms the earth, in the dungeon it is always cold, and the dampness there is cruel, for all around the castle is water. I thought I should moulder away completely. There is no air to breathe either, and as a result of all that, my wound has re-opened—the one, you know, from which the splinter came out at Bogdaniec after the beaver's fat."

"I remember," said Zbyszko. "I went for the beaver with Jagienka. So the curs kept you here in a dungeon?"

Macko nodded and answered:

"To tell you frankly, they weren't pleased to see me, and I was in danger of my life at their hands. There is great hatred here against Witold and the Samogitians, but still greater against those of us who aid them. In vain I told them why we went among the Samogitians. They would have cut off my head, and if they did not, it was only because they would have been sorry to lose my ransom, for as you know, money is more agreeable to them even than vengeance, and, furthermore, they wanted to have in their hands evidence that the king of Poland was sending aid to the pagans. We, who have been there, know that those pitiful Samogitians beg for baptism, if only not from German hands; but the Teutonic Knights pretend not to know this, and accuse them at all the courts, and along with them our king."

Here Macko's breath failed. He had to stop for a few moments, continuing only when he had recovered it.

"I might have died in the dungeon. It is true Arnold von Baden spoke on my behalf, for he also cared about the ransom. But he has no dignity among them, and they call him a bear. Fortunately, however, de Lorche heard of me from Arnold and straightaway raised a mighty tumult. I don't know whether he told you about it, as he likes to conceal his good deeds. They hold him in esteem here because a de Lorche once held high office in the Order, and because he comes of a distinguished family and is rich. So he told them that he is himself our captive, and that if they cut my throat here, or if I die of hunger and dampness, you will certainly cut his throat. He threatened the chapter that he would proclaim through all the courts of the West how the Teutonic Knights treat belted knights. So they grew afraid and put me in the hospital, where both the air and food are better."

"I will not take a single mark from de Lorche, so help me God!"

"It is pleasant to take money from an enemy, but it is right to let off a friend," said Macko. "And since, as I hear, an agreement has been made with the king for the exchange of captives, you will not need to pay for me."

"Why! What about our word of honor?" asked Zbyszko. "An agreement is an agreement, and Arnold might put us to shame."

Hearing that, Macko was troubled, reflected a little, and then said:

"Maybe we can bargain it down?"

"We fixed it ourselves. Are we now of less value than we were?"

Macko became still more troubled, but his eyes reflected admiration and still greater love for Zbyszko—if that were possible—than before.

"He watches out for his honor!" he muttered to himself. "That's the way he was born."

And he sighed. Zbyszko thought it was from grief over the marks they had to pay to the von Badens, so he said:

"You know how it is! Money we have enough; if only our misery were not so great."

"God will relieve yours," said the old knight with emotion. "I am not long for this world."

"Don't say that! You will be fine if only the wind blows through you."

"The wind? Wind bends a sapling, but breaks an old tree."

"Pooh! Your bones are not yet mouldering, and you have far to go to reach old age. Don't be sad."

"If you were cheerful, I would be merry also. However, I have another reason to be sad; nay, to speak the truth, we all have."

"What is that?" Zbyszko asked.

"Do you remember how I scolded you at Skirwoillo's camp for talking of the power of the Teutonic Knights? In the field our people are indeed tough, but I've never seen these curs up close until now!" Here Macko lowered his voice, as if in fear he might be overheard: "And now I see that you were right, not I. God help us! What strength, what power! Our knights' hands itch, and they are eager to be at the Germans as soon as possible, but they do not know that all nations and all kingdoms aid the Teutonic Knights, that they have more money than we, better training, stronger castles and more efficient implements of war. God help us! Both among us and here also they say that it must and will come to war; but when it comes, God have mercy on our kingdom and our nation!"

He took his greying head between his palms, rested his elbows on his knees, and fell silent.

"Now you understand," said Zbyszko. "In single combat we have many knights tougher than they. But as for a great war—well, you've seen with your own eyes."

"I have indeed! And God grant that the royal envoys may see too, and particularly the knight of Maszkowice!"

"I saw how his face clouded. He is a great expert in the affairs of war, and they say that no one in the world understands war as he does."

"If that is true, then I suppose there will be none."

"If the Teutonic Knights perceive that they are the stronger ones, then there certainly will be war. And I will say frankly: I wish that choice were already made, for we cannot go on living like this!"

And now Zbyszko lowered his head, as if overcome by his own and the general misery, while Macko said:

"I am sorry for our famous kingdom, and I fear lest God punish us for our excessive audacity. You remember how the knights in front of the cathedral at Wawel—before Mass, when your head was to be cut off, but was not—challenged Timur the Lame himself, though he is lord of forty kingdoms and has made a mountain of human heads. The Teutonic Knights were not enough for them. They wanted to challenge everyone at once, and that may be an insult to God."

Zbyszko caught his fair hair at the memory, for he was unexpectedly overcome with grief, and cried:

"Who but she rescued me from the headsman that time? O Jesus! My Danusia! O Jesus!"

And he began to tear his hair and then to bite his fists, with which he was trying to stifle his sobs, so torn was the heart within his breast by sudden pain.

"Boy, have God in your heart!" Macko cried. "Don't carry on so! What good will this do? Control yourself. Please!"

But Zbyszko was unable to calm himself for a long time, and it was only when Macko, who was really sick, grew so weak that he tottered and fell on a bench in a daze that Zbyszko came to his senses again. Then the young knight laid him on the bed, comforted him with wine sent by the bailiff, and watched over him until he fell asleep.

Next day they awoke late, rested and refreshed.

"Well," said Macko, "it seems my time has not come yet, and I think that if only the wind blew through me from the fields I could even mount a horse."

"The envoys will stay a few days longer," Zbyszko replied, "for more and more people keep coming to them to beg for captives who have been caught robbing in Mazovia or in Great Poland; but we can start when you like and when you feel strong enough."

At that moment Hlawa came in.

"Do you know what the envoys are doing?" the old knight asked him.

"They are visiting the High Castle and the church," replied the Czech. "The bailiff himself is conducting them, and then they are going to the great refectory to dinner, to which the master is intending to invite your graces also."

"And what have you been doing since the morning?"

"I have been looking at the German mercenary footmen whom the captains are drilling, and I have been comparing them with our Czech footmen."

"Do you remember the Czech footmen?"

"I was only a stripling when Sir Zych took me captive, but I remember them well, for I was always interested in such things since I was a little boy."

"And?"

"And nothing! The Teutonic Knights' footmen are indeed tough and well drilled, but they are oxen, whereas our Czechs are wolves. If it came to something, why, your graces know that oxen do not eat wolves, but wolves have a tremendous liking for beef."

"True," said Macko, who apparently knew something about this. "He who comes up against your countrymen recoils as if from a porcupine."

"In battle a mounted knight is worth ten footmen," said Zbyszko.

"But Malbork can only be taken by foot," replied the squire.

And with that the talk of footmen ended, for Macko, following his own thoughts, said:

"Listen, Wisehead! Today, after I have eaten and regained my strength, we will start."

"Where to?" asked the Czech.

"To Mazovia, of course; to Spychow," Zbyszko said.

"And shall we stay there?"

Macko looked questioningly at Zbyszko. Up until now, there had been no talk between them of what they would do next. The young man had perhaps already made his decision, but he evidently did not want to distress his uncle with it, so he said evasively:

"First you must get well."

"And then what?"

"Then? Then you must go back to Bogdaniec. I know how you love the place."

"And you do not?"

"Of course I do."

"I'm not saying that you should not go to Jurand," said Macko slowly, "for if he dies, he must be handsomely buried; but pay attention to what I am going to say, for you are young and your wit is not equal to mine. Spychow is somehow an unlucky place for you. Whatever good has befallen you has been elsewhere, while there nothing but heavy trouble and grief has been your lot."

"You're right," Zbyszko replied. "But Danusia's little coffin is there. . . ."

"Please!" Macko exclaimed, in fear lest Zbyszko should be seized by the same unexpected grief as on the preceding day.

But the young man's face reflected only tenderness and sorrow.

"There will be time to take counsel," he said presently. "Whatever the case, at Plock you must rest."

"Your grace will not lack care and attention there," Hlawa remarked.

"True!" said Zbyszko. "Do you know that Jagienka is there? She is a lady-in-waiting on Duke Ziemowit's wife. But you know, of course, for you brought her there yourself. She was at Spychow too; I am surprised that you did not tell me anything about her when we were with Skirwoillo."

"Not only was she at Spychow, but without her Jurand would either be still groping his way along the roads with his staff, or he would have died somewhere by the wayside. I brought her to Plock

on account of the abbot's inheritance, and I did not say anything
about her to you, for even had I done so, it would not have
mattered. You paid no attention to anything at that time, poor
man."

"She loves you dearly," said Zbyszko. "Thank God no letters
were needed, but she got one from the duchess on your behalf and,
through the duchess, from the Teutonic envoys."

"God bless the girl for that! There is no better maiden on the
earth," Macko said.

Further talk was interrupted by the arrival of Zyndram of
Maszkowice and Powala of Taczewo, who had heard of Macko's
fainting-fit of the previous day, and had come to visit him.

"Jesus Christ be praised!" said Zyndram, stepping across the
threshold. "How are you today?"

"God reward you! A little better. Zbyszko says that if only the
wind were to blow around me I should be perfectly well."

"Why not? All will be well," said Powala in reply.

"I have had a good rest too," replied Macko. "Not like your
graces, who, I hear, rose early."

"Folk from hereabouts came to us to give us the names of
captives," said Zyndram, "and after that we looked at the Teutonic
Knights' stronghold: the lower-castle and both the castles."

"A powerful stronghold and powerful castles!" muttered Macko
gloomily.

"Most certainly. In the church are arabesque ornaments; they say
they learned the art of constructing them from the Saracens in
Sicily; while in the castles are wonderful apartments, their roofs
supported either on single pillars or on colonnades. You will see the
great refectory for yourselves. And the fortifications are everywhere
so elaborate that nowhere will you find anything like them. Such
walls are not to be breached even by the largest cannonballs. Verily,
it is a pleasure to look at them."

Zyndram spoke so cheerfully that Macko looked at him in
surprise and asked:

"And have you seen their wealth and their equipment, and their
army and guests?"

"They showed us everything, ostensibly from hospitality, but
really to impress us and depress our hearts."

"And?"

"Well, God will grant that when war comes we shall drive them over the mountains and seas and far away—from where they came."

Macko, forgetting his illness momentarily, sprang up in astonishment.

"How so, lord?" he said. "They say that you have a keen wit. As for me, I felt faint when I saw their power. Great God! How can you make that conclusion?" He turned to his nephew: "Zbyszko, have the wine they sent us put on the table. Sit down, your graces, and talk, for no doctor has invented a better balsam for my illness."

Zbyszko was himself very curious, so he put the jug of wine on the table, and mugs by it, after which they sat around the table, and the Lord of Maszkowice began to speak:

"All this fortification is nothing, for what is built by human hands can be destroyed by human hands. Do you know what holds bricks in their place? Mortar. And do you know what holds men together? Love."

"By God! Honey flows from your lips, lord!" Macko exclaimed.

Zyndram's heart rejoiced at this praise, and he went on:

"Of the folk from hereabouts, one has a brother in fetters with us, another a son, another a kinsman, and another a son-in-law or somebody. The border commanders bid them go pillaging among us—so more than one is fated to fall, and more than one to be caught by our men. But as the people here have already learned of the agreement between the king and the master, they have been coming to us since early this morning to give us the names of captives, which our clerk has written down. First there was a local cooper, a wealthy burgher—a German—with a house at Malbork, who concluded by saying: 'If I could do your king and kingdom a service in anything, I would give not only my property, but even my head.' I sent him packing, for I thought he was a Judas. But then came a parish priest from Oliva, asking for his brother, and saying: 'Is it true, lord, that you are going to make war on our Prussian lords? Know, then, that when our nation says, "Thy kingdom come!" it thinks of your king.' After that, two noblemen holding fiefs near Sztum came about their sons; merchants from Danzig came, craftsmen came, the bell-founder of Kwidzyn came, and a number of different people—and all said the same thing."

Here the Lord of Maszkowice broke off, got up, and looked

whether there might not be someone listening behind the door; then he came back and continued in a lower tone:

"I questioned them long about everything. The Teutonic Knights are hated throughout Prussia by the clergy, gentry, burghers, and yeomen. And they are hated not only by those who speak our language, or Prussian, but even by the Germans too. He who has to serve, serves; but every one of them prefers the plague to a Teutonic Knight. So it is."

"Yes, but what has that to do with the Knights' power?" asked Macko uneasily.

Zyndram passed his hand over his broad forehead and reflected a while, as if seeking a fitting comparison; finally he smiled and asked:

"Have you ever jousted in the lists?"

"Yes, more than once," Macko replied.

"Then what do you think? Will not even the strongest knight be overthrown at the first encounter if his saddle-girth and stirrup-straps are cut?"

"Assuredly."

"Well, you see: the Order is like such a knight."

"By God," Zbyszko exclaimed, "you will certainly find no better comparison even in a book!"

Macko was moved and said in a rather quavering voice:

"God reward you! The armorer must surely make a helmet specially for your head, for there is not a ready-made one anywhere to fit it."

CHAPTER LXVII

MACKO and Zbyszko had promised themselves to start from Malbork at once; but they were not able to leave the day on which Zyndram of Maszkowice had cheered their hearts so much, for there was a dinner in the High Castle and then a supper in honor of the envoys and guests, to which Zbyszko was invited as a royal knight, and Macko because of his kinship to Zbyszko. The dinner was attended by a smaller number of people and held in the splendid great refectory, which was lighted by ten windows, and whose vaulted roof was supported, by a unique architectural device, upon a single pillar. Besides the royal knights, the only strangers who sat down to table were a Swabian and a Burgundian count, the latter of whom, though feudatory to a rich overlord, had come in his name to borrow money from the Order. Of the Teutonic Knights, besides the grand master, there were present four dignitaries, called "Pillars of the Order," namely, the grand commander, the almoner, the keeper of the wardrobe, and the treasurer. The fifth pillar, the grand marshal, was at that time on the expedition against Witold.

Although the Order was sworn to poverty, they ate off dishes of gold and silver, and drank malmsey, for the master desired to dazzle the eyes of the Polish envoys. But despite the number of courses and the abundance of drink, the guests found the banquet somewhat irksome, because of the difficulty of conversing and the dignity all were required to maintain. On the other hand, the supper in the huge conventual refectory (*Convents Remter*) was a much more cheerful affair, for gathered there were the whole body of monks and all those guests who had not yet had time to join the marshal's army marching against Witold. Their merriment was not disturbed by any quarrel or dispute. It is true that the foreign knights, foreseeing that they would some day have to meet the Poles in battle, looked at them askance, but the Teutonic Knights had enjoined them beforehand most earnestly to keep the peace, lest in the persons of the envoys they should insult the king and the whole kingdom. But even so the Order manifested their lack of goodwill, for they warned their guests against the hot temper of the Poles, saying that, "for a single sharp word they will pull out your beard or stab you with a knife." So the guests were subsequently surprised by the good nature of both Powala of Taczewo and Zyndram of Maszkowice, and the keener-witted concluded that it was not the customs of the Poles which were rude, but the tongues of the Teutonic Knights which were malicious and venomous.

Some of them, accustomed to the elegant entertainments of the polished courts of the West, carried away no very high opinion of the customs of the Teutonic Knights themselves, for the banquet was accompanied by excessively loud instrumental music, coarse gleemen's songs, rude jokes by the jesters, dancing bears, and dancing barefoot girls. And when surprise was expressed at the presence of females in the High Castle, it was explained that the prohibition had been long neglected, and that even the great Winrich von Kniprode himself had danced here in his time with the fair Mary of Alfleben. The brethren stated that women were forbidden only to live in the castle, but that they might come to banquets in the refectory, and that last year Duke Witold's wife, who stayed in the royally furnished Old Armory in the Lower Castle, had come here every day to play checkers with golden pieces, which were given as a present to her every evening.

That evening also there were games of checkers, and games of chess and games with dice; indeed, these things occupied the guests' attention even more than conversation, which was drowned by the noise of the songs and loud instrumental music. Still, amid the general uproar there came moments of relative silence, and Zyndram of Maszkowice took advantage of one of these to ask the grand master innocently whether the Order was greatly beloved by its subjects in all its territories.

Conrad von Jungingen replied:

"Who loves the Cross ought to love the Order also."

This answer pleased the monks and guests, so they praised him for it, and he was encouraged to continue:

"Whoso is our friend feels at home among us, but whoso is not our friend—for him we have two methods."

"Which are . . . ?" asked the Polish knight.

"Your honor may not know that I come from my apartments to this refectory down a small flight of stairs in the wall, and that next to these stairs is a certain vaulted chamber, to which if I were to conduct your grace, you would recognize the first method."

"He would indeed!" the brethren shouted.

The Lord of Maszkowice guessed that the master was referring to that "tower" full of gold, of which the Teutonic Knights boasted, so he reflected a moment and answered:

"Once upon a time—oh, very long ago—a certain German emperor showed such a treasure-chamber to a Polish envoy named Skarbek and said: 'I have the means to beat your lord!' But Skarbek cast into it his own costly ring and replied: 'Gold to gold! We Poles are more in love with iron.' And does your honor know what came after that? After that came Hundsfeld."

"And what was Hundsfeld?" asked a dozen knights at the same time.

"Hundsfeld," replied Zyndram calmly, "was a field where there were not enough hands to bury the Germans; eventually, dogs finished the job."

Both the knights and the brethren of the Order were taken aback by such an answer and knew not what to say, while Zyndram of Maszkowice concluded:

"You will do nothing with gold against iron."

"Why!" exclaimed the master, "that is precisely our second method—iron. Your honor has seen the armorers' shops in the Lower Castle. Night and day they forge hammers there, and such breastplates and swords as are not to be equalled elsewhere."

Powala of Taczewo stretched out his hand to the middle of the table and took up a meat-chopper, a cubit long and more than half-a-handbreadth wide, which he easily twisted into a cornet shape, as if it were a piece of parchment. He held it up for all to see and then gave it to the master.

"If the iron in your swords is like this," he said, "you will not be able to do much with them."

And he smiled in self-satisfaction, while monks and laymen rose from their places and crowded around the grand master. They began to pass the twisted chopper from hand to hand, but none of them said anything, being amazed and struck dumb at the sight of such strength.

"By the head of St. Liborius!" the master finally exclaimed. "You have iron hands."

"And better iron than this," added the Count of Burgundy. "He twisted the chopper as if it had been made of wax."

"His face did not even redden, and his veins did not swell!" exclaimed one of the brethren.

Powala replied:

"Our nation is simple, for it knows not such wealth and comforts as I see here, but it is robust."

Then the Italian and French knights approached him and began to address him in their musical language, of which old Macko said that it was like the beating of tin dishes. They admired his strength, while he clinked glasses with them and answered:

"Such things are often done among us at banquets, and sometimes a smaller chopper is twisted even by a girl."

But the Germans, who loved to boast before strangers of their stature and strength, became ashamed and angry, so old Helfenstein called down the table:

"Shame upon us! Brother Arnold von Baden—show everyone here that our bones are not also made of church wax. Give him a chopper!"

A servant quickly brought one and laid it before Arnold, but, either because he was flustered in the presence of so many witnesses, or because his fingers were really weaker than Powala's, though he did indeed bend it in the middle and fold it, he could not twist it.

So several of the foreign guests, to whom the Teutonic Knights had more than once previously whispered that war with King Jagiello would begin in the winter, became quite thoughtful and reflected that the winter was usually terribly severe in this country and that perhaps it would be better to return, while there was yet time, to a milder climate and their native castles.

It was surprising that they should begin to think of this in July, at a time of fair and hot weather.

CHAPTER LXVIII

AT Plock, Zbyszko and Macko found no one at court, for the duke and duchess had gone, with their eight children, to Czersk at the invitation of Duchess Anna Danuta. They learned from the bishop that Jagienka intended to stay at Spychow with Jurand until his death. This news pleased them, as they wanted to go to Spychow themselves. Macko took the occasion to praise highly Jagienka's goodness in choosing to go to a dying man, who was not even her kinsman, rather than to the entertainments at Czersk, where there was sure to be dancing and pleasures of all kinds.

"Maybe she did it partly so as not to miss us," said the old knight. "It's been a long time since I saw her, and I shall be glad to look on her again, for I know that she is fond of me. The girl must have grown, and she certainly must be more beautiful than before."

And Zbyszko said:

"She has changed considerably. Beautiful she was always, but I remembered her as a simple girl, and now she is fit for a king's palace."

"She has changed so much? Ah, they are an old line, those Jastrzebcy of Zgorzelice, whose war-cry is 'To a Feast!'" A moment of silence followed, and then the old knight spoke again: "Doubtless it will be as I told you, and she will want to go to Zgorzelice."

"I was surprised that she ever left it."

"She wanted to look after the sick abbot, who had no proper care. Besides, she was afraid of Cztan and Wolf, and I told her myself that her brothers would be safer without her than with her."

"Verily, it would be impossible for them to attack orphans."

Macko reflected:

"But I wonder whether they did not avenge themselves on me for having taken her away, and whether there will be a single beam left at Bogdaniec. God alone knows! Nor do I know whether I shall be able to defend myself against them when I return. They are young and sturdy fellows, while I am old."

"Ha! tell that to someone who doesn't know you," Zbyszko replied.

Macko had not, indeed, been quite sincere in what he said, for he was concerned about something else, but for the time being he only waved his hand.

"Had I not fallen sick at Malbork," he said, "things would not have been so bad. But we will talk of that at Spychow."

And next morning, after a night's rest at Plock, they set out for Spychow.

The days were clear, and the road dry and easy to travel, as well as safe, for after the recent agreement the Teutonic Knights had restrained the border robbers. Anyway, the two knights belonged to that class of travellers whom it was better for a robber to bow before from a distance than to accost close at hand, so the journey passed quickly, and on the fifth day after leaving Plock they reached Spychow in the morning without any difficulty. Jagienka, who was attached to Macko as to the best friend in the world, greeted him as if he were her father; while he, though not a man easily moved, was deeply touched by the beloved girl's goodwill; and when Zbyszko, after asking about Jurand, went to him and to his "loved one," the old knight drew a deep breath and said:

"Well! Whom God wished to take, He took, and whom He wished to leave, He left; but I think that our adventures and our wanderings through swamps and forests are now ended." A moment later, however, he added: "Hey! Where did the Lord Jesus not lead us in the course of these last years!"

"But the divine hand guarded you," Jagienka replied.

"True. It did indeed watch over us; but, to speak frankly, it is now time to go home."

"We must stay here as long as Jurand lives," said the girl.

"How is he?"

"His head is raised heavenwards and he smiles: he must already be seeing paradise, and Danusia in it."

"Are you attending him?"

"Yes, but Father Caleb says that angels are also. Yesterday, the housekeeper here saw two."

"They say," Macko answered, "that it is most fitting for a nobleman to die in the field, but to die as Jurand is dying is also good—in one's bed."

"He eats nothing, he drinks nothing, he only smiles continually," said Jagienka.

"Let us go to him. Zbyszko should be there."

But Zbyszko had stayed only a short time with Jurand, who recognized no one, and then he had gone to Danusia's coffin in the vault. There he stayed until old Tolima came to fetch him to a meal. As he was going out, he noticed by the light of the torch that the coffin was covered with little wreaths of cornflower and marigold, while the cleanly swept floor round about was scattered over with sweet flag, mallow, and lime blossom, which gave out a honeyed perfume. The young man's heart swelled at the sight.

"Who has decked my loved one like that?" he asked.

"The young lady of Zgorzelice," Tolima replied.

The young knight said nothing, but a few moments later, when he caught sight of Jagienka, he suddenly bowed to her knees and embraced them, exclaiming:

"God reward you for your goodness and for those flowers for Danusia!"

And he shed bitter tears, while she took his head between her hands like a sister trying to comfort a mourning brother, and said:

"Oh, my Zbyszko, I would gladly console you still more."

After that, abundant tears flowed from her eyes also.

CHAPTER LXIX

JURAND died a few days later. For a whole week Father Caleb celebrated Masses over his body, which did not in the least decay—by a miracle, it seemed to all—and throughout the week Spychow was thronged with guests. Then came a period of quiet, as usual after a funeral. Zbyszko went regularly to the vault and sometimes with his crossbow to the forest, but he did not shoot at any beast—he walked as if in a daze. Until one evening he entered the chamber where the girls were sitting with Macko and Hlawa, and said unexpectedly:

"Listen to what I am going to say! Sorrow is good for no one, so it will be better for you to return to Bogdaniec and Zgorzelice than to stay here in sorrow."

Silence followed. They all understood that it would be a very serious talk—and it was only after a while that Macko spoke:

"Better for us, but better also for you."

Zbyszko shook his fair hair.

"Nay," he said. "I too, God grant, shall return to Bogdaniec, but now I must do something else."

"Alas!" Macko exclaimed. "I said that it would be the end, but there is no end. For God's sake, Zbyszko!"

"But you know that I made a vow."

"Is that a reason? There is no Danusia, so there is no vow. Death has absolved you from your vow."

"My death would have absolved me, but not hers. I swore to God on my honor as a knight. What would you have? On my honor as a knight!"

The least mention of knightly honor had an almost magical

effect on Macko. Apart from the commandments of God and the Church, he had not followed many others in the course of his life, but those few he followed unswervingly.

"I'm not saying that you should not keep your oath," he said.

"Only what?"

"Only this, that you are young and have time for everything. Come now with us; you will have a rest—you will shake off your grief and pain, and then you can go wherever you like."

"Then I will tell you as sincerely as at confession," Zbyszko replied. "You see that I go where I'm needed. I converse with you. I eat and drink, like everyone else. But I tell you honestly that in my heart and soul I cannot get over it. There is nothing but sorrow within me, nothing but pain; nothing but these bitter tears, which freely flow from my eyes."

"Then it will be worst for you precisely among strangers."

"No!" Zbyszko replied. "God knows I should waste away completely at Bogdaniec. When I tell you that I cannot, I cannot! I need war, for in the field it is easier to forget. I feel that when I have fulfilled my vow, when I am able to tell that redeemed soul: 'I have fulfilled all that I promised you,' then only shall I be relieved. But not before. You would not be able to keep me at Bogdaniec even on a rope."

After these words such a silence fell in the chamber that the flies could be heard buzzing under the ceiling.

"If he would only waste away at Bogdaniec, then he had better go where he must," said Jagienka at last.

Macko put both hands on the back of his neck, as he usually did in moments of great perplexity, and then sighed deeply, and said: "Almighty God!"

Jagienka continued:

"But Zbyszko, you must swear that if God preserves you, you will not stay here, but will come back to us."

"Why should I not come back? I shall not avoid Spychow; but I shall not stay here."

"For," the girl went on in a somewhat lower voice, "if you are concerned about Danusia, we will take her coffin with us to Krzesnia."

"Jagna!" Zbyszko burst out.

And in the first moment of transport and gratitude, he fell at her feet.

CHAPTER LXX

THE old knight was very eager to accompany Zbyszko and join Duke Witold's army, but Zbyszko would not hear of it. He insisted on going alone, without any troop of armed men, without wagons, but with only three mounted attendants, of whom one was to carry food; the second, armor and clothing, and the third, bearskins for bedding. In vain Jagienka and Macko implored him to take at least Hlawa, as a squire of proven strength and devotion. Zbyszko persisted in refusing, saying that he must forget the pain gnawing at him, whereas the presence of his squire would remind him of all he had been through.

Before his departure there was a serious discussion as to what to do with Spychow. Macko advised the sale of the estate. He said that it was an unlucky piece of ground which brought nothing but misfortune and misery. There was much wealth of every kind: money, armor, horses, garments, sheepskins, costly furs, expensive implements, and cattle; and Macko was, as a matter of fact, anxious to put that wealth into service at Bogdaniec, which was dearer to him than any other piece of ground in the world. So they discussed the question for a long time, but Zbyszko firmly refused to agree to any sale.

"What!" he said. "Shall I sell Jurand's bones? Is it thus that I am to repay him for the benefits he has heaped on me?"

"We have offered to take Danusia's coffin with us," Macko replied. "We can take Jurand's also."

"No; he is here with his fathers, and without his fathers he would find it dreary at Krzesnia. If you take Danusia, he will be left here far from his child, and if you take him also, his fathers will be left here alone."

"You forget that Jurand sees them all every day in paradise, and Father Caleb says that he is in paradise," replied the old knight.

But Father Caleb, who was on Zbyszko's side, said:

"His soul is in paradise, but his body is on earth until the Judgment Day."

Macko reflected a little and then added, following his own line of thought:

"Yes; I suppose Jurand does not see anyone who was not redeemed by accepting the Lord; there is no help for that."

"What is the good of trying to understand God's judgments?" Zbyszko replied. "But God forbid that a stranger should live here over that sacred dust! It's best to leave them all here. I will not sell Spychow, were they to give me a duchy for it."

Macko realized that further argumentation would be fruitless. He knew his nephew's obstinacy, and in the bottom of his heart, he admired it, as he did all of the young man's qualities.

So presently he said:

"It is true this lad rubs me the wrong way, but there is truth in what he says."

And he was perplexed, for indeed he did not know what to do.

But Jagienka, who had said nothing hitherto, now offered fresh advice:

"If we could find an honest man to administer the estate here, or to become tenant of it, it would be the perfect thing. Best would be to let it on a tenancy, for thus you would have ready money without any trouble. Maybe Tolima? He is old and knows more of war than of estate management, but, if not he, then perhaps Father Caleb."

"Dear young lady!" Father Caleb replied. "There is a piece of earth ready for both Tolima and me, but to cover us, not for us to walk upon." Then he turned to Tolima: "That's true, is it not, old man?"

Tolima put his hand to his pointed ear and asked: "What is the matter?" And when it had been repeated to him more loudly, he said: "It is the sacred truth. I am not an administrator! The axe ploughs deeper than the ploughshare. I should be glad to avenge my lord and his child. . . ." And he stretched out his lean but sinewy hand, with its crooked, talon-like fingers, and then, turning his grey, wolf-head towards Macko and Zbyszko, added: "Take me with you against the Germans, your graces. That is what I am fit for."

And he was right. He had contributed not a little to Jurand's wealth, but only by warfare and booty—not by management of his estate.

So Jagienka, who had been thinking meanwhile what she should say, spoke again:

"Here there ought to be a young man, and one who is not afraid, for the Teutonic wall is close by; one, I say, who will not only not hide from the Germans but will go out and look for them. If I may say so, I think that Hlawa is the man for the job."

"Listen to her wisdom!" exclaimed Macko. Despite all his love for Jagienka, he could not conceive of a woman having anything to say on such a matter, much less a raven-haired girl.

But the Czech rose from the bench on which he was sitting.

"As God is my witness," he said, "I would gladly go to the war with Lord Zbyszko, for we have already given the Germans a little drubbing, and we should again. But if I have to stay behind, then I would rather stay here. Tolima knows me; he is my friend. The Teutonic wall is close by. So what? That's just it! We shall see who will be first to tire of the neighborship. If I am to be afraid of them, let them be afraid of me. May the Lord Jesus forbid, also, that I should do your graces any wrong in the administration of this place and take everything for myself. In this the young lady will bear me witness, since she knows I would rather perish a hundred times than show her a dishonest face. Of management I understand as much as I picked up at Zgorzelice, but I think there is more need here of the axe and the sword than of the plough. And all this is greatly to my liking, except that—you know—to stay here alone. . . ."

"Yes?" Zbyszko asked. "Why do you hesitate?"

But Hlawa was quite embarrassed, and he continued in a halting voice:

"You see, if the young lady goes away, everyone will go with her. Fighting is good, and managing estates also. But it is so lonely— without any help. . . . It would be terribly dreary here without the young lady and without . . . what I just wanted to say . . . and besides, the young lady was not travelling alone. So if no one helped me here . . . I don't know. . . ."

"What is the fellow talking about?" Macko asked.

"You have a keen wit, and yet you have noticed nothing," Jagienka replied.

"Well?"

Instead of answering, she turned to the squire:

"And suppose Anulka were to stay with you, could you hold out?"

Thereupon the Czech flung himself down at her feet, so that the dust rose from the floor.

"I would hold out with her even in hell!" he cried, embracing her feet.

Zbyszko, hearing this cry, looked at his squire in amazement, for he had not known of anything and had not guessed anything; while Macko wondered at the importance of a woman in all human affairs and at the way in which every matter may succeed or completely fail through her.

"God is gracious," he muttered, "that I am not interested in them any more."

Jagienka, turning to Hlawa anew, said:

"Now all we have to know is whether Anulka can hold out with you."

And she called her, and Anulka came in, evidently knowing, or guessing, what was in question, for she came in shielding her eyes with her arm, and with her head bent so low that only her parted fair hair could be seen, lit up by a ray of sunlight. At first she stopped near the doorway, and then, rushing to Jagienka, she fell on her knees before her and hid her face in the folds of her skirt.

And the Czech knelt beside her and said to Jagienka:

"Give us your blessing, young lady."

CHAPTER LXXI

THE time for Zbyszko's departure came the following day. He sat high on a big war-horse, his friends around him. Jagienka, standing by his stirrup, silently raised her sorrowful blue eyes to the young man, as if wanting to look her fill before he left. Macko and Father Caleb stood by the other stirrup, and nearby were the Czech and Anulka. The young knight turned his head to one side and the other, exchanging with them such short words as are usual before a long journey: "Farewell!" "God conduct you!" "It is time now!" "Alas, time! time!" He had already taken leave of everyone earlier, and of Jagienka, whose knees he had embraced in gratitude for all her goodness. But now, when he looked down on her from his high knight's saddle, he felt a desire to say some additional good word to her, since her raised eyes and face said to him so clearly, "Come back!"—that his heart swelled with genuine gratitude.

And, as if answering her unspoken appeal, he said:

"Jagienka, I feel towards you as I would to an only sister. You know! I won't say more."

"I know. God reward you!"

"And don't forget my uncle."

"And don't you forget him."

"I shall come back, if I do not perish."

"Don't perish."

Once before, at Plock, when he had spoken of his expedition, she had said the same thing to him: "Don't perish." But now the words came from still deeper within her heart, and perhaps to hide

her tears, she leaned forward so far that for a moment her brow
touched Zbyszko's knee.

Meanwhile the mounted attendants by the gate, holding the
pack-horses all ready for the road, began to sing:

> *"The ring will not be lost,*
> *The golden ring will not be lost.*
> *The raven will come with it,*
> *Will come with it from the meadow,*
> *And bring it to the girl."*

"Let us start!" Zbyszko called out.

"God conduct you!"

Hooves resounded on the wooden drawbridge, one of the horses
gave a prolonged neigh, the others snorted noisily, and the train set
off.

Jagienka, Macko, the priest, and Tolima, together with the
Czech and his girl and those servants who were staying behind at
Spychow, went out onto the bridge and looked after the departing
travellers. Father Caleb made the sign of the cross behind them
repeatedly, until at last they disappeared beyond some high alder
bushes, and then he said:

"Under this sign no ill hap will befall them."

And Macko added:

"Certainly, but it is good, too, that the horses snorted the way
they did."

But they did not remain long at Spychow either. At the end of a
fortnight, the old knight, having settled matters with the Czech,
who was to stay as a tenant on the estate, set out with Jagienka for
Bogdaniec at the head of a long train of wagons surrounded by
armed attendants. Father Caleb and old Tolima were not exactly
pleased to see those wagons, for, to tell the truth, Macko had rather
plundered Spychow; but as Zbyszko had left the administration
entirely in his hands, no one dared to oppose him. As a matter of
fact, he would have taken still more had he not been restrained by
Jagienka, with whom he argued, indeed, talking scornfully of
"woman's wit," but whom, all the same, he obeyed in almost
everything.

Danusia's coffin, however, they did not take with them. Because
Spychow had not been sold, Zbyszko preferred that she should be

left with her fathers. On the other hand, they took a quantity of money and various valuables, which had in considerable part been plundered from the Germans in the many battles fought by Jurand against them. Accordingly, Macko, gazing at the laden wagons covered with wicker hurdles, rejoiced to think how he would benefit and administer Bogdaniec. Nevertheless, his joy was poisoned by the fear that Zbyszko might die. But knowing the young man's knightly skill, he did not lose hope that he would return in safety, and he thought with delight of that moment.

"Perhaps God desired," he said to himself, "that Zbyszko should first get Spychow and afterwards Moczydoly and everything which the abbot left. Let him just return in safety and I will build him a worthy castle at Bogdaniec. And then we shall see!"

It occurred to him at that moment that Cztan of Rogow and Wolf of Birchwood would assuredly not be too glad to welcome him and that perhaps he would have to fight them; but he did not care about this any more than an old war-horse cares when the time comes to go to battle. His health was restored, he felt strength in his bones, and he knew that he could easily deal with those two bullies, who, dangerous though they were, lacked any kind of knightly training. He had, indeed, taken another tone in his recent talk with Zbyszko, but that was only because he wanted to persuade him to return.

"Hah! I am a pike, while they are only gudgeons," he thought. "It will be better for them to keep out of my way."

On the other hand, he was disquieted by something else: Zbyszko would return God knew when, and meanwhile he regarded Jagienka only as a sister. Suppose the girl were also to look on him only as a brother, and suppose she did not want to wait for his uncertain return?

So he turned to her.

"Listen, Jagienka," he said. "I'm not speaking of Cztan or Wolf, for they are coarse fellows and not for you. You are now a court lady, after all! But you are growing up. Your deceased father said that you already were feeling the urge, and that was some years ago. I know about these things! They say that when a girl's maiden-wreath is too tight for her, she will find someone herself to take it off her head. Of course, we're not talking about Cztan or Wolf. But what do you think?"

"Whatever are you asking about?"

"Will you give yourself in marriage to just anyone?"

"I? I shall become a nun."

"Don't talk nonsense! And if Zbyszko returns?"

But she shook her head:

"I shall become a nun."

"Well, and if he were to fall in love with you? If he were to beg you to marry him?"

Thereupon the girl turned her blushing face to the fields, but the wind, which was blowing precisely from there, bore to Macko her soft answer:

"Then I would not become a nun."

CHAPTER LXXII

THEY spent some time at Plock, in order to settle matters connected with the inheritance and the abbot's will, and then, with the necessary documents in their possession, they continued their journey, resting but little on the road, which was easy and safe, since the drought had baked the mud and narrowed the rivers, and the highway ran through a quiet countryside, inhabited by a kind and hospitable people. Nevertheless, the cautious Macko sent on an attendant from Sieradz to Zgorzelice to let them know of his and Jagienka's impending arrival; in consequence of which, Jagienka's brother Jasko rode half-way to meet them, and conducted them home at the head of armed farm-hands.

There was no little joy and no few greetings and shouts on the occasion of this meeting. Jasko was still so similar to Jagienka as one drop of water is to another, but he had already grown taller than she. He was a sturdy lad: valiant, merry like the deceased Zych, whose love of continual singing he had inherited, and as lively as a spark. He felt himself already grown-up in years and strength, and regarded himself as a man, commanding his attendants like a real leader, and they carried out all his orders in a twinkling, evidently fearing his authority and power.

So Macko and Jagienka were surprised at his development, and he also was surprised and greatly pleased with the beauty and courtly manners of his sister, whom he had not seen for a long time. He told her that he had been on the point of going to her, and that in a very short time they would not have found him at home, for he, too, needed to see the world and mix with men, gain knightly experience, and find opportunity here and there to fight with errant knights.

"To know the world and the customs of men," said Macko to him in reply, "is a good thing, since it teaches how to bear oneself and what to say in every situation, and strengthens one's native wit. But as for fighting, it is better that I should tell you that you are still too young, than have you hear it from a strange knight, who would certainly laugh at you for your pains."

"He would weep after such laughter," Jasko replied, "or if not he, then his wife and children."

And he looked straight forward with mighty boldness, as if he would say to every knight errant in the world, "Prepare for death!" But the old knight of Bogdaniec asked him:

"Did Cztan and Wolf leave you in peace? For they liked to look at Jagienka."

"Hah! Wolf was slain in Silesia. He wanted to capture a German castle there, and he did so, but he was struck down by a log of wood hurled from the walls. Two days later, he breathed his last."

"I am sorry to hear that. His father also used to go to Silesia and fight against the Germans who oppressed our nation there, and he took booty from them. The capturing of castles is the hardest thing, for neither armor nor knightly training are of any avail. God grant that Duke Witold will not have to take castles in his campaign, but will only have to crush the Teutonic Knights in the field. And Cztan? What about him?"

Jasko began to laugh:

"Cztan has married! He has taken the daughter of a yeoman from High Bank, a girl famed for her charms. Hah! she is not only pretty, but capable too. More than one man yields to Cztan, but she strikes him in his shaggy face and leads him by the nose like a bear on a chain."

The old knight was amused when he heard that.

"You see! All women are alike! You, too, Jagienka, will be like that. Praise God that you had no trouble with those two bullies, for, to tell the truth, I am surprised that they did not give vent to their malice against Bogdaniec."

"Cztan wanted to, but Wolf, being wiser than he, would not let him. Wolf came over to us at Zgorzelice to ask what had happened to Jagienka, and I told him she had gone to make arrangements about the abbot's inheritance. And he said: 'Why did Macko not tell me anything about it?' So I replied: 'Do you think Jagienka is yours, that he had to tell you?' Then he reflected a while, and at length said: 'True! she is not mine.' And since he had a keen wit, he evidently concluded at once that he would gain your confidence and ours if he defended Bogdaniec against Cztan. So they fought at Lawica, near Piaski, and wounded one another, and then they got dead drunk, as they always did."

"Lord, light Wolf's soul!" said Macko, and drew a deep breath, glad that he would find no unexpected damage at Bogdaniec.

And he found none. On the contrary, the flocks and herds had multiplied, and from the small herd of mares, there were now two-year-old foals, some of them by the Frisian war stallions and, therefore, unusually big and strong. The only loss was that a few captives had escaped, but not many, for they could only get away to Silesia, and there the German or germanized robber knights treated captives worse than did the Polish gentry. The huge old house, however, was considerably on its way to ruin. The floors had cracked, the walls and roofs were leaning, and the larch beams, hewn two hundred years or more ago, had begun to rot. In every room, where the numerous swarm of Hailstones of Bogdaniec had once lived, water dripped during the heavy summer rains. The roof was full of holes and was covered with great tufts of green and reddish moss. The whole building was settling down and looked like an immense, decaying mushroom.

"With care, it would have still lasted, for it has only recently begun to fall into disrepair," Macko said to the old foreman, Kondrat, who had looked after the estate in the absence of its lords. "Even so, I can live here until my death, but Zbyszko ought to have a castelet."

"Great God! A castelet?"

"Well! Why not?"

It had been the old man's favorite idea to leave Zbyszko and his future children a castelet. He knew that a nobleman who lived, not in a usual manor-house, but behind a moat and a palisade, and who had, besides, a watchtower, from which a watchman observed the surrounding area, was immediately regarded as "something" by the neighbors, and that it was easier for him to obtain an office. Macko desired little for himself these days, but for Zbyszko and his sons he did not want to be limited, particularly now, when their property had grown so considerably.

"Let him take Jagienka as well," he thought, "and with her Moczydoly and the abbot's inheritance. No one in the neighborhood would rival us—which God grant."

But everything depended on whether Zbyszko would return— and that was uncertain and dependent on the grace of God. So Macko told himself that he must now be on the best possible terms with God, and offend Him in nothing, but win His favor by all possible means. With this desire, he did not begrudge either wax or grain or game for the church at Krzesnia, and one evening he came to Zgorzelice and said to Jagienka:

"I am going to Cracow tomorrow, to the grave of our sainted queen Jadwiga."

She sprang up from her seat in terror:

"Have you had bad news?"

"There is no news at all, for it's too soon. But do you remember that time when I was lying sick with the splinter in my side—that time you went with Zbyszko to find a beaver? I vowed then that if God gave me back my health, I would go to that grave. Everyone praised my desire at that time. As they should have! God has enough saints to serve Him in heaven, but, after all, no ordinary saint is of as much significance up there as our lady, whom I do not wish to offend, particularly since I am anxious for Zbyszko's safety."

"True, as I live!" said Jagienka. "But you have only just returned from such an exhausting journey."

"Well, I would rather finish everything at once, and then sit around at home until Zbyszko's return. If only our queen intervenes on his behalf with the Lord Jesus, then with his good armor, even ten Germans will not be able to deal with him. After that, I shall build a castle with greater hope."

"You are indeed tireless."

"Certainly I am still hale. I will tell you something else. Let Jasko, who is burning to take to the road, come with me. I am experienced and shall be able to restrain him. And if some adventure should befall—for the lad's hands itch—you know that combat is nothing new to me, whether on foot or on horseback, with swords or axes."

"I know. No one will guard him better than you."

"But I don't think it will come to combat. As long as the queen lived, Cracow was full of foreign knights, who wanted to look at her beauty—but now they prefer to make for Malbork, where the kegs are bulging with malmsey."

"But there is a new queen now."

Macko made a wry face and waved his hand.

"I have seen her—and I will say no more—you understand." Presently he added: "In three or four weeks, we shall be back again."

And so it turned out. The old knight first made Jasko swear on his honor as a knight and on the head of St. George that he would not insist on a longer journey—and they set out.

They reached Cracow without incident, for the country was peaceful and was protected from attacks on the part of the germanized border dukes and robber German knights by the fear of the royal power and the valor of the inhabitants. After fulfilling their vows, they were received at the royal court on the introduction of Powala of Taczewo and Duke Jamont. Macko had thought that at court and in the various offices he would be eagerly questioned about the Teutonic Knights, as a man who knew them well and had had a look at them from close quarters. But after his conversation with the chancellor and the sword-bearer of Cracow, he realized with amazement that they knew as much or more of the Teutonic Knights than he did. They knew everything, down to the smallest detail, of what was happening both at Malbork itself and the other castles, however distant. They knew the state of the commands, the number of the soldiers in each place, the amount of artillery, the time required to gather the armies together, and the designs of the Knights in the event of war. They knew even the character of each commander: whether he was impulsive and ardent, or cautious. And everything was written down as carefully as if war were to break out on the morrow.

The old knight was quite delighted by this, for he concluded that they were preparing for war at Cracow far more cautiously, intelligently, and formidably than at Malbork. "The Lord Jesus gave us equal or greater valor," Macko said to himself, "and obviously more intelligence and more foresight." And so it was at that time. He soon learned, also, the sources of their information: it had been furnished by the inhabitants of Prussia themselves, from people of every station, Germans as well as Poles. The Order had been able to rouse such hatred against itself that everyone in its dominions looked for the coming of Jagiello's army as if for the soul's salvation.

Then Macko remembered what Zyndram of Maszkowice had said previously at Malbork—and repeated to himself:

"That man has a head on his shoulders! So full of wisdom!"

And he recalled his every word, and once he even borrowed his wisdom, for when the young Jasko began to question him about the Teutonic Knights, he said:

"They are strong indeed, but what do you think? Will not even the strongest knight be unhorsed if his saddle-girth and stirrup-leathers are cut?"

"He will be unhorsed as sure as I stand here," replied the youth.

"Ha! You see!" Macko shouted. "I wanted you to understand this."

"Why?"

"Because the Order is like such a knight." And he added after a moment: "You won't hear that from just anyone—never fear!"

And when the young man could still not grasp what he meant, he explained it to him, forgetting to add that he had not thought out the comparison himself, but that it had come, word for word, from the powerful brain of Zyndram of Maszkowice.

CHAPTER LXXIII

THEY did not stay long at Cracow. They would have stayed a still shorter time had it not been for Jasko's eagerness to look at the city and the people, for it all seemed to him a marvellous dream. None the less, the old knight was in a great hurry to get back to his domestic comforts and to the harvest, so Jasko's begging was of little avail, and by the Assumption of the Virgin they were already back—Macko at Bogdaniec, Jasko at Zgorzelice with his sister.

Thenceforth life for them flowed on monotonously, filled with farming work and the usual rural occupations. The harvest at Zgorzelice, which was situated on a plain, and even more at Jagienka's Moczydoly, turned out excellent, but at Bogdaniec, in consequence of the dry season, the fruits of the soil were poor, and not much trouble was required to gather them in. In general, there was a dearth of cultivable land at Bogdaniec. This land was situated on the edge of the forest, and in consequence of the lords' long absence, even those plots which the abbot had cleared and brought under the plough had been neglected again for lack of hands. The old knight, however sensitive he might be to every loss, did not take this too much to heart, since he knew that with money it would be easy to get everything into good working order—if there were only someone for whom to toil and work. But it was just this doubt which embittered his labor and his days. He did not, indeed, give up. He rose at dawn, visited the flocks and herds, inspected the work in field and forest, and even chose a site for the new castelet and prepared building material; but when after a tiring day the sun melted into golden and red splendor, he was frequently seized by such intense yearning and, with it, by such anxiety, as he had never known before. "I toil and labor here," he said to himself, "while my boy is perhaps lying on the battlefield transfixed by a spear, and wolves are tolling his funeral bell with their teeth." At this thought his heart was constricted with great love and great pain. At such times he would listen attentively for the sound of hooves announcing the daily arrival of Jagienka, for when he pretended before her to be full of hope, he became more cheerful himself and gained comfort in his sorrow.

She used to come every day, usually towards evening, armed for the return trip with a crossbow at her saddle and a spear. There was no real possibility of her one day unexpectedly finding Zbyszko at home, as Macko did not expect him back for a year, or even a year and a half; but evidently the girl cherished hope, for she always came, not as of old in a shirt fastened at the neck with a ribbon, and a sheepskin coat with the wool outside, and leaves in her dishevelled hair, but with a beautiful plait of hair down her back and a tight-fitting bodice of colored Sieradz cloth. Macko would go out to meet her, and her first question was always the same, as if prescribed: "Well?" And his first answer was: "No news!" Then he would take her into the chamber, and they would talk by the fire of Zbyszko, of Lithuania, of the Teutonic Knights, and of the war—always in a circle, always on the same themes—and neither of them was ever wearied with this conversation; indeed, neither of them ever had enough.

So it went on for months. Sometimes he went to Zgorzelice, but more often she came to Bogdaniec. Occasionally, however, if there was unrest in the neighborhood, or at the bears' rutting-time, when the old males, madly following a she-bear, were inclined to attack, Macko would accompany the girl home. Well-armed as he was, the old man was not afraid of any wild beasts, for he was more dangerous to them than they were to him. At those times they used to ride stirrup to stirrup, and threatening sounds often came to their ears from the depths of the forest; yet they forgot everything which might happen to them and talked only of Zbyszko. Where is he? What is he doing? Has he already slain, or is he close to slaying, as many Teutonic Knights as he vowed to the dead Danusia and her dead mother? Will he come back soon? On these occasions Jagienka used to ask Macko questions she had already put a hundred times before, but he answered with the same consideration and thought as if he were hearing them for the first time.

"You say," she said, "that a battle in the field is not so terrible for a knight as the storming of castles?"

"See what happened to Wolf. No armor avails against a log of wood hurled from ramparts, but in the field, if a knight has the necessary training, he can hold out even against ten men."

"And Zbyszko? Has he fine armor?"

"He has several fine suits; the best is the one he took from the Frisians, for it was forged at Milan. A year ago it was still rather loose on Zbyszko, but now it fits him perfectly."

"Then no weapon is any good against such armor, true?"

"What human hands have made, human hands can find a means to deal with. Milan mail is matched by Milan swords—or English arrows."

"English arrows?" asked Jagienka anxiously.

"Did I not tell you? There are no better archers in the world—except perhaps the Mazovians of the forests, but they have not such excellent bows. An English crossbow will pierce the best mail at a hundred paces. I have seen them at Wilno. And none of them ever misses, and there are some who can hit a hawk in flight."

"Oh, those sons of pagans! However did you deal with them?"

"The only thing we could do was to rush at 'em! Those doggies handle their halberds well too, but at close quarters our men can deal with them."

"The hand of God was over you, that is certain, and it will be over Zbyszko now."

"I often say: 'O God, who created us and settled us at Bogdaniec, take care now that we do not die out!' The matter is now in God's hands. It is true, it is no small thing to attend to the whole world and forget nothing; but firstly, a man may somehow call attention to himself by not begrudging anything to the Holy Church, and secondly, God's head is not as man's."

Thus they frequently talked together, inspiring one another with hope and good cheer. Meanwhile days, weeks, and months passed by. In the autumn Macko fell into a dispute with old Wolf of Birchwood. Some time ago there had been an old boundary quarrel between the Wolfs and the abbot concerning the fresh plots in the forest which the latter had cleared and kept for himself when he held Bogdaniec in pledge. Once he had even challenged both Wolfs to fight him at the same time, with lances or long swords, but they were unwilling to fight a churchman, and in court they could get nothing. Now old Wolf remembered those fields, but Macko, who was greedy for nothing in the world so much as for land, and who was excited by the thought that the barley was coming up splendidly in the freshly cleared soil, would not hear of giving them back. They would most certainly have gone to the authorities, had they not met by chance at the parish priest's at Krzesnia. There, when old Wolf suddenly said at the end of a fierce quarrel, "Before men decide, I will appeal to God, who will take vengeance on your family for my wrongs," the obstinate Macko suddenly softened; he became pale and momentarily silent, and then exclaimed to his quarrelsome neighbor:

"Listen! It was not I who began this dispute, but the abbot. God knows who is right, but if you are going to curse Zbyszko, then take the clearings, and may God grant Zbyszko health and happiness as I yield them to you with my whole heart."

And he extended his hand, while Wolf, who had known him long, was amazed beyond measure, for he had never guessed what love for his nephew was hidden in that apparently hard heart and what anxiety concerning his fate now filled it. So for a long time he could not utter a word, and it was only when the priest of Krzesnia, delighted by the turn the affair had taken, blessed them with the sign of the cross, that he replied:

"If it is so, that is different. I was not thinking of profit, for I am old and I have no one to whom to leave my property, but only of justice. If a man shows me goodwill, I will give him even what is mine. May God bless your nephew, so that in your old age you may not have to weep for him as I have to weep for my only boy!"

They threw themselves in one another's arms, and then they argued for a long time as to who should take the clearings. In the end, Macko was persuaded to do so, since Wolf was alone in the world and had indeed no one to whom to leave his estate.

Afterwards, Macko invited the old man to Bogdaniec, where he entertained him abundantly with food and drink, for he himself was rejoiced greatly at heart. He was also pleased with the hope that the barley in the clearings would come up strongly, and at the same time by the thought that he had turned away God's displeasure from Zbyszko.

"If he returns, he will not be short of land or cattle," he thought.

Jagienka was no less satisfied with their reconciliation.

"Now," she said, when she had heard how everything had gone, "if the Lord Jesus in His mercy wishes to show that reconciliation is dearer to Him than quarrels, He must give you back Zbyszko safe and sound."

Macko's face brightened, as if a ray of sunlight had fallen on it.

"I think so too," he said. "God is almighty, for He is almighty, but there are methods for even dealing with the heavenly powers; one must only have intelligence."

"You never lacked cunning," the girl replied, raising her eyes. And after a moment, as if she had thought of something, she went on: "My, you do love that Zbyszko of yours. You do indeed!"

"Who would not love him?" the old knight replied. "And you? I suppose you hate him?"

Jagienka made no direct answer; but, sitting on the bench by Macko's side, she drew still nearer to him and, turning away her head, nudged him with her elbow:

"Leave me alone!"

CHAPTER LXXIV

THE war for Samogitia between the Teutonic Knights and Witold interested people in the kingdom too much for them not to ask plenty of questions about its course. Some were convinced that Jagiello would come to the aid of his cousin and that there would soon be a great expedition against the Order. The knighthood rallied to it, and in all the seats of the nobles it was repeated that a considerable number of Cracow lords who belonged to the royal council were inclined towards war, thinking that it was necessary once and for all to finish with an enemy who was never satisfied with what he had, but thought of robbing others even when fearing royal power. But Macko, who was an intelligent man, and had seen and learned much of the world, did not believe in the near approach of war; and he frequently spoke thus to the young Jasko of Zgorzelice and other neighbors whom he met at Krzesnia:

"As long as Grand Master Conrad lives, nothing will come of it. He is wiser than the others and knows that it would be no common war, but like saying: 'Your death or mine!' And knowing the king's power, he will not let it come to that."

"Yes, but suppose the king declares war first?" asked the neighbors.

Macko shook his head:

"You see, I have looked at everything from up close and have been able to draw more than one conclusion. If he were a king of our former line, Christian kings for centuries, then perhaps he would strike at the Germans first. But our Wladyslaw Jagiello—I do not want to withhold from him his due honor, for he is a noble lord, whom may God maintain in health—before we chose him king was Grand Duke of Lithuania and a pagan; he has only just received Christianity, and the Germans bark throughout the world that he is still a pagan at heart. So it is not at all fitting for him to declare war first and shed Christian blood. This is the reason he does not go at once to Witold's aid, although his hands are itching to do so, for I know he hates the Teutonic Knights like leprosy."

By words like these, Macko won the reputation of being a keen-witted man who could clarify any issue. So at Krzesnia, people eagerly gathered around him every Sunday after Mass, and it became the custom for one or another neighbor, if he heard any news, to go to Bogdaniec, where the old knight would explain what a common nobleman's head could not grasp. For his part, Macko received everyone hospitably and talked with each person gladly, and when the visitor had finally finished his business, Macko never forgot to take leave of him with the following words:

"You wonder at my wits, but if Zbyszko—God grant it!—returns, then you will have something to wonder at. He deserves to sit even in the royal council, such a clever, sensible rascal he is."

And trying to persuade his guests of that, he at last persuaded himself, and Jagienka too. Zbyszko seemed to them both like some fairy-tale prince. When spring came, they could scarcely sit at home. The swallows and the storks returned; the corncrakes began to call in the meadows, and the quails could be heard in the green corn; flocks of cranes and wild duck had already passed overhead—Zbyszko alone did not return. But as the birds were migrating from the south, a winged wind brought news of war from the north. Tales were told of battles and numerous combats, in which the resourceful Witold was sometimes victorious and sometimes defeated; tales were told of great losses among the Germans caused by winter and disease. Until finally the whole country rang with the joyful news that the valiant Kiejstut's son had taken New Kowno, or Gotteswerder, and had destroyed it, leaving not one stone and not one beam upon another. When this news reached him, Macko mounted his horse and rode posthaste to Zgorzelice.

"Hah! I know those parts well," he said, "for we thrashed the Teutonic Knights there thoroughly, Zbyszko and Skirwoillo and I. The honest de Lorche was captured by us there too. God granted that those Germans slipped-up there, for the castle was difficult to take."

Jagienka, however, had already heard of the destruction of New Kowno before Macko's arrival, and she heard even more: namely, that Witold had begun negotiations for peace. This last piece of news concerned her even more than the former, for if there were to be peace, Zbyszko, if he were alive, would certainly return home.

So she questioned the old knight as to whether the report was credible, and he considered the matter and answered her as follows:

"With Witold everything is possible. He is a man quite different from anyone else and assuredly the most cunning of all Christian lords. If he desires to extend his rule towards Ruthenia, then he makes peace with the Germans, but when he has gained what he set before himself, then he is pounding the Germans again! They cannot deal either with him or with Samogitia. One day he takes it from them, another day he gives it back—and not only gives it back, but himself helps them to crush it. There are some among us—yes, and in Lithuania too—who take it ill of him that he plays thus with the blood of that unhappy people. And I, too, to tell the truth, should think it shameful, if he were not Witold—for sometimes I think: suppose he is wiser than I and knows what he is doing? I heard from Skirwoillo himself that he has made of the country an abscess ever-festering in the Teutonic body, so that it may never regain its health. The mothers in Samogitia will always bear children, and blood is not to be regretted, as long as it does not flow to waste."

"The only thing I care about is whether Zbyszko will return."

"If God permits—but God grant, girl, that you may have said it in a lucky hour!"

Several months passed, however. Rumors arrived that peace had actually been made; the corn became golden and heavy with ears; the small fields sown with buckwheat had already lost their rich color, but of Zbyszko not a word was to be heard.

Finally, after the corn-harvest, Macko could hold out no longer, and he announced that he was going to Spychow to gather information, since Lithuania was not far from there, and at same time to look into the Czech's management.

Jagienka insisted on going with him, but he was unwilling to take her, so a quarrel began between them that lasted a whole week.

And then one evening, when they were arguing together at Zgorzelice, there burst into the courtyard like a hurricane a lad from Bogdaniec, barefoot, riding barebacked and capless, who shouted to them from in front of the terrace on which they were sitting:

"The young lord has returned!"

Zbyszko had indeed returned, but he was somewhat strange in his behavior. He was not only lean and parched by the wind in the open field and haggard, but at the same time indifferent and laconic in speech. The Czech, who with his wife had arrived with him, spoke for him and for himself. He said that the young knight's expedition had evidently been successful, since he had laid a whole bunch of peacock and ostrich crests on the coffins of Danusia and her mother at Spychow. He had also brought back with him captured horses and armor, two suits of which were extraordinarily valuable, though terribly dented by blows of sword and axe. Macko was burning with curiosity to learn all the details from his nephew's own lips, but Zbyszko only waved his hand and answered unintelligibly—and on the third day fell sick and had to take to his bed. It appeared that his left side was badly bruised and that two ribs were broken, which, having been badly set, hindered his walking and breathing. Moreover, the old injuries which had troubled him after his adventure with the aurochs were now renewed, and his strength had been finally exhausted by the journey from Spychow. Nothing was actually dangerous in itself, for he was a young and stalwart fellow, like an oak, but for the time being he was the prey of such measureless weariness that it seemed as if all the fatigues he had undergone were only now making themselves felt. At first Macko thought that after two or three days' rest in bed it would all pass, but actually the opposite was the case. No ointments were of any avail, nor censings with perfumed herbs, recommended by the local shepherd, nor herbal brews sent by Jagienka or the Krzesnia priest: Zbyszko grew continually weaker, continually wearier, and continually more dispirited.

"What is the matter with you? Perhaps you want something?" the old knight would ask him.

"I want nothing," Zbyszko would reply.

Thus passed day after day. Jagienka, who began to think that it was perhaps something more than an ordinary illness, and that the young man might have some secret which oppressed him, urged Macko to try once more to find out what it could be.

Macko agreed without hesitation; but, after a few moments of reflection, he said:

"And suppose he would prefer to tell you? For he—yes—he likes you, and I have noticed that when you are moving about the chamber, he follows you with his eyes."

"You've noticed this?" Jagienka asked.

"If I said 'follows,' then I meant 'follows.' And when you are away for some time, he keeps looking towards the door. So you ask him."

And there the matter stood. However, it transpired that Jagienka did not know how to ask him and had no courage to ask. She realized that she would have to somehow speak of Danusia and of Zbyszko's love for the dead girl—and such things refused to pass her lips.

"You are shrewder," she said to Macko, "and you have greater sense and experience. You speak to him; I cannot."

So, whether he liked to or not, Macko undertook the task, and one morning, when Zbyszko seemed somewhat fresher than usual, he began to talk to him:

"Hlawa told me that you laid a splendid wreath of peacock feathers in the vault at Spychow."

But Zbyszko, lying on his back, merely nodded, without taking his eyes off the ceiling.

"Well! the Lord Jesus blessed you, for in war it is easier to meet foot-soldiers than knights. . . . You can slay as many men-at-arms as you like, but you often have to really look around before you find a knight. . . . Did they find their way of themselves to the edge of your sword?"

"I challenged several to combat on beaten ground, and one time they surrounded me in battle," the young man replied lazily.

"And you have brought a good amount of booty. . . ."

"Duke Witold gave me part of it."

"Is he always so generous?"

Zbyszko nodded again, evidently being disinclined for further talk.

But Macko did not give up and decided to come to the point.

"Tell me frankly," he said; "when you covered that coffin with those crests, you must have felt wonderfully relieved. . . . One is always glad when one has fulfilled a vow. . . . Were you glad? Eh?"

Zbyszko took his sorrowful eyes off the ceiling and turned them to Macko—and answered as if with a certain surprise:

"No."

"No? Great heavens! I should have thought that when you had consoled those spirits in heaven, it would have been the end."

But the young man closed his eyes for a few moments, as if in deep thought, and at last replied:

"Evidently human blood is no consolation to souls in paradise."

A few moments of silence followed.

"Then why did you go to that war?" Macko finally asked.

"Why?" Zbyszko replied with a little more animation. "I also thought that it would bring me relief. I thought that I should console Danusia and myself. But afterwards I felt quite strange. I left the coffins in the vault, and my heart was just as heavy as before. So it is evident that human blood is no consolation to souls in paradise."

"Someone must have told you that, for you would never have thought it out for yourself."

"I did come to that conclusion myself, because the world seemed no more cheerful to me afterwards than before. Father Caleb confirmed it."

"To slay an enemy in war is no sin; nay, it is even praiseworthy, and these are the enemies of our whole race."

"I have no sin on my conscience, and I do not mourn for them."

"But continually for Danusia?"

"Yes. When I think of her, I feel mournful. But everything is God's will! She is better off at the heavenly court, and I am already accustomed to it."

"Then why do you not shake off your sorrow? What do you need?"

"Do I know?"

"You have no lack of rest, and your illness will soon leave you. Go to the baths, bathe, drink a tankard of mead to make you sweat—that's what you need!"

"And then what?"

"You will soon grow cheerful again."

"Where am I to find the source of cheerfulness? I find none in myself, and no one can lend me any."

"You are hiding something!"

Zbyszko shrugged his shoulders.

"I cannot be cheerful, but I have nothing to hide."

He said this so sincerely that Macko immediately ceased to suspect him of having any secret. He passed his broad palm over his grey hair, as he was accustomed to do whenever he reflected earnestly on any subject, and finally said:

"Then I will tell you what you lack. One stage is finished in your life, and another has not yet begun—do you understand?"

"Not very well, but it may be," the young man replied.

And he stretched himself like a man who is sleepy.

Macko, however, was sure he had guessed the real cause. He was quite happy, for he ceased entirely to be anxious. He put even more confidence in his own wit and intelligence than before, and told himself: "It is not surprising that people come to me for advice!"

And when Jagienka arrived that same evening, before she had time even to dismount, he told her that he knew what was wrong with Zbyszko.

So the girl leapt from the saddle and asked:

"Well? What? Tell me!"

"It is you who have the right medicine for him."

"I? What medicine?"

He took her by the waist and whispered something in her ear, but not for long, since she sprang back from him as if she had been burnt, and hiding her blushing face between the saddle-cloth and the high-saddle, she exclaimed:

"Go away! I can't stand you!"

"As God is dear to me, I am speaking the truth!" Macko said, laughing.

CHAPTER LXXV

OLD Macko had guessed the truth correctly, but only half of it. One stage of Zbyszko's life was indeed finished. At every mention of Danusia, he mourned for her, but he said himself that she must be better off at the heavenly court than she had been at the duke's. He had by now accustomed himself to the thought that she was no longer on earth, and he considered her death inevitable. Formerly at Cracow he had greatly admired the figures of various holy virgins cut out of glass and framed in cames of lead in the church windows—bright-colored, translucent in the sun; and now he pictured Danusia in the same way. He saw her heavenly, translucent, in profile, with folded hands and raised eyes, or playing on the lute, amid various divine musicians who play in heaven for the Mother of God and for her Child. There was nothing earthly in her any more; she had become a spirit so pure and incorporeal that when he sometimes recalled how she had waited on the duchess at the hunting-lodge, and had laughed and talked and sat down with the others to table, he was overcome with surprise that such a thing had been possible. Even during his expedition, at the side of Witold, when war and battles had claimed his whole attention, he had ceased to yearn for his deceased wife as a man yearns for a woman, but thought of her only as a pious man thinks of his patron saint. Thus his love, gradually losing its earthly elements, had changed more and more into a sweet memory, pure as a cloudless sky—and, quite simply, into worship.

If he had been a man frail in body and inclined to deeper thought, he would have become a monk—and in the quiet life of a monastery he would have preserved and enshrined that heavenly memory until the moment when his spirit would have escaped from its corporeal bonds into limitless space, like a bird from a cage. But he had only just begun the third decade of his life—and he could squeeze the sap out of branches in his hands and the breath out of a horse between his thighs. He was like the usual nobleman and gentleman of those days, who—if he did not die in infancy or become a priest—knew no bounds nor measure in his bodily impulses or his strength, and either gave himself up to robbery, lechery, and drunkenness, or else, marrying young, went, when the call came around to war, with twenty-four sons, or even more—sons as strong as wild boars.

But he did not know that he was like that—particularly because he had been sick from the beginning. Slowly, however, his badly-set ribs grew together, leaving only an insignificant lump in his side, which gave him no discomfort and could be well concealed, not only by a breastplate, but by an ordinary garment. His weariness passed. His abundant, fair hair, which he had cut short in mourning for Danusia, had grown anew and fell half-way down his back. His former unusually good looks had returned. When, over a decade ago at Cracow, he had gone to meet death at the executioner's hand, he had looked like a scion of some great family, but now he had become still more handsome, a real prince, with gigantic shoulders, chest, arms, and thighs, but a young girl's face. Strength and life boiled over in him like soup in a pot and now, raised to a still higher degree by chastity and long rest, coursed like fire through his veins. Not knowing what it was, he thought he was still sick, and he continued to lie in bed, glad that Macko and Jagienka attended on him, cared for him and divined all his wishes. At times he felt that he was as happy as if he were in heaven, and at other times—particularly when Jagienka was not at his side— that he was badly off and that life was sad and intolerable. Then he would be seized with yawning, shivering, and feverish fits, and would declare to Macko that when he was restored to health he would go anew to the ends of the earth, against the Germans, or the Tartars, or similar savage folk, if only to pass the time, which pressed upon him cruelly. And Macko, instead of opposing, nod-ded and agreed—but meanwhile sent for Jagienka, upon whose arrival Zbyszko's thoughts of new expeditions melted immediately like snows in the summer sun.

She, for her part, came readily, both when she was summoned and of her own will, for she had fallen in love with Zbyszko with the whole strength of her heart and soul. During her stay at the episcopal and ducal courts at Plock, she had seen knights equally handsome, equally renowned for strength and valor, who more than once had knelt before her, vowing faith to her till death; but he had been her chosen, him she had loved in the dawn of her youth with her first love, and the misfortunes through which he had passed served only to strengthen her love—to such a degree that he was a hundred times dearer to her than not only all knights, but even all dukes and princes of the earth. Now, when he was recovering health and growing every day more handsome, her love changed almost into a daze and veiled the whole world before her eyes.

She did not admit it, however, even to herself, and concealed it from Zbyszko as carefully as possible, out of fear lest he scorn her again. Even with Macko, ready as she had been to make confidences before, she now became cautious and silent. The only thing which might have betrayed her was the care she showed in nursing Zbyszko, but she endeavored to give it the appearance of something else—and, to this end, she once expressed herself artfully to Zbyszko:

"If I look after you a bit, it is only out of affection for Macko, and you thought—what? Tell me!"

And, pretending to adjust the hair on her forehead, she covered her face with her hand and studied him through her fingers, while he, taken by surprise at her question, blushed like a girl and only after some time replied:

"I thought nothing. You are different now."

And once again there was silence.

"Different?" asked the girl at last in a quiet, soft tone. "Well, of course I am different. But God forbid that I should now hate being with you!"

"God reward you for that!" Zbyszko replied.

And from that time they got on well together, though they were somewhat awkward and ill at ease. Frequently it might have seemed that both of them were speaking of one thing and thinking of another. Silence frequently fell between them. Zbyszko, lying all the time in bed, followed her with his eyes—as Macko had said—wherever she moved, for, at certain times, she seemed to him so beautiful that he could not look enough at her. Sometimes their glances suddenly met, and then their faces flushed, and the girl's deep breast moved with a sudden breath, and her heart beat as if in expectation that she would hear something which would cause her soul to melt away within her. But Zbyszko said nothing, for he had lost all his old boldness with her and feared to frighten her by a careless word, and despite what his eyes saw, he persuaded himself that she was only showing him sisterly affection out of regard for Macko.

One day he began to talk of it to Macko. He tried to speak quietly and even indifferently, but he did not notice how his words sounded more and more like a half-bitter, half-sorrowful complaint. Macko, however, listened patiently to all he had to say, and at the end said but one single word:

"Fool!"

And he went out of the room.

But in the cow-shed he began to rub his hands and smack his thighs in great joy.

"Ha!" he said to himself. "When you could have had her cheaply, you would not look at her. So now have your fill of fear and anxiety, for you are a fool. I will build a castelet, and you can lick your lips meanwhile. I will not say anything to you and will not lift the mist from your eyes, though you neigh louder than all the horses at Bogdaniec. When twigs lie on glowing coals, sooner or later a flame will break out, but I am not going to blow on the coals, for I think there is no need."

Indeed, he not only did not blow on the coals, but he even opposed Zbyszko and vexed him, like a cunning old man who likes to play with an inexperienced youth. So, one time when Zbyszko told him again that he would go on some distant expedition to rid himself of his intolerable life, he replied:

"As long as you had no hair under your nose, I used to direct you, but now—follow your own will. If you must at all costs trust your own sense and go—well, go."

Zbyszko sprang up in surprise and sat on the bed.

"What? You're not going to oppose me even on this issue?"

"What have I to oppose? I am only very grieved for the family which would die out with you, but even for that perhaps a solution can be found."

"What solution?" Zbyszko asked in alarm.

"What solution? Well, there's no denying that I'm old, but none the less I have strength in my bones. It's true that some younger fellow would be better suited for Jagienka, but, seeing as how I was a friend of her dead father—who knows. . . ."

"You were a friend of her father's," Zbyszko replied, "but for me you never showed the least goodwill—never, never!"

And he broke off, for his chin began to quiver; but Macko said:

"Pooh! If you are determined to die at all costs, what can I do?"

"Good! Do what you like—but I shall leave this very day!"

"Fool!" Macko repeated.

And again he went out of the room, this time to inspect the peasants: both those from Bogdaniec and those whom Jagienka had sent him from Zgorzelice and Moczydoly to help in digging the moat that would surround the castelet.

CHAPTER LXXVI

ZBYSZKO did not indeed fulfill his threat and go away, but after the lapse of a week his health was completely restored and he could no longer continue to lie in bed. Macko told him that he now ought to go to Zgorzelice and thank Jagienka for her care and attention; so one day, after scalding himself thoroughly in a bath, he determined to go without further delay. To this end, he had beautiful garments brought from his chest, which he changed into, and then he busied himself with combing his hair. This was no small or easy task, and not only because of the abundance of hair which fell down his back, like a mane, below his shoulder-blades. Knights in daily life wore their hair in a net shaped like a mushroom, which had this advantage: that on expeditions their helmets hurt them less; whereas for festivities, at weddings, or on visits to houses where there were young ladies, they arranged it in beautiful curls that were often smeared with white-of-egg to make them shine and to give them consistency. This was the way in which Zbyszko now desired to do his hair. But the two women who were summoned from the kitchen were not accustomed to such a task and were unable to do it properly. Zbyszko's hair, dry and dishevelled after the bath, would not lie down, and stuck out like badly-laid thatch on a hut roof. Neither the ornamental combs of buffalo horn which he had captured from the Frisians were of any help, nor even the curry-comb which one of the women fetched from the stable. Zbyszko finally grew cross and impatient, when into the chamber came Macko, accompanied by Jagienka, who had arrived unexpectedly in the meantime.

"Jesus Christ be praised!" said the girl.

"For ever and ever," Zbyszko replied, his face lit up with joy. "How wonderful! We were just coming to Zgorzelice, and here you are!"

And his eyes brightened, for now every time he saw her, his heart grew as light as if he had been looking at the rising sun.

But Jagienka, seeing the worried women with combs in their hands and the curry-comb lying on the bench by Zbyszko's side and his dishevelled hair, burst out laughing.

"Why, you look like a scarecrow!" she exclaimed, showing her beautiful white teeth between her coral-red lips. "You ought to be set up in the hemp field or in the cherry orchard!"

But he became disheartened.

"We wanted to come to Zgorzelice," he said. "There you could not have offended a guest, while here you can make fun of me as much as you like, and, verily, you are always fond of doing so."

"I fond of doing so?" asked the girl. "Almighty God! I came here to invite you to supper, and I am not laughing at you, but at these women, for if I were in their place, I should know what to do."

"Even you could do nothing!"

"And who do you suppose does Jasko's hair?"

"Jasko is your brother," Zbyszko replied.

"Of course he is!"

At this point the old and experienced Macko determined to come to their aid.

"In houses," he said, "where a knightly lad's hair grows long again after being cut, his sister combs it; and in the case of a married man, his wife; but the custom is that where a knight has no sister or wife, a noble damsel may attend on him, even if they are complete strangers."

"Is there really such a custom?" asked Jagienka, lowering her eyes.

"Not only in manor-houses, but even in castles; yes, even at the king's court," Macko replied.

Then he turned to the women:

"Since you are of no use, get back to the kitchen!"

"Let them bring me some warm water," added the girl.

Macko went out together with the women, ostensibly to see that they did not waste time—and presently he sent in some warm water. After it was put in the chamber, the young people were left alone. Jagienka, dipping a towel in the water, wet Zbyszko's hair with it thoroughly, and when it was no longer dishevelled but lay flat with the weight of the water, she took a comb and sat down on the bench by the young man's side to continue with her work.

And so they sat side by side, both of them unusually handsome and beyond measure in love, yet shy and silent. Jagienka at length began to arrange his golden hair, and he felt the nearness of her raised arms and of her hands, and trembled from head to foot, restraining himself with the whole force of his will from catching her by the waist and pressing her with all his strength to his breast.

In the silence, their quick breathing could be heard.

"Are you sick?" asked the girl presently. "What's the matter?"

"Nothing!" the young knight replied.

"You are panting so."

"And so are you."

Again silence fell. Jagienka's cheeks blossomed like a rose, for she felt that Zbyszko never took his eyes off her face for a single moment; so, to hide her embarrassment through conversation, she asked:

"Why are you looking at me like that?"

"Does it disturb you?"

"It does not disturb me; I'm just asking."

"Jagienka!"

"What? . . ."

Zbyszko drew a deep breath, sighed, and moved his lips as if getting ready for a long talk, but evidently his courage was not yet sufficient, for he only repeated anew:

"Jagienka!"

"What?"

"I'm afraid to say. . . ."

"Don't be afraid. I am a simple girl, not a dragon."

"Most certainly you are not a dragon! But Uncle Macko says that he wants to take you. . . ."

"So he does, but not for himself."

And she fell silent, as if frightened by her own words.

"By the dear God, my Jagienka! And what have you to say to that?" Zbyszko cried out.

But her eyes filled unexpectedly with tears, her beautiful lips began to quiver, and her voice became so low that Zbyszko could scarcely catch her words:

"Papa and the abbot wanted . . . and I—well, you know."

At these words, joy burst out in his heart like a sudden flame. So he caught the girl in his arms and lifted her up as if she were a feather, shouting excitedly:

"Jagna! Jagna! My golden girl! My little sunbeam! Hurrah, hurrah!"

And he shouted so loud that old Macko, thinking something strange had happened, rushed into the room. But, seeing Jagienka in Zbyszko's arms, he was amazed that everything should have gone so quickly, and exclaimed:

"In the name of the Father and of the Son! Control yourself, boy!"

Zbyszko went towards him, set Jagienka down, and was about to kneel with her; but before they could do so, the old man caught them in his bony arms and pressed them with all his strength to his breast.

"Jesus Christ be praised! I knew it would end like this, but what a joy it is! God bless you! Now it will be easier to die. A girl like the purest gold. In the eyes of God and in the eyes of men. Truly! And now let come what may, since I have lived to experience such joy. I must go to Zgorzelice and tell Jasko. Oh, if only old Zych were alive—and the abbot! But I will take the place of both, for, to tell the truth, I love you both so much that I am ashamed to talk of it."

And although he had a heart in his breast like tempered steel, he was so moved that something constricted his throat. He kissed Zbyszko again, and then Jagienka on both cheeks, and muttering, half-choked by tears, "Honey-sweet, that girl," he went to the stables to have the horses saddled.

When he had got outside, he staggered in his joy onto the sunflowers growing in front of the house and began to stare at their dark circles, surrounded with yellow petals, exactly as if he were drunk.

"Yes, there's a lot of you," he said, "but God grant that of the Hailstones of Bogdaniec there will be still more."

Then, on his way to the stables, he began to mutter again and to count:

"Bogdaniec, the abbot's estates, Spychow, Moczydoly. . . . God always knows what He is doing, and when old Wolf's time comes, it will be worthwhile buying Birchwood. Fine meadows! . . ."

Meanwhile Jagienka and Zbyszko had also come out. They stood in front of the house, joyous, happy, and radiant like the sun.

"Uncle!" cried out Zbyszko from a distance.

And Macko turned to them, opened his arms and shouted, as if he were in a forest:

"Hey! hey! Over here!"

CHAPTER LXXVII

THEY lived at Moczydoly while old Macko was building the castelet for them at Bogdaniec. He was building it laboriously, for he wanted the walls to be of stone and mortar, and the watchtower to be of brick, which was scarce in the vicinity. In the first year he dug out the moat, which was fairly easy, for the eminence on which the castelet was to stand had once been surrounded with a ditch, possibly in still pagan times, and so all that was needed was to clean this of the trees and the hawthorn bushes with which it was overgrown, and then to deepen and strengthen it as required. In the course of this work, they discovered an abundant spring, which soon filled the moat so full that Macko had to devise an outlet for the surplus water. After that, he erected a palisade on the rampart, and he began to collect material for the walls of the little castle: oak beams so thick that three men could not embrace one and larch wood which would not rot either under the clay floor or when covered with turf. He set about raising these walls only after a year, despite the constant help which he had from the peasants of Zgorzelice and Moczydoly; but when the time came, he set about it with all the more energy because Jagienka had already born twins. Then the heavens opened before the old knight, for he now had someone for whom to work and strive; he knew that the line of the Hailstones would not die out, and that the Blunt Horseshoe would still from time to time be steeped in hostile blood.

The twins were given the names of Macko and Jasko. "Sturdy lads," the old man said. "There are none like them in the kingdom; and it is not yet evening." And he loved them immediately with a

great love, and Jagienka became everything in the world to him.
Whoever praised her in his presence could get anything from him.
But men genuinely envied Zbyszko for having such a wife, and
they praised her not merely for what they could get, as she truly
shone in the neighborhood like the loveliest flower of the field. She
had brought her husband a large dowry, but more besides: namely,
great love and dazzling beauty, and a courtesy and valiancy such as
more than one knight might have been proud to show. It was
nothing for her to get up and attend to her housekeeping only a
few days after her confinement and then ride hunting with her
husband, or to dash on horseback from Moczydoly to Bogdaniec
in the morning and return to Jasko and Macko before noon. So her
husband loved her like the apple of his eye; old Macko loved her;
the servants, for whom she had a kindly heart, loved her; and at
Krzesnia, when she went to church on Sundays, she was greeted by
a murmur of admiration and worship. Her former suitor, the
quarrelsome Cztan of Rogow, who was married to a yeoman's
daughter, used to drink after Mass with old Wolf of Birchwood at
the inn, where he would say, raising his glass: "Your son and I
fought over her more than once, and wanted to marry her, but it
was like reaching for the moon."

Others declared loudly that someone like her might only be
found at the king's court at Cracow. For besides her wealth, charm,
and courtesy, her vigor and strength were admired beyond measure. There was but one opinion concerning this: "What a woman!
She can prop a bear in the forest with her spear, and she does not
need to crack nuts with her teeth, but lays them on a bench and
suddenly sits on them, and then they are all crushed as if under a
millstone." So they praised her in the parish town of Krzesnia and
in the neighboring villages and even in the voivode's town of
Sieradz. None the less, while envying Zbyszko of Bogdaniec, they
did not wonder too much that he had got her, for he was surrounded with such a halo of military glory as no one in the vicinity
could equal.

The young nobles and gentry used to tell one another many tales
of the Germans whom he had "cracked" in battles under the
leadership of Witold and in single combats on beaten earth. They
said that no one had ever escaped from his hands; that at Malbork
he had unhorsed twelve knights, among whom was the grand

master's brother, Ulrich; and, finally, that he had been admitted to joust even with the Cracow knights and that the invincible Zawisza the Black himself was his affectionate friend.

Some refused to believe such extraordinary gossip, but even they, if there was a discussion as to whom the neighborhood would choose if the Polish knights had to go and measure themselves with foreigners, said: "Most certainly Zbyszko." Only afterwards did they name the shaggy Cztan of Rogow and other local fighters, who in knightly training fell far behind the young owner of Bogdaniec.

His great affluence joined with his fame to win him men's respect. It was no merit that he had obtained Moczydoly and the abbot's large estates by marrying Jagienka; but, before that, he had inherited Spychow with the enormous treasures gathered by Jurand; besides, it was whispered that the booty taken by the knights of Bogdaniec alone, consisting of armor, horses, garments, and jewellery, amounted to three or four good villages.

So it was regarded as a special favor of God for the line of the Hailstones, with the Blunt Horseshoe for their coat-of-arms, that, though until recently they had been sunk so low that they possessed nothing but an empty Bogdaniec, they had now outgrown all others in the vicinity. "Why, at Bogdaniec after the fire there remained only that old hunchbacked house," old people said. "The estate itself, owing to lack of hands, had to be mortgaged to a kinsman—and now they are building a castle." Accordingly, people's amazement was great, but being accompanied by an instinctive feeling that the whole nation was also advancing with irresistible impetus to measureless prosperity, and that the course of things had to be so by divine will, this amazement was not accompanied by malice or envy. Nay, the vicinity boasted and was proud of these knights of Bogdaniec. They constituted visible proof of what a nobleman might attain by strength of arm in combination with a valiant heart and a knightly lust for adventure. At the sight of them, many a man felt that it was too narrow for him amid the comforts of home and within the borders of his inheritance, and that beyond the wall there was great wealth and broad lands in the power of evil lords, which might be conquered with measureless advantage for himself and the kingdom. And this excess of vigor in the various noble families permeated and stirred the whole community, and was like hot water, which must boil over the edge of the pot. The shrewd Cracow lords and the peace-loving king might restrain these forces for a time and put off the war with the eternal enemy for many years, but no human power could stifle them completely, nor check the impetus of a people advancing toward greatness.

CHAPTER LXXVIII

MACKO had fallen on happy days. Indeed, he frequently told the neighbors that he had got more than he had ever expected. Even old age only whitened his hair and beard without so far taking from him either his strength or his health. His heart was full of such good cheer as it had never known before. His once stern face became ever more kindly, and his eyes smiled brightly at whomever he met. He was deeply convinced that all bad things were gone forever, and that no anxiety, no misery, would now disturb the days of his life, which flowed along peacefully like a placid river. To go on fighting until old age, and then to administer the estate and increase it for his "grandchildren" had been his deepest desire at all times, and now everything had been splendidly fulfilled. The work of the estate was going smoothly. Large clearings had been made in the forests, and the new land was fresh and green each spring with the verdure of various crops; the fruits of the earth increased; on the meadows were forty mares with foals, which the old nobleman inspected every day; flocks of sheep and herds of cattle pastured on the fallow fields and in the open underwoods. Bogdaniec was completely transformed. The abandoned settlement had become a populous and well-to-do village, and anyone who approached it was dazzled by the far-seen watchtower and the still unblackened walls of the castelet, shining gold in the sun or purple in the evening glow.

So old Macko rejoiced at heart in the riches and prosperity and all the work of the estate—and did not deny it when folk said he had a lucky hand. A year after the twins, a boy came into the world, whom Jagienka called Zych in honor and memory of her father. Macko received him with joy and was not in the least distressed by the thought that if it went on like this, the property amassed with such trouble and effort would have to be divided into small holdings. "For what did we have?" he once remarked to Zbyszko. "Nothing! Yet God made us prosperous. Old Pakosz of Sulislawice," he said, "has twenty-two sons and only one village, and yet they do not die of hunger. Is there but little land in the kingdom and in Lithuania? Are there but few villages and castles in the hands of the Teutonic dogs? Hey! Supposing the Lord Jesus were to grant you more sons! There would be room enough, since there are whole castles of red brick in those regions, of which our gracious king would make us castellans." And it was worthy of note that, though the Order was at the height of its power and surpassed all the kingdoms of the West in wealth, strength, and the number of its trained soldiers, yet this old knight thought of Teutonic castles as future seats for his "grandchildren." And many others doubtless thought the same in the kingdom of Jagiello, not only because the castles were on old Polish land, which the Order had occupied, but because they were conscious of that mighty power which was boiling in the breast of the nation and seeking outlet on every side.

It was only in the fourth year after Zbyszko's marriage that the castelet was finished, with the aid not only of local hands from Zgorzelice and Moczydoly but also of hands lent by the neighbors, and in particular by old Wolf of Birchwood, who, left alone in the world as he was after the death of his son, had become very friendly with Macko and then with Zbyszko and Jagienka. Macko had adorned the rooms with booty which he and Zbyszko had either taken themselves or had inherited from Jurand of Spychow; he had added furniture and other things inherited from the abbot or brought by Jagienka from her home; he had introduced glass windowpanes from Sieradz. Thus, he had arranged a splendid residence. Still, it was only in the fifth year that Zbyszko moved with his wife and children into the castelet, when the other buildings, such as stables, cow-houses, kitchens, and baths, were finished, as well as the underground store-chambers, which the old man had made of stone and mortar, so as to last an infinite time. He himself, however, preferred to remain in the old house, declining all of Zbyszko's and Jagienka's invitations with such arguments as these:

"Here I will die, where I was born. You see, during the war between the Grzymala and Nalecz clans, Bogdaniec was burnt to the ground—all the buildings and all the huts—nay, even the fences, and only the house was left. People said that it did not burn because of all the moss on the roof, but I think the hand of God had a part in it, and His will that we should return here and grow up anew from here. During our warfaring, I complained more than once that we had no place to which to return, but that was not quite true, for, though verily there was no estate to administer and nothing to put in our mouths, there was shelter for our heads. You, young people, are different, but I think that since the old house did not fail us, it is not fitting for me to fail it."

So he stayed. None the less, he liked to go over to the little castle and compare its size and splendor with the old former dwelling, and at the same time to look at Zbyszko and Jagienka and the "grandchildren." Everything he saw there was in considerable part his own work, and yet he was struck with surprise and amazement. Occasionally old Wolf came over for a chat by the fire, or else he himself went over to Birchwood, and once he expressed his thoughts to him about "the new order of things" as follows:

"You know, sometimes I amazed! Of course, Zbyszko was at Cracow in the castle with the king—yes, they very nearly cut off his head—and in Mazovia, and at Malbork, and at Duke Janusz's, while Jagienka also was brought up in affluence, but they had no castle of their own. But now it is as if they had never been accustomed to anything else. They walk about, I tell you, in the rooms, they walk about and walk about and give orders to the servants, and when they are tired, they sit down. A real castellan and chatelaine! They also have a room in which they dine with the headmen, foremen, and servants, with seats in it, higher for him and her, while the rest sit lower down, waiting until the master and mistress have suitably filled their dishes. Such is court custom, but one must remember that they are not a great lord and lady, but only my nephew and his wife, who kiss my old man's hand, seat me in the first place, and call me their benefactor."

"That is why the Lord Jesus blesses them," old Wolf observed. Afterwards, shaking his head sorrowfully, he drank his mead, stirred the coals on the hearth with an iron poker, and said: "But my boy is dead!"

"God's will."

"True! The elder brothers, of whom there were five, fell long ago. You know. Yes, it was God's will. But this one was the stoutest of all. A real Wolf, and if he had not fallen, maybe he would have been sitting in his own castle today."

"It would have been better if Cztan had fallen."

"Cztan! He can supposedly carry millstones on his back, but how many times did my son knock him about! My son had knightly training, but now Cztan is led around by his wife, for though he is a strong fellow, he is a fool."

"Hey, he's all harnessed up!" Macko declared.

And he took the opportunity to praise not only knightly training but also Zbyszko's sound sense, and to boast how he had fought with sharp weapons at Malbork against the foremost knights, and how with dukes "he will talk as familiarly as if he were eating nuts." He also praised his orderly mind and his energetic administration of the estate, without which the castelet would soon have eaten up his wealth. Not wishing old Wolf to think, however, that such a thing might actually happen, he concluded in a lower tone:

"Yes, by God's grace there is enough of all kinds of goods, more than people think; but don't speak of it to anyone."

None the less, people guessed and knew and told one another in exaggerated terms of all the riches which the knights of Bogdaniec were supposed to have brought from Spychow. It was said that they had brought money in salt-kegs from Mazovia. Macko had also agreed to lend some dozen marks to a well-to-do landowner of Koniecpole, which absolutely convinced the neighborhood of his possession of "treasure." Accordingly, the importance of Bogdaniec grew, as did the respect in which it was held, and the little castle never lacked for guests; at which Macko, careful with money though he was, was not displeased, for he knew that that, too, increases a family's fame.

The christenings in particular were splendid, and once a year, after Assumption, Zbyszko held a great banquet for his neighbors, to which the noble ladies also used to come to look at the knightly exercises, listen to the minstrels, and dance with the young knights by the light of resinous torches until morning. On these occasions old Macko used to feast his eyes and rejoice his heart with the sight of Zbyszko and Jagienka, so elegant and lordly did they look. Zbyszko grew manly and filled out, and though in comparison with his powerful and tall figure, his face always appeared youthful, yet, when he tied his abundant hair with a purple band and put on a fine garment embroidered with silver and gold, not only Macko but more than one nobleman said to himself: "Great heavens, he looks like a real duke sitting in his castle!" And frequently knights who knew the Western custom knelt before Jagienka and begged her to consent to be the lady of their thoughts—such was the splendor radiated by her health and youth, her strength and beauty. The old Master of Koniecpole, the voivode of Sieradz himself, was astonished at the sight of her and compared her with the glow of dawn and even with the "kindly sun, which gives light to the earth and fills even old bones with a livelier warmth."

CHAPTER LXXIX

NEVERTHELESS, in the fifth year—when exemplary order had been introduced into all the villages, when the watchtower was finished and the banner of the Blunt Horseshoe had been flying over it for several months and Jagienka had happily borne a fourth son, to whom was given the name of Jurand—old Macko said to Zbyszko:

"All is going well, and if the Lord Jesus grants a happy end to one thing more, then I will die at peace."

Zbyszko looked at him questioningly, and presently asked:

"I suppose you are speaking of war with the Teutonic Knights, for what else could you need?"

"Then I will say what I told you before," Macko replied. "As long as Grand Master Conrad lives there will be no war."

"Will he live forever?"

"No, but neither shall I, and therefore I am thinking of something else."

"Of what, then?"

"Eh! better not to say. Meanwhile I am going to Spychow, and perhaps I shall meet the dukes at Plock and Czersk as well."

Zbyszko was not too greatly surprised at this answer, for in the course of the last few years Macko had repeatedly gone to Spychow, so he only asked:

"Shall you be away long?"

"Longer than usual, for I shall stop at Plock."

So a week later Macko set out, taking with him several wagons and a good suit of armor, "in case I have to joust in the lists." At parting he announced that perhaps he would be away longer than usual, and he was indeed, for there was no news of him for half a year. Zbyszko finally began to worry and sent a messenger to Spychow, but the man met Macko at Sieradz and came back with him.

The old knight was rather gloomy on his return, but after questioning Zbyszko in detail as to all that had happened during his absence, and satisfying himself that all was well, he brightened up a little and began to tell the story of his expedition.

"You know, I have been at Malbork," he said.

"At Malbork?"

"Where else should I have been?"

Zbyszko looked at him for a few moments in amazement, then suddenly slapped his thigh and said:

"Oh, heavens! And I completely forgot."

"You might forget, for you have fulfilled your vows," Macko replied, "but God forbid that I should sit here and forget my own honor! It is not our custom to fail in anything, and so help me God, I will not fail in this as long as I breathe!"

Here Macko's face darkened and became so threatening and obstinate as Zbyszko had not seen it since the days when they went to battle against the Teutonic Knights with Witold and Skirwoillo.

"Well, what happened?" he asked. "Did he escape you?"

"He did not escape my hands because he did not face me."

"Why is that?"

"He has become grand commander."

"Kuno Lichtenstein—grand commander?"

"Yes. Maybe they will elect him grand master too. Who knows? But even now he thinks himself the equal of princes. They say that he manages everything, and that all the affairs of the Order are on his shoulders, while the master does nothing without him. How will such a man accept a challenge to combat on beaten earth? You will only be laughed at."

"Did they laugh at you?" asked Zbyszko, whose eyes flashed with sudden anger.

"Duchess Alexandra of Plock laughed. 'You might as well challenge the Roman emperor! He,' she said, meaning Lichtenstein, 'as we know, has received challenges from Zawisza the Black and Powala and Paszko of Biskupice, and yet he sent no answer even to men like these, for he may not. It is not that he lacks courage, but he is a monk, and he has an office so honorable and dignified that he doesn't even think about such things; besides, he would lose more honor by taking up a challenge than by paying no attention to it.' So the lady said."

"And what did you reply to that?"

"I was most grieved, but I said that I still must go to Malbork, so that I could say to God and man: 'What was in my power, I have done.' Then I asked the lady to devise some kind of embassy for me and to give me a letter to Malbork, for I knew that otherwise I would not get my head out of that wolves' den again. In my heart, however, I thought: 'He was unwilling to fix a term either for Zawisza or Powala or Paszko, but if I catch him by the beak in front of the master himself and all the commanders and guests, and pluck out his moustache and beard, then surely he will meet me in combat.'"

"Ah, what a cunning man you are!" exclaimed Zbyszko with enthusiasm.

"Hey!" replied the old knight. "There is a way for everything, if one only has a head on one's shoulders. But in this case the Lord Jesus failed to be gracious, for I did not find Lichtenstein at Malbork. They said he had gone on a mission to Witold. So I did not know what to do: whether to wait or to go after him. I was afraid I might miss him. But as I had been acquainted with the master and the grand keeper of the wardrobe in former times, I admitted them to the real reason why I had come, but they cried out that it could not be."

"Why not?"

"For the same reason as the Duchess of Plock had given. And the master said: 'What would you think of me if I were to meet every knight from Mazovia or from Poland who might challenge me to combat?' Well, he was right, for he would long have been gone from this world if he had. Then he and the keeper of the wardrobe marvelled, and told the story at supper. I tell you, the hall buzzed like a beehive! Particularly among the guests. A number of them rose at once, shouting: 'Kuno may not, but we may!' So I chose three with whom to fight in turn, but the master, though I had begged him repeatedly, allowed me to fight with only one, whose surname was Lichtenstein and who was a kinsman of Kuno."

"Well, what happened?" cried out Zbyszko.

"Well, I have brought home his armor, but it is so full of holes that no one will give even a single mark for it."

"Dear God, you did indeed fulfill your vow!"

"At first I was glad, for I thought so myself, but afterwards I thought: 'No! It is not the same!' And now I have no rest, for it is really not the same."

But Zbyszko began to console him:

"You know me, and you know I would not let either myself or anyone else off lightly in such a case; but if the same thing had happened to me, I should have had enough. And I tell you that the greatest knights at Cracow will support me in this. Even Zawisza, who knows best of all what is required by knightly honor, will certainly say nothing different."

"You believe so?" Macko asked.

"Just think. They are famous throughout the world, and they challenged him too, but none of them accomplished as much as you have done. You vowed death to Lichtenstein, and you have indeed slain a Lichtenstein."

"Maybe," said the old knight.

But Zbyszko, who was interested in knightly matters, asked:

"Come, tell me. Was he young or old? And what sort of combat was it? On horseback or on foot?"

"He was about thirty-five years old with a beard down to his belt, and the combat was on horseback. God helped me to unhorse him with my lance, and then we went at it with swords. I tell you, the blood gushed from his mouth so that his whole beard seemed like a crimson icicle."

"And you have complained more than once that you are growing old!"

"When I am sitting on horseback or have my feet firmly planted on the ground, I can hold my own; but I can no longer leap into the saddle in full armor."

"Even Kuno would not have escaped your hands."

The old man waved his hand contemptuously, as if to say that with Kuno it would have been considerably easier; and then they went to look at the captured armor, which Macko had brought away only as evidence of his victory, for it was too smashed up and, therefore, of no value. Only the beautifully-wrought cuisses and knee-pieces were undamaged.

"Yet I should have preferred them to be Kuno's," said Macko gloomily.

"God knows what is best," replied Zbyszko. "You will not get Kuno if he becomes grand master, unless it be in some great battle."

"I listened carefully to what people were saying," Macko replied. "Some say that Conrad will be succeeded by Kuno, and others say that it will be Conrad's brother, Ulrich."

"I should prefer it to be Ulrich," said Zbyszko.

"So should I, and do you know why? Kuno has more wit and cunning, while Ulrich is the more impetuous. He is a true knight, who will observe the rules of honor, but he quivers with eagerness for war with us. They say, too, that if he becomes grand master, there will soon come such a storm as was never yet seen on the earth. And Conrad is supposed to have frequent fits of faintness. Once he lost consciousness even when I was there. Hey, maybe we shall live to see it!"

"God grant it! And are there any new disputes with the kingdom?"

"There are disputes both old and new. A Teutonic Knight is always a Teutonic Knight. Even though he knows that you are stronger and that it is bad to start a quarrel with you, he will lie in wait to get what he can that is yours, for such is his nature."

"They think that the Order is more powerful than all kingdoms."

"Not all of them think so, but many do, and Ulrich among them. In point of fact, their power is enormous."

"But remember what Zyndram of Maszkowice said."

"I remember, and every year it gets worse for them. No brother welcomes his brother as they welcomed me when no Teutonic Knight was looking. They all have had enough of them."

"Then it will not be a long wait!"

"Not long, and yet long," said Macko. And after a moment of reflection, he added: "Meanwhile we must labor hard and increase the wealth of the estate, so as to be able to appear worthily on the field of battle."

CHAPTER LXXX

GRAND Master Conrad, however, did not die until a year later. Jasko of Zgorzelice, Jagienka's brother, who was the first to hear at Sieradz the news of his death and of the election of Ulrich von Jungingen, was also the first to bring it to Bogdaniec, where, as in all the seats of the nobility, it made the most profound impression on hearts and minds. "Times are coming such as we have never seen," said old Macko solemnly; while Jagienka immediately brought all her children to Zbyszko and began herself to take leave of him as if he were setting out on the morrow. Macko and Zbyszko knew, indeed, that war would not flare up all at once; nevertheless, they believed that it would come, and they began to prepare for it. They chose horses and suits of armor, and trained in the craft of war the squires, the servants, the headmen of the villages settled "under German law," who were obliged to present themselves on horseback for expeditions, and the impoverished gentry, who gladly gathered around the more wealthy. And the same activity went on at all the other manor houses. Everywhere hammers beat in smithies, everywhere old breastplates were cleaned and smeared with bear's fat melted in cauldrons, wagons were fixed, and stores of provisions—groats and smoked meat—were gathered together. After church on Sundays and holy days, eager inquiries were made for the latest news, and there was general regret if it was of peace, for every man was deeply convinced that an end must be made once and for all of the terrible foe of the whole Polish race, and that the kingdom would not flourish in power and peace and work until, according to the words of St. Bridget, the teeth of the Teutonic Knights had been broken and their right hand cut off.

Particularly at Krzesnia a crowd of eager listeners surrounded Macko and Zbyszko, who were regarded as men who knew the Order and were experienced in war against the Germans. They were questioned, not only for news, but also regarding methods of dealing with the Germans: how best to fight them, what was their custom in single combat, in what respect they were superior to the Poles and in what respect inferior, and whether after breaking lances it was easier to smash their armor with axe or with sword.

They were indeed experienced in such matters, so they were heard with great attention, especially since there was a general conviction that the war would not be an easy one, that the Poles would have to measure themselves with the foremost knights of every country and not be content with breaking the enemy here and there, but do it thoroughly, or else themselves perish utterly. The impoverished gentry said to themselves: "If it must be, then it must be—either their death or ours!" And a generation which was inspired by a feeling of future greatness was not discouraged by that thought; on the contrary, men's courage grew from day to day; they set about their work without vain boasting, but rather with a certain stubborn concentration and a genuine contempt for death.

"For us or for them, death is fated."

But meanwhile time passed and lengthened, and there was no war. Stories were indeed told of disagreements between King Wladyslaw Jagiello and the Order—and of the district of Dobrzyn, though it had been redeemed years before, of border quarrels, and of some place called Drezdenko, which many heard of now for the first time and which both sides were said to be claiming. But there was no war. Some even began to doubt whether there would be any at all, for there were always quarrels, and they usually ended in conferences, agreements, and the sending of embassies. So the report circulated that this time also some Teutonic envoys had come to Cracow while Polish envoys had gone to Malbork. Mediation by the kings of Bohemia and Hungary, or even by the pope himself, was spoken of. Away from Cracow, nothing was known with certainty, so various rumors, often strange and impossible, circulated among the people. But there was no war.

At length even Macko, who could remember no few threats of

war which had ended in agreements, did not know what to think of it all, and betook himself to Cracow to gain more certain knowledge. He did not stay there long; in the sixth week he was already back again—with a greatly brightened face. When the usual group of nobles surrounded him at Krzesnia, eager for news, he answered their numerous questions with another question:

"Are your spearpoints and axe-edges sharp?"

"Why? Come on! Great heavens, what news have you? Whom have you seen?" cried voices from all sides.

"Whom have I seen? Zyndram of Maszkowice! And what news do I have? Such that you will have to saddle your horses very soon."

"By God! How so? Tell us!"

"Have you ever heard of Drezdenko?"

"Of course we have heard of it. But there are many small castles such as that, and it has no more land than you have here at Bogdaniec."

"A poor cause of war, isn't it?"

"Certainly it is a poor one; there have been greater ones, and yet nothing has happened afterwards."

"But do you know what parable Zyndram of Maszkowice told me in connection with Drezdenko?"

"Tell us quickly; we're burning with curiosity!"

"Well, he told me this: 'A blind man was going along a road and stumbled over a stone. He stumbled because he was blind, but the stone was the cause of his fall.' Well, Drezdenko is such a stone."

"How so? The Order is still standing."

"Do you not understand? Then I will tell it to you in another way. When a vessel is too full, a single drop will cause it to overflow."

The knights were filled with such enthusiasm that Macko had to restrain it, for they wanted to mount and ride to Sieradz straightaway.

"Be ready," he told them, "but wait patiently. We will not be forgotten here."

So they waited in readiness; but they had to wait long; so long, indeed, that some began anew to doubt. But Macko did not doubt. As the arrival of birds proclaims the coming of spring, so various signs enabled him, with his experience, to recognize that war was approaching—and a great war.

In the first place, orders were given for the organization of hunts in the royal forests, on such a scale as even the oldest folk could not recall. Thousands of beaters were collected for the hunts, at which whole herds of bison, aurochs, stags, wild boars, and various mixed game fell victims. The forests smoked for weeks and months, and in the smoke was dried salt meat, which was afterwards sent to the voivode towns and, from there, to warehouses at Plock. It was obvious that supplies for great armies were being prepared. Macko knew very well what to think of that, for similar great hunts had been ordered by Witold on the eve of each of his great expeditions. But there were other signs as well. The villeins began to escape in whole bands "from under the German" to the kingdom and into Mazovia. To the neighborhood of Bogdaniec there came chiefly subjects of the German knights in Silesia, but it was known that the same thing was going on everywhere, particularly in Mazovia. The Czech, Hlawa, who was administering Spychow in Mazovia, sent from there a dozen or more Mazovians who had fled from Prussia and taken refuge with him. These folk begged him to let them take part in the war as footmen, for they desired to avenge their wrongs on the Teutonic Knights, whom they hated with their whole hearts. They said also that certain villages on the Prussian border were almost completely depopulated, since the yeomen had gone over with their wives and children into the Mazovian duchies. The Teutonic Knights hanged any runaways they caught, it is true, but nothing could now keep the unhappy population back, and many a man preferred death to life under the terrible Teutonic yoke. Following this exodus of people, another exodus arrived. Poor church menials from Prussia began swarming the whole countryside. They all made for Cracow. They came from Danzig, Malbork, Torun, even from distant Konigsberg, from all the towns, and from all the twenty commanderies. Among these people were also sacristans and organists, various monastic servants, and even clerics and parish priests. It was supposed that they brought news of everything that was happening in Prussia: of the preparations for war, the fortification of castles, of their garrisons and the status of the mercenaries and foreign knights. It was whispered that the voivodes in their administrative towns and the royal counsellors at Cracow shut themselves up with these people for hours at a time, questioning them and writing down the information they gave.

Some returned secretly to Prussia and then appeared again in the kingdom. There came reports from Cracow that the king and the lords of his council knew of the Teutonic Knights' every step from them.

At Malbork, the opposite was the case. A certain ecclesiastic who had escaped from that capital, stopped with the landowners of Koniecpole and told them that Master Ulrich and the other knights were not anxious about the reports from Poland, being certain that with one attack they would defeat and overthrow the whole kingdom forevermore, "so that not a trace of it will be left." He further repeated the grand master's words, pronounced at a banquet at Malbork: "The more of them there will be, the cheaper will be the price of sheepskin coats in Prussia." So they were preparing for war with joy and intoxication of spirit, confident in their own strength and the aid which was being sent them by all, even the most distant kingdoms.

But, despite all these warlike signs, preparations, and efforts, the war did not come as quickly as people wished. The young Master of Bogdaniec was now irked even at home. All had long been ready; his spirit within him was eager for fame and battle; so every day's delay weighed heavy on him, and he often made reproaches to his uncle, as if the issue of war or peace lay with him.

"You promised for certain that it would come," he said, "and nothing ever happens at all!"

To which, Macko replied:

"You are wise, but not too wise! Do you not see what is happening?"

"Suppose the king comes to an agreement at the last moment? They say he does not want war."

"True, he does not, yet who but he shouted: 'I should not be king if I were to allow them to take Drezdenko'? And the Germans have taken Drezdenko and hold it to this day. Yes, the king does not wish to shed Christian blood, but the lords of his council, who are keen-witted and who feel the superiority of Polish might, will push the Germans to the wall, and I tell you only one thing, that if there were no Drezdenko, something else would be found instead."

"I heard that it was Grand Master Conrad who took Drezdenko before his death, yet he surely was afraid of the king."

"He was afraid of him, for he knew the power of Poland better than the others, but even he was unable to restrain the Order's greed. At Cracow they told me that old von Ost, the owner of Drezdenko, at the time when the Teutonic Knights occupied the New Mark, did homage to the king as a vassal, for the land had been Polish for centuries, and he wanted to belong to the kingdom. But the Knights invited him to Malbork, made him drunk with wine, and obtained from him a document leaving it to them. Then the king's patience was entirely exhausted."

"For sure!" exclaimed Zbyszko.

"But it is as Zyndram of Maszkowice said: Drezdenko is only the stone over which the blind man stumbled."

"But if the Germans give back Drezdenko, what will happen?"

"Then another stone will be found. But a Teutonic Knight will not give back what he has once swallowed unless you open his stomach, which God grant we may soon do!"

"Yes!" exclaimed Zbyszko joyfully. "Conrad might have given it back, but Ulrich will not. He is a true knight on whom there is no spot, but he is terribly hot-headed."

Thus they talked together, and meanwhile events rolled on, as stones dislodged on a mountain-side by the foot of a traveller roll with ever greater momentum into the abyss.

Suddenly the whole kingdom resounded with the news that the Teutonic Knights had attacked and pillaged the old Polish town of Santok, which had been mortgaged to the Knights of St. John. The new grand master, Ulrich, who had purposely left Malbork when the Polish envoys arrived to express their congratulations on his election, and who at the beginning of his rule had ordered German to be used in place of Latin in all dealings with the king and with the Poles, at last showed his true colors. The Cracow lords, who were quietly pressing for war, understood that he was pressing for it loudly and, at the same time, blindly, and with an arrogance which the grand masters had not permitted themselves towards the Polish nation even when their power had been greater and the kingdom's power had been less.

Nevertheless, the dignitaries of the Order, less impetuous and more cunning than Ulrich, and knowing Witold well, endeavored to win him over with gifts and with flattery so excessive that its like would have to be sought in those ages when shrines and altars were raised to Roman Caesars in their lifetime. "There are two benefactors of the Order," the Teutonic envoys told Jagiello's governor with low bows; "the first one is God, and the second one is Witold; therefore, Witold's every wish and every word is sacred to the Teutonic Knights." And they begged for his arbitration in the matter of Drezdenko, thinking that if he, a feudatory of the king, were to undertake to judge his sovereign lord, he would thereby offend him, and their good relations would be broken, if not forever, at least for a long time. But as the lords of the council knew all that was done and planned at Malbork, the king also chose Witold as his arbitrator.

And the Order regretted their choice. The Teutonic dignitaries, who had thought they knew the grand duke, found out that their knowledge was incomplete, for he not only assigned Drezdenko to the Poles, but knowing at the same time and divining how the affair must end, he stirred up Samogitia again to revolt and, showing the Order an ever more threatening countenance, began to help the Samogitians with men, arms, and grain from the fertile Polish lands.

When that happened, everyone, in all the districts of the huge state, concluded that the fatal hour had struck. And indeed it had.

One day at Bogdaniec, when old Macko, Zbyszko, and Jagienka were sitting before the gate of the castelet, enjoying the fine weather and the warmth, there suddenly appeared an unknown man on a foaming horse, who, after reigning in his horse before them, threw at their feet something like a wreath plaited of reeds and osier twigs, and shouted: "The call to arms! The call to arms!" Then he was off again.

They all sprang to their feet in great excitement. Macko's face grew solemn and threatening. Zbyszko rushed to send a squire further on with the summons, and then returned with fire in his eyes and cried: "War! At last God has granted it. War!"

"And such a war as we have never seen before," added Macko gravely.

Then he turned to the servants, who had gathered in a twinkling around their lords:

"Blow the horn on the watchtower to the four corners of the world! Let others hurry to the villages to summon the headmen!

Bring out the horses from the stables and harness them to the wagons! Be quick about it!"

His voice had not yet ceased thundering when the servants rushed in different directions to carry out his commands, which was not difficult, as everything had been prepared long since: men, wagons, horses, arms, armor, provisions. All that was needed was to mount and go!

But first Zbyszko asked Macko one more question.

"Will you not stay at home?"

"I? Whatever is in your head?"

"For according to the law you may do this, being a man advanced in years—and there would be someone to guard Jagienka and the children."

"Now listen; I have been waiting for this hour until my hair has turned white."

It sufficed to look at his cold, stubborn face to realize that words were useless. Anyway, despite his seventy years, he was still as sound as an oak, and his arms moved easily in their joints, and his axe whistled when he brandished it. He could no longer, it is true, leap full-armed into the saddle without using the stirrups, but even many young knights, particularly in the countries of the West, could not do it either. On the other hand, he was a master of knightly training, and there was no more experienced warrior in the vicinity.

Jagienka evidently was not afraid of remaining alone. When she heard her husband's words she got up and said, kissing his hand:

"Do not trouble about me, dear Zbyszko, for the castle is strong, and you know I am not inclined to panic, and neither crossbow nor spear is strange to me. This is not the time to think of us, when the kingdom must be saved, and God will watch over us."

Suddenly her eyes filled with tears, which rolled in great drops down her lily cheeks. Then, pointing to her band of children, she continued in a voice quivering with emotion:

"If it were not for these tots, I should lie at your feet until you took me to the war!"

"Jagna!" Zbyszko exclaimed, clasping her in his arms.

And she embraced his neck and began to repeat, nestling to him as close as she could:

"Only come back, my golden one, my only one, my dearest!"

"And thank God every day for giving you such a wife," added Macko in a thick voice.

An hour later the standard on the watchtower was hauled down in token of the absence of the lords. Zbyszko and Macko allowed Jagienka and the children to accompany them as far as Sieradz, so after an abundant meal they all set out together, with their men and the whole wagon-train.

The day was clear and windless. The forests stood motionless in the quiet air. The herds of cattle on the fields and fallow land were also enjoying their midday rest, slowly and thoughtfully chewing the cud. Because of the dryness of the air, there arose at places along the roads whirls of golden dust, over which gleamed little sparks of fire, immeasurably bright in the sun. Zbyszko pointed them out to his wife and children, saying:

"Do you know what it is that shines there above the dust? The points of lances and spears. Evidently the war-summons has passed everywhere, and from all parts the nation is marching against the German."

And so it was. Not far beyond the boundary of Bogdaniec, they met Jagienka's brother, the young Jasko of Zgorzelice, who as a well-to-do landowner rode with three lancers and took with him two score of armed footmen.

Shortly afterwards, at a crossroads, the bearded face of Cztan of Rogow peered at them out of the clouds of dust; he was indeed no friend of the Bogdaniec folk, but now he called out: "At those Teutonic curs!" And bowing to them in goodwill, he galloped away through the grey cloud. They met also old Wolf of Birchwood. His head already shook a little from old age, but he was going too, to avenge the death of his son whom the Germans had slain in Silesia.

And as they drew nearer to Sieradz, the clouds of dust became ever more frequent on the roads, and when the towers of the town loomed up afar, the whole highway was filled with knights, village headmen, and soldiers, all making for the appointed muster-place. So when he saw that mass of men, sound and stalwart, stubborn in battle, and hardened above all others to endure discomforts, wet, cold, and all kinds of fatigues, old Macko's heart rejoiced, and he told himself that victory was certain.

CHAPTER LXXXI

WAR finally broke out, not abounding in battles, and at the beginning not too favorable in its course for the Poles. Before the Polish forces arrived, the Teutonic Knights captured Bobrowniki, levelled Zlotorya to the ground, and occupied anew the unhappy district of Dobrzyn which had been recovered with such effort not long before. Then the mediation of the Bohemian and Hungarian kings put out the conflagration for a time. There followed a truce, during which Wenceslas, King of Bohemia, was to judge the dispute between Poland and the Order.

There was no pause, however, in the gathering of armies, which continued to approach one another throughout the winter and spring months, and when the venal Bohemian king issued a judgment in favor of the Order, the war perforce broke out again.

Meanwhile summer came, and together with it advanced the "nations" under Witold. After crossing the Vistula at Czerwiensk, the two armies united with the forces of the Mazovian dukes. On the other side, in camp at Siecie stood a hundred thousand iron-clad Germans. Jagiello wanted to cross the Drweca and advance directly on Malbork, but when that proved impossible, he turned back from Kurzetnik towards Dzialdowo and, after destroying the Teutonic castle of Dabrowno, or Gilgenburg, encamped there.

Both he and the Polish and Lithuanian dignitaries knew that a decisive battle must soon occur, but no one thought it would come until a few days had passed. It was supposed that the grand master, having checked the king's progress, would choose to give his forces a rest, so as to bring them to the mortal struggle unfatigued and fresh. Meanwhile the king's armies stopped for the night at Dabrowno. The capture of this fortress, although without orders, and even contrary to the will of the council of war, filled the hearts of King Jagiello and Witold with joy and confidence, for the castle was a strong one, surrounded by the waters of a lake, and possessing thick walls and a numerous garrison. Nevertheless, the Polish knights had taken it in the twinkling of an eye with such irresistible impetus that, before the whole army came up, there already remained nothing of the town and castle but burning ruins, amidst which Witold's wild warriors and the Tartars under Saladin cut down the last survivors of the desperately-resisting German soldiers.

The fire did not, however, last long, for it was quenched by a short but heavy shower of rain. The entire night of July fourteenth was remarkably changeable and stormy. A strong gale brought one storm after another. At times the whole sky seemed to be on fire with lightnings, and thunder rolled with terrible reverberations from east to west. Frequent thunderbolts filled the air with the smell of sulphur, and then all sounds were drowned out once more by a heavy downpour. Afterwards, the wind dispersed the clouds, and among their shreds came out the stars and a large, bright moon. Not until after midnight did the gale subside, sufficiently at least for fires to be lit. Then thousands and thousands of them shone out in a moment all over the enormous Polish-Lithuanian camp, and the soldiers dried their drenched clothes by them, singing battle songs.

King Wladyslaw Jagiello also was awake. He had taken refuge from the storm in a house at the very edge of the camp, and there the council of war was sitting and listening to the report of the capture of Gilgenburg. As the Sieradz division had taken part in the attack, its leader, James of Koniecpole, was summoned with others to explain why he had captured the town without orders and had not recalled the storming party, even though the king had sent his adjutant and several of his attendants to hold them back.

For this reason, the voivode, not being certain whether he would not be reprimanded, or even punished, took with him a dozen or more of the foremost knights, among them old Macko and Zbyszko, to bear witness that the adjutant had only reached them when they were already on the walls of the castle, engaged in the stiffest fighting with the garrison. And as for the fact that he had attacked the castle at all: "It is difficult," he said, "to ask about every detail when the army is extended over several leagues." Having been sent ahead, he concluded that it was his duty to destroy obstacles in front of the army, and to fight the enemy wherever he might be found. Hearing these words, King Jagiello, Duke Witold, and the lords, who at the bottom of their hearts were pleased with what had happened, not only did not reprimand the voivode and the Sieradz men for their action but praised their valor "in having so quickly taken the castle and overcome its brave garrison."

On this occasion Macko and Zbyszko were able to see some of the wisest heads in the kingdom, for in addition to the king and the Mazovian dukes there were present the two leaders of all the forces: Witold, who was at the head of the Lithuanians, Samogitians, Ruthenians, Bessarabians, Wallachians, and Tartars; and Zyndram of Maszkowice, with "The Same as the Sun" for his escutcheon, Sword-Bearer of Cracow, chief inspector of the Polish armies, who surpassed all the rest in his knowledge of military matters. Besides them, there were in the council great warriors and statesmen: the Castellan of Cracow, Christian of Ostrow; the Voivode of Cracow, Jasko of Tarnow; the Voivodes of Poznan (Sedziwoj of Ostrorog) and of Sedomierz (Nicholas of Michalowice); the Rector of St. Florian's parish and also the Vice-Chancellor, Nicholas Traba; the Marshal of the Kingdom, Zbigniew of Brzezie; the Bailiff of Cracow, Peter Szafraniec; and finally Ziemowit, the son of Ziemowit, Duke of Plock, the only young man among them, but remarkably skilled in war, so that the great king himself valued his opinion highly.

In a large adjoining room, some of the greatest knights, whose fame resounded far and wide in Poland and beyond, were waiting to give their advice as might be required; so Macko and Zbyszko saw there Zawisza the Black and his brother Farurej; Abdank Skarbek of Gory, and Dobko of Olesnica, who in his day had overthrown twelve German knights in a tournament at Torun; the huge Paszko the Thief of Biskupice, and Powala of Taczewo, their good friend of Cracow days, and Krzon of Goat's Head; Martin of Wrocimowice, who bore the great standard of the whole kingdom, Florian Jelitczyk of Korytnica, Lis of Fair-Ground, terrible in hand-to-hand encounter, and Staszko of Charbimowice, who could leap over two horses in full armor.

There were also many other famous knights who fought in front of the standards, from various districts and from Mazovia. These acquaintances, and particularly Powala, were glad to see Macko and Zbyszko, and began straightaway to talk with them about old times and adventures.

"Hey!" said the Lord of Taczewo to Zbyszko. "You certainly have a heavy reckoning with the Teutonic Knights, but I think now you will be able to repay them for everything."

"I shall repay them, though it be with blood, as we all shall pay them!" Zbyszko replied.

"Do you know that your Kuno Lichtenstein is now grand commander?" remarked Paszko the Thief of Biskupice.

"I know, and my uncle knows too."

"God grant I may meet him!" Macko interrupted. "I have a special matter to settle with him."

"We challenged him too," said Powala, "but he replied that his office forbade his engaging in combat. Well, now I suppose it will no longer forbid him."

Thereupon Zawisza, who always spoke with great dignity, said:

"He will be his to whom God has destined him."

Out of pure curiosity, Zbyszko asked for an opinion on his uncle's case: whether he had not satisfied his vow by meeting a kinsman of Lichtenstein who offered himself in his place, and slaying him. And all cried out that he had. The obstinate Macko alone, though he was pleased by the judgment, said:

"Yes, but I should be surer of salvation if I could meet Kuno himself."

Then they began to talk of the capture of Gilgenburg and of the coming great battle, which they expected shortly, for the grand master could do nothing else but block the king's way.

Just as they were trying to guess the precise day of the upcoming battle, a tall, lean knight, dressed in red cloth and with a red cap on his head, came up to them. He stretched out his arms and said in a soft, almost feminine voice:

"Greetings to you, Sir Zbyszko of Bogdaniec!"

"De Lorche!" Zbyszko exclaimed. "You here?" And he threw his arms around him, for fond memories of him had remained, and when they had kissed one another like dear friends, he asked him joyously: "You here? On our side?"

"Many Guelders knights are perhaps to be found on the other side," replied de Lorche, "but I owe my lord, Duke Janusz, service for Longwood."

"Then you are master of Longwood now that old Nicholas is dead?"

"Yes. For after the death of Nicholas and of his son, who was slain at Bobrowniki, Longwood passed to the fair Jagienka, who for five years has been my wife and lady."

"Great God!" Zbyszko exclaimed. "Tell me, how did it all happen?"

But de Lorche greeted old Macko and said:

"Your former squire, Wisehead, told me you were here; he is waiting in my tent and watching over supper. It is, indeed, a long way off, at the far end of the camp, but one can get there quickly on horseback, so come with me."

Then, turning to Powala, whom he had known in former times at Plock, he added:

"And you, noble lord. It will be a joy and an honor for me."

"Good!" replied Powala. "It is pleasant to chat with acquaintances, and on the way we will take a look at the camp."

So they went outside to mount their horses. However, before they did so, a servant of de Lorche's threw cloaks over their shoulders which he had evidently brought on purpose. Then, approaching Zbyszko, he kissed his hand and said:

"My respects to you, lord. I am your former servant, but in the dark you cannot recognize me. Do you remember Sanderus?"

"By God!" Zbyszko exclaimed.

And for a moment there came back to him memories of the sorrows, pains, and misery which he had formerly endured, just as a few weeks earlier, when, after the junction of the royal armies with the companies of the Mazovian dukes, he had met his own squire Hlawa after a long absence.

So he said:

"Sanderus. Heh! I remember those old times and you! What have you been doing since then, and where have you been wandering? I suppose you are not still hawking relics?"

"No, lord. Until last spring I was a sacristan at the church of

Longwood, but as my late father had occupied himself with the craft of war, when war broke out I was immediately disgusted with the bronze of church bells, and I got a hankering for iron and steel."

"What do I hear?" exclaimed Zbyszko, who somehow could not imagine Sanderus going to battle with sword, lance, or axe.

But Sanderus said, holding Zbyszko's stirrup:

"A year ago, by command of the Bishop of Plock, I went to the Prussian lands and did him a considerable service; but I will tell you about that later, and now, your greatness, mount your horse, for that Bohemian count whom you call Hlawa is waiting for you with supper in my lord's tent."

Zbyszko accordingly mounted and rode beside Sieur de Lorche so as to be able to talk freely with him, for he was curious to hear his story.

"I am very glad," he said, "that you are on our side, but I am surprised. I thought you were serving with the Teutonic Knights."

"Those serve who take pay," replied de Lorche, "but I did not take it. No. I only came among the Teutonic Knights to seek adventures and win my knight's belt, which, as you know, I got from the hands of a Polish duke. After spending long years in these countries, I came to see on whose side was justice, and when I married and settled here as well, how could I be against you? I am now a man of this country. See how well I have learned your language? Why, I have even begun to forget my own."

"What about your estates in Guelders? I heard you were a kinsman of the ruler there, and owner of many castles and manors."

"I ceded my inheritance to my kinsman, Fulk de Lorche, who paid me for it. Five years ago I visited Guelders and brought great wealth from there, with which I bought an estate in Mazovia."

"And how did it happen that you married Jagienka of Longwood?"

"Ah," replied de Lorche, "who can divine the hearts of women? She always made fun of me, until one day, when I had enough of it, I told her I was going away to the wars in Asia to drown out my grief and would never return. So she unexpectedly burst into tears and said: 'Then I shall become a nun.' I fell at her feet for those words, and a fortnight later the Bishop of Plock gave us his blessing in church."

"Have you any children?" Zbyszko asked.

"After the war Jagienka is going to the tomb of your Queen Jadwiga to get her blessing," replied de Lorche with a sigh.

"Good! They say that that is a sure method, and that in these matters there is no better intercessor than our sainted queen. The decisive battle in this war will come in a few days, and then there will be peace."

"Yes."

"But the Teutonic Knights doubtless call you a traitor?"

"No," said de Lorche. "You know how sensitive I am on the point of knightly honor. Sanderus was going to Malbork with commissions from the Bishop of Plock, so I sent a letter by him to Grand Master Ulrich, in which I informed him that I was terminating my service, and set forth the reasons I had for taking your side."

"Ha, Sanderus!" Zbyszko exclaimed. "He told me that the bronze of church bells disgusted him, and that he had a hankering for iron. This seems strange to me, since he always had the courage of a mouse."

Sieur de Lorche laughed and replied:

"Sanderus has this much to do with iron and steel, that he shaves me and my squires."

"Is that so?" asked Zbyszko in amusement.

For some time they rode on in silence, and then de Lorche raised his eyes to the sky.

"I invited you to supper," he said, "but it seems as if it will be breakfast time before we get there."

"The moon is still shining," Zbyszko answered. "Let us make haste."

So they caught up with Macko and Powala and rode on together four abreast along the broad camp street, which was always laid out by order of the leaders between the tents and the fires, so that the passage might be free. As they wanted to get to the Mazovian companies stationed at the far end of the camp, they had to cross the whole length of it.

"Since Poland has been Poland," declared Macko, "it has never yet seen such armies, for the nations have marched from the ends of the earth."

"No other king could put such armies in the field," replied de Lorche, "for none rules over so powerful a state."

The old knight turned to Powala of Taczewo:

"How many companies did you say came with Duke Witold?"

"Forty," replied Powala. "Of our Polish and Mazovian there are fifty, but no so strong as Witold's, for with him sometimes several thousand men serve under one banner. Ha! We heard that the master said they were a rabble better at handling spoons than swords, but God grant he said it in an evil hour, for I think the Lithuanian spears will be deeply stained with Teutonic blood."

"And these men we are passing now, who are they?" asked de Lorche.

"They are Tartars, led by Witold's vassal, Saladin."

"Good men in battle?"

"Lithuania knows how to war against them, and defeated a considerable part of them, which is the reason they have had to come to this war. But Western knights have difficulty with them, for they are more dangerous in flight than in actual battle."

"Let us look more closely at them," said de Lorche.

So they rode up to the fires, which were surrounded by men with bare arms, clothed, despite the summer heat, in sheepskin jackets with the wool outside. The majority of them slept on the bare ground or on damp straw steaming in the heat, but many were squatting by the burning piles; some passed the night hours humming strange songs and striking in accompaniment one shin-bone of a horse against another, thereby making a strange and disagreeable clatter; others thumped on tabors or strummed on tight-stretched bowstrings. Still others were devouring smoky, yet bloody pieces of meat just taken from the fire, while blowing on them with puffed, blue lips.

In general they looked so wild and menacing that it would have been easier to take them for some dreadful forest monsters than for human beings. The smoke of the fires was acrid, owing to the horse and mutton fat melting over them; besides this, an intolerable stench of burning animal hair and scorched sheepskins permeated the air, together with the nauseous odor of fresh-stripped hides and blood. From the other, dark side of the street, where the horses stood, the wind brought the smell of sweat. These riding ponies, several hundreds of which were kept ready to start in any direction, had eaten off all the grass under their feet and now bit one another, squeaking shrilly and snorting. The grooms stopped their fighting by shouts and blows with rawhide whips.

It was dangerous to go alone among the Tartars, for the barbarians were extraordinarily thievish. Right beyond them were the not-much-less barbarous Bessarabians, with horns on their heads, and the long-haired Wallachians, who instead of breastplates wore painted wooden boards on their breasts and backs, and awkward masks representing monsters, skeletons, or wild beasts; further on were the Serbians, whose camp, now sunk in sleep, resounded during daytime halts with the music of flutes, balalaikas, multankas, and various other instruments.

The fires shone brightly, and in the sky, between the clouds being dispersed by the strong wind, shone the large, bright moon, by whose light our knights observed the camp. Beyond the Serbians were the pitiful Samogitians. The Germans had deluged their land with blood, and yet at every call from Witold they rushed to fresh battles. And now, as if conscious that their misery would shortly end forever, they came here, emboldened by Skirwoillo, whose mere name filled the Germans with rage and fear. The Samogitian campfires burned side by side with the Lithuanian, for they were the same nation, with the same customs and the same speech.

But at the entrance to the Lithuanian camp, a gloomy sight fell upon the knights' gaze. On a gallows constructed of round posts hung two human corpses, which the wind rocked and swung and turned and shook with such force that the frame creaked mournfully. The horses snorted at the sight of these corpses and sat back somewhat on their haunches, so the knights crossed themselves piously, and when they had passed, Powala said:

"Duke Witold was with the king, and I was at the king's side, when they brought those culprits before him. Our bishops and lords had already previously made complaints that the Lithuanians waged war too ruthlessly and that they did not even spare churches. So when these men were brought before him—they were important men, but they had outraged the Holy Sacrament—the duke was so transported with rage that it was terrifying to look at him, and he ordered them to hang themselves. The poor men had to put up the gallows themselves and hang themselves upon it, and one urged on the other: 'Make haste, or the duke will be still more angered!' And all the Tartars and Lithuanians were struck with fear, for they are not afraid of death, but of the anger of their duke."

"Yes, I remember," said Zbyszko, "that when the king was angry with me that time at Cracow because of Lichtenstein, young Duke Jamont, who was a royal page, also advised me to hang myself. And he gave me the advice in all sincerity, though I would have challenged him to combat for it on beaten earth, had it not been that they were to cut off my head anyway, as you know."

"Duke Jamont has learned knightly customs since then," replied Powala.

Amid this conversation they passed the great Lithuanian camp and three fine Ruthenian regiments, the strongest of which was from Smolensk, and then they entered the camp of the Poles. In it lay fifty companies—the core and at the same time the spearhead of all the armies. Their armor was better, their horses bigger, their knights more practised and not inferior to the Western knights. In strength of limb and endurance of hunger, cold, and fatigue, these landowners of Great and Little Poland even surpassed the more comfort-loving warriors of the West. Their customs were simpler, their breastplates thicker, and their endurance greater, while their contempt of death and their measureless stubbornness in battle were frequently the wonder of the knights who came from distant France and England.

De Lorche, who knew the Polish knighthood well, also said as much:

"Here is the whole strength and the whole hope of this great army. I remember how they complained more than once at Malbork that in battle with you every handbreadth of ground had to be bought with a river of blood."

"Now blood will flow in a river too," replied Macko, "for the Order likewise never brought together such a power before."

Powala added:

"Sir Korzbog, who bore letters from the king to the master, said the Teutonic Knights claimed that neither the Roman emperor nor any king has such a power, and that the Order could subjugate all the kingdoms of the earth."

"Bah, there are more of us!" Zbyszko said.

"Yes, but they think little of Witold's army, saying that the men are but poorly armed and will break at the first impact, like a clay pot under a hammer. Whether it is true or not, I do not know."

"It is true and it is not true," declared the cautious Macko. "Zbyszko and I know them, for we have fought by their sides. Their armor is certainly worse, and their horses rough and shaggy, so they frequently give way under the pressure of knights. But they have hearts as bold as, or even more valiant than, those of the Germans."

"We shall know before long," said Powala. "The king's eyes constantly fill with tears at the thought of the shedding of so much Christian blood, and up until the last minute, he would gladly conclude a just peace, but the pride of the Teutonic Knights will not allow it."

"Indeed not!" exclaimed Macko. "I know the Teutonic Knights and we all know them. But God has already loaded the scales on which He will weigh our blood and that of the enemies of our race."

They were now not far from the Mazovian companies, among which were pitched the tents of de Lorche, when in the middle of the "street" they caught sight of a number of men gathered in a group and looking up at the sky.

"Halt there, halt!" called a voice from amidst the crowd.

"Who is speaking, and what are you doing here?" asked Powala.

"The Rector of Klobuck. And who are you?"

"Powala of Taczewo, the knights of Bogdaniec, and Sieur de Lorche."

"Ah, it is you, lords," said the priest in a strange tone, coming up to Powala's horse. "Just look at the moon and see what is happening on it. What a prophetic and wonderful night!"

So the knights raised their heads and looked at the moon, which was already pale and near the west.

"I cannot distinguish anything," said Powala. "And you, do you see anything? What do you see?"

"A cowled monk is fighting with a crowned king. Look! Oh, there! In the name of the Father and of the Son and of the Holy Ghost! How fiercely they are struggling. God, be merciful to us sinners!"

Silence fell, for they all held their breath.

"Look, look!" cried the priest.

"True, there is something of the kind!" exclaimed Macko.

"True! true!" assented the others.

"Ha! the king has overthrown the monk," cried the priest of Klobuck suddenly. "He has put his foot on him. Jesus Christ be praised!"

"For ever and ever!"

At that moment a large black cloud obscured the moon, and the night became dark. The light of the fires quivered in blood-red stripes across the road.

The knights moved on, and when they had left the group behind, Powala asked:

"Did you see anything?"

"At first nothing," Macko replied, "but afterwards I saw both the king and the monk clearly."

"So did I."

"And so did I."

"A sign from God," declared Powala. "Ha! Now, despite our king's tears, it is evident that there will not be peace."

"And the battle will be such as the world does not remember," said Macko.

And they rode on in silence, with full and solemn hearts.

When they were not far from de Lorche's tent, the wind rose again with such force that in the twinkling of an eye it scattered the fires of the Mazovians. The air was filled with thousands of brands, burning splinters, and sparks, and it was thick with coils of smoke.

"Hey, it's smoking terribly!" exclaimed Zbyszko, pulling down the cloak which the wind had blown over his head.

"And it seems that one can hear human groans and weeping in the wind."

"The dawn is not far off," added de Lorche, "and no man knows what the new day will bring him."

CHAPTER LXXXII

THE storm not only did not cease towards morning, but it actually increased in force to such an extent that it was impossible to pitch the tent in which Jagiello had been accustomed to hear three Masses daily ever since the expedition began. Witold finally hastened to him with prayers and entreaties that he would put off divine service to a more convenient time in the shelter of the forest and not hold up the march. His wish was granted, for there was no possibility of doing otherwise.

At sunrise the armies moved off in one massive body, like a wave, and behind them trailed an endless supply column of wagons. After they had marched an hour, the wind fell, so that it was possible to unfurl the standards. And then, as far as eye could see, the fields appeared to be covered with multicolored flowers. No eye could take in all the forces or that forest of various banners under which the regiments advanced. The province of Cracow marched under its red banner with the while eagle coronate, which was also the principal ensign of the whole kingdom, a great standard for great armies. It was born by Martin of Wrocimowice, with the Half-Goat for his coat-of-arms, a powerful knight and famed throughout the world. Behind it followed the court troops, one under the double cross of Lithuania, the other under the Grand Duchy's "knight-in-pursuit" banner. Next, under the sign of St. George, marched the powerful force of mercenaries and foreign volunteers, mainly composed of Czechs and Moravians, many of whom had come to the war; indeed, the whole forty-ninth company was composed exclusively of them. They were wild, undisciplined folk, especially the footmen who followed the lancers, but so skilled in battle and so stubborn in fight that all other infantry which came into contact with them recoiled in haste like a dog from a porcupine. Their arms consisted of halberds, scythes, axes, and particularly iron flails, which they wielded with truly terrible effect. They were ready to serve any who would hire them, for their element was war, pillage, and slaughter.

At the flank of the Moravians and Czechs, marched sixteen companies from the Polish districts under their own standards: one from Przemysl, one from Lwow, one from Halicz, and three from Podolia; and, behind them, the footmen of the same regions, armed for the most part with pikes and scythes. The Mazovian dukes, Janusz and Ziemowit, led the twenty-first, second, and third companies. Close by, came the bishops' and then the lords' companies to the number of twenty-two, led by Jasko of Tarnow, Jedrek of Teczyno, Spytko of Leliwa, and Krzon of Ostrow; Nicholas of Michalowice, Zbigniew of Brzezie, Krzon of Goat's Head; James of Koniecpole, Jasko Ligeza, Kmit, and Zaklika; and, besides them, the family companies of the Gryfits and the Bobowskis and the Kozli Rogows and various others, who gathered in battle under a banner with a common coat-of-arms and shouted a common war-cry.

The earth blossomed under them, just like the meadows blossom with flowers in the spring. A wave of horses and a wave of men moved forward, a forest of lances above them with colored pennons, like smaller florets, and behind them, amid clouds of dust, the burghers and the yeomen on foot. They knew they were going to a terrible battle, but they knew it had to be, so they advanced with willing hearts.

On the right wing advanced Witold's units, under banners of different colors, but all alike with the representation of the Lithuanian "knight-in-pursuit." No eye could take in the whole of these forces, for they extended amid the fields and forests over a front of more than a league.

Before noon, the armies approached the villages of Logdau and Tannenberg, where they halted at the edge of the forest. The place seemed suitable for the midday rest, being protected against any sudden attack by the overflow of Lake Dabrowski on the left and by Lake Lubiecz on the right, while in front there was a stretch of open country a league in breadth. In the middle of that stretch, rising gently westwards, lay the green meadows of Grunwald, and somewhat farther were the grey thatched roofs and melancholy empty fallows of Tannenberg. An enemy advancing to the forests and knolls could easily have been seen, but it was not expected that he would appear earlier than the morrow. The armies accordingly made only a temporary halt at this point, but since the experienced Zyndram of Maszkowice kept military order even on the march, they stood so that they might be ready for action at any moment. By command of the leader, scouts were even sent out on light, swift horses far in front towards Grunwald and Tannenberg and beyond, to reconnoitre the vicinity; and meanwhile, as the king was anxious to hear his usual Mass, the chapel tent was set up on the high shore of Lake Lubiecz.

Jagiello, Witold, the Mazovian dukes, and the council of war proceeded to the tent. In front of it, the foremost knights had gathered, both to recommend themselves to God before a terrible day and to have a sight of the king. They saw him walking in his grey camp dress, with grave face expressive of serious anxiety. The years had little changed his figure, and had not covered his face with wrinkles, nor whitened his hair, which he still used to push behind his ears with a quick movement, just as when Zbyszko had seen him first at Cracow. But he walked as if bent under the load of the terrible responsibility weighing on his shoulders, as if plunged in deep grief. In the army it was said that the king wept continually for all the Christian blood which was about to be shed, and so he did, in truth. Jagiello shuddered at the idea of war, particularly against men who bore the Cross on their cloaks and on their standards, and with his whole heart he desired peace. In vain the Polish lords, and even the Hungarian mediators, Scibor and Gara, represented to him the pride and overconfidence of the Teutonic Knights, which was such that Grand Master Ulrich was ready to challenge the whole world to war; in vain his own envoy, Peter Korzbog, swore on the Cross of Our Lord and on the fishes of his escutcheon that the Order would not listen to a word of peace and that the commander of Gniew, Count von Wende, who alone urged peace, had been heaped by the others with mockery and insult. He still cherished the hope that the enemy would recognize the justice of his demands, would grieve for the shedding of human blood, and would end the terrible feud by a just settlement.

So even now he went to pray for that in the chapel, for his simple and kindly soul was moved by grave disquiet. Jagiello had indeed visited the lands of the Teutonic Knights with fire and sword in the past, but he had done it as a pagan Lithuanian duke; whereas now, when as King of Poland and a Christian he saw the burning villages, the ashes, blood, and tears, he was filled with fear of divine wrath, particularly since the war as yet was just beginning. If it could only stop at that! But today or tomorrow the nations would clash, and the earth would be drenched with blood. "The enemy is indeed unrighteous in his dealings, but he bears the Cross on his cloak and is guarded by relics so great and so sacred that the mind recoils from them in fear." Throughout the army they were thought of with alarm, and it was not the spearpoints, nor the swords, nor the axes of which the Poles were apprehensive, but these sacred remains. "How shall we raise our arm against the master," said these knights who knew no fear, "if he has on his breastplate a reliquary containing holy bones and wood from the Cross of the Redeemer?" Witold, it is true, burned with eagerness for war, pressed for it, and hastened to the battle, but the devout heart of the king was constricted at the thought of these heavenly powers, with which the Order strove to shield its unworthiness.

CHAPTER LXXXIII

FATHER Bartosz of Klobuck had just finished one Mass, and Father Jarosz, the Rector of Kalisz, was about to begin the second, and the king had gone outside the tent to stretch his legs, which were rather cramped with kneeling, when the nobleman Hanko Ostojczyk galloped up on a foaming horse and shouted, before he leapt from the saddle:

"The Germans are advancing, Your Majesty!"

The knights sprang up, and the king's expression changed instantly. He was silent for a second, and then cried out:

"Jesus Christ be praised! Where have you seen them, and how many companies?"

"I saw one company at Grunwald," replied Hanko, out of breath, "but a dust-cloud rose from behind the hill, as if more of them were on the march."

"Jesus Christ be praised!" repeated the king.

Meanwhile Witold, whose blood had rushed to his face at Hanko's first words and whose eyes had begun to glow like coals, turned to his courtiers and cried:

"Cancel the second Mass, and bring my horse!"

The king laid his hand on his shoulder.

"You go, cousin," he said, "but I will stay and hear the second Mass."

So Witold and Zyndram of Maszkowice leapt on their horses; but just as they were about to set off to the camp, there rode up a second scout, the noble Peter Oksza of Wlostowo, shouting:

"Germans! Germans! I have seen two companies!"

"To horse!" shouted voices among the courtiers and knights.

But Peter had not yet ceased speaking when the beating of hooves was heard anew, and a third scout rode up, and after him a fourth, a fifth, and a sixth—they all had seen German companies advancing in ever greater numbers. There was no longer any doubt. The whole Teutonic army was blocking the way of the royal forces.

The knights scattered in a flash to their companies. With the king, in front of the chapel tent, remained only a handful of courtiers, priests, and pages. But at that moment the bell sounded as a sign that the rector of Kalisz was beginning the second Mass, so Jagiello extended his arms, clasped his hands piously, and, raising his eyes to heaven, went with slow steps into the chapel.

But when he came out of the tent upon the conclusion of the second Mass, he could convince himself with his own eyes that the scouts had spoken the truth, for on the edges of the extensive, sloping plain there was something black, as if a forest had grown up suddenly on the empty fields, and over that forest a rainbow of banners played in changing colors in the sun. Still farther away, far beyond Grunwald and Tannenberg, a huge cloud of dust rose towards the sky. The king took in the whole of the threatening horizon at a glance, and then turned to the sub-chancellor, Father Nicholas, and asked:

"Who is today's patron saint?"

"It is the Day of the Sending Out of the Apostles," replied the reverend sub-chancellor.

The king sighed.

"So the Day of the Apostles will be the last day of life for many thousand Christians who will meet on this field."

And he pointed to the wide, empty plain, on which in the middle, half-way to Tannenberg, rose a few immemorial oaks.

Meanwhile his horse had been brought, and a short distance away appeared sixty lancers, whom Zyndram of Maszkowice had sent as bodyguard for the king.

This bodyguard was commanded by Alexander, younger son of the Duke of Plock, and brother of that Ziemowit whose special capacity for war had given him a seat on the council. His lieutenant was the Lithuanian Sigismund Korybut, nephew of the monarch, a youth of great expectations and great destiny, but of restless temper. Among the knights, the most famous were: Jasko Mazyk of Dabrowa, a real giant, in stature almost equal to Paszko of Biskupice and in strength not much inferior to Zawisza the Black himself; Zolawa, a Bohemian baron, small and lean, but of measureless skill, famous for his single combats at the Bohemian and Hungarian courts, in which he had defeated a dozen or more Austrian knights; a second Czech, Sokol, a champion bowman; Bieniasz Wierusz of Great Poland; Peter the Milanese; the Lithuanian boyar Sienko of Pohost, whose father, Peter, led one company from Smolensk; the king's kinsman, Duke Fieduszko; Duke Jamont, and also many Polish knights, "chosen out of thousands" and sworn to defend the king to the last drop of their blood and shield him from every mishap of war. Close by the king's side were the reverend sub-chancellor Nicholas and the secretary Zbigniew of Olesnica, a learned youth, skilled in the arts of reading and writing, but at the same time as strong as a wild boar. The king's armor was guarded by three esquires: Czajka of New Manor, Nicholas of Morawica, and Danillo the Ruthenian, who held the royal bow and quiver. The train was completed by fifteen or sixteen men of the court, mounted on swift horses, who carried the king's orders to his armies.

The esquires clad their lord in splendid shining armor and then brought him a yew-black steed, likewise "chosen out of thousands," which snorted—a good omen—from under its steel frontlet and, filling the air with its neighing, crouched somewhat, like a bird about to fly. The king, when he felt a horse under him and a lance in his hand, suddenly changed. Sorrow vanished from his face, his small, black eyes began to flash, and flushes passed over his cheeks; but this change lasted only a moment; when the reverend sub-chancellor blessed him with a crucifix, he became grave again and humbly bent his silver-helmeted head.

Meanwhile the German army, coming down from the highest part of the plain, passed Grunwald, passed Tannenberg, and halted in full battle array in the midst of the field. From the Polish camp below, there was an excellent view of the compact mass of iron-clad horses and knights. Keen eyes could even distinguish the various emblems embroidered on the standards flapping in the breeze:

crosses, eagles, griffins, swords, helmets, lambs, and heads of bison and of bear.

Old Macko and Zbyszko, who had warred against the Teutonic Knights before and knew their forces and their blazons, pointed out to their Sieradz men the two companies of the grand master, in which served the very flower and elect of the knighthood; the leading company of the whole Order, commanded by Frederick of Wallenrod; the mighty squadron of St. George, with its banner showing a red cross on a white field—and many more. The only ensigns they did not know were those of various foreign knights, of whom thousands had come from all corners of the world: from Austria, from Bavaria, from Swabia, from Switzerland, from chivalrous Burgundy, from rich Flanders, from sunny France—of whose knights Macko had once said that even when overthrown and lying on the ground, they still would utter brave and boastful words—from overseas England, home of first-rate archers, and even from distant Spain, where amid incessant struggles with the Saracen, blossomed a valor and sense of honor unsurpassed.

The blood began to course more quickly through the veins of these tough nobles from Sieradz, Koniecpole, Krzesnia, Bogdaniec, Rogow, Birchwood, and many other Polish lands, at the thought that the moment had come for them to join battle with the Germans and all that splendid knighthood. The faces of the older men grew grave and stern, for they well knew how hard and cruel would be the work. But the hearts of the younger men began to strain like hunting dogs on a leash when they see the game afar. So some grasped their lances, sword-hilts, or axe-handles more firmly, and sat back on their horses as if preparing for a jump, while others breathed rapidly, as if their breastplates had suddenly become too tight. But the more experienced warriors consoled them, saying: "It will not pass you by; there is enough for all. God grant there may not be too much!"

Meanwhile the Teutonic Knights, looking down on the wooded plain, saw on the edge of the forest only a dozen or so companies of Poles, and were not at all sure whether the whole of the royal army was there. On the left, it is true, near the lake there were also grey groups of warriors to be seen, and in the dust glittered something like the points of the light javelins which the Lithuanians used. It might, however, be nothing more than a strong Polish advance guard. But fugitives from captured Gilgenburg, some dozen of whom were brought before the master, declared that all the Polish and Lithuanian armies faced them.

It was in vain, however, that they spoke of their strength. Grand Master Ulrich would not believe them, for from the beginning of the war he had believed only what was convenient and what foreshadowed certain victory. He had sent out no reconnaissance or scouts, concluding that even without them it must come to a general battle, a battle which could only end in the terrible defeat of the enemy. Confident of his strength, which was such as no grand master yet had ever mustered, he was contemptuous of the foe, and when the commander of Gniew, who had reconnoitred on his own account, informed him that Jagiello's armies were, after all, more numerous than his own, he replied:

"What armies? It is only against the Poles that we shall have to use some effort; the rest, even though they be more numerous, are common folk, better at handling spoons than swords."

And marching as he was with great forces to battle, he now grew radiant with joy when he suddenly found himself in presence of the foe and when the sight of the general standard of the whole kingdom, the red field of which showed up against the dark background of the forest, left him no longer in any doubt that the main body of the enemy was before him.

But it was impossible for the Germans to charge the Poles at the edge of the forest and within it, for the knights were deadly fighters only in the open field, and neither liked nor were able to fight in woodland brakes.

So a short council was held at the master's side, to discuss means for enticing the enemy out of the thickets.

"By St. George!" cried the master. "We have marched ten miles without a rest, the heat is oppressive, and our bodies are dripping with sweat beneath our armor. We will not wait here until it pleases the enemy to come out into the field."

Then Count von Wende, respected for his years and for his wisdom, said:

"It is true my words have been laughed at, and laughed at by such as God grant may escape from this field, where I shall fall," and here he looked at Werner von Tettingen; "yet I will say what my conscience and my love for the Order bid me. The Poles do not lack courage, but, as I know, the king is hoping until the last minute to receive proposals for peace."

Werner von Tettingen made no reply, save only for a contemptuous snort, but the master also was displeased at Wende's words, so he said:

"Is this the time to think of peace? There is something else we have to discuss."

"There is always time for God's work," von Wende replied.

But the ruthless commander of Czluchow, Henry, who had sworn that he would have two naked swords borne before him until he had soaked them in Polish blood, turned his fat, sweaty face to the master and cried in unbridled rage:

"I prefer death to shame, and though I be quite alone, I will charge the whole Polish army with these swords!"

Ulrich frowned somewhat.

"Your words are contrary to discipline," he said. And then to the commanders: "Discuss only how to draw the enemy out of the forest."

So various men gave various advice, until at last the commanders and the foremost guests accepted the proposal of Gersdorf to send two heralds to the king with a message, to the effect that the master sends him two swords and challenges the Poles to mortal combat, and if they have too little space, he will withdraw his army somewhat to give them more.

Jagiello had just come from the lakeshore and was on his way to the Polish companies on the left wing, where he had to belt a whole group of knights, when he was suddenly informed that two heralds were riding out from the Teutonic army.

His heart beat with hope.

"Perhaps they are coming with a just peace."

"God grant it!" replied the clergy.

The king sent for Witold, but the latter could not come since he was already occupied with preparing his armies; meanwhile, the heralds approached the camp without any haste.

In the bright sunshine they could clearly be seen riding on

enormous caparisoned horses; one man had on his shield the imperial black eagle on a gold field, the other, who was a herald of the Duke of Stettin, a griffin on a white field. The ranks opened to let them pass. Soon they dismounted and were before the great king. Bowing a little to show him honor, they discharged their mission thus:

"Grand Master Ulrich," said the first, "challenges Your Majesty and Duke Witold to mortal battle, and in order to rouse your courage, which seems to have failed, sends you these two naked swords."

Thus saying, he laid the swords at the king's feet. Jasko Mazyk of Dabrowa interpreted his words to the king, but scarcely had he finished when the second herald with the griffin on his shield advanced, and said:

"Grand Master Ulrich bids us also inform you that if the field of battle seems too small to you, he will withdraw his armies somewhat so that you need not loiter in the thickets."

Jasko Mazyk again interpreted his words. Silence fell, while the knights in the royal train ground their teeth at such arrogance and scorn.

Jagiello's last hopes went up in smoke. He had hoped for a mission of concord and peace, whereas it was actually a mission of arrogance and war.

So he raised his watery eyes and thus replied:

"Of swords we have enough, but I will take these as an omen of victory sent me by God himself through your hands. The field of battle will be marked out by Him. And it is to His justice that I now appeal, making complaint of my wrong and your lawlessness and pride. Amen!"

And two great tears rolled over his sunburnt cheeks.

Meanwhile the knights in his train began to shout: "The Germans are withdrawing! They are making room!"

The heralds retired, and presently they were to be seen riding uphill on their enormous steeds, with the silk tabards which they wore over their armor shining in the sun.

The Polish armies came out of the forest and the thickets in battle array. In the front were the so-called spearhead squadrons, composed of the most formidable knights; behind them came the main body, and then the footmen and mercenaries. Between the

companies, two long lanes opened up, through which passed Zyndram of Maszkowice and Witold, the latter without a helmet on
his head, in shining armor, and looking like an evil-boding star or
a wind-blown flame.

The knights took deep breaths and sat more firmly in their
saddles.

The battle was about to begin.

Meanwhile the grand master looked at the royal armies coming
out of the forest.

He looked long at their great force, at their wide-spread
wings, like those of a gigantic bird, at the colorful standards
waving in the breeze, and suddenly his heart was constricted by
some terrible, unknown feeling. Perhaps in his mind he saw piles
of corpses and rivers of blood. Though he feared not man,
perhaps he now feared God, holding the scales of victory up
there in the high heavens.

For the first time, he thought what a dreadful day had dawned;
for the first time, he felt what measureless responsibility he had
taken on his shoulders.

So his face paled, his lips quivered, and from his eyes flowed
abundant tears. The commanders looked with amazement at their
leader.

"What is the matter, lord?" asked Count von Wende.

"It is indeed a fit moment for tears!" exclaimed the ruthless
Henry, commander of Czluchow.

And the grand commander, Kuno Lichtenstein, pouted and then
said:

"I openly reprimand you, grand master. It is your duty now to
raise the hearts of the knights, not weaken them. In truth, we have
never seen you like this."

Despite all the master's efforts, tears fell continually on his black
beard, as if someone else were weeping in him.

At length he restrained himself somewhat and, looking sternly
at the commanders, cried:

"To your companies!"

Then each man hastened to his own, for the grand master had
spoken with great authority. He then stretched out his hand to his
esquire, and said:

"Give me my helmet."

The hearts of the warriors in both armies were already beating like hammers, but the trumpets had not yet given the signal for battle.

A period of waiting followed, perhaps harder to bear than actual battle. On the field, between the Germans and the royal army, there grew, on the side towards Tannenberg, a few immemorial oaks, onto which the peasants of the place had clambered to look at the extent of these enormous armies, such as the world had not seen for ages. But apart from that one clump, the whole field was empty, colorless, and terrifying, like the dead waste of a steppe. Only the wind passed over it, and above it hovered Death. The eyes of the knights turned involuntarily to that ill-boding, silent plain. Clouds passing over the sky hid the sun from time to time, and at those moments a deadly dusk fell.

Suddenly a windstorm arose. It roared in the forest, tore off thousands of leaves, fell on the field, caught dry blades of grass, raised clouds of dust, and threw them in the eyes of the Teutonic hosts. At the same moment the air was split by the shrill sound of horns, bugles, and whistles, and the whole Lithuanian wing detached itself like an enormous flock of birds aflight. According to their custom, they rode immediately at a gallop, their horses' necks outstretched and ears laid back; and thus, brandishing their swords and spears, they advanced with a dreadful shout against the left wing of the Teutonic Knights.

The grand master happened to be there. His emotion had now passed, and his eyes flashed sparks instead of dropping tears. When he saw the rushing mass of Lithuanian troops, he turned to Frederick Wallenrod, the leader on that flank, and said:

"Witold has advanced first. Now begin, you too, in God's name!"

And with a wave of his right hand, he set fourteen companies of iron knights on the move.

"*Gott mit uns!*" shouted Wallenrod.

The companies lowered their lances and started at a walking-pace. But as a rock rolled from a height falls with ever increasing impetus, so they: from a walk, they increased to a trot; from that, to a gallop, and then they rushed forward with the terrible, irresist-

ible force of an avalanche, which must crush and wipe out everything that lies in its path.

The earth groaned and bent underneath them.

At any moment the battle would extend and flare along the
whole line, so the Polish companies began to sing the old battle
hymn of Saint Wojciech. A hundred-thousand iron-clad heads
looked up to heaven, and from a hundred-thousand breasts, there
issued one thundering voice:

> *"Mother of God, blessed virgin,*
> *Mary, famed by God himself!*
> *From thy Son, O gracious lady,*
> *Mother stainless, mother only,*
> *Gain us pardon for our sins!*
> *Kyrie eleison!"*

And straightaway strength came into their bones, and their
hearts prepared for death. There was measureless victorious force
in those voices and in that hymn, as if thunder had really begun to
roll in the sky. The lances quivered in the hands of the knights;
their standards and pennons trembled; the air shook, the branches
in the forest shook, and in its depths, awakened echoes answered,
as if repeating to the lakes and meadows and to the whole world far
and wide:

> *"Gain us pardon for our sins!*
> *Kyrie eleison!"*

And the warriors continued:

> *"Through the Son, the crucified One,*
> *Hear our voice and fill our thoughts;*
> *Hear our prayer with which we pray thee;*
> *Give this to us, thus we beg thee:*
> *Grant on earth a pious sojourn,*
> *After life grant rest in heaven!*
> *Kyrie eleison!"*

And echoes repeated in answer: *"Kyrie eleison!"* Meanwhile on
the right wing a fierce battle had already commenced, and it moved
ever closer to the left.

The clash of arms, the squeals of horses, and the dreadful shouts of men mingled with the hymn. But at times the shouts were not so loud, as if the men were short of breath, and in one of these pauses the thundering voices were to be heard yet again:

> *"Adam, Adam, God's yeoman,*
> *You sit with God in His high council;*
> *Find a place for us, thy children*
> *There where holy angels reign!*
> *Where joy is,*
> *Where love is,*
> *Where one sees the Creator,*
> *Throned mid angels, without end.*
> *Kyrie eleison!"*

And again echoes bore the words *"Kyrie eleison!"* throughout the forest. The shouts on the right wing grew still louder, but none could know or distinguish what was happening there, for Grand Master Ulrich, who was watching the battle from the hill-top, had just hurled twenty companies against the Poles.

But Zyndram of Maszkowice rode like a thunderbolt to the Polish spearhead, in which were the foremost knights, and pointing with his sword to the approaching cloud of Germans, he shouted so loud that the horses in the front rank actually recoiled on their haunches:

"At them! Strike!"

So the knights advanced, leaning over their horses' necks with lances levelled.

The Lithuanians bent under the terrible onset of the Germans. The first ranks, which were the best armed and composed of the wealthier boyars, fell in heaps on the ground. The next strove stubbornly against the Teutonic Knights, but no valor, no endurance, no human power could save them from defeat and disaster. How, indeed, could it be otherwise when on the one side fought knights completely clad in steel armor and mounted on horses shielded by steel, and on the other a people, tall, certainly, and strong, but on small ponies, and covered only with skins? In vain the stubborn Lithuanians strove to reach German flesh. Spears, swords, the points of pikes, or clubs studded with flints or nails, recoiled from the iron plates as from a boulder or the walls of a castle. Witold's unfortunate units were overwhelmed by the weight of men and horses, cut down by axe and sword, pierced and broken by halberds, and trampled under the feet of horses. In vain Duke Witold hurled fresh forces into the jaws of death, vain was their resistance, useless their stubbornness, useless their contempt of death, for naught all the rivers of blood they shed! The Tartars, Bessarabians, and Wallachians fled first, and soon the Lithuanian wall broke, and wild panic seized all the warriors.

The greater part of the armies fled towards Lake Lubiecz, pursued by the main body of the Germans, who mowed them down so terribly that the whole shore became covered with corpses.

However, the other and smaller part of Witold's armies, including the three Smolensk companies, withdrew towards the Polish wing, hard pressed by six companies of Germans and, afterwards, by those returning from the pursuit. But the better-armed Smolensk men offered a more effective resistance. The battle here took on the character of a slaughter. Every step, almost every inch of ground had to be bought by rivers of blood. One of the Smolensk regiments was cut down almost to the last man. The two others defended themselves with desperate obstinacy. But nothing now could check the victorious Germans. Some of their companies were seized with the wild fury of battle. Single knights, urging on their horses by sharp strokes of their spurs, threw themselves blindly into the densest thicket of the enemy, brandishing sword or axe aloft. The strokes of their swords and halberds grew almost superhuman, and the whole line—pressing, trampling, and crushing the Smolensk horses and knights—at last reached the flank of the spearhead and the main body of the Poles, both of which had been engaged for over an hour with the Germans led by Kuno Lichtenstein.

Kuno had not found it so easy, for his opponents were more equally armed and horsed, and equal in knightly training. The Germans were stopped by Polish lances and thrown back, particularly since they were first charged by three formidable companies: the Cracow, the scouts under Andrew of Brochocice, and the king's guards, led by Powala of Taczewo. However, the battle flamed up most fiercely after the lances had been broken. Shield then dashed against shield, man closed with man, horses fell, standards were overthrown, helmets, hauberks, and breastplates split under the blows of swords and battle-axes, iron dripped with blood, and knights were hurled from their saddles like uprooted pines. Those

of the Teutonic Knights who had had experience at Wilno of battle
with the Poles knew how tough and unyielding that people was,
but the novices and foreign guests were overcome with an amazement akin to fear. More than one, indeed, reined in his horse
involuntarily and looked around uncertainly and, before he had
decided what to do, was struck down by a blow from a Polish hand.
And just as hail falls mercilessly and thickly from a leaden cloud
onto ripening fields of corn, thus fell the terrible blows inflicted by
the combatants. Sword and axe and hatchet hewed and struck
without breathing-space or pity; iron plates rang like anvils; death
blew out lives like candles, groans were torn from breasts, eyes
became glazed, and pale youths sank into everlasting night.

Sparks from iron flew aloft, together with fragments of lance-
shafts, pennons, ostrich and peacock plumes. Stallions' feet slipped
on bloody breastplates lying on the ground and on horses' bodies.
Whoever fell wounded was crushed by their iron shoes.

But none of the foremost Polish knights had fallen as yet, and
they went forward in the noise and press—shouting the names of
their patron saints or their family war-cries—as a fire goes forward
over a dry steppe, devouring grass and bushes in its course. Lis of
Fair-Ground was the first to engage the valiant commander of
Osteroda, Gamrath, who had lost his shield and wound his white
cloak in a bundle around his arm, the better to ward off blows.

With the blade of his sword, Lis cut through his cloak and
hauberk and severed his arm, while with a second thrust he pierced
his belly until the sword-point grated on his spine. The men of
Osteroda shouted in terror at the sight of the death of their leader,
but Lis threw himself among them like an eagle among cranes, and
when Staszko of Charbimowice and Domarat of Kobylany rushed
to his aid, the three of them began to shell out lives as a bear shells
young peas in a field.

There, too, Paszko the Thief of Biskupice slew the famous
brother Conrad of Adelsbach. The latter, when he saw before him
a giant with a bloody axe in his hands, to which clung matted
human hair, was struck with terror and wanted to yield himself
captive. But Paszko, not hearing him amid the uproar, rose in his
stirrups and split his head together with his steel helmet as one
might split an apple in twain. Right afterwards he slew Loch of
Mecklenburg, and Klingenstein, and the Swabian Helmsdorf, who

came of a wealthy count's family, and Limpach from near Mayence, and Nachterwitz from Mayence too, until finally the terrified Germans withdrew before him to the left and right, while he beat upon them as on a tottering wall. Every moment he could be seen rising in the saddle, and then his axe flashed and a German helmet would fall down between the horses.

There also the mighty Andrew of Brochocice, having broken his sword on the head of a knight who had an owl on his shield and an owl's-head visor, caught him by the arm and crushed it, and then snatched his battle-axe and straightaway took his life with it. He also took the young Sir Dunnheim captive, for seeing him without a helmet, he was sorry to slay him, since he was scarcely more than a child, and looked at him with childish eyes. Then Andrew threw him to his squires, not guessing that he was a future son-in-law, for the young knight afterwards took his daughter to wife and remained in Poland to the end of his days.

The Germans, however, attacked fiercely in an attempt to rescue young Dunnheim, who came of a wealthy family of counts on the Rhine, but the knights of the advance company—Sumik of Nadbroze, and two brothers from Plomykowo, and Dobko Ochwia, and Zych Pikna—stopped them on the spot as a lion may stop a bull, and pressed them towards the company of St. George, spreading disaster and destruction among them.

Meanwhile the king's guards, led by Ciolek of Zelichowo, had engaged the knightly guests of the Order. There Powala of Taczewo, possessed of superhuman strength, overthrew men and horses, crushed iron helmets as if they were eggshells, and charged whole groups alone; while beside him went Leszko of Goraj, another Powala, this one of Wyhucze, Mscislaw of Skrzynno, and two Czechs, Sokol and Zbislawek. The battle here lasted long, for that one company was attacked by three, but when Jasko of Tarnow's twenty-seventh regiment came to its aid, the forces became more or less equal, and the Germans were thrown back almost half a crossbow-shot from the point where they were first encountered.

But they were thrown back still farther by the great Cracow company led by Zyndram of Maszkowice himself, with the most formidable of all the Poles, Zawisza the Black, at its head. At his side fought his brother Farurej, and Florian Jelitczyk of Korytnica, and Skarbek of Gory, and the famous Lis of Fair-Ground above-mentioned, and Paszko the Thief, and Jan Nalecz, and Staszko of Charbimowice. Valiant warriors fell one by one under the terrible hand of Zawisza, as if in his black armor death itself had come to meet them, while he fought with frowning brow and distended nostrils, calm and intent, as if doing but his usual work. At times he moved his shield steadily and parried a blow; but every flash of his sword was followed by the dreadful cry of a man struck down, while he did not even look around, but went forward in his task, like a black cloud from which every moment falls a bolt.

The Poznan company, its emblem a crownless eagle, also fought to the death, and the archbishop's and three Mazovian companies rivalled its energy. But the rest also surpassed themselves in obstinacy and stubborn valor. In the Sieradz company, young Zbyszko of Bogdaniec threw himself like a wild boar into the thickest of the fray, and at his side went the formidable old Macko, fighting cautiously, like a wolf who only bites to kill.

He looked everywhere for Kuno Lichtenstein, but not being able to find him in the press, he contented himself meanwhile with others, particularly such as had splendid armor, and woe betide any knight who chanced to meet him. Not far from the two knights of Bogdaniec, the ominous Cztan of Rogow fought desperately. At his first conflict his helmet had been smashed, so he now fought with bare head, terrifying the Germans with his bloodstained, shaggy face, which made him appear like some inhuman monster of the forest.

And so hundreds and then thousands of warriors on either side fell and covered the earth with their bodies, until at last, under the strokes of the obstinate Poles, the German line began to waver. Then something happened which might have decided in one moment the fate of the battle.

The German companies that had pursued the Lithuanians were now returning, inflamed and intoxicated with their previous victory. Considering all the royal armies as already scattered and the battle decisively won, they were returning in large disordered groups, with shouts and song, when suddenly they perceived a fierce and bloody fight to their front, and the Poles almost victorious, surrounding the German forces.

Lowering their heads, they looked in amazement through the slits of their visors at what was happening, and then each man as he stood struck spurs into his horse and charged into the melee.

So group charged after group, until soon thousands were pouring against the now-fatigued Polish companies. The Germans shouted with joy at sight of the approaching aid, and began to strike at the Poles with fresh ardor. A dreadful battle began to rage along the whole line; torrents of blood flowed over the ground; the sky darkened and dull rolls of thunder were heard, as if God himself desired to mingle with the struggling combatants.

Victory began to incline towards the Germans. Confusion was on the point of showing itself in the Polish line, and the frenzied Teutonic fighters began with once voice to sing the hymn of triumph: *"Christ ist erstanden!"*

Meanwhile something had happened yet more dreadful.

A Teutonic Knight, lying on the ground, had stabbed the belly of the horse on which sat Martin of Wrocimowice, holding the great Cracow standard with the crowned eagle, sacred to all the armies. Horse and rider suddenly went down, and with them tottered and fell the standard itself.

In a moment hundreds of iron hands stretched out to grasp it, and a howl of joy was drawn from every German breast. It seemed to them that this was the end: that terror and panic would now possess the Poles, that the moment of defeat, murder, and slaughter was at hand, and that all they had to do was to hunt and cut down the fugitives.

But a terrible and bloody disappointment awaited them.

The Polish armies cried out like one man, it is true, at the sight of the falling standard, but this shout and this despair was a sign not of terror but of rage. You would have said that living fire had fallen on their armor. The most formidable men of both armies rushed like furious lions to the spot, and you would have thought that a storm had burst around the standard. Men and horses fought and kicked in one monstrous confusion of waving arms, ringing swords, growling axes, steel biting on iron, clatter, groans, and wild cries of felled men—all mingled into one most ghastly sound, as if the damned had suddenly cried out from the abyss. A cloud of dust arose, and from it rushed out horses blind with fear, riderless, with bloodshot eyes and wildly waving manes.

But this did not last long. Not a single German came out alive from that storm, and presently the rescued standard waved anew above the Polish forces. The wind stirred it and blew it out, and it blossomed splendidly, like a gigantic flower—a sign of hope, a sign of divine wrath against the Germans and of victory for the Polish knights.

The whole Polish army greeted it with a shout of triumph, and fell upon the Germans with such ardor and impetus that each company seemed to have doubled in numbers and in strength.

And the Germans, attacked and pressed without mercy, without a pause for drawing breath, driven in from all sides, battered unpityingly by hatchet, sword, axe, and club, began anew to waver and give way. Here and there cries for mercy could be heard. Here and there some foreign knight rushed out of the melee pale with shock and terror, and fled in whatever direction his no-less-terrified charger was taking him. The majority of the white cloaks, which the brothers of the Order wore over their armor, were now lying on the ground.

Grave alarm took possession of the hearts of the Teutonic leaders. They concluded that their only hope of safety was now in the grand master, who was standing ready at the head of sixteen reserve companies.

He, too, looking down on the battle, concluded that the moment had come, and set his iron companies in motion as a gale moves a heavy hail-cloud, pregnant with disaster.

But still earlier than this, Zyndram of Maszkowice appeared on his wild stallion in front of the third Polish line, which up to now had taken no part in the fight. He had been following carefully the course of the entire battle.

There were among the Polish footmen several units of Bohemian mercenaries. One of these had wavered even before the battle began, but recovered itself in time, remained on the spot, and got rid of its leader. It now burned with the lust of battle, desiring to make up by valor for its temporary weakness. But the main force consisted of the Polish companies, which were composed of small landowners, mounted, but not clad in armor, and footmen— burghers and mostly yeomen, armed with pikes, heavy spears, and scythes, the blades straight with the handles.

"Make ready! Make ready!" shouted Zyndram of Maszkowice in stentorian tones, galloping along the ranks with the quickness of lightning.

"Make ready!" repeated his subordinate leaders.

So the yeomen, understanding that their time had come, rested the handles of their pikes, flails, and scythes on the ground, crossed themselves piously, and spat upon their huge, calloused hands.

The ominous sound of spitting was to be heard all down the line, and then each man caught hold of his weapon and drew breath. At that moment a messenger rode up to Zyndram with an order from the king, which he whispered, panting, into his ear; whereupon Zyndram turned to the footmen, waved his sword, and shouted: "Forward!"

"Forward! In line ! Evenly !" reverberated the voices of the leaders.

"Come on! At the curs! At 'em!"

They advanced. So as to keep step and not break ranks, they all began to repeat in unison:

"Hail—Ma—ry—full—of—grace—the—Lord—is—with—thee!"

And they went forward like a deluge: the mercenary troops and the burgher formations; yeomen from Little and Great Poland; Silesians who had taken refuge in the kingdom before the war, and Mazovians from the neighborhood of Elk, who had fled from the Teutonic Knights. The whole field glittered with their spearpoints and their scythes.

Until they reached the foe.

"Strike!" shouted the leaders.

"Ugh!"

Each man grunted like a sturdy woodman swinging his axe for the first blow, and then they laid on as long as strength and breath permitted.

The uproar and the shouts rose to high heaven.

The king, who was surveying the whole battle from a height, sent out messenger after messenger, and grew hoarse with shouting orders, until at last he perceived that all his armies were engaged, and he prepared to throw himself also into the battle.

But his courtiers would not let him, fearing for the sacred person of their lord. Zolawa caught his horse by the bridle and would not let go though the king struck his hand with his lance. Others also barred his way, begging and imploring, and declaring that his presence would not decide the fortunes of the battle.

But meanwhile the greatest danger suddenly impended over the king and the whole of his train.

The grand master, following the example of those who had returned from the pursuit of the Lithuanians, and proposing himself also to charge the Poles at their flank, had made a circuit, as the result of which his sixteen chosen companies were about to pass near the eminence on which Wladyslaw Jagiello stood.

His men observed the danger, but there was no time to withdraw. They merely furled the royal standard, while at the same time the royal scribe, Zbigniew of Olesnica, galloped to the nearest company, which was just preparing to receive the foe and was commanded by Nicholas Kielbasa.

"The king is in peril. To his aid!" shouted Zbigniew.

But Kielbasa, who had lost his helmet, tore his sweaty and bloodstained cap from his head and showed it to the messenger, shouting in furious rage:

"Look whether we are wasting our time here! Madman! Do you not see that that cloud is driving at us, and that we should bring it on the king? Go away, else I will run you through with this sword."

And forgetful with whom he spoke, panting and enraged, he actually advanced toward the messenger, but the latter, seeing with whom he had to do and, what was more, that the old warrior was right, rode back to the king and told him what Kielbasa had said.

Then the king's bodyguard moved forward like a wall, to shield their lord with their breasts. This time, however, the king was not to be restrained, but took his place in the front rank. Scarcely were they drawn up, however, before the German companies were so near that the blazons on their shields could be clearly distinguished. The sight of those forces might cause the most valiant hearts to quake, for they were the very flower and elect of the knighthood. Clad in shining armor, mounted on horses huge as aurochses, and unfatigued by battle, in which as yet they had borne no part, they rode like a hurricane, with beating hooves and clash of arms and flapping of banners and pennons, with the grand master himself at the front, his broad, white cloak flying in the wind, like the wings of an enormous eagle.

The master now passed by the royal train and made for the principal battle, for what were a handful of knights standing at one side to him, a man who never guessed and never recognized the presence of the king? But from one of his companies a gigantic German turned aside, and whether he recognized Jagiello or was lured by the royal silver armor, or merely desired to distinguish himself by knightly daring, he bent his head, lowered his lance, and rode straight for the king.

The king in his turn set spurs to his horse and likewise rode straight for him before he could be restrained. And they would undoubtedly have met in mortal combat had it not been for the same Zbigniew of Olesnica, the young secretary of the king, who was equally skilled in Latin and in knightly crafts. Having a fragment of a lance in hand, he rode at the German from the side and struck him a thundering blow on the head, crushing his helmet and hurling him to the ground. "At that moment the king himself struck him with his lance-point on the bare forehead and deigned to slay him with his own hand," the chroniclers say.

Thus perished the famous German knight, Sir Diepold Kikieritz von Dieber. Duke Jamont caught his horse, while the Teutonic Knight lay mortally wounded in his white cloak over his steel armor, and his gold-embroidered belt. His eyes were rolled up, but his feet still for some time kicked the earth, until death, the greatest quieter of man, covered his head with night and quieted him forever.

The knights of the Chelmno company were dashing to avenge the death of their comrade, but the grand master himself barred their way, and shouting *"Herum! herum!"* drove them where the fate of that bloody day was to be decided: that is, to the main battle.

And again a strange thing happened. Nicholas Kielbasa, who was nearest the field, had recognized the enemy, but the other Polish companies failed to do so in the dust and, thinking it was the Lithuanians returning to the fight, made no haste to receive their charge.

It was only Dobko of Olesnica who rode out to meet the grand master galloping in front and recognized him by his cloak, his shield, and the large reliquary he wore on his breastplate. But the Polish knight did not dare to strike with his lance at the reliquary, though he was greatly superior to the master in strength, so the master struck up Dobko's lance and slightly wounded his horse, after which they passed each other, wheeled around and rode their ways, each to his own men.

"Germans! The grand master himself!" shouted Dobko.

Hearing that, the Polish companies straightaway rode at full gallop against the foe. The first to make contact was Nicholas Kielbasa with his men, and the battle raged anew.

But whether it was that the Chelmno knights, among whom were many of Polish blood, did not put their hearts into their charge, or that nothing could now check the fury of the Poles, this fresh attack did not result in the success the master had intended. He had thought that this would be the last blow to the royal power, but he soon saw that the Poles were pressing on, advancing, striking, wounding, squeezing his troops as if with iron pincers, and that his knights were defending themselves rather than attacking.

In vain he urged them with his voice, in vain he drove them on with his sword. They defended themselves, indeed, and defended themselves well, but they did not display that impetuosity or ardor which inspires victorious armies, and which filled the hearts of the Poles. These latter, in battered armor, despite blood and wounds, with splintered weapons, and no breath left to shout, still rushed in a frenzy against the thickest press of Germans. The Germans, on the other hand, began to rein in their horses and look around, seeking a chance to escape from these iron pincers which were getting them ever more tightly in their grip; they gave ground, slowly indeed, but continually, as if striving to escape unnoticed from the murderous melee. Suddenly, from the direction of the forest, fresh shouts were heard. It was Zyndram, who had brought up the yeomen and sent them into the fight. Soon scythes grated against iron, breastplates clanked under the blows of flails, corpses fell ever more thickly, blood flowed in streams on the trampled earth, and the battle raged like one immense flame; for the Germans, realizing that their only salvation was the sword, defended themselves with the energy of desperation.

And they struggled thus, with victory in doubt, until huge clouds of dust rose unexpectedly on the right flank of the battle.

"The Lithuanians are returning!" shouted the Poles in great joy.

They had guessed right. The Lithuanians, whom it was easier to scatter than defeat, were now returning, and with inhuman uproar dashed like a whirlwind on their swift horses to the fight.

Then some of the commanders, with Werner von Tettingen at their head, rode in haste to the master.

"Save yourself, lord!" cried the commander of Elbing with white lips. "Save yourself and the Order before you are encircled."

But the knightly Ulrich looked at him gloomily and, raising his hand towards heaven, cried:

"God forbid that I should leave the field on which so many valiant men have fallen! God forbid!"

And shouting to his men to follow, he threw himself into the heat of the battle. Meanwhile the Lithuanians came up, and so confused and boiling became the melee that no human eye could distinguish in it anything whatsoever.

The grand master, struck by the point of a Lithuanian pike in the mouth and twice wounded in the face, for some time parried blows with his weakening right hand; but at last a spear pierced his neck and he fell like an oak to the ground.

A swarm of skin-clad warriors completely covered him.

Werner von Tettingen fled with some companies, but all the rest were encircled by the royal armies. The battle changed into a massacre, and a disaster for the Teutonic Knights so great that in the whole of human history there have been few like it. Never in Christian times, since the wars of the Romans and the Goths with Attila, and of Charles Martel with the Arabs, had such mighty armies faced and fought each other. But now one of them already lay for the greater part like a field of mown corn. Those companies which the grand master had brought up to the battle surrendered. The Chelmno men stuck their pennons in the ground. Other German knights leapt from their horses in token of surrender and knelt down on the bloodstained earth. The whole squadron of St. George, in which served the foreign knights, together with its leader, did the same.

But the battle still continued, for many companies of Teutonic Knights preferred death to begging for quarter or captivity. The Germans now fought, according to their custom, in a huge, closed circle, and defended themselves like a herd of wild boar surrounded by packs of wolves. The Poles and Lithuanians wound around the circle as a snake winds around the body of a bull, and constricted it more and more. And again arms swung, flails clanked, scythes grated, swords cut, spears pierced, and hatchets and axes struck home. The Germans were cut down like a forest, and died in silence, huge and unafraid.

Some raised their visors and took a last leave of one another, giving each other a final kiss before they died; some threw themselves blindly into the fray, as if seized with sudden frenzy; others fought as if in a dream; while still others killed themselves, driving their misericords into their throats, or throwing away their neckpieces and turning to their comrades with the prayer to "Thrust."

The unrelenting Poles soon broke up the great circle into a dozen or more smaller groups, and then it became easier for single knights to escape. But in general even these scattered groups fought with desperate fury.

Few knelt down and begged for quarter, and when the terrible onset of the Poles at length broke up these smaller groups, even single knights disdained to surrender themselves alive into the hands of the victors. It was a day of disaster most terrible for the Order and for all the Western knighthood, but it was also a day of the greatest glory. Under the gigantic Arnold von Baden, who was surrounded by the yeoman foot-soldiers, rose a pile of Polish corpses, on which he stood, mighty and invincible, like a frontier post firmly planted on a hill, and whoever approached within a sword's length of him fell as if struck by a thunderbolt.

At last Zawisza the Black himself approached him, but seeing that the knight was without a horse, and not wishing to attack him unchivalrously from the rear, he dismounted and shouted to him:

"Turn your head, German, and yield, or else fight with me!"

Arnold turned around, and recognizing Zawisza by his black armor and the Sulima escutcheon on his shield, he said to himself:

"Death is approaching and my hour is at hand, for no one can escape from his hands alive. Yet if I were to overcome him, I should win undying fame and perhaps save my own life."

So he sprang to meet him, and they rushed together like two storms on the corpse-laden earth. But Zawisza so greatly surpassed all other men in strength that unhappy were the parents whose sons' lot it was to meet him in battle. The Malbork shield broke under the stroke of his sword, the steel helmet broke like an earthen pot, and the valiant Arnold fell, his head split in two.

Henry, the commander of Czluchow, that most bitter foe of the

Polish race who had sworn to have two swords borne before him until he had dipped them both in Polish blood, now tried to slip away unobserved from the field, as a fox slips away from a brushwood surrounded by hunters, but Zbyszko of Bogdaniec blocked his way. The commander, seeing the sword raised over his head, cried out: *"Erbarme dich meiner!"* (Spare me!) and folded his hands in the attitude of prayer; but the young knight was unable to check the impetus of his blow, though he managed to turn his sword half around, so the flat of it struck the commander in his fat and sweaty face. Then Zbyszko threw him to his squire, who put a rope around his neck and dragged him away like an ox to the place where all the Teutonic captives were being gathered.

Meanwhile old Macko sought everywhere on the bloody battlefield for Kuno Lichtenstein, until fate, kindly on that day to the Poles in everything, gave him into his hands in the bushes where a handful of knights had concealed themselves, fleeing from the terrible defeat. The sunlight reflecting from their armor betrayed their presence to the pursuers. All fell together on their knees and yielded at once, but Macko, learning that the grand commander of the Order was among the captives, had him brought to his presence, and taking off his helmet, he asked him:

"Kuno Lichtenstein, do you recognize me?"

He knit his brows and fixed his eyes on Macko's face, and said after a moment:

"I saw you at the court at Plock."

"No," replied Macko, "you saw me before that. You saw me at Cracow, when I begged you for the life of my nephew, who for a thoughtless attack on you was sentenced to lose his head. Then I vowed to God and swore on my honor as a knight that I would find you and meet you in mortal combat."

"I know," replied Lichtenstein, pouting proudly, though turning very pale at the same time, "but now I am your prisoner, and you would bring shame upon yourself if you raised your sword against me."

Macko's face twitched ominously and became just like the muzzle of a wolf.

"Kuno Lichtenstein," he said, "I shall not raise my sword against an unarmed man, but I tell you that if you decline to fight with me I will have you hung on a rope like a dog."

"I have no choice—stand!" cried the grand commander.

"To the death, with no quarter!" Macko reminded him.

"To the death!"

In a moment they were fighting in the presence of the German and Polish knights. Kuno was younger and more agile, but Macko so far surpassed his opponent in strength of arm and leg that he overthrew him in a twinkling and put his knee on his stomach.

The commander's eyes bulged out of their sockets with terror.

"Spare me!" he groaned, foam and saliva coming from his lips.

"No!" answered the inexorable Macko.

And putting his misericord to his opponent's throat, he stabbed twice. Kuno gurgled horribly. A wave of blood burst from his lips, mortal spasms shook his body, and then he relaxed, and the great quieter of knights quieted him forever.

The battle changed into a massacre and pursuit. Whoever would not yield, perished. There were many battles and conflicts in the world in those times, but no living man could recall such a disaster as this. There fell under the feet of the great king not only the Teutonic Order, but the whole of Germany, which had aided with its most splendid knights that outpost of Germanism that was eating ever deeper into the Slavonic body.

Of seven hundred "white-cloaks" who were the leaders of this Germanic flood, scarcely fifteen survived. Over forty thousand bodies lay in everlasting sleep on that bloody field.

The innumerable standards which at noon still waved over the immense Teutonic army had all fallen into the bloodstained and victorious hands of the Poles. Not a single one was saved, and now the Polish and Lithuanian knights threw them at the feet of Jagiello, who raised his eyes devoutly to heaven and repeated with emotion: "God so willed!" The chief captives were also brought before the majesty of the king. Abdank Skarbek of Gory brought Kazimierz, Duke of Stettin; Trocnowski, a Bohemian knight, brought Conrad, Duke of Olesnica; and Przedpelko Kopidlowski brought George of Gersdorf, wounded and fainting, who had been at the head of all the foreign knights.

Twenty-two nations had taken part in the battle on the side of the Order against the Poles, and now the king's scribes wrote down the names of the captives, who knelt before his majesty and begged for mercy and permission to ransom themselves and return home.

The whole army of the Teutonic Knights had ceased to exist. The Poles in their pursuit took the huge Teutonic camp, and in it, besides the remnant of the army, a countless number of wagons, laden with fetters for Polish captives and wine for the great banquet after the victory.

The sun inclined towards the west. A brief, heavy shower of rain fell and laid the dust. Jagiello, Witold, and Zyndram of Maszkowice were just preparing to ride to the battlefield when the bodies of the fallen leaders were brought before them. The Lithuanians brought the body of Grand Master Ulrich von Jungingen, pierced with pikes and covered with dust and blood, and placed it before the king; but he sighed mournfully and, looking at the huge corpse lying on its back on the ground, said:

"This is he who this very morning thought himself superior to all the powers of the earth."

Then tears began to roll like pearls down his cheeks and presently he spoke again:

"But as he died a brave death, we will do honor to his valor and give him a worthy Christian burial."

And straightaway he gave command for the body to be carefully washed in the lake and dressed in fine clothes and covered, until the coffin should be ready, with a cloak of the Order.

Meanwhile ever more corpses were brought and identified by the captives: the grand commander Kuno Lichtenstein, his throat horribly cut with a misericord; marshal of the Order, Frederick Wallenrod; the grand keeper of the wardrobe, Count Albert Schwarzberg; the grand treasurer Thomas Merzhein; Count von Wende, who had met death at the hand of Powala of Taczewo; and more than six hundred bodies of distinguished commanders and brethren. The attendants placed them side by side, and they lay like trunks of fallen trees, with faces turned to the sky and white as their cloaks, with open, glazed eyes, and frozen expressions of rage and pride, fury and terror.

At their heads were planted the captured standards—every one. The evening breeze furled and unfurled their colored cloth, and they soughed a lullaby for the fallen. Far away in the twilight,

Lithuanian divisions were to be seen, dragging captured cannon, which the Teutonic Knights had used for the first time in open battle, but which had done no damage to the victors.

On the eminence around the king were gathered the greatest knights, who breathed heavily in fatigue, and looked at the standards and the corpses lying at their feet as tired reapers look at cut and tied-up sheaves. Hard had been the day and dreadful the fruit of the harvest, but now had come the evening: great, joyous, a gift of God.

So measureless happiness brightened the faces of the victors, for all understood that it was an evening which marked the end of misery and hardships, not only for that day, but for centuries.

The king, though he fully realized the extent of the defeat, looked in front of him in seeming amazement, and at length asked:

"Is the whole Order lying here?"

To which the sub-chancellor Nicholas, who knew the prophecy of St. Bridget, answered:

"The time has come when their teeth have been broken and their right hand has been cut off."

Then he raised his hand and made the sign of the cross, not only over those who lay nearest, but over the whole plain between Grunwald and Tannenberg. In the rays of the setting sun and the rain-cleared air there was a wide view of the huge, smoking, bloody battlefield, bristling with broken lances, spears, and scythes, and heaps of dead bodies of men and horses, among which stuck up dead hands and legs and hooves. And that mournful field of death, with its tens of thousands of bodies, extended farther than eye could see.

The attendants scattered over this measureless cemetery, collecting weapons and stripping armor from the dead.

And up above, in the reddening sky, there whirled and circled flocks of crows, ravens, and eagles, croaking and rejoicing noisily at the sight of food.

And not only did the hostile Teutonic Order lie now prostrate at the king's feet; the entirety of German power, which had hitherto been overspreading the unhappy Slavonic regions like a flood, was broken against Polish breasts on this day of redemption.

So to you, sacred past, and to you, sacrificial blood, be praise and honor for ever and ever!

CHAPTER LXXXIV

MACKO and Zbyszko returned to Bogdaniec. The old knight lived long thereafter, and Zbyszko waited in health and strength to see that happy hour when at one gate of Malbork the grand master of the Teutonic Knights rode out with tears in his eyes, while at the other entered the Polish voivode at the head of his armies, to take possession, in the name of the king and the kingdom, of the city and the whole region up to the blue waters of the Baltic.

THE TRILOGY,
by Henryk Sienkiewicz

Available from Hippocrene Books

"Kuniczak's modern translation is brilliant, timely and necessary...If you are going to read only one literary work in your life about Poland, read the Sienkiewicz Triology."
—*Christian Science Monitor*

THE TRILOGY tells a tale of war and adventure, recounting the violent fall of the Polish-Lithuanian Commonwealth in the 17th century after 200 years as the leading power in Europe. The first book, WITH FIRE AND SWORD, is set during the Cossack rebellions and bloody Tartar wars which cost Poland its hold on its eastern lands. THE DELUGE plays out against the Swedish invasion of 1655 and the dynastic wars in which Poland lost its Baltic territories. FIRE IN THE STEPPE concludes the Triology with the Polish-Turkish wars, hastening the rise of the Russian Empire.

"The Sienkiewicz Triology...stands with that handful of novels which not only depict but also help to determine the soul and character of the nation they describe."
—James Michener, from the Introduction to *With Fire and Sword*

WITH FIRE AND SWORD

"Most highly recommended." —*Library Journal*, starred review

"In this robust, modernized translation by Polish-born American novelist Kuniczak, we feel the Poles' resilient spirit of freedom and their national pride as the same spirit sweeping Eastern Europe today." —*Publishers Weekly*

"A suspenseful tale of bloody insurrection, heroism and romance in the best Dumas tradition...Kuniczak succeeds in producing a novel that is considerably more vivid, gripping and contemporary." —*Milwaukee Journal*

    1130 pages   *$24.95*   *ISBN 0-87052-974-*

THE DELUGE

"Old fashioned fiction of the highest order." —*New York Times Book Review*

"The convincing translation by Polish-born American novelist Kuniczak adds luster to a robust populist epic...Around the constants of love and war, Polish novelist Sienkiewicz weaves a fugue of betrayal, redemption, faith and passion." —*Publishers Weekly*

"The Deluge is historical fiction at its best...This massive epic of love, war and adventure comes to life in English in an innovative modern rendering...The Deluge is literature in the grand manner." —*The Chicago Tribune.*

    1,762 pages   *$45.00 (2 vol. set)*   *ISBN-87052-004-0*

FIRE IN THE STEPPE

"Fast-moving action...often mingles with genuine tragedy as well as with lighthearted humor, all those hallmarks of a perfect, realistic novel." —*World Literature Today*

"Like Volodyovski himself, this work champions romance through his enduring love for Basia, the impish soldier/princess. Then together these lovers command the martial stage, standing against the Turks' surging might and the Tartar Horde, standing firm on the rock of Kamyenetz in defense of Poland, church, and God. Great literature stands on such enduring themes and in this inspiring work, Sienkiewicz taps the essence of not only a nation but all people." —Starred review, *Library Journal*

    750 pages   *$24.95*   *ISBN 0-7818-0025-0*

The World's Greatest Bestseller for nearly a century in an American translation and in paperback!

QUO VADIS?
Henryk Sienkiewicz

The celebration of a reborn Poland and the rediscovery of its literary heritage coincide with this first new English translation in nearly 100 years: Nobel laureate Henryk Sienkiewicz's immortal classic QUO VADIS? is now brilliantly translated by Polish born Reverend Stanley F. Conrad. QUO VADIS? is not only a Polish national treasure, it is also a phenomenon of world literature, an epic set in the Ancient Rome of Nero's time which has garnered both critical and popular acclaim as the bestselling book of fiction published in the last century.

"This story is sure fire, and the new translation improves it." —*Amarillo Sunday News-Globe*

"If you do not have a copy of this famous novel in your library, here's the opportunity to get one worthy of being passed on to the next generation." —*Abilene Reporter-News*

QUO VADIS? is immensely readable and without equal, a sweeping saga of love, courage, and devotion, set against the background of Rome at the very dawn of Christianity. Just as the modern translation of The Trilogy became an instant success in the United States. QUO VADIS? is destined to be an American classic, cherished for years to come.

"[Conrad's translation] is likely to revive its popularity. The message of QUO VADIS? is universal. Contrasting as it does the early Christian message of love and reconciliation with the debauchery of a corrupt Roman empire that sensed its own demise, it speaks to the present as once it did to the tumultuous years that opened the 20th century." —*St. Louis Post-Dispatch*

500 pages	*$22.50c*	*ISBN 0-7818-0100-1*
	$14.95p	*ISBN 0-7818-0185-0*

Also from Hippocrene Books:
THE TRILOGY COMPANION: A Reader's Guide to the Trilogy of Henryk Sienkiewicz
Edited by Jerzy Krzyzanowski.
With index, map, and chart.

80 pages	*$10.00p*	*ISBN 0-87052-221-3*

HENRYK SIENKIEWICZ: A Biography
Mieczyslaw Giergielewicz

192 pages	*$7.95p*	*ISBN 0-87052-118-7*

Polish Literature and Folklore from Hippocrene

THE DOLL
Boleslaw Prus

Prus's legendary portrait of Polish society in the 19th century celebrates its twentieth year in English translation. "A fine novel, clearly in the tradition of Dickens, Balzac, Zola, and Peréz Galdós. *The Doll* would undoubtedly be a classic in America if it had been translated 50 years ago....The lively, idiomatic translation is a real achievement." —*Library Journal*

Anniversary Paperback Edition
700 pages   *$16.95p*   *ISBN 0-7818-0158-3*

PHARAOH
Boleslaw Prus; translated by Christopher Kasparek

First published in 1896, and now recently translated, *Pharaoh* is considered one of the great novels of Polish literature, and a timeless and universal story of the struggle for power.

691 pages   *$25.00c*   *ISBN 0-87052-152-7*

THE DARK DOMAIN
Stefan Grabinski; newly translated by Miroslaw Lipinski

These explorations of the extreme in human behavior, where the macabre and the bizarre combine to send a chill down the reader's spine, are by a master of Polish fantastic fiction.

192 pages   *$10.95p*   *ISBN 0-7818-0211-3*

TALES FROM THE SARAGOSSA MANUSCRIPT, or, Ten Days in the Life of Alphonse Van Worden
Jan Potocki

The celebrated classic of fantastic literature in the tradition of *The Arabian Nights.* "A Gothic novel, quite an extraordinary piece of writing." —Czeslaw Milosz

192 pages   *$8.95p*   *ISBN 0-87052-936-6*

THE GLASS MOUNTAIN: Twenty-Six Ancient Polish Folktales and Fables
Uretold by W.S. Kuniczak; illustrated by Pat Bargielski

"It is an heirloom book to pass on to children and grandchildren...A timeless book, with delightful illustrations, it will make a handsome addition to any library and will be a most treasured gift." —Polish American Cultural Network. 8 illustrations.

160 pages   *$14.95c*   *ISBN 0-7818-0087-0*

OLD POLISH LEGENDS
retold by F.C.Anstruther; wood engravings by J. Sekalski

Now in its second printing, this fine collection of eleven fairy tales, with an introduction by Zygmunt Nowakowski, was first published in Scotland in World War II, when the long night of the German occupation was at its darkest. 11 woodcut engravings.

66 pages   *$10.00c*   *ISBN 0-7818-0180-X*

PAN TADEUSZ
Adam Mickiewicz; translated by Kenneth R. MacKenzie; Polish and English text side by side
Poland's greatest epic poem in what is its finest English translation. Originally published in England, this volume is now available in North America. For English students of Polish, for Polish students of English, this classic poem in simultaneous translation is a special joy to read.
553 pages   *$19.95p*   *ISBN 0-7818-0033-1*

To order these or any other Hippocrene Books, contact your local bookstore, or send a check or money order for the price of the book plus $4.00 shipping and handling for the first book, and $.50 for each additional book to: Hippocrene Books, Inc., 171 Madison Avenue, New York, NY 10016. Prices are subject to change.

Hippocrene International Literature

TALES OF THE WANDERING JEW
edited by Brian Stableford

"This homage to one of the world's great stories collects the Wandering Jew's many English-language manifestations, a fascinating journey down the tangled roads of European literature, as infinite as those Ahasuerus is still walking. This collection offers you the chance to hitch a lift on the immortal sufferer's back. It's not the sort of offer anybody should turn down."
—*City Limits*

384 pages   *$14.95p*   *ISBN 0-7818-0215-6*

SENSO AND OTHER STORIES
Camillo Boito

Translated by Rod Conway-Morris and Christine Donougher

Boito's stories combine decadence, the macabre, the demoniac and depraved. They were an immediate success in fin de siècle Italy.

This selection contains Boito's most celebrated novella, "A Corpse," the bizarre tale of rivalry between an artist and a student of anatomy for the beautiful body of the artist's dead mistress.

192 pages   *$9.95p*   *ISBN 0-7818-0005-6*

THE MANDARIN (and other stories)
Eca de Queiroz

Eca de Queiroz (1845-1900) is considered to be Portugal's greatest nineteenth century novelist. His sharply satirical work aimed to expose the hypocrisies of his age. In *The Mandarin*, his lascivious anti-heroes are dragged from their narrow Lisbon lives into exotic encounters with Chinese mandarins, the Devil and Jesus Christ himself. In all three tales, the collision of provincial egotism and greed with higher or darker forces produces a very distinctive blend of social satire and fantasy.

160 pages   *$11.95p*   *ISBN 0-7818-0214-8*

THE DEDALUS BOOK OF BRITISH FANTASY: The Nineteenth Century
Brian Stableford, editor

Beginning in 1804 with Nathan Drake's "Henry Fitzowen," this anthology traces the development of the genre through the stories and poems of Coleridge, Keats, Dickens, Disraeli, William Morris, Christina Rossetti, Tennyson and Vernon Lee until the end of the century and Richard Garnett's "Alexander the Ratcatcher."

416 pages   *$14.95p*   *ISBN 0-7818-0212-1*

New
MONSIEUR DE PHOCAS
Jean Lorrain

His first taste of opium takes Phocas on a sweeping Dantaesque tour. After passively observing two men slash a woman's throat, he himself is caught up in the violence. He plunges to oozing depths, where vampires suck his blood.

Monsieur de Phocas ranks with *A Rebours* as the summation of the French Decadent Movement. Modeled on the *Portrait of Dorian Gray*, it drips with evil

320 pages   *$14.95p*   *ISBN 0-7818-0210-5*

BELGIUM
THE CATHEDRAL
J.K. Huysmans

This tale of aestheticism, decadence, spirituality and art, woven around the Chartres Cathedral, was hailed by the Symbolists as a major step forward for the novel.

339 pages   *$9.95p*   *ISBN 0-87052-615-4*

EN ROUTE
J.K. Huysmans

This second volume in a largely autobiographical triology portrays Durtal oscillating between former allegiance to the devil (*La-Bas*) and his quest for salvation, which he attains in *The Cathedral.*

313 pages   *$9.95p*   *ISBN 0-87052-616-2*

LA-BAS (Lower Depths)
J.K. Huysmans

This first volume in a trilogy (*En Route, The Cathedral*) is a classic work of nineteenth century Satanism which launched Huysman's reputation as one of the major novelists of his time.

356 pages   *$11.95p*   *ISBN 0-7818-0007-2*

THE GOLEM
Gustav Meyrink

This version of the traditional Hebrew tale of a clay figure endowed with life was first published in 1915, to great acclaim.

304 pages   *$11.95p*   *ISBN 0-946626-12-X*

CHINA
THE NEW REALISM: Writings from China After the Cultural Revolution
Edited by Lee Yee

The finest examples of the vivid, realistic protraits of modern Chinese society unleashed by the fall of the Gang of Four, collected by the founder of the most respected Chinese-language intellectual journal, *The Seventies.*

350 pages   *$14.95p*   *ISBN 0-88254-810-7*

                         $22.50c   *ISBN 0-88254-794-1*

ENGLAND
THE DEDALUS BOOK OF DECADENCE: Moral Ruins
Brian Stableford, editor
   A striking anthology which plumbs the depths of perversity, this unique collection features over 40 stories by such authors as Baudelaire, Poe, Wilde, Mirbeau, Rimbaud and Flecker.
   288 pages   *$14.95p*   *ISBN 0-7818-0109-5*

THE SECOND DEDALUS BOOK OF DECADENCE: The Black Feast
Brian Stableford, editor
   Huysmans described *decadence* as a "black feast" and this hearty anthology offers a veritable banquet, with contributions from the major practitioners and their precursors from France and England.
   356 pages   *$14.95p*   *ISBN 0-7818-0110-9*

THE DEDALUS BOOK OF FEMMES FATALES
Brian Stableford, editor
   These tales center on a favorite motif of the Romantic movement, the femme fatale, whose sexual magnetism draws men to their destruction.
   288 pages   *$14.95p*   *ISBN 0-7818-0108-7*

MEMOIRS OF A BENGAL CIVILIAN
John Beames
   With a keen eye for local color and human detail, Beames portrays rural eastern India at the height of the British Raj.
   250 pages   *$12.95p*   *ISBN 0-90787-175-5*

ACTS OF THE APOSTATES
Geoffrey Farrington
   Set in the time of Emperor Nero's dark reign, the book is an odyssey undertaken by mystics, charlatans and sorcerers through occult mysteries and madness.
   272 pages   *$11.95p*   *ISBN 0-94662-646-4*

REVENANTS
Geoffrey Farrington
   A family curse reaches through time to damn a young man in Victorian Cornwall in this masterpiece of classic Gothic horror.
   170 pages   *$4.95p*   *ISBN 0-94662-601-4*

MR. NARRATOR
Pat Gray
   Set in the surreal world of England, this Kafkaesque fantasy presents a corporate landscape which is at once sinister and comic.
   167 pages   *$6.95p*   *ISBN 0-94662-631-6*

ARABIAN NIGHTMARE
Robert Irwin

This original edition of "the best fantasy novel in the last hundred years," (*Fantasy Review*) was greatly acclaimed in Europe.

302 pages　　　*$11.95c*　　　*ISBN 0-94662-614-6*

HOLDING ON
Mervyn Jones

"A remarkable evocation of life in the East End of London...fakes nothing and blurs little." —*The Guardian*

309 pages　　　*$12.95p*　　　*ISBN 0-90787-156-9*

SCUM OF THE EARTH
Arthur Koestler

Arthur Koestler was living in the south of France at the beginning of World War II when he was interned in Vernet by the Nazis. "A memorable story, vivid, powerful, and deeply searching." —*Times Literary Supplement*

288 pages　　　*$12.95p*　　　*ISBN 0-90787-107-0*

IDEAL COMMONWEALTHS: More's *Utopia*; Bacon's *New Atlantis*; Campanella's *City of the Sun*; Harrington's *Oceana*

Contains four exercises in dream politics: social programs which are also early works of science fiction.

420 pages　　　*$16.95p*　　　*ISBN 0-94662-626-X*

FAROE ISLANDS

THE BLACK CAULDRON
William Heinesen

A work of magic realism which traces a series of boisterous, tragi-comic events in one of the more unusual western European societies.

304 pages　　　*$14.95p*　　　*ISBN 0-7818-0000-5*

LOST MUSICIANS
William Heinesen

The first English translation of this fascinating Faroese novel.

364 pages　　　*$3.95p*　　　*ISBN 0-87052-770-3*

FRANCE

THE DEVIL IN LOVE
Jacques Cazotte

French fantastic fiction, as engrossing today as it was when it was first published in the 18th century.

128 pages　　　*$9.95p*　　　*ISBN 0-7818-0009-9*

LES DIABOLIQUES
Barbey D'Aurevilly

Scandal made the book an immediate success in 1874, and it is now firmly established as a classic.

384 pages　　　*$7.95p*　　　*ISBN 0-946626-13-8*

QUEST OF THE ABSOLUTE
Honoré de Balzac

In this masterly study of obsession, a chance meeting with a Polish emigre introduced Balthazar Claes to alchemy and changes his life.

240 pages   *$7.95p*   *ISBN 0-94662-654-5*

ANGELS OF PERVERSITY
Remy De Gourmont

These tales are key examples of early Symbolist prose, shaped and inspired by the French decadent consciousness and must rank among the best short stories of the 1890s.

192 pages   *$9.95p*   *ISBN 0-7818-0004-8*

UNDINE
Fouqué De La Motte

Set in the Golden Age of Nordic chivalry, this Romantic classic, extolled by Goethe and Heine, draws out the mystical and the erotic from traditional folklore.

224 pages   *$8.95p*   *ISBN 0-94662-657-X*

THE PHANTOM OF THE OPERA
Gaston Leroux

The chilling tale of an opera house ghost, this is one of the most outstanding fantasy works of the 20th century.

300 pages   *$9.95p*   *ISBN 0-87052-937-4*

MICROMEGAS AND OTHER STORIES
Voltaire

A delightful collection of 18th century science fiction, in the form of fantastical travelogues.

192 pages   *$8.95p*   *ISBN 0-87052-614-6*

DIARY OF A CHAMBERMAID
Octave Mirbeau

Mirbeau brings a journalist's eye to Celestine's adventure as she loses her innocence and sinks to the level of the lascivious and depraved men who exploit her.

356 pages   *$14.95p*   *ISBN 0-7818-0008-0*

THE TORTURE GARDEN
Octave Mirabeau

In the empty "decency of an urban drawing room, in the exquisite artifice of a Chinese garden," the characters are confronted with the horror of their own secret selves.

296 pages   *$9.95p*   *ISBN 0-87052-933-1*

THE MYSTERIES OF PARIS
Eugene Sue

Written by an internationally acclaimed author sometimes called the French Charles Dickens, this novel presents a fantasy world rich in melodrama and sensational events.

467 pages   *$9.95p*   *ISBN 0-946626-30-8*

THE WANDERING JEW
Eugene Sue

The legend of Ahaserus, the Jew who was condemned to wander the world until the Second Coming of Christ.

850 pages   *$22.50p*   *ISBN 0-94662-633-2*

LAW
Roger Vailland

"It is and does all that a novel should—amuses, absorbs, excites and illuminates not only its chosen patch of ground but much more of life as well." —*The New York Times*

256 pages   *$12.95p*   *ISBN 0-90787-111-9*

GERMANY

SIMPLICISSIMUS
Johann Grimmelhausen

Portraying the plight of the German peasantry at the hands of troopers during the Thirty Years War, this picaresque novel was written by one who fought in the Imperial Army at the time.

400 pages   *$9.95p*   *ISBN 0-946626-32-4*

OBERAMMERGAU: A PASSION PLAY
Eric Lane & Ian Brenson, editors

232 pages   *$7.95p*   *ISBN 0-946626-05-7*

BARON MUNCHAUSEN
Rudolph Erich Raspe

This hilarious travelogue spoof is a delectable concoction of the fruits of the classics, medieval romances and fairy tales.

268 pages   *$11.95*   *ISBN 1-87398-235-6*

ARCHITECT OF RUINS
Herbert Rosenorfer; translated by Mike Mitchell

Four men, led by the architect of ruins, construct an armageddon shelter in the shape of a giant cigar so that when the end of the world comes, they can enter eternity in the right mood, while playing a Schubert string quartet.

384 pages   *$14.95p*   *ISBN 0-7818-0001-3*

GREECE

THE HISTORY OF A VENDETTA
Yorgi Yatromanolakis

This intricate, magical tale, rich in peasant myth, describes a murder in a small Cretan village. The *History of a Vendetta* won the Greek National Prize for Literature in 1983.

172 pages   *$11.95p*   *ISBN 0-7818-0002-1*

INDIA

THE KAMA SUTRA OF VATSYAYANA

This work of philosophy, psychology, Hindu dogma, and sexual customs and techniques is so important in its influence on Indian civilization that it survives as an indispensible key. *The*

Kama Sutra justly deserves its reputation as the most explicit, most descriptive and a totally fascinating book ever written on social and sexual customs.

Sir Richard Burton's eloquent and readable translation has long been recognized as a classic of Victorian writing.

252 pages   *$8.95p*   *ISBN 0-7818-0184-2*

ITALY

A CHILD OF PLEASURE
Gabriele D'Annunzio

The story of a corrupt young count and a woman even more infernally expert than himself established the author as a master of decadent fiction at the turn of the century.

326 pages   *$11.95p*   *ISBN 0-94662-660-X*

L'INNOCENTE (The Victim)
Gabriele D' Annunzio

Published in 1892, the lush settings and sensuous nature of the novel were captured brilliantly in Visconti's last film

356 pages   *$14.95p*   *ISBN 0-7818-0006-4*

TRIUMPH OF DEATH
Gabriele D'Annunzio

A heroic rendering of the Nietzschean aestheticism crafted in 1894.

332 pages   *$9.95p*   *ISBN 0-87052-934-X*

LA MADRE
Grazia Deledda

Instinctive passion is depicted beautifully in this treatment of the primitive communities of Sardinia, the Nobel Prize-winning author's native land.

404 pages   *$7.95p*   *ISBN 0-946626-20-0*

A CURE FOR SERPENTS: An Italian Doctor in North Africa
The Duke of Piranjo

The author describes his fascinating experiences as a doctor in Libya, Ethiopia and Somaliland in the 1920s and 30s.

263 pages   *$12.95p*   *ISBN 0-90787-116-X*

LATE MATTIA PASCAL
Luigi Pirandello

Published in 1904, this fascinating novel marks the beginning of Pirandello's preoccupation with the relativity of human personality.

484 pages   *$22.50p*   *ISBN 0-87052-377-5*

NOTEBOOKS OF SERAFINO GUBBIO
Luigi Pirandello

Written in 1915, this novel offers the clearest exposition of the relativity of human personality which later informed the author's plays.

356 pages   *$9.95p*   *ISBN 0-87052-938-2*

CAVALLERIA RUSTICANA
Giovanni Verga; translated by D.H. Lawrence
> The hopeless and violent world of the Sicilian peasantry sets the scene for these short stories.
> *250 pages*   *$4.95p*   *ISBN 0-946626-25-1*

I MALAVOGLIA (House by Medlar Tree)
Giovanni Verga; translated by D.H. Lawrence
> "One wonders why this moving and tragic tale is so little known." —the London *Observer*
> *272 pages*   *$14.95p*   *ISBN 0-87052-481-X*

MASTRO DON GESUALDO
Giovanni Verga; translated by D.H. Lawrence
> A peasant who has the audacity to marry an aristocrat, Gesualdo falls foul in the rigid class structure of mid-19th centry Sicily.
> *272 pages*   *$5.95p*   *ISBN 0-946626-03-0*

SHORT SICILIAN NOVELS
Giovanni Verga; translated by D.H. Lawrence
> "The *Short Sicilian Novels* have that sense of the wholeness of life, the spare exuberance, the endless inflections and overtones, and the magnificent and thrilling vitality of major literature."
> —*The New York Times*
> *171 pages*   *$7.95p*   *ISBN 0-946626-04-9*

RUSSIA

THE RED LAUGH
Leonid Andreyev
> Written in the wake of Russia's ignominious 1905 defeat at the hands of the Japanese, this is the feverish monologue of a Russian officer who ultimately seeks refuge in insanity.
> *232 pages*   *$8.95p*   *ISBN 0-946626-41-3*

THE DEDALUS BOOK OF RUSSIAN DECADENCE
Natalia Rubenstein, editor
> Capturing the excitement and iconoclasm of Russian decadence in the turbulent decades preceding the 1917 Revolution, this new anthology spans the decadent period in Russian literature—from Valery Bruysov, Fedor Sologub, and Zinaida Gippius and on through the work of Alexander Blok, and Andrei Bely to the last great flowering of decadent writers: Mandelstam, Tsvetaeva, Akhmatova, Patsternak and Mayakovsky. Inspired by their Western models, the Symbolists set out to shock their bourgeois public as they rejected socially-aware literature for a more experimental and provocative mode of writing.
> *400 pages*   *$16.95p*   *ISBN 0-7818-0107-9*

SPAIN

BLANQUERNA
Ramon Lull
> Written in Catalan by a mystic and martyr of the 13th century, this "Catholic's Pilgrim's Progress" was the first novel in any romance language.
> *540 pages*   *$14.95p*   *ISBN 0-87052-376-7*

UNITED STATES

THE KING IN YELLOW
R.W. Chambers

Chambers, who has been described as the missing link between Poe and Nobokov, weaves a strain of horror throughout this collection of bonechilling short stories.

255 pages   *$11.95p*   *ISBN 0-94662-651-0*

ROUGHING IT
Mark Twain

Setting out from Missouri, the young Samuel Clemens encountered the Wild West. His adventures led him to discover himself and the world, and in the process, to transform Western tall-tale into a literary form. 300 illustrations.

592 pages   *$9.95p*   *ISBN 0-87052-708-8*

A TRAMP ABROAD
Mark Twain

Twain's account of his rambles through Europe in 1878 is travel writing at its funniest and liveliest.

448 pages   *$14.95p*   *ISBN 0-87052-931-5*

To order these or any other Hippocrene Books, contact your local bookstore, or send a check or money order for the price of the book plus $4.00 shipping and handling for the first book, and $.50 for each additional book to: Hippocrene Books, Inc., 171 Madison Avenue, New York, NY 10016. Prices are subject to change.